THE ESTATE SERIES COLLECTION

BOOKS 1-3

MEL SHERRATT

WHY NOT JOIN MY READERS GROUP?

Did you know you can get 4 free pieces of writing? There's a catalogue of all my books as Mel Sherratt and Marcie Steele, a pen name I write under too. There's a short crime story, a Secrets on The Estate ebook (my best selling series) and a Coffee with Marcie ebook with more short stories.

Why not join? I keep you up to date with when the next book will be out, run regular competitions to win books and goodies, and talk about other books I've read and enjoyed.

SOMEWHERE TO HIDE

THREE MONTHS AGO

Liz McIntyre woke with a start when she heard the front door slam shut. She glanced at the clock: it was just gone midnight. A further check around assured her that the room was tidy. She jumped to her feet and rushed into the hallway.

'Hi, had a good night?' she asked her husband.

'No.' Kevin pushed past her. 'Make me a drink. Coffee will do.'

In the kitchen, Liz's hands shook as she filled the kettle with water. She hated Kevin when he was sober. Sober Kevin was far nastier than drunken Kevin. Quickly, she reached for his Super Dad mug.

'I'll have some toast while you're at it,' he shouted through to her.

When she went back into the living room, Kevin was sprawled on the settee, flicking through the television channels.

Liz placed the mug and plate on the coffee table. 'Is it okay if I go to bed now?' she spoke quietly.

'No. You can stay here until I tell you otherwise.' His eyes came up to rest on hers. 'Right here, next to me.'

Liz willed her legs to bend and sat down. Twenty minutes later, Kevin had finished his meal, finished his drink and finished with her as he fastened his trousers.

'Not very exciting, but at least you're clean and tidy,' he said as he stood up.

Liz wrapped her dressing gown around her body. Maybe now he'd let her leave the room.

'Why did you do that?'

Before she could reply, he grabbed her hair and pulled her to her feet. Liz gasped as dark menacing eyes glared at her.

'Answer me!'

'I – I don't understand what –'

'The minute I got off you, you covered yourself up. Do I repulse you that much?'

'No. I was cold, that's all.'

'Liar.' Kevin tugged at the belt. 'You don't look so good yourself.' Through the thin material of her nightdress, he squeezed her breast, causing her to gasp out in pain. 'Look at you. Not even a decent handful. You're nothing but skin and bones. I wonder what other people would think of you. Take them off.'

A moment's hesitation.

'Take them off or I'll rip them off.'

Liz shrugged off the gown, letting it drop to the floor.

'And the rest.'

'Please, Kevin.'

'Please, Kevin,' he mimicked. 'Take it off.'

In silence, she removed her nightdress. Standing naked before him, she covered her breasts with a forearm.

Kevin pulled her by the elbow, marching her into the hallway. 'Let's see what other people think of your pathetic, skinny body.' He opened the front door and pushed her outside.

Liz lurched forwards, landing with a thud on the front path. The gravel embedded itself into the skin of her palms and knees but she stayed quiet.

'Down on all fours. That's a great pose for you,' Kevin sneered. 'You're nothing but an ungrateful bitch anyway. So if you act like a dog, expect to be treated like one.'

Hot tears welled in Liz's eyes as she tried to stay calm. It was the middle of March and although it wasn't too cold outside, she was vulnerable. She had two people to think of right now; she didn't want Chloe to wake up. If she didn't play it cool, Kevin would make her stay outside all night. As if that wasn't bad enough, from the corner of her eye she noticed a curtain moving in the bedroom window of the house next door. Pushing her humiliation to the back of her mind, she looked up at him.

'I'm sorry,' she whispered, tears coming freely now.

Kevin leaned on the doorframe, one foot crossing the other, arms folded. His eyes seemed to be mocking her, daring her to come back at him and stand up for herself. Then he came outside.

Liz flinched as he drew near but gently, he helped her to stand up. He turned over her hands, checking the bleeding palms.

'Ouch, they look sore.' He smiled. 'Come on in and I'll see to them.'

He took her into the kitchen and pulled out a chair at the table. While he rummaged around in the cupboards, she sat shaking. Finally, he found what he was looking for and held it up.

'TCP.' His grin was almost manic. 'It'll hurt but it's for your own good.'

Fear gripped Liz as she realised his intention. She moved away but he grabbed one of her hands, turned it palm up and poured the liquid over it.

By now an expert on pain from slaps, punches, even the odd bite, Liz braced herself. Waves of heat radiated through her hand and up her arm. She did the worse thing possible.

She screamed.

Kevin slapped her across the face, the whole weight of his body behind it. Her head reared to the right, knocking her off balance and she fell to the floor. She scrambled towards the door. Kevin grabbed her ankles and pulled her back towards him. She kicked out, still thinking she could get away if she was quick. But the pain in her palm was nothing like the agony of his heel digging into the top of her hand. She screamed again.

'Shut up,' he warned. 'If anyone alerts that stupid bitch from the housing association, you'll get more like this.' He punched her in the stomach.

'Please, stop,' she sobbed.

As his fists started to fly, Liz curled up into a ball. She fought for breath with every blow but she had to keep quiet until it was over. It was the only way she knew she would survive.

1

Life on the Mitchell Estate was never dull. Of the fifteen hundred houses, some were owner-occupied, some were rented from the local authority but the majority belonged to Mitchell Housing Association. Split down the middle by Davy Road, the top half of the estate was known locally as The Mitch, housing families who tried hard to keep their properties respectable. Gardens were tended, rubbish put in the bins and cars were taxed and parked in their drives or by the kerbside. Tenants usually felt safe popping to the shop for a loaf of bread. Some of the neighbours greeted each other with a wave and a nod. Most of them watched out for each other when strangers were on the prowl.

The bottom of the estate, however, had a reputation for being the worst place in the city to live. It was referred to as living on the hell. There the cars were lucky to have any wheels left in the morning. Abandoned vehicles on the lawns were more prominent than garden shrubs. Rubbish was piled up in the middle of the pavements and tenants fought to be heard over the thud, thud of the music – that's if they weren't fighting among themselves.

In Christopher Avenue, only just on the bottom of the estate, Cath Mason had answered her door to many a strange request over the past three years. A knock at nine a.m. could mean a bailiff with an eviction warrant pending. It could be someone wanting to administer a slap or a punch to a person inside the house. It could mean an early morning raid by a drugs squad or even, on one occasion, armed police. Several times, it had been a husband returning from an all-night bender wanting to speak to his estranged wife – or a wayward teenager the worse for wear after a night on the tiles.

This morning she pulled back the bolts, keeping the chain in place before removing it when she saw who was standing on her doorstep.

'Josie! To what do I owe this pleasure?' She smiled. 'Or is this a business call?'

'It's always a pleasure to see you,' Josie Mellor replied. 'But I do have business to discuss as well. Is that the sound of the kettle boiling?'

They went through to the kitchen where Josie let out a huge sigh.

'For a Mitchell Housing Association property, Cath, your house is so welcoming,' she told her.

'What do you mean?'

'For starters, your rubbish hasn't been chucked to the floor and left to rot for months.' Josie pointed to the table. 'This isn't piled high with a metre of dirty washing. I can see your worktops too, not a single food product festering in a dish anywhere.'

Cath wrinkled up her nose as Josie continued.

'No congealed greasy residue in the sink, no pyramid of used teabags that's threatening to reach the ceiling. And it smells... clean.'

'Good – glad to hear it.' Cath flicked on the kettle. 'I can't imagine what it's like to do your job.'

'You know better than anyone what the Mitchell Estate is like. It's had its fair share of weirdos over the years.'

'Yeah, and you've visited most of them, Ms Housing Officer Extraordinaire.'

'It gives me a chance to send the worst of them to you though, doesn't it?'

'And don't I know it.' Cath tutted. 'My hair is turning grey far earlier than it should. You'll have me old before my time.'

Cath was one of the women on the estate who took pride in their appearance. Looking far younger than her thirty-nine years, with long dark hair and enticing brown eyes framed by the longest of lashes, she had hardly a wrinkle underneath her natural-look make-up. She was slim, yet curvy where necessary, wearing immaculate yet simple clothing. And she had a compassionate side, never missing a thing.

'Heavy caseload?' she asked, noticing Josie's drooping shoulders. She handed her a mug of tea and sat down at the table.

Josie nodded, following suit. 'Not enough hours in the day, as ever. How's Jess?'

'Jess is Jess.' Cath huffed. 'That girl will always think of herself and no one else. Did you hear what she did last week? She whacked one of the Bradley twins.'

'Oh dear.'

Gina Bradley was another tenant on the estate. She had three out of control children but the twins, fifteen-year-old girls, were by far the worst.

'I had their mother on the doorstep after my blood. That Gina thinks those girls are blameless, the silly cow. They're always in the thick of things but she won't have it.' Cath pointed at Josie. 'You should do something about it.'

'You're right. I wish I could get rid of the whole Bradley clan. I can't understand how we allowed them to take on so many properties in the same street. We should have split them all over the estate. Now I can't go down Stanley Avenue without getting accosted by mother, father, sister or grandmother.'

'Jess came home drunk again last week, too,' Cath continued, 'making all kinds of noise. Archie Meredith was over like a shot the next morning. Honestly, I have more visitors than Crewe Station. And they never see the good in anyone. They should try looking in a mirror once in a while.'

Josie smiled her gratitude. 'What would this estate do without you, Cath Mason? You are one special lady.'

'Stop trying to get on my good side. I know you're buttering me up for something. What brings you to my humble abode so early in the morning, anyway? I haven't seen much of you lately.'

Josie tucked her shoulder-length mousy hair behind her ears. 'I need a favour,' she replied.

Cath raised her eyebrows.

'Okay, okay. I need *another* favour. Remember when I asked if you'd be able to take on a woman with a young child, when she was ready to admit defeat?'

'That was some months ago now.'

'Liz McIntyre came to see me yesterday. She was in a terrible state and had the remnants of some pretty nasty bruises. I've put her and her daughter up in a hostel overnight but I was wondering...'

'Is she after somewhere to stay?'

Josie took a sip of her drink before nodding. 'It's only until I can fix her up with a place of her own. But it's better than her returning to him, which I know she will do if she has to stay in the hostel.' She paused. 'I'd feel so much better knowing that she was here with you. I've already asked her to move away, maybe to another area, but she won't leave the estate. I know I can trust you to look out for her and her daughter. Chloe is only eight. And you have room at the moment, don't you?'

When Cath's husband, Rich, died three years ago, her life had changed dramatically. Dragged up through her childhood, her marriage had been unstable, sometimes to the brink of nasty and back, but Rich had grounded her with his love.

She'd been thirty-six when the accident happened. And, as if that wasn't bad enough, she was made redundant the month after and again six months later with the next job.

Around that time, her friend's daughter, Nicola, came to stay. She wasn't getting on with her parents at home so it was a good idea all round. They had peace, quiet and assurance; Cath had someone to look after, company in a quiet house.

It hadn't all been fun: some of it was hard work. Nicola's mood swings were volatile but when she was happy, Cath had enjoyed her company.

Once Nicola felt able to return home and try again, Cath decided to see if there was any kind of fostering she could do involving young, perhaps even vulnerable, women.

It hadn't been easy but Josie managed to persuade the right people and Cath hadn't looked back. She'd completed a few general courses and had then been set up with a case worker from social services, with monthly supervisory meetings and one-to-ones to keep her up to date with the necessary requirements and legislation. It had given her something to work at: something she was good at; something to ease the pain.

'Of course,' she replied. 'Have I ever let down a damsel in distress?'

Josie smiled at her. 'Thanks, I'm sure Liz McIntyre will be grateful.'

'I meant helping you out, you dope.'

Cath disconnected the phone and sighed in spectacular fashion. Not only was Josie's earlier request about to end her peace and quiet, but it seemed there was a sixteen-year-old girl in need of her help too. Jess was going to be furious.

Seventeen-year-old Jess Myatt had been with Cath for near on a year now. She'd managed to keep her at school for the last few months of her final year but since then Jess had been reluctant to get a job. Cath kept encouraging her to enrol for college in September but Jess wasn't keen. What chance did she stand nowadays with so many skilled workers on the dole, she insisted?

To a certain point, Cath knew she was right. Jess had come away from school without an exam to her name, in steep competition with a lot of her friends who had achieved nothing either. And, as she rightly said over and over, who would take her on? There were only so many small back street shops and factories that would employ cheap labour.

To Cath's mind, someone coming to the house with a young child would take away the top spot Jess had gained due to the length of time she'd been there. Cath needed to prepare herself mentally for the inevitable ructions that the next few days would bring. She had to prepare Jess too. It wouldn't be fair to blame everything on her, despite her big woman attitude.

'Jess.' Cath knocked on the bedroom door before entering. 'I need to talk to you.'

'It's only quarter to ten,' a voice could be heard from beneath the duvet.

Cath drew back the bedroom curtains, staring out onto the street for a second before turning back. 'I've had a couple of calls today. One from social services and one from–'

'There's someone coming to stay, isn't there?'

Cath pulled back the duvet to reveal a scowling face. 'Yes,' she replied. 'But it's not someone. There are three people.'

'Three!' Jess sat up, short, red hair sticking up everywhere.

'I've had more than this before, and I'll do it again if I have to.'

'But –'

'There are no buts. You don't have the monopoly on me, even though it seems like you've been here forever now.'

'If things carry on the way they are,' Jess got out of bed and pushed past Cath, 'it looks like I'll be moving out anyway.'

Moments later, the bathroom door slammed.

Although Cath flinched at the bang, she wasn't really worried by it. Jess always came around eventually, even though it wasn't pleasant to witness her reaction.

When it was clear that Jess wasn't going to run back and put her point across more poignantly, Cath left the room and went back downstairs. Not yet ten o'clock and already she could feel a headache coming on. No wonder she felt like the weight of the world was on her shoulders at times.

And if past experiences were anything to go by, three people arriving at the same time meant a whole raft of problems coming with them. Life wasn't going to be quiet for the foreseeable future.

2

Josie Mellor had been working for Mitchell Housing Association for seventeen years. Even though she was small in stature and didn't look like she was capable of standing up for herself in any type of sticky situation, she'd been a housing officer for the past seven years. More recently, she'd been splitting her hours between on-going cases and working in the community house set up by one of the residents' associations.

And every day she thanked her lucky stars that there were people like Cath Mason who she could rely on.

'Hi again, Cath!' Josie's voice rang out with false brightness as she stood on the doorstep less than three hours after her last visit. 'I'm so sorry to put pressure on you, but you know this game by now. Like buses: there isn't one for ages and then two at the same time – or rather, three. This is Becky Ward.'

Cath held the front door open and ushered the two women inside. They went through to the kitchen and Cath sat Becky down at the table. She tilted up her chin. 'Lovely blue eyes you have there but I can't see them for the swelling. You've got a great shiner coming too. What did you do to get that?'

'Nothing.' Becky jerked her head away.

'She was caught shoplifting over on Vincent Square last night, at Shop&Save,' explained Josie. 'Andy – PC Baxter, I mean – tried to caution her but she gave him the slip. He spotted her again just after six this morning when he went back on duty. She was walking up Davy Road.'

'I can speak for myself,' Becky muttered before folding her arms.

Josie didn't doubt that for a second. She also believed that Becky would clam up the moment any awkward questions were asked of her.

'Have you eaten?' she said next.

'No.'

'Would you like some toast?' said Cath, 'and a cup of tea?'

Becky nodded. 'Thanks.'

Josie checked her watch. 'No tea for me. I've another appointment in ten minutes. No rest for the wicked, I suppose. Cath, can I leave Becky in your capable hands while I make enquiries?'

Becky's eyes widened. 'What kind of enquiries?'

'To see where you can stay. Cath can help for the short term but we have a duty of care to place you somewhere more permanent. Are you sure you can't go home?'

'I'm never going back.'

Josie's heart went out to the young girl. Becky might be sixteen but at the moment she had the look of a middle-aged woman who'd seen more than her fair share of worry. Her skin was pale except for the odd blemish and group of spots. Wavy, blonde hair rested halfway down her back, looking in desperate need of a good shampoo. Yet, other than the mud stains on the knees of her jeans, her clothes were clean. She didn't look like she had been on the streets for long.

Cath glanced around. 'Don't you have a bag?'

'She only has the clothes she's in now,' Josie explained when Becky didn't say anything. 'No possessions, no bags, no spare knickers, no toothbrush.'

'Well, it just might be your lucky day.' Cath smiled at Becky. 'You can stay for a while, if you like?'

Becky shrugged.

'I thought you could speak for yourself,' she teased. Then she looked up at Josie. 'Leave her with me. She can have the box room next to Jess's.'

Once Josie had left, Cath sat down at the table again. Noticing that Becky was crying, she reached for a box of tissues, pulled out a couple and handed them to her.

'I always find a good cry makes me feel better,' she said.

'I'm so screwed.' Becky blew her nose loudly. 'I don't know what to do.'

'About what?'

'Everything.'

Cath smiled at her theatrical tone. 'Have you fallen out with your parents?'

'No.'

'Brother? Sister?'

'No.'

'That's the reason why most young girls end up here. Take Jess, for instance. She's seventeen and her mother kicked her out because she couldn't cope with her mood swings. She's a feisty soul but treat her like an adult and she's not much to handle. I suppose your mother thought the same of you, hmm?'

'My mum's dead.'

'Oops. Trust me and my big mouth. I'm not known for my tact.' Cath decided to change the subject. 'Where's that accent of yours from? Manchester?'

Becky nodded. 'Salford.'

'So why Stockleigh?'

'It was the first bus that left from the station on Saturday. I – I didn't know where to go really.'

'Was that when you left home? On Saturday?'

'No, eleven days ago. I stayed around Salford but I started to get pestered by this creepy guy.'

'Don't worry. You're safe here for now.'

Cath didn't want to push Becky into talking so early on. She knew it was vital that she gained the girl's trust as soon as possible but prying too quickly was one lesson she'd learned during her first few months taking young girls in. She ran her right hand subconsciously over the scar on her left. Sarah Draycott had taken a pair of scissors to her after she'd asked her one question too many.

'You would have been better going south of Manchester rather than north,' she continued. 'This estate wouldn't have been my first choice – not my choice at all, actually. Even the stray dogs wander around in threes.'

'I don't think I'll ever feel safe again,' Becky whispered.

'It's not that bad, I suppose,' Cath relented. 'It's just that I've been born and bred here. The place is rife with the usual social housing problems – drugs, fighting, and thieving. I don't know how long you'll be here but you don't ever go to Vincent Square after dark by yourself or you're asking for trouble. Other than that, it's a great place to live.' She forced a smile. 'You could have done much worse.'

Becky looked like she was going to cry again so Cath stood up and opened the key cupboard. 'Your room is number two. It's the smallest one I have but it'll be fine. You don't have to use the key but if you feel safer that way, it's up to you. If you leave during the day, it stays here, understand?'

Becky nodded.

Cath knew she wasn't going to get any more out of her today. The girl needed some space. There were bound to be a lot more tears before the day was out.

'Right then,' she said. 'Let's get you settled. I bet you could do with a bath and a sleep. I'll introduce you to Jess later. She stormed out earlier so you'll have a bit of peace and quiet while she's not here. But be warned. The minute she's back, she's bound to create an atmosphere. She's really good at it.'

3

The next morning, Liz McIntyre woke up in unfamiliar surroundings. Disorientated, she sat up quickly before flopping back down on the bed. The room at Cath's house was welcoming, its walls painted a calming lavender. As well as the double bed she and Chloe were in, there was a wardrobe, a dressing table and an old school chair on the far wall. Two canvas paintings and a small blue vase filled with white carnations made the room look a little more homely.

Chloe was asleep for now but had woken up three times during the night, screaming out about a monster coming to get her. Liz hoped she hadn't woken anyone else; she'd tried to calm her quickly. Yet as Chloe had drifted off after each occasion, soothed by her mum's arms, it had taken ages for Liz to drift off again afterwards.

She turned slightly, Chloe's gentle snores the only sound in the room. Liz would do anything to protect her but how could she think they'd be able to escape from her husband's clutches, just like that? Then again, other women got away sometimes, didn't they?

Awake now, she slipped out of the bedroom and went downstairs. It was six thirty but Cath was already in the kitchen. She smiled when she saw her.

'Morning,' said Cath. 'Did you sleep much last night?'

'A little.'

'And Chloe?'

'On and off.' Liz thought better of sharing the story of the nightmares. 'I thought I'd come downstairs, make a cup of tea and go back before she wakes. Do you always get up this early?'

'Yes.' Cath closed the washer door quietly and reached for the powder. 'It's always the same, isn't it? When I was younger, I never wanted to get out of bed when the alarm clock went off at six for work. Now I don't even have to use an alarm clock. I'd love to have a lie in once in a while.'

Liz moved to the left, away from the glare of the early spring sun streaming through the large window at the far end of the room. Cath had the same standard fitted kitchen that Liz had left behind when she'd fled her home in Douglas Close but that was its only similarity. The white wooden units looked clinical there but here, beside the huge notice board covered in photos of young teenage girls, and the buttercup yellow walls, they looked warm.

She sat down at the pine table, wondering how many women had done the same with Cath Mason. Josie Mellor had told her that Cath took in young females but she would also take on anyone if she thought she could help.

How many had told her their secrets? How many lives had she'd helped to mould, hoping to send women off in another direction entirely than where they'd thought they were heading? Liz doubted she'd be able to help her though. The average age of the girls in the photos was that, girls. She was twenty-eight.

Cath joined her at the table. She was dressed in dark jeans, a white long-sleeved T-shirt and a multi-coloured scarf knotted at the nape of her neck. She wore make-up; her hair looked as if it had been straightened that morning.

Liz's shoulders drooped. How did she find the energy? She barely had the strength to get Chloe ready and off to school.

'How long have you lived on the estate?' Cath asked her. 'I can't say I've noticed you around.'

'I was in Douglas Close for eight years. We kept ourselves to ourselves.'

'And your fella? Married, were you?'

Liz nodded.

'I've been around here since I was sixteen.' Cath sat down opposite her. 'The estate's got worse since then but I wouldn't live anywhere else. It was where I met Rich – my late husband. When he died, I thought of moving away but I just couldn't. I had a lot of good people rallying around me. No matter what people say about the Mitchell Estate, there are some good ones here. It's just the troublemakers that make it worse for everyone else.'

'But there's not much to do around here, is there? I mean, is it any wonder the kids are bored? The clubs have closed down; most of the shops and the pubs are boarded up. I'm surprised everyone hasn't moved away. There must be more to life than this wretched routine all the time.'

Cath nodded. 'There's plenty going on at the community house. I'm a volunteer there. Josie Mellor helps to run it. We do all kinds of sessions, like job interview techniques, basic computer skills, that type of thing. Do you work?'

'No.'

That awkward silence filled the room again.

'How long were you married, Cath?' Liz broke into it.

'Sixteen years. Rich died three years ago. He fell down a flight of steps on his way back home from the pub one night and suffered fatal head injuries. Can you believe that? It was so senseless. What about you?'

'We married in 2004. I remember it as a good and a bad year. It was the year I gave birth to Chloe too.'

'I met Rich when I was seventeen. He was my real first boyfriend.' Cath pointed to a photo in the middle of the notice board. 'That was taken a few years ago, when he was best man at a wedding.'

Liz looked across to see a picture of two people. A smile lit up his face as Rich posed in a dark three-piece suit, Cath's arm linked through his as they stood in front of the church. Cath looked striking in a navy blue and cream shift dress and a wide-brimmed hat.

'You look so happy together,' said Liz.

'Oh, we weren't always like that.' Cath grinned. 'You need to ask Josie about the goings-on at Rich and Cath Mason's house. Time and time again I'd tell Rich to sling his hook when he'd come home from the pub absolutely blind drunk. He always said he was going out for the last hour, in the days when last orders meant eleven p.m. on the dot – and he'd always end up late, at some lock-up or another after hours.

'I do miss him still,' Cath added after a pause. 'It was really hard work at times but the more we were together, I suppose, the more it seemed to click.'

'Did the rest of your family like him?'

'I don't have any family. My father left my mother and me when I was six and my mother took to drink. She died when I was sixteen and I was put into a hostel for homeless teens.'

'Oh... I...' Liz sensed she'd put her foot in it again. 'Josie mentioned that you don't have any children, is that right?'

'Yes, that's right.' Cath sighed. 'Anyway, now that you've learned all there is to know about me, when you're ready to talk, I'm always here to listen. I've seen and heard everything in this house but what is said inside these four walls stays inside these four walls. You have my word. So if you ever need a shoulder to cry on, someone to rant at or a bit of friendly advice, don't be afraid to ask. I'm here to listen, not to pass judgement. There are things about my life that aren't so rosy either. I'm sure –'

Somewhere to Hide

'I can't believe it's only quarter past seven,' Jess said, barging into the room. She marched across the floor, her dressing gown flying wildly behind her, and pointed at Liz. 'That brat of yours has been snuffling for the past few minutes. She's kept me up half the night as well. Can't you gag her or something?'

'Hey!' Cath snapped. 'We'll have less of that talk. Chloe is entitled to make as much noise as she wants. Besides, you're seventeen and you make far more of a racket. You don't hear me complaining, do you?'

'I'd better go to her,' said Liz, quickly finishing her drink.

'Yes, do.' Jess made a shooing gesture. 'Run along and tend to the young miss before I knock her head off.'

Cath saw Jess give Liz an evil glare as she scuttled away.

'You'd better watch your step,' she told her once Liz had gone. 'You know I won't tolerate rudeness. And if your sleep is so important, where were you until midnight last night?'

'Out.'

'Out where?'

Jess folded her arms and rested against the worktop. 'Bloody hell, it's like being back at school.'

'You know you should be in by eleven during the week.'

'Rules, schmools.'

'They protect you as well as ensuring that you show consideration to others.'

Jess sighed dramatically. 'I'm sick of having to do this every time someone new arrives.'

'Then you know what to do about it, don't you?' Cath challenged.

*L*iz walked with Chloe across the estate and into Adam Street heading for the primary school. The weather was overcast and a tiny bit drizzly so she pulled her coat into her chest as it billowed in the wind.

Her eyes flitted over the crowd of parents gathered at the school gates, praying that she would spot Kevin if he was there so she could be ready to react. Even though she knew he was on the early shift at work and would most likely be waiting for them in the afternoon, her heart still pounded in her chest. She held on tightly to Chloe's hand.

'Will you be okay on your own today, Mum?' Chloe asked when they arrived at the entrance.

Liz ran a hand over her daughter's head. Chloe had a similar shade of mousy hair to her own, the same button nose and chubby cheeks. Unfortunately, Chloe had her dad's deep-set eyes, a constant reminder. They were looking up at her now.

'Of course I will, sweetheart.' She smiled. 'And I'll be here to pick you up as usual. There's nothing to worry about.'

'I could look after you. I'll make you some dinner and lots of cups of tea.'

Liz squatted down to her daughter's level. 'Please don't worry,' she said, giving her a comforting hug. 'I'll be fine.'

Liz waved until Chloe was out of sight and then sighed. They would get through this mess, she tried to reassure herself. It was only a matter of time.

'That's a huge sigh,' said a voice by her side.

Liz turned to see Maxine Rothbourne standing next to her. She was in her late thirties with short, bleached hair, far too much make-up and wearing the Shop&Save uniform of garish green trousers and tunic with matching ballet pumps. Liz saw her often because her daughter, Abby, was one of Chloe's friends.

She tried to muster a smile for her. 'Hi, Maxine.'

'Oh, dear. Rough weekend?'

'You could say that.'

'My two have been playing up all morning. I couldn't separate the little buggers, fighting over the free gift in the cereal, they were. I tell you, a piece of red plastic that's supposed to be a dog. I don't –'

An arm encircled Liz's waist, warm breath next to her ear. 'Hello, darling. Sorry I missed you this morning.'

Liz froze as Kevin kissed her cheek. Aware that Maxine was waiting to be introduced, she tried to keep the tremble from her voice.

'This is my husband,' she said.

'Ooh, hello.'

'I'm very pleased to meet you.' Kevin's smile was cheesy. 'It's Maxine, isn't it?'

Maxine ran a hand through her hair and beamed. 'That's right,' she nodded. 'I'm Abby's mum.'

'Ah.' Kevin nodded in recognition. 'She's a pretty little thing, isn't she, Liz?'

Liz managed to nod back but she needn't have bothered. She watched as Maxine's face and neck flushed under Kevin's constant gaze. Couldn't she see that he'd read the name from her work badge? That he was using his charm to make her feel special?

After a few seconds of small talk, Maxine left them. Most of the other parents had been and gone: there was only the odd one or two who were still rushing in late.

Kevin grabbed Liz's wrist and swung her round to face him.

'So, my lovely,' he hissed. 'Where the fuck did you disappear to?'

4

Becky crashed down on the length of her bed, her eyes flicking around the tiny room. It was barely big enough to hold the wardrobe and chest of drawers on the opposite wall. But then again, what had she to put in the room? What had she to hang up in the wardrobe?

She glanced down at the pink T-shirt and black jeans that she was wearing. Cath had given her two bags of clothes when she'd shown her to her room yesterday, left behind by some other girl.

She couldn't believe she was still free. She couldn't understand why there was no one coming after her: Rebecca Louise Ward wanted for the murder of James Michael Ward. Even though it was nearly two weeks since she'd ran away, she'd watched *Central News* last night but there hadn't been anything so far about a murder. She'd scanned the local newspaper but they weren't running the story. There wasn't even anything in the small print.

Perhaps she was too far away now. Her photograph must have been circulated everywhere but at least she'd had the sense to dump the knife. Even so, she didn't dare risk going out yet in case the police were still after her.

To alleviate her frustration, she pummelled the mattress over and over.

'What are you doing that for?' A voice came through the half open door. 'If you really want to vent your anger, you need to kick something and damage it.'

Becky looked up to see Jess standing on the threshold.

'How old are you?' Jess continued.

'Sixteen.'

'What're you running away from?'

'I've murdered someone.'

Jess snorted. 'Don't make me laugh. If the force of that punch is anything to go by you haven't got murder in you.'

Becky played with a loose strand of cotton on the hem of the curtains. 'That's what you think.'

Jess ventured in a step. 'Okay, then. Tell me who you're supposed to have killed.'

'My uncle.'

'What did you do to him?'

'I stabbed him.'

'No way!'

'Yes way.'

'You're lying.'

'No, I'm not.' Becky paused. The last thing she needed was to bring attention her way. What if Jess went to the police and told them where she was hiding? She'd end up in prison, or worse, on the run again.

Jess turned to leave but then stopped. 'I don't suppose you want to come out with me tonight?'

Becky shook her head. What if the police spotted her if she went into town?

'You'll soon change your mind. You'll have to find something to do or else Cath will have you making coffee at the community house every day. Besides, when you've been here for a few days, you'll get fed up of doing nothing.'

'I'm not going out ever again.' Becky's tone was defiant.

'You can't stay in here forever.'

'I'm not getting caught and going to prison. I'd kill myself first.'

'Ooh!' Jess raised her hands and wiggled her fingers. 'Big talk for such a small person.'

'I'm taller than you.'

'Skinny thing though, aren't you?'

'I won't be soon.'

Jess's mouth dropped opened. 'Don't tell me you're up the duff?'

Becky gnawed her bottom lip and looked away.

'Oh, you stupid bitch. Have you never heard of using a condom?'

'Leave me alone. It's got nothing to do with you.'

'It has if you want me to keep quiet about it.' Jess ran a finger over her top lip. 'What's it worth for me not to tell Cath? She'll have you out in a flash. You can't stay here if you're preggers. She won't allow it.'

'Piss off and leave me alone.' Becky turned her face towards the wall.

Jess grabbed her hair and pulled hard, yanking back her head. 'Don't turn your back on me, you silly cow.'

'Ow! Let me go, you bitch!'

'Who are you calling a bitch?' Jess cried. 'Look, I can make your life very uncomfortable if you don't play ball. So you're either with me or you're not.'

Becky grimaced. This was getting worse. All she wanted to do was lay low for a while until she could move on to somewhere better, away from this dump.

'I think you and me need to get to know each other better,' Jess went on. 'We *will* go out tonight and have some fun. Be ready for eight and I'll introduce you to some people.'

'I don't want to go out.'

Jess shrugged a shoulder. 'I'm not really bothered what you want to do.'

'But I –' Becky lowered her eyes as Jess glared at her again.

'I'll knock on your door when I'm ready.'

After she'd heard Jess run down the stairs, followed by the slam of the front door, Becky fell back on the bed and let her tears fall.

How the hell was she going to get out of this one? She couldn't say she was ill because Jess would come into her room and see that she was lying and if she stayed downstairs with Cath, then she would be in trouble when Jess caught her alone again.

There was only one thing to do. She would have to play the game. Be ready for eight o'clock and see where Jess took her. Maybe it would be fun.

Becky cried even harder then. Who was she trying to kid? This was her life now, her nightmare. She would have to toughen up or be eaten alive. She only had herself to rely on.

But that was the thing that scared her. She wasn't sure that she *could* rely on herself. Look at the mess she'd landed herself in: sixteen years old, pregnant and wanted for murder. If Cath found out, she'd send her packing and what would happen to her then?

Cath was in the back garden pegging out a load of washing. She jumped at the sound of the side gate slamming shut. When she looked around, Liz was leaning against it. She watched as she slid down to the floor before going to her quickly.

'Liz, whatever's the matter?'

Tears welled in Liz's eyes as she fought to catch her breath. 'My husband was waiting for me at Chloe's school. I thought he was on the early shift today. At first he was all nice, like come home, love, we can sort things out.' A sob escaped her. 'But when I said no, he started shouting. He said – he said –'

'Did he hurt you?'

Liz shook her head. 'I was waiting for Chloe to go into her classroom before I went to see the headmistress, to explain what had happened and see if I could collect her earlier for a few afternoons. I was hoping to settle her a little bit before I had to deal with him.'

Cath gently manoeuvred her to a bench at the side of the garden. 'How did you get away?'

'One of the teachers came out to lock the gates. She took me inside but I could see a blue Ford Focus and I knew it was Kevin's car. It was still there twenty minutes later. That's when the secretary gave me a lift home. I had to duck down in the back seat so he couldn't see me. What am I going to do?'

'You'll have to face him some time.' Cath wasn't one to jazz up the future. 'Do you think he'll be there this afternoon?'

'I'm not sure – most probably, if he hasn't gone to work. I'm picking Chloe up half an hour early. But I'm scared that he'll follow me here.'

'Don't you worry about that. I've dealt with far worse than him on my doorstep, on numerous occasions. That's why I'm linked up to a twenty-four-hour alarm system. If I have any type of trouble, the police will respond as soon as possible.'

'What if they don't come quick enough?'

'They've never let me down so far.'

'But they might. They're always going on about it on the television. Most of the time they're too late. And if he follows me here, where will I go then? I don't want to spend my life on the run from him, always having to look over my shoulder.'

Past experience told Cath that Kevin would probably arrive on her doorstep if not today, then over the next few days. It was usually during the first week. Apart from one man who'd held a knife against her throat until she'd told him where his wife was, she'd never had cause to worry. The men were only interested in getting their women away to hurt them again. They didn't want to deal with her, just find a way past her. But still, she'd stand her ground as always.

'He hit you, didn't he?' she asked.

Liz nodded, tears welling again.

'Often?'

Another nod.

Cath took Liz's hand and gave it a quick squeeze. 'You did the right thing to leave him. Did Chloe ever witness it?'

'No, we kept it from her.'

Cath studied Liz's face as she looked away. Liz had clear skin but prominent dark rings around each eye. Her brown hair, to her shoulders in length, was tied back off her face with a red band. She wore no make-up. Cath wondered when she'd stopped making the most of herself and whether it was her choice or Kevin's.

'Try not to worry,' she said. 'I've had men turning up on my doorstep since I started this game but they don't hang around forever. Most of the time they like the chase. You just need to learn to stick up for yourself.' Cath held up a hand as Liz began to protest. 'I know, I know. It's easy for me to say that but the quicker you do, the more he'll lose interest, once the power of the relationship has shifted. They always do.'

Liz glanced around the garden as if Kevin was going to jump out on her at any minute.

'You will get over things and move on,' Cath told her knowingly. 'I've seen lots of women who have made more of their lives. Obviously it hasn't always worked out but most of the time it has.'

'I don't know what I would have done without being able to stay here. You've probably saved my life.'

'Get off with you. There's no need to be so dramatic.'

'You think I'm joking?' Liz shook her head. 'One day he's Dr Jekyll: the next Mr Hyde. It always won me over, made me think that I could answer back, maybe reason with him and be a person with an opinion. He'd use it to lure me into a false sense of security, even though I knew what he was capable of after the sweet-talking had finished. It still scares me to think what might have happened if I hadn't left him.'

'There must have been someone you could confide in?' said Cath.

'I had a few acquaintances when I was at school and when I worked at the post office for a few months but when I hooked up with Kevin, I didn't see them much more after that.'

'Don't you have any close family?'

Liz scoffed. 'When my sister was born six years after me, it was like I didn't exist. She was the pretty one: I was always the clever one. She's always been the favourite. The year after I had Chloe, my parents moved to Devon. A year later, my sister and her family moved there too and I haven't seen them since.'

'That's such a shame,' said Cath.

'Don't get me wrong, I find out everything that my sister does in my mother's emails,' Liz explained. 'Mum can't wait to gloat. And she rings me every few months, though I think out of duty. She mostly goes on about how well Shauna's doing and how she goes out with *her* family all the time. She doesn't realise how hurtful it is. Last year, my parents even came to stay with friends in Congleton but they didn't call to see us.'

'Do you think it was because of Kevin?'

Liz shook her head. 'I know they never wanted me to marry him. They made it perfectly clear how much of a mistake I was making. But it isn't that. I'm just not the favourite daughter. It's really that simple.'

'It does explain why you stayed with Kevin for so long though. You might want to think about going to some of the courses run at the community house,' she said when Liz looked her way again moments later. 'I help out there too, with Josie Mellor. She's a fabulous housing officer; she has such a way of bringing out the best in people. I'm sure there's a lot more she can do for -'

'Why do you do this?' Liz interrupted her. 'It can't be an easy job, looking after waifs and strays with all the problems that we bring with us.'

Cath smiled. 'I have my reasons.'

'You could have got a job doing anything.'

'Around here?' Cath shook her head. 'Besides, I enjoy this, most of the time. The training was tough, and the money I get from social services doesn't run to much but at least I get a different challenge every day.'

'Some days are more challenging than others, no doubt,' Liz attempted a smile.

'And I get to work from home. I save a fortune in petrol. And, without any shops nearby to tempt me, I don't spend much money. It works out quite well.'

'But don't you ever get lonely? You're too young to be on your own.'

Cath laughed then. 'Who would have me, with a house full of hormonal women?'

That afternoon Cath had joined Liz as she collected Chloe from school. As they walked along Christopher Avenue on their way back, Liz was barely listening to her daughter as she chatted away. She was trying to swivel her head 360 degrees to look for Kevin. So far, thankfully, she hadn't seen him. Maybe he'd changed his shift to catch her this morning and was at work now.

'Cath, are you going to fetch me from school every day?' Chloe asked as she skipped into the garden holding on to her hand.

'Oh, I don't think so, sweetheart,' Cath replied. 'I wouldn't have time but I thought I'd make a special effort today. And I've bought you a cake, with lots of strawberry jam and pink icing.'

'Why? It isn't my birthday until next year now. I'll be nine in March. Mum says I can have my ears pierced when I'm nine.'

'I said you *might* be able to have your ears pierced, Chloe,' snapped Liz.

'Emily Baker had hers done last summer. She's in my class.' Chloe turned to her mum excitedly. 'Mum, Mum, can Emily come for tea at Cath's? Can she, please?'

'I don't think –'

'Of course she can come,' Cath told Chloe, smiling at Liz. 'You should treat my home like your own. Everyone's welcome, as long as I know in advance.'

A minute after they had all gone inside the house, a blue Ford Focus drove past slowly before speeding away.

5

*L*ater that evening, Becky agonised over what to wear as she rummaged through the bag of clothes she'd been given. She finally picked out a long-sleeved T-shirt with a red love heart emblazoned on the front and a pair of faded jeans that were a bit too long. She wore her own trainers; they were scruffy but what did she care? She didn't want to go out anyway.

A few minutes before eight o'clock, Jess came into her room. In contrast to Becky she wore skinny jeans, black heels and a fashionable lemon short-sleeved shirt with a white vest underneath. Her hair was spiked to perfection, make-up a little too brash.

She took one look at Becky and gasped. 'Jeez, you look like a ten-year-old.' She left as quickly as she'd arrived, returning moments later with a red top. 'Put that on. You've got to look presentable if you're coming out with me.'

Jess's stare eventually wore Becky down. The top had short sleeves, with a low, sweetheart neckline, and a black skull-and-crossbones emblem sewn on beneath it. Becky reckoned it looked like a designer brand but it could well be off a market stall for all she knew about labels.

Jess looked her up and down, frowning when she spotted her footwear. 'What size shoes do you take?'

'Five.'

Jess ran to her room again and came back with a pair of black high heels. 'Here. I can't be seen with you wearing those manky trainers. It would ruin my street cred.' She opened the window and took her own shoes off. 'Climb down onto the porch roof. Then use the sill on the window and jump onto the lawn. It's easy. I've done it loads of times.'

Jess disappeared and Becky stuck her head out of the window. Seconds later she saw her on the grass, beckoning her down. Becky took off her shoes, knowing that she would likely fall in them. She climbed out and joined Jess, put her shoes on again and sneaked over the back fence into the alley behind.

As they reached the main road, Becky glanced around taking in her new surroundings. Davy Road had the same style properties they'd left behind in Christopher Avenue. A row of identical semi-detached houses, parked cars squashed into every available space along the pavements on each side. Some of the gardens were tidy, some unkempt. For the most part, the properties looked spotless, and then, every now and again, a doss-hole would reveal itself, mostly hidden behind overgrown hedges, piles of rubbish along the path, yellow netting – or closed curtains that were too small for the window.

'Where are we going?' she asked, biting the skin at the side of her thumbnail.

'You and me are going to get lashed,' said Jess. 'We'll have to go to Shop&Save first to get some vodka.'

'I haven't got any money. Have you?'

'We don't need money, do we?'

Becky turned to her quickly, understanding her meaning. 'I can't steal anything. I nearly got caught when I first got here.'

'You'll be okay. Anyway, it's your test to join the gang.'

'What gang?'

'Our gang – you and me.'

Even though the spring night wasn't too cold, Becky shivered. 'I'll do time if the police catch me.'

'Don't give me that tall tale again. The police are no more looking for you than my parents are looking for me and they only live around the corner.' Jess grabbed her arm and kept a firm hold. 'Come on, it'll be a laugh.'

Minutes later, Becky stood in front of the alcohol shelves inside Shop&Save. Most of the expensive liquor was behind the till, and out of their reach, but there were a few cheaper bottles nearer to them.

Jess walked up and down the aisle, pretending to look for something while covertly watching the woman assistant. As the woman reached behind her for a packet of cigarettes, she whispered. 'Now!'

Becky grabbed a bottle of vodka and shoved it under her top. She held it in place with her arm by her side and moved away quickly. Her heart was beating fit to burst as she walked out of the shop and across the car park, faster and faster, not looking back until she'd crossed over Davy Road again.

Jess joined her a minute later. 'Hey, good work!' She took the bottle and swigged a huge mouthful, then passed it to Becky.

Becky did the same but coughed at the burning sensation in her throat.

Jess's eyes narrowed as she wiped her mouth. 'Don't tell me you've never drunk vodka before.'

'Of course I have,' Becky lied. Apart from cans of lager, there had never been any alcohol in her house. Her dad was always at the pub so there was no need to buy anything stronger. Trying to hide her naivety, she knocked back another large amount. 'What shall we do now?' she asked.

Jess checked her watch. 'We're meeting Danny Bradley in fifteen minutes. I said I'd be here about nine. He's coming to pick me up.'

'Is he your boyfriend?'

'I wish.' Jess urged Becky to drink some more vodka. 'He's not interested in me. I'm too young. He says he likes his ladies to be more experienced. I told him I'd had practice but he meant skills that come with age, I suppose. I'll keep on trying, though. He's gorgeous. You can see for yourself soon.'

'Does he have any friends?'

Jess laughed. 'None that would be interested in a virgin like you.'

'I'm not a virgin.' Becky replied, but then stopped. What did she care if Jess didn't believe her?

Both girls turned as a car came screeching to a halt inches from the kerb at the side of them. An electric window dropped down. Jess moved forwards and Becky followed, intrigued to see who had captured Jess's heart.

'Hey, Danny.' Jess pushed her chest out as she leaned on the car door. 'Feel like a good time tonight?'

'I might do. What're you drinking?'

'Vodka.' Jess threw a thumb over her shoulder. 'The new girl lifted it. Want some?'

'I've got my own stash.' Danny flapped his fingers. 'Move out of the way and let me have a look at her then.'

Jess pulled Becky nearer. Becky practically fell through the window with the force.

There were two men in the car. The passenger was about eighteen, with a skinhead and a bad case of acne, which was just as well because Becky couldn't take her eyes off the driver. His hair was cut short and he sported designer stubble. His skin was olive, his eyes as black as the mood he was trying to portray. But then he smiled, and Becky noticed that one of his front teeth was chipped. She felt her cheeks burning as he stared at her.

Suddenly, she was pushed aside.

Jess ran a hand across the paintwork of the car. 'Nice motor you've thieved.' She leaned further forwards this time. 'Where're you off to?'

'Around.' Danny revved the engine. 'Are you getting in or not?'

Jess opened the back door and slid along the seat. Becky followed suit but Danny turned, his hand on the back of the seat in front.

'Not you, lovely one. You can sit in the front with me. Parksy, shift your arse into the back.'

*C*ath switched on the kettle and checked her watch again. It was twenty minutes past eleven. She'd swing for Jess when she finally came home.

Why hadn't she thought to look in on Becky earlier? She'd knocked twice before half past nine, with no reply either time before going in on the third. Finding the room empty, Cath had been on tenterhooks since. She'd texted Jess straightaway but hadn't had any reply. She made a mental note to buy a pay-as-you-go phone for Becky.

Where would Jess take Becky? And would she keep her out all night? She wouldn't put it past Jess to try and get Becky into trouble straight away.

And why had they sneaked out in the first instance? Yes, she would have lectured them if they had gone out the front way but she wouldn't have stopped them. Despite what had been thrown at her over the past three years, as well as being paid to look after the girls, she was no one's keeper. There were only certain things she could get them to do.

Aware that she wasn't going to settle until she knew they were home safe and sound, she parted the curtains and stared out onto the street.

Cath hadn't really known her mother, Carole. Even before her father had left when she was six, Cath had learned to fend for herself. School was only two streets away, no main roads to negotiate, so she was capable of making the short journey alone. She made jam sandwiches for her lunch, soup for tea, then oven chips and fish fingers as she grew older.

Her clothes were always shabby, always worn that extra day before they were washed. Socks were grey, shoes were scuffed and she was teased for it at school. Reeking Riley she was called by the kids in her year. By the time she was ten, she was known as the quiet one without any friends.

As the years went on, Carole turned to drink to blot out her non-existent life and her daughter turned into herself to block out hers. Cath managed to look after herself. It became routine to get up early, clean the house, leave her mother in bed while she went to school.

Afterwards, she would wash and iron and cook tea before starting on her homework. If Carole was home for her return, she'd more than likely be sleeping off a hangover before going out again.

After a third spell in hospital, Carole's liver failed. Cath was sixteen when her mother took her last breath. The housing association claimed their house back and moved her into a block set up for homeless teenagers on the Mitchell Estate. The rooms were filled with girls, two in each. A woman in the flat downstairs was meant to look out for them. She was a type of warden, if Cath remembered rightly, but she didn't do a very good job of things. Luckily, it was here that she met Tina Unwin.

Tina told Cath she was only intending on staying for a few weeks until she got her life sorted. But five months later, she'd still been there. Cath settled in too and they became good friends, which she really enjoyed. It was nice to have someone to laugh with, cry with, come home to and care for even.

Yet in some ways, they were the worst months of Cath's life. It could be quite rowdy at the block. She learned to fight to defend her few possessions. There was a huge turnover of tenants so there were always ructions as another girl moved in and tried her luck in becoming top of the pile.

She'd been there for six months when she met Rich. He was nineteen and one of the Mitchell Estate's notorious scallies. He was known for getting his own way. He would fight for it, steal for it. Some people said he would kill for it, but Cath had never seen that in him.

Three months later, when Tina decided to try her luck with a guy she'd met in Preston, Cath moved in with Rich and life had been good for a few months – until he'd been sent to prison for three years for robbery. She was evicted from his place and went off the rails but they'd still kept in touch.

When he came out of prison after serving just over two years of his sentence, they hooked up again and married a year later. If it weren't for that one stupid mistake she'd made while Rich was inside, life until he died would have been more than she had deserved.

Cath sighed loudly and glanced up the street again but there was nothing. Where were they?

6

Becky held on to Jess for dear life as she negotiated her way along Christopher Avenue. It was half past eleven and she knew she was in for it from Cath when they finally got home.

'Watch out, you stupid cow!' Jess said for the umpteenth time as Becky fell forwards, taking her along too. Jess fell to the pavement, grazing her knee on the kerb. 'Ow! Anyone would think you've never had a drink before.'

'I can't go any further,' Becky slurred. 'I don't feel very well.'

'No more puke.' Jess took a step away. 'I'm never going to look Danny Bradley in the eye EVER again. You made a right mess of the car. It's a good job he dumped it.' She laughed. 'I bet the owner wouldn't want it back. Do you think they'll catch you because of your DNA in the spew?'

Becky threw up again. Then she began to cry.

'Jeez,' Jess moaned. 'I can't believe you have anything left in you.'

A window opened across the road. 'Will you two shut your mouths and get off home? Some of us are trying to sleep!'

Jess turned and raised her middle finger. 'Wind your neck in, Archie Meredith,' she shouted. 'Weren't you ever young, free and single? Why don't you get a life?'

'Why don't you get a job, you scrounging cow? I work a ten-hour shift to pay for the likes of you to lie in bed all day and get pissed every night.'

'Ooh, chill out fat bastard and cop a load of this.' Jess pulled up her top and flashed her bra. 'There you go. Think of me while you get yourself off.'

'Jess!' Cath spoke quietly as she walked up to them. 'That's enough!' She placed a hand on Becky's back. 'Where the hell have you two been?'

'Don't... feel... very well,' Becky managed to slur. 'My head's spinning.'

'She's such a lightweight,' said Jess. 'I wish I'd never bothered with her.'

'You shouldn't have taken her out at all,' Cath hissed.

'She's making all the noise, not me,' Jess shouted.

'Move them on, Cath, or I'll ring the association tomorrow,' a voice yelled across again.

'I'm doing my best, Archie,' Cath replied. 'Go in and I'll deal with them.'

'Yeah,' shouted Jess. 'Run along to wifey.'

'Enough, Jess! Get in the house, right now!'

'Okay, I'm going.' Jess staggered a few steps further. 'You can bring cheap-date along. It's pathetic that she can't take her ale. She's sixteen.'

'And you're seventeen. Neither of you should be drinking yet.' Cath pulled Becky to her feet. 'Let's get you home.'

'I can't,' Becky sobbed, dropping to the floor again.

'Yes, you can.'

'No, I...'

Cath pulled on Becky's arm. 'You'll have to help me, Jess,' she said.

'Who do you think I am?' Jess marched off as quickly as she could. 'I'm not her babysitter.'

Cath finally got Becky into the house, closing the front door behind them with a sigh. She guided her up the stairs and into her bedroom, all the time wondering if she would get a phone call or a letter from the housing association. She hadn't had either for a while so it was bound to happen soon. Not all of the residents in Christopher Avenue were thrilled about Cath helping out young girls in trouble.

She pushed open the bedroom door and Becky collapsed on top of her bed. Cath took off her shoes, pulled the duvet from underneath her and covered her up. She ran a hand over Becky's forehead. The poor child was white, her lips dry. Mascara ran in lines down her cheeks; red lipstick smeared around her mouth.

She watched her for a few moments before heading back out of the room. One thing was certain: she'd be having words with both of them in the morning.

She'd reached the door when Becky screamed.

'Don't leave me! I feel sick again.'

'You'll be fine once you've slept it off.'

'No... I...' Becky sat upright, a look of horror contorting her face. 'My baby! I've killed my baby!'

Cath closed her eyes for a moment. Did she say – oh no. Please, not that.

'Lie down,' she told her, 'and get some sleep.'

'But my baby! What have I done to my baby?'

*C*ath had just drifted off to sleep when she was awoken by a loud noise. She flicked on the light as someone banged on the front door.

'Liz!' Another bang. 'Liz! Get out here now.'

Cath flung her bedroom window open and peered down. 'Will you be quiet?' she cried. 'It's Kevin, isn't it?'

'So what if it is?'

'She doesn't want to see you.'

'I want to hear that from her.' Kevin peered up. 'And who the hell are you? Where's my daughter? CHLOE!'

'Be quiet!' From her position up high, Cath could see exactly how Kevin McIntyre could intimidate his wife. He was tall, broad and, in his drunken rage, neither attractive nor unsightly, just plain old nasty.

'I don't give a fuck if I wake up the whole universe! Liz! LIZ!'

'Will you lot ever shut UP!' The window opened across the street again. 'It's two a.m. and I've got to be up at five thirty. At this rate, it won't be worth going back to sleep.'

'Mind your own business, you nosy bastard.' Kevin yelled across to Archie Meredith. 'I'm staying here until I see my wife. LIZ!'

'I'm warning you, Cath. I'll be on the phone tomorrow. I'm sick of this every bloody night.'

'Look, Archie. I –'

'Piss off, you wanker.' Kevin shouted and then turned back to Cath. 'Tell her to come down or I'll kick the door in.'

'Come back in the morning when it's light and you're sober.'

Kevin shook his head and yelled. 'LIZ!'

'I'll have to go down to him. He won't stop shouting until I do.'

Cath turned to see Liz standing in her pyjamas, a cardigan clutched tightly around her middle.

'He's really drunk at the moment. Maybe you'd be better speaking to him tomorrow, when he's calmed down.'

'He knows where I am now.' Liz shook her head, close to tears. 'He won't give up until he's seen me. And I don't want him to upset Chloe. She's still asleep but she won't be if he carries on.'

Cath threw on her dressing gown. 'I'm coming down with you but you're not to open the door.'

'But –'

'You know full well what he's capable of. Don't give him the chance.'

'If I don't see him now, he'll come back again and again. Then where will I go?'

'I've said that you can stay here for as long as you want. I've dealt with his kind before and –'

Kevin shouted through the letterbox, making them both jump. 'I know you're in there. I just want to talk.'

Liz flew down the stairs and ran to the front door. She yanked across the bolt and opened it the inch the chain allowed. 'Leave us alone!' she shouted through the gap.

'Liz!' Cath followed quickly behind.

Kevin kicked at the door and it shot out of Liz's hands. He grabbed her by the throat and slammed her up against the wall.

'You fucking bitch,' he seethed. 'You can't leave me.'

Liz put her hands over his, trying to loosen his grip. 'Stop!'

'Let her go.' Cath grabbed the hockey stick that she kept behind the door and whacked it across the back of his knees.

Kevin cried out as his legs buckled and he sank to the floor.

Liz gasped for air as he let her go.

Cath stood with the stick poised to strike again. 'Thought you'd like a taste of your own medicine. It hurts, doesn't it?'

Kevin stepped towards her but she stood her ground.

'Come any nearer and I'll use it again,' she warned. 'You can't control me like you've controlled her.'

Kevin rushed towards Cath and she swung the stick again, this time cracking him on his shoulder.

'Are you going or am I calling the police?' She stood poised to strike again.

Kevin glared at her. 'I'm going,' he said, rubbing at his shoulder. 'But I'm warning *you*,' he pointed at Liz, 'I'll be back and when I am, I'm not leaving without you or my daughter. You have no right to take her from me.'

'I have every right!' Liz screamed. 'I won't let you see her.'

'You can't watch me every minute of the day.' Kevin grabbed Liz's arm.

'Mummy!'

Chloe was sitting on the landing, her arms wrapped around her knees. Tears poured down her face.

Kevin smiled. 'Chloe! Come down here and give your daddy a kiss.'

Chloe shook her head fervently.

Liz pushed past Kevin and ran up the stairs. 'Please leave us alone,' she said as she took Chloe into her arms. 'Look at what you're doing to her. She's so traumatised by what's happened that she's having nightmares.'

Kevin raised his arms in exasperation. 'I'll go,' he said. 'But I will be back. You can count on that.'

'I wouldn't count on anything if I were you.' Cath held open the front door. 'Time to leave, I think.'

Twenty minutes later, after checking again on Becky, Cath lay in her bed, wondering if that would be the last time she'd have to get up tonight. What a week, and it wasn't over yet.

Thank goodness it was Thursday tomorrow. There was nothing more grounding than a visit to the cemetery. Maybe she should take Jess and Becky with her. If they continued to behave as they had done tonight, either one of them could be joining her husband six feet under.

She switched off the bedside lamp and lay awake in the darkness, relishing the silence. The room was lit by a pale glow from the lamppost outside the bedroom window. It gave everything an eerie glow but she didn't care. All she wanted to do was sleep.

7

Despite the nocturnal goings-on, Cath was still up at six thirty the following morning. She frowned when she spotted an envelope on the mat. It was too early for their usual postman to have completed his round.

The envelope was blank. Inside, a handwritten note on white paper, the kind found in any newsagents or stationery shop. The message was clear and simple, written in capital letters.

'I AM WATCHING YOU'

Cath sighed. She wondered how long it would take Liz's husband to give up. Already, she had a gut feeling that this was going to be a long drawn-out affair. She decided to hide the note for now. It wouldn't be wise to let Liz see it yet. She'd been through enough last night. In the kitchen, she took out her diary, lodged the note inside and pushed it to the back of the drawer.

A while later, when she heard sounds of someone awake upstairs, Cath left for the cemetery. She wanted to be alone with her thoughts before drowning in everyone else's, once their days started and they unburdened their problems on to her.

But the quiet roads gave her more time to think about the night before. She couldn't stop seeing the angry snarl on Kevin's face as he had his hands around Liz's neck. Equally, she couldn't rid herself of Liz's sheer look of terror.

Finally, she arrived at the cemetery and parked up. Emerging into the sun, she breathed in the unmistakable smell of freshly cut grass. It had become customary for her to count the rows as she walked slowly along the pathway, turning right at number seven. Rich had been laid to rest in the sixth grave along.

'It's another lovely day, Rich,' she spoke aloud with no awkwardness. 'We're having quite a run of them for April.' She dropped to her knees in front of the gravestone, cleared away last week's flowers from the base, rinsed out the steel water holder and carefully arranged the fresh blooms in their place, all the time chattering on.

'We've got a really lively bunch in the house right now,' she added. 'I'm beginning to feel nearer to sixty years of age than forty – won't I get a roasting at my next one-to-one case study meeting with social services.

Still, I must admit I was feeling low when Cheryl Morton got sent down – you remember the last girl who stayed, she got six months – but now it seems I might have bitten off more than I can chew. Becky – she's one of the new girls - is barely sixteen and she told me last night that she's pregnant. If that's true, it means appointments with doctors and trips to the hospital. I'll be lumped with all that, I bet. Not that I mind for now, as Josie will have to find her somewhere suitable to stay.

'Then there's Liz. She has a daughter Chloe, who's only eight. She's such a quiet little girl. Her father has been handy with his fists. I don't know all of the details – I don't want to know them really – but I have to be there to listen if needs be, don't I? And sometimes that means asking awkward questions, but I suspect he's been hitting Liz for a long time, the bastard.' She paused for a moment before grinning. 'I gave him a good seeing to last night. No one messes with Cath Mason, do they?'

Her thoughts out in the open, Cath kneeled for a while in the peaceful surroundings. A couple with a baby in a pram walked past and she smiled at them. How she wished she were still part of a couple.

As the light wind played around with her hair, it almost seemed as if Rich was standing right beside her. She often felt that way. Sometimes she even turned her head expecting him to be there; expecting him to reach out and place a hand on her shoulder. She wished she could talk to him one more time, so he could tell her that everything was all right – that what she'd done was only to protect him. Only Rich could put her mind at ease. After all, there were no secrets between them now.

Half an hour later, she stood up. Raising her hand to her lips, she kissed her fingertips and gently touched the top of his headstone.

'I'd better be getting back to see what those girls have to say for themselves about last night's escapades. Wish me luck. I have a feeling I'm going to need it.'

. . .

It was half past ten when Becky showed her face later that morning. Cath and Liz were sitting at the kitchen table and she sat down across from them. After some thought, Cath had decided not to be too heavy on her. It had been her first night after all and she knew Becky was only partly to blame.

'You look a little green,' she said. 'Are you okay?'

Becky nodded. 'Sorry.'

'You should have told me you were going out.'

'I forgot.'

'And have you forgotten now that you had a drink? And that I had to put you to bed because you could barely stand up?'

'I told Jess that I'd drunk vodka before and I hadn't.' Becky began to pick at the raffia placemat on the table. 'It wasn't her fault.'

Cath raised her eyebrows. 'How long did it take you to think of that when you woke up this morning? I know Jess put you up to it. The one thing I can't fathom out is *why* you did it. You have a tongue in your head. You should have told her to back off if you didn't want to go out. Or you should have come to me.'

Except for the sound coming from the small television over on the far wall, the room descended into an awkward silence. Liz pointed at it as the news came on.

'I knew he was guilty,' she said. 'He has the look of a serial killer. I'd love to get my hands on him. What he did to those –'

Becky burst into tears.

'What's the matter?' Cath tried again to get her to talk. 'There's obviously something troubling you and the sooner you get it out in the open the better, don't you think?'

'You mean the baby?' said Becky.

'Baby?' Liz paled. 'You're pregnant?'

'Is that what I told you last night?' Becky looked at Cath.

'Was there something else that you might have meant?'

Becky gulped. 'I... I –'

'Whatever is going on inside that screwed up head of yours, you shouldn't be drinking if you're pregnant!' Liz raised her voice. 'How irresponsible can you be? Do you know the damage that you could cause to an –'

'That's enough, Liz,' Cath tried to calm her, slightly alarmed at her outburst.

'No, it isn't! You might have to be soft with her but I don't. I can't believe –'

'I said that's enough! If you can't find anything constructive to say, then I think you should leave and let me speak to Becky in private.'

Liz left the room without another word.

Once she'd gone, they sat in silence.

Somewhere to Hide

Becky's tears stopped but she still looked scared about something. And if Cath's instinct was right, it was more than just the baby.

'Do you want to tell me about it yet?' she coaxed her gently a few minutes later.

'About the baby?'

'About anything really.'

'I think I'm three months gone.'

'And does the father know?'

Becky shook her head.

'Are you going to tell him?'

Becky shook her head again.

'Is that why you ran away?' As Becky went to shake her head for the third time, Cath intervened. 'This needs to be a two-way conversation. You can't keep hiding behind the fact that I don't know anything about your background. You have to trust me or there's nothing I can do for you.'

Another silence.

'The housing association will find you a placement soon because you can't stay here. Are you sure you're pregnant? Have you had a test done?'

Becky shrugged. 'I peed on one of those sticks. There were two blue lines.'

'I'll get you tested again, to make certain. But you have to let me know what's happened to you or else I won't be able to fight your corner.'

'I don't know who the father is,' Becky said at last.

'You don't know because you've been sleeping around or you don't know because you're afraid to tell me who it is?'

'I don't sleep around.'

Another silence.

'So was it only the once?'

'No.'

'Was it someone that you know from school?'

Becky shook her head.

Cath could feel her frustration building up - why wouldn't she tell her? Then a hideous thought struck her.

'Becky, someone didn't force you to have sex, did they? I know some boys can be frisky but you have a right to say no. And if you did say no and he continued, then that's a different matter entirely.'

'Cath,' Becky leaned forwards, 'will you promise to keep it to yourself if I tell you a secret?'

'That secret had better not be about me,' Jess said as she barged into the room. She reached for a mug before turning back to Becky with a look that said, 'just you dare say anything'.

41

'Can you leave us for a few minutes?' Cath asked. 'We're having a private conversation. It won't take us long to finish.'

'I'm entitled to get a cup of coffee. And besides, I had a good long chat with Becky last night. I know her secret too, don't I?'

'You do?' Cath frowned, knowing that this could be dangerous.

'Yeah. So anything that's being said can be in front of me, can't it?'

'I'm never going to drink again,' Becky spoke quietly.

'Which brings me to my next question,' said Cath. 'If you did know Becky's secret, I'm appalled at you, Jess, for letting her get into that state. And why did you sneak out last night? I specifically told you to leave Becky alone but you couldn't resist, could you?'

'It wasn't my fault. Did she say it was?'

'Actually, she didn't. But I'm not stupid. I told you the other day to watch yourself or else.'

'You're worse than my mother at times.' Jess banged down her mug.

'Where did you get the money for alcohol?' Cath added. 'I didn't know that you had any.'

'I'm sorry, all right! I messed up. I shouldn't have taken Becky out with me, but believe me, it won't happen again. I can't stand snitches.'

'I didn't snitch!' said Becky.

'You must have. She knows far too much.' Jess began to walk away.

'Sit down, Jess,' said Cath.

'No, I'm not staying for another bloody table meeting.'

'I said sit down!'

Jess dropped heavily into the seat and folded her arms.

'You are not going to take advantage of Becky now that she's come to stay,' Cath said once she had Jess's attention again. 'I have a duty of care towards her, just as much as I do to you and I will not tolerate any late-night escapades, do you hear?'

'Yeah, yeah. I hear you.'

'I mean it, Jess. If Archie Meredith gets on to Josie, I'll be in trouble. So I want you in at eleven for the next two weeks – even weekends.'

'But –'

'No buts. Eleven o'clock or it's back to your mum's. I need Chloe to settle as well as Becky so I can't have you thinking that you can come and go as you please. I have my livelihood to think of too. I don't want any more nights like last night.'

'But we weren't the only ones making a racket,' Jess retorted. 'I heard that man shouting for Liz. He made as much noise as us.'

'I know he did and I can deal with that. But this is about you – both of you. Is that clear?'

Becky nodded straightaway. Cath continued to glare at Jess until she gave in and nodded too.

'Can I go now?' Jess stood up again.

'Yes. And try stopping off at The Academy,' Cath shouted after her. 'At least make an effort to look like you want to do something.' She turned back to Becky. 'Right, where were we? Weren't you about to tell me something?'

'What's The Academy?'

'It's a community college we have on the estate. It might be useful for you to pop in there, if you're sticking around. Aren't you due to take exams soon?'

Becky shrugged her shoulder.

'Shall I look into that for you?'

Another shrug. 'Is it okay if I go back to my room now?'

Cath watched her forlorn figure as she left. She sighed: why wasn't anyone looking for her? Someone should be missing her. Or else they didn't want anyone knowing that she was gone.

Whatever it was, she vowed to get to the bottom of it before too long. Secrets destroyed the soul.

8

Austin Forrester lit a cigarette and took a deep drag of it. He glanced up and down the road again before checking his watch. Twenty to one: Danny Bradley was late. He'd give him another ten minutes before he left.

It had worked out well for him hooking up with Danny. He'd met him at the dole office as he'd registered for benefits. Danny had been mouthing off while they'd both filled in another set of forms. Austin had liked his attitude enough to start a conversation.

Over the past few days, Danny had become his unofficial driver. The more he saw of him, the more he realised that the youth was in awe of him. And why? Because he liked the sound of his background. Danny couldn't work out the peppered truths from within Austin's elaborate lies. It was the one thing he enjoyed about sleeping rough. No matter which town he turned up in, he could be whoever he wanted to be.

A car horn peeped and he looked up to see a clapped-out Vauxhall Astra pulling in to the kerb. Hiding his look of contempt, he climbed into the passenger seat with a yank of a stiff door handle.

'All right, mate?' Danny nodded.

Austin nodded back. 'Surely you haven't nicked this?' Before he got in, he pushed aside empty cigarette cartons, crisp packets and cans of lager so that there was somewhere to put his feet.

Danny patted the steering wheel. 'This heap is all mine. I use it when I can't be arsed to get anything else. And I've lifted a twenty off the old woman so I've filled her up a little. What's the plan for today?'

Austin frowned, annoyed that Danny expected to spend time with him for the honour of being his driver. He swallowed down the words ready to spew out of his mouth. He needed to keep Danny on side, for a little while at least.

'No plan,' he said.

They turned off Alexander Avenue and onto Winston Road. Austin stared at the properties they passed.

'You robbed any of these?' he asked.

Danny changed gear noisily before replying. 'No, don't tend to shit on my own doorstep. I go on to the private estate – far more for the taking there. I do have a fence on here though, Mick Wilkinson. He takes most things from me.'

Austin made a mental note to find out more about Mick Wilkinson. It might be worth his while to get involved with some of the locals while he was here.

Danny sped up as a young girl tottered across the road in front of them, shoes too high and unintentionally making her wiggle provocatively. Austin sniggered causing Danny to check out why.

'Hey, Becky,' Danny shouted to her as he drew level. 'Fancy a ride and I don't mean of the motor?'

Becky stuck two fingers up to him.

Danny laughed. 'What a cracker, and so ripe.'

Austin watched in silence as Becky continued on her way. She didn't look much older than sixteen or so with her blonde hair tied away from her face. When she turned back and saw they were still watching, she pulled up the collar of her scruffy denim jacket to conceal her face.

'I fancy some fun with her,' said Danny. 'She'll most probably be up for it too. She's the new girl at Cath Mason's.'

'Cath Mason's?'

'She takes in all these homeless girls. Great for us single boys. They're always gagging for it. Most of them are already hooked on drugs so we get a fair trade off them as well. And if they aren't hooked, they usually are by the time they leave.'

'Sounds like a shit place to live.'

'I reckon it's okay. Cath Mason's a right looker too. I'd give her one anytime. Her old man copped it a few years back. I've never seen her out with another bloke since so I bet she's gagging for it too.'

'Yeah, she sounds more like my type.' Austin was still following Becky's disappearing form though.

Danny grinned. He papped his horn and waved as Becky looked back before vanishing around the corner out of view. 'She'll do for me. I'll have her by the end of the week.'

As Danny sped off up the road, Austin remained silent. For now he would let

Danny keep Becky warm for him. Then when the timing was right, Becky would be his.

Sitting on her bed, Liz logged on to her email account and sighed when she saw three new messages from Kevin. None of them had a subject heading but each of them had the same content in the body. She flicked onto the first one and scanned it quickly. *You will come back... I need you here with me... you won't stop me from seeing my daughter...*

She flipped down the lid of her laptop. Would he ever get fed up of harassing her? Earlier that morning, she'd been researching domestic violence. This obsession he had with her could go on forever. She couldn't bear the thought of it.

Yet again she wished she'd noticed the signs before she'd married him. What she'd seen as gestures of love and affection were really ways of controlling her, possessing her, making her into his own. From the first day she'd met him, Kevin had been protective. When was it that everything had gone wrong? All she had wanted was to be loved, not controlled. Not bullied, not owned.

As she looked down, she noticed Chloe's pink Barbie notepad tucked under the mattress. She pulled it out and flicked through the pages, smiling at the handwriting of a child who was trying hard to make it look grown up. There were lots of loops and letters joined together to make it more exciting.

But, just as quickly, her smile dropped as she read the words on one particular page:

My dad has found out where me and my mum are living. Cath, that is the lady whose house we are living in. She hit him with a sport stick. I wish my mum had hit my dad with a sport stick. I wish my dad would leave us alone and let mum be happy again. Mum used to smile and laugh. Now Mum is sad. I hear her when she cries at night. She thinks I am asleep but I am not. I think my mum is very brave. Mrs Johnston at school says that mums and dads are splitting up all the time but she didn't say that dads hit mums. Mum does not know I have seen Mum and Dad arguing a lot. Dad shouted at Mum all the time. Mum tried to make Dad happy. I hate my dad. I wish he would leave my mum alone. I wish we could stay at Cath's house forever.

It took Liz a long time to stop crying after she had finished reading. Without a doubt, her daughter's words would haunt her forever. What image of marriage could they have caused her to carry through her life? How could they have let their relationship have such an impact on her? There was no way she could go back to Kevin now. She needed to be strong for Chloe's sake.

She gazed around the bedroom. It had been a week since they'd arrived and despite the lack of space, it had become comfortable to her already. When she had been with Kevin, there was nowhere to hide. Here she could deal with it. As long as he couldn't get his hands on her, maybe she would grow stronger every day. Maybe he would get fed up of hanging around for her. And if he didn't then she would move to somewhere else. Chloe was her future, just as her future plans needed to be for Chloe.

Liz wiped her eyes and prayed that she could follow through with her thoughts. Despite feeling safe, she also knew they'd have to move out soon. Josie Mellor said that she'd find her something as quickly as she could and indeed, she was grateful for that. Chloe needed stability after what had happened recently. That essay certainly said as much. She read the words again before slipping the notebook back into its place. Then she thought about what to do next.

Should she confront Chloe? But Liz had tried to talk to her about things last night and she'd said she was tired and wanted to go to sleep.

She ran her hand through her hair, recalling how secretive she'd been as a child. It might do more harm than good if she were to admit to reading it. She decided not to do anything for now.

And at least she hadn't had to dodge Kevin on her way back from school that morning. She hoped that he'd get tired of hanging around the school gates. And as long as she didn't give him the chance to get her alone, she would be okay. The longer she stayed away, the stronger she would become.

Wouldn't she?

9

It didn't take long before Becky found the courage to venture out again after her first lone visit to Shop&Save went without incident. As she began to explore her new surroundings, it was obvious now, even to her, that she hadn't killed Uncle James as she'd originally thought – or if she had, her father must have buried him in the garden and said nothing, which was even more unlikely. Yet it was really weird that she hadn't heard anything.

She wondered if her dad was still missing her. It had been nearly a month since she'd legged it that night. In the next breath she doubted that very much, but she still liked to think he would. Because, funnily enough, she still missed him. No matter what he did – or didn't do – he would always be her flesh and blood. But then too, so was Uncle James. She shivered. Maybe it was best not to think about either of them.

Becky headed across to the shops. She walked along Davy Road for a few minutes and then over the grass and down the steps, through the middle of two blocks of flats and past the community house out onto Vincent Square. In Shop&Save, she noticed that she didn't know any of the women who were working that shift. By the time she came out, her pockets had a few edible goodies inside them that she hadn't paid for.

'Excuse me, Miss,' a voice said from behind. 'May I check your pockets?'

Becky began to run.

'Hey, wait up, you daft cow! I'm only messing.'

She turned to see Danny Bradley grinning at her. Despite what Jess had said about her making a fool of herself the other night, his eyes lit up as if he was pleased to see her.

'You mad fool.' She pressed a hand to her chest. 'You nearly gave me a heart attack.'

'You should be more careful.' Danny gave her a smile. 'I couldn't take my eyes off you in there. With a face like that, you're not going to go unnoticed. Where's your loopy mate?'

'I haven't seen her this morning.' Becky assumed he was referring to Jess. 'I'm sorry about the other night. I didn't mean to sick up over the seat of your car.'

'That's okay. It wasn't my car anyway, remember? You're not the only one that's good at nicking things. Where are you off to?' Danny took her hand and walked on with her. 'Anywhere exciting?'

'No, not really,' Becky managed to say as she felt the blood rush to her cheeks.

'How about doing nothing with me for a while then?'

'I wouldn't have thought walking was your style.'

'It's not, most of the time. But sometimes I want to do something different. And most of the time, I get to do what I want.' He looked at her pointedly. 'Do you fancy going for a ride somewhere tonight?'

For a second, she wasn't sure what to say.

Jess would kill her.

Cath wouldn't be too impressed either.

She glanced at him, enough to see the flicker of want in his eyes. An idea popped into her head: maybe she could kill two birds with one stone. She smiled shyly and nodded before she could change her mind.

'I feel like I'm starting school again,' Liz told Cath as she followed her up the path towards the community house. 'I'm so nervous.'

'It'll be fine,' Cath soothed as she opened the front door. 'Josie will sort you out. Besides, it's usually quieter in here around lunchtime.'

The community house had originally been two semi-detached properties. Doorways had been knocked through from kitchen to kitchen, giving the house six rooms and two bathrooms upstairs, two kitchen areas and two meeting rooms downstairs. The inner wall between the hallways had been removed making a double staircase with one entrance.

Liz spotted the signs on the wall in front of her: *Kids* with an arrow to the right and *Adults* with an arrow to the left. She could hear the deep base thud of the music in the background as they went through the door on the left.

49

A young man with short, spiked hair and an abundance of tattoos and piercings was sitting behind a desk.

'Hi Justin,' Cath greeted him. 'Is Josie in? She told me she'd be around this morning.'

'She is.' Justin pointed to a table by his side with a drinks machine. 'Help yourself and I'll get her for you.'

Liz sat down on one of two settees pushed back against the wall, a computer terminal at a desk to her right. The room was painted a pale yellow, making it welcoming but not enough to hide scuffmarks here and there, and causing her to wonder how many people came through it every day. Over the fireplace, a noticeboard advertised local college courses, imminent meetings and places to find advice. A radio played low in the background.

A few minutes later, Josie came towards them.

'Hi, Cath.' She smiled as she drew level and held out a hand. 'And Liz! We've finally got you here.'

'Hi.' Liz shook it timidly, unable to stop from shaking.

'There's no need to be nervous about anything while you're here,' she reassured. 'We're one big happy family.'

'Actually, she's right.' Justin joined them again. 'She's like my mother – a slave driver.'

Josie raised her eyebrows. 'I suppose you've met the apple of my eye.'

'Apple of your eye, my arse,' Justin quipped before grabbing a ringing phone.

'I'm off next door to see what's going on.' Cath checked her watch. 'See you back here in half an hour?'

'What can I do for you?' Josie asked Liz after they'd gone upstairs into her office and made themselves comfortable. 'Please tell me you want to attend one of my women in crisis sessions.'

'Is that okay?' Liz asked. 'You don't do them in batches, do you?'

'No, you can join in whenever you like.' Josie took a folder from a drawer in her desk and handed it to Liz. 'I made the course that way purposely. You can also come for one week or one hundred weeks. It's up to you.'

'Will I have to talk about anything in particular?'

'Oh no. Not unless you want to.'

'It's hard sometimes.' Liz looked out of the window for a moment, concentrating on a young mum walking by, dragging her toddler along by the side of another child in a pushchair. 'I'm so embarrassed, having to say all of this,' she added.

Josie sat forwards. 'Please don't be. Once you get to know some of the women here, they'll open up and tell you their stories. The important thing is that you're not the only one that something bad has happened to. And I think it'll do you good to hear that. And to talk to people who've been through it. I'll introduce you to Suzie: she'll tell you her story. It's a heart-breaking tale but Suzie has come out fighting. She's a different woman from the one I met last year.'

Josie paused a minute. 'I'm glad you came at last.' She smiled warmly when Liz didn't speak. 'I knew something was going on, even though you couldn't tell me. I remember the last time when I visited –'

Liz held up a hand for her to stop. Tears welled in her eyes as she recalled the situation Josie was referring to. Josie had been called out from the housing association because someone had complained about the noise again. She and Kevin had been arguing then too. But when he answered the door, Kevin had denied everything being suggested.

Liz heard Josie ask to see her and eventually Kevin called her through. Her face had clear marks where his fingers had pressed into her cheeks. Luckily for her, Josie had known better than to question Kevin there and then.

'I'm sorry,' said Josie. 'I didn't mean to stir up bad memories.'

'I just don't want to be reminded of it,' she explained.

'Then are you sure you're ready to come to the sessions? Sometimes they can be pretty distressing. Very up-lifting as well, but often sad. Will you be able to deal with that?'

'I have to. I need to build up my confidence. I'd like to get a job, something part-time maybe, to work around Chloe's school hours.'

'This will certainly get you on that road to recovery.' Josie smiled encouragingly. 'Is there anything else that you need to know for now?'

'Yes. I'm sure when I move from Cath's that Kevin will find out where I am. And I don't want to move out of the area just yet. So...' Liz glanced down for one split second before sitting upright with assertion. 'How do I go about getting an injunction or a harassment order or whatever?'

*B*ecky stood in front of her tiny wardrobe mirror checking her appearance meticulously. She wore Jess's lipstick. She wore Jess's mascara, Jess's blusher and eyeshadow and she had Jess's black and white top on too. She also still had the shoes that she'd been lent. The only thing she could call her own was her trashy underwear.

She pulled up the top and stared down at the once-white bra, one of the only items of clothing she'd arrived at Cath's with. It certainly wasn't seducing material: she'd have to remember not to take off her top. Either that or she'd have to whip her bra off if Danny did.

Everything had to be just perfect if she was going to have sex with him tonight. If she didn't look her best, she knew he'd swap her for the more experienced Jess in an instant.

Her hands shook as she ran her fingers over her hair again, trying to tame down a few unruly hairs. Had she got enough guts to go through with her plan? It was quite simple really. She would sleep with Danny Bradley and then she would forget everything her uncle had done to her. The memory would be erased. Then maybe she wouldn't feel so cheap.

Hearing a horn peep outside, she ran to the window. She caught sight of Danny pointing to the end of the street as he drove past quickly. Becky opened the window and jumped out onto the roof. Despite the trouble she'd be in with Cath, there was no way she wanted to be seen by Jess. She'd risk a telling off.

10

Cath was in the living room that evening when Liz joined her. She noticed her weary footsteps, her pale skin giving her a sickly flush. In need of a wash, her hair was tied back from her face, almost hidden out of the way.

'Has Chloe gone off yet?' she asked as Liz flopped down beside her on the settee.

'She's in bed but she isn't asleep. I've left her reading a book, although I know she should be settled by now. Where is everyone?'

'Jess is out, probably causing havoc somewhere, and Becky's in her room.' She pointed to an open bottle of red wine. At Liz's nod, she poured her a glass and they sat in companionable silence while *Coronation Street* came to its conclusion.

'Has Chloe said anything about Kevin lately?' Cath opened the conversation again.

Liz sighed long and heavy. 'I've been trying to talk to her tonight about it.'

'And?'

'She says she doesn't want to see him. She says he's a monster.'

'Hmm – she got that right.'

'I miss my home,' said Liz. Then, 'Oh, I didn't–'

Cath raised her hand. 'Don't mind me. I try my best with this place but it can only be a temporary substitute. There's only so much training I can do to help you, too. Home should always be special.'

'Please don't think that I'm ungrateful,' Liz tried to explain. 'I can't thank you enough for taking us in. If you hadn't, I don't know what would have happened.'

'I do. You would have gone back, taken a little bit more and then found another way out. And another until you'd got away again.'

There was silence for a moment.

'He turned into a –' Liz struggled for words to describe Kevin, 'a monster. Chloe was right. It's the perfect description.'

'I bet he didn't want you to go to work either?'

Liz shook her head. 'He said he earned enough for me to stay at home and look after Chloe.'

'So he had control over the money?'

'He gave me enough for the shopping. He paid all the bills though.'

'Did you ever go out?'

'Not as a family. Kevin used to meet up with his friends but I lost touch with all mine.'

Cath nodded. 'He controlled you. That's a form of domestic abuse in itself. Some men get their kicks out of it. It makes them feel superior, taking their inferior thoughts and hiding them away so that no one can mock them for being a coward. Because that's what they all are, cowards.'

Liz took a sip of wine before replying. 'I didn't have any choice. If I let him have his own way, then Chloe was sheltered from it. It worked until a month ago.'

'Were you with anyone before you met him?'

'Not anything long term.'

'That's a pity. If he's the only one you can compare a marriage to, then it's no wonder you stayed with him for so long. Do you think he'll ever leave you alone for good?'

'I doubt it. Though if I'd had the courage to leave sooner, I probably wouldn't be in this mess. I wish there were more places like this. Instead, all battered women get are scummy bed and breakfasts. No wonder women go back to the life they know yet hate.'

'And is that the only reason you would go back?'

'That and the promises he'd make.' Liz looked shamefaced. 'I believed him because I wanted to go home, get Chloe settled again. When Josie said that a hostel might be our only choice, I was halfway out of the door. Then she suggested you might be able to help.'

Cath smiled. 'I'm glad to be of assistance. I've told you before, you and Chloe can stay here for as long as you want. My house is always open to you – although I can't promise there will be a bed for you if you leave. Unfortunately someone else will probably want it.'

Somewhere to Hide

'All the same, it's good to hear. I want to feel safe before I can think about what to do next. The more I keep away from Kevin, the better I'll become. His hold on me will weaken. It will, won't it?'

Cath sighed. 'I hope so. We can try and help you – me and Josie – but you have to do the hardest part of it yourself. Then again, I think you already know that, don't you?'

'I was pregnant,' Liz said, her eyes brimming with tears. 'The last time he hit me. I was pregnant and he knew.'

'Was?'

'I lost it. He took my baby. I can never forgive him for that.'

'Is that why you were so upset about Becky?'

'Yes.' Liz sniffed. 'How can she be so thoughtless when all I wanted was another child?'

'She didn't know you had lost yours.'

'But she talked about it as if it wasn't real. She should–'

'She's just gone sixteen. And don't tell me you haven't noticed she has some sort of secret. I've been trying to get it out of her since she arrived. She won't even talk to her case worker.'

'What do you mean?'

'Something isn't right, but she'll only tell me when she's ready to. Unless... could you try and get it out of her?'

'I doubt she'll confide in me.' Liz shook her head.

'It was just a thought.'

'You'd think she'd want to talk to Jess with them being about the same age.'

'Are you mad? She's more mixed up than Becky ever will be.'

Liz smiled a little but it soon faded. 'I wish I could get through to Chloe. I know she's protective towards me but I don't really know what that's doing to her. She doesn't want to talk about it.'

'Maybe she feels allegiance towards you and doesn't want to speak ill about Kevin. Shall we try a different approach?' Cath offered.

'What do you have in mind?'

'You try and talk to Becky, see what you can find out. And I'll have a chat with Chloe?'

Liz shrugged. 'It's worth a shot, I suppose.'

'Smoke?' Danny reached in the glove compartment for his cigarettes.

'No, ta, not for me,' said Becky.

Danny started the car engine.

55

'Where're we going?' she asked, after they'd been driving along a main road for a few minutes.

'Just along the lanes, by the fields off the estate. We can find a quiet spot. No one will interrupt us there and we can have a bit of fun. That's what you want, isn't it?'

'If that's what you want too,' she replied, trying to sound self-assured.

'Sure. And don't worry, I won't be rough.'

'I'm not bothered.'

'Could have fooled me.' Danny stopped at a junction before turning right. 'By the look on your face, you're shit scared. You're not a virgin, are you?'

'No!'

'Shame. I like a challenge.'

'Well, you're not going to get one.'

Becky tried to look sexy but really, she didn't know how. Instead, she leaned over and placed her hand at the top of his thigh. Danny moved it to his crotch and pressed down hard. He groaned.

'See what you've done to me already?'

Becky pressed her hand down harder. 'Plenty more where that came from,' she said, her nerves hidden behind a faint smile.

As they continued on their way, she prayed she'd find the courage to go through with her plan. If she didn't, she realised she would have a long walk home. Danny Bradley would almost certainly dump her. She couldn't play around with his feelings: she'd heard girls at school being called dick teases.

This was for real now. Danny Bradley was more of a man than a boy. He wouldn't want to be messed around. Hadn't he already told her that he got what he wanted, when he wanted it? Imagine how he'd feel if she told him to stop.

In the midst of her panic, Danny turned down an unused dirt track, switched off the engine and moved towards her. He ran a finger over her lips, her chin, down her chest. It stopped at the seam of her top.

'It's a perfect spot here,' he told her. 'No one will see us, don't worry.'

Becky felt herself relax into their first kisses. Her skin tingled more at his touch. Her mouth responded to his as he probed with his tongue deeper and deeper. Her hands roamed over his clothes, inside his clothes, urging him closer.

But within seconds, she felt the customary terror rise up inside her. She closed her eyes but past images made her open them again. She had to get this over with, rid herself of those ugly memories. With urgency, she reached for Danny's belt and tugged at the buckle.

Danny gently eased away her hand and put it behind his back again. 'No rush, little one,' he said, not taking his eyes from hers. His hand then found its way up the front of her top.

Becky froze.

Danny stopped kissing her. 'What's up?'

'Nothing.' She pulled him near again.

How could she tell him what was flashing through her mind as he touched her skin for the first time? How another one had been there before but hadn't been so gentle?

'Let's go into the back,' Danny whispered moments later.

They climbed over and lay out on the seat. The night was warm, the air in the car was hot with anticipation.

Becky blinked away tears as he pushed into her. She turned away as he thrust, moving quicker and quicker. Then she grabbed hard onto his buttocks, pushing him in deeper and deeper. It hurt, how it hurt. But maybe that would make him come quicker. Still he continued for longer than she could bear.

When he was all but there, she tuned out. And then it was over.

But Becky had seen the look on his face. She'd seen it before, the disgust as she'd allowed someone to use her.

'Didn't you like it?' she whispered, her lower lip trembling.

'Whatever gave you that idea?'

'I saw the look on your face, as you, you know.'

Danny grinned. 'That was my sex face. Maybe I'll see yours one day. You didn't come, did you?'

Becky shook her head, unsure if she had reached her peak or not. How would she know?

'Have you never?'

'Of course I have,' she muttered, pulling down her top.

'Yeah, right.' Danny shoved his hand up her skirt but Becky pushed it away.

'Piss off!'

'Hey, don't get stroppy. I was only asking. Because if you haven't, I could do something else that would *guarantee* that you would.'

Becky had had enough for one night. She felt the wetness between her legs and tried desperately not to gag.

'I thought...'

As Danny touched her lightly on her shoulder, she jumped and inched away from him.

'Whoa.' He threw up his hands in surrender. 'You look really scared. What the hell has happened to you?'

'Nothing.' Becky tried to smile, hoping to throw him off the scent. The less people that knew about her problems, the more she could keep them a secret. 'I got scared, that's all. I did like it.'

Danny reached for his fags. 'Thank Christ for that. I thought my reputation was going to get trashed!'

Later, after she'd said goodnight to Danny, Becky ran upstairs and locked herself in the bathroom. She stripped off quickly and stepped under the shower. In frustration, she began to cry. She felt dirty, trashy, cheap. Scrubbing her skin until it was sore to the touch didn't make her feel any better.

She let the water cascade over her head as she tried not to scream out loud. Why couldn't she have enjoyed sex with Danny? Would she always be haunted by what had happened to her? Always feel disgusted, like she did now, every time someone else touched her? Would she never be able to fall in love because men would repulse her?

Her skin was stinging when she went back to her bedroom. As she changed into pyjamas, she heard a rap at her window. She pulled back the curtain to see Jess standing there.

'Let me in!' Jess whispered loudly.

Becky opened the window wide enough for her to climb through.

'Why didn't you use the front door?' she asked. 'It's not late.'

'Cath will still tell me off, the stupid old fart.' Jess yanked down her denim skirt. 'What's the matter with your face? Have you been crying?'

'No.' Becky wiped at her eyes.

'Where did you get to tonight? I was going to take you out with me. You missed out on some gear. I've had loads to drink and I've had some whizz.'

'Whizz?'

'Billy?'

Becky looked on blankly.

'Phet?' Jess tutted. 'Speed, you dozy moron.'

'Oh.'

'You're so naïve.'

Becky clicked in. That was the reason Jess was being so nice.

'Can you feel the love tonight?' Jess began to sing loudly. 'If you want a feel, I'm you...our...rrrrssss!'

'Be quiet.' Becky pushed Jess towards the door. 'You'll get into trouble, remember. You go to bed and I'll say you were with me last night, until I ran off or something. I'll say you were looking for me.'

Jess grinned at her. 'Would you do that?' she said. 'Aw, you're so sweet.'

'You have to be quiet though,' Becky warned. 'Cath's still up. You don't want to start her off.'

Jess put a finger on her lips. 'I will be oh so quiet,' she whispered loudly. She took another step then turned back. 'Will you be my special friend, Becks? I need a special friend.'

'Yes but go to bed.'

'I would, if I could remember where my room is.' Jess snorted. 'Oh, what am I like?' She sat down on Becky's bed with a thud. 'I can sleep here.'

'No, you can't.'

Becky pulled her to her feet again with so much force that Jess fell, nearly knocking both of them over.

'Watch out!' Instinctively, she put an arm across her stomach. Luckily, Jess kept moving forwards. Becky heard her bedroom door open and bang shut a few moments later, then peace resumed again.

She splayed her hand over her stomach, realisation sinking in. The baby growing inside her meant that she'd be stuck with what that monster had done to her for the rest of her life, and in more ways than one.

'Why did this happen to me?' she sobbed quietly.

11

'Are we going to stay at Cath's for a long time?' Chloe asked her mum as they turned into Christopher Avenue on their way home from school.

'I'm not sure,' said Liz. 'Why?'

'I like it here.'

'Don't you miss your room? And your toys?'

'Toys are for babies, Mum. And I can have new ones when I need them, can't I?'

If only it were that simple, Liz thought. But now that she wanted to include Chloe in more decisions, and she'd had a word with Josie who had boosted her confidence tremendously, at least it gave her the opportunity to discuss another idea she'd mentioned.

'Would you be okay if I went to work? Only part-time, while you were at school?'

'So you can still walk with me?' Chloe began to skip at her side.

'Of course,' said Liz. 'And it means that we might be able to have a treat every now and then. Things are going to be tough now that Dad isn't around.'

Chloe took hold of Liz's hand in her own smaller one. 'We'll be okay, Mum. Just you and me.'

Liz held back tears as they walked the last few metres to Cath's house. With such an old head on young shoulders, she was frightened that Chloe's childhood had gone already.

The footsteps from behind were upon her before she had time to react. A

60

Somewhere to Hide

hand on her shoulder pulled her back with force. Liz barely managed to stay on her feet as she was spun round, coming face to face with Kevin.

'What do – do you want?' she stuttered, her newfound confidence slipping away.

Kevin ignored her. Instead, he smiled and reached down to tweak Chloe's chin. But Chloe moved her head out of the way.

'What's the matter, angel?' he asked. 'You're not scared of your dad, are you?'

'No,' said Chloe sharply. 'And neither is my mum.'

Liz looked down at Chloe. 'Run along to Cath's and I'll be with you in a minute.'

'But I don't want to leave you.' She took her mother's hand again.

Liz gave it a reassuring squeeze. 'I think Cath said she was making cakes to sell at the community house. Maybe you could help her?'

'I'll be back in five minutes if you're not there,' she said, reluctantly walking away.

'What do you want now?' Liz turned to Kevin.

'You know what,' he replied. 'I want you to come home, both of you.'

Liz shook her head. 'I can't. Especially after what happened the other night.'

'That woman is a lunatic.' Kevin rubbed at his shoulder. 'You should see the bruise I have.'

'It's probably similar to the ones you left me with.'

'What did you say?'

'I... I...' Liz pushed her hands deep into the pockets of her coat so that he couldn't see how much they were shaking.

'I told you I was sorry, what more do you want me to do?'

'And that makes it okay, does it? I lost my baby – our baby.'

'We can make another one.'

'It isn't like a Lego building. We can't pick up the pieces as if nothing has happened.'

Kevin faltered. 'I miss you, and Chloe. I promise it won't happen again.'

'You followed me here and tried to strangle me.'

'I was drunk!'

Liz glanced down the road towards Cath's house, hoping that Chloe was safe in the garden. Cath was standing at the gate, looking on. It made her feel so much better. She turned back to Kevin.

'I won't let you hurt me ever again.'

Kevin grabbed her arm. 'Who the hell do you think you are with your threatening tone?' His spittle peppered Liz's cheeks.

'You killed our baby.'

'I DIDN'T KNOW YOU WERE PREGNANT!'

'Would it have made a difference?'

'You always push me too far.' Kevin gripped her arm harder still. 'It's time you stopped messing about. I want you home by tomorrow. If you're not there by the time I get off the late shift, there'll be trouble like you've never known before.'

'Everything all right, Liz?' Cath's voice came from behind as she drew near.

'Mind your own business, you nosy bitch.' Kevin let go of Liz.

Cath ignored him and linked her arm through Liz's. 'Come on.'

'You can't hide forever,' Kevin shouted after them.

Liz could almost feel his eyes burning a hole in the back of her head. She tried not to run as she drew closer to the safety of the gate, all the time struggling to hold back tears. Just being near to him again had brought back all the fear, all the pain, all the control he'd had over her. How could she think she was able to stand up to him?

Becky and Jess were in Jess's bedroom getting ready to go out. Since she'd covered for Jess the other night, they'd spent a bit more time together. Becky knew Jess was using her but she didn't mind so much. She'd rather not be on her own anyway.

'Can I borrow your white T-shirt, the one with the punk woman image on it?' she asked her.

'No, I'm going to wear it.' Jess stopped straightening her hair for a moment. 'I'm going to shag Danny tonight. I've decided to make myself as accessible as possible.'

As Jess turned back to straightening her hair, Becky felt the heat from her cheeks. What would Jess do to her if she found out that she had slept with Danny? She'd probably have no teeth left by the time she'd finished with her.

Yet, even though she couldn't tell her what had happened, Jess might be consoled by the fact that Danny had barely looked at her since the night they'd slept together in his car. Just yesterday, he'd papped his horn and driven past when she'd been going to the shops. She thought he might have come back to ask her out again but she'd watched his car until it had gone from her view.

'I think he treats women like shit anyway,' she told Jess. 'I bet he shags them once and then loses interest. His type usually do.'

Jess laughed. 'He would if it was you he was sleeping with. Whereas me, well, I've got hidden talents. I'll get him one day. And I bet he's sooo worth the wait.'

Becky said nothing as Jess rummaged through a pile of clothes on her bedroom floor. She watched as she sniffed the armpits of a blue T-shirt before throwing it at her.

'Try this one, but spray plenty of perfume on it. It reeks of smoke.'

'I haven't got –'

Jess gave her a bottle of Thierry Mugler's eau de parfum. 'It's Angel. It's my favourite. I think he should bring one out called Urban Angels, don't you reckon? It's a good name for us down and outs.'

'I'm not a down and out,' muttered Becky.

'Of course you are. That's why the likes of Danny Bradley won't have us. We're too common. Not that he'd have you anyway. It's getting more and more obvious that you're up the duff.'

Despite being fed up of all the appointments Cath had dragged her along to since she had told her she was pregnant, Becky had tried to keep on top of things, as well as hide it from others. But Jess was right. As she glanced down at her stomach, she noticed that her jeans were getting tighter. Already, she was having problems fastening the zip. Another week and she'd have to abandon them.

Keeping her pregnancy a secret from others was going to become harder still over the next month. But then, she knew if she could get Danny interested again, he wouldn't be bothered about a bit of weight on her belly. All he'd want is what was between her legs, there for him to take whenever he fancied it. Because she would let him if he wanted to – again and again. One of those times must erase the memories. Surely the more she did it and the more boys she did it with, she would finally replace its power?

A car horn beeped.

'Suppose we'd better go out the front way tonight,' said Jess. 'Come on, or else he'll be on his way without us.'

Giving herself the once over in Jess's wardrobe mirror, Becky turned sideways and ran a hand over her bump. It wasn't too noticeable yet but it wouldn't be long. She pulled down the blue T-shirt just as Jess grabbed her hand.

'Come on!'

'Where are you two off to in such a hurry?' Cath asked as they whooshed past her in the hallway downstairs after hanging up their keys in the kitchen.

Becky stopped in her tracks. 'We're going ...'

'... Out for a walk,' Jess finished off for her.

'Yeah, for a walk.'

'Behave yourselves this time. I don't want any more trouble brought to my doorstep. I've had enough grief off the housing association lately over the noise.'

12

When the girls got to Danny's car, Becky would have been annoyed at his lack of interest if it wasn't for the youth sitting in the passenger seat. Lush was the perfect word to describe him: tanned skin due to the recent spate of warm weather, brown hair and eyes, with a fashionable amount of designer stubble. He wore black denims, his light blue T-shirt the only smidgen of colour that she could see.

As he turned towards them with a smile that did things to her heart, she noticed a faint scar down the right side of his cheek. It was about two inches in length, serving to add a little bit more to his bad boy image. She wondered how he'd got it.

He winked as he caught her staring. Becky looked away immediately, her skin reddening as she slid along the seat.

Tonight Danny was in a different car, another old wreck. Jess said he'd nicked it but she couldn't understand why as it didn't seem any better than his own.

'Budge up, Parksy,' Jess told the youth in the back seat. 'Make room for two little ones. Hi, I'm Jess.' She leaned forwards to inspect the new arrival, pushing out her chest. 'And you are?'

'Austin.' He looked behind her. 'And you are?'

'Becky.' She smiled shyly.

Danny screeched off and they rode around the estate for a while before heading up towards the city centre. But twenty minutes later, Danny pulled the

Somewhere to Hide

car over to the side of the road. In temper, he banged his hands on the steering wheel.

'Not again!'

'What's up?' said Jess.

'Run out of petrol.'

'What are we going to do?'

Becky looked out of the window. On one side there was a row of non-descript terraced houses; on the other, a large area of painted boards showing coloured murals. She wondered what they were hiding: she hadn't seen them before. In fact, she hadn't got a clue where they were. They could be miles away as far as she knew.

'Got any money on you?' Danny asked them.

Jess shook her head. 'I might have a fiver in change but that's it.'

Danny turned to Becky. 'You?'

'No.'

He banged his hands on the steering wheel again. Blushing, he turned to Austin. 'I don't suppose...?'

'No,' Austin smirked. 'You'll have to get another car and make sure it's got a full tank this time.'

'A fiver between us?' Danny laughed loudly to hide his embarrassment.

They sat in silence while the radio blasted out some dreary tune. Suddenly, Danny opened his door. 'Come on, you lot.'

Becky and Jess wriggled across the back seat and into the cool night air. Parksy followed. Danny retrieved his crowbar, tucked it inside his jacket and the five of them stood on the pavement.

'Are you going to do another one?' Jess asked, wide-eyed with excitement.

Danny nodded and strode off up the road. 'I'll have to. I don't get my giro 'til later in the week so unless I can thieve a bit off the old lady again, my car's got to stay put.'

They all followed behind. Danny finally spotted a small hatchback parked in the alleyway between two rows of terraced houses. He pointed at it.

'This'll do,' he said. 'No one will see me if I'm quick.' He pulled the crow bar out from underneath his jacket. 'You two carry on walking,' he told the girls. 'We'll meet you around the corner.'

'Do you think we should be doing this?' Becky said to Jess as they walked towards the end of the street. 'Cath will kill us if she finds out.'

Jess linked her arm. 'Relax. No one will find out.'

'It's not nice, though. To have your car nicked.'

'Needs must.'

Becky wasn't sure she liked Jess's attitude. If they nicked a car, someone would miss it.

'Danny's done it lots of times,' Jess told her. 'It's not as simple now though. Most of the modern cars have alarms and immobilisers. That's why he picks older models. He'll run this one around for a while and drop us off.' She grinned. 'Well, drop you off actually. I'm hoping to stay with him, have me some fun.'

'That Austin's a bit of all right,' said Becky, trying not to blush as she said his name.

'Isn't he just! Actually, I might try him out and you can have Danny, if you like.'

'Jess, I need to tell you –'

Danny screeched to a halt beside them in the stolen car. 'Get in,' he said, looking directly at Becky.

'It's that easy?' Becky was shocked.

'Of course it's not *that* easy.' Jess made for the door handle first. 'He just does it all the time.'

'Not you,' said Danny. 'You're going nowhere. Parksy, you can get out as well. Becky, you can get in.'

'But I –'

'Couldn't you at least drive us home first?' Parksy pleaded. 'We're miles away from the estate.'

Danny leaned over and patted his friend's stomach. 'The walk will do you good,' he grinned. 'Besides, you might be able to kop off with her, if you're desperate.'

'I heard that!' said Jess.

'You were meant to. Now come on you lot, get your arse into gear. I'm not in the mood to get caught tonight.'

'No, just laid, you dirty bastard.' Parksy glared at Austin. 'So why does he get to stay? He's only been around for a few weeks and already you're –'

The look Austin gave Parksy made him get out of the car.

'What did he mean about getting laid, Becky?' asked Jess.

Becky tried to shrug it off. Unsure what to do, she waited. Austin ushered her forwards with a nod of his head. She climbed back in.

'Becky.' Jess pointed at Parksy. 'You can't leave me with him.'

Becky moved to get out but Danny slammed the door lock down.

'Oi, let me out!' she said. 'I thought you were joking. I'm not staying without Jess.'

Danny looked at her with a mixture of lust and menace. Then he laughed and after a quick wink at an irate-looking Jess, he screeched off again.

'Ciao for now,' he shouted through the window.

'Stop.' Becky looked back as they rode away, this time heading down the main road and away from the city centre. 'Let me out of the car.'

'Quit whining.' Danny flashed a glare through the rear-view mirror.

'I will not. Let me out!' Becky's mind started to work overtime. Not only was she stuck with Danny who she knew would expect sex, but there was another man in the car. Someone who none of them knew well at all. If he was nasty, two men could do anything to her. Fear flooded her veins. For a second, she thought about opening the door and flinging herself into the road to escape. Stupid, stupid cow to get herself into this situation.

But then Austin turned and gave her a smile. She wasn't sure why but its warmth was reassuring. She settled down again. Danny was trying to work the CD player.

Austin held up a ten-pound note. 'Found this in the glove compartment.'

'Cool.' Danny took it from him. 'There's enough petrol in this one so we can get a few cans.'

Austin snatched the note back. '*I'll* decide what to do with it.'

'Of course, boss. Whatever you say.'

They stopped off at an off-licence and Austin went inside. He came back out minutes later with a few cans and they sat outside while she and Austin drank it.

'Want a tinnie?' Austin offered a drink to Danny.

Danny shook his head. 'I don't drink and drive. I'd rather have my freedom.'

By this time, Becky had begun to calm down and once the booze was finished, she felt in control of the situation again. Danny drove off towards the disused track they'd been to before. Once there, he stilled the engine and climbed into the back with her. Austin got out, lit a cigarette and walked a few metres in front.

Danny began to kiss her and for a short while they did nothing else. She became increasingly turned on as he pushed his tongue into her mouth, exploring her deeply. His hand went up the back of her T-shirt, his fingers teasing the bare skin up and down her spine. She followed suit, pulling him towards her so that there was no room between them. He shoved his hand down the front of her jeans. And that was when the panic began to take over. If she let Danny do this, then what would Austin want?

Danny's hand moved further down, cupping her, trying to get his fingers inside her.

'No, stop,' she cried.

'Ah, come on, Becks. Don't do this again. You'll get a rep as a tease.' Danny pressed her hand down onto his erection. 'You know you want it really.' He sniggered, glancing at Austin who had walked back to the car. 'You know you want it from both of us.'

Becky suddenly became very sober. 'Leave me alone.' She pushed Danny away and, with the force of a tornado, lashed out.

Danny grabbed her wrists and held her down. 'What's wrong with you? You were quick to give it away the other night. I'm only after a repeat performance.'

'No, I –'

Before she could protest again, Danny was lifted from her and thrown from the car. He fell to the ground on his back, scraping across the gravel.

'What the –'

'Leave her alone.' Austin stood over him. He flicked open a knife.

'Whoa!' Danny retreated a few feet backwards. He held his hands up in surrender. 'There's no need for that, mate. She's my girl, you know. I don't just shag anyone.'

Austin turned to Becky with a look in his eyes that she would never forget. It was danger personified. She held her breath as he stared at her.

'Is that right?' he asked her. 'Is he your man?'

Becky shrugged slightly, not wanting to admit anything. She flinched as he took a step towards Danny.

'Yes!' she cried. 'Yes, he's my man.'

Austin stood still for a moment. Then he put the knife away and helped Danny up as if he'd simply tripped over.

'I suggest you treat your girl with a little more respect.' He clasped Danny's shoulder. 'Take her home. I think she's had enough for one night. And I need this car for something else later.'

13

'You're home early,' Cath said looking up from her magazine as Jess flopped beside her on the settee and folded her arms. 'It's only half past nine. Are you feeling okay?'

'No. I've had a terrible night, if you must know.'

'Where's Becky?'

Jess shrugged her shoulders.

'But you left with her. Where did she get to?'

'*She* got into a stolen car with Danny Bradley, leaving me to make my own way home.'

'What?' Cath put down her magazine.

'I would never have done that. Mates don't leave other mates behind. And she knows I fancy Danny Bradley. She's dead when I get hold of her.'

'But you shouldn't have left her on her own! Where did you last see her?'

'I've told you,' Jess snapped. 'She got into a stolen car with Danny Bradley and some other bloke called Austin. How the hell should I know where they took her?'

'But I trusted you to look after her and –'

'This isn't my fault. I told her not to get into the car but she ignored me. And then they left me to walk home! Do you think I wanted to walk miles? My feet are killing me.' She took off a shoe. 'Look at my blisters. I won't be able to walk tomorrow. But what sympathy do I get for doing the right thing? All you do is moan at *me*.'

Cath touched her arm gently. 'Sorry, I'm just worried about her. I never expected Becky to go off the rails.'

'Like me, you mean.'

'No, I didn't say –'

'If you're so bothered about your precious Becky, then maybe you'd better start looking for her.'

Cath stood up. 'I think I might do that.'

She was outside in the driveway when a police car pulled up in the street. PC Andy Baxter got out of the driver's seat. She and Andy had known each other for some years. She'd been lucky to have him on side since Rich had died too.

'I believe I have something – or someone – that belongs to you.' Andy opened the rear door and a sullen Becky climbed out.

'Where the hell have you been?' cried Cath.

'I'm not late,' Becky retorted.

'I picked her up not far from where a stolen car was abandoned,' Andy explained. 'We'd been following it for a while: two males and a female inside it. Looked suspiciously like Becky but she's denying it.'

'It wasn't me!'

'She won't tell me who was driving it and I didn't get a good look at him. But I have my suspicions about that too.'

Cath shook her head. 'You've only been here five minutes yet every time you go out, you bring trouble home. I –'

'I didn't have any choice. And – and Jess left me, you should be mad with her too.'

'Don't try and put the blame on me, you cow,' said Jess.

'That's enough.' Andy nodded towards the house. 'Shall we go inside rather than argue on the doorstep?'

Becky marched past Cath to go into the house. But Cath pulled her back.

'I thought so.' She grabbed Becky's chin and sniffed. 'In your state, you shouldn't be drinking. I told you to be careful. What were you thinking of?'

'You're pregnant?' Andy shook his head.

'I don't want to be.' Tears pricked at Becky's eyes.

Cath calmed a little at this remark. Maybe this could be an opportunity to get to the bottom of her little secret.

'Kitchen. Now,' she demanded.

Andy followed them in. Close on his heels was Jess.

Cath stopped her in the doorway. 'I'll handle this.'

'But –'

She closed the door, leaving Jess protesting in the hall. Then she sat down beside Becky at the table.

'You and I need to talk,' she said. 'And I'm willing to sit here all night if I have to.'

'I've got nothing to say.'

'I have.' Andy sat down next to Cath. 'I'm going to let you off with a caution this time,' he took out his notebook, 'because you're new around here and because, technically I can't prove whether you were in the car under your own volition. But if there is *one* more next time, I won't be so lenient.'

'Thanks, Andy,' said Cath.

'But it wasn't my fault. They locked the doors and I –'

'Will you shut up and listen to him! He's giving you a second chance. Not that you deserve one but –'

Becky stood up, scraping her chair noisily across the floor. 'Leave me alone, both of you. I don't need your help, or your concern. I can look after myself, and my baby. I'll go to the housing association first thing tomorrow, get myself a flat and move out of here. You can wash your hands of me. That's what you want to do, isn't it?'

'Of course not.' Cath touched her arm.

'No, I mean it! I'll pack my things now. You won't see me again after tomorrow.'

She stormed across the room. This time, Cath left her to it.

Andy shook his head. 'I still don't know how you do this, Cath. You have far more patience than I'll ever have.'

'I don't always feel patient but I have to keep my wits.' Cath sighed. 'What else is out there for them? I can only take in four of these girls at a time. God only knows what happens to the ones that I miss.'

Becky paused when she saw Jess waiting outside her bedroom door. That was all she needed. After the mix up with Danny, they'd been on their way to drop her off. It was when they were driving past Vincent Square, heading for Christopher Avenue, that they'd first heard police sirens. Through the back window, Becky noticed an unmarked car, only a few feet behind them.

Danny had raced around the estate for several minutes trying to lose them. But in the end, he'd driven into a large fenced yard and he and Austin had got out. They'd legged it up and over a row of garages and dropped into the field behind. Becky had sneaked through a privet hedge and ended up in someone's garden. She'd run down the path and was out in the street when Andy had collared her.

'You're dead when I get you on your own,' Jess told her. 'Don't think you can treat me like a piece of shit.'

'Leave me alone.'

Becky pushed past her and into her room. Jess grabbed for her arm but she was too quick. In a flash, the door was shut and locked.

Sliding down to the floor as Jess hurled a torrent of abuse from the other side of it, she held her head in her hands. What was it with her lately? Was this how her life was going to pan out? Getting into trouble all the time and then what? Drugs? Prison? If she carried on like this, they'd take her baby into care. Then she'd be alone again.

She rested a hand on her stomach. That was laughable really. What could she give a baby when she couldn't look after herself?

More to the point, what had got into Danny Bradley? Becky might have let him sleep with her but he didn't own her. And now Austin thought they were an item, it looked like she'd lost her chance with him. He was much cooler than Danny Bradley would ever be.

She would have to toughen up.

Exhausted and emotional, she dragged herself across to the bed and flopped down onto it.

'Stuff you all,' she said, bursting into tears. 'Stuff the lot of you. I don't need anyone else.'

14

'I will not tolerate this kind of behaviour,' Cath repeated to Becky over breakfast the next morning. 'It's bad enough that you came in drunk and woke up the whole street when you first arrived but to be brought home by the police? Well, it raises eyebrows and I don't want any of that.'

'But I told you, it wasn't my fault,' Becky said. 'They wouldn't let me out of the car. They left Jess behind.'

'*They* left you behind to take the blame.'

'*They* are going to kill you when they get hold of you,' said Jess as she joined them in the kitchen.

'I never grassed them up,' said Becky.

'You're both as bad as each other,' said Cath. 'I was so sure that you two would become friends.'

'Just because we're both teenagers, it doesn't mean we'll get on.' Jess slumped down next to Becky and rested her chin on the heel of her hand. 'And friends would look out for each other, not leave them in the lurch to walk miles home on their own.'

'I'm sorry, okay!' said Becky. 'I didn't know they'd leave you behind.'

Cath sighed. All she wanted was a bit of peace and quiet every now and then. But while she had the two of them together, it seemed a perfect time to keep the conversation going.

'I want you – both of you – to start thinking of other people for a change and show some respect,' she said. 'It isn't much to ask.'

'I don't know why you've dragged me into this,' Jess remarked. 'It wasn't me who was brought home by the rozzers last night.'

'Not this time, but it has been on occasion.' Jess opened her mouth to complain but Cath didn't give her the chance to speak. 'You know I can't settle until you're home because I worry. What do you want me to do? Buy a notice board and get you to write on it where you are and what time you'll be back?'

'I'm not doing that. It'd be like being at school.'

'If you act like children, then I'll treat you the same. This talk is again to remind you of the rules.'

'Not those frigging rules.' Jess folded her arms. 'You don't have control over our every waking minute.'

'Of course I know that,' said Cath. 'But while you are here, you will show me some respect. You came in late the night before last and I turned a blind eye as you were coherent.'

'So?'

'Put yourself in my position. I have four people to think about. Can you imagine what that is like?'

'Five,' said Becky quietly.

'What?' Cath turned towards her.

'There are five of us to look after.' Lightly, she ran a hand over her stomach.

'At least you'll get out of here if you have a baby. Single woman with a child gets further up the list. You'll have a flat in no time when some other poor slapper does a runner. That Josie Mellor will be round here soon, trying to move you on.' Jess pointed at Cath. 'That's what she likes to do, move you on so that you're someone else's problem.'

'That's a lie!' Cath banged her hand down on the table. 'You know I always do what I think is best for you – the best for you all.' She pointed at her. '*You* had better watch your step and be a good friend to this one, and you,' she pointed to Becky, 'need to get streetwise pretty sharpish or you'll be shat on from a great height and used for God only knows what.'

'Like me,' said Jess.

Cath gave her a sarcastic smile. 'Yes, like you.'

Jess scraped back her chair and stormed out of the room.

The kitchen door slammed and finally there was peace. Becky stayed quiet for a moment.

'You won't make me leave, will you?' she asked then.

Cath shook her head. 'No, I won't. But you, as well as Jess, need to show some respect. I can only do so much to protect you. You've been here a while now and for the most part of it, you've behaved yourself. But I don't want you getting in too deep with the wrong crowd. And you need to start looking after yourself, and your baby.'

'I don't really know a crowd.'

Cath gave her half a smile, not sure if she was trying to make light of the situation or not. 'All the same, I don't want to ruin my relationship with PC Baxter. It's a good job I have him. Do you hear me?'

Cath pulled her arms high and stretched. It was nearly one a.m. She felt exhausted but was glad that she'd managed to see the end of the film, have a bit of time alone. She switched off the television and listened.

Silence. The house was quiet and there was nothing going on out in the garden. Since their little chat that morning, both girls had been behaving themselves. This evening, Becky hadn't gone out at all but had stayed in her room and Jess had come in at ten, not a whiff of alcohol. She'd apologised for her outburst that morning and they'd talked for a while before she'd gone off to bed. All in all, it had been a better day.

She sat still for a while. This was her favourite time of night, when everyone was home, safely tucked up in their beds, and she could switch off completely.

Ten minutes later, she yawned loudly. She picked up the empty mugs and went to draw the bolts across the front door. But her high mood was short-lived when she saw another envelope on the mat. Like the last one, it was blank on both sides.

Cath ripped it open. Again there was a piece of cheap lined paper, the writing on it the same as the first note.

'YOU WILL NEVER BE SAFE.'

Cath screwed up the note in anger. Stupid, stupid man. How dare Kevin McIntyre put her in this predicament! He must have sneaked up to the house while she was watching the film. She shuddered: what a creep.

But, just as quickly, she smoothed out the paper. Now there were two of them, the matter became a little more serious. Should she show them to Liz or would it have the desired effect of putting the frighteners on her? Liz was trying to get on with her life: it was just a shame that stupid prick of her husband wasn't.

Cath sighed. She'd speak to Andy as soon as she could. Maybe talking it through would make more sense of it.

The next day, Cath was over on Vincent Square in the newsagents, flicking through a magazine when someone nudged her. She turned to see Josie and smiled warmly, pointing at the female model she'd been looking at.

'I was looking to see how I could give the impression of being twenty years younger in a day,' she told her. 'I mean, what do they do with these models? Believe me, no amount of Botox or tummy tucks would get rid of the crisps and chocolate that I stuffed down me last night. Mind you, it did give me some exercise this morning. I had to run to the loo several times because I ate too much. Oh, hello...'

Cath looked on in embarrassment when she noticed that Josie wasn't alone. The man standing to her right was tall, thin but not to the point of being skinny. His hair was dark, receding slightly and cropped short, his clothes clean and stylish. She noted that he could easily fit in the magazine alongside Miss Twenty Something Trollop, although it would have to be a spread on sugar daddies: he looked like he was in his mid-forties. As well as the upturn of his lips, bright blue eyes were smiling at her too.

All at once, she felt heat rise from her chest, up her neck and spread swiftly across her face.

Josie noticed it too and grinned. 'This is Matthew Simpson – Matt,' she introduced. 'He's the new maintenance officer I was telling you about.'

Cath thrust out her hand. 'Pleased to meet you, Matt.'

'Likewise,' Matt replied, letting his hand linger in hers for a second longer than necessary.

'Those youths have been hanging around again, Josie,' said an elderly lady carrying a small dog underneath her arm. She pushed past them all to grab the three-for-a-pound chocolate bars on offer. 'It's been chaos in my street lately. How many times do I have to complain before anything gets done about it?'

'We do our best, Mrs Weston,' Josie replied. 'But sometimes it's hard to get the right results for everyone.'

'And you're no better,' Mrs Weston vented her anger on Cath next. 'That girl of yours, that Myatt girl, has been causing trouble too.'

'Wind your neck in, Vera,' Cath replied. 'Your grandsons aren't so perfect, are they?'

Mrs Weston walked off muttering to herself.

'Wow, is it always this eventful when you buy a bag of crisps?' Matt wanted to know. 'There seems to be so much happening on this estate.'

Cath and Josie shared a smile.

'Wait 'til you've been here for a month,' said Josie. 'You'll soon want to go back to where you came from.

'Which is where, exactly?' Cath was intrigued.

'Buxton.'

'And you chose to come and work *here*?'

Matt laughed at the outlandish look on her face. 'It's not that bad, surely?'

'Ever watched *Shameless*?'

'Yes.'

'And *The Sopranos*?'

Matt nodded slowly, his eyes flicking quickly between them.

'How about *Dexter*?' Josie smirked.

'Who?'

'*Dexter*. It's an American series. He works in forensics and he's a serial killer.'

'Or even *Taggart*. There's always a *mur-da* going down on the Mitchell Estate.'

Josie nudged Cath sharply. 'Bugger off. You'll scare him away before I've told him the rest.'

'The rest?' Matt's eyes widened but he finally realised he was being had when the women burst into laughter.

'You're playing with me,' he grinned. 'Right?'

'Actually,' said Josie, 'I'm afraid we're not.'

Becky lay on her bed, her hand resting on her tummy. While she urged her baby to move, she wondered how big it was. And was it okay in there? Was it safe to have sex or should she stop Danny from touching her? That was when she could stand him pawing at her: her breasts were swollen and sore to touch which made it unbearable at times.

She couldn't believe how many check-ups and appointments that she'd been given to go to over the next few months. There were even more where she was scheduled to see Cath's caseworker who had been allocated to her, too. But even she knew she shouldn't have been running around like a lunatic. What would have happened if she had fallen?

After she'd ran from the stolen car, Danny had texted her to apologise for his actions. Becky had sulked for a while before making up with him. Without Jess and Cath knowing, they'd met up again and they'd had sex, four times so far. Twice she'd closed her eyes and imagined that it was Austin Forrester kissing her, Austin Forrester touching her. Austin Forrester with his smouldering eyes, his strong features, his sexy bum she'd been staring at the other day when he'd been checking the oil on Danny's old wreck.

She wondered – if she had sex with Austin, would everything be okay? Would the memories fade quicker? Was it only because Danny was rough and he wasn't the right one for her? Or maybe he was the right one for her. How would she know?

There was a knock on the door. Becky looked up to see Liz.

'I thought you might like this.' She came into the room and handed her a book. 'It's a bit old but it has some useful tips and such.'

The paperback was called *Baby Knowledge – From Conception to Birth*. Becky took it from her, wondering if she had secret psychic powers.

'And if there's anything that isn't in there, just ask,' Liz added. 'I bet there's something you'd like to know.'

At Becky's continued silence, Liz turned to leave.

'Does it hurt a lot?' Becky whispered softly.

'Like hell,' Liz nodded. 'I can't tell you otherwise. It wouldn't be fair.'

'How long did it take?'

'Just over eight hours.'

'Will it take me that long?'

Liz sat down on the bed beside her. 'Everyone's different,' she said. 'When I went to the baby clinic, I spoke to a woman who only realised she was having the baby when she went to the loo and saw the baby's head coming out.'

Becky paled in an instant.

'Sorry.' Liz grimaced. 'I'm not helping, am I?'

'I want to know, though.'

'Anything else?'

'How big will it be now?'

'It'll probably be about the size of a pear. That's why it's so important to look after yourself. The baby needs you at the moment. You are its lifeline. Whatever you do now could possibly have a profound effect on its future.'

Becky looked up, drinking in Liz's every word.

'It's you it's relying on,' she continued. 'You and no one else. Do you get what I'm trying to say?'

Becky nodded. Liz was right. This was her baby: *her* responsibility. She would look after it as best she could, make sure that no one hurt it. Eager to learn more, she opened the book and began to look through the pages.

Liz stood up. 'Why don't you read some of it and then see if you have any questions afterwards? I'm always around for a chat.'

Once she'd gone, Becky lay back on the bed, her legs flat on the mattress this time. No swinging her ankles about like a trapeze artist. Until she'd checked the book, she was going to stay in this position.

An hour later and she was clued up enough to know that things had to change. From now on, there would be no more drinking. No more risk-taking in stolen cars. No more cigarettes here and there that could easily turn into a bigger habit. She wouldn't do anything that may harm her baby.

The book said that having sex was okay too. So if she wanted to do it with Austin, she'd have to do it quickly before she decided who to have as her boyfriend. She liked Danny but she really liked Austin. Maybe he would be the better father, if he were boyfriend-staying-around material.

And he was so mature. Look how he'd sorted Danny out for her when he'd gone too far. That was the trouble with Danny. He didn't know when to stop, when enough was enough. But Austin, well, Austin was more of a man.

She recalled his face, something that had played a big part in her dreams over the past few nights. She remembered every little detail: fiery eyes that often glanced up and down her body, the silver loop earring hanging from his left ear. Yet again she wondered how he'd acquired the scar on his cheek. So far she'd been too shy to ask him.

She rested her hand on her stomach again as she considered how to go about her plan. She had to sleep with Austin soon or else he'd guess that she was pregnant. She wouldn't be able to keep it to herself for much longer, even if she wanted to anyway. It didn't take much to work things out. She was bursting out of her clothes even more now, especially her jeans – she couldn't fasten the waistband at all. Cath had bought her some maternity leggings and a few baggy T-shirts but she didn't want to wear them yet.

But how would she tell Danny that she didn't want to see him anymore? And how was she going to tell Austin that she fancied him when he was always with Danny?

Becky pondered for a while. Maybe it would be better to keep things sweet with Danny in case Austin didn't like her as much as she thought. Although from the looks he kept shooting her way, she doubted that very much.

She smiled. It was then that she realised, despite being sixteen and scared stiff, she really did want to keep her baby. So what if everyone thought she was young and naïve. She'd show them she was mature and ready for anything.

15

Cath was running late for her session helping out at the community house. She'd tried three outfits on before she settled on her favourite flirty-swishy skirt, cream wedge heels and a knitted sleeveless top. The recent run of warm weather had continued into May, long enough for her to gain a bit of a glow to her skin which the top showed off as subtly as a tiny bit of cleavage. Now she was frantically searching for her car keys. She slapped her forehead more firmly than she'd intended.

'Think,' she told herself. 'Where did you have them last?' She cast her mind back to the day before, as if her mind had wandered far from thinking about Matt Simpson after they'd been introduced.

Oh, yes: they'd just come back from the shops. She raced over to the fruit bowl. There next to the apples, oranges and bananas was a bunch of keys.

'Girls,' she shouted through to the living room. 'I've left a list of jobs for you to do before I get back. Make sure they're done.'

Checking herself one last time in the hall mirror, she rushed outside. Then she stopped abruptly.

'Shitty, shitty, shit!'

There was a huge scratch down the near side of her car. Both tyres had been slashed and the wing mirrors had been pulled off and slung onto the grass. She rushed round to the other side, only to find the same had been done there.

'No!' Cath gulped back tears. 'Who did this to my car?'

Archie Meredith, who was putting rubbish into his wheelie bin, came rushing over. He gasped. 'That's such a mess. I didn't hear anything out of the ordinary last night. Did you?'

'I – just – I –' Cath ran both her hands through her carefully prepared hair and pulled it enough to hurt. 'Why is it always me?'

Archie walked around the car slowly. 'It might not be anything to do with you. Though it is probably *because* of you,' he said as Cath inspected the damage. 'I reckon you must have a long list of culprits. Well, because of whom you have staying with you, anyway.'

Not wanting to be drawn into a confrontation, Cath went back inside. She'd have to change her shoes: there was no way she could rush in the ones she was wearing.

Half an hour later, she hurried into The Den at the community house. She found Suzie, another volunteer helper, in the kitchen.

'I'm sorry I'm late,' she said, plonking her bag down in a flurry. 'My car's been vandalised and I've –'

The small, blonde woman held up a hand. 'It's okay. Matt's told me all about it. Not too much damage caused, I hope?'

'Matt?' Cath was taken by surprise.

'Josie reckons he's good with cars so she thought he might be able to help out. He's calling in later, once the rabble quietens down.'

The rabble Suzie was referring to began to arrive in dribs and drabs during the next hour. The Den was frequented by approximately fifty youngsters from the estate. They were teenagers like Jess who had left school without qualifications, had no aspirations and no chance of ever getting off the Mitchell Estate to improve their outlook.

For every one of them who came through the door twice a week, Cath saw a little bit of hope. When The Den had opened six months ago, the kids on the estate had avoided it, teasing anyone who had the audacity to attend a session there and generally blackballed the place without even stepping over its threshold.

But as the buzz about the place intensified and The Den became the place to be, a place to meet up, catch up and get a free mug of coffee and a seat to crash down on, Cath had seen the numbers slowly increasing. Once she'd got them on side, she'd then been given funding for laptops and set up meetings writing CVs, creating simple IT sessions and gradually raising awareness that there was more to life than sitting back and waiting for it to bite you.

Some of the teenagers had responded well, gone on to get themselves jobs and moved on with their lives. Some of them had stayed exactly the same as the first day they'd walked in. But the main thing was that they were still coming every week. And, surprisingly, the laptops hadn't been stolen. Cath had no doubt that she would crack some of them eventually. Success breeds success, she hoped.

Today, if she hadn't been running late, Cath would have done a session on what to wear for a job interview but there was no time for that now. Besides, she didn't feel like she could stand up and present anything positively today. Instead, the group would have to be content with the usual drop-in session with no particular structure other than coffee and a catch up.

As promised, Matt came by about eleven. Cath brightened at the sight of him walking towards her and gave him a wave. She glanced down at her feet, now sporting ballerina pumps and sighed. Why didn't she bring her shoes with her to change into?

She was sitting at the table, encouraging Katie Stedson to have a go at taking her GCSE maths again. Cath was prepared to help out as much as she could, although that wouldn't be a great deal as maths hadn't been her strong point either.

'I hear you've had a spot of trouble?' Matt said.

Katie looked up, waiting to get all the details. Cath pointed towards the door.

'There might be a better place to discuss things.' She spoke to Katie next. 'Think about what I said. It would be good for you to have something to focus on other than baby Teagan.'

Katie looked a little disgruntled as Matt and Cath left. They went upstairs to Josie's office, open to anyone when she wasn't there. Cath unlocked the door with her key.

'Sorry about that,' she referred to their earlier conversation as they sat down. 'But news travels fast around here. I don't want too many people to know that my car has been vandalised.'

'I'm sorry, too. I'm not used to the estate etiquette yet.' Matt smiled, the skin around his eyes wrinkling.

Cath smiled too. Then as the air crackled with expectancy, she felt colour rising in her cheeks again.

'Josie mentioned you might be able to help me out.' She opened the window and wafted a hand in front of her face, hoping that he'd think she was flushed because of the weather. 'I'm lost without my car.'

'Yes. I have a small trailer. If you like, I can remove the tyres and take them to be sorted. The mirrors I can fix back and replace; same too with the wipers. But I have to draw the line at a re-spray. I can't get scratches out. Unless they'll come out with a bit of elbow grease?'

Cath shrugged. 'I can't remember how deep they are. I was so angry that I didn't take too much notice.'

Matt checked his watch. 'Shall I pop by this evening?'

'Would you? Thanks.'

'I'll ring around during my lunch break for some prices and see if I can get a good deal anywhere. Then I can –'

There was a knock on the door and Josie walked in. 'Suzie told me you were here, Matt. When you have a moment, could you change the strip light in room seven please and see if you can do something with that squeaking door in the kitchen?'

Matt stood up and saluted Josie. 'Yes, boss. I'm on my way.'

'Later will do,' Josie grinned, 'if you're busy now.'

'No, I –'

'We were just finished,' said Cath, feeling her cheeks burning again.

Matt turned to her. 'See you later.' And then he was gone.

Josie perched on the corner of the desk. 'You're blushing like an infatuated teenager,' she said to Cath.

'I am not!'

'You are too. He is gorgeous, though, isn't he?'

Cath nodded, knowing better than to think she could hide her feelings from Josie.

'So would you?'

'Would I what?'

Josie winked. 'Touchy feely. Hide the sausage?'

Cath picked up a ruler from the desk and rapped Josie on the thigh. 'Don't be so childish.'

Josie leaned towards her and whispered. 'I'm not the one playing games.'

16

As Cath and Liz dished out dinner, and another missed opportunity to discuss the notes had passed, they heard a scream. Liz tore across the kitchen and up the stairs and Cath followed quickly behind. Chloe stood outside her room, holding up her baby doll. It had an arm missing.

'What happened, angel?' asked Liz. But Chloe was crying too much to tell her.

Cath could hear running water from the shower, and the sound of Becky singing softly in the bathroom. Jess's room, however, was occupied.

'Where the hell do you get off?' She grabbed Jess by the arm and dragged her out onto the landing.

'Get off me!' Jess tried to shrug her off.

Cath pushed her in front of Chloe and picked up the doll's arm from the floor. 'Is this your doing, you peevish cow?'

'No! I never touched it.'

'Then who was it?' Cath twirled round 360 degrees in a comical fashion. 'I don't see anyone else around here that would do such a cruel and thoughtless thing.'

'I told you, it wasn't me. You're always blaming me. What would I want with breaking her stupid doll?'

'Sometimes I could slap your legs for you,' she told her. 'You are such a bully.'

'I'd like to see you try,' Jess goaded. 'I'd have you reported to social services in a shot.'

Somewhere to Hide

Before anyone else could speak, there was another scream. But this time, it was more of a wail, like an animal in distress; a long and harrowing sound which stopped them all in their tracks.

Becky emerged from the bathroom, one hand at her chest clasping a towel covering her body, the other clutching her stomach. 'I'm bleeding,' she sobbed, 'and it hurts.'

Cath looked down at Becky's legs. There was a line of blood trickling down the inside of her thigh. Liz rushed across to help while Jess hovered around in the background and Chloe stood in the doorway of her bedroom.

Becky clung onto Cath. 'Please don't let me lose my baby.'

'Let's get you to your room. Can you walk?'

'I –' Becky folded over in agony, collapsing on the floor.

Cath stooped down and ran a hand over Becky's forehead. She was hot and clammy.

'We need to get you checked out,' she said.

'Won't she need an ambulance?' Jess asked.

'Ambulance!' Becky looked fraught with fear. 'But that book says –' She looked up at Liz. 'That book says it's the first sign of a mis – miscarriage.' She looked at Cath then. 'Please help me! Please stop the pain!'

With Cath on one side and Liz on the other, they helped Becky to climb down the stairs.

They were nearly halfway down when there was a knock at the door. Jess ran to open it.

Matt stood on the doorstep. 'Hi, is Cath - what's wrong?'

'It's Becky,' said Jess. 'I think she's having a miscarriage.'

'NO!' Becky gave out another loud scream and dropped to the floor again.

'Come on.' Cath tried to pull her back up. 'We're nearly there.'

'Let me help.' Matt moved past Jess and gently scooped Becky up in his arms. 'Hang on to my neck,' he told her. 'We'll get you sorted.'

He carried her down the stairs to his car, Cath following close behind. They both helped her into the back seat. Then Matt held the door open for Cath.

'I'll drive you there and you can sit in the back,' he said. 'She needs you with her.'

*I*t had been three days since Becky had been to the hospital. She had been inconsolable for the first twenty-four hours and lay on the settee in the living room. After that, she'd refused to come out of her room.

Cath had taken food and drink up to her but hardly any of it had been touched. She wished she could help her more, but she knew Becky would have to deal with it in her own way. Grief affected people differently.

The miscarriage had brought painful memories crashing back into Cath's mind. She'd tried to push them away, instead concentrating on looking after the distraught girl who had turned into no more than a child herself. But still they kept coming.

At lunchtime, she placed a sandwich and a mug of coffee on a tray and went upstairs. She knocked on Becky's bedroom door before she went in.

Becky was lying on her bed curled up in the foetal position. She held a pillow in her arms. Greasy curls stuck to her pale face, her eyes were puffy and her nostrils red and cracked.

'I've brought you something to eat,' Cath said, using her best singsong voice. 'Do you think you can manage a bite or two?'

'I'm not hungry.'

She slid the tray onto the bedside table. 'I'll leave it here for a while, just in case.'

'How can I eat when my baby is DEAD?'

Cath visibly jumped. 'You nearly gave me a heart attack, shouting out like that.'

'Sorry.' Becky paused. 'I don't know what to do now that... now that...'

Cath sat down beside her and pulled her into her arms.

'Why did it happen to me?' Becky sobbed. 'I'm not a terrible person.'

'Of course you're not, but sometimes it's just nature's way. There could have been something wrong with the baby that meant it couldn't survive.'

'That means it's my fault.' Becky's sobs became louder. 'Did I reject it? Why would I do that?'

'I didn't say that.' Cath tried to back pedal. 'I meant that maybe it would have suffered if it had been born.'

'But they can do so much these days. They could have saved it, those doctors. But they didn't because it was me. They looked down their noses but they don't know what I've been through. I wish I'd died as well.'

'Please don't speak like that.' Cath held Becky closer, as if she could protect her from the pain. 'Life is too precious.'

'It isn't.' Becky sniffed.

'It is. I know how you're feeling. I –'

'You haven't got any children so how would you know?'

'I –'

'It was *my* baby!' Becky began to cry again. She pushed Cath away.

Knowing when she was beat, Cath stood up. Her hand hovered over Becky's head as she contemplated trying again but she dismissed the thought as soon as it happened. She couldn't reach her yet.

Liz woke up with a start. She sat up in bed, half-expecting to hear a baby cry. Chloe stirred by her side but didn't wake.

It was one fifteen in the morning. She pulled back the duvet, crept out of the room and across the landing to the bathroom. There she sat on the edge of the bath and let her tears go.

Since Becky's miscarriage, Liz had been having recurring nightmares of losing her own child. Her baby would have been eighteen weeks old now, as big as an orange. It would have had eyelashes, maybe even some hair. It may have been able to hear her singing in the shower. It would have been growing rapidly and she would have been growing with it.

She rested her hand on her empty stomach. Either a boy or another girl would have been fine with her. She'd wanted another child so desperately.

She ran a hand through her hair, hating herself for even thinking it but secretly she was pleased that Becky had lost her baby. It would have been agony if she'd had to stay at Cath's and watch her grow, watch her give birth, see her walk around with a child that she didn't want.

Liz ran the cold water tap and swilled her face. How selfish was she? She knew how much Becky would be hurting because she'd been there. She could still feel the longing to sense the baby move, to wish that it were still part of her. She'd tried talking about it to Becky but twice she'd been rebuffed. She couldn't blame her for being angry. She had felt angry too, still did.

Flashbacks of a fist plunging into the soft flesh below her chest made her gasp and she began to cry again. Why had he done that to her? What had she done to deserve such treatment? Kevin should have loved her, protected her. He shouldn't have killed their baby.

She swilled her face again and then went back to her room. Chloe was still asleep, her arms above her head on the pillow. Liz got into bed, trying not to disturb her.

She lay there, gazing at her child, feeling the pull to hold her, protect her from the outside world. At least there was one thing she could be grateful for. She had Chloe, she would always have Chloe.

No one, not even Kevin, could take her away.

17

Cath was in the kitchen with Liz doing the dishes when Jess stormed in.

'I don't know what to do,' she said to them.

'About what?' asked Cath, perplexed.

'About Becky. She won't talk to me. She won't even come out of her room.'

'She's had a terrible loss. It's not like breaking a leg or having a stomach ache.'

'But she was too young to have a baby. I keep on telling her that.'

Liz reached a wet mug from the draining board. 'It's not a question of whether she wanted it,' she said. 'It's a question of losing something that was a part of you and now isn't. You need to realise that.'

'Says the voice of experience,' mocked Jess. 'Just because you're older than me doesn't mean that you know everything. You've never lost a baby, so how would you know?'

Cath saw Liz get ready to defend her corner. 'That's enough, Jess,' she interjected, not wanting another argument to start. She threw a tea towel at her. 'You can help to dry the dishes while you're sitting doing nothing.'

'That's not fair. Why do I –'

The door opened and they all turned to see Becky standing in the doorway. Her skin was blotchy, her eyes barely visible due to the dark circles beneath them. She wore an over-sized, over-stretched T-shirt and slippers, a cropped cardigan pulled close as if trying to keep out the pain.

Cath was the first to react. She ushered her into the room and sat her down at the table.

'Would you like a warm drink?' she asked. 'Jess, put the kettle on and then be on your way.'

'But –' Jess complained.

'I thought you were going shopping.'

'Not on my own.'

Cath raised her eyebrows.

'Fine! I know when I'm not wanted.'

Ten minutes later, coffee and toast had been made. But Becky hadn't touched either.

'I...' She looked up at Cath through watery eyes. 'I... can I talk to you?'

'I'd better get going,' said Liz. 'I need to –'

'No, please! Will you stay?'

'Okay.' Liz sat down at the table.

Cath followed suit, waiting patiently for Becky to compose herself.

Eventually she spoke.

'My baby was the only thing I had that was mine. I can't rely on my dad. I'll probably never see him again.' She looked at them both. 'I bet you've been wondering why he hasn't come after me?'

Cath nodded, unable to tell her that fathers hardly ever came after the girls that she looked after.

'My mum died when I was seven and I went to live with my granny.' Becky smiled. 'I never knew my Pops but I loved my granny, she was the best. I saw my dad every Sunday. He always came around after he'd been to the pub and most of the time he'd fall asleep when he'd had his Sunday dinner. But I didn't care. When she died, I had to go and live with him.'

'How old were you then?' asked Cath.

'Eleven. That's when everything changed for me. It was like... like living with a stranger. I spent most of the time on my own. My dad would be either at work or at the pub. All of my friends from school lived too far away for me to visit so I used to be in my room a lot. Then Uncle James started coming around.'

Cath froze as she feared what was coming next.

'He used to make such a fuss of me at first. I remember him buying me lots of nice things – toys, comics, sweets. Then one night when they'd both come in from the pub, he came up to my room. I was asleep and he woke me up when he tried to get into bed with me. I thought he was drunk and I pushed him away but he kept trying to kiss me and run his hands all over my body. Then he grabbed my chin really hard and told me to shut up or else he'd tell my dad how naughty I was. That was the start of it all. It just got worse from there. I –'

'You mean –' Liz started, 'you mean, he *touched* you.'

Becky laughed, a cackling sound that made Cath cringe.

'He did more than touch me,' she said. 'Whose baby do you think it was?'

'I didn't mean it to sound as if it wasn't true.' Liz sounded distraught.

Cath gave Liz's arm a reassuring squeeze as Becky continued.

'The first time I thought I might be pregnant, I chucked myself down the stairs because I didn't want to have his baby. I was fourteen and he'd been coming in to my room once a month since that first time. I didn't have anyone to talk to then either but I just knew.'

'Didn't your dad suspect anything?' asked Cath.

Becky shook her head. 'I hardly ever saw him, remember? So it was easy really. I didn't go to school while he was at work sometimes anyway, so I stayed off a little longer. But I hurt my arm when I fell and it was so painful that I went to the hospital. Before I had it X-rayed, I told one of the nurses about the things that were happening to my body. She asked me how old I was. I said I was sixteen. They did some tests and she told me that I wasn't pregnant anymore. I never told anyone else.'

'Oh, Becky.' Tears streamed down Liz's cheeks.

'When I thought I was pregnant again, I knew I had to do something about it. So I got a knife.'

Liz gasped.

'I wasn't going to hurt myself,' Becky explained. 'But I was going to make sure he never came near me again. On the night I left home, I let my uncle come into my room as usual and just before he, you know, I – I stabbed him in the leg.

'He fell against the wall and didn't wake up when I shook him. I made a run for it. I had to get away. I thought I'd killed him.' She shuddered. 'That's why I was so scared to come out of my room when I first got here. I thought the police would be looking for me. I swear he was dead when I left him. But he must have been so drunk that he passed out.

'I took off because I thought he'd stopped breathing. I couldn't have killed him though, because it would have been on the news, wouldn't it?'

'Becky,' said Cath gently. 'None of it was your fault.'

'It was! Don't you see? I could have stopped him doing it but I was a coward. I thought he'd tell my dad and then I'd have to go into a home because there was no one else to look after me. I didn't want to go into care. So I stayed quiet. I did try once or twice to stop him but he made sure that I didn't try again. He was too strong for me.'

Cath swallowed. How could this still happen? There were supposed to be laws to protect the young innocents but every time she opened a newspaper, every time she switched on a radio or television, she'd hear about another victim. She wished she had enough money and a bigger house to help them all.

'I meant what I said,' she reiterated, knowing that she had to get the message across. 'It wasn't your fault. This was some pathetic, bastard of a man who used and abused a child for his own purposes.'

'I – I should have stopped him.'

'You were raped.' Cath reached across the table for her hand and gave it a squeeze. But Becky pulled it away.

'No! I *let* him do those things. Don't you see? I let him do it to me again and again and again. He said... he said it was all I was good for.'

'Did you ever talk to your dad about it?'

Becky paused, her memory flicking back to the night she had left her family home. The night she saw her dad pretending to be asleep when she'd tried to talk to him. She shook her head.

'I didn't think he'd believe me.'

She started to cry then, her sobs ringing around the kitchen, getting into the bones of both women. Cath rushed to her and it was in her arms that she finally gave in.

'It was horrible. And every time I think of my baby, I think of what he did to me. That's why I was punished. That's why I lost my baby!'

'It wasn't your fault.' Cath held her close. 'You had no control over things. You were taken advantage of, clear and simple.'

'No... I...' Becky's words became inaudible.

'It wasn't your fault. And it will never happen to you again. Do you hear me? Never!'

Eleven thirty that night, Cath was curled up on the settee. The television was on in the background: she hadn't watched it since switching it on an hour ago when Jess had come in. Becky had been in her room for most of the night.

Even though she'd talked it through with her caseworker, Cath was still disturbed by Becky's revelations that morning. She'd thought she'd heard it all over the past three years but what Becky finally told her had been really shocking. How could her father condone what was happening? Becky's uncle was abusing her while, it seemed to Cath, reading between the lines, her father knew perfectly well what was going on.

How could he let someone, his brother, violate his daughter? And from such an early age, and for so long. No wonder Becky had been hard to crack since she'd arrived. First her mum had died, then her granny. Since then, it didn't seem like she'd had anyone to trust. Plus she also carried with her the fear that no one would believe her even if she did confide in someone.

Cath recalled how it had shocked Liz too. She'd caught her crying an hour later, wondering how Becky's father could have turned a blind eye. Put his child at risk. Cath had to agree. If he were standing in front of her now, she would gouge his eyes out. No, more than that, she'd like to knee him in the balls and then ram her elbow in his back. Then, while he was on his knees, she'd like to kick him in the face as hard as she could. Then she'd cut off his brother's dick with something serrated, taking her time to extend the pain.

In reality, what she really wanted to do was contact Becky's father and get her uncle charged with rape of a minor. It was obvious to her now that he hadn't been in touch because of the problems it would cause. His brother would be known as a sex offender. Becky would most probably be dragged through the courts as well.

But, Cath sighed and stretched her arms high above her head, Becky wouldn't give anyone her address. She had tried on several occasions to get it from her. Maybe she would tell them later but for now, she'd chosen not to do anything. Put it all behind her now that the baby had gone. Poor kid. Perhaps there was something else she could do for her. She would speak to her case-worker again. She couldn't just let it ride.

When Rich had died three years ago, part of Cath had died with him. She knew that looking after these women gave her a purpose to continue. But the worry it caused her sometimes became too much.

'Am I doing the right thing by these girls, Rich?' she whispered into the room. 'Do I do enough for them? Or is it what they do for me? I hate myself for what I did. Why did I do that, Rich? Why?'

Cath sat in silence, waiting for an answer that wouldn't come. But she knew the reason why she did this. It was because she could never turn her back on another person.

18

It was nearing the end of May and it had been a while since Liz had seen or heard from Kevin. Cath kept thinking that every extra day he kept away was a bonus. After the notes however, which she still hadn't mentioned to her, she doubted that he would leave things be. Even so the banging on the door that evening took them both by surprise.

Liz jumped up from the settee. 'Oh, no, he's here. What am I going to do?'

'Liz!' Kevin rapped hard on the living room window next. He cupped his hands and peered through. 'I can see you. Get out here, right now!'

Cath opened the front window slightly. 'I thought we'd seen the last of you. What do you want this time?'

'Keep out of this, you interfering bitch.'

'Oh, please, if I had a pound for every time someone called me that, I'd be worth a small fortune now. Go home.'

'You can't keep her from me forever.'

'I don't want to talk to you,' Liz said, appearing at Cath's side.

Kevin held up Chloe's bike. 'I've come to bring this actually. My Chloe loved this.'

'Men often do this,' Cath whispered to Liz. 'Bring something for the child to make the mother feel guilty. Leave it on the front then,' she shouted to Kevin. 'I'll get it later.'

'No, I want to give it to her.'

'She's in bed,' said Liz. 'I'll come and get it.'

Cath closed the window. 'I'll go. He might be playing the wounded father but he is still capable of hurting you.' She pressed the red emergency call-out button at the side of the telephone unit. 'Let's see if there's anyone on shift that can help us first.'

Kevin banged on the window again. 'Liz!' he yelled. 'Where are you? What are you doing in there?'

'I'm coming.'

'Liz, no,' Cath cried.

But Liz was out of the front door before she had time to pull her back.

Kevin threw the bike down onto the ground and grabbed her arms. 'You think you can say what you like because you're hiding in there, don't you?' he hissed.

'Let her go,' said Cath.

Kevin forced Liz to her knees. 'Back off,' he told Cath. 'You're nothing without the stick.'

'I can get it if you want to meet it again. My stick loves cowards. Now take your hands off her.'

'I'll do as I wish.' Kevin leered at his wife.

'You're hurting me,' said Liz.

'I –'

'Leave my mum alone.' Chloe screamed as she appeared in the doorway. She ran across the garden, arms out in front, her pink nightdress flailing around her legs.

At the sight of his daughter, Kevin let go of Liz immediately. Chloe ran into her arms and burst into tears. Liz held on to her tightly.

'Hey.' Kevin bent down to Chloe's level. 'Me and Mum were only fooling around.' He opened his arms wide. 'Haven't you got a kiss for your old dad?'

'Get lost,' sobbed Chloe. 'I'm not a baby. I know you're trying to hurt Mum and I won't let you.'

'Christ, what have you been telling her? She can't be scared of me. I'm her father.'

'I haven't said anything to her,' said Liz, truthfully.

'She's old enough to see things for what they are,' added Cath.

'Yes, but –'

'Go away!' shouted Chloe. 'I hate you. You hurt my mum.'

As she turned her head away, Liz stared at Kevin with a mixture of fear and hate. Fear of what he might do to her when he eventually did catch up with her: hate for the man she had given her heart to at such a tender age and all he'd done was pummel into it and knock out all her hopes and dreams for a happy life.

Cath glanced towards the road as a police car stopped at the kerb. Moments later, a policeman got out of it.

'You called the police?' Kevin glared at Cath. 'What the hell did you do that for?'

'You can't keep coming round and threatening her. Liz has to move on with her life and so do you.'

'Like hell I do.' Deciding to change tactics, Kevin walked slowly towards Liz. 'Please come home. Listen to me. I'm nothing without you. I'll change.'

'You said that last time.'

'But I promise! I'll do whatever you want. I'll –'

'– stop bothering her.' PC Mark White came through the gate. 'That would be a good place to start. Hi, Cath, nice evening.'

'It was until he showed up.' Cath smiled, relieved to see Mark standing in her garden. 'I wonder if you might sort out a little problem we have.'

'I don't know why she called you,' Kevin pointed a finger at Cath, 'but there was no reason to. I'm having a quiet conversation with my wife and then I'm going home.' This time he looked pointedly at Liz. 'Alone again.'

'Do you want to go with him?' Mark spoke to Liz.

Liz shook her head. Chloe was still holding on to her for dear life, her tiny frame shaking as she sobbed.

'Then I think you'd better call it a night.' Mark indicated towards the gate with a nod of his head. 'On your way.'

'I'm not going yet,' said Kevin. 'I don't see why I should.'

'You'll have to stay outside all night then.' Cath walked over to join Liz and Chloe. 'Because we're all going in now, aren't we?'

Liz nodded. 'Come on, Chloe. Let's get you back into that warm bed of yours.'

But Chloe clung to Liz's waist. 'Not until *he* goes.'

'Chloe.' Kevin reached out to touch her but Chloe screamed. She continued to scream until he held up his hands. 'Okay, okay, I'm going.'

'Finally, he gets the message,' Cath said sarcastically. 'And I wouldn't bother coming back too soon either. If at all.'

'You can't stop me.'

'You're right.' Mark reached for his notepad. He walked to the gate and pointed to a blue car. 'Is this his?' When Liz nodded, he noted down the number plate and then addressed Kevin again. 'I can't stop you, but a harassment order can. And I think I have enough evidence to get one against you. You're harassing your wife, you're scaring your daughter and you're making a general nuisance of yourself in the street.' He glanced around. 'There are three people that I can see watching what's going on.'

'That's because they're all nosy bastards.'

'Swear again and I'll lock you up. You might be able to get away with it when I'm not here but now that I am, you can add breach of the peace to your list, if you're not careful. Now, move! I want you out of this street or I'll arrest you.'

'I'm going,' Kevin snapped.

Cath shook her head as she followed Liz indoors. What the hell had got into her? Stupid woman, putting herself in danger like that.

As soon as she came downstairs again after settling Chloe, Cath ripped into her.

'The next time he comes here – because there will be a next time,' she told her, 'I don't want you to go running out to him. You know what he's capable of. Whatever possessed you?'

'Sorry.' Liz wouldn't look at her.

'I have an alarm system for a reason. I have backup from the police for a reason. When I say do not go outside, I mean do NOT go outside. That should never have happened. You put yourself in danger.'

'You don't know him like I do. He won't give in until he's done what he came to do. He would have been outside all night if I hadn't gone out to him.'

'No, he wouldn't. The police would have moved him on. Instead you let Chloe see him attack you. Mark's right. You should think about getting a harassment order or you're never going to get rid of him.'

'Don't you think he'll get tired of it soon?'

'I don't know,' she replied. 'I thought he'd gone when he stayed away for so long since the last time. Now he's back on the scene. Unless something drastic is done, he'll do it all the time.'

'I should never have said anything to him.'

'No, you shouldn't have.'

'I – I just felt brave because I thought he couldn't get at me. Now I've antagonised him again, I've left myself open.'

Cath could see how upset Liz was so she held her tongue. 'I'm – what's that racket?'

Cath and Liz followed the noise to its source. There were loud bangs coming from Becky's room. When Cath opened the door, she saw Becky standing on the roof outside her window. She was pummelling on the glass.

'Cath!' Becky banged hard again. 'Cath, let me in!'

'Be quiet, will you!' Cath pushed up the window and reached for her arm. 'I thought you were already in here.'

'Nope... I snuck out.'

'Can't I ever have a night of peace?' She managed to pull Becky through the window.

'That cow!' Becky slurred, pointing at the windowsill. 'I left a book there, so I could get in again. She must have moved it.' She peered down at the floor, swaying as she tried to remain upright.

'What are you wittering on about?' Cath sat her down on the side of the bed.

'That Jess. I left the window open.'

Cath wafted her hand in front of her face. 'What have you been drinking? And more to the point, where did you get the money from?'

'Who needs money when I have pockets?' Becky laughed at her own joke. She pointed to her jeans. 'I have *biiiiiiiiiggg* pockets, Cath.'

Cath sighed. 'Let's get you into bed before you do anything else.'

'I shagged Pete Freeman tonight. Around the back of the old White Lion.' Becky waggled her little finger. 'That's what I think of Pete Freeman. What a weenie.'

Cath wanted to tell her that she shouldn't be having sex yet, that it was too soon after the miscarriage, but she knew Becky wouldn't take anything in. Instead, she pulled off her shoes while Liz removed her jacket. They tried to get her into bed but Becky had other ideas. She began to sing.

'*Baby you're the one. You still turn me on. You can lick my hole again!*'

'Becky, that's enough,' Cath scolded.

Behind them, they heard Chloe giggle.

Liz went to her. 'You should be in bed, young lady, or I'll never get you up for school in the morning.'

'Chloe?' said Becky, trying to focus on the small figure standing in the doorway. 'Chloe, is that you?'

'Hiya, Becks,' Chloe said before being whisked away by Liz.

'Chloe, don't let the boys touch you. They'll do evil things to you and fu –'

'Becky! That's enough now. Show some respect. Chloe is just a child.'

'But you said I was only a child, didn't you?' Becky stopped. Suddenly the drunken giggles turned to tearful wails. 'You mean baby, don't you? My baby, I lost my baby. Cath, why did I lose my baby?'

19

Cath always enjoyed her time at the community house, both in The Den with the teenagers and helping out with the adult courses. It was a time when she felt she could leave all her cares and worries behind at the front door, for a few hours at least. She'd usually be too busy to think about anybody else. But Becky kept popping into her mind.

That poor girl had so much going on. Was it any wonder she was going out with boys and drinking to ease the pain? She wished she could get through to her, talk to her somehow. She'd have to think what to do.

This week there'd been a volunteer teaching the women simple self-defence moves. Out of everything, Cath enjoyed helping out with the self-assertiveness courses best. She loved to see someone change from a caterpillar into a butterfly as the weeks attending the courses flew by. Some sessions were for anyone to attend but some were purely for the women to discuss and share their different stories. Sometimes they were harrowing; sometimes inspiring. So wherever possible, she and Josie would ensure there was a bit of light-hearted fun within a serious message.

'I wasn't really expecting to learn anything,' Josie said afterwards as she and Cath tidied up the room. 'But you never know when you might have to defend yourself in day-to-day life.'

'I don't often go out after dark, if I can help it.' Cath stacked a chair on top of a pile underneath the window. 'But some of those things would be useful if I didn't feel safe.'

'And there were so many tips. I particularly liked the one where she said to yell fire if you felt threatened. How many people would come running then rather than if you just screamed?'

'Do you need any help in here, ladies?' Matt popped his head around the door.

'I think we can manage to move a few tables,' Josie teased. 'After what we've been taught, we no longer feel like the weaker sex, do we, Cath?'

Cath grinned.

'Oh, you've been to the self-defence class. Tell me more.' Matt came into the room. 'You have me intrigued.'

Josie gathered together two plastic cups that had been left on a table and put them in the bin. 'Shall we show him what we've learned?'

Cath pursed her lips, trying to stop the grin from looking maniacal. How come she always acted like a tongue-tied teenager whenever Matt came on the scene? It had happened when he'd called to sort out her car again after the vandalism. She'd gone bright red every time he'd spoken to her. In the end, after handing him a cuppa, she'd headed back indoors for fear of making a total idiot of herself.

She glanced at Josie. 'Shall we show him the elbow jab?' Cath moved to Matt's side, pulled her left elbow up high and across towards her right shoulder.

'Move your hips too,' said Josie.

Cath gave a slight nod and swivelled her hips, allowing her elbow to move further to the right. Then with all her force, she swung it round towards Matt. She caught him straight in his chest.

Matt grunted and dropped to a stoop.

'Are you okay?' Cath bent down to his level. 'I thought I'd swing and miss you.'

Josie had a hand over her mouth. Suddenly she lost control, laughter bursting out raucously.

Matt clutched a hand to his chest, his breathing rapid. 'Jesus, I wouldn't like to cross you in a dark alleyway. I'm going to have a right bruise there.'

'I'm so sorry.' Cath tried to look concerned, but it was impossible as Josie was still laughing at the top of her voice. She felt a smile forming and gnawed at her bottom lip to try and stop it.

'It's a good job she didn't catch you in the temple or the throat as we were shown next,' Josie managed to say between sniggers. Tears were pouring down her face. 'She might have killed you.'

'I didn't realise he was that close,' Cath hissed, embarrassment creeping in.

Matt raised a hand. 'It was my fault,' he explained. 'I saw a piece of cotton on the back of your jumper and I was going to remove it. I doubt it will still be there with that force,' he added as Cath checked her sleeve.

'Sorry, Matt,' Josie said, wiping at her eyes. 'I haven't laughed so much in ages. It was the look on your face.' She started to giggle again.

Matt stood up slowly. Still holding onto his chest, he spoke to Cath. 'You owe me one for that. I reckon you need to suck up to me big time.'

Josie burst into laughter again. Cath blushed. Matt looked bewildered. But then his eyes began to twinkle and his mouth twitched.

'Ah, yes, sexual favours will do nicely. Your place or mine?'

Cath lowered her eyes from his intense stare. How could she get out of this one?

'Coffee.' She pointed to the door. 'I'll just go and make a fresh batch.'

Later that evening, Becky and Jess were in Becky's room, sitting on her bed. Jess was trying to get Becky to go out with her but so far she'd had no luck. Becky would much rather stay in. She didn't feel like company at all, not even having a giggle with Jess. She wasn't sure she'd ever laugh again.

'Come on,' Jess coaxed. 'It'll do you good to get bladdered and forget everything for a while.'

'I got bladdered two nights ago and that didn't help.'

Jess snorted. 'The Pete Freeman night. Crap lay, isn't he?'

'Oh, have you –?'

'Yeah. Not much to talk about there. Anyway, forget about Pete. We might bump into Austin. I know how much you fancy him. Now that you're not, well, you know, you can enjoy yourself more, can't you?'

'I don't want to.'

'I'll blag some vodka.'

Becky stared at herself in the tiny mirror on her dressing table. She'd do anything to get rid of this empty feeling. It was as if her life had come to a halt, a crossroads even. She didn't know what she was going to do next.

'It might block out your pain, make you feel better.'

'I doubt it.'

'Please!' Jess pulled out a small plastic bag from her pocket. 'You can have some of this.'

Becky eyed it warily. 'Is that what I think it is?'

'Yep. It's whizz.'

'What does it do again?'

'It makes you feel happy, more lively, like everyone is your friend.'

'But aren't all drugs dangerous?'

'I suppose so but this is tame, really. I try to keep away from the heavier stuff.'

Becky gasped. 'You mean you've tried other things?'

Jess nodded. 'I've done ecstasy loads of times and coke a few times. But whizz doesn't make me as angry as coke.' She dipped her finger into the bag and then held it out to Becky afterwards.

'Go on,' she urged. 'You'll love it. It will make the night more interesting.'

Becky gave in. Tentatively she dipped in her index finger and copied Jess, running it over her top gums. She stood there for a moment.

'What?' said Jess, moments later as Becky remained rooted to the spot.

'I don't feel any different.'

Jess sighed. 'Give it a chance. You'll feel it soon.'

'If I come out with you, can I wear your red shoes?'

'Red shoes, no knickers,' said Jess, grinning.

'What?'

'It's a saying or something.'

'I thought that was fur coat, no knickers.'

'Oh, yes. I think you're right.'

Becky smiled.

'So you'll come out then?'

Half an hour later, they headed for Vincent Square and joined the throng of kids huddled around the Shop&Save car park. Becky became louder and louder as the night wore on. She laughed, she danced and she drank whatever she could scrounge.

Danny, Austin and Parksy strolled up an hour later. Becky was singing an Adele song at the top of her voice. She stopped as they walked past, noticing Austin looking at her. She couldn't work out if he was pleased to see her or sick of the sight of her so she turned her attention to Danny instead.

'Hey, Dan,' she smiled seductively. 'Do you fancy a little bit of hanky panky?'

As Danny turned back with a grin, Jess nudged Becky sharply. 'Oi! Behave yourself, slag.'

'Piss off. I can have whoever I want. It's not up to you.'

'Back off, Becks, or –'

'Ooh,' said Danny, thrilled at the attention. 'There's a fight brewing, lads.'

'Shut up,' said Jess.

'Chill out, woman. I'm stocking up on booze and then going for a drive. Want to come?'

'Did you hear about Pete Freeman?' Danny asked later when the five of them were driving around the estate in his car. Austin had taken the passenger seat again. Becky and Jess were squashed in the back with Parksy.

'No, what happened?'

'He got beat up. He's in hospital. Broken nose, broken arm. His ankle had been stamped on so much that it needed plating.'

Jess and Becky looked at each other and started to giggle.

'Did they catch who did it?' Jess eventually asked after they remembered that the matter didn't warrant their laughter.

'He never saw who it was. He said he came out of the pub and was ambushed.'

'Ambushed.' Jess and Becky giggled again.

Austin looked back with a smirk. 'You two pissed already? Or are you on something else?'

'Us?' Jess feigned disgust. 'Becky and I would never partake of such a thing.'

'Yeah, right. And my dick is two inches long.'

'Two inches!' Jess shrieked. 'I hope it's longer than that.' She nudged him. 'Fancy showing me later?'

'In your dreams, wild one.'

Jess pretended to swoon. She nudged Danny. 'I prefer to dream about you, though.'

Becky bit down hard on her bottom lip. She had to remain calm, make sure she didn't spit out her secret while she was loaded. She also prayed that Danny and Austin wouldn't let it slip either. Luckily, they didn't. Danny pushed Jess's hand away as she leaned forwards.

'How about you, Becks?' Parksy joined in. He grinned lasciviously and pressed his hand to his crotch. 'Who do you dream about?'

'Not you, that's for certain.' She heard Austin snigger. Then he turned around and looked at her.

'Do you dream about me, Becks?'

'Would you like me to?' she dared to say.

Austin ignored her question. 'Do you?'

'I might do.'

'I wouldn't blame you. I am worth dreaming about.'

Their eyes stayed locked together as if no one else was in the car, as if time had stood still and there were only the two of them.

'Sloppy seconds your style, then?' Danny turned to Austin with a scowl.

Austin turned towards him, very slowly. 'Shut the fuck up, Bradley.'

Jess looked on in confusion. 'What does he mean by sloppy seconds, Becks?'

20

After a thankfully uneventful morning at the community house, Cath had hardly set foot on the driveway before Jess and Becky were out of the front door and running towards her.

'We've been robbed,' Jess told her.

Cath's heart sank. She rushed into the house expecting to see a mess but nothing seemed to be out of place.

'I thought you said –'

'Nothing's been touched downstairs except the photo of you and Rich.' Jess handed her the photograph in the frame. The glass was broken, the corner of the frame hanging together by a small tack. 'And the tin that you keep all your notes in.'

Cath frowned. 'How did you know about that?'

'I've always known about it, since I moved in.'

'Ever taken anything from it?'

'No!'

'Me neither,' added Becky quickly. 'But it's empty now.'

Cath went through into the kitchen. The drawers on the unit were all open, the contents thrown across the floor. She stepped carefully over to the tin. Lifting the lid, she saw it was empty.

'Damn and blast!'

'It's that cow, Cheryl, isn't it?' Jess answered herself with the nod of her head. 'I bet she's got out of juvie and come straight round here.'

'Don't call her names, Jess. And I don't think she's out yet,' said Cath. 'Have you both checked your rooms?'

'I've got eighty quid missing,' Jess said quickly.

Cath rolled her eyes. 'Nice try, but you're not getting that from me. Besides, where would you get eighty pounds? And what about you, Becky?'

'No. But I've got nothing to take really.'

'What about Liz's room?'

'It's locked. There's a muddy footprint on the door. Well, a bit of one anyway.'

Cath thanked the Lord for small mercies as she rushed into her own room. Nothing seemed to have been touched in there either. She picked up the huge toy rabbit that sat on the bed. Rich had bought it for her. To everyone else, Roger the Rabbit was a stuffed toy: to Cath, Roger the Rabbit was where she stashed her rainy-day fund. She checked the pocket of his blue corduroy trousers and smiled when she saw the four hundred pounds was still there.

'I hope you give her a good leathering when you next see her,' Jess moaned behind her.

'Who?' asked Cath.

'Cheryl! It must be her. You let her get away with things before so she thinks she can do what she likes.'

'Sounds like someone else I know.'

Jess tutted.

Cath went back downstairs. 'Come and give me a hand,' she shouted to them. 'Help me clear up this mess.'

'Oh, no.' Jess put her arm out in front of Becky. 'You and me aren't setting foot in the kitchen until the plods are called. Our DNA will be over everything and then who will she blame?'

Becky stopped in mid step.

'You've been watching too much television.' Cath shook her head and picked up a pile of papers from the floor.

'Aren't you reporting it?' Jess sounded bewildered.

'Of course I am, but I suppose it will be another unsolved crime reference number to add to the others.'

Two days later as Cath and Liz were on their way home from the community house, Liz dropped a bombshell.

'Moving out?' said Cath. 'Aren't you happy staying with me?'

'Yes, of course,' said Liz. 'I just think it would be good for Chloe to settle down somewhere now.'

'I know, but –'

'She needs her own room, her own space.' Liz looked on with pleading eyes, willing Cath to understand. 'She can't have that at your house.'

'But what about Kevin?' Cath thought back to the last time they'd seen him. 'I'm sorry if I was sharp with you. I just didn't want him to get the upper hand. I don't want you to leave because of it, though.'

'Don't be silly. That hasn't anything to do with my decision.' Liz shook her head. 'Kevin will find me wherever I go. But I've spoken to Josie and she's setting us up in a flat. She's going to reinforce the doors and locks as part of the domestic violence programme initiatives. She's also going to set up a telephone system like yours so I can contact the police if I need to.'

Cath was astounded. 'You've certainly thought it through,' she said.

'Yes, but only because you gave me the confidence to do so. You've become my friend, I hope, as well as my confidante. And if you're up to it, I'm going to need your friendship much more when I leave.'

Cath felt herself blushing at Liz's straight talking. She wasn't used to compliments; that someone liked to spend time with her. She smiled. Putting aside all selfish thoughts of how she'd enjoyed having the two of them around, she hugged Liz.

'You don't get rid of me that easily,' she told her. 'Has Josie got anything lined up for you?'

'There's a flat come empty in Preston Avenue. It's near to Suzie Rushton, you know, from the community house? Josie says we can keep an eye out for each other.'

'That's great.' Cath tried to sound enthusiastic but if Josie had a flat empty, she knew the system. Liz would have to be out of there within a fortnight.

'Would you like to come with me to view it?' Liz asked. 'I'm going tomorrow afternoon, half past two. I'd really like your opinion.'

Cath nodded. 'Sure, why not?'

Later back at home, Cath sat quietly sipping hot coffee. In just under three months she'd watched Liz start to believe that a life without Kevin was possible. That she could do this by herself – fend for herself and Chloe. Still, she might have helped her to gain confidence, but inwardly she cursed herself. It had been great having Liz around to talk to. She was nearer to her age than anyone else. She could have a laugh with her; discuss stupid, light-hearted things, like the men in their shorts when there was only football on the television. Or the latest gossip in *Heat* magazine and last night's episode of *EastEnders*.

More importantly, she'd really enjoyed having Chloe around. That little girl had brought extra rays of sunshine into the house. She was everything that Cath would have hoped for in a daughter: bright, intelligent and caring. Chloe was always asking Liz how she was, always using her manners. Her parents might not have got along but between them they had done a great job of bringing up Chloe. If only Liz could keep Kevin from getting his claws into her, she might not be too damaged by what she'd been through so far.

Yet although she didn't doubt for a second that Liz thought she was confident enough to live alone without Kevin's interference, Cath had seen it all before. She'd helped no end of women who had moved on from there to a new place, only to let their men move back in with them again. A few of them had learned the hard way, ending up with more bruises and mental scars. A few had even come back to stay before moving on again. Each time the women were adamant that their men were going to change; most of the time they never did.

Cath stood up and stretched her arms above her head. No matter what happened in the future, she would be there for her.

A few minutes later, Liz joined her. She turned to Cath with a smile and held up a box of chocolates. 'Got these for tonight. And I thought I could treat you to a takeaway?'

Cath rubbed her hands together. 'Fantastic. As long as it all comes with a bottle of red, I'm good with it.'

Liz laughed. 'You and your wine. At least I won't turn into an alcoholic in my own place.'

'Just promise me that you won't let that useless shit back into your life, once my back is turned.'

Liz tried to look insulted at the suggestion but broke out into a smile eventually. 'I am scared about going it alone but I have you, and Josie, to help me out. Even if it's just for someone to talk things through with, I don't feel so alone anymore.' She held a hand to her chest. 'And I promise you faithfully that I will do my best not to let him get to me.'

21

'Is this it?' Cath sounded exasperated as she looked around the tiny flat.

'Yes.' Josie wasn't put off by her tone as she followed her back into the living room. 'What do you think, Liz?'

Cath didn't give her time to answer before replying. 'And you want to swap my house with its range of rooms for this tiny shed?'

'Of course she does.' Josie prodded Cath lightly in the chest. 'Don't take any notice of her, Liz. She's feeling low because you're moving on.'

'No, I am not,' Cath snapped.

Liz touched her lightly on her forearm. 'She's winding you up. Even I can see that.'

Cath relaxed a little and stuck her tongue out at Josie as a means of apology. If truth be told, she was still smarting over the quickness of everything. If she took this property, Liz would have to be moved in by next weekend or pay rent until she did. The property had to be occupied as soon as benefits were registered against it. But, as Josie had rightly guessed, Cath had started to feel lonely already.

'It's okay, I suppose,' she offered reluctantly. 'Preston Avenue is one of the better streets on the estate.'

'I must admit it's a far cry from my house in Douglas Close,' said Liz as she gazed around the square living room with its dowdy wallpaper and peeling skirting boards. 'But it's much better than moving in to one of the high-rise blocks.' She smiled at Josie. 'A lick of paint and a fair bit of elbow grease and it will be home in no time. When can I have the keys?'

'Are you sure?' Josie searched Liz's face for the slightest glimmer of doubt but didn't see anything. 'You can stay at Cath's for a while longer.'

'I'm sure,' nodded Liz.

'How does a week on Monday suit you?' asked Josie.

'What do you think, Cath?' Liz twirled round to face her. 'Can you put up with us for that long?'

'Suppose I'll have to,' she muttered. Then she winked at her. 'I am going to miss you, though.'

'See,' cried Josie. 'What did I tell you?'

'I just love having you and Chloe around,' Cath stated. 'Much more than anyone else I've had to stay.'

'I'm sure I'll be in your kitchen as much as mine,' Liz soothed. She ran a hand over a bare wall, feeling the bumps and knocks of years gone by. 'Besides, you're going to help me to decorate, aren't you?'

Cath tutted. 'Trust me to get lumbered with that one!'

Later that night when she was certain she could hear Jess in the shower, Cath knocked on Becky's bedroom door.

'You going out tonight?' she asked.

Becky shook her head. 'Jess has a date. I hate playing gooseberry.'

Cath marvelled at how mature she sounded. It was nothing like the young, frightened slip of a girl who had turned up on her doorstep at the end of March.

'I have something for you.' Cath sat down on the bed and gave her the pink bag.

'What is it?'

'Open it and see.'

Becky reached inside and took out a small box covered with purple velvet. She flipped open the lid. Inside was a ring, a simple silver band with a tiny pearl and a moonstone.

'Do you like it?'

Becky pulled it out of the box. 'It's lovely.'

'When my husband died, I bought this.' Cath held a silver necklace away from her neck and showed it to Becky. It had a small locket threaded through it. 'This heart reminds me of him. I feel like his love is locked away inside. When I feel sad, I clasp my hands around it and remember his love for me.'

'I've seen you doing that lots of times,' said Becky.

Cath smiled. 'I thought you could do the same with the ring. When you feel sad, twirl it around your finger. When you're ready to move on, if you feel like it, you can take it off.'

Becky had tears in her eyes. Cath touched her face gently.

'It's okay to be upset, Becks, but it's not okay to get drunk, take your anger out on your body. Sometime soon you will stop hurting. And then you will only have the memory.' She took the ring and slid it onto Becky's middle finger. It was a little loose. 'You can come with me to get it altered. I just wanted to buy it for you. I got you this as well.' Cath opened another bag and took out a candle in a glass container. 'Whenever you feel sad, light this and think of your baby. I light one up every year on my wedding anniversary and to mark Rich's birthday.'

'What about –'

Cath shook her head. 'I don't want to remember the day he died. I want to remember the happy times.'

Suddenly Becky was crying. 'I don't want to forget it,' she sobbed, 'but it hurts to remember it.'

'You have to think about things before they fade.'

'How long will that take?'

Cath sighed, wishing she had the answer to that one. She still hadn't got over it yet.

'I don't know,' she said. 'Some people get through it quicker than others. Some don't get over it at all. You are the only one who can decide how it goes.'

Becky sniffed. 'I don't want to.'

'I know.' Cath nodded. 'Believe me, I know. But life needs to go on.' She paused for a moment. 'Don't think I'm being callous but maybe you should think about coming to do some more lessons at The Community House now? It's too late, really, to go back to school - but you could think of sitting your exams at college in September. Having something in the future to focus on might help.'

'I don't want to think of the future without my baby.'

Cath hugged her. There was so much more she wanted to say but for now she chose to abstain. Becky didn't need to hear anything else.

Cath went to her own room. By the side of the bed, she dropped to her knees and pulled out an old-fashioned toffee tin from underneath it. She sat down and, with a deep breath, took off the lid.

The tin was full of mementos. Photos of times gone by, birthday cards, anniversary cards, tickets for her first concert to see Take That and tickets for last year's concert to see Take That where she'd nearly lost her voice by shouting 'I love you, Gary'.

The first photo she came to had been taken on her wedding day. As she picked it up, a lone tear rolled down her cheek. Although she could clearly see his smile, clearly hear his laughter, she couldn't remember Rich's touch. She ran a finger over the image. The picture had aged but the twinkle in his eye was still plain to see.

When he'd died, one by one, all their friends had dropped away. Friends she'd thought would stay around forever had deserted her. It had hurt at first: had they only come to see her because of Rich? Why did everyone love Rich and not her?

But then she'd come to realise that they were uncomfortable around her now that she was no longer part of a couple. They'd done so much together that it was hard for people to accept her alone. Without him, she was a reminder of what had been and his friends couldn't cope with it. It was easier for them not to acknowledge her, she could see that now. But it still hurt and three years later, it left her with no one to confide in.

Quickly, she flicked through the box to find something that would make her smile. She found another photo of Rich. Bare-chested, he was sipping a beer at a beach café. They'd been in Ibiza. Cath closed her eyes for a moment, almost feeling the breeze rustling through her hair as she recalled the two of them running along the beach hand in hand, getting drunk on sangria and skinny-dipping at midnight. With so many dreams and wishes, they'd planned their lives down to the finest detail. At least some of it had turned out as they'd expected.

Rich's memorial card was next to surface. The funeral service had been a mixture of pride and pain. Pride for the man she had spent most of her life with: pain because losing him had torn her apart.

There was nothing of Cath's childhood in the tin except her birth certificate. She picked it up. Underneath it was what she was looking for. Folded up inside an anniversary card was another birth certificate. Inside that was a small photograph. She gazed at it sadly before turning it over to read the word she'd written on the back of it when she was eighteen.

Simon.

The blue ink of the lettering had faded over time but the image was as sharp now as the day it was taken. It was her most treasured possession, a photograph of her son, provided by the hospital. Simon's tiny hands were up by the side of his head. He had a bush of dark hair, her long fingers, and her stubby nose. Painfully, she recalled she hadn't had time to notice anything else before he'd been whisked away.

Why hadn't she told Rich about him? It had been her one stupid mistake and it haunted her now just as much as it had then.

Cath's tears wouldn't stop this time. She cursed. Why had she made herself look at the photos? Hadn't she cried enough over the past few days?

But really, she knew why she had opened the tin. It was because, as she'd gone through Becky's trauma with her, she'd been thinking that now was the right time to do something about making amends for her own mistake.

She was going to look for her son.

22

Josie and Liz were sitting together during a break in the latest self-assertiveness session. They'd both sat through a harrowing discussion, listening to Alison Bennett. Alison had fled from her husband four times so far. Each time he'd found her and each time he'd dragged her back to their marital home and beat her to within an inch of her life. But she'd still left again. After the last time, she'd pressed charges and he got eighteen months.

Instead of looking forward to the six months Alison had left before he got out, she was counting down the weeks until he would find her again. She was certain that he would. Josie hoped that wouldn't happen to Liz. Despite her professional role, she'd become quite fond of having her around.

'So are you all set for the big move?' she asked Liz.

'I think so,' Liz replied. 'Although I'm pretty scared after listening to Alison just then.'

Josie had no answer to that. 'At least the security pack is in place now,' she said instead. 'I do wish I could offer you more in the way of safety but a personal alarm, property alarm and a reinforced front door is about my limit.'

'It's a start.' Liz nodded gratefully. 'And you never know, maybe Kevin will get bored after a while.'

'That is when he eventually finds out that you're not at Cath's anymore. Oh, I nearly forgot. I have something for you.'

Josie rushed out of the room and came back dragging a black plastic bag behind her. She plonked it at Liz's feet.

'Curtains, cushions and covers,' she explained. 'One of my tenants, Dot, brought them in yesterday. Don't worry – she's one of my better tenants so they're clean. They're yours, if you like them.'

Liz opened the bag and looked inside, expecting to see some garish sixties flowers or gingham checks but was pleasantly surprised to see modern aqua blue, coffee and chocolate swirls on a cream background.

'They're really nice.' She smiled her gratitude. 'I'll take them, thanks.'

'There are a couple of framed pictures in there too, and some decorative candles.'

'I never checked to see if there were any curtain rails.' Liz delved into the bag again and pulled out two church candles and an unopened bag of pot-pourri.

'Two minutes ladies, and we'll get back together.' Josie waved a hand in the air to signify that the break was nearly over and then turned back to Liz. 'That's not a problem. I'll get Matt to come over, if not. He'll brighten any place up. And he's such eye candy, isn't he?' Josie raised her eyebrows in a comical fashion.

Liz shook her head. 'Don't even think about it. I've had enough of the one I've left. I don't want to get involved with –'

'Not you,' Josie interrupted. 'I would never suggest that after what you've been through. I was thinking more along the lines of Cath.'

'Oh?'

'It's never right that she's on her own after so long. Rich died three years ago now. She gives so much of herself to other people that it's time she found someone to look after her for a change.'

'I wonder what's stopping them getting together. I know she likes him. She talks about him often – quite often, in fact.'

'I'm not sure, really.' Josie paused for a moment. 'Maybe we should think about setting them up. What do you think?'

'It's very kind of you to do this,' Liz said to Matt.

'I didn't have much choice,' Matt replied. 'That Josie is a right slave-driver. Not that I mind, though,' he added hastily. 'As long as I get a cuppa and a chocolate biscuit as a reward, I'm content.'

Liz smiled. 'It doesn't take much to make you happy, then?'

'Man of simple taste, me.' He grinned. Then he glanced through the window. 'Hey, there's a pretty woman walking down your path.'

Liz followed Matt's eyes and smiled. Time to put Operation Cath into place. She rushed to the door.

'Cath, how lovely to see you.'

Cath smirked. 'I only saw you this morning, you dope. What are you going to be like when you desert me and move in here? And after all I've done for... oh.'

Matt jumped off the steps and moved backwards, pretending to cower. 'Don't hurt me,' he cried. 'I promise I'll be good.'

'Hello, again to you, too,' Cath grinned. 'I had a feeling that the elbow in the chest would be a standing joke for a long time to come.'

As Matt took the box she was holding, Liz watched with interest. Was Cath blushing? She sensed tension mounting but it was shot down by the arrival of Becky.

'Christ, this box is heavy,' she moaned. Spotting Matt, she hauled it on top of the one he'd taken from Cath.

'Anyone for coffee?' Liz asked. She grabbed Becky by her shoulders and marched her across the room towards the tiny kitchen. 'You can help me.'

Once Matt had put down the boxes and gone up the ladder again, Cath opened the lid of the top one and busied herself unearthing some mugs that she'd decided to give away. Sneakily, she stole another look at him. He had his back towards her, showing her his shapely, muscular legs and buttocks that fitted his jeans just so. As he reached up to secure a bracket, his white T-shirt rose up slightly to reveal bare skin at the waistline. Her hand reached out of its own accord and she pulled it back speedily. Her eyes continued upwards. No unsightly curly neck hair on show.

Matt must have sensed her staring and suddenly turned her way. Cath was caught.

'How are you finding your new job?' she asked him quickly.

'It's great.' He pointed to another bracket on the floor. Cath passed it to him. 'The duties are really varied, keeps me busy. Mind you, I've heard your job keeps you busy too.'

'Oh?' Cath didn't know whether to be pleased that he'd asked about her or curious to know why.

Becky came through with a tray of drinks. 'Tea for the workers,' she said. 'Although from where I'm standing, there doesn't seem to be much work being done.'

'Cheeky,' said Matt. 'Men take their time to make sure things are done right.'

'More likely they take their time full stop,' Liz remarked as she joined them again.

'I can see that no matter what I say, I'll be outnumbered.' Matt jumped down to their level again. 'Three to one's no good for any man.'

'Especially when we hate men more than most women,' said Becky.

Matt opened his mouth to speak but thought better of it.

Becky laughed. 'Joking,' she admitted. 'I know all men aren't losers.'

'Most are,' muttered Liz.

'Now, now,' Cath chastised. 'Don't give Matt a hard time. He's being a saint today. I know I'm a dab hand with a paintbrush but I'm hopeless with a drill. Some things you do need a man for.'

'Like sex,' Becky giggled.

'Not necessarily,' Cath and Liz said simultaneously. Then embarrassment set in. They looked at each other, then at Matt, who now had the colouring of tomato ketchup, and burst into laughter.

'I'm getting back up my ladder,' said Matt. 'There are too many hormones at this level for my liking.'

The next morning, Cath couldn't believe her eyes when she found another note sitting on the doormat. In annoyance, she swiped up the envelope and tore it open.

'I'M COMING AFTER YOU'

She sighed with frustration. That was the third one now. She couldn't keep it from Liz any longer.

But Liz was so happy about moving out. Did she really want to spoil that happiness? She knew it wouldn't take Kevin long to find out where she and Chloe had moved to but maybe by then he would have given up on this stupid note writing thing.

As she made her first coffee of the day, yet again she wondered how much risk she was putting Liz in by not telling her about them. She decided it was time to speak to PC Baxter. Andy would know what to do. Maybe he could warn Kevin off with a stern word. That way, she wouldn't have to tell Liz, and Kevin would get his comeuppance and perhaps be more wary of leaving notes. Liz didn't need anything to distract her from the move. Because Kevin hadn't been around, Cath had watched her soften a little more. Since she'd seen the flat and started to move her things in readiness for the move this weekend, she'd seen a sparkle come back to her. It was a sign of hope. Who was she to dash it for her? Quickly, she hid the note and made a mental reminder to catch up with Andy.

23

'You must have heard the kettle boiling,' Cath said to Andy as she opened the front door to him later that afternoon. He followed her through into the kitchen.

'Sorry I couldn't ring after I got your message. I've been busy on a bit of business,' he explained as he sat down at the table. 'Still trying to get my mitts into that thieving Mick Wilkinson but the scrote, as always, is evading me. What's up?'

'I need your advice on something.' Cath retrieved her diary from the drawer and showed Andy the hand-delivered notes.

'It does seem a bit suspect,' he said after studying them. 'They're obviously from the same person: they all have a threatening tone to them. Even so, we have no proof unless there are fingerprints that we could match up to our database.'

'It's him.'

'The ex-husband?'

Cath slid a mug of tea across the table and sat down opposite him. 'I think so. But what about you?'

Andy nodded. 'It's more than likely. You don't think they're for either of the other girls? Jess or Becky?'

'No. I think what needs to be said to them would be said direct.'

'You mean with a slap rather than a grown-up taunt.'

Cath grinned. 'Precisely.'

Andy read the notes again, spreading them out on the table. 'Do you want me to warn him off?' he asked.

Somewhere to Hide

'Will it work?'

'I can't be certain of it.' He held up a hand for silence as a voice came through over his radio but then continued to drink his tea when he realised it wasn't for him. 'But sometimes it does the trick. I'll mention harassment warnings again to see if he gets the message. Most of the time they do.'

'Thanks.' Cath felt her shoulders relaxing as her problem was shared. 'Will you keep it to yourself, though?'

Andy raised an eyebrow inquisitively.

'I haven't said anything to Liz.'

'Ah.'

'I don't want to worry her,' Cath spoke out defensively. 'She's trying to forget him and move on, not be reminded of his every move. I don't want to worry her any more than is necessary.'

'You're getting too close, Cath,' Andy pointed out gently. 'She has a right to know.'

'Yes, but –'

'How would you feel if someone had kept it from you?'

Cath looked down at the table. Andy was right: she'd be mortified.

'And what if there are more to come? If he thinks they aren't being taken seriously, he might move on to other things.'

'I don't follow.'

'If he thinks that the notes don't bother Liz, then,' Andy shrugged a shoulder, 'who knows what else he might do to get her attention.'

They sat in silence while Cath mulled it over.

'I still don't know what to do,' she said eventually.

'Yes, you do. It's Liz who needs to decide. You should show them to her.'

'Please, just try to sort it first.'

After a moment's contemplation, Andy nodded. 'If we can sort it out, then it will be better all round.' He pointed to the notes. 'I'll keep these safe for now and see what my wonderful persuasive tactics can do.'

*B*ecky rearranged her skirt and climbed back into the front of Danny's car. She pulled down the visor and applied a generous layer of Strawberry Burst. The sickly scent invaded the small space but it didn't make it smell any better.

Since Jess was now seeing Mickey Grainger three nights a week, Becky had become a regular in the back of Danny's car.

After her talk with Cath, she'd stopped sleeping around but Danny seemed to always be available when she was tired of waiting for Jess. And Austin had gone slightly off radar. Twice Danny had picked her up on her way to the shops and both times Austin hadn't been around.

'I want you to do something for me,' Danny said as he tucked his shirt back into his trousers. 'You like sex, right?'

Becky rolled her eyes. 'That's so obvious,' she fibbed. She didn't so much like the sex, as the attention that it gave her but he didn't need to know that.

'I'm doing a job tonight and I need to make sure the security guard is... kept busy.'

Becky flicked her eyes to his. 'You are joking.'

'Nope.'

'You want me to have sex with a security guard?'

'No... yes... no... well, actually whatever it takes for me to get in and out unnoticed.'

'Get stuffed!' Becky folded her arms and turned away. 'I'm nobody's whore.'

'You're a whore when you want to be,' Danny smirked. 'Austin's told me how you've been giving him the come on.'

'I have not.' Becky turned back so quickly that she cricked her neck. She rubbed at it angrily.

'All right, keep your hair on.' Danny lit a cigarette. 'I just need you to flirt with him really. There's money in it for you, if you do.'

'How much?'

'Twenty quid.'

'I'm doing nothing for a twenty.'

'Thirty then?'

Becky paused. 'How come you're not including your new best friend, Austin?'

'That's none of your business.'

'It is if you want me to do a job for you.'

Danny exhaled loudly. Becky wafted her hand in front of her face as the smoke engulfed her.

'All I need you to do is keep the guy on the gate busy, long enough for me to get in and give you a signal when I'm out.'

'What are you going in after?'

'Someone's given me a tip off that there's money to be had. If you can keep the guard sweet once I'm in, it'll be a doddle. Then do the same while I get out again.'

'I don't know, Dan.'

Danny leaned across and pulled her top down lower to show a little more cleavage. 'Use these,' he said. 'Shove them in his face and he'll probably come in his pants.'

Becky had huge doubts of that working. 'What if he's old and manky?' she asked.

'Then use your mouth.' Danny sniggered snidely. 'You're good at one thing. I'll give you that much.'

'I am not going down on some old man just so you can rob somewhere.'

'Fifty quid?'

'Not for a hundred.' Becky opened the car door and scrambled out.

'Becks.' Danny shouted after her. 'Come back!'

'Piss off and do your own dirty work,' she yelled before disappearing through an alley and back into the estate.

Hidden behind a row of industrial bins a few metres away, Austin watched the drama unfold. It had been a good idea to steal a car and follow them tonight: he'd sensed something was going down with Danny. Danny had been way too preoccupied that afternoon. Four times they'd driven past Cookson's Factory. On the third, Austin had asked Danny if he had anything planned. But Danny had flatly denied it.

He grinned when he saw the indignant look on Becky's face as she marched off. Austin hated how Danny made a fool of her, one put down after another when she wasn't around. She was a sweet girl really. She could do far better than hang around with that prick.

As Becky made her way home, Austin watched Danny roll a balaclava over his face and, with a quick glimpse around to check the coast was clear, sling a rucksack over the fencing away from the main gate and climb over after it.

Austin threw his cigarette to the ground, stubbed it out with his heel and followed him. When he got to the fencing, he pulled himself up and jumped to the other side. Grinning, he followed after Danny. What a stupid bastard he was. He'd handed things to him on a plate.

24

As usual when Cath had things on her mind, she found herself up early, sitting in the kitchen drinking tea while everyone in the house slept around her.

She couldn't get Liz from her mind. The house was going to be so different after today when she and Chloe moved out. She was going to miss Chloe belting around as only an eight-year-old can do and asking for bunches in her hair as 'Cath doesn't pull as much as Mum'. Yet she couldn't tell anyone that. Liz had made a momentous step towards gaining her independence. Who was she to come over all self-pitying and sulky because she was going to be left alone again?

She'd caught up with Andy yesterday. He'd told her he'd had a word with Kevin McIntyre who had denied sending the notes. Andy had said he'd try and keep an eye out for Liz as much as he could.

It was then that she thought of Matt. Cath really liked him and she knew the feeling was mutual, but was that all there was to it? And as much as she didn't want to make a fool of herself, she also didn't want to think of anyone taking Rich's place. Rich hadn't left her for someone else. He'd died. Of course he'd want her to move on and stop being lonely but she couldn't. Not yet anyway.

She pushed Matt to the back of her mind again. It was the only space she could muster for him right now. Because at the forefront of it was Simon. After instructing a solicitor to help track him down, she was due to go in and see him soon. She was so nervous about the outcome. What happened if he'd come to a dead end and couldn't find Simon?

Somewhere to Hide

'Morning,' said Liz as she came into the kitchen. 'I can't believe it will be my last one waking up here.'

'Morning, traitor.' Cath smiled as she pulled out a chair for her to sit on.

'Have you been up long?'

'I couldn't sleep. I didn't expect you to be awake yet, though.'

Liz yawned and stretched her arms above her head. 'Chloe kept me awake for most of it. She's as excited as if it was Christmas Day. Now she's fast asleep and *I* am wide awake.'

'And are you all set?'

'I'm still scared to death about it,' Liz admitted candidly. Then she came across all shy, blushing as she spoke. 'Talking to you is like having my own personal counsellor. You're like my fairy godmother really. Even after knowing you for such a short space of time, I'm going to miss you so much.'

'Oh, I'm not far away and always at the end of the phone.'

'At least I have Chloe on side. She's been an angel, as usual. I don't know what I did to deserve such a good little girl.'

Cath smiled at the memory of Chloe when she'd first seen the flat. She hadn't taken any notice of the peeling wallpaper, the smelly kitchen cupboards, the overgrown jungle of a garden, the rubbish that had to be removed before they could move in. Even having her own bedroom again had been second best. The main thing that had swung it for Chloe was that her best friend, Emily, lived three doors away.

'I know,' Liz agreed. 'She can't decide where to put her bed in her new room. That was mainly why she couldn't sleep last night.'

'What time is your furniture arriving?'

'Anytime from nine until midday. I'm so grateful for Josie's help.'

Josie had put Liz in touch with a place that sold second-hand furniture. For a small fee and proof that she was claiming benefits, she could take away as much as she wanted. Josie had warned her that sometimes the donations weren't up to much but other times she'd seen people come away with some wonderful items.

Liz had trotted off with a list and apart from a coffee table had got the lot: double bed, single bed, wardrobes, drawers, small table and chairs that folded up out of the way, bookcase for Chloe and a wall unit for the living room, washing machine, cooker, small television and a nearly-new, grey, Dralon three-piece suite. Not exactly the colour she would choose but the quality was superb. And although most things weren't up to much in the fashion stakes, everything was clean and tidy. She'd even spotted a mirror and a couple of table lamps.

'Praise the Lord for decent people who donate what they no longer require,' she added with a grin.

'I'm going to miss you so much,' Cath said suddenly. 'It's been great having you around.'

'Even though I brought along an eight-year-old maniac and a wayward husband?'

'Works both ways.' Cath nodded. 'Didn't I say welcome to the mad house when you first came to stay?'

Liz faltered. 'Do you think I was right to get away, Cath?' she asked, in a voice similar to Chloe's when she was at fault.

Cath sat forwards and covered Liz's hand with her own. 'Of course! It took a lot of courage to do what you did. Why do you think it was wrong?'

'I thought I could forget him if he wasn't around to remind me. But the memories came with me – not to mention the man himself at times. I can't stop thinking about him, yet I know that I don't want to be with him anymore. It's like his ghost is following me around. Watching my every move in case I do something he disapproves of. Every time I go out, I keep looking over my shoulder, expecting him to pounce on me. Do you think he'll ever give up?'

Cath shrugged. 'I don't know, Liz. My experience over the years hasn't taught me how to anticipate these things because every man I've dealt with has been different. I've only had a couple who have gone on for a while, though. Maybe Kevin will get fed up eventually.'

'You're such a good listener,' Liz told her, which brought her neatly onto the subject that was intriguing her. 'I think you would have made a great mum. It's a shame you and Rich didn't have any children.'

Cath endeavoured not to look too sad as she tried to explain some of the pain in her heart. 'We did try for years before he died but nothing happened.' She went off into a world of her own, her eyes glistening as she thought about what might have been. Especially if she had told him about Simon. Why hadn't she told him!

Liz gave Cath a sympathetic smile. 'Thanks for listening to me going on. I'm still getting used to everything changing. It's good to have someone to confide in.'

Cath stood up and suddenly Liz was hugging her.

'You're only moving five minutes away,' she said, wiping away a tear. 'You can come back as often as you like.'

'Don't say that,' said Liz. 'If you say it too many times, I might have to stay here. It will be much – what's the matter?'

'Sorry.' Cath had gone to turn the radio up. 'There's something going on at Cookson's Factory down the road. I'm sure I heard that someone's been murdered.' As the hourly broadcast moved on to the next story, she switched on the television to see if the story had caught the morning's news.

. . .

*B*ecky had heard Liz going downstairs but hadn't wanted to get out of bed just yet. But ten minutes later, when she heard Liz go back to her room, she stretched and decided that she might as well get up.

'Morning, Cath.' She yawned loudly before plonking herself down beside her at the kitchen table.

'Morning.' Cath kept her eyes on the television.

'What's up?'

'Someone has been murdered. I'm looking to see if it's anyone I know.'

'Cath!' said Becky. 'That's so morbid.'

'Everyone's interested in something when it happens on their doorstep. It's a local factory – Cookson's. It's not far from here. A security guard was shot last night.'

Becky gulped. She knew exactly how far away it was.

They sat in silence, both engrossed as they watched *Sky News*. The man was reported to be in his forties, had worked at the factory for nine years and was rumoured to come from Stockleigh. He'd been shot twice, once in the chest and once in the leg.

A few minutes later, the news bulletin changed to another story. Cath stood up.

'Suppose I'd better get ready for my shift at The Den,' she said. 'Do you want me to leave this on?'

Unable to speak, Becky nodded. She began to shake. This time it was she who kept her eyes peeled to the screen. But they soon filled with tears as it all became too much for her. Her skin tone changed to a sickly grey colour, eyes deep pools of horror.

'What's the matter?' asked Cath, catching her eye.

'I know who killed that security guard.'

Cath caught her breath. 'Don't tell me that you were involved?'

'No. Danny Bradley wanted me to help him but I wouldn't. I left him there, I swear.'

Cath sat down again. 'Tell me everything,' she said.

Once Cath knew what had happened, she went to ring the police. Becky dragged her knees up to her chest and balanced precariously on the chair. Stupid, stupid cow. What was wrong with her? First there was the business with Uncle James. Then there was the trauma of losing her baby. Now Danny Bradley had murdered someone. Would she always attract trouble?

'What did they say?' She looked up as Cath came back into the room, trepidation plain to see in her eyes.

'They already have Danny in custody. Andy says he can't say much right now but Danny was found injured on site. He claims that he had nothing to do with the shooting, and he has come up with some cock-and-bull story. He says he was hit over the head and passed out. When he came round, the gun was in his hand. What the hell were you doing –?'

'He had a gun?' Becky stood up, her eyes widening in horror. 'He had a *gun*!'

'Yes, a flipping gun! Have you any idea who you've been messing around with? Danny Bradley is a troublemaker and –'

'He had a gun?' Becky repeated. 'I – what happens if they think I'm involved? They'll lock me up too and then I'll get hooked on drugs and end up like that Cheryl. I –'

'Becky!' Cath placed her hands on the young girl's shoulders to calm the hysteria that was mounting. 'If you're telling the truth, you have nothing to worry about.'

'But if I grass him up, I'll have all the Bradley family coming after me. They scare me.' She began to hyperventilate. 'What if –'

'Becky, calm down.' Cath looked her directly in the eye again. 'Danny's prints were all over the gun. And they've found his rucksack. Andy says he'll need to talk to you.'

But Becky could only register one thing.

'No.' She shook her head furtively. 'He's a bit scary at times but he hasn't got murder in him. He must have panicked or something.' She shook her head again. 'No, not Danny Bradley.'

25

Becky was on her way to the shops to get a few things for Cath when she heard footsteps behind her.

'Hey, gorgeous.'

She swivelled round to see who was addressing her and smiled, her heart giving a flutter when she saw Austin running towards her. She hadn't seen him since Danny had been charged last week.

'I heard about Dan,' he said. 'Are you okay?'

'No. It's doing my head in. People keep thinking I was involved.'

'But you weren't, were you?'

'No!'

'Hey, just checking.'

Austin gave her a smile that made her insides do something most peculiar. She leaned on the garden wall of a nearby house.

'Bet you never thought he'd do someone in.' Austin sat down too. 'Want to talk about it?'

Becky shook her head. She didn't think it was possible, even now. At first, she'd blamed herself. If she'd flirted with the security guy, he might not be dead. But eventually she'd realised that this was Danny's fault, nothing to do with her.

'I didn't even know he had a gun,' Becky admitted. 'I've never seen it.'

'He showed me lots of times.'

'Did he?'

'Yeah. He bragged about how he'd use it one day. I thought he was all talk.

Just goes to show how wrong I was. Do you miss him now that he's banged up on remand?'

'Not anymore. He's evil to do that.'

'I know that he should have treated you better.'

'Really?'

'Yeah. He had the chance to be your man and he blew it. I would never waste an opportunity to get to know you better.' Austin reached for her hand. 'I think you're beautiful.'

'Really?' Becky repeated, this time with a giggle.

'Can I say something? You won't get upset?'

Becky shrugged.

'I always thought he was too good for you.'

Becky smiled. 'Really?' she said again.

Austin grinned back. 'Really.'

'Oh.'

'So how about you and me going out some time soon?'

In the city centre, Liz crossed over at the traffic lights on the high street and made her way to the shops. She had a few bills to pay, she needed a small piece of netting for the bathroom window from the indoor market and Chloe had asked for the latest *Bratz* magazine. Although she'd had a few expenses lately, she reckoned she could run to that. Chloe had been a good girl: she deserved a treat.

It had been ten days since she'd moved into the flat. The place was beginning to look welcoming at last and even though she'd spent a great deal of time at Cath's, she was beginning to feel like she could make it into a home for her and Chloe.

Bills paid and netting purchased, she decided to catch the bus home rather than walk the half hour back to Preston Avenue. The day was especially warm and she held her face up to the sun for a moment, still relishing her freedom. It was good to be out on a day like this. Maybe she should take Chloe to the park again this afternoon – that is if she could tear her away from Emily's house, which is where she'd left her this morning. They'd become inseparable since the move. It was good to see her so happy.

When she looked back down again, Liz gasped. Kevin was walking towards her. He was with a young woman: she looked no more than a teenager. They were laughing about something, the woman talking enthusiastically with her hands.

Liz's legs felt as if they were made of something heavy. In desperation, she looked around for somewhere to hide and dived into the nearest shop. Much to the astonishment of the till assistant, she pressed herself up against the wall.

She watched as Kevin walked past the doorway, his arm now slung around the girl's shoulders. He hadn't seen her.

Liz gulped, her hand covering her mouth as she began to dry-retch. She could hear their laughter taunting her. As she stood like a statue, paralysed by fear, Kevin pulled the woman closer and gave her a squeeze. Then she heard giggling.

They walked further away and Liz's breathing took on a life of its own again. She moved across to the window, staying hidden behind a post, continuing to watch until they were out of sight.

'Are you okay, love?' the till assistant asked with genuine concern. 'You look like you've seen a ghost.'

'I – I...'

'Ex-partner was it?'

Liz stared at her but the woman smiled.

'Don't worry, I'm not psychic. I followed your gaze. Would you like to sit down for a while, until you get your colour back?'

'No, I'm fine.' Liz's breathing was calming down now; she wanted to get home as soon as possible. 'But thanks for your concern.'

With that she was out of the shop, heading for home on foot, in the opposite direction to Kevin McIntyre.

26

'I can't believe he's with someone else,' Liz said as she relayed her ordeal to Cath. 'What if he does the same things to her that he did to me?'

'That shouldn't concern you now.'

'I can't just switch off after what he did.'

Cath sighed. 'Sorry, I didn't mean that to sound harsh. What I meant to say is there will always be victims in this world. Maybe he won't hit her –'

'So you think it was my fault that he treated me like that!'

'– Until he gets to know her better,' Cath finished off her sentence.

Liz lowered her eyes. She should have known that whatever Cath said would make sense. As soon as she'd got back to the flat and bolted the door, she was the first person she'd contacted. Cath had been there in minutes. Now she was here, Liz doubted her words.

'Men like Kevin will always get the upper hand with their women,' Cath continued regardless. 'The woman he was with has two choices, just like you did. You chose well. Maybe she will too. But that doesn't mean that you have to feel sorry for her. We make our own mistakes.'

'Yes, but what if he hurts her like he hurt me?'

'You got over it, didn't you? You got away from him.'

'It still doesn't make it right.'

'Of course it doesn't. But in my experience, a lot of women around here are regularly abused by their husbands. It's part and parcel of their lives.' Cath

Somewhere to Hide

raised her hand when she saw Liz was about to interrupt again. 'I'm not saying that it's right. But some of the women don't know any better. They've watched their mothers being punched and kicked by their fathers. They've seen man after man come along and abuse them. None of them chose it, but sometimes it's a way of life for them. Heartless to hear, I know, but some of the women think they deserve it. They –'

'How can you say such things? I never thought I deserved it!'

'Will you let me finish before butting in, woman? Their men drag them down; make them feel insignificant, like they have done wrong. That's what Kevin did to you, didn't he?'

Liz nodded reluctantly.

'He made you feel that you were worth nothing. Like no one else would want you. Now imagine that you confided in your mother and she told you that it was your duty to take a good beating every now and then as par for the course. What would you do?'

Liz didn't know what to say to that.

'Nature versus nurture, Liz. That's what I meant. It wasn't intended to make you feel that you didn't do your best to get away. You are one of the lucky ones. There are too many women out there who go unheard.'

'What would you have done if Rich had hit out at you every now and then?'

'He did.'

Liz gasped. 'What did you do?'

'I hit him back, twice as hard. That's what Josie meant by the shenanigans going on when Rich was alive. He gave me a backhander twice but, luckily for me, Rich was remorseful. And boy, did I make him pay.'

Liz's lower lip started to tremble.

'I'm sorry. I didn't mean it to sound like I was making fun of you.'

'You didn't,' said Liz. 'I'm just so scared.'

Cath hugged her. 'Look around you, Liz. Look what you've created. You have such a lovely place here, a new, safe home. I bet it feels like that already?'

Liz glanced around. The walls were coloured pale aqua, woodwork a slightly darker shade now. To lighten it up, there was a huge mirror hanging over the fireplace. It made more of a focal point than the cheap pine fire surround that had taken hours to strip of its dark chocolate gloss paint. Add to that the curtains and paraphernalia that Josie had given to her and the overall feel of the place was warmth.

She sniffed before nodding. 'It's getting there.'

'And you?'

Liz nodded again. 'We're getting there too, me and Chloe.'

'You'll be okay here.' Cath hugged her again, trying greatly to ease her pain. But when they pulled away, Liz stood with tears running down her face.

'Things will get better, right?'

'Off out with lover boy again?' Jess stood in Becky's bedroom door, watching as she applied her make-up.

'Yep,' said Becky.

'He only wants you because you spread your legs so easily.'

Becky turned her head slightly, enough to stare back. 'Don't be so nasty. You're only jealous.'

'I know.' Jess threw herself down onto Becky's bed. 'Now that Danny's off the scene, it's left me with no one but the local idiots. Bloody marvellous.'

'So Mickey Grainger's off the scene too?'

'Defo. I'm not going anywhere near him now I know he's been shagging around behind my back.'

Not long after they'd become an item, Jess had caught Mickey snogging the face off Lucinda Chapman as she'd been on her way to the toilet in The Butcher's Arms. She'd pulled them apart but instead of taking her anger out on Mickey, she'd punched Lucinda in the eye. A fight had erupted – Becky had become embroiled in it too – but Jess hadn't spoken to Mickey since, despite the constant barrage of text messages and phone calls from him.

'That's precisely why I'm going out with Austin,' said Becky.

'You've only been out with him a few times.'

'So?'

Suddenly Jess's demeanour changed. 'Be careful, Becks. I've heard a few things around the estate about him.'

'Like what?'

'He gave Trevor Watson a right good pasting the other night. Apparently, it was because he looked at him the wrong way.'

'Rumours schmumours,' Becky repeated one of Jess's favourite slang terms. Satisfied with her eye shadow, she started applying mascara. 'And Trevor Watson is a right knob anyway. Everyone knows that.'

'And he slapped one of the Bradley twins because they wouldn't move out of his way.'

This had Becky's attention. 'What were they doing hanging around him? Wait 'til I get my hands on them.'

'Chill out, will you?' Jess sounded horrified.

'Says the one who told me to toughen up.'

'Yes, but that was only to wise up to how things work around here.' Jess frowned. 'Do what you want, but Becks?' She waited for her to look up again. 'I'm here if you want to talk, yeah?'

Becky checked her appearance one more time and grabbed her key.

'Time to go,' she said and pushed Jess out of her room. Austin would be waiting around the corner for her.

27

There had been talk for a while about a crowd of them going bowling. Josie said she'd invited Andy Baxter and his wife and Suzie Rushton from the community house. Liz had said she'd try to get a babysitter and Jess and Becky had said they'd come along too. They had arranged it for that evening but during the day, one by one they'd cried off until there was only Josie and Matt meeting Cath.

When Cath had arrived ten minutes early, she'd spotted Matt in the foyer. Josie hadn't answered her mobile when Matt tried to contact her. They'd then waited a further half an hour before realising that she wasn't going to show. Embarrassment turned to laughter and they'd decided to go it alone. And it had been great, once the awkwardness had gone. Cath hadn't enjoyed herself so much in a good while.

'I can't believe you've thrashed me,' Matt said as they zigzagged through the milling crowds in the foyer of Super Bowl and then out into the night.

'I promise I wasn't fibbing when I said I was useless at it.' Cath grinned, failing to hide her delight: she had beaten Matt four games to two, including five strikes.

Matt folded his hand around hers. 'You'd better not relay any of this to Josie. She'd beat me up for lesser things.'

Cath tutted. 'You mean our friend who set us up?'

They fell into a steady pace along the path that led to the car park. Matt stopped as they drew near a burger van.

'Fancy a hot dog?'

'Why not?'

They joined the small queue and within minutes had put in their order.

'How long have you known Josie?' Matt asked as they waited for it to be prepared.

'Since she started working on the Mitchell Estate.'

'So were you a naughty girl then? Josie only deals with unruly tenants –'

Cath thumped him playfully on his arm.

'Or so I heard.'

'My husband had a flat and once we were married, she helped us to get a bigger place. We didn't have any children so we were bottom of the list for a house. Josie persuaded one of the old girls with a large three-bedroom house to do a swap with us. We had a downstairs flat with hardly any garden to maintain so it was perfect for her. Turns out it was more perfect than I thought once Rich had gone. The largest bedroom was converted into two small box rooms, giving me four bedrooms, and there's a separate dining room, which I use as a spare bedroom in emergency situations. I sometimes sleep on a sofa bed in the kitchen on the odd night if necessary, too - if someone needs a bed in a hurry for a night.'

'Wow, that's impressive.'

She smiled with affection. 'I love doing what I do. I've always admired Josie for the work she does, too.'

'She is remarkable,' Matt agreed. 'I suppose she's always been so passionate?'

Cath nodded. 'Not many things get her down, although I thought we'd lost her last year when the community house opened. But luckily for us, she splits her time between there and the office.'

'She still does support calls?'

'Yes. She wanted to keep in with the women on the estate. She's a born helper. Anyway, less about Josie. What about you? What really brought you here? Marriage break up?'

Matt looked on in astonishment. 'How did you know?'

'It was a lucky guess.' Cath grinned. 'Do you have any children?'

'No, we never got around to it.' Matt sniggered harshly. 'We were always too busy arguing to think of the better things in life. And I'm not sure that I want children now. I'm forty-five.'

'That's not old.'

'It's old enough to be set in my ways.'

Cath frowned. He seemed so sure about it that it was almost too sad to hear.

'And you don't have any regrets about moving?' she asked, deciding to change the subject. 'Now that you've been here for a while, I'm sure you must be as mad as the rest of us?'

Matt laughed. 'I still don't think the Mitchell Estate is that bad.'

'It is.'

'It was strange at first, I must admit, but now I wouldn't want to be anywhere else.'

'You're definitely as mad as the rest of us then,' Cath teased.

'I must be. But the best thing about moving here so far is that it's given me a chance to get to know you.' Matt moved towards her and lightly kissed the corner of her mouth.

He moved back, staring intently at her.

Cath pulled him close again.

When Cath got home and let herself into the house, Jess and Becky were huddled together on the bottom step of the stairs.

'Did you hear my car?' she asked, amused to see they were waiting for her.

'Yes, we wanted to know how the date of the century went,' said Jess.

'I'll kill that Josie Mellor when I get my hands on her,' Cath told them. 'She set us up.'

The girls only had to glance at each other before bursting into laughter.

Cath turned her head sharply. 'Did everyone know?' she asked, feeling the start of a smile.

'Yeah.' They spoke in unison.

'I will definitely kill her when I see her.' Cath grinned as they stared at her, waiting for more details she presumed. 'But it was worth showing up. I had a great time.'

'And did you have a snog?' Jess followed her through to the kitchen. Becky was right behind her.

'Never mind, young lady.' Cath busied herself making coffee.

'Didn't he try to feel you up?'

'Jess!' said Becky. 'People as old as Cath don't get felt up.'

'What do you mean, people as old as me?' Cath came to her own defence. 'I'll have you know I haven't reached forty yet.'

Becky grinned. 'You know what she meant. Sex for us teenagers is a boy seeing how far a girl will let her go.'

'You should know that one,' whispered Jess.

Becky glared at her but relaxed when she saw her grinning too. Now that they were getting on much better, the snide remarks had stopped. But every now and then, Becky couldn't fathom out what was intended and what wasn't. This time she saw it was meant as a joke.

'Did you go bowling eventually?' Becky asked.

'Yep.'

'And did you get a strike?' Jess taunted.

'Yep.' Cath bit her lower lip to stop from smiling at the double meaning of the sentence. But then she decided to back it up. 'Five times actually.'

Becky and Jess looked on wide-eyed. Cath smiled: two could play their silly games.

'I had a hot dog as well,' she also volunteered.

Jess and Becky smirked at each other.

'Is *that* what you called it in your day?' Jess teased. 'We'd call it –'

'I had a hot dog of the *food* variety, you cheeky mare. In *my* day, we never did anything untoward on a first date. Yes...' Cath paused. The night had been fun, even though it had felt really strange to kiss another man after so long. All at once, it had made her realise how lonely she was. So when Matt had suggested they meet up again, she'd agreed without hesitation.

'Yes, I do admit to going on a date with Matt,' she said sweetly. 'And what's more, I'm going out with him again.'

Even though Cath had enjoyed herself immensely that evening, she ended up having a fidgety night. Images of Rich and Matt flashed up intermittently and she tossed and turned in her bed. First she'd be kissing Rich and then pushing him away. Then she would do the same with Matt. Then she would wake up breathless, wrestling with the duvet, pummelling the pillow to stop from screaming out.

What was wrong with her? The first man she'd shown any affection to and she was reacting like this. She should be remembering Matt's touch, Matt's tender kisses. Surely after three years she had nothing to feel guilty about? Yet she couldn't help feeling at fault – which left her with one burning question. Was she really ready to go out with Matt?

But she knew the lack of sleep was more to do with the appointment she had with the solicitor that morning. He had rung to ask her to call in. She was dreading knowing what he had found out, if anything, but also she was so desperate to know.

Finally, she could bear it no longer. Even though it was only five thirty, she got up. It didn't make sense to try and force sleep.

Going downstairs, she noticed there was another note waiting on the doormat. Annoyed, she ripped it open.

'STINKING WHORE'

Cath sighed. How dare Kevin write that about Liz, especially after Andy Baxter had warned him of the consequences if he sent any more messages.

Although she could be grateful for one thing, she supposed. Obviously,

Kevin didn't know that Liz wasn't living there anymore. She hoped he'd moved on when Liz had seen him out with that young girl in town but it looked like he was back on the scene. She would have to brace herself for another torrent of abuse. Kevin wouldn't give up until he knew where Liz had gone. She could keep him off the scent for a few days, a week at the most, but he'd want to see Liz. Come what may, there was no way Cath would ever tell him where she had moved to.

She tucked the note away to give to Andy. Why couldn't Kevin accept that Liz didn't want that kind of life anymore and leave her and Chloe alone? What was it with some men these days, she wondered? Why did they think they had the right to interfere in a woman's life and leave her with nothing but turmoil?

She sat down at the table with a thud and rested her head in her hands. In the space of a few short hours, her life had turned upside down. Wait until she got hold of Josie Mellor.

But she was smiling.

28

'It's your fault,' Cath told her when she collared Josie in her office later that same morning. 'You started this whole sorry fiasco.'

'*You* needed a helping hand,' said Josie. 'You shouldn't have to be alone at your age. I know Rich wouldn't have wanted that.'

'Talk to the dead, can you?'

'Oh, Cath, I'm sorry. I didn't think.' Josie raised her hands in surrender. 'You're right. I was a nerd head. I just thought that you and Matt were a good fit. He's single, a nice guy and so attractive. You're single, a nice woman and well... I knew he would find you attractive. You deserve some fun, some loving in your life. What are you so afraid of?'

'Afraid of?' Cath looked on in wonder.

'Starting again, in case it doesn't work out? In case it doesn't measure up to you and Rich?'

'Our marriage wasn't that perfect, as well you'll remember.'

'You see?' Josie smiled encouragingly as she picked up a bundle of files. 'So don't make out that it was all sweetness and light and that you will never find another Rich. No one is expecting you to do that. I want you to find a Matt.'

Despite herself, Cath smiled. She knew that Josie was right – she had been over-analysing her marriage. But she was wrong about one thing.

'I'm not afraid,' she told her. 'I just feel guilty after... after...'

'Cath Mason, surely you didn't give out on your first date?'

'No. I meant I haven't been kissed by anyone else for years. That's the reason behind all this crap I've been tormenting myself with.'

'Then it's about time you caught up and moved on.'

Cath spotted the clock. 'Will you look at the time. I'm going to be late!'

'Yes, where are you off to, dressed up all posh?' Josie asked as she rushed to the door.

'I'm going in to town.' Cath was non-committal. 'Nowhere in particular.'

Rushing through the pedestrian-only shopping area an hour later, Cath got to her appointment with ten minutes to spare. She sat down in the roomy reception area and reached for a magazine. Steele, Barrett and Co had been the first solicitor she'd come across in the local phone directory. Now that she was here, she recalled looking inside it many times on her trips into town.

She casually thumbed a gardening magazine as she recalled what Josie had said about Matt. She knew she'd put Rich on a pedestal and left him there too long. Would he really have wanted her to be alone forever? Not likely. And Matt was a nice guy to mess around with. It didn't have to be anything serious.

A door opened to her right and a man she was sure wasn't old enough to have passed any exams, came towards her. If first impressions really did count, he had to score top marks. All smart pin-striped suit and shiny black shoes, his hair, although cut in a choppy style, looked like he'd spent hours getting it just right. He strode towards her, his large hand outstretched.

'Mrs Mason?' He shook hers firmly. 'I'm David Barrett. Come on through. Zoe, could we have drinks, please?'

The office she was ushered into was vast, modern and tidy. Even its minimalist décor seemed inviting. Cath sat down, realising that if the business was as good as the overall appearance of everything she'd seen so far, this was going to cost her a fortune.

'Mrs Mason, I won't beat about the bush. I did some digging around after you called to arrange this meeting,' Mr Barrett started once he'd settled into his seat. 'I know the details you gave me were scarce but no one can change their date of birth, now can they? Unless they don't want to be found, that is.'

Mr Barrett laughed a little. Cath smiled faintly to play along with him but she didn't find it funny. What planet was he on? People changed their identity with plastic surgery these days, so changing a date of birth to get lost in the system would be a doddle.

She looked up as Mr Barrett had paused. He had the most captivating of eyes, but Cath could see apprehension in them. She held her breath, studying his face, desperately looking for some sort of clue.

'What is it?' she prompted.
'Mrs Mason, I've managed to track down your son.'

29

'But how?' Cath's hand clutched her chest. 'I only gave you a few details. Where is he? Does he want to see me? Oh, don't be so pathetic, Cath. Of course he doesn't want to see you. Not after all these years.'

Mr Barrett held up his hand for her to stop but she continued as if not seeing it.

'And abandoning him like that as a –' She sat forwards. 'He does want to see me, doesn't he?'

'Mrs Mason.' Mr Barrett spoke straight yet with a soothing manner. 'I'm sorry but, no, he doesn't.'

'What?' Cath faltered, trying hard to keep her composure as the man sitting before her shattered her dreams.

'I tracked down his adoptive parents. He was with them until he was ten. They told him about you then. They thought it best to be honest with him from an early age but it backfired. He started to become disruptive, uncontrollable. Eventually they had no choice but to put him back into care. He spent the rest of his years in a council run home and that is all they can tell me. He rings them sporadically – he does have a tendency to go off radar for long periods. During his last call, they told him you were trying to contact him but he said that he didn't want to see you. I could keep on digging, if you'd rather hear it from him?'

Cath felt like she'd lost the ability to speak.

'People change, Mrs Mason,' Mr Barrett added, noting her distress. 'He was only sixteen when they last saw him. Would you like me to continue with my enquiries?'

'No, thank you.'

Without remembering how, Cath got into her car and began to drive. The sky was an inviting clear blue but her mood was sombre. Passing the city's central park, she decided to pull over and take a walk.

With every step she took, she didn't notice anyone who passed her by. The flowers were out in bloom, the perfectly mowed lawns and the preened hedges were wasted on her. All she could see was her baby being taken away, Mr Barrett's words running continuously through her mind.

She carried on until she found herself by the side of the lake. Spying a bench that was as empty as she felt inside, she sat down. Before long, tears poured down her face. For years, she had dreamed of this moment and, now it was here, it had all turned out wrong.

Why wouldn't Simon see her, let her explain the situation? Let her explain that she thought she'd done the best for him.

It hadn't even crossed her mind during last night's thoughts of Rich and Matt. She'd thought the meeting today would be a matter of formality, sorting out further details or finalising others so that Mr Barrett could then begin his search. Cath didn't think for one minute that he would have acted so quickly.

For three hours, she watched the world go by while inside she was breaking. Her mind replayed every single detail of the time when she had given Simon up for adoption. Even now she could clearly recall the tiny curls of hair stuck to his face as he took his first few breaths and found out that he could scream.

She could still see his tiny squashed nose, his long, yet perfect fingers which wound round her thumb so tightly. Like that one treasured photograph, she only had a memory. She couldn't remember anything else because he had been taken away.

But all too well, Cath remembered that feeling of inadequacy and longing. How she cried as the nurses looked on. She'd wanted to scream at them, make them understand that she wasn't in a good place, that she couldn't look after him. That she was scared, alone, vulnerable.

Now it was like losing him again. After all this time, all the years she had yearned to see her son's face, longed for forgiveness, he didn't want to know, and she couldn't blame him.

For a while, she found herself hating Rich. If he hadn't been sent to prison, this would never have happened. And she should have been able to talk to him, air her concerns. Things might have been so different then. Why hadn't she trusted him? If he loved her as much as he said he did, then surely he would have understood her dilemma?

But she knew she couldn't blame Rich for any of it. It was all her fault. She'd chosen not to tell him because she didn't want him to leave her. She couldn't risk losing him so instead she'd stayed quiet. She was the stupid one.

Cath jumped back to reality as a man too old to be riding a bicycle rode past, narrowly missing her feet as he wobbled about perilously. It was the first week of the school summer break and the park was busy. Children ran around the outside of the lake. Mothers fed the ducks with their toddlers. A group of boys with nets and buckets were shouting so loud they would frighten off anything they might catch. A man was walking towards them, no doubt to tell them to be quiet. She began to cry again. How could life go on all around her?

She must have gone off in a daze again because the next thing she saw was a stout man wearing green overalls standing in front of her. He had kind eyes and a warm smile.

'Are you okay?' he asked gently. 'You've been sitting there for hours.'

'I'm admiring the beautiful view,' Cath said, knowing that he'd see right through it.

'Troubles are better when they're shared. Haven't you got anyone to talk to?'

'Sometimes the words won't come out, no matter how many people are waiting to listen.'

The man sat down beside her, not close enough to cause offence. 'Whatever you have done, or indeed what someone else has done, can always be rectified,' he said.

Cath sniffed. 'If only it were that simple. I've ruined someone's life.'

'I doubt it. We humans do a pretty good job of that ourselves.'

They sat in silence for a minute or two before he put his hands on his knees and pushed himself up straight.

'I was about to have a coffee before I leave for the day.' The man smiled warmly. 'There's a spare one going, if you'd like it?'

Cath burst into tears. His kindness was more than she deserved. She wiped at her eyes quickly.

'Thank you but I need to go home. I need to hate myself for a while longer yet though.'

'Don't make it too long, then, hmm?'

He tipped his cap, a gentlemanly gesture that Cath admired in him immediately. Manners didn't cost anything and they were hardly ever reciprocated nowadays. God bless the older generation.

Finally, she headed home. Just before five thirty, she parked in the driveway and switched off the engine. How the hell she was going to get through the rest of the evening she didn't know.

'Cath! Where have you been?' Liz cried as she came through the front door.

Jess and Becky followed quickly behind her. 'The girls rang me when you weren't answering your phone so I came around. We've all been trying. Have you switched it off?'

'You look like crap,' said Jess. Liz nudged her sharply.

To their amazement, Cath walked past them into the living room. All three trouped behind her and watched as she poured a large drink of whatever was first to hand and knocked it back in one go.

'We've been really worried about you,' said Becky.

'I've only been gone for a few hours.' Cath looked at them, each in turn. 'Surely you can survive without me for that long? I'm not responsible for everyone. I can't be responsible for – responsible for –'

She began to fill the glass again but her hands started to shake uncontrollably. Liz took the bottle from her.

'Cath, what's going on?' she asked gently.

Cath looked up. 'I... I...' It was no use: if she started to speak, she would cry. She picked up her bag and left the room.

'Cath!' Liz called after her.

Upstairs, Cath closed the door quickly so they couldn't see the tears streaming down her face. It was all she could do to stop herself turning back to them. She couldn't tell them. She felt so ashamed. But she needed to talk to someone.

In the safety of her bedroom, she switched her mobile phone on and dialled a number. A welcome voice rang out.

'Hello, Josie Mellor speaking.'

30

Cath sunk into Josie's embrace as soon as she saw her but at first she couldn't speak. How could she find the right words to explain what had happened? She was going to show herself for what she was: a fraud, a fake, a useless human being.

But she *had* to tell someone. The secret was eating her up, churning her insides. She took a deep breath before she began.

'I went to see a solicitor today. He's been trying to track someone down for me and...' Cath looked at Josie as she said the words she'd never spoken to anyone before. 'I lied when I said I couldn't have children. I had a son by another man, when I was with Rich.'

'What?' Josie stared at her, wide-eyed.

'I – I was so lonely when he was in prison, and so young and naïve. Three years was such a long stretch. When one of his friends started to call around more than was necessary, I began to look forward to his visits. One day he kissed me and... and I kissed him back. One thing led to another...' Cath clung to Josie as she continued to speak. 'Two months later, I found out I was pregnant.'

'So you had the baby?' Josie sounded puzzled. 'I had no idea.'

'Neither did he. I didn't tell anyone.'

'But how did you –?'

'How could I tell him? It was my fault that I got into such a mess. If Rich had found out, I would have lost him.'

'No, surely not.'

'Of course I would! Rich was a right Jack-the-lad then. It was only prison that changed him for the better as he swore he'd never go back once he got out. Imagine how he would have felt if I'd turned up on his release. "Oh hi, darling. This is Simon. He was born while you were inside. No, Rich I wasn't unfaithful, not once."'

'Your son was called Simon?' Josie said without thinking.

'Yes.' Cath began to cry again. 'And I let him down. I let him down so badly.'

'So you had him adopted?'

Cath nodded. 'I always thought that one day I might meet up with him. But I've just found out that he... he doesn't want anything to do with me, ever. Now I won't be able to t – t – tell him how much I – I loved him. How I made the biggest mistake of my life; how I should never have given him up.'

Josie grabbed a handful of tissues from the cube by the side of the bed and passed them to Cath.

'How come Rich never found out?' she said, wiping at her eyes too. 'You can hardly explain a bump like that away.'

'I kept it hidden for a long time with baggy clothes. Then when it came to the time that I couldn't hide it any longer, I stopped seeing him. I told him that I was ill, kept in touch by phone and letter. I still don't know to this day how I got away with it. I guess he must have trusted me. I rang a friend I'd made when I was in care. She was the only person that knew about Simon; the only one I knew I could trust to help me out and keep quiet. I knew she wouldn't judge me either. Tina let me stay for two months, until I'd had him. Then I came back home and started to see Rich in prison again.'

'I can't believe he didn't find out, given how quickly rumours fly around this estate.'

'He wasn't suspicious about it, I suppose, because no one he knew saw me around so he *could* think I was holed up somewhere with a dreadful bug. And Terry Lewis – that's the father's name – kept his mouth shut.'

'He would, the low life.' Josie knew of Terry and his family. 'He'd be scared of what Rich would have done to him.'

Cath sniffed before blowing her nose loudly. 'I couldn't risk losing Rich if he found out the truth.'

'Oh, *Cath*. Is that why you didn't have any more children?'

'No! I knew I could get pregnant so I assumed there must have been something wrong with him. It might have been me: some sort of complication at the birth, though I can't recall anything going wrong. That's why I didn't push the fact that he didn't want to go for tests. If he had ever found out –'

'And you've kept this to yourself for all those years? That's so brave.'

'It's not brave at all.' Cath shook her head. 'I was a coward, afraid to face up to my responsibilities.'

'No, that's not how it was,' Josie disagreed. 'You were young and frightened. You did what you thought was best at the time.'

'No. I did what was best for me.'

'And what about now? You must feel better that you've told someone about it?'

'No, I feel like I've been robbed of the chance to say I'm sorry,' she said. 'In the back of my mind, I've lived for the day that I can see his face again. I prayed that his new family would love him but he became too much of a handful and they gave him away. How must he feel now? That must seem like a double whammy – the boy that nobody wanted.

'Every year on his birthday, I light a candle for the baby that I lost. Somehow, I always believed I'd meet him when the time was right. It was selfish of me really. All I want to do is to say sorry to him, so that my conscience is clear. But it never will be. He hates me, Josie. He'll never forgive me.'

She started to cry again. This time it took her a long time to stop.

Cath didn't sleep much that night. She'd switched off her mobile phone when a few texts arrived and she hadn't left her room since. Becky had brought coffee and toast up twice but she'd left them all untouched. Even now as a new day was breaking, she was still going over and over the events that led to the ache in her heart.

She was so grateful that she had Josie to talk things through with. As usual, she'd been right there for her. Cath knew she was lucky. Josie was someone she could call a friend, no matter what her job involved. She was the salt of the earth. She would tell her whether she was right or wrong, even if it wasn't what Cath wanted to hear.

It had felt so good to share her secret after all those years. Time after time Josie had said she shouldn't blame herself for what had happened to Simon. Cath told her how she'd often prayed that he would turn up, out of the blue, having tracked her down. There was no doubt that Rich would have been shocked at first but she'd always hoped that he would have accepted the situation, once he'd had time to digest the facts.

She began to cry again. Oh, why hadn't she told Rich the truth? She'd betrayed both of them, her son and her husband. But Rich had been betrayed the most. She'd been deceitful to him every day, until the day he'd been so cruelly taken from her.

She punched the pillow. Then again, and again.

Why, why, WHY?

Why had she lied to the man that had meant everything to her?

31

Jess popped her head round the kitchen door to find Becky sitting at the table busy clicking buttons on her phone. 'Do you fancy coming out tonight?'

'I can't.' Becky didn't lift her head up. 'I'm seeing Austin.'

'But I haven't seen you for ages!'

'I wasn't supposed to be going out with him tonight. He said he was busy but he's texted me, so I am now.'

Jess sighed dramatically, sitting down next to her. 'Can't you cry off and come out with me?' she begged.

Becky relented. Hadn't she said that she would spend more time with Jess? But the thought of seeing Austin again made her insides go all peculiar.

'I hate being on my own,' Jess continued, watching Becky's finger hover over the send button. She grabbed her free hand. 'Please! Knock him on the head and come out with me instead.'

'Okay, okay.' Becky pressed the delete button and began to write another text.

'Yay.' Jess punched the air. 'I've missed having you around.'

'I'll have to tell him that I'm sick or something. I don't want to get him mad.'

'You can't say that.' Jess shook her head quickly. 'If you do, we won't be able to go to The Butcher's Arms in case he's there. And you don't want to make him mad. He might give you a backhander.'

'He'd never do that to me. He's not a scrote like Danny Bradley. Austin knows how to treat a lady properly.'

Jess sighed. 'I hope we can get into The Butcher's. I heard it was raided last week because of us under-agers. We might have to stick to lemonade or have a drink before we go.'

'Whatever.' Becky started to write another text message.

'What are you going to tell him?'

'The truth – well, almost. I'll say I'd already arranged to go out with you.'

'That won't work. He'll be pissed off that you've dropped him for me then.'

'Austin doesn't own me.'

Both of them shot to their feet as they heard the front door open. Jess reached for a tea towel as Becky turned on the hot water tap and quickly squirted washing up liquid on top of the pile of dishes left to soak.

Cath came through with two bags of shopping. 'That's what I like to see, girls.' She put them down on the table and smiled knowingly. 'And once those dishes are done, perhaps you wouldn't mind making me a cuppa before you finish off. I'm parched.' She pulled out a pack of vanilla slices. 'I have cakes too.'

'Have you been to the community house?' asked Becky.

'Yes. I've been with the rabble.'

'I bet they've missed you since you've been ill?'

After her devastating news, Cath hadn't told anyone but Josie about tracking down Simon and finding out that he didn't want to meet her. They'd spoken over the phone since but it had been nearly a week before she'd felt like getting back to her routine again. So she'd faked a sickness virus and stayed at home. She hadn't even told Matt yet.

Before she'd left the community house, she'd collected a few leaflets for Jess. She handed them to her once they'd finished the dishes.

'What's this?'

'New college courses, starting this September. Thought you might like to know what days –'

'Have you seen the time?' Jess shoved the leaflet in her pocket. 'Must dash. Off to see a man about a dog.'

And with that she was gone. Becky wasn't too far behind.

Cath smiled. She wasn't sure if she was more annoyed that Jess wouldn't take her advice or grateful for a bit of peace and quiet to enjoy her drink now they'd gone. And her cake.

*L*ater that evening, Cath was having a girl's night in over at Liz's. Liz had made a huge bowl of chilli con carne for them to eat. Once Chloe had gone to bed, Cath had opened the bottle of wine she'd brought with her.

'I'm glad to see that you're feeling a little more settled,' she said as she passed Liz a glass. 'I do hope Kevin has finally given up now.'

'I hope so, although I'll always have my doubts, I suppose.'

'Maybe he's with that woman you saw him with?'

Liz shrugged. 'Who cares as long as he's not anywhere near us. He told me about her.'

'Really?'

'She's called Charlotte Heyburn and apparently she's a far better shag than me.'

Cath stopped, her glass halfway to her lips. 'He said that? Was he trying to make you jealous? Make you see what you've been missing?'

'I don't know but I ignored him anyway. I haven't seen him since.' Liz lowered her eyes, not wanting Cath to dig any deeper. It had been a traumatic experience when Kevin had collared her at the shops again. He'd waited for her to come out of Shop&Save, taken her arm and marched her over to his car before she'd had time to protest. She wouldn't get into the car with him and so they'd had a heated argument right there in the car park. That was when he told her about Charlotte Heyburn and a couple of others that he didn't even know the names of.

Liz chinked her glass with Cath's. 'Here's to a better future for us both. So come on, spill. Have you done the dirty deed with Matt yet?'

'Don't be so nosy.' Cath tried to look shocked but failed dismally by bursting into laughter.

Liz grabbed a cushion from the settee and threw it at her. 'I need details.'

'It's complicated.' Cath sighed.

'Why?'

'Well, I know that Matt wants to.'

'Hmm, that's a little obvious. He can't keep his eyes off you whenever you're around.'

'Really?'

'Don't try and change the subject.'

'Me? I would never be so devious.'

Liz picked up another cushion. Before she threw it, Cath continued.

'Okay, okay. Where were we? Oh, yes, I was telling you that he wants to and...'

'And?'

'... I want to.'

'And?' Liz was practically hyperventilating by now.

Cath shrugged her shoulders in reply but it wasn't good enough.

'It's like trying to get the truth out of Chloe! What are you so embarrassed about?'

'I'm afraid that I'll have healed up, I'll be totally useless at it, that he won't want to do it again – not to mention, all those embarrassing slurps and slips – that I have to touch another man's...' She ran a hand through her hair. 'I feel like I've forgotten what to do.'

Liz sat there, mouth agog. Then she smiled. 'They're only nerves. I'm sure they'll go once you get down to it.'

'You're sure about that?'

Liz paused for a moment. 'I'm no expert but they do liken it to riding a bike. Once learned, never forgotten.'

'But my bike is an old battered Chopper type from the seventies and I want to be a new type of mountain bike – one with twenty-four gears that can cope with any terrain.'

'You have nothing to worry about on that score.' Liz dismissed her words with a flick of her wrist. 'Get it done and then let me have this conversation with you. I'm sure you'll be fine.'

'You reckon?'

'Yes, I reckon! Stop thinking about it or you'll never do it. There will never be a right time, a right frame of mind or a right state of happiness. Life isn't like that. You have to grab these opportunities...' She stopped then and grinned. 'I was going to say, grab them by the balls.'

Cath grinned too. She raised her glass in the air. 'Right then, I'll do it.'

'What? Grab him by the balls?' Liz raised her glass too. 'Thank goodness for that. Now when shall I ring you for all the gory details? I still want to know everything!'

Becky and Jess were returning from their night out.

'I've had a great time.' Jess slung an arm around Becky's shoulders as they approached the house.

'I really enjoyed it too,' said Becky. 'I couldn't believe that Phipps ended up getting barred for dropping his trousers again.'

'I think he should be arrested after seeing the size of his prick. Did you clock it? It was *huge*. I don't think I'd like it anywhere near me.'

'He wouldn't put it anywhere near you.'

'Only because it's probably already been in you, you cheeky cow.' Jess went to push her but Becky moved out of the way.

'Ha, missed me,' she yelled before tripping and falling back into the flower border. She landed on the lawn with a thump. 'Ow.'

Jess laughed. She pulled Becky up and they walked into the house.

'Cath not home yet then? The dirty stop out. At least she won't know that we've been drinking.' She grinned. 'She must still be out with Matt the Magnificent.'

'She went over to see Liz, remember?' Becky followed her through to the kitchen. 'I'm glad she's seeing Matt though.'

'I know. She seems happier already. Although we still don't know why she was so upset last week, do we?'

'She seems to have got over it now.' Then Becky giggled. 'Imagine how pissed off she must feel that she can't just bring him back to her place because of us cramping her style.'

'I hadn't thought of that. Maybe we should make ourselves scarce some nights.'

They went upstairs a few minutes later. Becky had only just got into her room when she heard a tap at the window. She turned her head quickly. There was another tap. It sounded like a pebble hitting the glass. She looked down to see Austin in the garden. She waved before running downstairs to join him on the back lawn.

'Hiya, you!' She flung herself unsteadily into his arms. 'Have you missed me?'

Austin pushed her away. 'Where the fuck have you been?'

'I told you I was going out with Jess.'

'She's a right slapper: got a reputation for giving out. I don't want you mixing with her, do you hear me?'

Becky wanted to say so many things in reply but she was too drunk to get her head around it all.

'But –' she began.

Austin grabbed her wrists and pulled her nearer. 'When I tell you to do something, you do it. You don't argue. Got that?'

'But –' She stopped. Austin was staring at her in a scary way. 'What did I do wrong?'

'You went out with her when you should have been going out with me.'

'You were busy. You told me last night that –'

'I told you today that I had changed my plans.'

'But I'd already arranged to go out with Jess. Ow, you're hurting me. Let go.'

Austin squeezed her wrists tighter. He pulled Becky to within an inch of his face.

'You do not defy me.' He spoke through gritted teeth. 'Ever. Do you hear me? Or else I'll –'

'Stop it,' she wailed. 'You're really hurting me!'

Austin let go and Becky was pulled into his embrace.

'I'm sorry, my little one.' He ran his hand over her hair, as if to soothe away her pain. 'I'm overreacting again. I really missed you tonight.'

'I'm s – sorry too,' she replied, glad to feel his arms around her once more. 'I won't do it again.'

'I know you won't.'

Luckily for Becky, she couldn't see his menacing expression.

32

Jess and Becky came down for breakfast. Jess walked into the kitchen looking like an extra from a zombie film. Her hair was uncombed, remains of smudged make-up still clear around her eyes. Becky didn't look too much better, blonde hair like rat tails, luggy and unkempt.

'What were you two up to last night?' Cath asked.

'Nothing much,' Jess fibbed, sitting down with a thud. 'We hung around the square.'

'Really? I wasn't born yesterday. You both look like you've been dragged through a hedge backwards.'

'We haven't been drinking,' fibbed Jess, 'if that's what you mean.'

'I'm thirsty,' said Becky, looking away quickly.

As she reached up for a glass, Cath pointed at her. 'What have you done?'

Becky stared down at her wrist where purple-black bruising had begun to appear. She frowned. 'I'm not sure.'

'Were you with Austin? Did he do that to you?'

Becky pulled her hand down by her side.

'She was out with me last night,' said Jess. 'Let me have a look, Becks.'

'It's nothing!'

But Jess looked anyway. She balked. 'I didn't do that, did I? I know I pushed you and you landed on the lawn but I didn't mean to.'

Cath held up Becky's arm for further inspection. 'No, Jess. You wouldn't have done that. But someone did.' She looked Becky straight in the eye. 'Didn't they?'

'I – I can't remember.' Becky wouldn't meet her gaze.

Cath sighed in exasperation. Whatever had gone on last night, Becky wasn't about to confide in her. She would have to get it out of her in her own time.

But get it out of her she would.

The following evening when Matt pulled up outside her house, Cath wasn't looking forward to the night ending. They had been out for a drink and the time had flown by, even though it was still quite early. She had really enjoyed his company. So much so that she hadn't said a word of the prepared speech that she'd been going over in her head before meeting him.

Matt switched off the engine and turned towards her. 'I've really enjoyed myself tonight.'

'Me too,' said Cath. All of a sudden shyness enveloped her.

Gently, Matt removed a stray hair from her face and ran a finger down her cheek and over her top lip. Cath took a sharp intake of breath at his touch. His eyes bore into hers, causing her to shiver involuntarily.

'Matt, I need to tell you something.'

'Oh?'

'I –' She struggled to get her thoughts straight as his eyes pooled with lust. 'Things are complicated.'

'Aren't they always?' Matt moved an inch closer, his hand now cupping her chin. He tilted it upwards.

'It isn't that I'm not interested in you. It's – I have some excess baggage to deal with.'

'You need me to wait for a while?'

Cath nodded, scouring his face for clues of his reaction. 'Would you be willing to take things slowly?'

He let her stew for a few seconds before replying. 'And then you'll be all mine for the taking?'

Cath couldn't help but smile. 'If you'd like me to be yours.'

'That depends.'

For a split second, Cath felt herself physically droop until he continued.

'I'll need something to hang onto until I have your undivided attention.'

This time when he moved in to kiss her, she let him. When they finally broke free, he kept his face close to hers.

'So this time that you need?' He kissed the tip of her nose.

Cath was still lost in the kiss. 'Hmm?'

'A day? Two days? A week? Two weeks?'

'I'm not sure.'

'You take as long as you need. I'll still be –'

'No, you don't understand.' She pulled him nearer again until their lips were a hair width apart. 'I don't think I can wait that long? Would you like to come in for coffee?'

'If it means another half an hour in your company, then yes. I just need to use the little boy's room.'

Once inside, Cath dived into the kitchen. The house seemed quiet as she filled the kettle with water. She stopped to listen afterwards but there was nothing. Then again, it was only just after ten o'clock. She knew both Jess and Becky had gone out before her.

Matt came back. His arms circled her waist and he kissed her neck. She shivered at his touch. It didn't go unnoticed.

He turned her to face him. 'Even though I enjoy coffee, I was wondering if you'd fancy making me breakfast soon.'

Cath's heart felt like it had located into her throat. She could almost hear the roar of it inside her head.

'I'd really love to,' she said. 'But...'

Matt stuck out his bottom lip. 'But,' he pressed himself up against her so she could feel his erection, 'look what you do to me.'

'Typical man,' Cath muttered.

'I –'

She looked up at him with a grin. 'Only kidding.' She thought back to Josie and Liz's advice. Then she kissed him. 'It's because of the girls.'

'Oh!' Matt's smile was back.

Cath pressed her finger to his lips. 'Give me one minute?'

She ran upstairs. As she had suspected, both Jess and Becky's rooms were empty. For a moment outside her own bedroom door, she hesitated. Then she pushed it open. The room as ever was tidy but she left it like that. It was too soon.

Matt was sitting on the settee in the living room when she went downstairs. 'Everything okay?' he asked.

'It couldn't be better.' Cath closed the curtains and then, very bravely she thought afterwards, went to sit on his lap. He smiled as his hands slipped around her waist again.

'The girls are out at the moment but we need to be prepared in case either of them arrives home sooner than usual.' In one swift move, she pulled her T-shirt over her head and threw it to the floor. 'I can't offer you my bed because –'

'I wouldn't ask,' Matt replied, his voice soft.

'– it's too soon.'

His hand slid up behind her neck and he pulled her towards him. 'This will do fine,' he whispered before his lips touched hers again.

. . .

*T*wo hours later, Jess and Becky were home and in bed. They'd spent a fair bit of time chatting to Matt before they'd left him and Cath in peace to fool around again. Now they were trying to say goodbye on the doorstep.

'I need to go,' Matt said as they kissed again. 'It's late and if I stay here much longer, I'll have to stop over. And what would the neighbours say then, Cath Mason?'

'I don't give a stuff what the neighbours would say, Matthew Simpson.' She kissed him again.

'But you should be setting a good example for those girls of yours.'

'I do set a good example for them.' She ran her tongue suggestively over his top lip and he groaned. They kissed again.

Matt broke free. 'I'm going now.'

Cath stepped forwards. 'I'll walk you to your car.'

'It's only down the street.' He kissed her again. 'Go in and I'll call you tomorrow.'

As soon as she closed the door, Cath ran to get her phone. Feeling like she was fifteen again, she texted Matt a quick message and grinned as she thought of him reading it outside.

*M*att laughed out loud when he read the message. Cath had certainly blown more than his mind! He texted back a reply and then searched out his car keys.

A noise made him turn quickly but before he could focus on anything, he was hit from behind, a sharp knock to the back of his head. He fell to his knees. An elbow came down on his back, followed by a fist upwards into his face.

He bent forwards to protect himself as he was kicked in the stomach. Instinctively he curled up into a ball, trying to guard himself from the punches raining down on him.

Finally, it stopped. In the silence of the night, Matt struggled to get his breath.

'Keep away from her,' his attacker spoke. 'And if I hear you mention this to anyone, I'll get you again and next time I'll finish you off.'

Matt tried to speak but there was too much blood filling his mouth.

'Get in your car and drive away. And don't come back here or I'll be the death of her. Do you understand?'

Matt retched as he was kicked in the stomach one last time.

'Do you understand?!'

'Yes.' Matt pushed himself to his feet. Holding onto his chest, he staggered to his car, fumbled with the lock and clambered in. As he drove off, he could see the silhouette of his attacker, a black shadow that would look the part in any crime drama. The shadow was still there when he turned out of Christopher Avenue.

33

Cath woke up the next day feeling like the proverbial cat that had lapped up the cream. She stretched out lazily: the grin on her face wouldn't subside. Matthew Simpson had brought back so many feelings that had disappeared after Rich had died. She felt lustful, tingly and contented even. Like Sleeping Beauty, she'd been awakened from a very long sleep. Yet still she felt guilty.

She reached over to the framed photograph beside her bed and brought it closer. She ran a finger over the sharp jut of Rich's chin, looked into eyes that sparkled out from the image. It had always been her favourite photo. Rich seemed so happy, so... so alive, just like she was now.

'Please don't hate me,' she whispered. 'It's been such a long time without you. And I – I think you'd like Matt.'

She put the photo back before jumping out of bed. Then she sent a text message to Matt.

After she'd taken a shower, she checked to see if he had replied but there was nothing yet. Impatient for an answer, she sent another and then went downstairs. She'd most probably see him soon anyway. She was due at the community house in an hour.

Before that morning's session, Cath was searching out pens in the stationery cupboard.

'Need any help today?' she heard a voice behind her.

She turned to see Liz and handed her a box and two note pads. 'An extra pair of hands will do. Are you coming to join my session?'

'I am indeed.'

'Great.' Thinking back to their previous conversation, she couldn't help grinning but, alarmingly, she felt her skin start to redden.

'You're blushing,' said Liz. 'And by the look on your face... have you been up to something with our lovely maintenance officer?'

'Nothing that hasn't been done before. And you were right. It was like riding a bike.'

'You were definitely riding then?'

Cath blushed even more. She hid a yawn as she checked her phone but there were still no new messages.

'You're not waiting for him to text you?' Liz sniggered.

'Yes. Honestly, I feel like a teenager again.'

'I wish I'd made more use of mobile phones in my teens. It would have been so much fun to send and receive love messages.' Liz sighed. 'But, knowing my luck, I'd probably have been dumped by text.'

'It is good, I suppose, but it still leaves you hanging around waiting for a reply. I sent a message this morning and now I'm checking my phone every two seconds to see if he's got back to me. It's mad.'

'Perhaps he's in a meeting. Or maybe he doesn't do texting. It's definitely more of a woman thing, don't you think?'

Cath's phone beeped. Both women gasped in anticipation. But Cath tutted as she read who the message was from.

'It's Jess.' She shook her head in annoyance. 'I told her she had to help me out this morning. She's now saying she can't make it because she has to go into town. But she's sending Becky in her place. Un-bloody-believable. I can't even dock her any wages for not showing, either – as well she knows. I'll have to think of something else. She can't keep getting Becky to help out. It's only making coffee and doing a few dishes. It's not hard graft.'

'Well, I'd far rather work with Becky than Jess,' said Liz. 'She's a pleasure to be around, really gets stuck into whatever you give her. And talking of which, I've got a few hours working on the counter at Pete's Newsagents on the square. It's not much but I can fit it in around Chloe's school hours.'

'That's great news, Liz.' Cath snapped her phone shut. 'I just wish I could engage the same enthusiasm out of Jess.'

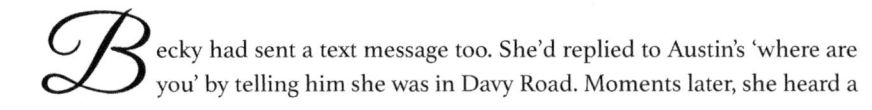

*B*ecky had sent a text message too. She'd replied to Austin's 'where are you' by telling him she was in Davy Road. Moments later, she heard a car pull up alongside her. Austin had commandeered Danny's heap when he'd been put on remand.

'Hey, gorgeous. Fancy a lift somewhere?'

With a smile, she slid into the passenger seat and threw her arms around his neck. He kissed her before starting the engine.

'Where are you off to so early?' he asked.

'I'm covering for Jess at the community house.'

'You shouldn't have to do her dirty work. Let someone else help out.'

'There isn't anyone else. And I don't really mind.'

'It's not your problem, though?'

Becky caught her breath as she felt Austin's hand creep up inside her skirt. 'But I don't think it's fair on Cath that she has to do it all.'

'I'm lonely,' he whined. 'I was hoping that you might keep me company. That's why I came to find you.'

'Can I meet you afterwards?'

As Austin withdrew his hand, she felt a curtain come down between them.

'I suppose I'll have to occupy myself then,' he sulked.

'It's only for three hours.' Becky checked her watch. 'I should be there until one but I'll try and get off before, if you like.'

Austin didn't reply. They were only a street away from the community house now. Becky was stuck. If she didn't turn up, she'd get the wrath of both Cath and Jess. But if she didn't spend time with Austin, he'd go into a sulk and maybe wouldn't want to meet her later.

She reached across to touch his cheek but he pulled his head away.

'I'll see if I can do two hours instead of three,' she suggested.

Still he didn't reply. He turned the corner and the car screeched to a halt. Becky shot forwards in her seat.

'Okay, okay. You win.' She raised her palms then let them fall heavily in her lap. 'I'll come with you.'

Cath's phone beeped and she reached for it again. Sighing heavily, it took all of her strength not to sling it across the room. Instead she began to stab at the keys as she sent back a reply.

'I take it that isn't Matt either?' Liz asked, trying hard to hide a smirk.

'No. Becky isn't coming now.' Cath pressed the send button before looking up. 'Honestly, kids these days.'

. . .

'Shall we go to your place?' Becky suggested casually to Austin. She was aware of the way his mood could change so quickly with a few choice words but she was curious too. Every time she'd suggested it so far, he'd refused.

'It's going to be a nice day.' Austin glanced up at the sky through the window. 'I've got a blanket in the back. I'm sure we can find a quiet spot somewhere.'

'Are you ashamed of me?' she blurted out.

'No.'

'Then why won't you tell me anything about yourself?'

'Nothing to tell. Been nowhere, done nothing.'

'But you clam up when I mention family. Or friends. Or... where do you live?'

'I told you, not far.'

'But why the big secret? You never –'

'Stop with the questions.'

Austin slammed on the brakes and took a sharp left. He screeched up the narrow street, crashing over speed humps, barely missing parked cars on either side. Becky held onto the door handle as he flew around another bend.

'Austin! I –'

The look he gave her silenced her immediately. The dark cloud had descended again. She held on for dear life as she waited for it to pass.

A few minutes later, he turned into the car park of The White Lion and drove round to the back. He parked the car with a yank of the handbrake.

'What have you come here for?' she asked. 'I thought we were going to lie out in the sun.'

Austin smiled then, as if none of the past few minutes had happened. He pulled the keys out of the ignition and turned towards her. 'Come on,' he said.

Becky scrambled out of the car, running to keep up with him. He pulled back the metal sheeting at one of the boarded-up windows. She could see an opening small enough to crawl through. She looked at him incredulously.

'You live *here*?'

'Nowt wrong in it.' He mistook her wide-eyed look for one of disapproval.

'No, I think it's cool,' she replied. 'It's probably where I would have ended up if I hadn't been caught by that copper and sent to Cath's.' She lifted her foot. 'Give us a leg up.'

Austin clasped his hands together and she stepped onto his palms. One quick push up and she was in. She jumped down onto the seating and then onto the floor. Austin was through after her before her eyes had adjusted to the gloom.

He grabbed her around the waist. 'Are you scared of the dark?' he whispered into her ear.

'Should I be?'

Becky pressed her body against his. He kissed her, pushing her backwards as he did so. She felt her feet slide over the odd beer mat. Before she knew it, her back was against the bar. She hooked one toe behind the trip rail. Austin had his hands inside her top, and then it was over her head and across the floor. She blanked out what it might have landed on – or in.

Suddenly, she heard a noise and stopped. 'What was that?'

'Only the rats.'

'Rats!' She pushed him away and began to stamp her feet.

Austin grinned. 'Relax, I'm winding you up. There's no one here but us.'

His lips found her neck and moved down her chest as she gazed around the room suspiciously. Her eyes were more accustomed to the dimness now: tiny shafts of light coming through some of the smaller windows here and there. The floor was covered in dirty red carpeting. Crushed velvet curtains hung redundant in front of the windows; the stools around the many tables sat as if waiting for opening time and the regulars to troop in. Apart from a layer of dust, Becky reckoned the place would clean up pretty quickly. She wished it would open so that they had more choice on the estate.

She heard another noise.

'What was that?'

'I told you. It's an old building.' Austin pulled down the zip to his jeans. Becky placed her hand over his as he undid his button.

'How do you know there's no one else here?'

'There wasn't when I left this morning.'

'But you got in through the window. Couldn't someone else do the same?'

'I thought you said the place was cool.'

'From the *outside*, yes. It gives me the creeps in here, though.'

Austin took her hand. 'If it makes you feel better, we'll check the rooms.' He headed towards a door on the right. 'Kitchen first: bedroom last.'

After a successful session with the teenagers in The Den, Cath was clearing the room when her phone rang. Disappointed to see it wasn't Matt, she grinned when she saw who it was, knowing that she'd be calling to get all the juicy details of her date.

'Hi, Josie, what's up?'

'You don't know then?'

'Know what?'

'You haven't heard from Matt this morning?'

Cath checked her watch: it was just gone midday. 'I texted him earlier but I haven't had a reply.'

'Oh.' Now Josie sounded really confused. 'Maybe I'd better tell you then.'

'Tell me what? Is Matt okay?'

'No, he was beaten up pretty bad last night.'

'But I was with him last night.' Cath's blood ran cold. 'He left around quarter to one, I think. How bad is he?'

'Pretty messed up by the sound of it but he says it's only superficial. He called in sick this morning, said he'd most probably be off for the rest of this week.'

Cath leaned on the wall. 'No wonder he didn't reply to my text.' Then another thought struck her. 'He's not in hospital, is he?'

'No, he's at home.'

'I'll ring him now and see if he answers. If he doesn't, I'll call around. No, I already have his address. Thanks for letting me know.'

As soon as she cancelled Josie's call, Cath rang Matt's mobile. It went unanswered before finally switching to voicemail.

'Matt? It's me, Cath. Josie's told me what happened. I hope you're okay. Give me a quick ring when you get this message, would you?'

34

Now that she'd been there for two hours, the smell and the dreariness of the disused pub had started to become less eerie to Becky. They were dozing, lying together on the single mattress that Austin called his bed.

'It's so cool in here and I love spending time with you.' She ran a finger up and down his chest. Getting no response, she looked up at him. Austin was staring at the ceiling in a world of his own. She sat up and folded her arms.

'What's up now?' she asked. 'You've gone all moody on me again.'

'I'm thinking.'

'About what?'

'Things.' He took a drag of his cigarette.

Becky tried again. She swirled a finger further and further down his stomach. But he pushed her hand away. She fell sideways off the mattress onto the dusty floor.

'What did you do that for?' Her palm had landed on something dirty but she didn't know what. She grimaced, rubbing at it carefully.

Austin stood up and pulled on his trousers. 'It's all sex with you. I don't want to do it all the fucking time.'

'But I thought you liked having sex with me.' She pouted seductively and, ignoring the stained floor now, walked towards him on all fours.

'Stop acting like a slut.'

Sensing the cloud looming over them again, Becky covered her chest with one hand and grabbed her T-shirt with the other. What was wrong with him? One minute he would be doing really intimate things with her: the next he'd be looking at her as if she was a pile of shit. It was as if he were two different people.

She dressed quickly and stood up to tuck her T-shirt into her jeans. Daring a quick peep at him, she was glad to see he smiled at her. The nice Austin was back.

'Let's get something to eat,' he said.

Becky followed behind him in total confusion but happy that his hand was holding hers at least.

Cath drove to Matt's address, pulling up outside a block of six private flats. She peered up at the one she thought might be Matt's to see if she could see any sign of life. But there was nothing. She parked her car and pressed the intercom. No reply from flat six.

She pressed it again: still no answer.

She stepped back, shielding her eyes from the glare of the sun and looked up at the window again. But she couldn't detect anything.

'Matt?' she shouted self-consciously. 'Matt, are you in there?'

Nothing.

She pressed the intercom again, leaving her finger on longer than last time. In desperation, she took out her phone and rang him once more.

Cath frowned. Since the last time she'd tried, Matt's mobile had been switched off. Even though it was out of office hours, she rang to speak to Josie instead.

'I haven't heard from him since this morning,' Josie told her.

'Do you think he's gone back to the hospital?' Cath's tone was one of desperation. 'Maybe he's hurting more than he thought and went for further treatment. The staff are so busy, they might have missed something and sent him home too soon. Maybe he can't use his phone?'

'You can leave phones on in hospitals now.'

'In some areas you can,' Cath replied.

'I must admit it is odd for him not to ring you back. Maybe you're right. I bet he was having treatment when you called and he switched it off when he saw the signs.'

'But he could have rung me earlier. I would have been straight up there, wherever 'there' is.'

'I'm sure he'll get back to you as soon as he can.' Josie tried to reassure her. 'He thinks a lot of you.'

Cath thought of the intimacy they'd shared the night before. She remembered how he hadn't wanted to leave. Something didn't add up.

'I just want to see that's he's okay,' she said.

And, she added to herself, to get all the details. Had it happened on his way home, or outside his block of flats?

Or had it happened outside her house?

Becky hadn't got through the front door before Jess flew at her.

'What are you playing at?' Jess snapped. 'You said you'd cover my stint, you cow.'

'You shouldn't ask me to cover for something that you can't be bothered to do yourself. That's not what friends are for.' Becky pushed past her and into the kitchen.

'Cut the crap. I know who you were with and where you were. You were with Austin.'

'I wasn't,' Becky lied.

'I saw you coming out of the car park of The White Lion.'

'What?'

'Gone round the back for a quick one, had you?'

'You're only jealous,' she replied, realising that she may have got away with it. Austin said she was to tell no one that he was squatting there or else they'd move him on.

'I'm not jealous of you.' Jess flopped into a chair at the table. 'What's happened to us, Becks? We were getting on really well. I can't believe you wouldn't cover for me.'

Seeing herself through Jess's eyes, Becky relented.

'I'm sorry. I was on my way,' she admitted, 'but Austin pulled up beside me when I got to Davy Road. He went all funny when I said I couldn't see him until after I'd been to the community house.'

'That's still no reason to cop out. Cath's going to go mad at me.' Jess folded her arms, knowing she'd got Becky's attention; she'd learned over the weeks how to get under her skin, make her feel guilty.

'Sorry,' Becky muttered.

'Is he always that intense?'

Becky shrugged, not meeting her eye for fear of giving her inner thoughts away. He *was* always that intense.

'You'd better hope that Cath doesn't give me too much of a hard time when she gets home,' Jess added.

Becky nodded. 'Sorry.'

Jess grinned and on impulse gave her a hug. 'You and me have got a lot to learn about friendship, but we'll get there.'

. . .

After tossing and turning in bed that night, Cath switched on the bedroom lamp and propped herself up. It was quarter past midnight. She checked her mobile phone again but the display showed no new messages. She sat up, hugged her knees to her chest and rested her chin on them.

What was going on? Matt still hadn't contacted her. She'd left him a handful of voice messages, along with half a dozen text messages. She'd even called back to his flat after she'd cooked and dished out something to eat, pushing a note through the letterbox outside the building when she hadn't got an answer again.

She stared ahead, by this time not knowing what to think. Was he ignoring her because he didn't like his appearance? She'd seen some bruises in her time so that wouldn't be a problem. Or was he ignoring her because he was embarrassed at being caught out? That was nothing to be ashamed of on this estate either.

But one thing kept running through her mind repeatedly. Was Matt ignoring her because he'd had his fun? Was that all she was getting? One quick bit of 'how's your father' and 'I had a great time, thanks'. A one-night stand.

Cath shook her head. She knew she was being irrational. Matt wouldn't ignore her. The signs were clearly there that he'd wanted to see her again. She reread the last text message he'd sent:

You really did blow me away. Can't wait for it to happen again... and to see you again of course! Mx

It didn't sound like he was giving her the elbow. There must be something wrong. But why would he let her worry like this? It didn't make sense.

Sighing loudly she turned off the light, hoping that sleep would come to her soon.

35

The next morning, Liz woke up to what seemed to be another promising day of hot weather. She'd washed and pegged out a load of washing before Chloe got out of bed at seven thirty. At eight thirty, she kissed her daughter goodbye when Emily's mum called for her. They were going to Chester for the day. It was mid-August and since the beginning of the school holidays, Chloe and Emily had become inseparable. It was heart-warming to see Chloe smiling.

Two more loads were done by lunchtime and just before she was due to leave for the community house, she decided to tackle a couple of bits of hand washing that she'd been putting off. She thought about this week's session as she scrubbed at them gently. It was going to be about self-confidence, something she was really looking forward to learning about. Last week, they'd been given homework to do. They'd been asked to think about what they'd like to change in their lives if they were more confident and to write it down. Liz grinned as she recalled Chloe's look of astonishment when she'd told her. She hadn't been so happy at her reply though. 'You're far too old for homework, Mum,' she'd said in the grown-up way that only a child could.

After her initial reservations about the sessions, Liz had started to look forward to getting together with the women at the community house. The group she'd been with were really friendly, especially Suzie Rushton whom she'd bonded with immediately.

Getting used to being with people again had been a huge hurdle, one she was still trying to conquer, but as Suzie had said, baby steps were all that was needed.

She folded a pair of Chloe's shorts and put them on the pile. As she reached over for the peg bag, she knocked a glass of juice over. It splashed over her top, down the washer and onto the floor.

'Bugger,' she cursed aloud: she'd only just put it on. Rubbing at it with a cloth made it worse. She glanced out of the window at the washing blowing slightly in the breeze. Perhaps her blue T-shirt would be dry now. In a tizzy, she yanked open the ironing board, unravelled the cord on the iron and plugged it in. She unlocked the door and went outside.

'Hiya, Liz,' she heard someone say. 'You okay?'

'Oh, hi there.' Liz could just about see her neighbour, Jackie, over the garden fence. 'Enjoying the weather?'

'I sure am.' Jackie shielded her eyes from the midday sun. 'I can't believe we've had it for so long. Hardly any rain at all. It's been wonderful, hasn't it?'

'At least your peace won't be shattered.' Liz un-pegged the T-shirt as she spoke. 'Chloe's out for the day so she won't be chitter-chattering.'

'I don't mind that. I like your Chloe. She's a real angel.'

Liz laughed as she walked back up the path. 'You should see her when she's after her own way. She's a right little madam.'

'Are you off out soon?'

'Yes, I'm going to the community house.' She checked her watch again. 'Oh, Lord, I'm going to be late. I'd better get going. See you.'

Liz ran into the flat and locked the door behind her. In her bedroom, she slipped out of the juice-splattered top. As she pulled her head through the clean T-shirt, she caught sight of a shadow at the door. Before she had a chance to react, she saw Kevin blocking the doorway. He had a knife in his hand. Fear she'd hoped never to feel again tore through her body.

'You – you shouldn't be here,' she managed to stutter.

Kevin stepped towards her. Liz moved back. She felt her heels hit the skirting board on the wall behind her. He stared at her unfalteringly.

'Please, Kevin... I ...'

Kevin touched the tip of the blade, glazed eyes never leaving hers. Then he grabbed her by the wrist and pulled her nearer. In one swift movement, the blade was against her throat.

Liz squeezed her eyes shut, sure he was going to kill her.

'I could waste you right here,' he said calmly. 'But I wouldn't want Chloe to see you if someone brings her home when they come looking for you.'

Looking for me? Liz gulped.

'So I figure, you walk out in front and I'll follow on behind.' He moved a smidgeon closer. 'Don't make a murmur, a sound, anything to indicate you are scared. You will smile why we walk down the path and then get into my car. Then we're going for a short drive. Do you understand?'

Liz's teeth began to chatter. She wasn't sure her legs would carry her that far. It took all of her strength to nod.

'Good. Let's go then, shall we?' Kevin stared at her with those dead eyes again. She had never seen him this calm, this desensitised before. Cautiously, she stepped past him.

'Wait there a minute.'

Through the pine mirror on the chest of drawers, she watched as he searched in her wardrobe. She wanted to make a run for it but she knew better than that. She had to stay strong for her daughter.

Kevin pulled down her long black cardigan and placed it over his wrist and hand, concealing the knife altogether. Then he came towards her.

'You can go now.'

Liz arched her back away from him and started to move. She unlocked the door, walked out of the flat and down the three steps to the path, all the time realising that he must have been watching her. When she thought he'd given up searching for her, he must have stayed hidden in the shadows, biding his time. Waiting for her to slip up, just like she had today. In her hurry, she'd left the door open while she'd rushed to get that T-shirt. Stupid, stupid, stupid!

When they got to the gate and it was locked, Liz realised that Kevin must have climbed over it – maybe lying in wait for a while. But where could he have hidden? Her eyes flicked to the small gap behind the bin stores. Was it possible he could have been there? And for how long?

She slid back the bolts and walked out towards the street. Kevin held on to her arm, the knife still pushing on her back, the tip of the blade staying in contact all the time.

Liz looked around the nearby gardens but apart from a man up ahead mowing his lawn, it was pretty much quiet. She'd have to do what Kevin said until she could get away.

As she got into the passenger seat of his car, she looked up to see Jackie watching from her front window. In desperation, Liz widened her eyes, hoping that this tiny movement would raise her suspicions. She didn't dare do anything else: one wrong move and she'd be dead, she was certain.

Jackie darted out of view. Liz gulped. She wasn't sure she'd seen her.

Oh Chloe, my darling. I'm so, so sorry.

36

Jackie Smythe had lived on the Mitchell Estate all of her life. At seventeen, she was married and had two children but the lout had done a runner three years later. At twenty-five, she married again. After two more kids, he left too and alcohol became her new best friend. Now in her late forties, the life she'd led had started to tell on her in more ways than one.

But PC Baxter liked Jackie. She had a spirit about her that was needed to survive on the estate and since Josie had moved her from the notorious Stanley Avenue, Jackie had calmed her drinking down. At least, he assumed she had: he hadn't been called out for a disturbance at her property for some time now.

So when she said she was worried about Liz McIntyre, Andy had driven round to see her immediately.

'It might be something and nothing,' Jackie told him. 'You know I'm usually not one for interfering, but I can tell she's had trouble with a fella. The look that she gave me was like a frightened rabbit. She was trapped. I was trapped. I wanted to run out to her but I didn't dare in case he did anything stupid.'

Andy took out his notebook. 'Can you tell me anything else? Colour, make of car? What they were wearing etc?'

'It was some kind of Ford, navy blue. It was a four door, I think. I'd only just seen her in the garden. I was talking to her and –'

Andy raised a finger as his phone started to ring. 'Hello? Yes. When? Where? I'm on my way.' He disconnected the call and stood up quickly.

'What's wrong?' Jackie stood up too. 'You've gone quite pale for a copper.'

'There's something I need to check out.' Andy shoved his notebook back into his pocket. 'I have to go.'

'You should finish with me before going off to deal with some scrote on the estate. Liz could be in danger and as usual you don't give a shit.'

'It's not like that.' Andy handed her a card and headed for the door. 'Can you call the police helpline, give them my badge number, explain the situation and tell them everything – anything – you know. I'll follow up from there.' Before getting into his car, he shouted to her. 'You've been a great help, Jackie. Thanks.'

Cath disconnected her phone. She tapped it on her bottom lip. It wasn't like Liz to be late for the sessions at the community house, let alone not answer her mobile. She looked to the door, any second expecting her to rush through, all apologies, and sit down at the back of the room.

'We're out of coffee,' Suzie shouted across to her. 'I'm going to see if I can pinch some from The Den.'

Cath moved to the door. 'You stay here. I'll go and look. Do you want to get the group started?'

Andy had seen plenty of horrors since he'd started working on the Mitchell Estate but luckily not too many deaths – and all of them had died through natural causes. This body, however, wasn't even cold yet. Kevin McIntyre still had faint colour in his cheeks as he hung from the tree in front of him.

'When did you find him?' he asked PC Mark White when he reached his side.

'About twenty minutes ago.' Mark nodded his head in the direction of an elderly man, a young Spaniel sitting at his feet. 'He does this walk every afternoon. When he went past earlier, he wasn't there. When he came back,' he pointed, 'he was hanging. Said it gave him the fright of his life.'

'Nothing prepares you for it, does it?' Andy looked around. There weren't many professionals at the scene yet, only two more police officers, but he knew that in less than half an hour, the place would be swarming with them.

He stared up at the body. There was only this one tree in the area that would support the man's weight and height: the rest were too small. Jackie Smythe had been accurate in her description of Kevin's clothes: jeans, blue and white striped T-shirt. A black baseball cap had been found a few feet away.

'He doesn't seem to have any ID,' said Mark. 'But I've seen his face enough times to know him. It's McIntyre, isn't it? Lived over in Douglas Close. We used to get called there on domestics. I saw him at Cath Mason's too.'

'Yeah,' nodded Andy. 'Kevin McIntyre. He was last seen walking his wife out of her property a couple of hours ago. Neighbour reckons she looked shit scared of him. They drove off in his car. I've circulated details of it.'

'Fuck!' Mark rubbed at his chin. 'I remember her too. Small, nice-looking, really nervy. They have a young daughter, don't they?'

Andy nodded. 'I'm going to drive around the streets nearby. He can't have got far with her in such a short space of time. I've got to find her.'

'I'll come with you.'

'Hi, Josie, it's Cath.'

'Hi, how're you doing? Have you heard from Matt?'

'No, but that's not why I'm calling you. Have you seen or heard from Liz McIntyre this morning?'

'No, why?'

'She didn't turn up for this afternoon's session. I've seen her twice since last week and she said she was really looking forward to it. I've tried her phone but it keeps ringing out.'

'I'm at a tenant's house but should be done in an hour. Would you like me to call by her flat then?'

'No, I'll pop round anyway. My mind won't rest now until I've seen her.'

'You don't think anything's happened to her, do you? After we've just got her back on her feet?'

'I hope not. I'll kill that Kevin McIntyre myself if he's done anything stupid.'

'I suppose you're off out with Austin the wonder boy tonight,' said a bored-looking Jess as she painted her toenails a bright shade of orange.

'Hmm-hmm.'

Jess tutted her annoyance. 'You two *are* joined at the hip. I thought you were into having a good time and going out with the girls before you settled down.'

'I am. It's just that –' Becky faltered then thought better of it. 'Jess, sometimes he scares me.' She told her what had happened the other day, when Austin had pushed her across the floor. But she pretended he'd made her get out of the car rather than tell Jess they were inside the disused pub. 'He caused such a stir about me using sex as a way to get affection.'

'Didn't stop him from having sex with you, though, did it?'

'He didn't want to know again.'

Jess laughed. 'You might have tired him out.'

Becky didn't laugh with her. Jess noticed.

'If he scares you that much, then why don't you finish things with him? There's plenty more where he came from. And,' she nodded, 'you should be looking forward to going out with him, not dreading what mood he'll be in when he turns up. He's a grown man!'

Becky sat in silence while she thought through what Jess had said. Maybe she had latched on to Austin on the rebound from Danny Bradley. After all, she'd been abused constantly for a few years. Maybe now she didn't really understand what was right and what was wrong behaviour. She mentioned this to Jess, being careful not to slip up about Danny.

'If you spoke to half of the women on this estate, they'd say that you should let your man do as he pleases with you, but I disagree.' Finishing her nails, Jess replaced the top on the polish and put it down onto the coffee table. 'I believe a fella shouldn't do anything that you don't want him to. If you let him get away with his moody sulks, he'll do it more and more. Then you're in the circle.'

Becky looked confused. 'The circle?'

'The circle of violence. Once he smacks you and then makes you feel like you deserve it, his next step is to go on and on at you until you believe his messages. That's the logic behind Josie Mellor's courses, so I've been told.'

Becky paused for thought. Austin had scared her twice but he had apologised straight afterwards. Maybe she'd caught him at his worst.

Surmising that she was losing Becky, Jess continued. 'Has he ever hit you?'

'Not as such.' When Jess raised her eyebrows, she continued. 'He's grabbed me a few times but he's always been sorry afterwards.'

'Like those bruises on your wrist?'

Becky nodded.

'Those are typical signs to watch out for. Maybe you should stay away from him for a while?'

'I can't do that. He needs me. We'll make it work, you'll see.'

'You'd better be more careful then. If I saw you coming out of the car park of The White Lion, who else might have?'

Becky gasped. 'I hadn't thought of that.'

'Now if it was Cath...' Jess left the sentence unfinished for more of an effect but she continued. 'Do you get down to it in the car or has he broken in to the pub?'

Becky felt herself blush. She turned away but Jess had noticed.

'You go inside? Ooh, I'm not sure if I fancy that. Is it creepy?'

'Not really, but it's a bit smelly.'

'I used to go in that pub until it shut down. Which rooms have you been in?'

'Most of them,' said Becky. Suddenly the secrecy was too much for her. 'Jess, if I tell you something, will you swear not to tell Austin that you know?'

'I promise,' she said, truthfully. Austin might have caused a rift between them but Becky needed to talk.

'Austin lives there.'

'What, in the pub?' Jess was shocked. 'No way!'

'Yes way.'

'So when you go to have sex there, really he's taking you back to his place.'

Becky nodded. 'You won't tell anyone, will you?'

'No, but why have you told me?'

'He gives me the creeps every now and again. Only for a moment or two,' she explained as she saw Jess recoil. 'And then the real Austin comes back to me.'

'He'd better not touch you. If anything happens –'

Becky laughed nervously. 'Nothing is going to happen to me, you great nerd. I've told you, I can look after myself.'

37

*A*ndy pulled up behind a blue Ford Focus. It was parked in Finlay Place, a row of one-bedroom bungalows for the elderly. An overgrown hedgerow followed the length of the pavement, the entrance to the adjacent playing fields was about ten feet away. The registration matched the one that Mark had taken down when Kevin McIntyre caused a commotion over at Cath's house a few weeks back.

The car was empty when they reached it. Andy quickly put on a pair of latex gloves and checked the driver's door. Finding it unlocked, he flicked the boot release. Then, holding his breath, he lifted the tailgate. But apart from a towel and an empty petrol can, the boot was empty.

'I'm going to walk back to the body, see if I spot anything on the way,' Andy told Mark. 'Then I'll go over to the community house. You stay here until forensics arrive.'

*C*ath was smiling as she chatted to one of the teenagers upstairs. Her face changed when she spotted Andy walking towards her. By the look of him, he'd had a shock. This couldn't be good. She ushered him into Josie's empty office and closed the door.

Through the window, Andy watched as the world went on with its business, as if nothing dreadful was unfolding. He hadn't been able to find anything on his walk back to the body so had come to see if Cath had seen Liz.

'Andy?' Cath touched him gently on the arm. 'What's happened?'

Somewhere to Hide

'Kevin McIntyre hanged himself this afternoon.'

'Oh no. I can't get hold of Liz. Please tell me he hasn't hurt her.'

Andy had tears in his eyes as he spoke. 'That's just it. I can't tell you anything. Her neighbour said he left with her this morning in his car. We've found it over on Finlay Place, not far from where we found him hanging. The car was empty.'

'And Liz? What's happened to her?'

'We don't know yet.'

'You haven't found her?'

Andy shook his head. 'I walked Kevin's likely path back from the car to the tree where he hanged himself but I couldn't see anything. It's mostly grass but I only did a quick scan. The guys are out in force now. I'm going back to join them.'

Cath was lost for words. She'd known something was wrong when Liz hadn't shown up. She picked up her phone and tried the number again. It rang three times and then it was answered.

'Liz?' Cath shouted excitedly.

'No, it's Josie.'

'I thought –'

'I'm at the flat. I couldn't get her off my mind after I'd spoken to you so I called round. The back door was unlocked. I knocked but there was no reply so I went in. There's no one here. Her phone's lying on her bed and the iron's still switched on. It's as if she's vanished into thin air.'

'Josie, there's something I need to tell you.'

Cath told Andy what Josie had said.

'I have to go,' he said. 'I'll keep you informed as soon as I hear anything.'

'And are you checking the hospitals?'

'Already on to it.'

His phone rang then. Cath held her breath while he listened to the caller. She could tell it was bad news before he'd said a word to her. The colour had drained from his face and he began to tap his toe on the skirting board.

'I'm on my way,' he said finally and disconnected the phone.

'Have they found her?' Cath asked, tears pouring down her face.

'They've found someone.' Andy thought back to Jackie Smythe's description of what Liz had been wearing: blue T-shirt, cropped jeans, strappy white shoes with a chunky heel and a white clip in her hair. 'Hidden well apparently, in the bushes at the edge of the walkway off Finlay Place, and on the way to where Kevin was found.'

'Hidden? What do you mean?'

Andy kicked the wall. 'Fuck!' He kicked it again.

'Andy, you're scaring me.' Cath grabbed his arm. 'Tell me, please. I have to know. Is she alive? Andy, is she alive?'

'Cath!' Chloe greeted her as she was dropped off there by Emily's mum. She looked around the kitchen before twirling back to face her. 'Where's mum?'

Cath smiled at Chloe and took her bag and cardigan from her. 'She's not feeling too well this afternoon, pumpkin, so I'm going to look after you. How do you fancy something to eat with us? Jess and Becky are cooking.'

'Cool,' said Chloe. 'I can show you my new gymnastics moves. I've learned how to do a crab today.'

Cath sighed with relief. It seemed Chloe didn't suspect a thing. At least they had some breathing space now until they heard from the hospital. Liz had been found alive but it was touch and go.

'That's great, honey,' she said. 'You can show us all.'

'Josie!' Chloe beamed as she came into Cath's kitchen an hour later. 'We're making pancakes. Would you like one?'

'No, I've got to...' Josie noticed Chloe's smile drooping. 'Go on, then. Just a little one, though.'

'We're having fun, aren't we, Chloe?' said Becky. She was standing next to Jess, watching the batter mix in the frying pan change to something edible.

Chloe grabbed Josie's clammy hand and pulled her towards the table. 'Sit down here,' she demanded, 'and I'll bring it over to you.'

'One minute.' Josie pulled her hand away gently. 'I need a word with Cath first.'

'She's out in the garden,' said Jess. 'You go out to her. Me and Becks will look after this one.'

Josie smiled with gratitude. People were always the same in a crisis, she thought. They forgot about hindering and just helped all they could.

To all intents and purposes, Cath was sitting on the garden bench, watching the sun disappear behind the hedge. In reality, all she could see was Liz's face flashing before her eyes. From what Andy had told them, it seemed that she'd been dragged out of sight, possibly left for dead. Luckily it hadn't taken too long to find her and she'd been rushed straight into surgery with internal bleeding.

Cath was blaming herself. How could she have let her move out to be attacked by that man? She should have insisted that Liz stay with her for longer.

'We let her down,' she said as Josie walked towards her. 'We knew he'd go after her and we let down our guard.'

Josie flopped down beside Cath and they sat in silence, neither of them wanting to start a conversation.

'Will you stay for a while?' Cath spoke eventually.

'Of course.'

'You're a good one.'

'I had thought you'd be saying that about Matt. What happened between you two? One minute you were all smiles: the next, it's as if it never happened.'

Cath shrugged. 'He stopped returning my calls after we slept together. He must have had his fill of me and moved on to pastures new.'

Josie shook her head. 'Matt wouldn't do that.'

'You obviously don't know him as well as you think you do.'

'But everything was hunky-dory until he was assaulted, wasn't it?'

'Who knows? I haven't seen him since then.'

'Not even at the community house?'

'Not in the last week. He's avoiding me completely. But I don't care anymore.'

'Now listen here, this is me you're talking to. I know you too well for bullshit. You were mad about him, even through your guilt!'

'He made a fool out of me.'

Josie shook her head again. 'That doesn't sound like Matt. Something doesn't ring true. I'm going to ask him in the morning.'

'You'd better not,' Cath retorted. 'If anyone is going to ask him, it'll be me. I can do my own dirty work.'

'But what if –'

'Forget it, Josie.' Cath stood up. 'I've got more important things to think about. Besides, he's a loser. He should have thought about what he was doing before he dumped me.'

'Maybe he did,' said Josie quietly, another thought crossing her mind as Cath walked away.

It was seven thirty that evening before Cath took a call from Andy. Jess and Becky were keeping Chloe entertained, watching television in the living room.

'Andy's on his way over,' Cath told Josie who had stayed there, waiting to hear any news. 'I know it's late for Chloe but I said I'd get the girls to take her out.'

Josie's eyes filled with tears. 'That poor child.'

They hugged briefly. Cath put on a happy face before going into the living room.

'Right, young lady, seeing as you are in my charge tonight, I think a chocolate treat is in order. Do you fancy a trip to the off-licence?'

'Can I ring my mum first?' Chloe asked. 'I want to see if she's feeling better.'

'Not right now, sweetheart. Let's leave her be for tonight. Now, I think I'll have some Minstrels and a Mars bar. What do you fancy, Jess?'

Jess stood up quickly. 'Ooh, I'll have to wait until I get there. I can never make up my mind.'

She nudged Becky who then reached for Chloe's hand. 'We'll race you to the end of the street.'

As the two girls disappeared through the door, Cath handed a five-pound note to Jess.

'She's so young.' Jess held back her tears. 'How could he... how could he do that to Liz?'

Cath threw an arm around her shoulder and gave her a quick squeeze.

'Are the police coming?'

'Yes. If there aren't too many youths hanging around, perhaps you can come back through the park? Keep Chloe out for about an hour – just in case.'

'What? You mean...?' Jess shook her head vehemently. 'She won't be dead. She can't be! She's just injured, that's all. She'll be okay.'

'I hope so, Jess,' said Cath. 'I really hope so.'

*A*ndy walked up to Cath's front door with a heavy heart. His shift had finished over an hour ago but it was what he'd seen during those hours that was playing on his mind. He really wanted to go home but he couldn't until he'd been to see Cath and Josie. They were the only people that knew Liz well.

Cath opened the front door before he got to it. He walked in silence through to the kitchen where they joined Josie.

Andy gulped as he looked from one to the other. 'She made it but barely,' he said quietly. 'Her prospects are good if she can fight everything but it's still touch and go.'

Cath held on to the edge of the worktop as she felt her legs go weak. Josie looked away unable to speak.

'It seems McIntyre drove her to Finlay Place and assaulted her. Then he must have dragged her out of sight. There was no way she could have got to where she was with the injuries she had.' Andy reached out a hand. 'Sit down, Cath, before you collapse.'

'She fought back,' he continued once they were sat around the table. 'There are defence wounds on her arms, and her face has some vicious bruising appearing around her eyes. But the main damage was to her torso. She was found with a deep stab wound to her stomach. I might as well tell you now as you'll probably hear it in the news tomorrow. The doctors have done all they could – she was in there for four hours – but it's up to her now.'

'We should have done more,' Josie whispered.

'We couldn't have done anything else.'

'Can we see her?' Cath looked up through eyes that glistened with tears.

'I'm not sure. You'd be better checking in the morning.' Andy handed a card to her. 'This is the ward phone number. I'll ring and tell them you're her next-of-kin, if you like? I hope they'll talk to you. But I do need to contact her family. Do you know of anyone?'

'She has parents in Devon,' said Cath, 'and a sister, although they don't seem to give a shit about her.'

'They still need to be told.' Andy stood up and jerked his head towards the door. 'I'd better be going.'

'When is your shift over?'

'A while ago but I couldn't go home without seeing you first.'

Cath smiled her gratitude. Andy Baxter deserved an award for what he had to put up with in his day-to-day life. All those people out there who thought he had a 'bobby's job' should do a couple of shifts with him. She was certain they'd change their tune about police officers being paid too much money.

'When are you going to tell Chloe?' Josie asked once he was gone.

'It can wait until the morning. The last thing she needs right now is to be told – told –' Cath broke down in tears. 'How could he do that to Liz, the selfish bastard!'

38

While Cath got Chloe ready for bed, Josie gave Becky and Jess an update before heading home.

'I didn't think he'd do anything like that,' said Jess afterwards, shaking her head. 'I know I was always ribbing her about him but I never thought he'd try to kill her.'

Becky sniffed. 'She was really nice to me when I lost my baby. I can't believe he'd leave her like that.'

Cath appeared in the doorway a few minutes later. 'Chloe's settled at last,' she said, taking the coffee that Josie had made for her. 'I've put her in my bed for now.'

Jess frowned. 'She'll be staying here, won't she?'

'We'll have to see how things go with Liz,' Josie explained. 'But let's not think about that now. There will be lots of questions to answer in the morning.'

Becky drew her knees up to her chest, her arms hugging them tightly. 'Do you think she felt much pain?' she asked.

Cath gulped. The million-dollar question which no one would ever be able to answer. Despite knowing what the newspaper would report, she wasn't going to tell them the gory details that Andy had shared with her earlier.

'I doubt it,' she said. 'Andy reckons that her injuries would have made her slip into unconsciousness quite quickly.'

'But she probably felt everything while he kicked the shit out of her first.'

None of them had an answer to that.

. . .

Somewhere to Hide

*O*nce Josie had gone, Cath checked in on Chloe and then went back downstairs to Jess and Becky. She found them sitting in silence. The television was blaring out a comedy but both of them seemed lost in their thoughts.

'I thought you two would be off out by now,' she said.

'Don't feel like it,' said Jess.

'Me neither,' said Becky.

'Coffee?' she asked. 'Or maybe a little something stronger? I know I shouldn't encourage you but a little tot in a hot drink won't hurt. And it may help you sleep.'

'Coffee,' said Becky.

'Something stronger,' said Jess at the same time.

'Let's do both, then.'

Cath flicked on the kettle. As she waited for it to boil, she stared out of the window. It was still hard to take in all that had happened. Was it only yesterday that she'd found Chloe's tennis racket at the bottom of the cupboard and put it in the outhouse ready to return it? Why couldn't she have done that this morning? Then Liz might not have been attacked.

Her mobile phone beeped. Cath slid up the cover.

'*I'm really sorry to hear about Liz. I know this is bad timing but when you're free, could we chat? Matt.*'

Cath slid the cover shut abruptly. How dare he try to get around her now, after what had just happened with Liz. That was sick, to use it to his own advantage.

But then again, maybe he was genuinely upset. Matt knew Liz too, not as closely obviously, but in circumstances such as these it didn't really matter. To even know a person who had been beaten up so brutally must be upsetting enough. Maybe she shouldn't be too harsh. It did, after all, show a human side to him, a side that she hadn't seen too much of admittedly.

What had happened between them, she wondered again. Why had he dropped off the face of the earth after they'd had sex? She'd been so convinced he'd enjoyed it too.

The kettle switched off and she cursed loudly. Now was not the time to think of herself.

*A*fter a restless night, Cath was awake early. Chloe lay sleeping soundly beside her. It pained her to think how she slept so peacefully now, oblivious to what was going on. How she didn't know that her life would be very different when she awoke.

She gazed at her, wanting to pick her up and squeeze her hard; wanting to protect her from what had happened; keep her wrapped up away from hurt and anger. Even though it was warm, she pulled the duvet up and over Chloe's bare arms. She gulped back tears.

How could she tell her what had happened? Chloe had only just started to accept that she and Liz were on their own now. Last week, Liz had been saying how much brighter she seemed since they'd moved into the flat. Now it was all going to be shattered. She hoped and prayed that Liz would pull through, for her daughter's sake.

She must have dozed off because when she woke up next, Chloe was sitting up beside her, playing with her baby doll.

'Hello, missy.' Cath prodded her gently in the arm.

Chloe turned to face her. 'Hello.'

'Did you sleep okay?'

'Yes. Can I ring Mum this morning?'

'It's still early yet. I think we need to get your breakfast first. What do you fancy? Toast with marmalade?'

'Yuck!' Chloe shook her head. 'I don't like marmalade.'

'Peanut butter?'

'No!'

'Jam?'

Chloe giggled. 'No.'

'How about I spread a cheese triangle over it?'

Chloe nodded enthusiastically. Cath pulled back the duvet. 'Right then. Race you downstairs!'

Later as she waited for the bread to toast, Cath contemplated what to say. She glanced at the clock: half past seven. Maybe she should ring the hospital first and get an update. But what would happen then if anything had happened to Liz? She'd have to tell Chloe and she wouldn't want to do that. Without realising, she banged the palm of her hand on her forehead three times.

'What's the matter, Cath?'

Cath turned to see Chloe looking at her strangely. She dropped her eyes. *Oh Chloe, I'm going to break your heart.* She gulped. But it had to be done. She slid over the toast, knowing that it had been impractical to cook breakfast beforehand. Chloe wouldn't be able to eat after what she was about to tell her.

'Is my mummy sick a lot?' Chloe's bottom lip began to tremble.

Cath sat down beside her. 'I – I – Chloe, a terrible thing happened yesterday.

I didn't want to tell you until I was sure of everything. Now that I am, I think you should know about it.'

'Has my dad hurt my mum?'

Cath cringed. How much violence towards her mother had Chloe seen to ask that?

'Yes, he has,' she said. 'Your dad found out where you were living and he was angry with your mum. So he – he got a little too rough with her and he – he...' Cath couldn't hold back any longer. She began to cry.

Chloe started to cry too. 'Is Mummy in heaven?'

'No, but she's very poorly in hospital.'

'So she might go to heaven and be with the angels?'

'She might but we don't know yet.'

'But I don't want her to be with the angels. I won't be able to see her.'

'Chloe, your mum is poorly but she might not go to heaven,' Cath reiterated. 'Your mum loves you very much and she is a strong lady. She would never want to leave you.'

'I want my mum. I want my MUM!'

Cath pulled her onto her lap and cradled her while she sobbed. Tears ran down her own face as she held on to Chloe's little body as it jerked and shook. She wished there was some way that she could soften the blow but there wasn't.

Life was cruel: it was a fact. But how would someone as young as Chloe get through this? She prayed that Liz would survive. She had to. The child had been through enough already.

Suddenly Chloe pulled away. 'Where is my dad?' she asked. 'Is he in heaven?'

'Yes.' Cath's heart sunk. 'He's in heaven. You won't be able to see him.'

'But that means I have no dad and no mum to look after me. What about me?' Chloe covered her hands with her ears and began to scream. 'I want my mum. I want my MUMMY!'

Cath let her vent her anger. After a few seconds, she fell back into Cath's arms again. She snuffled into her chest for a while.

'My dad loved my mum too much, didn't he?' she whispered.

Cath wiped at her cheeks. 'Yes, honey, he did.'

39

Cath could hardly breathe as she sat next to Andy in a small room off Liz's ward later that morning. She'd left Chloe with Jess and Becky, saying that she would come straight home if they texted her. She hoped Chloe would settle with them for an hour or so. So far, there had been no text.

'What if she's beaten so badly that she doesn't recognise anyone?' Cath shuddered. 'What if her brain has been damaged?'

'She's in good hands,' said Andy. 'Let's wait and see.'

'Yes, but what if –'

They looked up as a middle-aged woman came into the room. She was heavy framed with a round face and thick black hair tied in a ponytail. She pulled up a chair and sat directly facing them both. Cath didn't like the solemn look on her face. She braced herself for bad news.

'I'm Dr Morgan.'

'Is Liz… is she okay?'

'Are you next-of-kin?'

'No, but she's the closest person to Liz at the moment while we contact the family,' Andy explained.

The woman nodded. 'Elizabeth – Liz is out of imminent danger for now.'

Cath sighed dramatically. Then she burst into tears.

'She came through surgery well and we've since carried out a few tests. We're still waiting on some results but thankfully she has no damage to her brain.'

'Is she conscious?'

'Yes, but she'll be in a lot of pain today so I've given her something to help.

She might not be particularly lucid until tomorrow. As well as the knife wound she has a cracked rib, a dislocated shoulder and a gash on her wrist. Her left foot is badly sprained and three of her fingers are broken. She obviously fought to survive. You have the attacker, you say?' She looked at Andy for confirmation.

Andy nodded. 'He's lying on a slab in the mortuary.'

'Ah.'

'Can we see her for a few minutes?'

'No longer than that.' Dr Morgan stood up. 'But remember what I said. She may wake up and talk to you but she won't recall anything.'

They followed the doctor through into the ward and on to where there were four bays. Cath paused at the foot of one of them, staring at the still figure lying in the bed, wires and tubes coming from her attached to all kinds of machines. Beeps, lines and flashes. It was a sight Cath would never forget: it would be etched on her mind forever.

She stayed at the foot of the bed, not wanting to go any nearer, not wanting to get in the way. The ward had a surreal quietness to it – almost as if no one dared to speak. A nurse checking a chart smiled and urged her to step forwards. All at once, she was at the bedside.

'Hi there,' she whispered. Her hand hovered in mid-air over Liz's swollen cheek before she thought better of touching it. 'It's me – Cath.'

'Most of her injuries are superficial,' said Dr Morgan. 'They will heal in time. And now that you're here, I'm sure you'll help with her recuperation.'

*B*ack out in the waiting room, Josie came rushing in half an hour later.

'Sorry, I couldn't get here earlier,' she apologised. 'The traffic's terrible and it took me an age to find a parking space. Have you seen her? How is she?'

'She's going to be okay.' Cath burst into tears again.

The two women hugged.

Josie looked at Andy over Cath's shoulder. 'Did you manage to contact her family?'

'Yes. Kevin's too. His father hadn't seen him for years. They'd had an argument when he accused Kevin of mistreating Liz. He was quite angry at first, blaming himself for not doing more. Far different than when I spoke to Liz's mum. She went on and on about how she'd told her that there was something not quite right about Kevin. And then she started moaning about the time it would take to drive up from Devon and how she wasn't even sure that she would. Not once did she ask about Chloe. I had to hold my tongue a few times.'

They sat down on a row of chairs. The waiting room was spacious but open.

Relatives of loved ones in intensive care sat around too. Young and old. It was heart-breaking to see how everyone held their breath when a door opened and a doctor appeared. Hopes dashed or tears of joy. Fifty-fifty.

'And how's Chloe?' asked Josie.

'I have to make cakes with her later,' Cath spoke matter-of-factly.

'You haven't told her, then?'

'Yes, I told her. But she doesn't believe that Dad has gone to heaven and she wants to make cakes for when Mum is better. I suppose if it takes her mind off things…'

Cath shrugged, her eyes brimming with tears again.

With Cath at the hospital for most of the day, Jess and Becky had been looking after Chloe. Now she was back to take over, Becky had slipped out to see Austin. They were inside The White Lion, lying on the filthy mattress that she was so used to now. She rested her head on his chest.

'I can't stop thinking about it,' she said to him. 'Don't you think it's sad? Chloe's only eight. What would have happened to her if they'd both died? I –'

'Shut up with your rattle, will you?' Austin sat up and reached for his cigarettes. He lit one and took a long drag before lying back again.

Becky cuddled into his side. 'But it's such a shame.'

'How do you know she didn't deserve what she got?'

'That's not a nice thing to say.'

'I'm not a nice person.'

Becky smiled, even though she was a little unnerved by the tone of his voice. She tried to boost his mood.

'Of course, you are,' she replied. 'I think you're fab.'

'I'm not what you think I am.'

'How would I know? You still won't tell me anything about yourself.'

Austin took his arm from her shoulder and placed it behind his head. 'There's nothing to tell.'

'But I want to know *everything*.' Becky sat up on her elbow to face him. 'You just have to let me in. There's something eating you up. Maybe I can help if you talk about it?'

'I told you, all right. There's nothing to talk about. But I will say one thing.' Austin turned towards her. 'Everyone will know my name soon.'

The look on his face made Becky's skin crawl. 'What do you mean?'

'It's my birthday at the end of next week. My twenty-first, my coming of age. The day that I get to be a grown-up.'

'Why didn't you say?' Becky whined. 'It doesn't give me much time, does it? I'll have to go shopping, get something special for you. We have to celebrate.'

Austin nodded, looking happy for the first time that day.

'Yeah, let's celebrate,' he said. 'The day's going to end with a bang anyway. One way or another.'

Becky frowned: he was talking in riddles again.

Austin jumped up and pulled on his jeans. 'Come on, let's go. I've got things to do this afternoon.'

'Yeah, I've got lots to do now.' Becky stood up and flung herself into his arms. 'Austin Forrester, I love you so much.'

A bewildered-looking Austin gave her a smile. 'Really?'

'Yeah, really. I love you and I'm going to make this birthday one to remember.'

Austin smirked again. 'You don't need to go to any trouble. I'm capable of doing that all by myself.'

Josie and Matt were sorting out a storeroom that had gone haywire at the community house. There was all manner of things stacked on shelves, not to mention the floor, and she needed someone tall to reach the top shelves.

'Have you heard off Cath lately?' Josie asked. Despite being warned by her, she was determined to get to the bottom of what had happened between the two of them.

'No.' Matt stepped up onto a low stool and then handed a box down to Josie.

She took it from him and put it on the floor. She looked up at him, willing him to continue but he remained silent. She decided to move things along.

'What went on between you and her?' she asked bluntly. 'I thought you were getting on really well.'

'We were.' Matt handed her another box.

'And?' Josie said impatiently as he handed her another.

'And nothing.'

Josie sighed. 'Quit messing around, Matt. We sleep with someone and move on to the next conquest when we're sixteen, not at our age.'

'I never did that!' Matt sounded appalled.

'No?'

'No!'

'That's what Cath thinks.'

'Does she?' Matt ran his hand over his chin.

'What happened?' Josie questioned gently. 'One minute you're whistling all day, can't wait for your date with Cath. You sleep with her –'

'She told you that too?'

Josie nodded. 'She said she had a great time and couldn't wait to see you again.'

Matt sighed. 'It's – it's complicated.'

'I must admit, I can't understand why you haven't contacted her to see how she was after Liz was attacked.'

'I've sent dozens of text messages. I even called a few times, right after it happened, but her phone either rang out or it was disconnected after a few rings.'

Josie frowned. 'This man who attacked you. You didn't get a look at him at all?'

'No, I was completely taken by surprise.'

'What about his build? His hair? Even his shoes?'

Matt shook his head. 'I curled up in a ball. The bastard kicked the shit out of me.'

'Do you think it could have been Kevin McIntyre that attacked you?'

'Kevin McIntyre? You mean he thought I'd been seeing Liz and was warning me off *her*?'

'What do you mean, warning you off?'

'The guy who beat me up. He told me to stay away from her.'

'But Kevin didn't know that Liz had moved out then so he could have been on the watch for her. Can you recall any tone to his voice? Any accent?'

'I can't remember.'

'Was there anything else?'

'He said, "Don't come back or I'll be the death of her."' Matt froze. 'I could have stopped Liz being attacked, couldn't I?'

Josie shook her head. 'No one could have stopped that from happening. You mustn't blame yourself.'

'But if I had reported the attack, perhaps the police would have checked up with him.' Matt stepped back onto the floor. 'It was my fault.'

'No, it wasn't.'

'I thought he'd hurt Cath, if I didn't stay away. You don't know how much it's pained me, not being able to see her. I wanted to, so badly. But the way he hammered into me, I was scared he'd beat her too. And, maybe I was naïve in believing him but I don't know the estate like you do, nor its tenants. I didn't want anything to happen to her. What a wimp I've been.' He caught his breath while he looked at his watch. 'I'm going round to see her. Right now, if it's okay with you?'

'No,' said Josie. 'It isn't. She has too much to think about at the moment.' She paused. 'But she needs someone like you. More than she will ever know. More than she'll ever admit. You just need to convince her of that.'

40

While Chloe stayed with Cath, each day Liz became just that little bit better. She was moved from intensive care to a routine ward shortly after she'd been admitted, where she recuperated well. Finally she was on the mend and told she would be discharged shortly. That afternoon, she was sitting by the side of her bed when Cath arrived to visit.

'Hello, you.' Cath smiled, pleased to see her up and about. 'How are you feeling today?'

'I'm feeling good,' said Liz. 'I had a better night's sleep and I'm hoping to go home the day after tomorrow.'

'Really? Oh, that's great news.' Then Cath's smile dropped. 'Are you sure you want to go back to the flat? You can always come and stay with me for a while, until you find your feet again.'

Liz shook her head slightly. 'I could stay with you but I want to get back. I –'

Cath gave Liz's hand a quick squeeze. 'You don't have to explain anything to me. Although I'm always here to listen whenever you need me.'

Liz's silence told Cath not to pursue the matter. But it was after they'd settled down to their usual routine of vending machine coffee and afternoon TV that Liz started to talk.

'I ran out to the garden for ten seconds and left the back door unlocked,' she said quietly. 'Stupid, stupid. I can't believe I did it.'

'But you weren't to know he'd climbed over the gate.' Cath pulled her chair closer.

'He must have been waiting for me. One minute I was changing into a clean

T-shirt – I'd spilt orange juice down the one I was wearing – the next minute I turned around and – and he was there in front of me. Well, I went into panic mode. Before I knew it, I was up against the wall and he'd cornered me. All I could think of was that the iron was on and if he reached over and grabbed it...' Liz shuddered, tears spilling out of her eyes. 'He had a knife anyway. He covered it up and made me walk out to his car.'

'Why didn't anyone help you?'

'There was no one around – and to the outside world, he was just a man walking down the path with his wife. I hardly know anyone, anyway. Luckily for me, Jackie from next door noticed my distress.'

Cath sat quietly while Liz cried for a moment. She half thought she wouldn't be able to tell her any more for that day so was surprised when she spoke again.

'He drove me across to Finlay Place. He made me get out of the car and took hold of my hand, squeezing it so hard that my fingers went numb. All the time he was hurling abuse at me, muttering to me, saying I shouldn't have left and that what he was about to do was all my fault. All I kept thinking was that if I didn't antagonise him, he'd let me go. He tucked the knife in his pocket and covered it with his jumper. Then he marched me across the playing fields. As we were walking up the path, I realised there was no one around to shout out to so I decided to make a run for it. If I could get back to one of the houses behind me, maybe I could get away. So I shook off his hand and ran. But he caught me.'

Liz's sob was enough to tear a hole in Cath's heart.

'I – I thought he was going to kill me,' she cried, clinging onto Cath's arm. 'He stabbed me with the knife and I dropped to the grass. He kept on hitting me. I tried to crawl away but he kicked me in the back. It was a rage I hadn't seen in him before. He grabbed my arm and turned me to face him. I thought I was a goner.'

By this time, Cath was crying openly too. She held Liz close to her as she finally broke down.

'I said one word that stopped him. I shouted out Chloe's name.'

'You were so brave,' Cath whispered into her hair.

She was too. Cath couldn't begin to imagine how she would have reacted in that situation. Everyone thought she was strong because she could stick up for herself and the women she looked after but, in reality, she would have gone to pieces if she'd had to put up with what Liz had gone through.

Liz pulled away then and they sat in silence with their own thoughts. Shortly after, Cath looked over to see she was asleep. She left the ward quietly, deep in thought, only to find Matt sitting on a chair outside in the corridor. The awkward look on his face matched her discomfort at the sight of him; a few yellow-green bruises were all he had left to suggest he'd recently been attacked.

'Can we talk?' he asked.

'No, I don't think so,' she told him sharply. 'I think it's a little too late for that.'

A porter wheeled a bed past with an elderly patient lying in it, a nurse carrying his belongings. A man with his leg in plaster to the knee hobbled past on crutches. A male cleaner mopped a floor. Visitors coming and going: staff in varying uniforms walking up and down. Everyone around them was oblivious to Cath's personal trauma.

'You have some nerve,' she told Matt. She made to move past him but he touched her arm.

'Please! Let me explain.'

'Do you think you can say anything to take away the humiliation you caused because you thought of me as nothing but your latest conquest?'

Matt looked uncomfortable. 'Josie told me that you thought that.'

Cath glared at him. 'I might have known. Pray tell me, what lies did you tell her?'

'She made me realise how stupid I'd been but I did have my reasons.' He pointed to a row of empty chairs. 'Give me five minutes to explain. Please?'

The look that he gave her could have melted her heart had she been in the right frame of mind.

'Five minutes,' she told him.

Ten minutes later, Cath's head was in turmoil after he'd told her Josie's opinion about things.

'But why didn't you stand up for yourself?' she questioned

Matt bowed his head before raising his eyes to meet hers. 'I admit that he got to me. I've never been a fighter and I was terrified when he said he'd hurt you. Yet since I've had that conversation with Josie, I can't get it out of my head that it was that man, Kevin, who thought I was after his wife. I could have prevented Liz's attack.'

Cath instinctively touched his hand. 'You mustn't blame yourself for his actions,' she told him. 'He would have done that anyway. He wasn't of sound mind.'

'But I should have done something to protect her.'

'Actually I think I could have done something too.' Cath told him about the notes that had been pushed through her letterbox. 'Andy has told me now that Liz knew about them. He mentioned them to her because he had to, as part of his job, and she never said anything to me. But I should have shown them to her earlier,' she said afterwards.

'Most people would have done the same in your position.'

'I doubt that very much.'

Matt smiled shyly. 'Maybe neither of us should blame each other and realise that Kevin McIntyre would have got to Liz regardless.'

'That's what Josie said. But it doesn't make me feel any better.'

'I think we should listen to her.'

Cath paused for a moment while she looked into Matt's eyes. Honest, earnest eyes that were telling her so much more than what he was saying. Matt had kept away from her because he feared for her safety as well as his own. He'd taken a right old beating, had been scared enough to think that whoever attacked him would do her harm. He might not be as hard as Rich Mason but he cared for her all the same.

She kept her eyes trained on his as a porter wheeled a young boy in a wheelchair past them. 'Would it help if I said I was sorry?' she asked.

Matt shrugged like a petulant child.

Cath knew that he sensed victory and shrugged her shoulders too. 'That's that, then.' She stood up but he pulled her down again.

'Of course it would help.' He grinned. 'I think it would help more if you said that you were willing to try again. And then much more if you kissed me too.'

'Don't push your luck, matey.' She sighed loudly. 'Let's hope this is the last time anything happens for a while.'

'At your house?' Matt scoffed. 'Things will never be quiet with your lot.'

41

Becky had been out shopping in preparation for Austin's birthday in the morning. Luckily, she had managed to save up a few pounds from the pocket money Cath gave to her for completing chores around the house.

By four thirty, she'd bought him a striped shirt and a cheap CD player with rechargeable batteries. She was fed up with sitting in silence in the pub and if they were going to celebrate properly, they'd need some music. She bought a couple of CDs, chocolates and nibbles, a bottle of fizzy wine and two bottles of cheap vodka.

By five thirty she was in her room, rolling out wrapping paper on her bedroom floor. Of the presents she'd got, she hoped he'd like the shirt best. Maybe she could get him to put it on tonight rather than save it until tomorrow.

She broke a strip of tape with her teeth and fastened down one corner of the paper. But when she pulled again, the roll came to an end.

'Shit!' She rushed downstairs to search through the drawers. Cath must have some more somewhere.

'What are you after?' Jess asked as she walked in.

'Sellotape,' Becky cried. 'I've used the last of the roll I found this morning. And I can't find any more.'

'What do you need it for?'

'To wrap up presents.' She kept her back towards Jess as she continued to rummage. 'It's Austin's birthday tomorrow so I'm making a special effort. I want everything to be perfect.'

'He doesn't deserve you,' Jess taunted.

Becky turned her head to stare at her. 'Don't start that again.'

'You're all alone in that pub. No one can hear you scream.'

'I'm not that scared of him. He's just a lot more streetwise than Danny Bradley.'

'Danny's part of the scratty Bradley family. He was bound to do something stupid sooner or later. That's why he murdered that security guard. It was in his genes.'

'I know exactly what's in Austin's jeans.' Becky giggled this time. 'He makes me feel special, though. Not like Danny Bradley. He's all mouth when it comes to –' Suddenly she stopped.

'You cheap slag,' Jess cried out when she realised what she was about to say. She grabbed hold of Becky's hair and tried to slap her face.

But Becky fought back. Her first hit landed on the side of Jess's face.

'You told me that Danny never screwed you.' Jess slapped Becky. 'You lying bitch.'

'Girls!' said Cath as she walked into the room. She threw down her bag and keys. 'Girls, stop! I could hear the both of you the minute I got out of my car.'

Jess swung for Becky again but Becky lashed out with her feet. She caught Jess on the shin. Jess let go of her then.

'Ow! I'll kill –'

'I said break it up.' Cath pushed herself between the two of them. 'Right now.'

Jess pointed at Becky. 'She started it,' she accused.

'I did not,' said Becky, trying to catch her breath. 'It was you. You grabbed my hair.'

'Only because –'

'Girls!' said Cath. 'You're supposed to be friends.'

'Friends don't shag each other's boyfriends, do they, Becky?' Jess pushed past Cath and ran upstairs to her room.

Cath stared at Becky. 'Care to tell me what's been going on?'

Becky shrugged her shoulders, her reddening cheeks giving away her embarrassment. 'Do you have any more tape, Cath? This roll has finished.'

*J*ust after seven, forgetting all about her argument with Jess, Becky raced out of the door and down to the end of the street where she could see Austin waiting for her. They drove straight to The White Lion.

MEL SHERRATT

Half an hour later, she stretched out on the mattress. The smile on her face had grown to full capacity.

'I thought I'd give you something to remember me by.' Austin lit a cigarette.

Becky sighed. 'You're talking in riddles again. I'll never be able to work you out, will I?'

'It will all become clear soon.'

'Maybe the birthday boy would like some more loving first?'

Afterwards, Austin swigged back more vodka. He wiped his mouth with the back of his hand and burped loudly.

'Two more hours,' he said.

'Until your birthday?'

'Until I can unleash my plan.'

'What plan?'

Austin flopped down beside her, ignoring her question. 'Let's get wasted.'

'Becky?'

'Hmm?'

'Becky. Wake up.' Austin nudged her. 'It's midnight.'

Becky opened an eye. The few candles she'd lit earlier flickered in the gloom, disorientating her slightly. Then she realised what he'd said.

'Shit!' She sat up and pulled her top over her head quickly. 'Why didn't you wake me? Cath's going to kill me.'

'Don't I get my presents before you run off?'

Becky shuffled over to the carrier bag that she'd brought with her. Despite trying to get him to open anything earlier, Austin had declined. She pulled out a brightly coloured parcel and shuffled back to him.

'Happy birthday.' She planted a kiss on his lips. 'There are two pressies for tonight and two for tomorrow. Oh, it is tomorrow.' She giggled.

Austin sat up, back against the wall and brought up his knees. She rested her chin on them as he ripped open the present. He pulled out the shirt and held it up.

'Nice,' he said. 'At least I'll look well dressed for the final act.'

'Final act? You scare me when you talk like that. What do you mean? The final act of what?'

'Shut the fuck up.' Austin's face went dark again.

'But what's wrong now?'

'I said shut the fuck up!'

He leaned forwards and punched her in the face.

Becky fell backwards. Dazed, she placed her hand to her mouth. Before she could register that there was blood on her fingers, he punched her again. This time she disappeared into blackness.

42

When Becky came round, Austin was tucking the new shirt into his jeans. He threw her clothes onto the mattress.

'Get dressed.'

She lifted her head a little and then put it down quickly as the room began to spin. She squinted at him. What the hell had happened to her? Had she drank too much?

'Austin, I don't feel well,' she murmured. 'What did you–?'

And then she remembered what had happened. She tried not to panic. He was stronger than her, capable of anything. She needed to gather her composure. This was what Jess had warned her about. Jess had said he'd hit her eventually but she hadn't believed her.

'I said get dressed.' Austin pulled her roughly to her feet.

Becky struggled to get into her jeans. He threw her shoes across the floor towards her.

'Hurry up, for fuck's sake.'

'I'm trying my best.' She began to cry, feeling her lip beginning to swell.

Austin took hold of her arm, squeezing it hard. 'I said hurry up.'

She slipped her feet into her pumps but she still wasn't quick enough. He grabbed a fistful of her hair and pulled her upright.

'Ow.' She yelped like a puppy, trying to ease away his hands. But he was already dragging her out of the room. She lost her footing halfway down the stairs: he continued regardless. She scrambled back to her feet when she reached the ground floor. The pain in her head intensified.

Austin pushed her through the door into the lounge area. Apart from two further candles alight on the bar, the room was in darkness. But Becky could make out two chairs, side by side in the middle of the floor. He shoved her into one of them. Instinctively, she got up and ran towards the door. But he was quick on her tail. He yanked her back by the hair and pushed her down again with a thump. From underneath the chair, he produced a piece of rope.

'I knew I'd have to do this,' he said with a huge sigh. 'You always were a wild one.'

'No.' Becky fought hard but he held her down with the weight of his body. He took hold of her hands and tied them behind her back. Then he grabbed for her feet. She kicked out in defence. He slapped her hard again: her head lolled to the side with the force. It was enough to quieten her while he carried on. The next piece of rope went around her waist and secured her to the chair.

'Please,' she whispered, her teeth starting to chatter. 'Let me go home.'

'Sorry, I didn't quite hear you.' He brought his head down to her level and cupped his hand around his ear.

Becky's mouth felt dry but she still managed to speak. 'I want to go home.'

'What about my home?'

'I – I –'

'You wanted to know about my background? Now you can sit here and listen.' He laughed at the irony of his own joke. 'You can hardly leave until I say so.'

He picked up the other chair and placed it a short distance in front of hers. Facing her, he straddled it and began to talk.

'You think you were hard done by when your mother died? I never knew my mother. The bitch abandoned me as soon as she had me.' His eyes burned into her as he spoke. 'It was the not knowing that got to me. Can you imagine what that was like? Always wondering why the fuck she gave me away.'

Austin wiped at his brow. It was then that Becky saw he had a gun. She sat still, trying not to panic while he continued.

'I was fostered out for a few years and then social services told me I was too much of a troublemaker to be adopted so they put me back into a home. Well, that was all I needed, the stupid fuckers. I was wound up, like a wooden top. I was always in trouble for fighting but I became top dog. No one messed with Simon.'

'Simon?' Becky's brow furrowed.

'By the time I was sixteen and out on my own, I was into all sorts – drugs, alcohol. I tried glue a few times but didn't like it much.' He grinned. 'It made me look too much of a mess: put the girls off kissing me. And you know what that meant? No sex.' He nodded slightly. 'There is a reason why you and me like sex so much. It's because for a few moments in our pathetic lives, the pain of not being loved is replaced by someone wanting to be with you, someone wanting you to feel good.' He aimed the gun at her face. 'You ought to be careful of that, once I'm gone. You need to be more picky.'

Becky whimpered and squeezed her eyes shut. He was going to kill her! She started to shake. The room went quiet. When she opened her eyes again, the gun was back down by Austin's side. But his words were still up in the air.

'What do you mean, when you're gone?' she asked, struggling to find her voice. She coughed to clear her throat.

'Don't interrupt me. I haven't finished yet!'

Becky tried to loosen her wrists but it was no use. The rope was fastened too tightly for her to budge it.

'They kicked me out of my hostel eventually and I ended up living rough. That's when I first had an idea about finding her, my mother. It took me a while to track her down, but when I did find out her address, I ended up losing my temper and getting banged up for assault. It was only a two-month stretch the first time. Second time I got six months but they let me out after three. I came straight here and that's when I did my first kill.'

Becky began to cry then. 'Please let me go,' she begged. 'You're scaring me.'

Austin snorted vulgarly. 'Don't worry, my pretty one, I'm not going to do you in. I like you, Becks. You'll be spared, if you act quickly. There's a knife over on the bar, in between the two candles. If you get the chance, you should try to cut yourself loose.'

Becky's eyes flitted around until they landed on the knife. Austin was talking in riddles again. What did he mean if she got the chance? Panic engulfed her. She breathed deeply to keep it at bay. Inwardly she urged herself to focus, try to work out the clues he was giving to her.

'I didn't get caught for the murder,' Austin went on. 'It was made to look like an accident so no one came after me. I just wanted her to hurt, like she'd made me hurt. I took away the one person she loved more than herself. And I would have got to her sooner if I hadn't gone into a fucking rage as I watched her at his funeral being all upset and teary-eyed. Afterwards, I went ballistic. I got pissed and when I came out of the pub, there was a lad walking towards me. I felt so angry and he was, well, he was in the wrong place at the wrong time. But I got caught. Fucking CCTV cameras. I did three years for GBH. That's why it's taken me until now to finish off what I started.'

Becky stayed still as he pointed the gun down towards her stomach. Austin seemed to have slipped into a trance. He was waving it around now as if he'd forgotten its existence. One false slip and he could kill her.

'What about the people who fostered you?' She tried to keep him talking.

'Yeah, they were okay actually but they couldn't cope with me. I don't blame them. I only blame her. I've always kept in touch with them in case she tried to contact me. They told me all about the phone call from her solicitor when I rang. I nearly ran then, Becks, even though I was so close. The bitch was messing with my head. She wanted to see me. She thought she had the right to contact me after all I'd been through.'

Austin looked up again. Becky could see pain behind the anger but she knew she couldn't help him.

'I began to watch the house.' Austin smiled, almost kindly. 'You weren't supposed to be part of the plan, but you were there. Why not have a bit of fun?' He waved the gun around the room again.

'Stop,' Becky cried. 'Please. I don't want to hear anymore.'

Austin moved forwards quickly and sat down heavily, straddling her lap. Becky moved her head to one side but he squeezed her chin hard. It brought tears to her eyes. The whole of her face felt like it was on fire.

'You were the one who went on and on about knowing everything. Well, now I'm telling you.' Austin stopped for a moment, his breathing heavy. 'It was when I saw you that I knew I could get my plan going. But you were off screwing Danny Bradley.' He laughed nastily. 'It was easy to get rid of him too. What better way than to set him up for murder.'

Becky's eyes filled with tears. Austin squeezed her chin harder and she groaned.

'I was following you when you stopped outside the factory. I watched you storming off in a strop. I remember laughing at you: you went marching off in such a mood. That's when I had an idea of how to get you for myself. I followed Danny into the warehouse.'

Becky gulped. 'You murdered the security guard, didn't you?'

'Yes, the girl has got it!' Austin threw a punch in mid-air. 'And from then on you were mine. I gleaned every bit of information that I could from you. Don't worry. I know I used you but I did like you. It wasn't a chore. It was quite good fun actually. You're a right little goer.'

Becky's shoulders dropped, the clues were falling into place. It seemed like Austin wouldn't stop until he'd killed whom he had come after.

'You've worked it out,' Austin grinned excitedly. 'Haven't you?'

Becky nodded. 'Cath is your mum.'

43

*A*ustin clapped slowly but significantly. He stood up and threw the chair across the room. 'Give the girl a round of applause.'

'Austin, I –'

'Shut up.'

'But, I –'

'I said shut up!' Austin cracked her across the face again.

This time Becky did as she was told.

*C*ath had been waiting up for Becky. Just recently, Becky had been home on time but when eleven o'clock had come and gone, and Jess had arrived back on her own, Cath had asked her if she knew her whereabouts. Jess had told her it was Austin's birthday, so Cath had decided she'd give Becky the benefit of the doubt.

Jess had gone to bed at half eleven and she'd thought nothing more of it until Becky hadn't arrived home at midnight. She waited another ten minutes but still there was no sign of her. Finally, she sent her a text message to express her annoyance. But she didn't go to bed. Instead she dozed on the settee, half listening out for a knock on the door.

Now it was nearing eight thirty the next morning. She sat in the kitchen with a cup of coffee, wondering what to do next. Becky hadn't replied to the text message. Cath had rung her mobile phone too but it had gone unanswered. It was so unlike her. Some of the girls she'd had to stay had sneaked back in the next morning, not even thinking how worried she might be because no one had ever cared for them before. Today's date playing heavily on her mind, she decided to take a quick look around Becky's bedroom.

Upstairs, her eyes quickly skimmed around, trying to see if anything looked out of place. Becky's belongings were strewn everywhere: make-up left as she'd used it, hairdryer on the floor after she'd sat in front of the wardrobe mirror, used tissues scrunched up in a pile on the drawers. Two pairs of shoes looked like they'd been discarded at the last minute for a better choice, along with a denim skirt and a T-shirt thrown on top of the bed.

Cath stood still for a moment. There was nothing unusual about the room. She opened the wardrobe door and sighed with relief when she saw the rest of Becky's clothing still there. At least she hadn't done a runner.

She sat down on the bed and wondered if she was over-reacting. Maybe it was Becky's way of rebelling, growing up. After all, she'd been the same at her age. No, actually, she'd been far worse. But she had also been more streetwise.

Absent-mindedly, she picked up the greeting card standing on the windowsill. On the front was a sepia picture of a young boy and girl. They were holding hands and walking along a dusty lane into the distance. She opened it and read the message written inside.

'TO BECKY, HOPE YOU ENJOYED YOURSELF LAST NIGHT. HA, HA. LOVE A.'

Cath gasped. Images of other words flew across the front of her mind.

'I'M WATCHING YOU.'

'YOU WILL NEVER BE SAFE.'

She rushed downstairs to the kitchen, pulled out the last notes that Kevin had sent to Liz and looked at them carefully. Her hand covered her mouth as the reality sunk in.

'I'M COMING AFTER YOU.'

'STINKING WHORE.'

The handwriting on the card sent to Becky was the same as the handwriting on the notes. She'd – no, everyone – had thought that Kevin McIntyre was responsible for them. Everyone had thought they were meant for Liz.

Austin had written the card. Austin had written the notes. But he'd sent that card to Becky with affection so the notes couldn't have been meant for her. Now she knew they weren't meant for Liz, could they have been for Jess? But Jess didn't really know Austin so why would he watch her?

She sat down with a thud at the table. It couldn't be him, could it? Again she read the notes.

'I'M WATCHING YOU.'

'YOU WILL NEVER BE SAFE.'

'I'M COMING AFTER YOU.'
'STINKING WHORE.'

Cath cast her mind back to the strange goings-on over the past few months. Her car had been vandalised; the house has been burgled, the only thing smashed up had been a photograph of her and Rich. Could it have been Austin?

Then there were the notes.

Today's date was the fifteenth of August.

It all fitted into place.

The messages were meant for her.

*'J*ess!' Cath barged into her room. 'Wake up! I need to talk to you.'

'I'm awake,' Jess shouted through from the bathroom. 'I've been up ages actually. I'm going into town to –'

'Becky didn't come home last night.'

Jess opened the door. 'What?'

'I've texted her and rung her but there's been no reply.' Cath paused to catch her breath. 'Have you any idea where she would be? Please, Jess. This is no time to think you're betraying a trust. I need to know.'

'Austin's squatting in The White Lion.'

A look of fury crossed Cath's face. 'You knew where she was and you didn't tell me?'

'I didn't know she wouldn't come home.'

'Okay.' Cath tried to hide her panic. 'I'm going over to look for her.'

'I'll come with you.'

'No, I need you to stay here in case she comes back.' She wiggled her mobile phone in her hand. 'Will you ring me straight away if she does?'

Jess nodded. 'I'm sorry. Becky's grown up so much lately that I thought she could handle herself.'

'I'm sorry too, for snapping at you.' Cath gave her a reassuring hug. 'We all make mistakes,' she added, praying that her one big mistake wasn't about to catch up with her.

*J*osie was listening to a voicemail on her office phone.

'Anyone home?' Matt waved his hand in front of her face to get her attention. 'What's up with you? You're miles away.'

Josie looked up with a frown. 'Cath's left me a message to say she'll be late for this morning's session. Becky didn't come home last night. She reckons she's out with that lad she's been hanging around with.'

Matt raised his chin in recognition. 'That Austin fella? I saw her with him last week. He was in a clapped-out Vauxhall. I remember when I had one of those back in the day. I added extras to make it look like an SR. Can you remember those, Josie?' He paused. 'I'm not helping, am I?'

But Josie didn't seem to be listening. 'Matt, have you and Cath ever discussed her past?'

'I know she was widowed three years ago and I know about the baby that she gave up for adoption, if that's what you mean.'

Josie smiled. 'She's trusting you, then?'

'She was upset the other night because it's his birthday this week.'

'Did she tell you that she'd tried to make contact with him?'

'Yes. And that he didn't want anything to do with her. I wish he'd give her a chance. He'd love the Cath we know. And she was only young. Surely he can't hold that against her?'

Josie ran her hands through her hair and then rested her chin in her palms. 'Something's not right. I just can't put my finger on it.'

Matt smiled. 'You really care for her, don't you?'

Josie nodded. 'I care for them all. They're like my extended family.' Suddenly Josie sat upright. 'Oh shit!'

Matt looked on in bewilderment.

'I'm not sure but I think Cath could be in danger. And if Becky didn't come home...' Josie picked up her car keys.

'We'd better get over to Cath's.'

Becky hadn't got a clue what time it was but she reckoned that it must be morning. The room was a tiny bit lighter and she could see more than the shadows, which didn't help in the slightest. Every part of her body felt stiff from sitting in the same position for hours. Behind the double doors that led through to the kitchen, she could hear Austin banging about. Every now and then he'd come out, pick up a couple of stools and take them back into the room. When he next appeared, she tried to talk to him. She said the first thing that came into her head.

'Austin, I need to pee.'

'You're not getting me on that one. That's the oldest trick in the book. Even if there was a working loo, you'd only try and do a runner.'

'But, please, I –'

'Piss in your pants,' he told her without even looking her way. 'I had to do that loads of times when I was young. My foster brother used to tie me up in a chair and keep me there for hours.'

He disappeared into the back room again with another stool in each hand. Becky wanted to cry. One of her eyes had swollen badly, but she could still see out of it. In desperation, she glanced around the room. She couldn't see anything sharp except for the knife on the bar but she'd never reach that. She couldn't even stand up because her feet were tied together. One slight move and she'd topple over. That was the last thing she needed to do, to rouse his suspicion.

The double doors banged open again and Austin reappeared. Dust was smeared down his face and his shirt had dirty marks down its front. Much to Becky's dismay, the gun was tucked into the waistband of his jeans.

'Everything's in position now.' He held his arms up high as if saluting the air. 'Just one more thing to fetch until Mummy dear shows up.' He checked his watch. 'Not long now, I'm sure. She's bound to work things out soon.'

'What time is it?' Becky asked.

Austin switched on the CD player that she'd given him last night. As the music pumped out its beat, he turned it up louder and louder until the bass reverberated around the room.

'It's party time,' he shouted. 'And now for my party trick.'

He ran out of the room, laughing like a hyena. He was back moments later with a canister in each hand. He raised them high in the air before twirling round, letting the liquid pour out and splash over everything around him. As some dropped into Becky's lap, she let out a scream.

It was petrol.

44

Cath pulled up erratically in the car park of The White Lion and scrambled out of her car. She glanced at the metal sheeting covering the windows and doors but couldn't see any clear way in. She raced around the back. As she got nearer to the building, she heard the music. For a split second, she thought the pub had re-opened. But then she heard a scream. She pulled her mobile phone from her pocket and dialled Andy's number. As she waited for him to answer, she heard another scream. Shit: his phone went through to voicemail. She left a quick message but there was no time to call anyone else. She would have to go inside.

At the first bay window, she ran her hands over the metal sheeting but couldn't feel anything out of place. She tried the next bay window: nothing there either. On the third attempt, tears of frustration were threatening to fall when she noticed the jemmied corner. She climbed up onto the thin window ledge and pulled it up. The glass had been smashed, scattered over the seating inside. She stepped in carefully. Then she froze. Although she didn't know what he looked like, she was half expecting Austin to be waiting there with an axe, ready to chop her head off.

Her heart racing in time to the music's upbeat tempo, she edged towards its source. It took every ounce of courage but when she got to a door, she peeped through the tiny diamond window at the top. Knowing the layout of the pub having been there many times before it closed, she knew it was the lounge. In the dim light, she could make out a few tables and chairs, a long-forgotten dartboard hanging forlornly over on the far wall. Then she saw Becky. She was sitting on a chair, another empty one beside her. Cath could see her hands tied behind her back.

There was a man standing over her, waving his hands around. From where she stood, he seemed to be dancing. Her breath came in shallow bursts. For the first time ever, she was looking at her son.

She moved away from the door, hoping to calm herself while she thought what to do next. Should she just walk in and announce her presence? But what would he do when he saw her?

Should she go and get help or could she talk to him, see if he would let Becky go?

Would he hurt Becky?

Cath held back a sob as she realised she had no idea how he would react. She'd never spoken to him; she didn't know anything about him. She couldn't judge his character.

But it was Becky who decided for her. When Cath heard her screaming again, she pushed open the door.

'She isn't here,' Jess told Josie and Matt as they came down the path towards her. 'I took Chloe to her friend's house and when I came back there was still no sign of her. What shall I do?'

'We haven't come about Becky.' Josie moved past her. 'It's Cath we need to talk to. Is she in?'

'I meant Cath.' Jess frowned. 'What's going on?'

Josie had no time to answer questions. 'Do you know where she was heading?'

'The White Lion. Austin broke in. Becky told me he's been sleeping rough in there.'

'It's got to be him,' said Matt.

Josie nodded. 'He's holding Becky because he knows that Cath will go looking for her.'

'What's going on?' Jess repeated. 'Tell me! I need –'

Josie held up a hand for silence and spoke to Matt. 'What if I was wrong about Kevin McIntyre beating you up? What if it was Austin and he was warning you against seeing Cath?'

Matt gulped. 'If you're right, then Austin is out to hurt Cath, maybe Becky too. We need to get to them quickly.' He disappeared down the path towards his car.

'You think he's going to hurt them?' said Jess. 'Why would he do that?'

Somewhere to Hide

'I – I can't tell you,' said Josie, not wanting to betray Cath. 'I'm going with Matt. You wait here until –'

'I'm coming with you.'

'No. I need you to –'

'I'm not staying behind again. I have to know if they're all right.'

'But I want you on standby in case we have to call for backup from the police.'

'The police! You don't think –'

'Come on, Josie,' Matt urged her. 'We need to move fast.'

'I'm not staying here,' said Jess. 'I'll wait outside the pub and if I don't hear from you in ten minutes, I can ring the police on my mobile.'

Josie nodded and they ran to catch up with Matt. Within seconds, they were speeding towards The White Lion.

When Austin spotted Cath walking into the room, he ran to switch off the music. It left an eerie silence bouncing around the walls. He held out his arms as if to welcome her.

'I knew you'd come.' He smiled as if happy to see her. 'You've remembered what day it is.'

Cath couldn't speak. She was mesmerised by the man standing in front of her. His dark hair, his medium build, his good looks in a devil-may-care sense, the scar down the side of his face. A carbon copy of her eyes stared at her but on him, they looked mean, moody and menacing.

With dismay, she noticed his fingers curled around the handle of a gun. Tears sprang to her eyes. She wanted to reach out to him, but she knew it would be too antagonistic.

'Have you remembered what day it is?' Austin bellowed, bringing her out of her trance.

'Of course I've remembered,' she replied. 'I gave birth to you twenty-one years ago, at two twenty-five in the afternoon. I would never forget that.'

'You forgot me as soon as I was out of your belly, though, didn't you? Please, after all this time, tell me why you gave me away?'

'I was too young to cope with you. I –'

'LIAR!'

'I was! I swear.'

'You didn't care about me.'

'No.' Cath took a tentative step towards him. 'I've thought about you every day. You were always on my mind. I called you Simon.'

Austin's face contorted with rage. 'Do you think I'd want to stick with that name after you'd given me away with it, you stupid bitch?'

'Please, let me explain. I –'

'Don't speak to me.' He pointed the gun at her.

Becky screamed again.

Cath's face creased in anguish yet she dared to take another step forward. 'I tried to contact you,' she said. 'Just recently, through my solicitor. He told me –'

Austin crossed the room and brought the butt of the gun down onto her forehead. She hit the ground with a thud.

'Cath!' Becky began to cry again. 'Austin, this has gone beyond a joke now. Please let us go.'

'This isn't a *joke,* you silly bitch.' Austin grasped Cath under each arm, dragged her across the room and sat her on the chair next to Becky. He pulled out another piece of rope from underneath the chair, pushing her head back as it lolled forwards. He turned to look at Becky for a moment. 'Now you have someone to keep you company while I decide whether to let you go or let you burn in hell with my mother.'

'No!'

'She obviously cares about you because she came here but she never gave a fuck about me. So maybe we should all go out of this world together.'

'Austin, please.' Becky wriggled about in her chair, hoping to loosen off the ropes. 'You said you wouldn't hurt me.'

'Oh, dear.' Austin grinned as he bound Cath's legs to the chair. 'I lied.'

'There's Cath's car!' Josie pointed it out as they approached the disused pub. Matt pulled up beside it, got out and raced across the car park.

Josie turned to Jess in the rear seat. 'Wait here,' she told her. 'Give us ten minutes and if we're not back, call the police.'

'But –'

'Do as I say. Please.'

After looking over each downstairs window, Matt pointed to the side of the building.

'There's no way in at the front. I'll try around the back.' When Josie reached him, he was at the far window. 'Over here!' He pulled up the metal sheeting and climbed through.

Josie stood for a moment wondering what to do. Should she go in or should she call the police and wait outside?

'Come on!' Matt whispered loudly.

She didn't hesitate this time. Within seconds, she was through.

'What shall we –?'

He put his finger to his lips and they listened. Becky's crying could just about be heard above the ranting of a man.

'What are we going to do?' Josie whispered.

'I haven't got a clue,' said Matt.

Josie moved in front of him. 'Let me see if I can talk to him.'

'No, I'll go first.'

45

Josie followed closely behind Matt as they entered the lounge, shielded by him but trying to take in as much as she could about the room and the situation. They moved slowly forwards into the main area. She could see Becky and Cath, their hands and feet bound, ropes tying them to the chairs. Cath's head had been lolling to the right but now she seemed to be coming round.

Austin stood in front of them. Behind him, the door to the next room was ajar. Josie could see tables and stools piled up like a bonfire; curtains, cardboard and newspapers thrown on top. The whiff of petrol fumes became more apparent as they inched their way forwards. As she realised his intentions, Josie gulped, hoping she could keep her fear concealed.

'Ah, the cavalry has arrived.' Austin pulled his legs together sharply, stamping his right foot and saluting them both. Then in a quick move, he brought his face down millimetres from Cath's. 'I wish you'd told me that you'd invited other people. I thought the party was going to be an intimate affair with just the three of us.'

'Please.' Cath's voice was no more than a croak. 'Let Becky go. She has nothing to do with this.'

'That's where you're wrong.' Austin shook his head. 'Because I know that you care about her, don't you?'

'Yes,' Cath whispered.

'Don't you!'

'Yes!'

'That's better. Now, all I need –' He turned his head towards Josie and Matt and pointed the gun at them. 'Come any closer and I'll blow your fucking brains out.'

Matt froze in mid step. Josie walked into him with a thud.

Austin sighed loudly. 'Can't you see that I'm busy?' He circled the two chairs. Then he stopped in front of Cath and held the gun to her forehead.

'No!' Matt stepped forwards.

'I told you to stay where you were. But if you do insist on joining in, pull up a chair, why don't you? You can watch the show for free. You can even join in, if you so wish.' He flashed them a smile, using the gun to point out the seating. 'Sit.'

As they sat down, Josie wondered if she should reach for her phone and see if she could alert the police. They were several feet away: maybe Austin wouldn't see her.

But she didn't dare provoke him. There was no telling what he was capable of in his frame of mind. All she could do was hope that Jess would ring for her. And...

Stuff it. She decided to try and talk him down.

'Austin, my name is Josie,' she began, 'and I'm one of Cath's closest friends. She told me all about you. How she made a mistake when she gave you up. How she wished she'd never been so stupid. She's always wanted to meet you to apologise, get to know you so that you could become a part of her life now. Please, I think you should give her a chance to explain.'

'She doesn't deserve a fucking chance!' Austin bellowed across the room before lowering his voice back to normal. 'And she needs to listen to me first.'

'I'm listening,' said Cath. 'But I want to talk too. I need to tell you how sorry that –'

'You left me in care to rot.' Austin moved to the middle of the room again, the gun down by his side. 'Because of you, I didn't have a decent start in life.'

'I thought you'd be better looked after by someone else. Someone more stable, who could give you a good grounding. I couldn't do that on my own.'

'But you had a man then, didn't you? Why didn't you want me?'

Cath began to cry. 'Because I –'

'Say it.'

She shook her head.

'Just fucking say it!'

'Because I didn't want to lose him!'

'That's right.' Austin nodded. 'You thought more of him than you did of your own son, didn't you?'

'No,' she said. 'I – I was too young to realise how important you were.'

'But I knew how important Mr Mason was to you, didn't I... Mummy?' Austin bent down to her eye level. 'Which is why I can now take great pleasure in telling you that he didn't fall down the stairs on that fateful night. I gave him a helping hand – well, a helping shove, actually.'

'No.' Cath shook her head. She didn't want to hear what she knew was coming next.

'Once upon a time there was a man called Rich Mason,' Austin continued. 'He loved his wife, Cath, and she loved him. She loved him so much that she didn't tell him she had given away her baby.'

'It wasn't like that. I –'

'You didn't want him to know about me.'

'No. It wasn't –'

'He knew who I was before I pushed him.'

Cath felt bile rise in her throat. 'You... you killed my husband?'

'Of course *I* killed him. I wanted to take away the one thing that you loved, that would cause you the most pain. So I took his life in return for the life you refused to give me. It was easy really.'

'No,' Cath sobbed loudly.

'Austin,' said Becky. 'Please don't –'

'I watched him for a few weeks, learned his routine: what nights he went to the pub, which way he walked home. I must admit, the steps at Frazer Terrace were an added bonus.'

'No!'

'On the night I killed him, I hid behind some hedges until he'd staggered past. Then I called him back. I told him who I was.' He pointed the gun at Cath. 'Told him you were a fucking bitch. When he lunged towards me with his fists flying, I pushed him and down the steps he went. One, two, three, four, ten! But he didn't die straightaway.'

'No more. Please,' Cath cried.

'When I got down to him, he was lying in a huddle on his side. He'd taken a knock to his head, there was blood everywhere. His leg was twisted underneath him. I remember his arm hanging funny too. He spoke to me then.'

'You mean he was alive?' Cath gasped.

Austin nodded. 'Right until I kicked him in the head a couple of times. I'm not stupid, though. I only kicked him twice so that it wouldn't be noticed. And I could hardly make much more of a mess.' He laughed.

'Austin.' Becky tried again.

'There were others too. Tell them who, Becks, if you're so desperate to talk.'

'He killed the security guard at Cookson's. It wasn't Danny Bradley. He set him up.'

. . .

*A*s everything clicked into place, Cath felt distress like never before. Suddenly everything she stood for seemed like a lie. Her son, standing in front of her, was a killer. She wanted to hate him for what he'd done but she couldn't. She couldn't blame him because she had set the ball rolling.

In silence, she watched him cross the room to the double doors. She watched him flick open his lighter. Glancing over at Matt and Josie, she urged them to help. But what could they do? Austin had a gun. They'd all witnessed how unstable he was. She couldn't blame them for sitting this out.

She tried one last time to talk to him.

'Why now?' she shouted. 'Why come back now?'

'Because I watched you with him and it made me sick. And then you made me even angrier at his funeral. I could see how much you cared about him. You should have loved me that much!' Still he kept his back towards them. 'There was so much rage, so much *anger*, inside me that I stormed off: ended up kicking someone half to death. I got caught and did time, three years.

'While I was in there – every fucking day I was locked up – I thought of what I would do to you when I got out. It kept me sane, working out my revenge.' Austin flicked the lighter and ignited the flame. For a second, he turned back to them all, a smile on his face, his eyes darker still. Then he threw it into the room.

The flames took hold almost immediately. Cath gulped. She had created a monster. A demon that was not only hell-bent on destroying her but was prepared to take everyone she cared for down with her too. Feeling helpless, she writhed around, trying to free herself.

'If you want to survive, I'd leave now,' Austin turned towards Josie and Matt. 'The room back there will go up pretty sharpish. I reckon the smoke will become unbearable first and then... what the fuck are you doing?'

*J*osie looked up sharply. All the while Austin had been talking, she'd been trying to send a text message to Andy. She'd typed a letter at a time and was about to press send. Before she could finish it, Austin ran over and swiped it out of her hand.

Matt spied his chance and reached for the gun. As they grappled, Josie ran over to retrieve the phone. She pressed send, willing it to go faster. When the screen was clear again, she dialled 999. But instead of putting the phone to her ear, she left it connected and slid it underneath one of the tables. There wasn't enough time: she could see the flames catching hold in the other room, smoke starting to bellow out.

'Help me, Josie,' cried Becky, wriggling in her chair.

Matt tried to knock the gun from Austin's grip but he was too strong. Austin struck it across Matt's face. As he fell to the floor, Becky screamed.

'No, Austin! Leave him alone.'

'Matt!' Helpless to do anything, Cath screamed too.

Josie stayed poised. She had no choice. Austin had turned the gun on her.

'Did you send it?' he asked.

Josie nodded. 'The police will be here in minutes.' She hoped that he believed her. How was she to know if Andy Baxter was able to read the message straight away? Or if the operator had taken the call seriously and was busy trying to locate them – or if it had been dismissed as a nuisance call.

'You stupid bitch.' Austin took hold of Josie's arm and threw her at Cath's feet. 'You are not going to spoil my party!'

'Austin, I –' Cath tried one more time to reach him. The smoke was getting thicker now. She began to cough.

Austin glared at her. She blinked back tears as she saw the hatred he had for her.

'I'm sorry,' she managed to say.

But he wasn't listening anymore. 'I don't care about you,' he replied. 'Today is all about me. It's my birthday and I promised I'd go out with a bang. This isn't quite how I'd planned it as I was going to make sure you were dead first. But I figure it will hurt you more this way. And hey, I'll make sure you'll never forget the date.'

'Austin – Simon, I will never forget your birth date. Ever.'

'But this way I can make absolutely sure.' He turned the gun and aimed it at his forehead. 'It was because you made me do this.'

'No!' Becky screamed.

Austin gave Becky one final look. 'Bye, Becks.' He winked at her.

Then he pulled the trigger.

46

Cath cried out as Austin's body hit the floor. What was left of his face fell towards her: remnants of hair attached to a bloody mass of tissue. She squeezed her eyes shut tight to rid herself of the image. But even then, she knew it would haunt her dreams forever.

Josie covered her mouth with her hand and ran over to the room where the fire was. She managed to close the door, hoping to contain the flames and gain them a few minutes extra before the lounge was completely full of smoke.

'He left a knife,' Becky shouted over to her. 'Over there between the candles.'

Josie raced across to it and slashed at the rope around Becky's hands until it was loose. She handed her the knife.

'Cut your feet free and then untie Cath,' she cried, coughing. 'Then you'll have to help me drag Matt out.'

'He poured petrol everywhere,' Becky spluttered, hacking away at the rope.

'I know. We'll be okay if we hurry.' Josie touched Cath's shoulder. 'Are you all right?'

Cath nodded. 'Please help Matt.'

Josie ran over to him. Blood poured down his face from a gash over his eye and he was out for the count. Coughing again, she slapped him about the face to stir him.

'Matt, wake up!'

Moments later, Becky was at her side.

'We'll have to carry him,' she told her. 'Here, grab his arm.'

They picked him up and slowly moved across to the exit. Flames were licking at the door behind them, singe marks visible where the fire was taking hold. The smoke was increasing as quickly as the relentless noise from the roar of the fire.

'I'll get his legs,' Cath said as she reached them at last. She picked up one foot but just as quickly dropped it in order to wipe her eyes. 'I can't see,' she spluttered.

Matt groaned.

'Matt!' said Josie. 'I was beginning to wonder how we'd get you out.'

In the next room, the air was clearer. It gave them vital seconds to catch their breath and they headed towards the window. But Cath dropped behind.

'What about Austin?' she said.

'There's nothing we can do for him now,' shouted Josie.

'But I can't leave him in there. He'll burn to death.'

'He's already dead.'

There was a bang. Behind them, one of the doors swung open. Josie ran to close it again. She peered through the tiny window.

'We can't go back in there. It's too dangerous. We have to get out.'

'But –'

'He's gone, Cath,' said Josie again. 'And we need to go too. Come on. Come on!'

Becky climbed through the window to find Jess waiting on the other side.

'You're here!' Jess exclaimed. 'I rang the police.'

They helped Matt through and then Josie followed. Stepping down to the car park, she bent over, resting her hands on her knees as she gasped for air. When she stood upright and turned to see where Cath was, she wasn't there. Two police cars arrived in quick succession but she ran back to the window.

'Cath?' she shouted. 'Cath! You need to come out. Right now!'

'I can't leave him. I can't leave him again.'

Without thinking of her own safety, Josie climbed back inside. By now the smoke was coming underneath the doors in that room, enough for her to feel threatened. Cath was on her knees staring at the door, one hand raised in front of her. Josie grabbed her arm and pulled.

'We have to go,' she said. 'Now.'

Cath looked up at her, pain etched on her face as tears slid down her cheeks. 'I let him down,' she cried, gut-wrenching sobs coming from deep within. 'He was my son and I let him down.'

'But you helped a lot of other people because of it.' Josie coughed again. 'Come on!'

'I let him down.'

'Come on!'

Josie pulled her up and across to the window. Andy was climbing down from the seating. He helped them both to get back outside before jumping out himself.

When Matt saw Cath, he struggled to get to his feet. As she got to him, she fell into his arms.

'I let him down,' she repeated over and over.

To the sound of sirens getting closer, they walked to the front of the building.

'We made it,' laughed Becky, throwing her arms around Jess. 'We bloody well made it.'

Then she burst into tears.

47

It took a couple of weeks for the dust to settle down after they all escaped. Austin's body had been burned beyond recognition when the fire had finally been put out. Due to the amount of rubbish inside and outside of the property, it had burned for hours. The investigation had taken place, the cause of death had been established and the building was due to be demolished as soon as possible.

Once the bruises had started to fade and the media attention stopped, everyone could reflect on their stories. Cath, Josie and Matt were sitting around the table in Cath's kitchen.

'You were so brave coming after us,' Cath told them both, tears welling in her eyes again. 'If you hadn't worked it all out, Becky and I would have been toast. Literally.'

Josie smiled. She knew that joking was Cath's way of dealing with the reality of how close they'd all been to death.

'We could all have been toast if it wasn't for Austin,' she concurred. 'In his state of mind he could have booby-trapped doors, windows, anything to make sure we didn't have a way out. And if he hadn't left the knife, then we would all have struggled. And you,' Josie pointed at Matt, 'you need to lose some weight. You're too heavy to be carried.'

Cath patted Matt's tummy gently. 'You leave my man alone, Josie Mellor,' she told her. 'I like him exactly the way he is.'

'Yeah.' Matt pinched an inch of the skin around his waist. 'These are my love handles, if you must know.'

Josie held up her hands in mock surrender. 'I just meant that the next time you get stuck in a fire, don't –'

'*Excuse* me,' Matt interjected. 'I'll have you know, the next time I get stuck in a fire, I want to be the one doing all the rescuing. I missed out on all of the action.'

Cath blinked back tears as she looked around her kitchen. Everything could have been so different. Liz was on the mend now too. Apart from the mental scars, most of her injuries would heal fully over the coming months. She'd moved back into her flat as planned but Cath had insisted on cooking her a good meal every evening until she was able to stand for longer periods.

Jess and Becky arrived a few minutes later in a burst of colour and laughter.

'Guess what?' said Jess as she and Becky came into the kitchen. 'I've got a job.'

Cath stared at her wide-eyed. 'You?'

'Yes, me.' Jess folded her arms. 'Why are you so surprised? You're always on at me to get off my arse and do something.'

'I have one too,' said Becky. She sat down next to Matt.

'It was Becky's idea, if you must know.' Jess sat down as well. 'She saw the advert. The place is called Sparks.'

'That's the new bar opening in Stockleigh,' said Josie.

'Yeah, that's the one. We walked in as bold as brass, lied that we'd worked in a bar before. They took one look at us and wanted proof of age. We looked a right pair of stupid mares.' Jess giggled. 'But they took pity on us and we're collecting glasses. It'll be boring but we'll make it fun. We start tonight, eight 'til midnight. That's okay, isn't it, Cath?'

'That's fine by me as long as you look out for each other.'

'And fine by me as we'll get more time to spend alone,' whispered Matt loud enough for everyone to hear.

Becky and Jess rolled their eyes at each other. But Josie beamed. It was great to see the two of them together at last.

The next day, in her bedroom, Cath rummaged in her jewellery box for a necklace to wear. Her fingers fell upon Rich's watch. She picked it up, held it to her wrist. The hands displayed the time as twelve fifteen, the battery long ago run out.

She touched its face lightly, remembering when she'd given it to him. It had been his thirtieth birthday. Rich had gone mad; said she shouldn't have spent so much money on him. When she told him that she loved him enough to spend every penny she had, he'd laughed. He'd said he had meant that now she'd have to spend far more for his fortieth birthday. Sadly, she never got that chance.

She placed the watch back carefully, chose a necklace with a cheap glass pendant and fastened it behind her neck. Putting it straight in the mirror, she couldn't help but think back to the day she'd laid Rich to rest: the hymns they'd sung, the bright clear sky even though a bitter wind blew, the vicar's tribute to her wonderful man, the flower arrangement she'd ordered for him, the large congregation that came to say goodbye. Even years later, she could remember it like it was yesterday.

There was a knock on the door. Matt stepped into her room. He took one look at Cath, walked over and hugged her tightly.

'Come on,' he said. 'Let's go and say goodbye to your son.'

They'd made sure the house was empty before Matt had gone out into the garden and dug a small hole in the soil border at the bottom. Cath walked down with him now, one hand covered by his, the other carrying her memory tin.

As they stood by the side of the hole, Cath said a silent prayer, looked up to the sky and placed the box carefully in the ground. Matt covered it with soil and took her hand again. They stood in silence for a while.

Laying her memories of Simon to rest was the only thing she could do to ease the pain of the past. Her one mistake and she would live to regret it forever. But maybe it was time to look towards a new life.

And, for now, that future belonged to her and Matt.

***

A LETTER FROM MEL

First of all, I'd like to say a huge thank you for choosing to read Somewhere to Hide. I hope you enjoyed my first outing to the fictional town of Stockleigh and the Mitchell Estate. I had so much fun creating characters such as Cath, Josie and Becky and I hoped you enjoyed reading their stories as much as I did writing about them.

If you did like Somewhere to Hide, I would be grateful if you would write a small review. I'd love to hear what you think, and it can also help other readers to discover one of my books for the first time. Maybe you can recommend it to your friends and family.

Keep in touch,

Mel x

BEHIND A CLOSED DOOR

PROLOGUE

Of all the shenanigans that occurred on the Mitchell Estate, nothing sent shivers down Josie Mellor's spine more than a no-response call.

'Josie, it's Trevor. The alarm's going off at five Nursery Lane. No one's answering.'

'But that's Edie Rutter.' Josie grabbed her car keys, the phone still against her ear.

'Her son can't get there for about an hour,' Trevor continued. 'Any chance of you checking on her for me?'

'I'm already on my way.'

It took Josie less than five minutes to drive to Edie's home. She banged on the front door and lifted up the letterbox to shout through.

'Edie? It's Josie. Are you there?'

She looked through the window but could see no one in the front room. She raced around to the back and stood on her toes to look through the kitchen window. There didn't seem anything amiss, although she couldn't see the floor from where she was standing. She moved to the bedroom window, took off a woollen glove, and gave it a firm rap.

'Edie?'

Cursing her short legs, Josie moved aside a terracotta plant pot, jumped up onto the low wall and looked inside. She screwed up her eyes, trying to focus through the pattern of the netting.

In desperation, she began to lift up some of the pots around the tiny patio area. At her third attempt, she found what she was looking for.

Moments later, she unlocked Edie's front door and stepped in. Please God, she prayed, don't let it be gruesome. Let her be asleep.

The television was on low as she stepped into the tiny porch. Through the slightly open door, she could see a foot in a pink slipper. She pushed it open, her hand covering her mouth. Wide eyes stared straight at her. Edie was lying on her back, her head turned towards the door. There was a pool of blood around her ear.

Josie gagged. There was no life in Edie's eyes but she looked terrified. The buzzer for the lifeline system still hung round her neck; Josie had fitted it when Edie's husband had died. Alfred Rutter had left Edie broken-hearted and distraught – leaving Josie with the job of visiting her regularly to see that she was coping.

It was then that she noticed the mess. The living room was littered with Edie's possessions; the lamp and its occasional table lay on its side, photographs were ripped from their frames and discarded, glass shards sprinkled like confetti, and the mahogany sideboard stood with its doors wide open, its contents slung across the carpet. And what was that on the poker? She shuddered.

'God bless you, Edie Rutter,' Josie whispered into the silence of the room.

A noise behind her made her jump.

'Bloody hell, Andy, you scared the shit out of me! Couldn't you have knocked to let me know you're here?'

'Sorry, the door was open. I heard the call and then I saw your car outside.'

Tears streamed down Josie's cheeks. Her hand shook as she pointed at Edie. 'She's dead, and I don't think it was an accident.'

PC Andy Baxter took off his police helmet and a glove. He checked Edie's neck for a pulse. Then he held his palm in front of her mouth. But there was no sign of life.

'What the hell happened in here, Andy?' Josie asked. 'It's one thing to rob the old dears but another to take their lives as they try to defend what's theirs.'

'There are some nasty bastards out there. We can't protect everyone, no matter how hard we try.'

'How long do you think she's been there?' Josie glanced at the clock on the mantelpiece. It was nine thirty-two. 'All night, maybe?'

'Early hours, I suspect. She must have come round enough to raise the alarm before she died.'

Josie pointed to the poker lying on the rug, knowing better than to touch it. 'There's blood on that.'

Andy nodded before reaching for his radio. 'I'll get the team out, set the wheels in motion.'

When Josie didn't move, Andy placed a hand on her shoulder. She looked up at him with tears in her eyes.

'How can anyone do that?' she asked. 'Even if it was an accident, someone left her there to die. That's beyond belief. It's so cruel.'

Andy sighed. 'Aren't you forgetting something?'

'What?'

'This is the Mitchell Estate.'

1

Josie Mellor threw her car keys onto her desk and collapsed in a huddle on her chair.

'What is it with me and the Bradley family? That's five more complaints I've received in as many days. I was hoping after I'd been to visit Gina last week that the twins would behave themselves.'

'Your three-fifteen's here,' Debbie Wilkins shouted across the office. 'I've put her in interview cubicle one. She seems a bit stressed.'

'A bit stressed?' Josie retorted. 'She ought to try finding dead people and dealing with the aftermath like I did with Edie Rutter last month. And before I can take a minute to catch my breath this afternoon, I've got to deal with all *this*.' She pushed aside the pile of phone messages on her desk that had grown considerably since she'd left it two hours ago. 'I'm sure our tenants think I have the answers to all their problems.'

'Poor Edie,' Debbie said as she joined her. 'I really liked her. She was a lovely old sort.'

'Me too.'

Josie had been distraught when Edie had been found dead with head injuries in her bungalow a few weeks ago. The place had been trashed and a huge sum of money, among other things, had been stolen. But Mrs Rutter's daughter had been particularly upset that a pearl necklace with a clasp in the shape of a butterfly was missing. It had been a family heirloom. There had been no leads at all, not even with the press coverage it had received for a couple of weeks afterwards.

'It doesn't seem fair, does it?' Josie could feel tears forming again. 'People shouldn't die all alone. I met her son at Mr Barber's funeral. He thought a lot of his parents, not like some of the families on the estate.'

'Cluck, cluck, Mother Hen,' Ray Harman chirped up. 'It's a good job everyone has Josie Mellor to look out for them.'

Josie pulled a face at Ray. 'Yes, it is, because if it was up to you, there would be no Mitchell Estate, right?'

Ray nodded, pushing his glasses back up his nose. 'You got me.'

'Yes, I got you a long time ago, you smarmy git,' she muttered under her breath.

'You've only yourself to blame, though. If you would insist on spoon-feeding the morons, then what do you expect?'

Josie ignored him. She'd known a lot of people like Ray during her eighteen years working for Mitchell Housing Association. Ray was in his late forties and had been a housing officer for longer than Josie, yet he didn't mince his words when it came to job dissatisfaction.

Between the two of them, they covered the sprawling estate, along with Doug Pattison, the maintenance officer. Doug looked after reporting all the repairs needed at the properties but would always offer to help out if Josie didn't feel safe going to a visit alone. Ray, however, would be far too busy checking if garden hedges were an inch higher than they should be or whether Ms-Anderson-at-number-fifty-two's skirt needed to be an inch higher than it was.

Josie picked up two folders from her desk and wiped her eyes again. 'Right, then, I'd better get started on the next one. As the saying goes, no rest for the wicked.'

She put on her broadest smile as she walked into the glass-walled cubicle a few minutes later. 'Hello, Kelly.'

Kelly Winterton's face scrunched up with indignation.

'And, you,' Josie turned her attention to the young child sitting next to her, 'you must be Emily. Am I right?'

Emily nodded shyly.

'Do you remember me? I've met you before, at your house, and it's very nice to see you again. Now, if I give you some pens and a colouring book, do you think you can choose a picture to fill in with some bright colours while I speak to your mummy?'

'Have you got a red one?' asked Emily, wide brown eyes looking up expectantly. 'Please.'

Josie gave her one of the folders and watched her face light up when she saw the packet containing felt-tipped pens of every colour. Along with her mittens, her coat and scarf came off in a flash and she got down to work.

'Now then, it's your turn.' Josie pushed a thick form across the table towards Kelly. 'You'll need to fill in the bits I've marked with a cross while I go through your options.'

Kelly remained silent while she chewed on her nails.

'As the tenancy is in Mr Johnstone's name only, and due to his recent trip to Her Majesty's Services, the number one priority is to stay where you are now – at Patrick Street – while we set eviction proceedings in motion.'

'Eviction proceedings?' Kelly cried. 'What do you mean? He's only been sent down for six months.'

Josie flicked over a page and pointed to a box. 'Mr Johnstone isn't entitled to housing benefit if he's in prison for longer than thirteen weeks, and as he won't be able to pay the rent himself, we'll try and get him to give up his tenancy. Six months will give him a bill of at least two thousand pounds to pay when he gets released. And he'll have a criminal record – which will work in our favour.'

'But –' interrupted Kelly.

'We don't do evictions willy-nilly,' Josie continued. 'We feel we have a duty of care to offer you something else, and we have to follow procedures – take Mr Johnstone to court first, sign paperwork, so it's likely to take a while. You can stay at Patrick Street until that date, if you wish.'

Josie had Kelly's full attention now.

'But what if he only serves three months, half his time? Scott will keep his nose clean, you know him.'

'Not my rulings, I'm afraid. And if he doesn't assign the property straight back to us, for every week he's inside, he'll be liable to pay when he does get out.'

Kelly sat forwards. 'I'll claim benefits, then. I live there too.'

'Are there any bills in your name?'

'How the hell should I know?' They sat in silence until Kelly sighed loudly.

'I don't think so,' she replied.

'In that case, you have no proof that you've been living there. You're registered with the benefits agency from 18 Christopher Avenue.'

Kelly frowned. 'No, that's my mum's address. I left there five years ago when I shacked up with Scott.'

'Not according to our records.'

'But he filled the forms in for me!'

Josie raised her eyebrows questioningly.

'I had my money paid into my own account,' Kelly snapped. 'I didn't have to ask him for it if that's what you're getting at.'

'No, what I'm trying to tell you is that he lived at Patrick Street claiming as a single man. You were – unbeknownst to you, maybe – claiming as a single mother.'

'But why would he do that?'

'To get more money. Lots of couples scam that way.'

Kelly shook her head. 'He wouldn't do that, not to us.'

'Oh, he would,' Josie told her. 'And he has.'

As Kelly sat quiet for a moment, Josie could almost hear her brain trying to work out the logistics of the conversation. She hoped she'd got through to her about how different the rights of a tenant were once a prison sentence was handed out.

'Mummy, look at my picture,' said Emily, thrusting the drawing book at Kelly.

'It's very good.' Kelly glanced at it quickly. 'Can you do another one while I finish off? There's a good girl.' She looked at Josie and spoke quietly. 'And my other option?'

Josie pointed to another box. 'You could have your own tenancy. It would have to be another property, though – it couldn't be Patrick Street because that's in Mr Johnstone's name.'

Kelly quickly wrote down her national insurance number. 'Would Scott be able to move in with me when he gets out?'

'Yes, but you'll have to declare it to the benefits agency. No more single living.'

'*I* didn't know that I was.'

Josie turned the form over to the back page. 'If you do decide to have your own tenancy, there are two flats ready to view.'

Kelly narrowed her eyes. 'You never said anything about moving into a flat,' she hissed.

'There are only the two of you, and with you being classed as homeless now, you don't have much of a choice, I'm afraid.'

'But I'm not homeless – you're forcing me to leave my house! And there are three of us. You're forgetting Scott.'

Josie leaned forwards, aware how vital it was that she gained Kelly's trust. 'I don't feel good about doing this but Mr Johnstone played things really clever. By keeping your name off any of the household bills, as well as the tenancy agreement, it means that you can't prove you've been living there for the past twelve months. Therefore, you're not entitled to stay. If he won't sign the forms, we'll start eviction proceedings for non-payment of rent. Eventually, the property will come back to us.'

'But you know how long I've been living there.' Kelly's eyes pleaded to Josie. 'You could vouch for me.'

'It's not that simple. For all I know, you could have been staying over for a couple of nights whenever I've visited.'

Kelly sat back in her chair again and folded her arms. 'So I'm fucked, whichever way I look at things?'

Josie was used to tenants swearing at her when she told them something they didn't want to hear. Unlike some of the violent ones who'd come within an inch of her face to do so, she sensed that Kelly wasn't using it for the benefit of annoying her. Her anger seemed to be directed at the system.

'The other thing I need to tell you is that both flats are on the top of the estate.'

'You mean on the hell? It gets freaking worse.' Kelly kicked the table leg in temper. Emily jumped but with a quick, reassuring smile from her mum, continued to draw.

'It's only just off Davy Road,' explained Josie. 'Much better than being right at the top. And watch your language, please.'

The Mitchell Estate was mostly made up of rented accommodation, some properties owned by the local authority and the majority of the remainder belonged to Mitchell Housing Association. It was split down the middle by a main road. Everyone knew that the bottom of the estate was the worst place in the city to live. 'Living on the hell', it was known as: the top of the estate, The Mitch, wasn't much better, but was definitely the lesser evil of the two.

As Kelly's head fell into her hands, Josie's heart went out to her. The application form told her that Kelly was twenty-four and Emily was four. From her appearance, Josie could see that Kelly was capable of looking after herself. She could spot no obvious indications of self-neglect; no dark bags under her eyes, no sallow, spotty skin, so she wasn't doing drugs – always a good sign.

Kelly's dark brown hair was cut in a short and spiky style, and her iconic elfin face wore just the right amount of make-up to make Josie feel fifty-seven instead of thirty-seven. She wore stylish clothes, all clean and pressed, and her daughter was spotless.

'Both flats need decorating,' Josie forged ahead, regardless of Kelly's silence. 'Which we will give you an allowance for, but it probably won't cover the cost of all you'll need. I take it from your earlier comment that you'll be claiming benefits?'

Kelly slapped her hand down hard on the table top. 'Don't you look down your nose at me, you snotty cow, with your high and mighty attitude. Just because you work here doesn't mean that you're better than me. I used to have a job before I had Emily, but Scott wanted me to stay at home with her when she was little. What's wrong with that? Don't you think bringing up a kid is worthy of a job title?'

'You need to calm down, Kelly.'

'If you must know, I hate living off hand-outs. It makes me feel like crap.' She looked up again with a glare. 'Don't you think I wish I could get a job again? But it's been too long – who'd take me on? I've got no one to look after Emily. And if I did, I'd get a pittance that won't be worth getting out of bed for.'

'Don't knock yourself too much. You have as much chance as anyone.'

'But what can I do?'

'Lots, if you put your mind to it.'

Kelly stared at Josie, ready to protest again, but realised that she wasn't patronising her.

Josie pointed to the last empty box. 'You need to sign here as well. I also need to do a property inspection.'

'But I don't want to move out!'

'You don't have to move out straightaway, but you *will* be evicted and then I won't be able to help you.'

Kelly's shoulders drooped even further. 'I don't have a choice, do I?'

'Yes,' nodded Josie. 'You could always try and find yourself another property to rent. But you need to decide soon what is right for you – and Emily. I can't hold the flats for too long. There are other people on the waiting list.'

'Mummy, can we go now?' Emily asked. 'I want to see Nanny.'

Kelly smiled at her. 'Sure we can, poppet. You get your coat on, I won't be a minute.'

Josie sighed. Underneath the hard exterior, she could see a frightened young woman. Yes, she lived on a rough estate and mixed with a few rough characters, but this wasn't the East End of London.

Already she could feel herself warming to Kelly's plight as she watched her fasten up Emily's coat. Josie knew she could help her. It would be hard work trying to pierce Kelly's durable shell, but persistence was her middle name. How many hostile people had she befriended over the years? They hadn't all been success stories but she had a feeling that Kelly could be one of them.

'I can help you through this,' she offered.

'I don't need your help,' Kelly replied curtly. 'I don't need anyone's help. I can manage on my own.'

Hmm, thought Josie, maybe not. Even so, she wasn't perturbed by the tone of her voice.

'I'm sure you can,' she agreed. 'Now, you need to sign here and we're done. Then there are the flats to view.'

2

'So who else do you know on the Mitchell Estate?' Josie asked Kelly later that afternoon, as she walked down the path towards a block of four flats.

Kelly shrugged her shoulders as she followed behind her. 'I know loads of people but no one I'm close to. I see Lynsey Kirkwell every now and again.'

Lynsey was another of Josie's tenants. She was twenty-two, with three children each having a different father, and her family was notorious. Josie knew her brothers, too; Michael and Stevie were the elder two of three, Jay being the youngest by ten years.

'Funny choice of friend.'

'I met her in the health centre when I took Emily for her first weigh-in. She was nice to me. Scott's not keen on me having friends, but Lynsey was okay because he knew her brothers.'

'But she's so untidy.' Josie screwed up her face. She wanted to say 'filthy' but knew where her professional boundary lay. Lynsey had been one of her failures. She thought back to the last visit she'd made to her flat; wallpaper on most of the walls had been torn, crayon drawings and swear words prominent over the bottom half. The furniture and appliances were up-to-date and brand new but there wasn't really a need for the top-notch carpeting as there had been nowhere to stand without treading on someone's clothes. The smell of body odour and chip fat stayed with Josie for hours afterwards, clinging to her coat, no matter how much body spray she squirted on it.

'Is Emily with your parents?' she asked next.

'None of your business.'

Josie chose to ignore the hostility in Kelly's voice. 'Let's look at this flat first and the other one is further down.'

Kelly watched as Josie struggled to undo the frozen padlock on the steel door that covered the front entrance. 'Why are there so many boarded-up properties around here?' she asked.

'It's called vandaglaze.' The door gave out an almighty groan. 'It means the buggers can't damage it. It saves us thousands. You should see what they do to these places if they get in. Mind the step, now.'

Kelly waited for Josie to kick away the colossal mountain of junk mail and final demands. Then she followed her down a narrow, dark passageway. She wrinkled up her nose at the smell that assaulted her nostrils.

'New plaster,' Josie explained when she noticed. 'It smells like pee, doesn't it? But it'll go when the property has been ventilated.' She ushered her into a fair-sized room. 'Bedroom one. Needs a lick of paint and swift removal of the ghastly seventies swirls.'

One step to the right.

'Bedroom two... Emily's, maybe?'

Kelly dragged heavy feet behind her as she walked across to inspect the cupboard in the corner of the room. She tugged at a piece of stray wallpaper around the doorway. It fell onto the manky cord carpeting that had been left behind. She shook her head in dismay. How could this woman standing beside her think that *this* room was good enough for her daughter?

Josie sighed in irritation as they moved through into the living room. She could clearly see the damage caused by Mrs Corden's five dogs – which had been removed by the RSPCA – claw marks on both doors, teeth marks on the doorframe. The room hadn't been decorated in a good many years, the paintwork yellow and peeling. Even the UPVC windows had stains of nicotine imprinted in them.

Kelly went through the door leading into the small kitchen. Another overpowering odour emerged when she opened a cupboard door.

'It's due to have a re-fit next year,' Josie explained when she saw Kelly pull back her head. 'You'll be able to choose from three styles and colours.'

'Do people really live like this?' Kelly eventually found her voice. She kept her back towards Josie while her eyes flitted around in revulsion. 'I don't know how you do this job. It's gross in here.'

'This is nothing compared to some of the places I visit. This estate has a large number of social housing properties but, fortunately for me, the city council owns most of them. Mitchell Housing Association is a drop in the ocean. Besides, showing people around empty properties is the better part of my work.

I much prefer it to when people have been there for a while and made their mark, if you know what I mean.'

People were often confused with Josie's role of housing officer, especially the tenants, who thought she pushed her nose in where it didn't belong. For work purposes, the estate had been split into patches and she and Ray had 600 properties each to look after, no matter what the complaint.

One appointment could find Josie holding someone's hand as they cried for the loss of a loved one while she sorted out their benefits. The next she could be laying down the law with a noisy family hell bent on causing chaos for the rest of their street.

She could be sorting out an alleged dog barking complaint just as easily as reporting a dead cat run over on the main road; a mound of rubbish being dumped on the odd patch of grass or having a cup of tea with a new tenant.

On the odd occasion, Josie had to evict someone for anti-social behaviour, it was usually followed by showing a desperate family around a scratty property they'd have to make their home from now on, due to theirs being repossessed.

'Most of my tenants live respectfully,' she added, after Kelly had gone quiet again. 'We do have the odd ones who won't help themselves. That's why the property is in such a mess. There's only the bathroom left, do you want to see it?'

Kelly shuddered as she turned back to face her. 'I'm not looking in there after seeing the state of everywhere else.'

Josie smiled. 'That's my USP,' she said, leading the way to the newly refurbished room.

'Your what?'

Josie grinned, feeling awkward. 'My unique selling point. It's just had a makeover. You'll be the first one to pee in the toilet – unless the workmen beat you to it.'

As Josie made her short trip home at the end of the day, she couldn't get Kelly Winterton out of her head. It seemed a peculiar set-up, Kelly and Scott. Most couples on the Mitchell Estate who committed benefit fraud claimed they were living at separate addresses so that they could each get their hands on a single parent allowance. 41 Patrick Street had been set up as if Kelly didn't exist and it seemed intentional. But Kelly did exist. And she said Scott loved her. It didn't ring true to Josie.

She sat in the small queue of cars waiting for the traffic lights to turn green, all the time thinking that Kelly didn't seem right for the girlfriend of a thief. It was as if she'd given in to life at an early age. Yet she certainly seemed to love

Scott, so did he owe her in some way? Josie made a mental note to find out more background information about the couple.

The outside light shone brightly when she pulled into the driveway. Home for Mr and Mrs Mellor was a semi-detached house in a quiet, leafy cul-de-sac that Josie had been left in her mother's will. Inside, the pampas bathroom suite and drab, wooden kitchen units had been swapped for white enamels, chrome fittings and natural woods. Oppressive, worn carpets had been replaced with wooden flooring and rugs. Curtains that had hung at the single-glazed windows for years had been ripped down and, in their place, coloured-blinds and tag-topped linen had been put up, now in front of double-glazed units.

It still hadn't made the house into a home though.

'Finally, you're back.' Stewart's voice came booming from the kitchen as she walked through the front door.

Josie's heart sank at his tone. She pulled off her coat and decided to ignore it.

'Have you had anything to eat yet?' she asked him.

Stewart came from out of the shadows, his eyes as dark as his mood. 'Thought I'd wait for you. I wasn't sure what time you'd get home.'

Josie moved past him and into the kitchen, sighing loudly as she looked around the worktops. A knife stood erect in the butter tub, a dirty plate next to it and the bread by its side, fallen slices left out in the air. On the kitchen table, three mugs congregated around an empty crisp packet.

'You must realise how time flies when you're in all afternoon,' she replied as she set about tidying the room. 'Couldn't you at least clean up after yourself?'

Stewart gathered together the dishes and dumped them into the kitchen sink. 'It's not worth washing three mugs and a plate. You can do them after tea. What are we having, by the way?'

'It'll have to be something from the freezer, I suppose. I didn't have time to do any shopping today.'

Josie had planned to go to the supermarket to stock up during her lunch break, but an alleged complaint about a dangerous dog had come in that had taken an age to sort out. The tenant had insisted she call the police, which she wouldn't do before investigating further. Josie had to take both sides into consideration before she made a decision as to who was in the wrong. She'd arranged to see the dog's owner tomorrow to get their account. It was something she wasn't looking forward to: the owner's bark was far worse than the dog's.

'Not again.' Stewart sounded in pain. 'Why can't you come home earlier and cook something interesting? Like shepherd's pie or roast chicken and all the trimmings. You used to do that all the time.'

'*All the time* was when you would have been appreciative of it. Don't you realise that I work long hours, too?' Josie ferociously squeezed washing up liquid into the bowl and ran the hot water. 'Oh yeah, of course you do. You're always quick to rub that in my face.'

Almost sullenly, Stewart pushed past her. 'I'm going to have a shower and then I'll be on my computer. Shout me when it's ready.'

'Stewart, wait.' Josie called out, the compassionate side of her refusing to give up. 'What's wrong?'

'What's *wrong*?' he repeated her question with a sneer. 'As soon as you get home, you start moaning at me. The minute you walk through the door, it's 'why haven't you done this, Stewart' or 'did you remember to do that, Stewart'. I can't understand why though because you never do anything for me. You can't even cook something for me. Instead I have to make do with supermarket ready-meal garbage.'

'That's not fair,' Josie retaliated. 'You finished work at half past two; you could have gone to the shops this afternoon. You could have prepared some vegetables. You could have put a chicken in to roast so that I could finish it off when I got in.' She pointed to the worktop. 'And you could have tidied this mess up, so that I don't have to. There are two of us in this marriage.'

'You're always coming home later than you say,' Stewart added, ignoring her jibes. 'You seem to think that job of yours is far more important than me.'

'Of course it isn't,' Josie snapped. 'You know I like to come home as soon as I can.'

'To your house, not to me.'

'No, I –'

With him scuttling out of the room after slamming the door, things suddenly became brighter again. Josie rummaged in the cupboards for something to lessen his bad mood. At the same time, she couldn't help thinking that surely some women must be welcomed home with a meal on the table, a bottle of wine chilling and good conversation every night. Why did she always feel as though she'd be coming home and treading on eggshells? It seemed worse than being at work sometimes.

Half an hour later, Stewart emerged in the doorway again, smelling clean and fresh. At five-foot ten, he stood eight inches taller than Josie, but she often felt like it was eighteen as he towered over her. Thin build, with the beginnings of a paunch on his stomach, his fair hair hung down in waves and always looked as if it could do with a good styling. But then who was she to criticise?

Josie's brown hair was two different colours due to the blonde dye that she had fatefully tried out last year. It may tumble down below her shoulders but she hadn't the heart to get it dyed again. Neither was it worth hearing Stewart moaning about her wasting yet more money stripping it back to its natural colour professionally. Still, she supposed it didn't look too bad when it was tied up.

'I'm going out,' he informed her, grabbing his jacket from off the chair.

'But I've put some pasta on to cook. I remembered I bought some mince the other day. I'm making spaghetti bolognaise.'

'Can't be bothered to wait.'

'But… where are you going?'

'I told you – out.'

'Don't go, Stewart,' Josie cried. 'Please wait.'

The door slammed shut behind him.

'Piss off, then,' she shouted in frustration. 'See if I care.'

3

The following morning, Josie picked up her folder, fastened the zip on her work coat and stepped out of her car into Clarence Avenue. The January weather was continuing its cold snap and she pulled the collar in close to her neck, praying that Amy Cartwright would be in this time. Even though the appointment was pre-arranged, Amy often forgot she was coming.

The young girl that came to the door didn't look any older than thirteen, but in reality she was nineteen. Unfortunately, her mental age was still that of a thirteen-year-old when she'd been taken advantage of.

By the state of her appearance, it didn't look like she was coping very well this week. The heavily built teenager's face was fraught, her dark hair was unkempt, her eyes downcast. Most of her six-month-old son's breakfast had found its way down the front of her pyjamas.

'Hi, Amy.' Josie changed her worried face to a cheery one. 'Had a late start this morning?'

'Reece kept me awake all night,' Amy explained tearfully. 'He won't stop crying.'

'Let me take a look, see if I can figure out what's bothering him.'

Josie followed her through into the lounge. Her shoulders sagged at the state of it. Amy and the baby didn't have much in the way of clothing, but every piece of it seemed to be littering the floor. A disgruntled Reece was propped up on the settee, with a cushion under his arm to stop him falling.

'You need to put some of your clothes away,' Josie said matter-of-factly. 'Can you fold them up into a neat pile on the armchair for me first, please?' Amy

243

obliged and Josie picked up the baby. 'Hey, little man,' she soothed. 'What's wrong with you?'

'I've fed him this morning,' Amy spoke out, defensively. 'And I've changed him twice because he had a really stinky nappy.'

'He's probably cutting a tooth. I'm sure there's nothing else wrong with him.'

'But why doesn't he stop crying?'

Josie played teacher again. 'Have you ever had a bad tooth, Amy?'

'Yeah, loads. My dad said I ate too many toffees when I was a baby.'

Josie nodded. Baby Reece seemed fine to her. Although she didn't profess to be a midwife, she suspected he was just being a bit grouchy because he'd missed his sleep. His cheeks were tinged with red, he didn't feel exceedingly warm to the touch, he was dry and he'd been fed. She laid him back down on the settee and reached for his rattle.

'He's tired because he's been kept awake by the pain of his teeth coming through. Why don't you try him with a bit of teething gel and see if he settles then?'

Amy went through to the kitchen and Josie followed her. Apart from a small pile of dishes in the sink, the room was cluttered but clean. Josie opened the larder door and checked its contents; it was full of mostly canned foods, but there were lots of them, so there was no need to make a shopping list yet.

'How are you feeling this week? What did the doctor say about your asthma?'

'He gave me another inhaler.' Amy pulled it from her pyjama pocket. 'It's purple.'

Josie smiled at her innocence. Amy was still a child, looking after her own. Because she wouldn't tell her parents who Reece's father was, let alone Josie, Amy's father had thrown her out onto the streets. Josie had tried to talk him round but to no avail, and Amy had been put into a small flat in Clarence Avenue, on the opposite side of the estate from everyone she knew.

Her mum, afraid of what her husband would do to her, visited on the quiet every now and then, but other than her, Amy had no one to turn to. What a position to be in – nineteen, no family contact, no partner to help her, no future to look forward to. Still, if Josie made a difference to one young mum on the estate, it was something. Job satisfaction, she would call it.

Once Reece had been placated, Josie pulled out a blank to-do list and started to fill it in. Amy needed to pay an instalment on her electricity bill, sort her dirty washing into two piles ready to load, and take Reece to the clinic. She also wanted her to join in with the mothers' and toddlers' group on Friday over at the community house, a neighbourhood one-stop shop run by volunteers from the estate. Surprisingly, Amy was willing to give it a go this week. Shyness usually stopped her.

Confident that everything was in hand, Josie made her way to her next call. Charlotte Hatfield was twenty-three and had four children under the age of five. She also had a violent partner she'd fled from several times and was currently hiding out on the estate. Josie had seen Charlotte twice already but was finding it hard to break down the barriers.

Charlotte came to the door, cigarette in one hand, baby held firmly in the other. Like Amy, she was wearing pyjamas. Her greasy hair hung limp, the bags under her eyes as dark as liquorice. The skin from her bottom lip was peeling off.

Charlotte didn't speak, just left the door open for Josie to follow her. The living room they went into was sparsely furnished, with a tatty settee, chair and coffee table that Josie had managed to find for her, and bare plastered walls that had yet to be decorated.

Two large windows were at either end of the room, but only one set of curtains had been pulled apart. In the middle of the floor, the twins – four-year-old boys – raced cars along the bare floorboards. Two-year-old Joshua sat at his mum's feet.

'Shift out of my way, Callum,' said Charlotte. 'Jake, stop screeching at the top of your bloody voice, will you?'

'How are things?' Josie sat down on a stripy deckchair that would be better placed outside in the garden. She gathered together her paperwork and opened Charlotte's file. As she looked up, she noticed the remainder of a black eye. Charlotte's hair hid most of the bruising, but it could clearly be seen when she turned to face her more.

'Okay,' Charlotte answered. She sat down on the worn settee, resting the baby to the side of her chest.

'Has Nathan been in touch?'

'No!'

'Then how did you get that bruise?'

'I fell.'

Josie raised her eyebrows. 'Are you sure?'

Charlotte glared at her. 'I told you, didn't I? Don't you believe me?'

'Well –'

'He's not been here, okay? But he'll find me eventually. He always does.'

'Then how did you get the injury?' Josie knew she was pressing things but refused to back down. Sometimes it worked and people opened up to her. Sometimes it didn't and she'd be sent packing, but it was always worth a try.

'He rang my mobile,' Charlotte spoke eventually. 'I was having a lie down. I'd had a shit night with Poppy. She'd kept me awake for most of it and then Callum got me up at the crack of dawn with tummy ache. I found out later that when the phone rang, Jake had picked it up. It was easy to get the street name out of him. Nathan asked a woman who was in her garden if anyone had moved in recently and the stupid cow pointed me out.'

Josie sighed loudly.

'He threatened to take my kids!' Charlotte raised her voice.

'I wasn't blaming you.'

'No, but you're judging me, aren't you? Your sort always does.'

'Not all of us do that, Charlotte.'

The baby squirmed. Charlotte settled her into the crook of her arm. 'He's not taking my kids,' she said defiantly. 'I won't let him do that.'

'He wouldn't be able to do anything if you'd press charges against him,' Josie urged, raising her voice over the twins crashing their cars together. 'He'd be locked up for a long time, the injuries he's caused you before.'

'No, I won't do it.' Charlotte shook her head. 'What if he gets off with it? I'll be turfed to another new town, new neighbourhood, new everything with nothing from a previous life. No furniture, no money, no one to turn to.'

'But wouldn't you like it to be over?'

As the boys' cries became noisier, Charlotte cracked. 'Will you pair shut up with that racket before I smack both of your arses!' she screamed. 'What do I have to do to get some peace around here, for fuck's sake?'

'Hey, come on now,' Josie tried to calm the situation. Both Callum and Jake hadn't taken any notice of their mother's outbreak, but little Joshua had burst into tears.

Charlotte looked at Josie with loathing. 'You have no idea what it's like,' she said. 'I've moved three times in a year to get away from him and each time he finds me again. Each time, it gets worse. I can't keep moving and I'm sick of being the one who has to do everything. And it's not good for the kids.'

'So what *do* you want to do about him?'

Charlotte shrugged her shoulders in resignation. 'I don't know, but I'm fed up of running. Even a harassment warning doesn't stop him. I miss my family. Maybe I should go back to Leeds and settle down near them. Maybe Nathan wouldn't want to follow me there.'

Maybe, maybe, maybe. Maybe next time he'll give you one slap too many and there'll be no one to look after the kids. Josie shuddered and kept her thoughts to herself.

'I'll help you,' she said, 'whatever you decide to do. In the meantime, I'll fit you the panic buzzer I've brought with me that will link you to our control room. If Nathan arrives and you don't want to see him, press it, and if we can, we'll get a police officer to attend as soon as. And if it's office hours, I'll do my utmost to attend myself.'

Charlotte looked away. Josie knew she'd probably heard it all before. Lord knows, she wished there was more she could do about it, but there were only so many hours in a day.

And anyway, who was she to dish out advice? In some ways, she was no different from Charlotte – wasn't she ruled by the mood swings of a man?

4

'Mummy, can I watch the penguins?' Emily shouted up from the bottom of the stairs.

Kelly stretched out her legs. Through tear-swollen eyes, she stared at the clock on the bedside table. Half past seven: the day had hardly begun.

'Okay,' she shouted back, 'but be careful with the DVD.'

'I'm not a baby!'

Kelly had to agree. It didn't seem a minute since Emily had been born; now she was due to start school in September.

Moments later, Emily came running into the bedroom. 'Mummy! Where is it? I can't find it anywhere.'

'In a minute, Em.' Before she could complain, Emily tore off again.

Sighing heavily, Kelly pulled away the duvet and then promptly pulled it back again. What was there to get up for? It would have been different if Scott had been lying beside her. Usually she'd get up around eight, leaving Emily to climb into her empty space and flick on the portable television. But that had all changed since he'd been sent to prison.

'Mummy!'

'I'm coming! Have you looked under the settee?'

'I can see Jay's car.'

This time Kelly got out of bed quickly. She pulled on a pair of jeans and a jumper, wondering what he wanted this time. She'd refused to speak to him when he'd called around last week after the court hearing.

Kelly opened the front door. 'What do you want?' she snapped.

Jay hovered on the path for a moment, his hands thrust deep into his coat pockets. 'Can I come in?' he asked eventually.

'No, I don't want you calling when Scott isn't here.'

'I've got something for you,' his foot tapped on the doorstep, 'and I'd rather not give it to you here.'

Kelly sighed but held open the door.

'Hiya, Jay,' Emily greeted him as they went through into the living room. 'Daddy's not here. He's gone to work away, for a very long time.'

Scott had told Emily that she'd need to be a good girl if he had to go away for a while. He didn't want to see her if he was sent down and Kelly wouldn't take her anyway. She felt Emily was too young to go into a prison environment, even though it would be an open prison. In fact, she wasn't sure that she wanted to go there herself yet. Regardless, with any luck, he'd be out in three months – if he kept his nose clean.

'You'll just have to put up with me, little monster, won't you?' Jay told the little girl. He nudged her gently, almost knocking her over. Emily giggled loudly.

Jay Kirkwell was twenty-eight with stylish, dark spiked hair, olive skin and a tall, thin physique. Of the three brothers, Kelly liked him the most; she tolerated all of them, for Scott's sake, but Stevie and Michael were rough, more aggressive. Jay had a softer side to him. He would always use his mischievous grin to try and make her smile.

But he would get nowhere trying that technique today.

Work-shy hands pushed a white envelope into hers. 'There's five hundred quid. It's to help out, while you're on your own.'

Kelly reached inside and pulled out a handful of twenty-pound notes. All at once she realised that Scott even had a contingency plan. Just how big had that last job been?

She slumped down on the settee. 'Why weren't you caught?' she questioned Jay sharply.

'Because I wasn't there.'

'Come off it. Wherever Scott was, you were never far behind. And your brothers had been on the job, too. You'll be telling me it was your night off next.'

'No. I –'

'Don't tell me that you weren't involved – you went slinking off to the kitchen beforehand, to talk to him about *the job*.'

'That's not how it –'

Kelly held up her hand to quieten him but Jay continued anyway.

'I know you're angry with me. You're right, I couldn't stop them. But –'

'I lost count of how many times I begged Scott to go straight but once a thief there's always another better opportunity that's a dead cert. At least we managed to spend Christmas together as a family.'

'Three months is nothing, it'll go by in a flash. Scott will be ...'

Jay knew he wouldn't get through to her so he left the sentence hanging. She had every right to be angry with him. He hadn't been able to stop them.

Jay wasn't looking at her now, but Kelly still glared at him anyway. She was too angry to speak. It didn't seem fair; two of his brothers and her partner were in jail and he was free to do as he pleased.

'Is that all?' she asked, when they'd been sitting without conversation for a while.

Reluctantly, Jay got to his feet. 'Suppose so.' He turned back before reaching the door. 'You can ring me anytime you need help. Don't push me away.'

Jay had penetrating eyes, the deepest of blue irises that would make the harshest of women fall under his spell in seconds. But they were wasted on Kelly. She stared back until he lowered his gaze.

'I don't want to ring you, I don't want your help, and,' she thrust the envelope roughly back into his hands, 'I don't want the money.'

'Kelly, it's dog eat dog out there. You're going to need help, whether you like it or not.' Jay held out the envelope until Kelly reluctantly took it from him again.

'Give me a bell if you need me,' he reiterated.

Sinking down on the settee once he'd gone, Emily jumped up beside her mum and snuggled into her chest. She began to play with her hair.

'I like Jay, Mummy,' she stated. 'Will he come again?'

Kelly sighed. 'I don't know, Em, but we'll cope on our own.'

Content with this, Emily turned her attention back to the penguins.

Kelly's eyes glistened with tears as she realised how uncertain her future had become in the space of a few days. She knew the coming weeks would be tough but, despite what Jay thought, she could cope on her own until Scott was released. Well, she could as soon as she had the appointment with Josie Mellor out of the way.

*J*osie had to admit to being pleasantly surprised at the immaculate condition of 41 Patrick Street as she looked around the upstairs rooms. It never failed to amaze her how some families on benefits did better for material things than she herself did with two full-time wages coming in. Everything looked brand new: brown leather settees, a large widescreen television with built-in DVD recorder, modern wallpaper and curtains, the latest collection of vases, candles and picture frames. It would be tough for *her* to move out, never mind Kelly.

'This looks lovely,' she tried to jolly her up as they went from bedroom to bedroom. 'And downstairs is equally as nice.'

'I still can't believe you have to check it at all.' Kelly reached for Emily's hand. 'How can you live with yourself? I've been here for five years and I've never caused you any trouble.'

'You'd be surprised at the things I've seen when tenants have abandoned properties.'

Kelly rolled her eyes. 'Like what exactly?'

'Walls knocked down, doors blocked in, fires and kitchens ripped out,' said Josie. 'That's why we introduced the tenancy conditions. Anything done without permission needs to be brought back to standard or we'll re-do the work and issue a charge.'

'I hope you're not referring to me. Me and Scott wouldn't do –'

'No, I'm not referring to you at –'

'But you are going to make me move into that heap of junk you call a flat in Clarence Avenue?'

'I know it's not ideal,' Josie tried to sympathise without sounding patronising, 'but you can make it homely. Then, when you've lived there for a while as a registered tenant, you can go on the transfer list and move somewhere else.'

'And the chances of ever getting to the top of that list are...?'

'That will be up to you, and how Scott behaves when he comes out of prison.'

'Is Daddy in prison, Mummy?' Emily tugged on Kelly's hand.

'No, he's not, Em,' Kelly reassured her. She stared coldly at Josie. 'Can you at least try and be careful what you say?'

Josie didn't falter. 'This isn't my doing. Things have to change. I know you don't like it but that's the way it is. Scott must have known the risk with every job he did and you didn't say no to a life surrounded by material wealth because of it, did you? So you'll have to make the best of your time there.'

'But why Clarence Avenue? Can't we move to somewhere else?'

'No. When Mr Johnstone signed the tenancy agreement on Patrick Street, the only probable reason he managed to get a three-bedroomed house was due to low demand. We had a huge problem letting properties a few years ago but rising house prices have forced more people onto the renting ladder. Clarence Avenue is all we have for you at the moment.'

'They're both doss holes, if you ask me,' Kelly argued. 'I can't believe that you think I'd want to live in *any* of them.'

'Like I told you yesterday, you have no choice. It's either Clarence Avenue or you can find yourself somewhere to live. I think it's better if you go with the first choice, don't you?'

. . .

*L*ater that afternoon, Kelly walked briskly up Clarence Avenue, pushing against the freezing wind. She held on tightly to Emily's hand as she skipped along, singing a nursery rhyme.

They drew level with the first flat she'd seen yesterday and Kelly shuddered, remembering the inside of the property. The walls had been nicotine yellow, a shade she'd never seen on a colour sample chart from any DIY store and it had smelled like someone had used the place as a toilet.

Kelly chanced a quick look at the garden as she marched past. The weeds that had survived the winter had overtaken what looked like a rockery embedded in the middle of the postage-stamp sized garden. The obligatory mound of black waste bags formed another corner display, their contents shred across the path. Dried up baked beans, remains of a roast dinner and... ugh, she didn't want to think about the rest. At least the inside of the flat she'd decided to take had seemed a little more habitable.

She pushed her way through the overgrown hedges again.

'Mummy, I'm wet,' Emily wailed.

Kelly kept a hold of her hand as she guided her down the steps. 'Nearly there,' she gave her voice a singsong tone. 'Then we can see our new home, Emily. Isn't it exciting?'

Kelly opened the door and bent down to have a nosy at the mail that had been pushed to one side when she'd been shown around. Dozens of leaflets advertised two for the price of one pizzas and double-glazing. Red bill reminders for the previous tenant, the odd letter addressed to the new occupier and free newspapers aplenty.

'Pooh, it stinks.' Emily covered her nose with her hand.

Kelly encouraged her to climb the concrete stairs with a gentle nudge on her shoulder. A ninety degree turn to the left led them into a long hallway, made brighter by the vast but narrow landing window behind them. Four doors led off it. The first one on the right revealed the larger of the two bedrooms. Next to that was the bathroom. It was half the size of the one Kelly was leaving, with damp patches that needed to be papered over or, at the very least, painted. The door on the left led into the other bedroom.

Kelly walked the few steps towards the last door and pushed it open. It led into the living room.

'And it's cold,' Emily added, when Kelly hadn't answered her.

'It won't be, once we move our stuff here and put the fire on.'

'But it will be dark soon and I don't like the dark. I'm scared, Mummy. I want to go to Nanny's.'

'It won't be dark for ages yet, and I promise we'll be gone long before then.' Kelly squatted down to Emily's level and pulled her daughter into her arms. 'It's going to be fun living here, Em, wait and see. You can have your room decorated however you like. Do you want Barbie again? Or do you want something else now that you're growing into a young lady?'

'Can I choose my room first?'

While Emily raced around, determined on making as much noise as possible on the bare floorboards, Kelly checked the windows. Child locks had been fitted, but nothing to deter the thieves: at least they were on the first floor in this block. She ran a hand over the freshly plastered chimney breast. If only the other three walls were in the same state, she could get away with a lick of paint. But they weren't. The fresh plaster had been where the previous tenant must have ripped out the fireplace and hadn't put the damage right. The housing association had re-fitted another one, ripping off some of the wallpaper and plastering over a good deal of what was left.

Kelly looked out of the large window and surveyed the neighbouring properties. She was in a block of four flats: other than the two blocks above hers in Clarence Avenue, the rest consisted of semi-detached properties, similar to the one she was being forced to leave, but they were nowhere near as tidy. The garden in the house opposite had more rubbish bags there than in her new garden and a soggy, single mattress had been dumped on the path. On the patch of grass in front of a bay window, the shell of an old hatchback balanced precariously on piles of house bricks, the wheels having long ago vacated the body. The windscreen was missing and the number plates had been removed to claim anonymity.

Kelly tried to calm the fear mounting inside her. She'd spent six nights on her own since Scott had gone. Only now was it beginning to sink in that he wasn't coming home for a long time – wasn't coming home to Patrick Street at all, in fact. He'd made sure of that.

'I've picked me room, Mummy,' Emily shouted through, bringing Kelly back to the present with a jolt. 'Come and find me!'

'My room, Emily. I've picked *my* room.' Kelly raised a smile as she walked through to the bedroom. 'I can't see you,' she played along with her. 'Are you hiding from me?'

Emily giggled as Kelly flung open the cupboard door. In a fit of fun, she grabbed her daughter and began to tickle her.

As they collapsed into a heap of laughter, Kelly's nerves began to centre. Maybe it was inevitable that she'd be anxious about moving here, but what choice did she have? She had to live somewhere and here was as good as any place. It had a roof and four walls, much more than some people had, and she already had furniture – well, most of it would fit in.

It would keep her warm and dry, though, and that's all that mattered, really. And she would be safe, even on her own – if not entirely happy. Eventually she'd get used to every creak of the floorboards, every bang of the hot water system, without jumping out of bed to investigate the locked door.

'I think we'll go into town tomorrow morning, Em, and buy some roll ends of wallpaper. Then in the afternoon we'll start to pack up your things.'

'I have lots of things, don't I, Mummy?'

'Yes, you do.' Despite her reluctance, Kelly would have to ask Jay to lend a hand with some of the bigger items, but she promised herself it would only be this once. She looked around the room again. Number 33 Clarence Avenue, their new home. Well, it would be when she'd finished with it, Kelly resolved.

'Yoo-hoo! Anyone home?' There was a light rap on the door. 'Thought I'd come and see for myself as you said you'd be measuring up for curtains.'

'Nanny!' Emily rushed towards her.

'You call this home?' Kelly griped as her mum, Jill, came into the room. Their stature and height were the same and, apart from a few grey hairs instead of an all over brown, their resemblance was uncanny. Emily had the Winterton button nose too.

'Clarence Avenue isn't as bad as everyone makes out,' Jill tried to reassure her daughter.

'It'll do, I suppose. Looks pretty rough to me, though.'

Jill glanced around the bare living room. 'You can make it nice, love. You seem to have a flair for this kind of thing.'

'It's going to cost me a fortune to get it half decent,' Kelly continued, knowing that her mum really meant the inside and not the outside of the property. 'There's a stack of decorating to do, and cleaning. Everything needs to be scrubbed again before I'm moving one piece of furniture in. I can't believe the association let it out in this state.'

'Have you thought about what to do for money until Scott gets back from you know where?'

Kelly was confused. 'I don't follow,' she said.

'Your dad says they're advertising on the twilight shift at Miles's factory. Four 'til eight. It's a little unsociable but it could work out well for you. I could look after Emily.'

'Yeah, can we, Mummy?' Emily chirped in at the mention of her name. 'I can stay with Nanny.'

'And you know lots of people there. There's Pam, for a start.' Pam was Kelly's auntie. Her cousin, Estelle, worked at the factory too.

'I'm hardly going to have time to do anything else with all the decorating they're expecting me to do in this dump.'

Jill shrugged and walked over to the window. 'I just think there's more to you than a stay-at-home mum.'

'Actually, I was thinking of doing a college course.'

Jill turned back to her daughter and smiled. 'I think that's a great idea. What do you fancy doing?'

'I'm not sure, thought I'd suss it out.' Kelly back-pedalled slightly. 'I know that being a mum is the best job in the world but Em will be starting school in September. I don't know what I'll do with myself then. Maybe if I start a course while Scott is – erm,' she looked at her mum again, 'working away, I could always say I felt the need to fend for myself in case he went to work away again.'

'Maybe if you went to college during the day, you could manage the twilight shift?' Jill pulled a bag of sweets from her handbag and gave them to Emily. 'It's not rocket science and it's repetitive but you know the money will be good. And it beats scrounging off the social. I've always thought better of you than that.'

Kelly huffed. 'Knowing my luck, I'd probably be hopeless at it.'

'You won't know if you don't try.'

'But what if I'm not good enough?'

'Then you'll get better with practice. You're a smart woman, love, and not everyone on this estate needs to play the part of an extra in *Shameless*. Don't get dragged down with the rest of them,' she advised. 'You can get yourself out of this situation if you really want to.'

Kelly said nothing. She knew she needed to secure her future but she wouldn't make her mind up yet. There was so much changing in her life right now. She had all her furniture to pack up, her change of addresses to sort out, and she still had to go and see Scott, which was another thing she kept pushing to the back of her mind.

5

'Please tell me that's all of it.' Jay crammed two more boxes into the back of the van he'd borrowed. 'I don't know about you, but I'm knackered. I think you owe me a beer when we've shifted this load.'

'I think I can run to that,' Kelly answered. For all her misgivings, she wouldn't have managed today if it wasn't for Jay and his offer of a van. Her mum and dad had helped her to box up the remainder of their belongings yesterday, keeping Emily with them overnight so Kelly could shift the heavier items without her getting in the way this morning.

Jay pulled down the roller shutter and secured the padlock. 'I reckon we'll have this unpacked at the other end in a couple of hours. Do you want to see if we've forgotten anything?'

Kelly went back into the house and wandered around each room, checking cupboards, pulling out kitchen drawers, but she hadn't missed anything. Finally, she made one last trip to the living room. She held back tears. Never again would she open her curtains and feast her eyes on old Mrs Shelby across the road at number forty, who'd wave whenever she saw her; be woken up by the boys from number thirty-two coming home from the pub at the weekends; be able to nip in to see Sue, her mum's friend, at number seventeen to check on how her grandson was doing.

She had so many memories, good and bad: bringing Emily home from hospital, her first Christmas, her first birthday. Painting the living room walls buttercup yellow for two days until she and Scott couldn't live with it any longer and had to do it all again in pale lemon; the police knocking on the door every time there had been a robbery or break-in to check for stolen goods. Kelly had lost count of how many times that had happened during their relationship.

'Ready?' said Jay as he came back inside.

Kelly turned towards him. 'It's not fair.' She choked back tears. 'Why should I have to move out because of that thoughtless git? This is my home, too.'

'Don't worry. I'll help you in Clarence Avenue. It'll be like this place in no time – only don't try and badger me into any wallpapering. I'm crap at it. It always rolls down the wall again, no matter how much paste I put on.'

Kelly's lips twitched, thankful that he was trying to make her smile.

'Has Scott called again?' Jay asked.

'Yeah, last night.'

'And am I taking you to see him?'

'I'm not sure.'

Jay nodded. 'I thought you'd say that. But he needs you, Kel. I can't imagine what it's like in there but I know he'll be missing you.'

The lone tear that had trickled down Kelly's cheek now headed towards her neck. She wiped it away abruptly. 'He should've thought about that before he did that last job. I told him not to do it.'

'Don't you think he regrets that now?'

Kelly had asked herself that more than once over the past fortnight and it was eating her up inside. *Had* it all been a mistake? Had he been unaware of his actions? She needed to see Scott, ask him why he'd done it – to hear him say he hadn't realised that he'd put their lives into jeopardy. But it was too raw.

'I'm not ready to forgive him yet. Look what's happened because of his stupidity.'

'I know. You've every right to be upset.'

Yes, she did have every right to be upset. But Kelly didn't want Jay to see her like that. Despite her anguish, she held her head up.

'Upset is one thing, but feeling sorry for myself? I'm better than that.'

Jay flashed a smile. 'Of course you are, but everyone's entitled to throw a wobbler every now and then. It's only natural.'

Kelly sniffed, knowing that if she stood there much longer, she'd start crying properly. 'Let's get out of here,' she said, trying not to think that, as she walked down the path, it was for the very last time.

The following week, Josie was in the office, about to start on the massive task of clearing some of her paperwork. There were six people in that morning as she pulled out a bundle of files from her in-tray. Moments earlier, Debbie had finished her stint on the reception counter and was eating an apple while flicking through a pile of messages. A telephone went unanswered as Irene and Sonia argued over who was going to take over from her.

Where was the office manager when they needed her, Josie thought? Kay Whitehead had been their manager for the last seven years but most of that time had been spent working at their head office in Warbury on special projects – so special that none of her staff ever knew what she was doing. Sometimes the office ran okay without her being there: she was, she insisted, only a phone call away. Sometimes, however, things became a little lax and the staff started to rule the roost.

'Reception okay this morning?' Josie asked Debbie as she searched out a tenant's file from the large cabinet by her side.

Debbie nodded. 'Gets a bit boring, though, listening to everyone moaning.'

'Do you fancy coming out on the patch with me for a few visits? People will still moan but it's better than being inside – well, most of the time.'

Debbie nodded a little more eagerly this time. 'I'd love to.'

'Great. I'll sort it out. All you need to wear is trousers and flat boots or shoes. I'll find you some armour to change...' Josie grinned at the in-joke regarding their work wear. 'I'll find you a coat to wear.'

'Cluck, cluck, cluck, you're doing it again,' Ray teased, smirking at Josie as he sat down at his desk.

Josie stuck out her tongue.

'Whatever you do,' he shouted down the office to their new recruit, 'don't let her tell you the rules of a housing officer. They'll put you off our job for life.'

'Rules?' queried Debbie.

'Ignore him,' Josie soothed her as she frowned at a grinning Ray. 'I'll introduce you to them one at a time.'

When Josie next went out on her own, she spent a pleasant half hour with Amy and Reece Cartwright. As she left the property, she looked up the road. As she'd expected, Kelly Winterton had been hard at work. There was a pile of empty boxes crunched up neatly by the side of the wheelie bin and curtains were hanging in arcs at each of the windows.

As she drove past, Josie spotted Kelly on the pathway. She was quite a way through cutting back the hedge that separated the path from the small garden. Pleased to see her making an effort already, Josie decided to stop.

'Now that's what I like to see,' she said as she walked down the steps towards Kelly.

Kelly stood up straight and put a hand on the small of her back. 'It's bloody killed me to get this far, but I was sick of getting soaked when we moved in.'

'It looks great. And it's nice to see someone *doing* something rather than me having to enforce it with a dozen warning letters.' She was about to ask where Emily was when she appeared behind her mum.

'Hiya, lady,' Emily smiled a row of milky-white teeth. 'I'm helping Mummy clear the garden. I'm on litter duty.'

Kelly and Josie shared a smirk. Emily had numerous cuttings stuck to her red pom-pom hat, and a child's pink rucksack stuffed with crisp packets, toffee wrappers and the odd shrivelled leaf.

'What a good girl.' Josie bent down to her level. 'I think you can come and do my garden when you've finished here. You're doing a wonderful job.'

'Mummy says I have to leave the grown-up stuff for her to tidy up,' Emily pronounced, picking up the rucksack ready to return to her duties.

'Is she always that sweet?' Josie spoke to Kelly.

Kelly stopped mid-shear. 'You should've been here last night when she was crying for most of it.'

'Hello, ladies,' said someone behind them. They both turned to see a small woman. She looked to be in her sixties, with shots of grey running through her dark hair.

'Hello, Dot,' Josie smiled warmly. Dorothy Simpson had lived in the flat below Kelly since she'd lost her husband to lung cancer. She was the first tenant that Josie had taken on a viewing when she had started working for the association. 'This is Kelly. She and her daughter have moved in upstairs.'

'Yes, we met briefly earlier, and I like her already.' Dot smiled at Kelly. 'Especially if she's tackling the garden. I'd do it myself, but my arthritis is playing up at the moment.'

'There's no need,' Kelly told her. 'I'll keep it in order all the time from now on. I can't stand any kind of mess.'

Dot beamed even more when she spotted Emily. 'Hello. Would you like to see if I have any chocolate biscuits left in my tin?'

Emily shrugged shyly but took hold of Dot's hand anyway.

'If you ever need a babysitter for an odd hour here and there,' Dot said as she opened her front door, 'give me a nod. I'd love some company.'

'She seems nice,' Kelly said, as she continued to shear.

'Yes, Dot's one of my prize tenants. She's the chairman of Clarence Avenue Neighbourhood Watch, helps out at the church on Samuel Street. She's always running errands for people less fortunate than herself, too. I've never...' Josie stopped in mid flow as a black and white collie ran past on the pavement. She put her folder down on top of the low wall. 'I won't be a minute.'

Kelly couldn't resist going to investigate as Josie shouted Tess at the top of her voice and raced up the path.

Josie tore after the dog, grabbed for her collar and walked her back the way she had come. She marched Tess down the path and finally managed to tie her up in the garden again. As usual, Mr and Mrs Thomas weren't in to reprimand. Josie made a mental note to pop in next week when she called to see Amy.

Kelly had finished the hedge and was bagging up the last of the cuttings when Josie came into view again.

'You certainly have a varied role as a housing officer,' she grinned as she clocked the red glow of her cheeks.

'She's a good dog really, but she's always escaping. Between you and me, I've given up with her owners. I've had to tie her up in the back garden. It's not something I like doing but what else can I do? It'd be a trip with the dog warden if she's caught wandering the streets again.' Josie held up muddy palms. 'Don't suppose you'd take pity, offer me a cuppa and let me wash my hands?'

Kelly could hear Scott's scornful tone as he said 'absolutely no fucking way' quite clearly in her mind. But Scott wasn't here to say it aloud. Loneliness made her nod her head.

Once Kelly had checked that Emily wasn't badgering Dot too much, they went upstairs to the flat and into the living room. Josie glanced around. Although the floorboards had still to be covered, it was almost a replica of the room Kelly had left behind in Patrick Street: the large coffee and cream swirl rug, heavy ivory curtains hanging from a thick chrome pole. The settees had been placed in an L-shape on the back walls. Three wooden-framed photographs of Emily hung strategically above the tiled fireplace.

'It looks fantastic,' Josie enthused, before sitting down on the settee nearest to the window. 'It must have taken you ages to get rid of the yellow stains.'

Kelly ran her hand over the doorframe nearest to her. 'Three coats of white gloss. To be exact, it was three coats of one-coat gloss. And if you think this is bright, you should see Emily's room – Princess Pink.'

Josie unzipped her folder and pulled out Kelly's paperwork. 'Do you mind if I run through this while I'm here?' she asked when handed a mug. When Kelly didn't reply, she continued. 'Did you go and sort out your benefits last week?'

'Yeah.'

'What about your bills? Have you registered the suppliers in your name?'

Kelly nodded this time. Josie could feel her resistance to the questions.

'That's good,' she continued, 'because if you ever want to get out of here, you'll need to prove you've been a tenant long enough to qualify.'

'I told you I'm capable of surviving on my own,' Kelly muttered. She turned to stare out of the window.

Behind a Closed Door

Josie put her drink down on top of a coaster. 'I haven't called to spy on you. These are routine questions I ask all of my new tenants. I'm simply interested to see how the place is coming on. You have a real flair for making a home.' Her eyes raced around the room again. 'I'm genuinely amazed to see how much you've done in such a short space of time. Some of the tenants I signed up during the same week as you won't have moved in yet, let alone started any decorating. Now that you've done that, though, have you thought any more about getting a part-time job to tide you over?'

Kelly sat down on the other settee. 'Yeah, I need to do something. I don't know how people manage on benefits.' She grimaced, knowing how it would sound to Josie but when she'd lived with Scott, everything had been acquired without question; now she was fending for herself, she had to watch every penny.

'Why don't you come with me to look around Mitchell Academy?' Josie suggested. Mitchell Academy was a high school on the estate that had been used as a community college on its closure. Originally the building had housed six hundred pupils, but government cuts had insisted that it amalgamated with another school three miles away. 'What do you fancy doing?'

Kelly sighed. 'I don't know what I *can* do. It seems so long since I left school. My mum reckons I could get some work at Miles's Factory because my auntie works there. I might give it a go.'

Josie nodded. 'Great. It will alter your benefits if you do over eight hours a week but I think you could easily combine the two. My husband works at Miles's Factory; he does the day and noon shift.' She checked her watch and shot to her feet. 'I'd better get going. I need to call another couple of times yet though, just to see that you're settled. Is next Thursday morning okay for my next call?'

'Yeah, I suppose so. And I'd better rescue Dot from Emily.'

'Don't you mean rescue Emily from Dot?'

Kelly shook her head. 'I know exactly what I mean. That child can talk the hind legs off a donkey, given half the chance.'

Josie smiled to disguise her feelings. Her biological clock had been ticking for quite some time now but Stewart wanted to wait until the timing was right for him too. Then again, with the relationship how it was, there didn't seem much point in trying for a baby if they weren't more of a unit first.

'I'll show myself out and thanks for the drink,' she said. 'I don't accept such offers from everyone I visit, you know.'

*L*ater, as she went back outside to finish clearing up, Kelly recalled Josie's visit. She found herself warming to the woman behind the coat of authority. Josie had no airs and graces, no false chitchat. She was straight, to the point, yet never rude with it, and she didn't judge people. But it was her ability to care without being patronising that she really found admirable.

It also made Kelly realise how much she'd given up for Scott. She was twenty-four years old and not a friend to her name. Everyone she'd been close to had eventually been driven away in case they became too familiar and saw or heard too much. If she *had* had someone like Josie around all the time, to share her concerns and talk over her worries, maybe she might not have got into this mess.

Still, Kelly sighed, Josie was a housing officer. To her, a visit was part of the job. Kelly knew she must visit lots of tenants and make them feel that she was someone in authority that they could trust. But it did seem a pity that the arm of friendship she was offering came with strings attached.

6

It was nearing six thirty when Josie got home from work that evening. She knew she didn't have to rush because Stewart was on the noon shift, two 'til ten. It made her feel sad to realise how much she relished coming home to an empty house. Every other weekend she'd be thinking that the next week, when Stewart was on days – six 'til two – it would be different. But by each Friday night, she couldn't wait for his noon shift to start again.

She hung up her coat and checked the mail: a gas bill, two circulars, a bank statement for her and a bank statement for a Mrs S Mellor. She sighed. She'd rung the bank on several occasions to complain about the computer-generated error but still they kept coming. She left it on the kitchen table for Stewart, along with his monthly car magazine.

After running the Hoover around the living room, she ate a quick meal and then decided to savour the peace and quiet by finishing off the last three chapters of the romantic comedy she was reading, but she was also keeping one eye on the time, as there was a film she wanted to watch at eight.

At quarter to ten, she woke up with a jolt to see the film credits rolling. Damn and blast, she'd missed the ending again. She walked through to the kitchen, made a cheese and tomato sandwich for Stewart and two slices of cheese on toast for herself.

She was halfway through it as she heard his car pull up in the driveway. Automatically, she switched on the kettle and slid the sandwich across the table, reaching across to bring the salt and pepper nearer.

'Hiya, love,' she greeted him cheerily. 'It's a bit nippy. Have you had to scrape the ice off your car?'

'Yeah, it's not fit for a dog out there.' Stewart shrugged his coat off and threw it over the back of the nearest chair. He lifted up a corner of bread from the sandwich and frowned. 'Couldn't you have toasted it for me?'

Josie sighed. No rush to kiss her on the cheek, then. 'You had that last night. I thought you might like a change.'

'I'd rather have a curry.'

'Well, order a takeaway if you want to suffer with indigestion all night.' She pushed past him into the living room, taking her toast with her before he pinched it off the plate.

Fifteen minutes later, Stewart was still in the kitchen. Josie cocked an ear and yes, he'd turned on the portable television rather than come through and sit with her. Fuming to herself, she switched off the set she was idly watching, plumped up the cushions and took her dishes through.

'I'm going to bed,' she told him. 'You can slob out on the settee in the living room now that I've gone.'

Without waiting for his response, Josie slammed the dishes into the sink, noticing the chaos all around her. Honestly, how much mess could you make eating a cheese sandwich? But then her eyes flicked to the table to see the sandwich still there. Next to it was a bottle of tomato ketchup, Stewart's favourite – with cheese on toast.

'Bloody hell, Stewart,' she cried. 'Isn't anything I do good enough for you? What a waste.'

'Stop whining,' Stewart muttered, not taking his eyes from the TV screen. 'I'll have the sandwich for my dinner tomorrow.'

'That's hardly the point.' Josie reached for the washing liquid, then immediately put it down again. Stuff it: she wasn't going to wash them now. They could wait until the morning. After all, Stewart would never think to do them; it certainly didn't bother him when the bowl overflowed.

With every step she took up the stairs away from him, Josie's shoulders drooped a little more. She thought back to the nights when she used to rush upstairs half an hour before he was due home to change out of her sloppy joes and into fresh clothes to look nice for him, applying a little mascara and a smidgeon of lipstick and running a comb through her mass of hair. Come to think of it, Stewart had hardly noticed her then. That's why she'd stopped making an effort.

Her mind still whirred over an hour later as she tossed and turned in her bed. She knew Stewart had taken her advice and moved through to the living room because she could hear the television blaring out. He was watching some action film: she could clearly hear gunshots and every scream for mercy.

Josie lifted her head and pummelled her pillow before resting it again, wondering why things had become so difficult between them. You'd think they'd have so much in common, both of them losing their mums in their late twenties. Stewart had never known his father either. He'd died before he'd been born. His mother had taken care of his every whim until she'd died too, so when he'd moved in with Josie, she'd found herself back in her previous role of carer. Over time, it had become easier to give in to his demands, keep the peace – live the lie.

It had been the same with her mother. Was that all she'd ever be, she wondered, a skivvie to domestic chores? Ever since their wedding day, Josie had taken care of Stewart in the same way as her mother: cooking, cleaning, shopping, washing, and ironing. Maybe that's where she had gone wrong. But looking after people was the only thing she knew how to do. Josie's dad, Jack, had died suddenly of a heart attack when he was forty-two. Josie had only been two at the time so she had no memories of him at all.

Her mum, Brenda, had been distraught. Widowed at forty, she'd complained bitterly about her life being over. She had never remarried: there had been a few 'uncles' along the way that Josie could remember, but no one had moved in. They'd stayed in the same house – at least Brenda had been lucky enough not to have a mortgage weighing heavily on her shoulders.

A few months after Josie's fifteenth birthday, Brenda was injured in a car crash and was never able to walk unaided again. She wasn't confined to a wheelchair as such but, due to not using her legs as much as she was capable of doing, the muscles wasted away and she became housebound.

Depressed with her situation, Brenda became spiteful and jealous of her daughter's position. She constantly reminded Josie that she could go out whenever she wanted and that she didn't have to sit alone all day and all night too.

Trapped somewhere between pity and hate, Josie would stay in to keep the peace. Missing out on her carefree teenage years, she'd borrow books from the local library and read while her mother fell asleep on the settee. It was easier to give in and, after all the housework that she'd had, as well as finding time for homework, there hadn't been much time for anything else.

Josie hadn't been quick to make friends at college, and was glad of the receptionist job that came up at Mitchell Housing Association. The head office had only been minutes away in her car, giving her time to call home every lunchtime to see to her mother.

Things had become more difficult when she'd moved onto the Mitchell Estate as an administrative assistant, but she'd still managed the trip, most of the time eating a sandwich on the way.

When she was promoted to housing officer two years later, Brenda tried to talk her out of it. Although she still had office hours of nine to five, there had been lots of evening meetings to attend and Brenda didn't like anything that ate into the time her daughter should have been there to wait on her hand and foot.

But Josie, for once, stood her ground and at last gained some control in her life. She enjoyed her job. It had been tough at first, but once she got used to it, she found job satisfaction. She could see the results of her labour, she helped to improve people's lives and quite often was thanked for her efforts.

Not all of the tenants were bad news. There was a terrific display of community spirit. Ninety per cent of them were workers, law-abiding people who made up for the other ten per cent of rubbish.

Josie looked after her mum until Brenda had two strokes in quick succession and it became impossible for her to cope. It was then that she had to make the distressing decision to put her into a nursing home. Brenda needed constant care and attention, way beyond what she could give.

It broke her heart to let her go, but as soon as she settled her into Grove House, she knew she'd done the right thing. Josie had visited every other day until another, more severe stroke took her life eight months later.

As well as sorrow, Josie could remember feeling immense relief she'd been free at last to do what she wanted. She tackled some decorating and took a short break to York, her first ever time away from home, where she stayed in first-class indulgence.

As the weeks rolled into months, she started to go on the odd night out with some of the girls from work or they came to hers for a takeaway and a bottle of wine. She started to meet new people and her confidence was given a boost. Six months later, she met Stewart.

Now, memories of better times became overshadowed by a lack of passion. Perhaps this is how all marriages go, Josie considered.

She stopped in her tracks, her eyes opening wide in the dark of the room. Had she been aware of what was happening, just like Kelly Winterton? Had she turned a blind eye, even though she had done it unintentionally?

With that ugly thought, Josie switched off the bedside lamp and buried her head underneath the covers.

'Not again,' Kelly sighed, later that same night. Slowly she dragged herself to her feet, her daughter's wail for attention getting louder by the second.

'Hey.' Kelly pulled her into her arms. 'What's up with my little monster?'

'I want to go home. I don't like it here, Mummy.'

'Would it help if I sat here for a while?' she whispered, knowing full well that Emily would be asleep again soon. Her eyes had already started to close.

Kelly tucked the duvet closer around her daughter's body and looked at her watch. Eleven thirty: she'd only been in bed for an hour. She chewed lightly on her bottom lip. Even though Emily was safely tucked up in her own bed, the room was new, the place was new and the street was new. Through no fault of her own, her child had been dragged away from everything that she knew as her security. Kelly could understand her disorientation.

Her eyes scanned the room that she had struggled to decorate before she moved in. Emily had decided that she wanted everything as pink as possible: duvet, walls, curtains, and lampshades. Kelly had drawn a line at a fluffy pink carpet when the men from Kenny's Carpets had fitted flooring throughout.

Jay had told her Kenny owed him a favour and she could choose whatever she wanted for free. Kelly had resisted at first, but after a few days she couldn't bear to see those shabby floorboards any longer and gave in.

Most of Emily's toys had been hidden away in the cupboard above the stairs, making the bedroom look far tidier than it would have been at Patrick Street.

Peering down at her restless child, a perfect miniature of herself, Kelly couldn't help but feel a huge surge of love. Emily had certainly arrived at the wrong time in her life, but she was so glad that she had her now. She was her hope for the future, a ray of sunshine in an otherwise dull world – just like, Kelly supposed, she had been for her mum at one time.

Minutes later, sure that Emily was safely back in the land of nod, she left her room, made a coffee and dropped into the nearest settee. The living room was quiet except for the noise of the dripping tap from the bathroom. Even with the door shut tight, she could still hear it. Drip, drip, drip. She felt tears welling up in her eyes. Before long, she was sobbing like Emily.

The walls seemed to close in around her, suffocating her with their loneliness, dragging her down to despair. She hated it here in this flat and thought about her pending visit to see Scott. Jay was taking her in the morning. Even without the two-hour car journey, she wondered if she really wanted to go into that environment. She'd heard too many stories to think that any prison cell could be void of a mass murderer or some evil bastard ready to slit your throat at the mention of slopping out.

Kelly wanted to hate Scott for what he'd done, but she couldn't. What if Jay was telling the truth? What if Scott did need her more than she thought? Could she abandon him after five years together?

Questions, questions, questions.

Kelly's eyes had closed for all of ten minutes before she was jolted awake again by the sound of the techno beat bursting out from the flat next door.

Before her tears had started to fall for the second time, Kelly heard Emily beat her to it.

She sighed loudly. Would either of them settle in Clarence Avenue?

Over at Josie's house, it was an hour later that Stewart finally came to bed.

'I'm going in at six tomorrow,' he said, not bothering to kiss her goodnight. 'We've got lots of work on so I might as well do a few hours overtime while I can.'

'Okay,' Josie answered, before he dragged over the duvet and slept with his back towards her – the same thing he'd done for as long as she could remember now. She wondered why she thought it would be any different tonight.

The following morning, Stewart was up and out of the house before Josie got out of bed. Making all the difference to the start of the day, she set off to work with a spring in her step. Driving through the rush hour traffic, the radio belting out its tunes, she sang along to the lyrics at the top of her voice and wondered how long the feeling would last.

It was all of thirty minutes – enough for her to grab a quick cup of coffee – before the first phone call came in. There had been another burglary over at Wilma Place, a row of bungalows for the elderly. Someone had made another complaint about Gina Bradley's twins. That was the third one she'd had that week. Josie clicked on to the computer system and opened up the case. That was the beauty of hard drives, she surmised. If they were still using paper files, Claire and Rachel's files would be at least two inches thick. And that was one case of the Bradleys – for once, it wasn't their older brother, Danny. Nineteen-years-old and he'd already been into juvie twice for burglary and car theft.

Josie grabbed her car keys and coat. If she left now, she could see if Gina was in before she started her other appointments. She might as well get it over with first – it wasn't going to be pretty.

7

With all the courage she could muster, Josie unlatched the broken gate and walked slowly up the path towards Gina Bradley's front door. Every heavy step made her feel like turning around and running away. Although she knew Gina Bradley hated her with a passion, Josie tried hard not to show that the feeling was mutual.

She was about to knock on the door when it was yanked open. Gina stood there in all her splendour. She was a little woman but 'fat' and 'round' were too kind for her description. Looking like she hadn't seen a shower in weeks, she was wearing black leggings that threatened to walk off on their own, filthy white socks and a grey sweatshirt three sizes too small. Her hair had been dyed bright red this month, and with no make-up on her pale face, she reminded Josie of a matchstick – a jumbo matchstick.

'I suppose you're about due a visit,' Gina drawled, looking pointedly down at Josie from her advantage of being three steps up. 'What the hell do you want this time?'

'Morning to you too, Gina,' Josie replied, trying to sound confident. 'Can I come in?'

Gina turned away from her but left the door open. Josie squeezed her way through lager boxes stacked high in the hallway and followed her into the living room. From where she was standing, she surveyed the mess. At least a dozen dirty cups on the coffee table, piled next to them, plates containing the remnants of two different meals. Gossip and fashion magazines were scattered over the floor, beside nail varnish and bags of cotton wool pads. Clothes seemed to be strewn over every seat.

Gina flopped down onto the settee, not bothering to move anything.

Josie pulled her coat down as far as it would go to cover her bottom and perched on the edge of the chair. She didn't want to sit in anything suspect.

'I've had more complaints about the twins,' she began.

'Oh?' Gina lit up a cigarette and took two long drags before she spoke again. 'And which nosy bastard has reported them this time?'

'You know I can't tell you that.'

Gina glared at her. 'I can't see why not. I always guess who it is by the complaint. Anyway, what are they supposed to have done this time?'

'They've been causing a nuisance at the shops. They've –'

'Doing what?'

'Hanging around the outside, swearing at customers, begging for cigarettes and following people around in a threatening manner. On one occasion, a purse has gone missing.'

'I hope you're not saying that one of my girls nicked it.' Gina looked outraged.

'No, I don't have any proof but –'

'Then I'd shut your mouth if I were you or I'll have you for slander.'

Josie swallowed. Things were going no better than she'd envisioned, but she tried to stay calm.

'They've also been seen throwing eggs at Mrs Robson's bungalow,' she added.

Gina nodded and took another drag. 'So she's complained has she, the moaning old bag? I'll –'

'It wasn't her,' Josie told her truthfully. 'You know she keeps herself to herself.'

'She's a nutter.'

Josie ignored her, not wanting to be drawn into discussing anyone else. Just then, she heard the front door open and slam shut. She held her breath for a second, unsure what to expect, which member of this nasty family she would encounter next.

'What's she doing here?'

'Hello,' Josie greeted the scowling girl. She was followed by her identical twin sister, who ignored Josie and went into the kitchen.

'She's come about you two.' Gina stubbed out the remains of her cigarette and lit another one straight after. 'Do either of you know anything about a purse being nicked at Shop&Save. Claire?'

'No, we bloody don't.' Claire folded her arms across a blossoming chest. 'So don't start blaming me and Rach for it. We were home all night, weren't we, Mum?'

Gina snorted. 'That's right, love, you were.'

Josie sighed and stood up. It was like talking to a brick wall.

'I don't have any proof this time, Gina,' she said, 'but you can't keep on letting your girls rule the roost. Sooner or later, they're going to go too far.'

Gina pushed the pile of plates to one side and put up her feet. 'They're kids,' she yawned, stretching her arms above her head. 'They'll grow out of it.'

'Danny didn't.'

'Keep Danny out of this!'

'I was just saying.'

'Well, don't,' Gina warned. Her top lip curled up scathingly. 'If you've said what you've come to say, then sling your hook. Danny's still in bed, and if I start raising my voice, he'll wake up – and you don't want that, do you?'

Josie certainly didn't. Danny Bradley scared her more than Gina. An evil specimen of a young man, it gave her the creeps even looking at him.

'Yeah,' said Rachel. She sat down next to her mother. 'Get out of our house with your airs and graces.'

Josie stood her ground. 'Think about what I said, Gina. This can't keep happening.'

Gina did nothing but stare at her.

Feeling dismissed, Josie couldn't leave the house quick enough. Getting into her car, she drove to the next street, parked up again and took a breather. She held on to the steering wheel to stop her hands from shaking.

That bloody family. Who the hell did they think they were? She felt frustration rip through her. She was no match for them. They knew every benefit scam, every way to beat the system. Their father was no better; Pete Bradley was a complete layabout. Josie wondered if he'd ever done a day's legal work in his life.

The worst thing was, that was just the one house. Gina's mum and dad lived two doors further down. Three doors after that was Leah Bradley, Gina's younger sister. Stanley Avenue was overrun with that family because no one else wanted to live near any of the Bradleys.

Josie's nerves began to settle again. Although there were lots of decent people on the Mitchell Estate, there were plenty of badly-behaved families, too – yet none of them got under her skin as much as the Bradley's. The lot of them thought they were above the law.

But one day, one month, one year, one of them would do something, and she'd have the power to get them out. Until then, Josie would have to build up the evidence against them and bide her time.

. . .

The two-hour car journey to visit Scott had been a nightmare due to heavy rain and an overturned lorry on the motorway. Then there had been the humiliation of the search procedure and the intimidating atmosphere of the prison environment. But just seeing his face break out into a smile when he spotted her walking towards him in the visitors' room made it all worthwhile for Kelly.

For a minute or two, anyway.

'It's good to see you, babe,' Scott whispered, as he hugged her.

Kelly glanced over his shoulder cautiously, not daring to meet anyone's eye, fearing she wasn't allowed to touch him. But it seemed okay – lots of men were doing the same before they sat down.

There were approximately twenty tables arranged in rows up and down the room. The woman on the next table had two young children with her as she chatted excitedly to the man she'd come to visit. Luckily for Kelly, the 'working away' lie seemed to be doing its job. There was no need to confuse Emily.

People were talking, laughing, moaning, smiling – but Kelly couldn't find anything to smile about. Somehow a prison visiting room hadn't featured in her life plan.

Scott motioned to a chair. 'How's Em doing?' he asked.

'She's okay, I suppose,' Kelly replied. 'One minute she's fine about you not being there. Other times, she's upset. But I'm glad I've got her – I hate being on my own.'

'Is Jay keeping an eye on you?'

'Yeah, he brought me here today.'

'Good. I told him to look after the pair of you.'

'He shouldn't have to look out for us. That's supposed to be your job.'

Scott groaned. 'Don't let's go there, Kel. It's not like I can do anything about it now. Think of me, stuck in here, it's enough to drive any bloke loopy.'

Kelly ignored his self-pity and went straight to the main point. 'Did you get the letter from the housing association?'

Scott's top lip curled derisively. 'Yeah, but I'm not worried about it. You shouldn't be either.'

'But you'll have a bill for about two grand!'

'Which I can pay off at a couple of quid a week because I'm on the dole.'

Kelly frowned. 'You're not grasping the seriousness of the situation.'

'Rules are made to be broken.'

She folded her arms. 'But I don't want to live like that anymore. Besides, the house is still your responsibility while you're in here. Josie says empty properties are like a magnet on the estate. You'll have to pay for any damage.'

'Who the fuck is Josie?' Scott questioned. 'Not that interfering bitch from Mitchell Housing? And what do you mean by empty property? Don't tell me you've moved out?'

Kelly seemed surprised he hadn't realised sooner. 'Yeah, of course I have,' she said. 'I had to go and see Josie. She told me what would happen if I stayed at Patrick Street – they would have evicted us.'

Scott shook his head to protest. 'No, they wouldn't. She's trying to scare you. They can't evict me. They have to take me to court and I would've been out of here before that happened.'

'Maybe, but –'

'You should've stayed where you were. Now the house is empty, they've got more of a case – I could lose my tenancy rights! You've ruined everything, you silly cow.'

The icy look Scott threw Kelly chilled her bones. 'And how exactly have *I* done that?' she snapped. 'You being in here means that I *can't* stay at Patrick Street. They turfed me and Em out and it's *your* fault. How could you do that?'

Scott looked around the room as a couple of heads turned in their direction. One of the wardens started to walk towards them.

'Keep your voice down, Kel.' Scott cocked his head a little. 'Let me get this clear. The letter wasn't an empty threat?'

Kelly shook her head.

'They can't fucking do that. That's my home.'

'*Our* home,' corrected Kelly. 'At least it *was* our home until you got sent down. They've moved us to a flat – on Clarence Avenue.'

Scott's eyes bulged. 'Fucking hell, this is getting worse. If you're on Clarence Avenue, where am I supposed to go when I get out of here?'

'You haven't even asked how I am!'

Scott sniggered. 'I know you'll be coping. That's what keeps me going in here, knowing that you'll have everything under control. Well, it was until you told me about Patrick Street. Why didn't you stand your ground? They wouldn't have evicted you if you'd refused to go.'

'They would because I'm not mentioned on the tenancy agreement. My name isn't on any of the utility bills either. I'm registered for benefits from Christopher Avenue, my mum's address. Why did you do that?'

The warden had stopped a few feet away from them, content to linger for now. Scott settled back in his chair again.

'I didn't do it on purpose, if that's what you're thinking. I knew we could claim more money that way but I didn't know this would happen.'

Kelly huffed. '*You* said you'd never get caught. *You* said you'd never get sent down.'

'I say a lot of things. It doesn't mean everything always goes to plan.'

Kelly pushed her chair back with her feet but it didn't create enough space. Right now, she didn't want to be near him. All he seemed to be concerned about was his own welfare.

'What about me?' she asked him. 'And Emily – what about your daughter?'

Suddenly Scott's tone changed. 'Come on, Kel, this was never going to be easy, you coming to see me in here. I'm sorry, but when you're locked up, you do nothing but think of yourself.' He looked straight into her eyes, throwing her heart into turmoil. 'It's the thought of getting out and being with you that gets me through each day. Don't give up on me.'

'Then give up Patrick Street,' said Kelly. 'The longer you have it, the more rent you'll owe when you do get out. And you'll be moving back with me, anyway, won't you?'

'Yeah, course. Listen, I need you to do something – I need you to go and see Philip Matson, over in Bernard Place. He has some of my gear and I want you to get it back. I've been thinking and I don't trust him with it until I get out.'

Kelly narrowed her eyes. 'What kind of gear?'

'A bit of insurance.' Scott raised his hands in the air. 'Nothing to do with drugs, you know me.'

'Yes, I do know you. What have you been up to?'

'Something and nothing, babe. Nothing you need to worry about anyway, but I need you to keep it for me at Patrick – Clarence Avenue.'

'No way.' Kelly shook her head furtively. 'I am not doing your dirty work for you. What do you think I am, your lackey lad? Get Jay to do it.'

'I don't want anyone to know about it. It's a job I did on my own, so I don't want Stevie and Michael finding out. They'll only want a cut. And, I told you, it's not safe in Matson's hands.'

'A cut of what?' Kelly questioned further.

'Never you mind.'

'No, I won't fetch it unless you tell me what –'

'Just do it, Kel.' Scott's tone held a hint of menace. 'I don't –'

Kelly stood up. 'That's why you wanted me to come and see you,' she hissed. 'You're not bothered about me or Em.'

Scott stood up too. ''Course I am, babe. This money's for all of us, when I get out.'

'Money?'

'Yeah, I –'

'How come I didn't know about it?'

'I'm telling you now!'

The warden was on his way over again. Kelly turned to walk away. Scott reached up and lightly touched her arm.

'Please, Kel, do this one thing. Remember the good times ... didn't I always look out for you ... and Em?'

8

Jay was waiting for Kelly in the prison car park. He noted her red eyes as soon as she opened the door.

'I take it the visit didn't go to plan?' he remarked.

Kelly buckled up her seatbelt and shook her head. She didn't want to talk about it – least of all to a Kirkwell. Thankfully, Jay started the car and moved away from the building.

How had she let this happen? She asked herself the same thing over and over as Jay drove back onto the motorway. Her partner – the man she loved – had shown his true colours today. He didn't care about her. All he was bothered about was himself.

She turned to Jay at last. 'What a pushover I've been. Good old Kelly. Never one to make a fuss, always keeping the bloody peace. Fat lot of good that did me.'

'This isn't your fault,' Jay replied.

'Yeah, right. I should have been stronger, told him not to do that last job. I should have been more forceful, demand that he kept away from you and your bloody brothers. I should have told him –'

Kelly stopped sharply before she let slip about the parcel. She turned away to look out of the window again.

The landscape passed by in a blur. Kelly sensed that Jay wanted to carry on talking, but she wouldn't let him. She couldn't trust him – couldn't trust any of Scott's friends. And if she couldn't trust Jay, why should she try to make him feel better?

As they left Scott further and further behind, Kelly knew now that she would have to dig deeper to find the strength to rely on herself and herself only – regardless of whether she wanted to or not.

Before she made her next visit to Kelly, Josie dropped into Mitchell Academy to fetch two prospectuses. She'd been pondering whether to get a qualification in counselling for some time now. It could possibly help her with her work but, more importantly, it might make her find out more about herself.

However, there was one thing stopping her – or rather, one person. Stewart – Josie knew he'd hardly be pleased with the prospect of his wife being away from home for another night a week, even if it was only for two hours at a time. When he was working on the late shift, most nights he would ring to see if she was at home. It made her feel like a prisoner on a tag clocking on with her probationer.

No, Josie decided there and then that she was going to do this. She'd just have to think of something to throw Stewart off the scent.

Ten minutes later, she knocked on Kelly's front door. When she answered, Josie realised in dismay that Kelly had made more of an effort than she had. Fully made up, she wore dark jeans and a fashionable red sweatshirt. Consciously, Josie closed her coat to hide the fact that, to Kelly, with her extensive and stylish wardrobe, she would look like she only had a few outfits to her name.

'You must be psychic,' said Kelly, strangely glad to see Josie. 'I was about to flick the kettle on.'

Once upstairs, Josie's eyes swept over the living room, noticing that it was as tidy as it had been on her last visit. Emily lay on the settee, her feet waving in the air, her chin resting in her hands.

'Hello, Emily, what's Dora the Explorer up to today?'

Emily turned her head, her eyes opening widely. 'You know who Dora the Explorer is?'

'Of course I do. She's a very clever girl.'

'I like the penguins best.'

Josie was stumped at the mention of penguins. She turned as she heard Kelly behind her.

'I've brought you a prospectus from Mitchell Academy. I thought you might like to see what's available for you to try out.'

Kelly pushed Emily's legs along the settee and sat down. Emily put her feet into her mum's lap as Kelly flicked through the booklet.

'I'm thinking of enrolling on a counselling course,' said Josie, trying to start the conversation up again.

Kelly looked up. 'I thought counselling was part of your job?'

'I suppose it is,' said Josie. 'But I'd also like to be qualified to do it properly. And, although no two cases are the same, who's to say there isn't a better way to deal with a situation?'

'I think you're good at your job. You have a way about you. Scott warned me off people like you – people in authority.'

Josie smiled: praise indeed.

'Josie, will you read me a story before you go?' Emily came towards her with a book.

'Manners, young lady.' Kelly tapped her daughter's thigh lightly. 'It's rude to interrupt. Wait until we've finished talking, please.'

A knock at the front door interrupted their conversation for a second time. Emily rushed to her feet but Kelly pulled her back.

'What did I tell you about answering the door?' she scolded. 'That's always Mummy's job.'

An awkward silence descended as Jay followed Kelly into the living room.

'Jay!' shouted Emily.

'Hey there, maggot.' Jay picked her up and slung her over his shoulder. Emily started to squeal and giggle.

Ill at ease, Josie quickly got to her feet. She wondered why he was calling, although she wouldn't ask. Tenants were allowed visitors. It wasn't as if she had – or would even want – control over who came and went.

'Hello, Jay,' she said. 'How's your mother?'

Jay nodded. 'She's okay, ta.'

Josie spotted the flowers Kelly was holding.

'These are from Scott,' Kelly said. 'There's nothing sinister going on. It's my birthday tomorrow.'

'Happy birthday,' Josie offered, with a faint smile. 'Right, I'll be on my way. I was nearly finished anyway. One more visit in another four weeks and that'll be me done officially. It's obvious you're doing okay.'

Kelly sighed. What the hell would Josie think of her now? She must wonder if she associated with every villain on the estate. And it had been fun, she realised, talking to someone different for a change, even if she was a housing officer and therefore known as the anti-Christ.

Josie couldn't contain herself when they were alone, though. 'Does he come round often?' she said, as Kelly opened the front door to let her out.

Kelly shrugged a shoulder slightly. 'He's been a few times since Scott was sent down. Why?'

'Be careful, hmm? I really like Jay, but maybe you or I don't know what he's really capable of.'

'Like Scott, you mean.'

'No,' Josie faltered. 'I –'

'Keep your nose out of my business.' Kelly's eyes held a look of fury. 'You can't run my life for me – and don't bother calling again if you think you can.'

She closed the door. By the time she'd climbed the stairs again, her earlier thoughts about a friendship forming had been dismissed. It was Josie's job to see that she was settled. Maybe that was all she'd ever intended. Kelly now felt foolish thinking anything else.

Jay took one look at her face and thought better about mentioning his bad timing. Kelly marched past him into the kitchen, filled both rooms with the sound of water gushing out of the tap at full force, then switched on the kettle.

'It's not you that I'm mad with,' she shouted through to him. 'It's the situation I'm in.'

'Josie's all right,' said Jay.

Kelly sighed as she emerged in the doorway with a turquoise patterned vase for the flowers. 'I know. That's what I can't get my head around. She's a housing officer – the spawn of the devil, according to Scott.'

'Most people are the spawn of the devil according to Scott.'

'She seems different, though. Well, at least I thought she was.'

'I think she's really fair.' Jay casually flicked open the cover of the pink book on the table. Emily's eyes left the television long enough to register the information and he put it down quickly. 'I've never had a problem with her and I've known her for years,' he added. 'And she's someone you can trust not to spread your business. Mitchell's a great estate for rumour spreading. I should know, being a Kirkwell.'

Yes, thought Kelly, you being a Kirkwell is the reason why Josie wants to know my business in the first place.

Josie couldn't get Kelly's outburst out of her mind as she walked down the pavement towards Amy's flat. Sometimes she wished she didn't care so much, then she wouldn't get it in the neck when she interfered. Kelly was right: it was none of her business if Jay called round to see her every day – but that didn't stop her from feeling cynical about it.

She knocked on Amy's door but there was no answer. Josie checked her watch: she was ten minutes early. She bent down to check the lock. The key was still there on the other side of the door, meaning that Amy had to be in. Josie knocked again twice, waited for a couple of minutes.

When she still didn't come to the door, she pulled out her mobile phone, checked her file for a phone number and rang Amy. From inside the flat, she could hear the phone ringing. Concerned, she knocked again.

'Amy? It's Josie. I know you're in there. What's the matter?'

Still there was no answer. Josie quickly wrote a message on a calling card and popped it through the letterbox. Unable to do any more, she went back to her car.

Bloody typical, she thought.

Now she had Amy *and* Kelly to worry about.

For Josie, the day hadn't ended at five o'clock as the office closed its doors to the public. By rights, it wasn't her night to stay late for the monthly residents meeting, but Ray had conveniently had a memory lapse and left early straight from his last appointment. He'd rung in to speak to one of the admin staff rather than directly to her. Josie wasn't the type of person to shoot the messenger, so she'd had no choice but to step in.

'It's bloody ridiculous what we have to put up with around here,' Saul Tamworth said, as he slammed his fist down onto the table. 'I'm not paying a penny more in rent unless you get something done about it.'

'Yeah, too right,' nodded Muriel Tamworth. 'It's so flipping noisy, every night.'

Mr and Mrs Tamworth lived in Warren Street, on the outskirts of the estate. Over the past few months, they'd been plagued by a gang of teenagers tearing around on scrambler bikes across the open fields behind their property – a property they'd moved into *because* of the open fields they overlooked.

'Like I told you at the last meeting,' Josie reiterated patiently, 'this is a matter for the police to deal with. It's an anti-social behaviour issue and you need to contact them every time the boys come –'

'That's no bloody use. They can't do anything either! They're always far too busy to respond to the likes of us. Seven times I rang the switchboard last night.'

Mr Tamworth was a heavily built man in his late fifties, with grey hair and cheeks that matched the shade of his grubby red sweatshirt precisely. His wife was a fair bit younger, probably early thirties, built like a barrel with greasy hair and a face covered in acne. To Josie they seemed an odd couple, more like uncle and niece. They were two of nine tenants who had turned up for the monthly tenants' meeting – 'the gripe night', they called it back at the office. They sat on orange plastic chairs, squashed around a snooker table, in a room at the back of the community centre.

Josie tuned out of Mr Tamworth's rants and checked her watch as another

Behind a Closed Door

tenant, Mrs Roper, joined in. 'I think it's preposterous that you can't do anything about it,' she shouted across the room. 'The noise is atrocious, it's like having a hairdryer on high speed and I can't hear my television half the time.'

Josie wondered how she could hear anything above the full volume of her television. Mrs Roper had worn a hearing aid for the best part of thirty years now. Whenever Josie visited, it was sometimes minutes before she could get her attention, even banging on the front window after trying the door.

'Yeah, and it's always late when they –'

Josie held up a hand, trying to bring things back to the agenda. 'I'll have another word with PC Baxter and see what he can do. If he's on shift, maybe if he walks around the area every night for a couple of weeks, things might calm down.'

'That isn't the point.' Mrs Tamworth folded her arms across a huge chest that sat on an even larger stomach. 'They'll only move onto somewhere else.'

Josie raised her eyes to the ceiling and withheld her exasperation.

'Before *we* move on,' Mr Ashworth from number 92 William Precinct began to speak, 'I'd like to congratulate Josie on getting rid of most of the dog poo from in front of my house. It's been far more pleasant taking my daily walk.'

'Must be because you haven't let your own dog out to crap everywhere else,' muttered Mrs Pike from number 74.

Mr Ashworth sat forwards in his chair and turned his head to the right. 'You always have to say something detrimental, don't you, Mrs Pike? You can't say a nice word about anyone.'

Mrs Pike huffed. 'That's because I'm always right. You let that ratty thing of yours crap all over my pathway last month.'

'I cleaned it up, didn't I? Charlie had been poorly.'

'I bet it won't be long before it happens again.'

'It'll be a very long time, my dear. He passed away last week.'

'Moving swiftly on,' Josie interrupted. She checked the agenda for the next item on the list: number four of sixteen. Great, she sighed – the recent spate of burglaries. And considering there had been another two during the past fortnight, plus another attack on an elderly woman that had left her severely battered and bruised, Josie knew she'd be in for a roasting – even though it was nothing to do with her job.

9

By the time everyone had made sure they'd put their point forward, some more forcefully than others, Josie finally brought the meeting to a halt at five to seven. After stacking all the chairs and washing the coffee cups, she left for home ten minutes later. With hardly any traffic on the road, she'd just get back in time for *Coronation Street*. Quickly, she sent a text message to Stewart to let him know she was on her way.

She drove the short journey through the dark streets, wondering why her tenants always worried over the most trivial of matters. Didn't they have anything better in their lives to occupy their minds, apart from moaning about the little things or going on about other people's behaviour?

It was bound to be a case of the pot calling the kettle – Josie would love to get inside their homes at night to see what they really got up to behind closed doors. Then she thought of the huge age gap between Mr and Mrs Tamworth – hmm, maybe not.

Stewart was sprawled the length of the settee in the living room when she arrived home, but immediately jumped up to join her in the kitchen.

'Where the hell have you been until now?' he demanded.

'Let me at least take my coat off before you start ranting,' Josie said. 'I had to cover a tenants' meeting. Didn't you get my first text message? I sent it about half past four.'

'You never told me about it last night.'

'That's because I didn't know about it then. Good old Ray decided to bunk off and I was the only one left to cover it. Have you eaten yet?' Josie unzipped her fleece and moved through to the kitchen. 'If you haven't, I can cook you something while I catch *Corrie* on the portable.'

She'd only made it to the fridge when Stewart came up behind her. He slammed his palm on the wall by the side of her head.

'You're seeing someone else, aren't you?'

'What? Don't be –'

Stewart grabbed her arm, pulled her closer and sniffed. 'I can smell him on you. You've been with him tonight.'

Josie flinched as his fingers dug into her skin. 'I haven't been near anyone else. You know I wouldn't do –'

'*How* would I know? You could use that frigging job of yours as an excuse any time you want to. I wouldn't be any wiser. You could even meet him at one of your empty properties. You've got loads of opportunities, so don't deny it.'

'Stop it,' she cried. 'You're hurting me.'

'You don't see a problem with hurting me.'

'Let me go! I haven't been seeing anyone else.'

Stewart loosened his grip and bent forwards, his face an inch away from hers. 'No, you're right.' He sniggered. 'No one in their right mind would have you, would they?'

Josie let out her breath as she watched him shrug on his coat. There was so much that she wanted to say, but words wouldn't form. Instead, she watched him swipe up his car keys and leave the room.

As soon as the front door slammed behind him, she burst into tears. She sat down at the kitchen table, tentatively rolling her shoulder as she tried to ease the pain in her arm.

What had got into him now? If it wasn't the house, he'd be moaning about something else. Something trivial, just like most of her tenants. It was like being at work at times. Throughout their marriage, all she'd ever done for Stewart was her best, and now even that didn't seem good enough. But then again, no wonder he thought she was a good catch. He could see 'easy life' written all the way through her like the lettering inside a stick of seaside rock.

Josie had met Stewart after a night out in the town. One of the office girls was leaving and most of the housing staff had gone for a meal to send her on her way.

It was only after Josie had dropped the last of her passengers off that her car decided to splutter to a halt half a mile from home. Reluctant to walk alone in the dark, she'd rung Kay, the office manager, who had sent husband Richard to help. In the meantime, she'd opened the driver's door, released the handbrake and attempted to push it to the side of the road.

Stewart, with several of his friends, had rounded the corner on the way back from the pub to see a damsel in distress. They'd manoeuvred the car into a better position, locked it up and gone on their way.

Moments later, Stewart had returned to keep her company and by the time Richard had arrived, they'd arranged to meet up for a drink the following lunchtime. Josie could hardly believe her luck. He was the first man who'd shown an interest in her since her mum died.

Stewart had swept Josie off her feet. He called her beautiful and her confidence had grown. Josie knew she wasn't beautiful – far from it, with her pale complexion, wavy mass of hair and waif-like figure. But he took control of her, made her think that she needed him.

And, after losing her mum, that was exactly what she did need. It took her a long while to realise, however, that what she'd first mistaken for loving concern was actually his possessive manner.

Their wedding day a year later had been quiet. Josie wasn't one for a huge affair and Stewart had agreed with his bride-to-be. But it had been a lot quieter than she had at first anticipated. Stewart had booked the ceremony at the local register office for the month after he'd proposed. He said there was no point in waiting now that they both knew what they wanted.

There had only been the two of them. Stewart had managed to persuade a couple in their late fifties to witness the occasion, brought a disposable camera at the local chemist and a suit from the high street.

Josie wore a dress she'd found in the summer sales the week before and, late in August 2007, she became Mrs Josie Mellor. A quick meal afterwards – Stewart insisted on the witnesses tagging along too, giving them no time alone to celebrate – and that had been that.

It was when he came to live with her that things started to change. Like Josie, Stewart had never moved away from the family home, but his had been rented from the local council. Giving it up had been easy for him. There was no more rent to pay and what furniture he had he sold.

Before long, he began to question Josie's every move: what time was she coming home, what time did the meeting finish, could anyone else go instead? Josie soon realised he was a control freak, often behaving like a spoiled child if he didn't have things his own way. It wasn't long until she realised that she was in the same position that she'd been in with her mother.

She stared at her weary reflection in the window as she sat in silence. She wondered if this was really what marriage was about, what everyone raved about, what other girls had craved since puberty. Was this the 'worse' part mentioned in the wedding vows she'd taken, or did it get any better?

She wondered again if Stewart still loved her. Had he *ever* loved her or had he only ever seen her as a safe bet? Good old Josie; in her mind's eye, even she could see how much of a catch she'd been. She didn't have to be exceptional in the looks department to provide a roof over his head. She didn't need to keep up with the latest fashions to wash, dry and iron his clothes. She didn't have to have a confident manner to cook him a decent meal.

One lone tear trickled down her cheek. She left it to travel down her chin, her neck, her chest, as she wondered what she should do about things.

She knew what she *should* do. But she also knew what she *would* do – absolutely nothing.

'Hello, you.' Cath Mason flashed a welcoming smile as she opened her door to find Josie on her front doorstep. 'How's tricks?'

'Fine. I called by on the off chance you'd be in,' Josie explained, glad of a warm welcome for a change. 'I heard about the burglary. Are you okay?'

'Yeah, I'm fine, thanks.' Cath's shoulders sagged. 'Which is more than can be said about my TV. Whoever the bastard was, he put a hammer through the screen. I hadn't had it long.'

Josie pulled a sympathetic face. 'It's a good job you're insured.'

'Yes, and Matt has fitted better locks now, but it still pisses you off, doesn't it? Have you got time for a cuppa?'

'Sometimes I don't believe a word of what they say about this estate and its tenants. Some of them are salt of the earth.' Josie grinned. 'I'd love one please.'

'There's a packet of chocolate biscuits in the cupboard,' she pointed. 'Help yourself.'

'So, how are you and Matt getting along? Still good, I hope?' Josie enquired, as Cath bustled about making coffee. Cath's smile told her everything she needed to know. She sighed wistfully. 'I wish I could have a little more happiness every now and again.'

'Oh dear. That doesn't sound good.'

'Never mind me, I'm rambling.' Josie waved the remark away with the flick of a wrist. 'Something and nothing. Have the police got any clues as to who it might be?'

Cath shook her head. 'Nope, they just gave me a crime reference number. I'm yet again another statistic.'

'Do you think it might be linked to anyone you have staying here?'

'I don't think so, though I can't be certain.'

Cath Mason had been Josie's saviour many times over the past three years. She'd been widowed at thirty-six, four years ago now. Josie had always liked Rich Mason. Although a troublemaker in his early years, he'd left his reputation behind in the prison cell he'd spent three years in for armed robbery. Once out, he'd made an honest woman of Cath Riley.

But until a few months ago, everyone was under the assumption that Rich had stumbled coming home from the pub one night. One drink too many and he'd taken a tumble down a flight of steps on his way back. His neck had been broken and he'd died instantly.

Having found out since that the push had been deliberate and a couple of kicks to his head had finished him off, Cath had been left traumatised. But as always, only people close to her would know that.

It was a chance encounter that had started Cath on the caring route. A child of the care system herself, she'd taken in her friend's daughter after her friend had threatened to kick her out. The result had been a learning curve for Cath and, as she'd told Josie on numerous occasions, it had been nice to have company again. When she'd been made redundant for the second time in as many years, she'd opened up her home to more of the same.

Cath only had room for four girls at a time, but she'd always help Josie out as much as she could, even if it meant giving up her room to spend the odd nights on the settee. Sometimes the girls stayed a night, or sometimes a week. Often – like in Jess Myatt's and Becky Ward's cases – months at a time. But since Matt had come onto the scene and Cath had settled down with him, they'd been making enquiries into fostering children.

'I wish we could collar this dickhead who's been targeting the elderly on the estate. He's the bloody bane of my life at the moment.'

Josie sat down at the table and Cath pushed a mug over to her.

'I bet he is,' Cath said. 'But at least whoever did mine didn't take anything of sentimental value. Other things I can replace, but not photos or jewellery – not that I have any jewellery that's worth nicking. It's all cheap tat from Primarni.'

'And your window's been fixed, no doubt?' Josie's voice dripped with sarcasm.

Cath noticed it. 'You're joking, aren't you? You lot have put a piece of plywood over the pane but that's it. How's that supposed to make a woman feel safe?'

Josie reached for her folder. 'I'll make a note to chase it up when I get back. You know these things take time.'

'Bloody budgets,' said Cath.

The back door flew open and a skinny, young girl marched in, slamming it shut behind her. She peered across at them before getting a glass of water.

'Hello, Jess,' said Josie.

'Hi.'

'Did you get my shopping?' asked Cath.

Jess held up a carrier bag. 'They hadn't got any of that cheese that you wanted so I got cheddar instead.' She slung it down on the table and made for the door.

'Haven't you forgotten something?' said Cath.

Jess turned back with an exaggerated sigh. She pulled some coins from the pocket of her jeans.

Cath held out her hand as she gave them to her. 'Thank you.'

Jess smiled sweetly and turned on her heel again.

'And?' said Cath.

'And what?' Jess huffed.

Cath pointed to the bag on the table. 'It won't put itself away now, will it?'

Tutting, Jess grabbed the bag. 'What did your last servant die of?'

'Not doing as she was told. It's your own fault. You should have gone in to college this morning with Becky and you wouldn't have to do anything.'

'I didn't get up in time.'

'Becky did.'

'Becky's a swot. Besides, I don't like the lecturer this morning. He gives me the creeps the way he stares at me.'

'I'll give you a lift in tomorrow if you like?' Even though Jess had the odd day off here and there, Cath had been pleased that she'd stayed in college since September, and marks from some of her essays were good, surprising them both. Still, Cath didn't want to encourage her to skive off.

Jess muttered something indistinguishable under her breath as she opened the fridge. Cath rolled her eyes to the ceiling.

Josie grinned at her. 'Looks like another satisfied customer.'

Cath snorted. 'At least I have some.'

Kelly picked up the leaflet that Josie had left for her and shoved it into her coat pocket. Then she bundled Emily down the stairs and out into the morning air. One turn right and two lefts would take them onto Davy Road, the main road which chopped the estate in half more or less through its middle.

As February made way for March, the days were getting longer and lighter by the minute, and the weather had warmed up considerably after the past few weeks of frost and freezing winds.

'Will I meet lots of other kids?' Emily asked, as they made their way along Clarence Avenue.

'Yes, you will.' Kelly was pleased that Emily was looking forward to it. It wasn't her idea of fun to go along to a pre-school club, but now that she had so much time on her hands, it seemed a good idea. 'And it will be nice for you to have some friends ready for when you start school in September.'

At the pelican crossings, they crossed over Arnold Road and took a short-cut through the park at the back of the health centre. The gravel that covered the play area was scattered with litter and beer cans. The rubbish bin had been kicked off its holder and Kelly noticed that the street light at the entrance had been vandalised too.

The park was deserted but Kelly hurried through it anyway. A month ago, she never even knew this area existed. Now it amazed her how many streets on the estate she had never walked before, living at the bottom of the estate with Scott.

As they emerged from the park, they came across a group of youths sitting on the wall of the health centre. They were all wearing hoodies, combats and jeans, dark and menacing even in the light of day. One of them was messing around on a skateboard.

'Wha-hay, lads,' another one shouted as he spotted Kelly. 'Cop a look at the totty coming past.'

'What's totty, Mummy?' asked Emily as she skipped along.

'Never you mind.' Kelly frowned as the lad walked towards her, his mates egging him on.

'Totty is what I can't get enough of,' the lad said. He was quite an ugly fella up close: wide-set eyes, scabby skin and what looked like bum fluff on his chin made him appear more menacing than he was. He wore a black cap with the initials IA on the peak.

Idiot Arse, Kelly thought immediately.

He placed his hand on his crotch and thrust it forwards. 'You fancy some of this?'

'In your dreams,' replied Kelly, pushing past him. 'And they must be wet ones – what are you, fourteen?'

'Old enough to make you groan,' he replied cheekily.

Kelly glared at him before turning back to Emily.

'What's a wet dream, Mummy?'

Kelly groaned, hating this part of the estate already. Around the corner was Bernard Place. Two days ago she'd fetched Scott's package from Philip Matson's house. Kelly hadn't liked him on first impressions either, and was glad that he handed it to her without any fuss. The parcel looked like an old shoe box, and was completely covered in duct tape. Annoyingly, there was no way she could look inside it without Scott knowing.

Everything was good between them now. Scott had rung shortly after she and Jay had arrived home from the visit and apologised for being short with her.

He said he was looking forward to her next visit, but Kelly wasn't sure she could face going again.

'Will there be lots of books?' Emily broke into her thoughts.

'You'll have to wait and see,' Kelly told her with a smile. Emily had become obsessed with a set of pink teddy bear books that Dot had given to her.

It took them another ten minutes to walk to Mitchell Academy. Once she'd found the right way along the corridors, Kelly pushed open a door.

The room was as bright as you would imagine: toys piled high, spilling out of red and green plastic boxes. Above them hung a colourful collection of alphabet letters made out of cardboard and screwed up pieces of crepe paper.

Kelly spotted roughly fifteen children walking around in a circle, singing and shouting 'ring-a-roses' before stooping down on the floor. Emily's eyes lit up as one of the leaders let go of a child's hand and beckoned for her to join in. Immediately, her coat was unzipped and pressed into her mother's arms.

Feeling like a spare part as her daughter jumped up and down and pretended to sneeze, Kelly moved to the side of the room where there were four other women standing in a huddle. The one nearest to her nudged one of the others and they all turned to look. Kelly felt her stomach somersault until one of them smiled at her.

'Hiya, I'm Leah Bradley, Samuel's mum,' she said. Like most of the women in the room, Leah was in her early twenties. She had red hair tied in a ponytail and a freckly complexion. Kelly turned to look at the children, instantly recognising Samuel among the many blondes and brunettes.

'And I'm Sadie, Kurt's mum,' her companion said loudly over the shouting, as the children moved on to other things. On first glance, Kelly couldn't tell which boy would be Kurt. Sadie was at least six-foot-tall, with three-inch heels that made it painful for Kelly to look her in the eye. Her thin arms stuck out from the end of rolled-up sleeves.

Kelly smiled back shyly. 'My daughter's name is Emily and she's four. I'm Kelly.'

'Where are you from?'

'I've moved into Clarence Avenue.' Kelly caught the look of disgust that shot from Leah to Sadie. 'I used to be in Patrick Street, at the bottom of the estate,' she added quickly.

'Did I see you with Jay Kirkwell the other day?' Sadie's bird-like eyes flitted down to Kelly's toes and back up to her face before she nodded, now convinced. 'Yeah, it was you. At the DIY shop – he was carrying some boxes.'

'How come you moved out of Patrick Street?' Leah asked, before Kelly had time to reply to Sadie.

'It's a long story.'

'I'll bet it is.' In a flash, Leah had turned to the others and filled them in on her thoughts. Suddenly, they all turned away. Kelly was left to look awkward again.

'Who do I have to pay my money to?'

'I shouldn't think someone who lives in Clarence Avenue would have the money to pay,' said one of the other women.

'I always pay my way, you cheeky cow,' retorted Kelly.

'Hmm... and how do you manage that, I wonder?' Leah laughed snidely. The other girls laughed with Leah so she continued. 'Did Jay Kirkwell want paying too? What did you do for him in return for a favour?'

Kelly wasn't going to be judged by people who didn't know her. She moved to a chair at the far end of the room. While Emily had a waterproof apron popped over her head, she took off her coat and pretended to be interested in some of the paintings on the walls.

When they left the room an hour later, they stopped at the small coffee bar by the entrance. While they waited for their drinks, Kelly grabbed a prospectus. For the next fifteen minutes, with Emily engrossed in one of the books she'd brought along for her, she sipped her coffee and flicked through the pages. There was so much to choose from.

Basic computer skills – she had those, surely. She knew how to surf the net and navigate around search engines. IT courses – no, she wasn't technical.

Cookery courses wouldn't earn her any money. She'd never be able to rustle up anything spectacular on a regular basis and she wouldn't be able to put up with the mess. Maybe she should get a job as a cleaner instead, she mused. Kelly knew she was good at that.

But the course offering secretarial and general office skills was the one that caught her eye. It promised that she would be able to type properly at a fair amount of words per minute, lay out and present documents in a business-like manner and enhance her chances of getting an office job. Kelly was sold, and her head suddenly filled itself with all kinds of possibilities.

The course was on a Wednesday afternoon through to nine p.m. Now that the flat was decorated, Kelly would enquire into a few shifts at Miles's Factory. As long as her mum was still keen to look after Emily, Kelly could fit in four nights a week. While she brought a small amount of money in, it would give her the time she needed to gain some experience.

Then, when Emily was at school for most of the day, she'd be able to work in an office with other people, be part of a crowd. Maybe, eventually, she could work as a personal assistant for some bigwig and get paid lots of money. By the time she got to the registration room, Kelly was practically hyperventilating.

Full of renewed vigour, her steps home became lighter. Luckily, the gang of youths had moved on from the health centre to bother someone else. She even stopped off to push Emily on the deserted swings.

'Do you know what, Em? Your mum's going to college to learn how to be an office worker. I'm going to earn lots of pennies to buy nice things.'

'And books,' yelled Emily. 'I'd like my own pink teddy bear books.'

Kelly smiled. 'Yeah, and books.'

She pushed her daughter up towards the sky again and again, watching Emily stretching her little legs out to make herself go higher. She looked as free as Kelly felt.

From that moment, she resolved that the sky would be her limit, too. So what if Scott wouldn't approve of either of the things she was about to do? It was her life and she wasn't going to let him live it for her. As well, she vowed to show the likes of all the Leah's and Sadie's just what she was capable of.

10

Josie pulled the top off her pen with her teeth and wrote the date clearly at the top of her notepad. She was parked a few houses away from Mr Neblin's house, her first call of the day. She needed to see if he had moved the pile of rubbish in his back garden that was in danger of reaching the kitchen windowsill. Bonfire night had gone months before and his excuses for not burning it or getting rid of it were wearing thin.

As she drew level with number 78 Hector Walk, Josie let out a huge sigh in frustration. Even from the pavement, she could see that it was no better than the last time she'd visited.

She unlooped the string from the post which was holding the gate in place and walked carefully down the mud-covered pathway. Well, it wasn't a path as such, just an unofficial rut that Mr Neblin had made with the wheels of his car. No matter how many times she told him not to park his car on the garden area, he still left it rotting there.

Josie examined the wreck more closely. The tax disc was two months out of date. She doubted it was insured either, yet only yesterday she had seen him hurtling along Davy Road in it. She reckoned it was time to have a word with Andy. If she couldn't make him shift it, the law could impound it.

When she got closer to the mound of rubbish, Josie noticed the other items added to it since her last visit: a smashed-up wardrobe, a small television and more than a dozen rubbish bags.

Josie hammered hard on the back door.

'Fuck off!'

Unperturbed, she banged on the door, harder this time. Moments later, it was yanked open and a small man with a prominent belly stood scowling on the doorstep.

'Yes, it's that time again, Mr Neblin,' Josie said bluntly. 'I told you to shift that pile of rubbish by the time I called a week later.'

'Like I care.' Mr Neblin leaned on the doorframe and folded his arms.

'You will care when I –'

'Yeah, please tell me, Mrs Housing Officer, what are you going to do about it anyway? I'm all ears.'

'No, actually, Mr Neblin, you're all *talk*. I think I've given you enough rope to hang yourself. I'll get the association to remove this pile of crap and recharge it to you. It'll cost you a fortune but at least –'

'You won't get nothing from me. In case you haven't noticed, I haven't worked for seventeen years and you can't get blood out of a stone.'

'That isn't a problem. I can get it stopped out of your benefits on a weekly order. I'm sure you won't mind missing a few pints every week.'

Mr Neblin took a step forwards, his fists clenched at his sides. 'You can't do that.'

'I can and I will.'

'You're a right fucking bitch, aren't you? You think you're so bleeding clever but you won't get one up on me.'

Mr Neblin looked like he was going to blow up. If he squeezed his cheeks in any more, she could envisage steam coming from his ears. She decided to walk away.

'Do you know that people on this estate hate you?' he shouted after her. 'You haven't got a friend to your name in this place and one day it's going to come back and bite you right on your fucking fancy pants. Then what will you do?'

Josie walked away from the drivel spewing from his mouth. Her job was done there, no need to take any further abuse. If the nicey-nicey approach didn't work then she always had the option to hit him where it would hurt the most: his pocket.

The slam of a door never failed to make her jump, no matter how many times she heard it. She'd thought she'd dealt with everything working as an admin assistant back at the office, but it was nothing compared to what she sometimes faced out on the estate, with no counter to hide behind and no panic button to press. Out on the patch, if the going got rough, all Josie could do was walk away from the likes of Mr Neblin – and Gina Bradley.

. . .

Josie decided to call in at the newsagents for a bar of chocolate before heading back to the office. She smiled when she spotted Kelly flicking through a magazine, but wasn't surprised when her expression remained blank.

'Don't worry, I'm not with any of the heavy mob today,' Kelly muttered as she reached the cash desk.

Josie hid a smile: she was definitely not forgiven.

'On your own today?' she asked.

'Yes. Not that it's any of your business.'

'I meant without Emily.'

'Oh, I –'

'How's college?'

'Hey, John,' a loud voice boomed. Josie turned in time to spot Mr Neblin, before he disappeared behind the shelving. 'Do you sell black bin liners? I've got a load of rubbish that needs shifting pretty sharpish.'

The man behind the counter pointed to a shelf. 'They're the only ones we've got, Clive, above the envelopes. Will they do?'

'They'll have to do, especially if they get that stuck-up bitch from the housing office off my back.'

Kelly giggled as Josie's eyes flicked to the ceiling.

'I don't know what her old man must think of her,' Mr Neblin continued. 'She must definitely wear the trousers in that househo– oh, it's you.'

Kelly shoved her face into a magazine in order to stop from roaring with laughter.

'Yes, it's me,' said Josie. 'Glad to hear you're taking my advice, albeit a little late in the day.'

As soon as he'd gone, Kelly finally gave in. 'Did you see his face?' she laughed. Then she snorted. 'It was the colour of beetroot, he was so embarrassed.'

Josie got out her purse. 'I heard and saw everything that would shock me in my first year on this estate. Nothing gets to me now.'

Kelly relaxed a little. Maybe she had judged Josie as well as the other way around. From her actions with the man and the rubbish, it was clear she couldn't care less about his situation.

'College has been great,' she offered. 'And I got a job at Miles's Factory.'

'Well done you!'

Kelly nodded and then smiled. Seeing Josie today had made her realise how much she had missed her calling in. She'd only been to see her three times since she'd moved into Clarence Avenue but she'd been the only female company she'd enjoyed for a long time – even if she was a housing officer.

'I do my best,' she replied. 'Now, are you going to add a Kit-Kat to that stash of chocolate you're buying so you can call round some time for a quick break?'

Josie smiled. It had taken a while, but finally she was breaking down the barrier.

*L*ater that afternoon, Josie clock-watched from four o'clock onwards to ensure she left the office bang on five thirty, in order to beat most of the rush hour traffic. When she opened the front door to her home, she could hear noises coming from the kitchen. Unsure of what mood to expect from Stewart, she shrugged off her coat in a desperate attempt to gain more time.

But she needn't have worried. All was clear when she spotted the vase of her favourite flowers on the kitchen table. Propped up by the side of the lilies was a box of milk chocolates. She sniffed garlic in the air.

'I've been shopping,' Stewart informed her. 'I thought we could open a bottle of red, too.'

Josie frowned. Had he used psychic powers to read her mind last month?

'I'm sorry,' he said when she still hadn't moved moments later.

'You accused me of having an affair,' she spoke quietly.

'That's why I'm sorry.'

'You said no one else would want me! Have you any idea how much that hurt?'

Stewart urged her to take a seat. 'I was in a lousy mood. I shouldn't have taken it out on you.'

Josie sat down as Stewart poured her a glass of wine. As he moved to sit opposite her, she struggled to set her emotions straight. She wanted to feel relief that he was out of his dark mood, but she knew that it wouldn't last. She wanted to be content in her home, loved by her husband, but she knew that she never would.

She wanted to believe in Stewart, but something was telling her not to…

*A*fter college on Wednesday evening, Kelly walked the ten-minute journey home alone. She was so pleased that Emily had wanted to stay over at her nanny's. Emily had been griping for most of the day and Kelly's nerves felt ragged from trying to pacify her.

She hadn't been surprised – more faintly amused – to see that Emily had developed the Winterton stubborn streak at such an early age. Verbal battles and grumpiness had been the norm for the past couple of weeks. Emily had started to question when her daddy was coming home. For a child, Kelly assumed that the eight weeks Scott had been inside already must seem like eight years, and Emily's questions were getting more demanding, and upsetting. Everything Kelly had suggested, Emily had given a negative answer in response.

Halfway back, she decided to celebrate the opportunity of a night alone and grab a cheap bottle of wine. As she turned the corner onto Vincent Square, she found herself faced with a gang of teenagers. Two of them ran to block the shop doorway as she drew near.

'Excuse me,' she said, but they ignored her. After a quick dance in the doorway, Kelly pushed past them. The one who had the look of a serial killer followed her in. She walked down the first aisle, sensing his presence behind her. All at once, she imagined she could feel his breath on her neck. She wrapped a fist tightly around the handle of her bag.

'Spare us a quid then, lovely lady,' he said from behind.

Kelly turned quickly, taking him by surprise, and he bumped into her. The smell of ale clung to his breath. She pushed him away aggressively.

'Leave me alone.'

'Ah, come on sweetheart,' he lurched forwards. 'I'm only messing.'

Kelly pushed past him again and marched to the front of the store, praying that he wouldn't follow. By the time she'd paid for her goods, everything had gone quiet outside – until she stepped out of the door and saw the group reappear from behind the corner of the building.

'What've you got in the bag, then?' a small, plump lad queried.

'Nothing that you'll be allowed. Isn't it past your bedtime?'

The rest of the group laughed loudly but it didn't do Kelly any favours.

'Come on kids, let her past,' the shopkeeper said, in a resigned tone. 'Time you moved on to bother someone else.'

'Fuck off, oldie,' a girl with short red hair shouted, 'or you'll get a brick through your window.'

When they didn't move, Kelly had no choice but to push past them again. 'Stuck up bitch,' she heard one of them say, but she didn't turn around to see who. The lad who had followed her into the shop started to circle around her on a pushbike, each time moving a little closer. Kelly quickened her pace. Luckily, he lost interest as she left them further behind with each step.

A few minutes later, the panic inside her finally began to subside. Looking through the windows of the many houses she passed, Kelly saw family after family settled down for the night and wished she was safe at home too, getting a glass of wine down her neck as quickly as possible so that she could chill out.

She was turning into Davy Road when she heard a noise. Serial killer skidded to a halt on the pavement in front of her. Kelly moved to the side but he followed her. She tried to double back but he was too quick.

'Do you get a kick out of this type of thing or what?' she asked, almost praying that someone would drive past in their car, but knowing full well that no one would stop to help her if they did. 'Because I'm getting a little bit –'

'Give me your bag, bitch.'

'No, I bleeding won't.'

'Give me your fucking bag!'

Kelly clutched it to her chest. At the same time she noticed the sliver of steel in his hand. Instinctively, she moved backwards.

The bike was thrown down onto the pavement. 'Give it to me. Now,' he yelled.

Kelly froze with fear. He slapped her face, grabbed her hair and pulled her nearer. 'I'm not fucking messing this time.'

She gave him the bag. He pushed her away and she lost her footing, landing on the pavement with a sickly thud. She looked up at him, half expecting to get his boot in her face, but he got back on his bike. In a flash, he was gone.

Kelly began to retch. She managed to crawl to the kerbside where she threw up. Oh no, he had a knife. She could have been killed, all for the sake of a few pounds.

Tears streamed down her face when the fear of what could have happened replaced itself with the reality that it hadn't. She tried to remember what was inside her bag. Luckily, her keys and her mobile phone were in her coat pocket. But wait – would he have her address? Kelly sobbed uncontrollably as she tried to recall if anything had her details written on it. She prayed there was nothing in her purse that would lead him to her.

Then she ran.

The first thing Kelly did when she got home was ring Jay. When he arrived, she broke down in his arms and told him what had happened. He guided her into the living room and sat her down.

'Where were you?' he asked.

'At the – the – the shops.' Kelly sobbed as she clung on to him.

'Don't you know it's mad to go to The Square after dark? It's not only the kids –'

'I – I thought I'd be okay. It wasn't too late.'

'Did you get a look at him?'

'He was taller than me, really skinny, with horrible beady eyes. He had a black hoodie top... and a tattoo on his neck. Two boxing gloves, hanging down, tied together. And he stunk of booze.'

Jay stiffened. 'That's Ian Newton. He went to juvie about a year ago for assault. I thought he was still locked up.'

Kelly pulled away from him in a panic. 'I'm not sure if he has my address! You – you don't think he'll come and find me again, do you?'

Jay shook his head. 'No, he's a smack head. He'll be after a quick fix. Your bag's probably been thrown into someone's garden by now.'

'But he could have stabbed me, Jay, left me to bleed to death. He could have raped me. He could have done anything and I wouldn't have been able to stop him with a knife pointing at me. Emily's lost one parent for the time being. She could have lost both of them. How could I have been so stupid?'

Jay pulled her into his arms again. 'Hey, it's over now. Seeing as I hadn't finished my tea when you rang, do you fancy helping me with a takeaway? I could murder a chop suey.'

While Jay was gone, Kelly paced up and down the living room waiting for his return. Once she'd got home, she'd flew around in a panic, bolting the door behind her, checking all the windows were secure before shutting the curtains and sitting in the glow of the gas fire. It was only now that she dared put the light on – now that Jay had called round after she'd decided to ring him.

She touched her cheek. The redness was fading but it still felt numb. Stupid, stupid, silly bitch, she cursed herself. Was she the only person brainless enough to assume she was safe to go out alone at night?

When Jay returned, he had not one but two brown bags on his person. Kelly's face momentarily broke into a smile when her fake Louis Vuitton was handed to her. She unzipped the compartment and checked inside. Her purse was still there and so was the ten pound note she'd shoved in earlier, still folded into four behind her gas instalment card.

'Where did you get that?' she asked.

'I spotted Newton – or 'The Newt', as he prefers to be known as, stupid bastard – when I drove past the shops,' said Jay. 'After a little persuading, he told me where the bag was. Everything's there, isn't it?'

'I think so. I can't think of... what do you mean, after a little persuading?' Kelly's eyes bulged. 'You hit him, didn't you?'

Jay shook his head. 'Newton's a pussy. He only goes for women. He didn't put up much of a fight before coming clean.'

'Much of a fight? You said you didn't hit him.'

'It was a figure of speech. And he hit you, didn't he?'

'A slap is a bit different than a thrashing.'

'I didn't do much to him, if that's what you mean.'

All thoughts of the danger Kelly had put herself in went out of the window. As she'd got to know Jay more over the past few weeks, she'd started to think that maybe he was different. She took a step away from him.

'I want you to go,' she said.

'Don't be daft.' He moved past her and into the kitchen. 'The last thing you need is to be on your own.'

'Please, Jay. I've had a rough night. I want to be by myself.'

'Even more reason for me to stay. I'll keep you company while we eat. I'm not going to bite you.'

Kelly stood rooted to the spot.

Jay caught her eye. 'There's no need to look at me like that. I was only trying to help.'

'I don't need that kind of help!'

'Yeah, you do. You don't know who to trust at the moment.'

Kelly stood silent again and he finally got the message. She followed him down the stairs, drawing across the bolts once he'd gone. She slid down the door onto the mat and sat with her head in her hands, Jay's words ringing in her ears.

She should never have taken this flat. She should have moved back in with her aunty in Christopher Avenue. But no, Scott was only two months into his sentence and she'd been stupid enough to think that she could cope by herself. The phone call she'd had earlier from him had only added to her confusion. 'I've signed the papers, babe,' Scott had told her. 'No more Patrick Street. I've done it for you – it'll be different this time when I get back. You've got to trust me.'

See it was there again, that word: 'trust'. But how could Kelly trust anyone, let alone Scott? She wasn't even sure if she wanted him to come and live in Clarence Avenue when he was released. Life would only go back to how it was before. Kelly knew he wouldn't change his ways just to suit her. And to top it all, now she'd overreacted with Jay. Was her attempt at independence doomed?

She pulled back her head and banged it on the door three times in quick succession. She knew she could never knock enough sense into her thick skull, but it made her feel better by trying.

One thing was for sure, though. If Jay had spoken a word of truth tonight, it was that she didn't know who to trust anymore. She had never felt so lonely in her life.

11

'Right, that's the boring work questions out of the way,' Josie said, as she signed off Kelly's final support questionnaire. 'Is there anything else you'd like to know or can I leave you in the capable hands of Miss Emily?'

It was Wednesday morning, the third one the month of March had seen. Josie had been at Kelly's flat for half an hour now, ensconced far too comfortably in Kelly's settee. The rain lashing at the window gave her no incentive to move whatsoever. Phil and Holly were discussing fruit-shaped figures on daytime television.

Emily was playing dressing up, running from room to room and strutting her stuff before running off again. This time she had clattered across the living room floor in a pair of Kelly's high heels, wearing a stripy scarf around her neck like a feather boa and a belt that doubled as a hula hoop, which fell off twice before she got to them.

'Very nice.' Josie nodded her approval before Emily clicked-clacked off again. She turned back to Kelly who was in the middle of a yawn. 'She's so hard to keep up with, she always seems busy.'

The yawn turned into a sigh and Kelly stretched her arms above her head. 'Sometimes she's the only person I speak to during the day. She keeps me sane … It's been tough for me lately. I – I could really do with an ear, if you don't mind?'

'Go ahead,' Josie said. 'You know I was born to listen.'

Kelly took a deep breath. 'I was mugged a few nights ago and it scared the shit out of me.'

'Mugged?' Josie's eyes searched Kelly's body for injuries but there didn't seem to be any. 'Where did it happen? Were you hurt? Are you okay now?'

'I'm not too bad,' Kelly admitted. 'It takes more than a slap on the face to bring me down. I was scared though.' She began to unburden her tale.

'I know Ian Newton,' Josie broke in when Kelly mentioned his name. 'Lives on Gordon Street – his parents have no control over him. I thought he was still in juvie.'

'He's just got out.'

'Did you lose much?'

'No, see, that's the thing.' Kelly stalled. 'When I got home, I rang Jay.'

Josie raised her eyebrows slightly.

'I was petrified that Ian Newton knew my address. Jay went to get a takeaway and came back with my handbag and all of its contents, just like that. He must have picked a fight and I – I lost it with him.'

'Jay's usually the peacekeeper Kirkwell,' Josie came to his defence. 'He might use his reputation to gain control of a situation but I doubt that he would have used his fists unless he was provoked.'

'Two wrongs don't make a right,' Kelly shrugged, feeling embarrassed as she remembered how she had reacted. After her outburst she'd gone to bed and woken up the next day in a better frame of mind. There was no way she would give up her flat. She'd just suffered a setback that night and knowing that she'd been too hasty jumping to conclusions, she'd sent Jay a text message to apologise. Jay had made her suffer for two days until he'd sent one in return.

'How do you feel about Scott coming out of prison?' Josie dared to question. In recent conversations, just his name had been enough to shut down the barriers.

But Kelly didn't seem to mind this time. She pulled her legs up onto the settee and drew a cushion to her chest. 'He thinks he'll be out soon. I've only been to see him once, which was enough for me.'

'How long have you been with him?'

'He was my first real boyfriend. I met him when I was eighteen and then I was pregnant with Emily the year after.'

Kelly paused but Josie said nothing to ensure the conversation kept going.

'I'm a bit mixed up,' Kelly continued. 'I do miss him, but I don't miss the lifestyle. The constant worrying – whether he's coming home, whether he's been arrested again or who's knocking on the door next. I might have found it hard to start again by myself, but I've done it. I'm going to be earning some money soon – I start this Monday, by the way – and I'm going to college. Both of which Scott will go mad about.'

'You mustn't let him stop you doing anything,' said Josie, feeling guilty as soon as the words came out. Stewart had stopped her from doing lots of things over the years. How could she sit here and preach?

'What do you mean?'

'You can still go to work and complete your college course when he comes out.'

Kelly huffed. 'Yeah, right, and it's as easy as that.'

'Yes, it is. You'll have to think of some good reasons why you should continue, get your ammunition ready. Besides, surely he should want you to try and better yourself? He should be proud of what you've done under the circumstances. You wouldn't have lost your home if it weren't for him. You need to remember that.'

Kelly nodded. She would never forget how underhand Scott had been regarding the tenancy on Patrick Street – especially the position he'd put Emily in.

'I'm scared he'll want me to be the old Kelly,' she said, 'and I don't want to be her again.'

'No, you don't,' Josie agreed. 'What night is your secretarial course?'

'Tonight, six 'til nine.'

'I'm there every Wednesday too, so I can give you a lift home every week if you like? It's on the estate, before you say that I'm going out of my way.'

'Thanks, but I've managed to sort one out.' Josie didn't need to know that Jay had insisted on taking on the role of chauffeur.

'Fair enough,' said Josie, guessing rightly about what Kelly wasn't telling her. 'Just yell if you need me any time in the future.'

Kelly smiled with gratitude. Despite her job, Josie had turned out to be someone she liked. 'Are you married?' she asked, wanting to know a little more about her.

'Yes, just over five years.'

'Do you have any children?'

'No, we're quite set in our ways at the moment. We're both only children; both sets of parents died when we were young.' Josie knew it was a pathetic excuse. How could they bring a child into their relationship?

She checked her watch and jumped up quickly. 'I'd better be on my way. I've promised to cover the phones while some of the girls at the office go to the pub for their lunch.'

At the front door, Kelly thanked Josie for listening to her. 'I've enjoyed talking to you this morning – I hope I haven't said too much though.'

'I don't gossip,' Josie reassured her. 'Nor do I form opinions. What you've told me will stay with me only, if that's what you mean.'

Kelly smiled shyly. 'You change when you take off your coat. You lose your sense of authority.'

Josie was astounded at her perceptiveness. 'In this job, I have to be two different people at the same time. It's one of those things that only individuals who work with the general public face-to-face will understand. It stops you taking the insults personally.'

'You still ask too many questions for my liking,' Kelly continued, rolling her eyes to the ceiling.

'Force of habit, I'm afraid.'

'But I can run to a coffee whenever you can find a free minute in your full day?'

'You mean you'd like to be one of my regular 'tea-stops'?' Josie teased. 'Or 'pee-stops', as we often call them. I'm highly honoured. Most of them are above the age of seventy and only want me to call because they see no one else from week to week. But I suppose I can make an exception for you.'

'How are you getting on with the course?' Brian Walker asked, as he held open the door of Mitchell Academy later that night. He followed Josie out into the drizzle.

'It's great,' said Josie brightly. Brian was the course lecturer. Although she hadn't known him long, Josie had taken an instant liking to him. He was fair of face and nature and he spoke with a soft pitch.

'Really?' he continued. 'I was certain that tonight's topic had affected you more than you're letting on.'

'It is hard going. I know I'm only in my first month but it's very much like counselling for yourself,' Josie tried to explain. 'The group we have has gelled so quickly, I suppose due to the nature of the course and the things we have to share. It's quite draining actually, but very motivational when you hear what other people have gone through. Especially Tim.'

For part of the night's session, Tim had been talking about his ex-wife and how their marriage had fallen apart from his lack of trust. Sometimes Josie had had to stop her mind from wandering as she tried to listen to him, at the same time listing in her head all the similarities he had with Stewart.

Tim explained it was his need for control that eventually drove them apart – he had to be right every time. He found it hard to take criticism, found it hard to trust anyone, and so he pushed them away with his nastiness. Equally, he found it hard to communicate his love.

For Josie, it had been too close for comfort. When she'd met Stewart, she'd thought that her lack of self-belief would disappear, but now that she was married, it was worse than ever. She knew she had let him control her, just like she had let her mother do the same.

It was one of the reasons she'd enrolled on the course – to see if she could learn more about herself, as well as to pick up a qualification. She realised she had her limits, but she wanted to gain more confidence.

It had been enough for her to question Tim about it during their break. What Josie had learned had made her heart beat wildly. Eventually, Tim had got help for his problem and now he was much better. He'd lost his wife in the process: they'd divorced a long time ago, but he was with another partner and – for the first time in his forty-nine years – he felt content.

Josie hadn't been able to get the conversation out of her head. Feeling unable to ask him why he'd felt so insecure for the best part of his life, she wondered if Stewart could change if he got help, or perhaps she could find out exactly what was at the root of his problem. If she got him to admit there *was* a problem, she could help him, or try to send him in the right direction.

'That's the trouble with a small group, I'm afraid,' Brian nodded, understanding Josie fully now. 'We can only use ourselves as subject matter and sometimes it gets a little too close. I must admit, it's given me quite a lot of food for thought over the years.'

Josie delved into her handbag for her car keys. 'I thought we were going to learn *how* to be a counsellor, not to *be* counselled.'

Brian held up his hands in mock alarm. 'Hey, don't shoot the lecturer.'

Josie smiled. 'Can I offer you a lift anywhere?'

'I'm supposed to be meeting my son in The George and Dragon. No doubt he'll want some of my hard-earned cash. I don't suppose…'

'It's on my way home. Hop in.'

In the far corner of the car park, Stewart watched from the shadows as Josie stood deep in conversation with a man. He looked in his early fifties, dressed in a smart suit, small and round in stature with a mass of grey hair.

Stewart ground his teeth. Never taking his eyes from them, their laughter made his blood boil. Josie had lied to him last week. She wasn't at a meeting, like she'd told him. Neither had she been tonight. He'd already been into the reception to ask where she was, but they hadn't heard of any council meeting being held. They'd asked him if he had the right night, like he was an idiot. Of course he had the right night: Josie had gone to these so-called meetings for the last three Wednesdays.

It was obvious from what he'd seen – the bitch was having an affair.

As Josie reversed her car out of its space and onto the road, Stewart started up his engine. Not wanting to be spotted, he gave her a moment before pulling out after her. Maybe he could tail her in the dark, see where she was heading.

But then he stopped. He needed to think about this before he did anything too rash. Once he'd found out more details, she'd get his wrath.

There was no way he was prepared to lose everything after he had gone this far.

12

Kelly often wondered how her legs carried her through the gates of Miles's Factory on that first Monday afternoon. At quarter to four, Doreen, her supervisor for the shift, showed her to the locker room where she was given a key and some overalls. At five to four, Kelly followed her onto the factory floor with a knot in her stomach and a lump in her throat. The first thing she saw was Sally's welcoming smile. She had shown her what to do at her interview.

'Hi, again,' Sally shouted over the noise. A plump girl with blonde hair and freckles, she placed a cup on the conveyor belt and grabbed for the next one. 'You're sitting across from me – lucky you. Sometimes my talking can be drowned out by the racket in here.' She nodded to the girl who had joined them. 'That's Julia. She's okay for a laugh.'

Julia smiled at Kelly as she sat down behind Sally. She was in her late teens, with huge blue eyes almost hidden by her blonde fringe. Kelly smiled back and then glanced around the room. Women sat at most of the benches along the conveyor belt. There were three men in the far corner making up cardboard boxes and separators and a bunch of men playing air guitars while singing to the track belting out from the radio.

'Can you remember what to do or do you want me to show you again?' Sally offered moments later, when Kelly was sat still.

Kelly's shoulders drooped. 'Would you? Ta. You know how useless I was when I tried.'

'We do the same for everyone who starts – here.' She picked up another

Behind a Closed Door

cup, gave it to Kelly and walked round to join her. 'Dip your sponge into the water – not too much – and wipe it over one seam. Yes, that's right, not too hard or else you'll have to throw it. Then flick it round like this.' Sally took Kelly's wrist and turned it ninety degrees. 'Right, do the same down that seam. Good, that's much better. Quick, put it on the conveyor belt and grab the next one.'

'How long have you been doing this?' Kelly asked, once they'd finished a few cups together.

'Now, let me see ...' Sally scratched her head in comical fashion. 'Five, maybe six ... years.' She let the facts sink in before she burst into laughter again. 'It's easy once you get the hang of it. Too dry and the seam will still be visible; too wet and the cups will be soggy and have to be thrown. You're doing great,' she enthused.

Just then, Kelly noticed Doreen walking back towards the belt. She saw Sally slide a few of her own cups over towards her. Before Kelly could react, Doreen picked one up and examined it carefully. She ran a finger over the seam and raised a quizzical eyebrow.

'Not bad,' she said. Her eyes landed on Sally. 'I don't suppose you had anything to do with the quality of these?'

Sally feigned hurt. 'You've got the wrong idea of me, Mum.'

Doreen smirked.

'She's not too much of a slave driver, my mother,' Sally enlightened Kelly once Doreen had moved away again. 'You could do a lot worse. Some of the women are right bitches, especially that Estelle over on the day shift. She gets away with murder because her mum works here.'

Kelly stifled laughter and hid her face. Sally was talking about her aunty – who had helped her get the job – and her cousin.

Sally pulled a face. 'They're not family, are they? I should have guessed – everyone's related on here.'

Suddenly a young woman, her face as red as her long hair, rushed over to the bench and plonked herself down on the empty seat behind Kelly.

'Bloody typical, I missed the three forty-five bus again. I got a right bollocking last week for being late but is it my fault that Samuel won't run for ... oh fuck, don't tell me you're the new girl?'

Kelly looked up into the eyes of Leah, one of the women she'd met at the playgroup.

'You two know each other,' exclaimed Sally in delight.

'Know her?' Leah slipped quickly into her overall and sat down as if she hadn't been twenty minutes late. 'I don't think so – she comes from Clarence Avenue. You know, *the* Clarence Avenue –'

'Yeah, we all know Clarence Avenue, Leah,' Sally interrupted. 'Get to the point, what's wrong with it?'

Leah's eyes shot out as if on stalks. 'Where have you been hiding for the past few years? There are dealers and prostitutes and loads of anti-social behaviour going on. I wouldn't live there if my life depended on it.'

'Like your street is far better, then?' Sally turned to Kelly, who, by this time, had cheeks the same colour as Leah's hair. 'Leah lives in Stanley Avenue, two streets from you. Its tenants are – how shall I put it? – the devil's offspring. Isn't that what you usually call them, Leah?'

Leah huffed. She threw a scowl at Kelly before finally starting to work. Kelly bristled, but chose to ignore it for now.

Once they'd had a tea break at six fifteen, the night started to drag. Kelly lost count of the mugs she made a hash of, and the smirks that Leah threw at her every time she used too much water and the whole thing became too soggy.

At five past eight, she made her way back out of the factory gates with Sally. The young woman had taken an instant liking to her, which was more than she could say for Leah, who had stormed off in front of them. Kelly sighed as she realised that they'd probably be catching the same bus.

Sally said goodbye at the end of the street and Kelly crossed over towards the bus stop. A few minutes later, she rounded the corner to see Leah sitting down in the shelter. Leah folded her arms, then her legs, and threw Kelly a look that said, 'stay well away'.

Kelly was fine with this. She had more pressing things to occupy her mind – the first thing she was going to do when she'd collected Emily was relax in a nice, hot bath to ease her aching shoulders and neck. God knows how those women stooped forwards for so long during each shift.

Still, she sighed, while all the time feeling Leah's eyes boring into her head, *there's always tomorrow. Maybe things will improve.*

*J*osie stood in the middle of Philip Matson's living room for what seemed like a lifetime, but in reality was all of ten minutes. The room was a complete tip; papers, beer cans and takeaway cartons littering any available space – far too much of it for her liking. Three Rottweiler's sat at Philip's feet while he stubbed out a roll-up cigarette, before immediately lighting up the next. The thick plume of smoke curling around Josie's head started to make her feel light-headed. She wafted it away in vain.

Philip was a good-looking man – or he could be, if he ever took that scowl off his face. He was in his mid-thirties, with no work in him, no brain in him and no balls. Every time she saw him, he reminded Josie of one of the dirty detectives from any number of police television dramas.

They were in the middle of a stand-off. Josie had no time for Matson: Matson had no respect for Josie. The threat of eviction seemed the only weapon left to use, and it would hardly be a threat if he didn't pay something towards his rent in the next few days. She'd been trying for months to get him to understand the seriousness of his impending court hearing. She decided to try one more time.

'Mr Matson, if you can't be bothered to follow the correct procedure to claim your benefits, then how am I supposed to stop the eviction next week?'

Philip's head flipped up at the last moment. 'Eviction?' he frowned.

'I have the revenue team on my case. If you don't comply with the court order set up last month, they'll take you back to court and apply for an eviction order. Seeing as you haven't kept up with the simple repayment scheme of four pounds a week, the judge will grant it for us. You've only yourself to blame. You must understand that –'

Philip stood up abruptly. 'No, *you'd* better understand,' he said. 'I filled in the forms; *you* didn't do your job properly.'

'You didn't provide proof of your bank account,' Josie ticked off with her fingers. 'You didn't provide proof that you're claiming sick pay. We don't check all that out for you – you have to do some things for yourself. One of them is to get that lazy backside of yours out of that chair and to the office with the necessary paperwork.'

Philip scowled but Josie wasn't perturbed.

'You need to clear the account by 4 o'clock on Friday afternoon or we'll be applying for the order first thing on Monday morning. You've really left it late this time.'

Josie stepped back as Philip moved towards her. 'You won't kick me out.'

'If you pay what you owe, then –'

'Fifteen hundred quid?' he screamed.

Josie started. One of the dogs jumped onto the floor and began to prowl the room.

'Where the fuck am I going to get fifteen hundred quid?'

'It wouldn't have been anything if you'd taken the time to provide us with what we needed. That's the sad thing. We've been asking you for over six months now to provide proof of your bank details – all you had to do was bring it to the office for me to photocopy. Letter after letter, visit after visit. You've been to court four times and been given chances to co-operate with us. What more could we have done?'

'That's right.' Philip's tone was sarcastic. 'You're doing what you're paid to do, Mrs Jobsworth.'

'Yes, that is right.' Josie nodded. 'I am.'

'You chuck me out on Friday and it's you who I'll come after. It'll only take a few days to follow you around and I'll know where you live. You won't feel safe in your bed because you'll never know when I'll come calling.'

'Don't be ridiculous. If you lay one finger on me, I'll get *you* for it. It certainly won't take me long to find out where –' Josie's phone rang and she reached for it quickly. 'Hi, *PC Baxter*,' she almost shouted the words.

'Josie, it's Charlotte Hatfield,' said Andy. 'The control room have had a call from her every minute or so for the past few minutes, but there's no reply when they talk to her. All they can hear in the background is the kids screaming. I think her partner's got to her.'

Josie took a sharp intake of breath. 'Oh no. I – where are you?'

'I'm in Brian Road. You?'

'I'm in Bernard Place. Do you want to meet me there or do you want to come round to fetch me?'

'I'm on my way,' was all she heard before he disconnected the call.

Josie turned to Philip, who didn't seem to scare her anymore. 'I haven't got time for you, or your games. Pay up by Friday or we'll evict you. It's as simple as that. You've had enough chances now.'

Josie ran through the scratty jungle of a garden and jumped over the low wall. She could hear the police siren coming closer. Andy screeched to a halt beside her moments later.

'Get in,' he yelled.

The living room curtains were drawn when they pulled up outside Charlotte Hatfield's house. Andy banged hard on the front door while Josie ran round to the back. She fiddled in frustration with the bolts on the makeshift gate. Eventually, it gave way and she pushed it open.

She could hear the children crying. Through the rear window, she saw Charlotte lying on the floor, blood running from a gash on her head. The twins sat either side of her, Joshua hiding his face behind a cushion.

'Charlotte!' Josie banged on the window to get her attention. Charlotte turned her head slightly. She looked dazed; Josie knew that she wouldn't be able to recognise her. She banged on the window again.

'Callum! Jake! Go to the front door and let the policeman in.'

Callum ran towards the window and held up his hands. His tiny palms were smeared in blood. 'Mummy's bleeding,' he screamed.

'Go to the front door,' Josie urged him, her heart going out to the four-year-old.

Suddenly, she heard a loud bang and Andy appeared in the room. She watched him drop to his feet and talk into his radio before coming to her senses. Quickly, she ran round to join him and stepped into her worst nightmare.

Charlotte's injuries were more severe close up. Blood oozed out of the gash and down her neck. She wore only her underwear, the white cotton bra soaking up her blood. Her arms and torso were covered in cuts, her face a mass of swelling.

Andy spoke into the radio while the kids continued to cry. He threw Josie a latex glove. Josie pulled it on and knelt beside Charlotte.

'Charlotte?' she whispered. 'Charlotte? Can you hear me? Please say something.'

Charlotte's breath came quickly. Her mouth moved but there was no sound.

Josie reached inside herself for the strength she needed to deal with the reality. She picked up two-year-old Joshua, who threw his arms tightly around her neck. The little boy's complexion was white and he was shivering uncontrollably.

Glancing across the room, Josie could see that the baby was safe in her cot. She beckoned the two older boys towards her.

'I'll be back in a minute, Andy.'

If Sharon Watson, the next-door neighbour, was amazed to see Josie pushing past her with three small children in tow, she never batted an eyelid.

'I haven't got time to explain what's going on,' Josie told her, 'but I need you to look after the boys from next door. There's been an accident and I don't want them in the room. Will you help me?'

'Of course I will,' Sharon said, following closely behind. 'Come on, boys. I'm sure I have a packet of chocolate biscuits somewhere. Then we can see what's on the telly.'

By the time Josie ran back to the house, half the neighbours were out on the pavement and the paramedics were running in front of her. Andy moved away as they took over.

Within minutes, Charlotte was moved onto a stretcher. Two more police officers arrived and Josie sent one of them round to next door while she checked on the baby. Thankfully, Poppy had slept through most of the commotion.

Josie sat down on the settee and put her head in her hands. How many times would she be in this situation, feeling anxious, inadequate, and fearful? There was only so much she could do. She wasn't Wonder Woman, nor did she profess to be, but unlike the views of the Philip Matsons on this estate, sometimes what she did was more than a job. It was a lifeline.

Her mind flipped back to the previous summer when Liz McIntyre, another one of her tenants, had been beaten up by her husband. He'd left her for dead before hanging himself – fortunately, Liz had survived, but it was seeing Charlotte Hatfield in the same state that really upset Josie. Why do some men do this to women?

A tear spilled down her cheek. What the hell was she going to do with four kids under five? Charlotte's injuries couldn't be fully assessed until she got to the hospital, and there was no family near who could look after them. Someone from Children's Services was needed. Until then, she'd be left holding the baby herself.

Andy collapsed into the settee beside her. 'The reason I joined the force was that 'not a single day is the same' they say.' He shook his head. 'But days like these make you want to pack it in on the spot.'

Josie wiped at her eyes. It seemed strange to see Andy's face without his usual trademark grin, but today wasn't a day for smiles.

'There was nothing else we could have done,' she assured him. 'We set up everything, just in case, and it all went as planned: the telephone and pendant system that I fitted served its purpose, the control room staff reacted swiftly and you did your job brilliantly.'

Andy's eyes widened. 'You call that a good result?'

'Yes! We can't stop the bastards from doing what they do, but we can make it easier for the victims. If I hadn't fitted the emergency telephone, if you hadn't responded so quickly, Charlotte could have died.' Josie pointed a wobbly finger at the floor. 'Right there, Andy – she could have died right there. That's the reason we do what we do.'

13

It had taken Josie the rest of that day to deal with the attack on Charlotte Hatfield, and her children. Claire Tatton had arrived from Children's Services and taken all four. She'd arranged for them to be looked after until there was any news on how badly hurt Charlotte was.

Josie got back to the office a few minutes after five, thankful that, at least with the doors closed to the public, there would be no interruptions. She wanted to crack on with the paperwork before she left for the day, get down as much of her report as possible. That way she wouldn't have to go over it again tomorrow, although she knew she'd be thinking about it for a long time to come.

At five thirty, her mobile phone rang again. It would probably be Stewart: he'd called twice already to see where she was.

'I'm still at work,' she told him and then sighed, waiting for his torrent of abuse.

'You said you were finishing up ages ago. How long will you be now?'

'I'll be home soon, I promise. I'll bring something in with me to eat. Is there anything you fancy?'

Once she'd pacified him and made a swift call to Andy to learn that Charlotte was in a stable condition for now, she switched off her computer and headed for home.

As soon as she opened the front door, it was pulled from her grip. Stewart seized her arm, pushed her into the hallway and slammed it behind her with a crash.

'What took you so long? I told you to come home straight away.'

'And *I* told you I'd be home soon,' said Josie. 'Show a little compassion, I've spent most of the day dealing with a domestic violence incident.'

'Bollocks. You've been to college again, haven't you?'

Josie faltered. How had he found that out?

'No, I –'

'Liar! I saw you at Mitchell Academy on Wednesday. I checked at the reception and they said there weren't any residents' meetings that night.'

'Okay, okay. I have started a college course,' she admitted, 'although I haven't been there tonight. I wanted to tell you but I knew you wouldn't want me to go.'

'Too right, I wouldn't. You spend too much time away from the house as it is.'

'Stop saying that to me – you only want me here so I can be at your beck and call, to cook your meals, wash your clothes and clean up your mess.'

'That's what you should –'

'And I'm doing this course for me,' Josie retaliated, pushing him away. 'It has nothing to do with my work.'

Stewart huffed. 'So what's so important that you had to lie to me?'

Josie had already worked out what to say when Stewart eventually found out.

'I'm doing a computer course,' she fibbed. 'Spreadsheets, data input and the likes.'

'I wasn't talking about that,' Stewart answered. 'I was referring to the bloke who you were with when you left.'

Josie cast her mind back to Wednesday evening, then nodded in recognition. 'You mean Brian.' Then, after a moment's pause, 'have you been spying on me?'

'It's true though, isn't it? I can't stand it when you sneak around behind my back and –'

Josie pushed past him and went in to the kitchen. 'I'm hungry. I haven't had anything to eat all day except a bar of chocolate. I managed to get a cooked chicken and a pack of fresh salad on the way home. Shall we eat?'

Stewart quickly followed her through. 'So you're not going to deny it?'

Josie opened the fridge. 'There isn't anything *to* deny. Brian is my course tutor. I gave him a lift to The George and Dragon on Drury Street. He was meeting up with his son for a drink.'

'I don't believe you.'

Josie turned back to face him. 'Think about the logic of what you're insinuating, even for one minute. When have I ever got time to see anyone else? I'm always pandering to you. And, come to think of it, when was the last time that you did anything around the house?'

Stewart held up his hands. 'Not my problem.'

'It's your mess!'

'It's not my frigging house.'

'You've been saying the same thing now for the past five years. It's obvious this house isn't good enough for you. I'm surprised you find it in yourself to come through the front door at all.'

Stewart's face clouded over again. 'Trying to turn the tables now, are we? Trying to blame me for something instead?'

'Yes, I am,' said Josie, with annoyance. 'I don't want to come home to this every night. You treat this house like a hotel and I'm not having it anymore.'

Stewart moved across the room. Pushing her forcefully down into the chair, he sat opposite her at the table.

'What exactly do you mean by that?'

Josie looked behind him through the kitchen window while she tried to put her thoughts into some kind of order. After no more than a few seconds of silence, Stewart reached across and squeezed her chin.

'Get off.' Josie slapped away his hand. 'Why don't you tell me how you knew I was at college on Wednesday? And why you knew I gave Brian a lift. You followed me, didn't you?'

'Wouldn't you like to know.'

Josie felt disgust building up in her stomach as Stewart started to laugh. Not wanting to be near to him a moment longer, she stood up and walked towards the door. He reached for her arm again but she pulled it away from his grasp at the last second.

'Don't touch me,' she spat.

'Don't walk away from me, then. I'm not finished yet.'

'Not finished?' Josie shook her head. 'You think you can treat me badly and I'll stand there and take it? Well, I might have done yesterday, but after what I've seen today, I sure as hell won't. You don't own me.'

For a moment, Stewart recoiled at Josie's raised voice, but it didn't take him long to retaliate. 'You don't know how lucky you are to have me,' he threw back. 'No one else would want you, little miss housing officer.'

'Make up your mind. You've just accused me of having an affair.' Josie moved away again.

'I said don't walk away from me.' This time when Stewart grabbed for her, he didn't miss. He swung Josie round to face him. 'I think you'd better remember who you're talking to.'

'And who exactly *am* I talking to?' she seethed. 'A lazy bastard who can't be bothered to do anything for himself? A selfish bastard who thinks his woman should be his servant? An inconsiderate bastard who never does anything nice for anyone without expecting something back in return? Even worse than that – you're a bully.'

Stewart's grip on her arm tightened but Josie switched off from the pain.

'You've turned your own wife against you with your controlling ways. No – wait! What you're actually thinking is, shit, there goes my free meal ticket. Perhaps your plan was to use me until someone better came along.'

Stewart stared at her before pushing her away roughly. He went back into the kitchen but Josie followed him.

'But guess what, Stewart? I'm not going to do anything for you again until I get something done in return. It's about time someone looked after me for a change.'

'I would if you'd come home early for once.'

'Home to what exactly? You're hardly here to welcome me with open arms.'

'That's because you've always thought more of that fucking job than you have of me. What is it that turns you on, Josie? Do I have to smack you one before you take any notice of me?'

'You sick bastard. Do you think that's funny after what I've seen today?'

Whether it was the picture of an injured Charlotte lying unconscious on her living room floor that wouldn't leave her mind right now, she'd never know, but in that split second, Josie saw red. Stopping suddenly to catch her breath, she was left with a rush of energy as adrenaline sloshed through her veins. With both hands, she pushed him in his chest.

Stewart lurched forwards and punched her in the face.

Josie slumped to the floor. Trying hard to focus through watery eyes, she cautiously put her hand to her nose and pulled it back. It was covered in blood.

'Fuck... I...' Stewart's words failed to materialise.

Josie struggled to get to her feet, but her legs had other ideas. Stewart dropped to his knees in front of her, looking distraught as the realisation of what had happened – what he'd done – began to sink in. They sat on the floor for what seemed like hours. Neither of them spoke – how could they possibly put into words what had happened?

Finally, Stewart broke into the silence.

'Josie?' He looked into her eyes, frantic for some sign of reassurance.

'I'll be fine,' she eventually spoke.

'No, you won't. Let me...'

She flinched as he reached out to touch her. 'I can manage.'

'I don't know what came over me. I must have –'

'Leave me alone,' she whispered.

'No, I'm not leaving you like this.'

'Please, Stewart.'

'But I want to –'

Ignoring his offer of support, Josie managed to get to her feet. One arm stretched out in front, she walked slowly into the conservatory. Stewart joined her again when she sat down in the chair, his face racked with emotion. She couldn't be sure if it was concern for the pain he'd caused her or for the trouble he might be in now that he'd hit her.

'Go away,' she said again.

'At least let me –'

'Will you just leave me alone!' Josie screamed so loud that what blood was left in Stewart's face drained away rapidly. Getting the message at last, he made a swift exit.

14

*J*osie was still sitting in the conservatory two hours later. The last time she'd tried to get up, the agonizing pain that shot across her forehead had sent her reeling back into the chair. When she'd known for certain that Stewart's car had gone, she'd staggered into the hallway to inspect the damage he'd caused.

Peering into the mirror, painful though it was, she'd let the tears fall. Stewart's fist had caught her top lip as well as her nose. Tenderly, she'd touched the swollen mess and winced in pain. How she was going to explain it away at work was beyond her imagination. She might be able to hide the inevitable bruising, but no amount of make-up would get rid of the swelling. She'd have to book some time off.

Josie wasn't sure what hurt the most – her face, her heart or the humiliation. She should have seen that coming, especially after hearing Tim talk about his actions the other night, and how they had escalated. And she knew that if it were someone else with this problem, she'd be able to tell them exactly what to do – but herself? She wouldn't be able to take her own advice.

No wonder she sometimes felt inadequate to hand out guidance to the likes of Amy and Charlotte. How could she, when she wasn't prepared to practice what she preached?

Was it too much to ask for a show of affection now and then, for him to reaffirm his love? Stewart must have loved her at one time. Josie wanted to be wined and dined. The girls at work were always being treated to things. Only last month, Sonia had stayed in a plush hotel in the Lake District, drinking mugs of

Behind a Closed Door

hot chocolate in front of a roaring fire. The nearest she'd got to that with Stewart had been a walk around the local reservoir and that had been a very long time ago.

She moved back into the conservatory, wondering when the house had stopped being her home. Had it ever been a home to her? Sure, she'd felt safe when she was younger, but lately it had felt more like a prison, like she'd never be in control. Maybe she'd always feel like a fifteen-year-old here.

Perhaps you should leave.

Oh, what was she thinking? Josie began to cry again. It was okay for her to be brave at work as she wasn't dealing with her own problems. But here, the one and only time she'd stood up for herself, Stewart had lashed out.

She couldn't let the incident pass. For once in her life, she would have to take note of the advice that she dished out on a regular basis. Tonight she'd had a warning. She knew there could easily be a next time. Was she sure she wanted to stick around?

With thoughts of Charlotte rushing through her mind again, Josie reached for a cushion and pulled it to her chest. *What a mess you've made.* She wept hot tears through swollen eyes. *You bastard, how could you do this to me?*

Kelly woke up sharply as Emily nudged her arm.

'Mummy, your phone is ringing. I'll get it for you.'

Before she had time to respond, Emily had answered the call.

'Daddy! When are you coming home? I miss you. Yes, I'm being a good girl. I'm always a good girl. No, Mummy's been asleep. I'll give it to her.'

Emily ran over to the settee and gave Kelly the phone.

'Hello, babe. How're you doing?'

'I'm okay,' said Kelly. 'How are you?'

'I'm bearing up. Life isn't easy in here, but I'll cope. Are you missing me?'

'Yeah, of course.' She wasn't entirely sure that was true.

'Ah, but I'll be back soon enough.'

Emily came rushing over to Kelly's side. 'Can I speak to Daddy again?' she asked loudly.

'Wait a minute, Em.' Kelly needed some questions answered first. 'Scott, have you decided what you're going do when you get out yet?'

'But I want to speak to Daddy.' Emily pulled on her arm.

'Wait a minute. Have you thought –?'

'Let me speak to Daddy!'

'Put her back on,' said Scott.

Kelly handed the phone to her daughter with a sigh. Every time she

319

mentioned going on the straight and narrow when Scott was released, he changed the subject.

Emily put down the phone a minute later. 'Daddy had to go but he loves us lots and lots.'

Kelly lay back on the settee again and exhaled noisily. The word 'love' didn't always have the desired effect anymore.

*J*osie was in bed when she heard Stewart come back around eleven. Her mind in turmoil, with every creak of the stairs her heart skipped a beat. She held her breath as he quietly pushed open the bedroom door. Feigning sleep while he stood in front of her, he finally left. Josie blew out the breath she'd been holding. Minutes later, she heard him settle down in the spare room. At least he hadn't disturbed her.

She struggled to find sleep, switching the bedside lamp on as the still of the room got to her. Her head was pounding but she didn't want to fetch any more painkillers for fear of waking Stewart. Instead she lay alone, thinking alone, feeling alone, and questioning how long she had been feeling that way. Things couldn't go on like this.

The following morning, she sat at the kitchen table waiting for Stewart to come downstairs. Lying awake, she'd had time to make a lot of decisions. She knew he'd want to explain his actions, but she didn't care about him. It was about time she started to live life for herself. She was no one's slave. It was her own fault for allowing him to dominate her. In the forefront of her mind was Charlotte Hatfield. She couldn't let that happen to her.

When he came into the kitchen, Stewart's eyes widened in disbelief when he surveyed the damage he'd caused with one punch. The bruising around her eyes had darkened overnight and the cut on her nose from his ring was more visible as she turned her head towards him.

Stewart took a step closer. 'I'm sorry. I –'

Josie raised a hand. 'I don't want to hear your excuses, your apologies or even your despicable lies. Right now, I want you to understand that I don't forgive you for what you've done.'

'I know. I –'

'Don't interrupt me.' Josie flinched, her swollen face making it painful for her to talk. 'I'm not the same Josie as I was this time yesterday. You've made me realise a few things and one of them is that you've had your own way for far too long. It stops right now.'

Stewart frowned. 'It... it won't happen again. You've got to believe me.'

'You're damn right it won't happen again.' Even from where she was sitting,

Josie could see beads of sweat forming on Stewart's furrowed brow. With shaking hands, she picked up her mug of coffee. 'I want you to leave.'

'You can't be serious. I've said I'm sorry. What more –'

'Sorry isn't enough after the mess you've made of me. Look at me!' She pointed to her face. 'I can't live with a bully and I certainly can't live with a man who punched me.'

Stewart ran a hand through his hair before taking a step nearer. 'But I swear I won't do it again.'

'I know you won't because you won't be here.'

'You can't chuck me out. Where will I go?'

Josie had thought about this but had come to one conclusion. 'I don't care,' she said. 'I don't want to see you here again.'

There was silence in the room for a few seconds as her words sunk in. Then Stewart shook his head.

'No,' he said. 'I'm not leaving.'

Josie pushed herself up to her feet. She'd thought he'd react like this, try to talk her down into submission. But before she crumpled, she needed to let him know that she wasn't going to be a pushover this time. 'Then I'm going to ring the police,' she said. 'Maybe they can make you –'

'Wait.' Stewart touched her arm as she moved past him. He stared at her before his eyes narrowed. 'You're serious, aren't you?'

'I'm deadly serious,' she told him. 'Gullible Josie has gone forever. It's either the police or you leave – it's your choice.'

Stewart was silent for a few seconds in thought. 'Okay, I'll go for now – give you some time to yourself. I'll find someone at work who'll put me up for a few nights, then we can talk things through again.'

Josie nodded. If she could get him out of the house, then she could decide when she wanted to talk.

It wasn't until he left twenty minutes later with a few of his clothes packed into a holdall that she let her façade slip. Her shoulders dropped with relief that she'd had the courage to do what she'd set out to do, but inside she was breaking.

Was she strong enough to see this through?

As Kelly clocked on at the factory that night, she met Sally in the canteen for a drink before their shift began. It was something they'd quickly got into a routine of doing.

A guy called Robbie was doing his best to sing. He wasn't called Rob: Kelly had been informed by Sally when she'd started.

It had to be Robbie because he thought he looked exactly like the real version. It had taken a while before Kelly realised that Sally was being serious (the real Robbie Williams had nothing to worry about). Tonight, this Robbie was giving them a rendition of Angels, even though no one had asked him to.

Phil, one of the packers, covered his ears with his hands and grimaced. 'Jesus, Robbie, you sound like a whale. A whale in pain.'

Robbie threw him a smirk. 'That's not what the ladies tell me.'

'Where do you pick them up? At the deaf club?'

Everyone laughed.

'Maybe you're 'Misunderstood', Robbie,' said another fella Kelly vaguely recognised.

Some of the lads whooped.

'Wow,' said Phil. 'Mummy's boy's up on Robbie Williams' music. I'm stunned. Not many people remember that song from his greatest hits CD.'

'Mummy's boy' threw a screwed up crisp packet at him.

Everyone continued to banter until the clock approached four. Kelly slipped on her overall and sat down at her bench.

'Guess what I found out about little miss perfect, here?' Leah said, as she rushed in, late again. She pointed to Kelly. 'I know your secret now. Your fella's been sent down for thieving.'

Sally sighed loudly as she reached for a mug. 'Tell us something we don't know. That isn't a secret.'

'I didn't know!' Leah glared at Kelly. 'Anyway, what have you got to say about it?'

'There's nothing to say,' Kelly replied. 'He planned a break-in, he got caught and now he's doing his time.'

Leah folded her arms across her chest. 'He's a psycho. I heard it straight from the horse's mouth.'

The usually quiet Julia snorted. 'That's rich, coming from you – you look like a horse, Leah. Are you sure that you didn't tell yourself?'

As some of the other workers began to laugh, Leah reached over the belt, purposefully knocking over a whole batch of mugs.

'Oi!' Kelly cried out. 'It's taken me ages to do those, you bitch.'

Leah's hand covered her mouth but it didn't hide the smirk. 'Oh dear, I *am* sorry. It was an accident.'

'No, you did it on purpose.' Sally dropped to the floor to help Kelly pick up the damaged pieces.

'We'll help you to catch up again,' Julia told Kelly. She stared at Leah. 'We'll *all* help.'

Leah folded her arms. 'Don't count on it.'

Behind a Closed Door

'It won't matter much anyway.' Sally threw the pieces she'd collected into the bin. 'Kelly's only been here five minutes and she's far quicker than you anyway.'

'No, she's not.'

'And we don't have to make excuses up because she's never late.'

Kelly began to feel as though she was invisible. 'Come on, now,' she said. 'Let's not argue.'

'Who gave you permission to speak?' Leah barked.

Sally slammed down the bin lid. 'Why don't you shut up for once, Leah? What's the matter? Is your reputation as gossip queen faltering? Grow up or move down the line. You're boring us.'

'Thanks, Sal,' said Kelly, 'but I can hold my own.' She stared back angrily at the woman with the red hair who loathed her so much. 'I do think it's time you backed off, though. I'm getting sick and tired of your comments. You're no better than me. We're both in the same position – single mums doing the best we can for our kids. And at least I know where Emily's father is.'

Leah's face reddened by the second. 'Ooh, get you,' she managed to mutter. She didn't speak for the rest of their shift.

'Thank goodness that's over,' Kelly said as she left the building with Sally afterwards. 'I can't take much more of Leah's bitchy comments. If she carries on, I'll end up chinning her.'

'Don't worry,' Sally answered. 'She's backing down. Leah can't do much without an audience and even Julia isn't taking any notice of her now. You probably think I'm talking garbage but Leah's okay once you get to know her.'

Kelly smirked.

'It's true. For some reason you got off to a bad start. She'll come –'

A car beeped its horn and pulled up alongside them. Kelly smiled when she saw it was Jay.

'Need a lift?' he offered.

'Ooh, yes ta. See you tomorrow, Sal.'

'Things going well?' he asked as he pulled away from the kerb.

Kelly nodded. 'Getting better, I suppose.'

On the main road, Kelly spotted Leah sitting alone at the bus stop. Theatrically, she waved as they drove past. Leah's face was a picture.

15

Before Scott came out of prison, Kelly wanted to treat Jay to lunch for being so good to her over the past few weeks. That weekend, he drove them to a pub out in the country. Emily had been excited all morning because he'd told her it had a ball pit and a bouncy castle. Kelly knew there would be lots of children for her to play with, too. Once there, she and Jay hardly saw her, although they clearly heard her every now and then.

'I think I should have had more to eat before necking that wine,' Kelly said, taking another sip of her drink regardless of feeling a little tipsy. 'I'm such a lightweight. Two glasses of red and I'm under the table.'

'Got any room left for pudding?' Jay asked, as he grabbed for the dessert menu.

'Not even a tiny space.' She rubbed her stomach. 'Oh, go on then. I might just manage a banana split.'

'Care to share?'

'No. Get your own.' Playfully, Kelly poked him in the shoulder. 'Anyway, have what you want. You always pay for everything so it's my treat today.'

'But I don't mind –'

'What's the use of working if I don't get to spend *any* of it on luxuries? And Scott will be back soon so I won't have chance to thank you if I don't do it now.'

'Do you still miss him, Kel?' Jay questioned.

'Course I do.' Kelly lowered hers eyes, afraid of revealing her ever changing feelings for Scott. 'But you've been a massive help too.'

'Kel, I –'

Behind a Closed Door

'Mummy!' Emily shouted as she ran towards them. She stopped at the table and took a quick slurp of her drink through a straw. 'I've been hiding in the balls. Did you see me?'

'Yes,' Kelly fibbed. 'I bet the other children didn't though.'

'I'm going to hide again.'

'Ugh,' Jay shuddered as she ran back. 'Can you imagine what's inside that ball pit? I mean, underneath – jelly and custard, splodges of cream off the cakes, fizzy pop ...'

'Bits of fish fingers.' Kelly giggled, then grabbed Jay's hand. 'Thanks.' She leaned on the table with her elbow. 'I wouldn't have survived without your help – even though I didn't want your help at first.'

'I remember only too well. You were nasty to me no matter what I did.'

'I wasn't that bad,' Kelly protested.

'You were, but that's what mates are for. Look Kelly, are you sure that you –'

'Whoops.' Kelly's elbow slipped off the table and she fell forwards. 'What is it with me and lunchtime drinking?'

Jay sighed. He glanced over to where Emily was climbing a ladder ready to dive into the balls again. Then he looked at his watch. 'Jesus, have you seen the time? We'll have to go soon, Kel.'

'I suppose you're off to check up on your other woman, aren't you?'

Jay laughed. 'Me? I haven't got *time* for another woman.'

'You must have someone special in your life, though. I wonder what she thinks of all the time you spend with me and Em.' Kelly pointed an unsteady finger at him. 'You are a true... true friend. Scott should be vey – vey proud of you.'

In her inebriated state, Kelly didn't realise that Jay's smile didn't reach his eyes.

Surprisingly, but true to his word, Stewart stayed away from Josie. After a week on her own, she started to get over the initial shock of what had happened. Although the swelling around her nose had gone down in days, the black and blue of the bruising could still be seen. Her emotions had taken a battering too.

Stewart had sent her a few text messages, to which she'd responded with as few words as were appropriate. He'd even rung once, on Friday evening, to see if she would see him yet, but she'd told him it was too soon to start talking. She needed to be clear about what she planned to do next and she was nowhere near that stage yet.

By the time she went back to work, she was all thought out. More so, she needed to catch up with her case notes. It was hard for anyone not to have heard about Charlotte Hatfield over the past week. She'd been local front-page news for two nights, her story told in bold, graphic details.

Josie had been annoyed to be away from the office at such an important time. She wanted to make sure that all the paperwork was filled out correctly, that every t was crossed and every i was dotted, in case the statement was used as evidence in a court case.

She wanted to be sure they'd nail Charlotte's partner for it. After the damage Nathan had caused, he deserved no more than to rot in a ten-by-eight cell. However, reporting to work the next day looking the way she had wouldn't have been ideal.

Charlotte's children had been collected by their grandparents and ferried back to Leeds while Charlotte had spent two days in intensive care. She was now – thankfully – on the road to recovery.

It never failed to amaze Josie how much a human body could cope with in difficult situations. Her mind flipped back to her mum's last days. Brenda had hung on for what seemed like forever until her body, unable to take in food, slowly deteriorated and her heart stopped.

Arriving at the office, she boxed up her feelings and headed in. The first thing that greeted her was the report of another burglary.

'What's up?' Debbie asked as she passed over a mug of coffee.

'Mrs Lattimer's been robbed over the weekend,' Josie told her. 'Remember, we visited a couple of weeks ago?'

'Yes, she was really nice to me.' Debbie shook her head in disbelief. 'Is she okay?'

'I'm not sure. We only get the basics on the call-out logs. That's five now in the past couple of months. I'll have to pop in and see her.'

Debbie sighed. 'It makes it more personal when you know the tenant involved, doesn't it?'

'Yes.' Josie grabbed her keys and slipped her mobile phone into her coat pocket. 'It took me and her family ages to get her to move there in the first place. She didn't think she'd cope but she's been much more independent since. This will set her back big style. I'll have to pop round this morning, see if I can catch her in.'

'Send her my love,' Debbie shouted as she marched away. 'Let me know if there's anything I can do.'

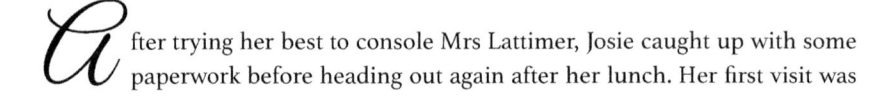

*A*fter trying her best to console Mrs Lattimer, Josie caught up with some paperwork before heading out again after her lunch. Her first visit was to Clarence Avenue. Rather than enjoying a mug of coffee with Kelly in her tidy, clean living room, she was crawling around the floor while baby Reece kicked his legs infuriatingly next to her. Josie was trying to make him laugh by waving a yellow rabbit in front of his face and then pressing it to his nose. He was niggling: Amy was heating some food for him.

'Has he been like this all morning?' Josie shouted through the open kitchen door, waiting for another loud yell as Reece took another breather. His angry little face was beginning to represent the colour of sun-ripened tomatoes.

Before Amy had time to reply, Josie's mobile started to ring. She rummaged around in her pockets until she found it. It was Craig from the office, wanting to know if she would get Irene's card on her way back. It was Irene's fiftieth birthday at the weekend and they'd had a bit of a collection. Although Irene wasn't particularly liked, it was astounding how much of a conscience people had when a collection went around the office. They'd collected quite a sum for her.

Josie disconnected the call, feeling herself shivering in the small room. Amy had reappeared with Reece's gooey delight and settled him onto her knee.

'It's a bit chilly in here, Amy. Have you got enough gas tokens?'

'Yeah, I took my card to the post office on Monday. It was on my to-do list.'

Josie smiled, watching her spoon in another mouthful, then carefully wipe the remainder from Reece's chin with his bib. She was such a good kid, it grieved her to see how she had been let down by her parents.

'Good. I wondered if the problem with your heating had been sorted.'

Amy looked up quickly. 'There's nothing wrong with my heating.'

'But Ray – you remember Ray, the other housing officer? – he said it wasn't working properly the other week. I thought that you were still having –'

'No, it's okay now.'

Josie wondered why Amy's body had tensed. For some reason, she wouldn't look her in the eye either.

'It's okay if you did something wrong,' she said, hoping to encourage Amy to open up. She decided it was time for a white lie. 'I know when I moved into my house, I was forever switching off things that should stay on or leaving things on that should be turned off.'

Amy began to relax a little but Josie had seen the signs and was worried. Amy seemed to be coping: the house was tidy and Reece, despite his grumbling, was looking well. Maybe there was something Amy was keeping to herself?

'Is there something else that you want to tell me?' Josie questioned, her voice soft.

Amy shook her head vehemently.

'I just wondered, because when I called the other day, I couldn't get an answer when I knocked. You were in, though, weren't you?'

'No, I was at the shops.'

'Are you sure?'

'Yes.'

Amy wouldn't look at Josie. Instead, she wiped Reece's face clean and pulled off his bib. Josie sighed and grabbed her file. There was nothing she could do when Amy was in this frame of mind. She was a stubborn little sod when she wanted to be – and she didn't have to tell Josie anything if she didn't want to.

For now, she'd have to be content that Amy was doing okay, even though there was clearly something on her mind. She'd have to dig deeper during her next visit.

The rest of the afternoon was quite successful for Josie, too. She'd been to see Mrs Baker from Russell Close, who had finished decorating the downstairs of her property: only another six months before the upstairs would be to a decent standard, no doubt. The new tenant in Winston Place had moved in on time and six of the eight garden checks had been tidied to a reasonable level.

After having a giggle at some of the extremely rude cards on display in the newsagents, she was making her way back to her car when she spotted a figure in the distance.

'Mrs Middleton!' Josie waved to catch her attention.

Ruth Middleton turned slightly but kept on walking.

'Wait a minute.' Josie had to run to catch her up. Finally as she drew nearer, Ruth stopped.

'How are you?' she asked, a hand held to her chest as she caught her breath.

'I'm fine, thanks,' Ruth smiled tightly.

'Good.' Josie knew instantly that the question was being avoided. Ruth didn't look well at all. A small woman, she was pale and thin, bags under her eyes denoting her lack of sleep. 'And how are things at home?'

The last time Josie had visited Ruth after a neighbour complaint about noise, she hadn't been faring well. Ruth seemed depressed, extremely subdued. It was almost as if she was in a trance.

Josie had wondered if she was on strong medication but Ruth hadn't come forward with the information. If it wasn't for the fact that she was living with her partner, she might have tried to get her some help – not that Martin was any use, but Josie did see him out a lot with Ruth's two young boys.

'Everything's fine,' Ruth replied.

'Right.' Josie stepped sideways to allow a woman with a double buggy and a toddler to get past. 'And the boys, are they doing okay? Looking forward to the Easter break coming up?'

Behind a Closed Door

'Look, I don't mean to be rude,' Ruth fiddled with the strap on her handbag, 'but I'm not sure that it's any of your business.'

'Sorry.' Josie wasn't taken aback by her tone. 'But you were upset when I last saw you and I thought –'

'You thought you'd come and stick your nose in again where it's not wanted.'

'No. That's not it at all. I'm worried about you.'

Ruth looked away. 'No, you're not. You're doing your job.'

'Maybe, but I'm trying –'

'Leave me be.' Ruth started to walk away. 'I don't need your help. I'm fine on my own.'

'Please, wait!' Josie grabbed her arm and was shocked when Ruth flinched. She pulled her hand away. 'You're not all right, are you?'

Ruth's eyes filled with tears.

'Let me help.' Josie tried desperately to connect with her. 'Please.'

'Sure, you can help. Do you know how? Leave me alone.'

Ruth turned away again. Josie had no choice but to let her go. Even so, she was still thinking of her when she got back to the office. She parked up next to Andy's police vehicle in the car park, wondering what he'd called in for.

'What's all the commotion?' she asked Sonia, who was practically sprinting up the corridor heading for the reception.

'Some dickhead's super-glued himself to the rent counter,' she said with a grin.

Josie pushed open the door into the office and Sonia turned back in astonishment.

'Aren't you coming to see? He's pissed off because his rent benefit has been stopped. One of the fraud officers caught him up a ladder cleaning windows on three separate occasions. He's meant to be incapacitated, unable to walk for ten metres without help.'

'I'm on my way.' Josie grinned: this she had to see. The dickhead in question must be Derek Maddox from Robert Place. Josie had contacted the fraud department six months previously and they'd been building up a file on him ever since. She plonked her things down on her desk – no surprise to see an empty office – and joined the rest of the staff as the party unfurled.

'That's her,' Derek shrieked as soon as Josie caught his furious eyes. 'That's the evil bitch that shopped me!'

Andy was having difficulty keeping his face straight as he looked over at Josie coming into view behind several housing staff. 'Mrs Mellor, do you have anything to do with this little incident?'

'Absolutely not, PC Baxter.' Josie shook her head. 'Contrary to popular belief, Mr Maddox, I don't know *everything* that goes on around the Mitchell Estate.'

'Then who the fuck was it?' Derek screamed again. 'When I find out who it is, I'll break every bone in their fucking body. I'll rip 'em up into pieces. I'll tear their balls off. I'll –'

'Calm down, Derek.' Andy failed to keep the snigger out of his voice. 'Swearing isn't going to help. It'll only stress you out, and you don't want to come unstuck now, do you?'

Derek's face turned a raspberry colour as laughter erupted from all around the reception area. An old lady Josie recognised from William Precinct pushed past him and handed the cashier her rent card through the slot in the glass. It seemed that she wasn't prepared to wait a minute longer.

'I'll leave you to it,' laughed Josie. She nudged Debbie. 'Get the digital camera.'

'Ooh, yes. We can laugh about him later, too.' Debbie grinned. 'What a knob.'

Josie smiled back. She'd known it would only be a matter of months before the job made Debbie as bitter and twisted as the rest of the staff. Once she'd been threatened a few times on the reception desk and verbally abused on the phone, she'd hardened up pretty sharpish.

She grinned. These were the times when she realised that some days on the Mitchell Estate *were* better than others. The rough was worth it for the smooth.

Just then, she noticed Ray scuttling into the office through the staff entrance.

'The photos aren't to show everyone, Debbie,' Josie told her as she moved towards him. 'It's further evidence that he hasn't got a bad back. Ray, have you got a minute?'

Ray turned towards Josie but continued to walk through into the office. 'Not enough of them in the day with scrotes like Maddox allowed to get away with benefit fraud.'

For once, Josie was in agreement with him. 'We got him in the end,' she said as she drew nearer to him. They walked through together into the main office. 'It's Amy Cartwright that I want to talk to you about.'

Ray stopped at his desk, picking up a message left for him on a notepad. 'Bloody pathetic.' He ripped it from the spine, crunched it into a ball and lobbed it at the waste paper bin. 'They always ring after you've arranged to see them yet there was no one in when I called. Well, no one who'd open the door, anyway. What about Amy Cartwright?'

'I saw her earlier and she was a bit off when I mentioned that you'd been out to sort her heating.'

Ray shrugged his shoulders. 'She caught me on one of my better days. She called in at the office to see Doug but he wasn't in so I went instead. Call me a Good Samaritan, if you want.'

Josie sat down at her desk in front of him. 'So why did she look so awkward when I mentioned your name? You didn't give her a hard time because she'd broken something, did you?'

Ray stretched his arms above his head before flexing his fingers noisily. 'Now, now, Josie, you know me better than that.'

Josie sighed. Yes she did, that was the trouble.

'What did you say to upset her?'

'Nothing.'

'Ray, you seem to forget, I've worked with you for years.'

'Amy's a thicko, she'll tell you anything. The only reason I went round at all was to stop me from having to go and see that Neblin bloke of yours. His son's been causing grief and the last time I called I had the whole street on my back moaning at me. So, if you must know, I went to save myself some aggro. Anyway, it's sorted now, so what's the problem?'

'The problem is you've upset her.' Josie reached for her phone to retrieve her voicemail messages as Irene, Sonia and Debbie burst in through the doors, still laughing about Derek Maddox. 'The next time you go to see her, let me know and I'll come with you. It's taken me ages to build a rapport with her. The last thing I need is for you to break the trust – and don't call her a thicko.'

Ray's chair scraped across the flooring as he stood up abruptly. 'Back off, Josie. Just because you look after all the waifs and strays doesn't mean I have to give the same customer care.'

'I –'

He threw his hands up into the air. 'No, don't worry, miss do-gooder. The next time Amy Cartwright needs something, I'll let you sort it out from the beginning. It's less hassle.'

Josie flicked two fingers up as he walked off. Sometimes it was like working in a nursery, not an office.

16

That Wednesday evening, Kelly slid a thin ham and mushroom pizza into the oven for herself and Emily and a crunchy pepperoni one for Jay. It was her first night off in ages, due to a change of shift with one of the early girls. Jay was due in fifteen minutes and Emily was helping her to arrange the salad in a bowl – or rather, she had been for a minute or so, before rushing off.

'Jay's here,' Emily shouted through the door. 'Can I let him in?'

'Only because I know it's Jay, young lady, else the rule still stands.'

As Emily bounded down the stairs to let him in, Kelly rushed across to the mirror and checked her appearance before he came into the room. He smiled and held out a bottle of wine. 'This calls for a celebration – your first night off.'

'That and the fact that the sun's been shining today. I actually took off my jacket this morning when I went to the shops.'

'We're having pizza,' Emily cried. She put both her tiny feet onto Jay's booted ones and balanced on them as he walked across the room. Laughing as she giggled, Jay lifted her up and threw her playfully onto the settee.

Once the pizza had been demolished, Jay topped up their glasses while Kelly got Emily into bed.

'At last,' Kelly sighed when she eventually joined him again. 'I tell you, that girl has got be the chattiest kid I know. I can't wait for her to start school to give me some peace.'

'Don't give me that, you'll miss her like crazy.'

Kelly sat down. 'I know. I'll – I'll miss you too when Scott gets back. I can't believe he'll be home in a few days.'

Behind a Closed Door

'I hope he keeps out of trouble this time. He needs to calm down and think of what he might lose if he gets caught again. I –'

'You think he's shit, don't you?' Kelly clipped. 'You thought he'd serve the full sentence because he wouldn't be able to stay out of trouble. Well, he's not a Kirkwell.'

'Ouch.' Jay turned away from Kelly's fierce stare for a moment. 'I didn't mean it to sound so nasty. It's just that I'm going to miss you.'

'Sorry.' Kelly grinned, instantly friends with him again. 'I was thinking earlier how it won't be the same. There'll be no more pizzas,' she raised her glass in the air, 'no more bottles of wine to share, no more nights watching *Cougar* or *Gossip Girl*. Scott hates that type of thing. He's into serial killers, blood, snot and the likes. It's rare I get to watch girlie things. It's been a pleasure to –'

Without warning, Jay leaned forwards. Time seemed to suspend as he stared directly into Kelly's eyes. His face contorted as if in pain. Quickly, he stood up and moved away.

'I can't do this anymore,' he said.

'Why? It's early yet.' Kelly picked up the bottle of wine, indicating that it was still half full.

'No, I mean I can't be with you anymore. This is killing me. I thought I could handle things but everything's gone weird now. I need to keep my wits about me. You're Scott's girl, my *mate's* girl. I've got no right to feel the way I do.'

All at once, the penny dropped for Kelly.

Jay sat back down again. He took her hands in his own. 'I can't help myself, Kel. I think about you all the time. I can't wait to pick you up from work every night, I go crazy over the weekends without you.'

'But you've taken me – us – out for the last two Sundays... Oh.' Kelly pulled her hands away.

'I shouldn't have, but I wanted to be with you. I thought I could handle it, but now I realise that... oh, fuck. I'm just going to come right out and say it. I realise that I love you.'

The last few words came out in a whisper but Kelly heard every one as if Jay had shouted them from the top of the Empire State building.

'I know I can give you so much more than Scott,' he continued. 'You're a great mum, you've started work to earn your keep to make a difference and you've *survived*. Some women would have sat cowering in a corner waiting for their partners to come back.'

Kelly sat in silence, unable to speak.

'You deserve far better than him,' Jay added.

She laughed harshly. 'Like you, you mean? Don't beat about the bush, Jay.'

He touched Kelly's cheek again, ever so slightly, like a feather floating past. 'I can't stop thinking about you.'

'But you're Scott's mate!'

Jay grimaced. 'I can't stop thinking about that either.'

'No,' Kelly shook her head, 'you can't. And you shouldn't.'

'But have you ever stopped to think about why I'm his mate? It's because I wanted to keep an eye on you. I know what Scott gets up to.'

'But you do it too.' Realising the living room door stood ajar, Kelly quickly closed it for fear of waking Emily. As she came back to stand in front of the fire, she shook her head, trying to rid it of all the confusion.

How could Jay sit there and make out that Scott was worse than him, just because he hadn't been caught that night? And why say it now? Was he only doing it to cover up his feelings – his guilt, perhaps? Taking her off the scent by trying to put the blame on Scott?

But it wasn't Scott's fault that his mate had fallen for his woman. And it wasn't Scott's fault that Kelly had led Jay on. Because that's what she'd done, hadn't she?

'You're just like him,' she said, if only to reassure herself.

Jay rubbed his hands over his face before looking up at her. 'But I'm not – you've got to believe me.'

'You've got a reputation on the estate for being a hard bastard. No one wants to start on a Kirkwell.'

'That's because I've had to defend myself because of who my brothers *are*. Men pick fights *because* of who I am. That's all it is. I've never stolen anything, and I've never done a job with Scott either.'

Kelly sat silent for a moment, puzzled by what he'd said. 'I thought you always went with him,' she said eventually.

Jay shook his head. 'No. How many more times do I have to tell you?'

'But you warned him off the last job. I heard you talking in the kitchen – you said it was too risky.'

'That's because it *was* too risky. I didn't want to see you suffer. I warned Stevie and Michael but they never listened either.'

Kelly was confused as she tried to work out the finer details. Scott had done lots of jobs with the Kirkwell brothers. Had she assumed that Jay was involved when he wasn't? She thought back to Josie defending his actions after she'd been attacked.

Had she been wrong?

She sat down next to him again. 'Tell me what's going on.'

'You know I'm the youngest brother,' Jay explained. 'I've had to live in their shadows for years. You're not the first person to think I'd be involved. But I swear to you, I'm not.

'What they do makes me sick. I haven't got time for petty thieves. They think they don't hurt people, people like you and me, but they do. For every factory they do over, hardworking people lose their jobs. For every car they steal to move on, someone's stranded. It's not as easy as the insurance paying out.

'When I heard about the last job, I tried to warn them all, but they wouldn't listen. I knew they wouldn't pull it off and it'd be up to me to pick up the pieces again.

'My mum's really upset about it. She never brought up four children for two of them to be drop-outs. Michael's been in the nick so many times, it'll be ages before he gets out.'

Kelly watched as Jay struggled with his emotions.

'You haven't got a clue what it's done to our family over the years. I didn't want that for you.' Jay chanced a quick glance at her. 'Nor Emily.'

For a split second, Kelly understood where Jay was coming from. Then she remembered something else.

'That money,' she said. 'That five hundred pounds – did Scott give it to you or was it yours to start with?'

Jay shook his head. 'It was mine. I thought it'd help you out.'

Kelly groaned. Finally she began to understand what he was talking about. Jay *was* racked with guilt: for what his brothers had brought on his parents, for what Scott had brought on her, and, most of all, for his feelings towards another man's woman.

She shuddered involuntarily. How had she not seen this happening, right underneath her nose? Stupidly, she'd enjoyed Jay's company more and more and, in the back of her mind, knew he was spending far too much time with her. Simply doing a favour for a mate wasn't what was happening.

And because she'd missed Scott so much, she'd taken Jay as a substitute, a replacement, until Scott was ready to return. She was entirely to blame for letting it happen, when it clearly shouldn't have.

As Jay pleaded with his eyes, begging her to talk, Kelly didn't know what to say. She couldn't give him what he wanted, yet she couldn't tell him what he didn't want to hear.

But staying silent did it for her. With one last look, Jay stood up and walked out of the room. Tears pouring down her cheeks, Kelly had no choice but to let him.

. . .

*A*t nine thirty, Kelly dialled Jay's mobile number again. She had to know that everything was all right. It was the last thing she wanted on Tuesday. Scott was bound to ask Jay to pick him up from prison and she needed no awkwardness between them. She had to make sure there was nothing that would make Scott suspicious, make him wonder what had been going on.

She knew she should be happy that Scott was coming home soon but all she could think about was Jay – how she'd hurt his feelings, betrayed his trust and, in a strange, yet totally unknown way, used him. She hadn't meant to – that had hurt the most.

As the call switched to voicemail yet again, Kelly flung her phone down onto the settee in a fit of anger.

*B*ut Jay was no more than a hundred yards away. He was parked a few houses down, on the opposite side of Clarence Avenue. Not for the first time, his thoughts switched to what could be going on behind the closed curtains. Was Kelly making herself nice, ready for Scott to come home?

He waited for his phone to stop ringing before he picked it up. Kelly's messages said that she wanted to talk, to clear the air. Jay wanted to talk to her so badly, even if his words would be empty.

Over the last few hours, his feelings had heightened, yet he fought with his conscience. Kelly belonged to Scott. He'd had no right to put her in that predicament, but he hadn't been able to stop himself.

Exasperated, he started the car engine and screeched away from the kerb.

*W*hen Josie's manager asked for some paperwork to be taken to their head office, Josie drew the short straw. After an age finding a space on the staff car park, she went into the main building. It hadn't changed much since she'd left it all those years ago, apart from a lick of paint here and there and a different corporate logo.

As she walked through the reception area towards the lifts, she saw someone she hadn't seen in years.

'Livvy?'

'Josie!' Livvy gave her a huge hug, looking genuinely pleased to see her. 'I haven't seen you properly in what, five years?'

Josie nodded. 'Yes, it must be. How are you?'

'Fair. I've split up with my partner but apart from that… How about you?'

'Same here. I've just separated from my husband.'

They both smiled half-heartedly, knowing there was now something else they had in common.

'I'm fine though,' Josie added. 'Apart from never having lived alone and jumping every time I hear a strange noise! Funny thing is, he worked shifts so I was often by myself in the house anyway. What are you doing here, though? It's a bit different from your usual role.'

'It's a long story.' Livvy smiled sadly. 'And one that makes me sound like an idiot. I'll never learn.'

'Tell me about it,' Josie joked.

'Hey, I might do that.' Livvy checked her watch. 'I'm on my way to a meeting so I have to go, but I'd love to catch up.'

'Yes, give me a ring when you're free.'

'How do you fancy pasta and wine with another single – maybe tomorrow after work? If we don't arrange something, you know we'll never act on it and it would be a shame not to after all this time.'

*A*t half past five the next evening, Josie pulled into one of two allocated parking spaces Livvy had told her about. Romney Court housed eighteen owner-occupied flats in three separate blocks. Number five was the one she was looking for. She pressed the buzzer on the intercom at the door entrance. After a moment, she heard a voice come through it.

'Come on up. You'll find me on the second floor.'

She went into a small lobby area, painted a welcoming lemon colour. Unlike the flats Josie was used to visiting, the area smelled clean, inviting, and fresh.

'I'm so glad you came.'

Josie looked up to see Livvy leaning over the balcony, her black hair hanging down like a curtain.

'Welcome to my humble abode,' she smiled.

Livvy's flat was so far removed from the style of Josie's house that she instantly felt old-fashioned. With every new room Livvy showed her, she had to stop her mouth from dropping to the floor.

The first room off the light hallway was the kitchen, which had a mishmash of stainless steel and beech units standing to attention along each side wall.

She gasped when she followed Livvy into the living room; plush cream carpeting mostly covered by a woollen rug barely a shade lighter, and two cream leather settees. The only colour in the room came from the vivid orange cushions and fresh lilies arranged in a vase on the glass-topped coffee table.

'It's beautiful,' said Josie. 'And so stylish.'

'Thanks. I have to warn you that it's much better than my cooking, though.'

Livvy pushed her gently into the kitchen and reached for a tartan oven glove. 'But I am a dab hand at putting pasta into a saucepan and a bag of salad into a bowl.'

For a long time, Josie had never felt as relaxed as she did that night in Livvy's kitchen. She and Livvy had met on an induction course when they'd both started at Mitchell Housing Association and had got on well since. They'd done various jobs together before going their separate ways, and only lost touch when Livvy had gone to work in the family business.

Their conversation flowed naturally, with no awkward silences as they caught up – despite Josie being in awe of Livvy's fabulous figure and the shine on her poker straight hair. Livvy could easily pass as a supermodel with legs reaching up to her ears, in wide-legged linen trousers, a white vest and an over-sized slash-necked baby-pink jumper. She padded around in bare feet, crimson toe nails peeping out every now and then. Josie sighed. She'd love to be that elegant.

'I love it here,' Livvy said over another coffee. 'The neighbours are great, I don't have any trouble from them and they don't mind when I have the occasional party. And that intercom system is a godsend.' She grinned. 'Especially being able to screen who is visiting. Great if you want to stand a guy up – not that I've ever done that. I think it'd be good fun to try though.'

'I bet you must have men falling at your feet.'

Livvy laughed. 'I have no intention of settling down in the near future. And when I do, I'm going to be moving into his palatial palace.'

'And you shouldn't let the last one put you off either. They're not all bad.' Josie couldn't believe she was saying that after her recent time with Stewart. But she knew it was true – and she hoped she wouldn't do the same either. This time she was going to take the advice she dished out to others.

'Honey,' Livvy said in a theatrical style that had Josie practically spitting out her drink, 'there isn't anything I can't deal with. If any man chooses to mess with me, and I see his face on my intercom screen, it'll be my pleasure not to let him in.'

'Oi, you two! Wait for me, will you?'

'What does she want?' muttered Sally. She had her arm linked through Kelly's as they made their way to the bus stop at the end of their last shift for that week. 'She's crawling around you lately like she wants to bury the hatchet.'

'More like bury a knife in my back, you mean,' Kelly muttered to her.

Leah drew up beside them with a puff. 'Do you fancy sitting with me on the bus tonight? Might as well, seeing as we're on speaking terms now.'

Sally stifled a laugh; Kelly nudged her sharply with her elbow. Leah's 'speaking terms' referred to the fact that she'd let Kelly join in a whole night's conversation without any type of sarcastic dig coming from her side of the bench.

'Suppose so,' said Kelly, her heart dropping when she noticed that Jay wasn't there to pick her up again. She hadn't seen him at all since Wednesday.

The three of them continued out of the factory gates and on towards the main road.

'I want to know *any* gossip she tells you,' Sally whispered, prompting Kelly to nudge her in the ribs again before she left them at the corner of the street. To her amazement, Leah linked an arm through hers as they continued to walk.

'I'm sorry we got off to a bad start,' she began.

Kelly turned to face her, completely bewildered by her turnaround.

Leah had the decency to look shamefaced. 'I suppose I was jealous of you. Look at you – you're gorgeous. Me, I'm fat and ugly.'

'I wouldn't say –'

'It's right though, isn't it? I hated you when I saw you at the playgroup so when I walked in here and found out you were the new girl – well, I kind of flipped.'

They reached the bus shelter and sat down on the empty bench seat.

'So why have you been so nasty to me?'

'I come from a shit family so I tend to stick up for myself by lashing out.' Leah shrugged. 'But I want you to know, if it's okay with you,' she looked up at Kelly through a heavy fringe, 'I'd like us to be friends.'

Kelly smiled. She knew how much of an effort it would have been for Leah to admit she was wrong.

'You have a deal,' she said, supposing she could give her the benefit of the doubt.

Moments later, as the bus drew up beside them, Leah got on first and turned to Kelly as they sat down. 'So, tell me, what's the story with Jay Kirkwell? Have you shagged him yet or can anyone have a go?'

Kelly's smile faltered.

*A*t work on Monday morning, Josie rushed to the reception when she received an internal telephone call from Sonia, saying that Charlotte Hatfield wanted to see her. She was curious to see how she was doing. It had been three weeks since Charlotte's attack and even though she had returned to the house on her release from hospital, now she'd decided to move nearer to her family. She'd come in to return the keys to the property.

'How are the boys coping?' Josie had enquired, after she'd accepted the flowers Charlotte had bought for her. She took her into an interview cubicle for the last time. Charlotte only had baby Poppy with her: she was fast asleep in her buggy.

'They're still with my mum in Leeds.'

Josie noticed that Charlotte's hair had been brushed over the gash that Nathan had left her with. Andy had told her she'd had seven stitches. Her front tooth was missing, but at least she was smiling again. She seemed in a lighter mood now that she had made up her mind to move on.

Charlotte delved into Poppy's carry-all bag and handed Josie a bunch of keys. 'Thanks for everything you've done for me,' she said. 'I don't think I'd be here today if it wasn't for your actions – and that copper as well.'

Josie shook her head. 'It wasn't just us. You played your own part in it.'

'Maybe, but it was you who made me think about the situation. You who made me realise I would be better going back home to my mum.' She paused. 'You who made me think about pressing charges.'

Josie looked up from the paperwork she was filling in.

Charlotte nodded her head. 'I've made a statement against Nathan.'

'Great,' said Josie. 'Me too.'

Charlotte smiled. 'Thanks. Nathan's on remand now anyway. They reckon he'll go down for GBH wounding with intent, but still...'

Josie reached across the desk and squeezed Charlotte's hand. 'That's fantastic news. I'm so pleased for you – and I'm proud of you for sticking up for yourself.'

Charlotte's eyes fell on the buggy. 'It's not only me that I have to look out for. I want my kids to have a better chance in life than I did. Poor Josh won't leave my side at the moment. He's become so clingy.'

Josie felt tears well in her eyes as she remembered the little boy's haunted look as she'd pulled him into her arms. It would stay with her for a long time. She prayed that he'd forget it as he got older.

'You'll all be fine soon.' She nodded her head in encouragement.

As they stood up, Charlotte lurched forwards and gave her a hug.

'Thanks for giving me my life back,' she said. 'I know the flowers aren't much.'

Josie hugged her back, pleased that there had been a happy ending to this case, albeit in the hard way.

'Are you kidding?' she laughed. 'Do you realise the forms I'll have to fill in because you've brought me a gift? We're not allowed to take anything from tenants in case it's misconstrued as bribery. I daren't even have a toffee off some people!'

Charlotte faltered. 'But that's pathetic! You do such an amazing job. I know I couldn't do what you do.'

'Stop it, you're making me blush.' Josie cried, feeling her cheeks warming.

'It's true though,' said Charlotte. 'I reckon you should change your job title to 'guardian angel'. It's perfect for you.'

17

For Kelly, Tuesday morning came around too quickly. Jay finally sent her a text message but it was only to back up what Scott had told her over the phone – Jay was to pick him up and they were due back around eleven.

She'd been waiting for this day for three months, where she had fended for herself and got by. But life had moved on and she wasn't sure if she wanted Scott to come back and insist that it reverted to the way it had been. She knew he'd want her to stop going to work and to college, but she couldn't do that – wouldn't do that.

Jay's revelation last week had sent Kelly's mind into a spin. Their disagreement had made her confused. How could she have been so stupid? How had she not seen the signs that his feelings towards her had changed? Was it because she didn't want to?

She'd really started to enjoy Jay's company, looking forward to the end of her shifts to see if he'd be waiting to take her home. She'd loved the fact that he cared enough to pick her up most nights. She loved the fact that he played with Emily, keeping her company while she prepared supper. The truth was that she loved everything about Jay.

And without meaning to, she'd hurt him. Now she was left to wonder how he'd react when he saw her. She'd missed him so much since they'd fallen out – alarmingly so, considering that Scott was coming home and she should be wondering how she would react when she saw him.

By half past ten, she was pacing up and down in her living room. She'd cleaned the flat from top to bottom. The fridge had been stocked up with as much food as she could afford, and Emily had jumped into the bath with her and they'd washed each other's hair. Everything was perfect.

Trying to contain her nerves as Emily stood on the settee looking through the window for Jay's car, Kelly flipped through the TV channels. She stayed on ITV, as *This Morning* was in full swing.

As much as she didn't want to hear about some woman's multiple birth going wrong, she needed to switch off. She was still feeling anxious about seeing Scott. What if they didn't like each other anymore after being apart? All too soon, there was no more time to worry.

'He's here!' shouted Emily. 'Daddy's back!'

Kelly jumped at the sound of her daughter's cries of excitement and moved to the spot where Emily had vacated. She saw Jay get out of the car first and then it was Scott's turn. His eyes searched the windows for her and her heart flipped as he spotted her and waved. She raised her hand as Emily threw herself at him.

'Daddy! Daddy! Daddy!' echoed down Clarence Avenue.

For the umpteenth time, Kelly checked her appearance. Her hand was shaking as she pulled at her fringe, her brown eyes energized yet fretful. She blew out a long breath. All of a sudden, she heard someone bounding up the stairs and there he was.

Scott smiled and Kelly's knees started to wobble.

'Hello, babe,' he spoke softly.

Kelly ran into his open arms. The relief of feeling his body close to hers was too much and she began to cry. All those mixed up thoughts instantly vanished. He was home.

Scott sat her down on the settee where she clung to him. 'Neat little place,' he admired, as he looked around. 'I see you haven't lost your flair for decorating.'

Kelly wiped her eyes while Emily showed Scott all of her new books. She smiled as Scott oohed and ahhed at the pink teddy bear series that Emily still read over and over.

Jay hung back in the kitchen doorway. Out of the corner of her eye, Kelly saw him trying to cover his emotions. She couldn't look at him; she felt so ashamed.

Now that Scott was here, she felt so... so different. It was as if all the feelings she'd struggled with had never existed. Scott was home. They were a family again – but where did that leave Jay?

Kelly tried to push away the guilt but the tears fell again. Scott pulled her nearer.

'Stop your crying, woman,' he teased, kissing her lightly on the tip of her nose.

Kelly gave him a watery smile.

'Because I'm going to take my two favourite women out for a bite of grub.' Scott pulled Emily onto his knee and looked across at Jay. 'Mate, you couldn't lend us a twenty 'til I get me benefits sorted and give us a lift to The Butcher's Arms, could you, youth?'

With time on her hands now Stewart wasn't there to make so much of a mess, Josie decided to clear out the loft, something she had been putting off for years since her mum died. She also wanted to see what things Stewart had put up there and move them to the spare room for him to collect.

She still hadn't seen him since she'd asked him to leave. He kept asking to meet up but she kept saying no. It seemed too rushed, too raw. It was much easier to keep putting it off.

Besides, she didn't want to think too far ahead just yet. Even though she knew she'd never take him back and the marriage was over, at the moment all she wanted to do was get used to being alone, and enjoy that feeling first.

Once she'd sorted out a few things for the charity shop, she took them out to her car.

'Hi, Josie,' a voice spoke to her bottom as she struggled to fit everything in the boot.

Josie pulled herself up to see her neighbour's brother standing by her side. He wore stylish glasses with a thick brown frame. Behind those glasses, Josie saw a pair of friendly blue eyes.

'Oh, hi, James,' she acknowledged. 'Been to visit Louise?'

'Yes, I called in after work. She's fed me to the brim, as usual. Can I help you with anything?'

'Thanks, but I can manage,' Josie declined his offer. She smiled at him, hoping she didn't sound too ungrateful. 'How is she, by the way?'

'She's good thanks. The baby's due next weekend. I can't believe it's gone so quickly.'

'Getting used to the sound of Uncle James, then?'

James laughed. An awkward silence fell between them.

'I –' he faltered. 'Louise told me that you and Stewart have split up.'

'Oh, yes –'

'I hope you don't mind,' he interrupted. 'I wasn't prying. I was just asking, well, you know.'

'No, not at all. It's fine, I'll get over it.'

'It's over for good, then?'

She nodded.

'Well, if there's anything you ever need a hand with, please, just ask.'
'Thanks, I will.' She smiled warmly.

That awkward silence again.

'Well, I'd better –'

'I must –'

They smiled again and James went on his way. Josie watched him for a moment. That was really sweet of him to offer help if she needed it, she realised. He'd seemed quite friendly over the few times she'd spoken to him, and she got on really well with his sister.

Once inside again, she moved Stewart's belongings to the spare room before making herself a well-earned cup of tea. Although it had begun to rain slightly, she threw open the conservatory door.

Sipping her drink, she marvelled at her luck. Even though she would have to take the rough with the smooth for a while – especially when she finally decided to talk things out with Stewart – maybe this was the point where her life might start to change for the better.

She smiled again, at nothing in particular.

The next morning, Kelly lay awake in bed. By her side, she could hear Scott breathing. She could just about make out his shape in the morning light – a strange shape she wasn't certain about yet.

Yesterday had been such a traumatic day. Emily had been sick after her dinner. Kelly knew it was bound to happen. She'd been so excited, running around like a puppy. Scott had spent the best part of the day teasing his little girl, kissing her, hugging her, loving her.

Once Kelly had finally got her off to sleep, it had been her turn. Awkward fumbles had turned into practiced foreplay and they'd made love on the rug in front of the fire. It had been familiar, like old times, like Scott had never been away. But she hadn't felt comforted as they lay in each other's arms afterwards. It had felt ... strange.

She sat up on her elbow and watched him while he slept. Scott had a complexion that only had to catch a ray of sun to deepen three shades. Unlike Jay, with his designer stubble, Scott was clean-shaven. She imagined how he would look with trendy facial hair.

Right now, although his stubble made him seem darker, Scott looked pasty. He'd lost weight, she'd noticed: about a stone, he'd told her. It didn't suit him; it made him look gaunt and a little scarier. But Scott liked his food and Kelly knew the weight would return in no time. And he was as tall as Jay, so he could carry it.

She turned back towards the wall and shut her eyes tightly to stop her tears. Why couldn't she get Jay out of her mind? Why did she keep comparing him to Scott? She couldn't help but feel that she'd let them both down. Now that Scott was back, Jay might not want to look out for Kelly anymore.

If Jay didn't want to see her, maybe he could move on quicker. Then maybe she could leave her awkwardness behind and concentrate on Scott. There could be no room in her life for Jay anymore.

Scott turned over and dragged her along the bed towards him. He spooned himself into her back and she felt the stirring of his erection.

'Morning, babe,' Scott whispered sleepily before yawning. 'Or should I say, 'morning glory'?'

Pushing Jay as far to the back of her mind as she could, Kelly reached behind her.

*L*ater that morning, Kelly was sitting with Emily on the floor. Scott was lying on the settee watching the television.

'Where's that box you fetched me from Phil Matson's, Kel?' he asked all of a sudden.

'It's in Em's room, hidden in with her toys,' she replied. 'Are you going to show me what's in it now?'

'It's nothing to worry your pretty head about.' Scott began to channel hop.

'You said that it was money.'

'I was kidding.'

Kelly frowned. 'I don't want anything dodgy in this flat.'

'Kelly, Kelly, Kelly.' Scott sighed loudly as he stretched his body. 'I've only just got back, but don't fret. I'll take care of you now. It'll be business as usual soon, you'll see.'

Kelly didn't want it to be business as usual. That box had been the bane of her life for the past few weeks. At first when she'd fetched it, she'd shoved it in the kitchen cupboard under the sink, but then she'd moved it in with Emily's toys and hidden it in the cupboard over the stairs, but still it seemed to call to her.

It reminded her of when she was the same age as Emily and she'd tried to peel the Sellotape off her Christmas presents while no one was watching. There had been times when she'd felt like ripping the tape off, looking inside and replacing it, but she knew he'd find out.

'Mummy, can I go and see Dot?' said Emily.

Scott turned his head towards Kelly. 'Who?'

'Dot lives downstairs and looks after me when Mummy goes to college. She doesn't look after me when Mummy goes to work, though. I stay with Nanny then.'

Scott nearly fell to the floor in his speed to sit up.

Kelly grimaced. 'Thanks, little lady,' she muttered.

'College?' Scott frowned. 'Work? What the fuck's she talking about, Kel?'

Emily giggled and covered her mouth.

Kelly tutted. 'Don't swear in front of Emily.'

'Don't tell me what to do,' he snarled, 'and don't change the subject. What's going on?'

Kelly wondered where to start. She supposed the beginning would be the best place.

'I've been learning secretarial and office skills. I've passed my first two assignments and my course tutor says I'll be able to take the next level in summer. Then I'm –'

'Whoa!' Scott held up a hand to silence her. 'What's with all the plans? And when had you planned to tell me about them? Was I even included in them?'

Kelly looked a little sheepish. 'Of course you were. I just wanted to surprise you, make you proud of me.'

'You don't have to go to college for me to be proud of you. Jesus, I'll be the laughing stock at the pub.' Scott moved his fingers in the air as if there was a keyboard in front of him. 'Did you think of that while you were typing your stupid letters?'

'You left me alone and I was bored,' Kelly pouted. 'I've always wanted to go to college but you talked me out of it. Now I'm doing something for myself, I feel better about things. I feel like I'm contributing to society.'

'You don't need to contribute to society. I provide for you.'

'Like you've provided for me over the past three months?'

'That was low.' Scott frowned. 'I've served my time.'

Kelly sighed. 'I know, but I was scared. I didn't think I'd cope with the bills on my own. That's why I've been working at the factory, too. I got a job on the twilight shift and –'

Scott turned to Emily. 'Em, go to your room for a minute, there's a good girl.'

'But I want to stay here with you.'

'Now!'

Emily shot off the settee.

'Don't shout at her.' Kelly came to her daughter's defence. 'It's not her fault that you're annoyed with me.'

'You told me not to swear in front of her – and don't change the subject. Who the fuck have you turned into while I've been gone? Not only are you going to college behind my back, but now you tell me you're working as well?'

'What's wrong with wanting to make something of myself?' Kelly began to pile up Emily's books and put them into the bookcase. 'I used to work before I met you, remember?'

'But you've not worked since, remember?'

'Only because *you* didn't want me to.'

'That's not the point. You don't work because we can claim more in benefits.'

Kelly placed her hands on her hips. 'As a single man and woman, you mean? If it wasn't for you and your stupid ideas, we'd still be in Patrick Street, so don't you dare blame that one on me. I would have been allowed to stay if I could prove that I'd been living there for over twelve months. But you saw to that, didn't you?'

'I didn't think I'd lose my house, for fuck's sake.'

'Don't give me that. You knew exactly what you were doing – screwing the benefit agency, as normal. Well, I'm halfway out of the benefit trap now and that's the way I'm staying.'

'Over my dead body.'

'Fine – I'll arrange that, shall I?'

Kelly marched past him but he grabbed her hand. She stopped.

'I've changed since you've been away,' she replied. 'I had to, so don't blame things on me. Maybe you should try working yourself – it might keep you out of trouble.'

'You must be joking. Working doesn't feature in my life plan.'

'I'm not stopping.'

'But you don't need to work now. I told you, I'll provide for you, like I used to. It was good enough before I was nicked. Besides, what am I going to do when you're not here?'

'That's simple. You can clean up; do the washing, a little ironing. Run the Hoover round, that kind of thing. Think of it as an investment for our future together.'

It was Scott's turn to sigh, but he did it more dramatically. 'Fuck, I've spent three months locked up. It's been torture without you, but if I knew I was coming back to this I'd rather have stayed inside.'

Suddenly, Kelly felt accountable. She'd expected a little griping while they got used to each other again, but Scott had only been back for a night and already she was nagging.

Seeing the distressed look on her face, Scott drew her into his arms. 'I've missed you, babe,' he told her. 'Don't let's row anymore.'

18

Because of that argument, Kelly's weekend had been hard to get through. She felt like she was tiptoeing on hot coals, trying to get used to having Scott around again. In such a short space of time, everything had changed so much.

After their disagreement on Saturday morning, Scott had gone on all day about her giving up her job at Miles's Factory. He'd sulked more than she would have expected Emily to at her age, creating a particularly charged atmosphere.

The day had been finished for her when he told her he'd invited Jay around for a takeaway on Saturday night. She'd feigned a headache at ten thirty, leaving the two of them to enjoy the rest of the bloodthirsty film they were watching. As ever, Scott seemed too pre-occupied with himself to notice the tense atmosphere between Jay and Kelly.

Sunday lunch had been a solemn affair at her mum's house. Neither of her parents were pleased that Scott had returned to Kelly's life, so the atmosphere was dicey. Things got decidedly worse when, after her dad questioned what prison life had been like, Scott had been only too happy to talk it up.

Kelly heard him sneering about one of the inmates who'd been slashed several times across his back during his first month there. With horror, she realised that he was bragging about his spell behind bars as if he had no problem returning.

After checking with her mum that it would be okay to leave Emily with her rather than with Scott when she was at work, they walked home. Within an hour, Scott's phone rang and he'd gone out to meet some guys in the pub, promising that it was only a little bit of business that he needed to sort out.

Ten minutes after he'd gone, Kelly and Emily sat together on the settee. They were reading the final pages of *Cinderella*.

'Mummy, will Daddy go away again soon?'

Kelly looked down into Emily's innocent brown eyes. She tried to hug away her worries. 'Of course he won't, monster.'

'I like it better when there's you and me.'

Kelly gulped away the tears threatening to fall and quickly turned to the next page of the book.

'Never mind, honey,' she said. 'I'm sure things will settle down again soon.'

Josie had been dreading Monday morning at work because she had an eviction lined up for ten o'clock. Philip Matson hadn't paid any money towards his rent since she'd last warned him on the day that Charlotte Hatfield had clung to life and, although the judge had been lenient that month, she wouldn't be this month when she realised that he hadn't kept to his arrangement again.

The first thing she did when she got to her desk was check that all the necessary paperwork had been completed. The bailiffs and the police had been booked and Doug was on standby to accompany her if the police were called away at the last minute – not that that was much comfort.

The joiner had been booked to change the locks if necessary, which she was sure would be the case. She knew Philip wouldn't have surrendered his keys.

The next thing was a cup of tea.

'Mondays always come around too soon, don't they?' Debbie remarked as she joined Josie and Craig in the tiny staff room. 'It doesn't seem a minute since we were leaving on Friday night.'

'My head certainly thinks so,' said Craig, rubbing at his left temple. 'I haven't recovered from Friday night yet, never mind Saturday and Sunday.'

'Tell me about it.' Josie shoved her lunch box into the overloaded fridge. 'Every neighbour and his dog seem to have rung up to complain about something or other and we've only been open for ten minutes. I'm sure our tenants see me as some kind of solicitor, the matters they think I'm responsible for.' She paused and turned to Debbie. 'I might have an eviction later this morning. Do you fancy coming with me?'

'Ooh, yeah.' Debbie's eyes lit up. 'Anything to get out of here for an hour or so.'

'I'll warn you now, though. Things might get a bit rough if the tenant shows up.'

'Rather you than me,' said Craig. He chinked his spoon on the side of his mug before chucking it into the sink. 'Those people out there are rough.'

'I can handle them,' said Debbie. 'Besides, there's nothing more I like than a good mur-der,' she added, *Taggart*-style.

Josie grinned. The young woman standing in front of her had the makings of a good officer when the opportunity arose.

Half an hour later, the call had been made and the curtains had started to twitch in Bernard Place. Their vehicles took up most of the tiny cul-de-sac: Josie's car, the marked Ford Focus belonging to the police, Paul the bailiff's Range Rover and the work van belonging to one of the joiners, bearing the Mitchell Housing Association logo along each side.

Josie knocked loudly twice on the front door before banging on the living room window three times.

'I bet he didn't turn up at court.' She peered through the letter box into an empty hallway. 'I can hear his dogs and there's no sign of any packing. He thinks the eviction isn't going to happen. Most people assume it's an empty threat.'

'What do we do now?' asked Debbie.

Josie gave the joiner the go ahead, as he stood waiting with his drill. 'Remove the lock. If he's in there, he'll be out once he hears that.'

Josie and Debbie sat on the wall chatting to Paul and PC Mark White while the joiner did his job. Although Mark was fairly new to the force, Josie had known Paul for eight years. She knew that his eldest daughter had gone to university and was doing extremely well. She knew that his son was getting married in October. But before she learned about all the things that had gone wrong so far in the planning, she was distracted by a shout as Philip finally showed up.

Josie turned to Debbie. 'Watch out for yourself. He's likely to kick off, so stay out of the way if anything happens.'

'Be careful,' said Debbie.

'Don't worry about me. This is bound to be the last time I'll have to deal with him anyway. The council are hardly likely to give him a place if we've evicted him for non-payment of his rent.'

Debbie stayed seated on the wall. Josie and Mark met Philip halfway up the path.

'Hello, Philip,' said Josie. 'Glad you could make it.'

Philip looked first at the joiner as he drilled through the lock of his front door, then back to Josie.

'What the fuck are you doing?'

What the fuck does it look like, Josie wanted to reply. Instead she kept calm. 'We're evicting you,' she said. 'I told you this would happen if –'

'You can't do this, you bitch.'

'Whoa there, cowboy, watch your language.' Mark held Philip at arm's length as he moved nearer to Josie. Paul handed Philip a copy of the eviction notice, which he promptly screwed into a ball and threw to the floor.

Even though Josie had taken a step backwards, she tried not to show concern. Philip was a troublemaker, but he seemed to be all mouth and empty threats, by all accounts. She knew the residents of Bernard Place would be glad to see the back of him.

'I warned you enough times,' Josie told him as she regained her composure.

'But... all my stuff... my dogs are still inside.'

'Then you'll have to remove them. I need vacant possession by the end of the day.'

Philip's eyes widened in disbelief. 'But I've got nowhere to go.'

Josie sighed. Evictions were always the worst part of her job, even if it was a low life such as Philip.

She should have been able to get through to him – show proof of income or else your housing benefits will be stopped. She should have carried out more than the fortnightly visits she'd made over the past few months, insisting that he brought the items she needed to the office, but there wasn't time to keep on chasing. Philip had hardly ever been at home for any of her pre-arranged visits *and* hadn't contacted her regarding any of her letters. Still, Josie felt like she had failed.

'I can give you until the end of the day,' she repeated. A battle of wills began as the two of them locked eyes.

Josie held out her hand. 'There's no going back now. If you give me the keys, we can stop any more damage and you can start to clear out your stuff.'

Once inside the property, Josie felt more at ease. The joiner and the Paul had left, their work finished. Philip used his mobile, trying to rally some friends to help him. Mark checked the rooms for stolen goods and Debbie took photographs with a digital camera.

'I still can't believe that tenants make-up imaginary items so that they can claim against the association,' she said, when Josie came into the living room.

'It's true, which is why, apart from the obvious safety reasons, there has to be at least two officers present at any eviction. Then they can't say we've nicked their brand-new widescreen TV, etcetera.'

Philip finished his call. 'I've got a mate coming over with a van. He'll help me move my stuff, though I don't know where the fuck it's all going to go.' He stared at Josie before pushing past them both into the kitchen.

'The steel doors will be fitted no later than three thirty,' Josie shouted after him. 'I'll leave you to sort things out and come back then.'

Desperate for fresh air, Josie followed Debbie out.

'Has he calmed down any?' Paul asked.

'Enough to get his arse into gear.'

'What if he can't do it all by this afternoon?'

'We'll let him in again by arrangement, but one of us will have to stay with him. We give tenants twenty-eight days to remove their belongings. If they don't, we clear it for them. It's such a shame to see good furniture go to waste, but there you have –'

'About bloody time you got rid of that scummy bastard,' a voice shouted from across the street. The unmistakable bubble of Mrs Myatt leaning on her garden gate opposite them assaulted their eyes. 'He's been causing trouble here since the day he moved in,' she continued. 'I can't believe it took you so long to get rid of him.'

'We'd get rid of a lot more people if we could,' Debbie told her. 'Our jobs aren't as easy as they seem.'

'Not that easy?' Mrs Myatt huffed and pointed to her overgrown lawn. 'If you stopped pestering people about keeping their gardens in pristine condition, you'd have plenty of time to do the important things. I'm surprised at you, Josie Mellor. I always thought you had more about you, never mind letting the likes of him get the better of you.'

Josie felt anger rising within her. 'Mrs Myatt,' she yelled across the cul-de-sac, 'why don't you –'

'Keep an eye on the situation here,' Debbie interrupted, before Josie could shout out the rest of the damning sentence, 'and ring us if anything kicks off before we call back at three-thirty?'

Mrs Myatt nodded and went inside with a slam of her front door.

'Stupid bitch. And you want to be a housing officer?' Josie shook her head in wonder.

After dropping Debbie back at the office, Josie texted Kelly to check if she was home – and that Scott wasn't.

'I'm not stopping,' she explained as she stood on the doorstep. 'I've got some books for Emily. Is she home?'

'No, she's gone to town with my mum. That girl has more of a social life than me.'

'How are things going?' Josie asked tentatively. 'I wanted to check that you were okay but I haven't liked to call unannounced since Scott's release from prison.'

Kelly shrugged. 'I suppose it'll take time to adjust again.'

A silence followed and Josie took this as her cue not to continue. She opened a bag and pulled out the first book she came to. It still tugged at her heartstrings to give them away, but she knew they were going to a good home.

'Aw.' She ran a finger over the cover. 'Enid Blyton was my favourite author. I've always wanted to write a book, especially about my job. People wouldn't believe what goes on here on the Mitchell Estate.'

'Got anything in there for me?' Kelly picked up another book. *Five go to Dorset*.

'Not unless you're seven. Some of them are going to be too old for now but she'll grow into them. And, I hope, grow to love them like I did.'

Kelly flicked through the pages. A photograph dropped onto the floor. Josie picked it up and pulled a face.

'One of my wedding photos.' She handed it to Kelly. 'Eek, I look so scared.'

Kelly looked at the photo of Josie and her husband standing on the steps of the register office. Josie looked like a child next to him. She was right, she did look scared. Then Kelly drew it nearer. She recognised the man.

'I know him.'

'Yes, you probably do,' nodded Josie. 'He works at Miles's Factory too. Do you remember me telling you? We've – we've split up recently.'

'Oh, I'm sorry.'

'No, don't be.' Josie smiled half-heartedly. 'There was nothing there to miss, if I'm honest. I'll get over it.'

'Josie. I –'

'Christ on a bike,' Josie interrupted, noticing the time. 'I have to go – I'll catch you later in the week. Bye.'

Kelly closed the door and made her way back up the stairs. Already she was searching her memory, running through previous conversations with Josie. Hadn't she said that they'd both lost their parents?

So that left one question: why did the men at work call the man in the photograph 'Mummy's Boy'?

19

At half past two, Josie was sorting out the eviction paperwork when she received a phone call to say that Stewart was in the main reception asking for her. A little bit taken aback, she rushed up to see him, but at the sight of him, she felt anger tear through her. She pointed to an interview cubicle and Stewart followed her in.

'I came to see how you were,' he said. 'I haven't seen you since...'

'Since you punched me in the face?'

'Sorry.' Stewart lowered his eyes for a moment. 'I got it into my head that you were seeing someone else.'

'So you thought you'd spy on me?'

'I was worried about you.'

'I don't think you'll ever worry about anyone other than yourself. And I can't see why you're so bothered. You haven't really liked living with me for a while now, have you?'

Stewart shrugged like a spoiled child.

'You've wanted out of this marriage for ages,' Josie continued into the silence that followed. 'So I've given you the opportunity. Now tell me the real reason that you're here.'

'What do you mean?'

'What do you want, Stewart?'

'I – I want to know what you're doing about the house.'

'My house?'

Stewart looked uncomfortable. 'I paid towards it too.'

355

The penny clicked and Josie gasped. 'You've come here to talk money?'

'I –'

'The house belongs to me. It was left to me by my mother. Granted, you paid towards its keep in the early years of our marriage, but you've hardly given anything towards the bills lately. I know you may be entitled to something – I'm not that heartless – but I'll be damned if you think you're getting thousands from me.'

'I'm entitled to half.'

'Oh, no you're not,' Josie raged. She lowered her voice before continuing. 'We need to talk but now isn't the time. I can meet you tonight in The Cat and Fiddle.'

'I'll come to the house.'

'No, you won't.'

'But –'

'I have work to do. I'll meet you in the pub later – six o'clock, take it or leave it.'

Josie let out a breath as she watched Stewart walk away. Tears filled her eyes and her hands began to shake uncontrollably. How dare he show up unannounced? She didn't like mixing her home life with her working days and he knew that.

She sat down for a moment to calm herself. After what they'd discussed, she felt totally let down. Seeing him now made her realise that she had no feelings left for him. She didn't love him; she didn't even like him anymore. Especially when it seemed he was more interested in the house than her welfare.

Finally, she stood up. She couldn't let him get away with treating her like this. If Stewart thought for a minute she was willing to bargain with him, he had another thing coming.

At ten to three, Kelly thought she'd given Scott enough time to return home. He'd promised to look after Emily that evening but, no sooner had he walked back into her life, the meetings he always used to go to had started up again. He'd been gone since he'd taken a phone call at eleven that morning.

Kelly grabbed her keys. 'Come on, Em. Let's see if Dot's in. Would you mind staying with her while I go to work, just for today?'

The grateful look on her daughter's face was enough to make Kelly blink away tears. Why had she thought she could leave Emily with Scott as soon as he returned? She'd known things were going to be rough while they got reacquainted but she hadn't thought they would be *this* rough. It was like living with a different person.

Or maybe he'd always been like this and she'd never noticed.

As she was about to fly down the stairs, Kelly heard the key turn in the door.

'I think she's gone,' she heard Scott say. Putting a finger over her lips, Kelly pulled Emily into the bathroom and quietly closed the door.

'Won't she go mental if you keep them in here?' someone else spoke. Kelly frowned, vaguely recognising the voice.

'She doesn't have any choice.' The bathroom door flew open. Scott freaked when he saw them both.

'What the fuck –'

'I might ask you the same thing.' Kelly pointed to the tank he was holding. 'What is that?'

Emily peeped out from behind Kelly's legs. She let out an ear-piercing scream. 'Spiders! Mummy, I hate spiders!'

'Stop your whining.' Scott placed the tank of creepy crawlies into the bath. 'They won't hurt you – well, most of them won't.'

Kelly stared at the man standing behind Scott. It was that Matson guy she'd fetched Scott's parcel from.

'Get them out of here,' she said, at the same time trying to console Emily by pulling her close.

'It's only for a few days. Since that bitch of a housing officer,' Scott turned towards Kelly with a sneer, 'you know, the one you're so friendly with – chucked him out of his house, he's nowhere to put them.'

'They can't stay in here.'

Emily was sniffling uncontrollably now.

'Em, don't be a baby.' Scott delved into the tank, picked up a spider and thrust it into her face. Emily turned away and screamed again. He laughed at her look of dismay.

'Grow up, Scott,' Kelly cried. 'She's frightened, for God's sake. Are you too bloody stupid to see that?'

'But where else can they go?'

'If they must stay, put them in the bin store outside. The key's hanging up in the kitchen.' Kelly pushed past them. Emily tightened her gip on her hand. 'They'd better not be in here when I get home.'

'Okay, okay. Keep your knickers on.' Scott knew when he was beat. 'I'll put them outside.'

Kelly managed to get down the stairs with Emily still clinging to her. She checked her watch after she'd pressed the tinny bell on Dot's doorframe. It was nearing quarter past three; she was going to be late for work now.

'One minute.'

Kelly's shoulders drooped, thankful for small mercies. At least Dot could keep an eye on Scott to see if anything else unpleasant found its way into her bathroom. God knows what that creepy guy had with him.

'I'm beginning to wish I'd kept hold of Patrick Street,' Scott muttered as he pushed past her rudely.

'That's funny,' Kelly replied sharply. 'So am I.'

Josie turned the dial up on the shower and stepped under the hot water, hoping to wash her troubles down the plughole along with the water. Sighing loudly, she stood for what seemed like an age as she recalled the last few hours.

What a day. When Philip Matson had eventually vacated the property, he'd also ripped the washing machine away from the wall, leaving damaged pipework and water pouring everywhere. Josie had had to call out the emergency plumber. Then there had been the meeting with Stewart that never was, as he hadn't turned up at The Cat and Fiddle. She hoped he'd come to his senses, that he wouldn't turn up unannounced again.

Luckily for her, she'd returned the favour and invited Livvy for something to eat that evening. She was glad to have some company.

'He's a right prick, messing you about like that,' Livvy said, as they sat down in the living room. 'What are you going to do now?'

'I'm not sure.' Josie handed her a glass of red wine. 'It's early days yet. I bet he thinks I won't be able to hack it in the real world without him.'

'Why don't you call his bluff and put the house up for sale?'

Josie stopped with the glass near her lips. 'I don't get you.'

Livvy shrugged. 'Let him know that you're moving on regardless.'

'But I don't want to sell it.'

'I'm not saying that you have to, but it might make him realise that you're serious about not taking him back. You won't change your mind about that, will you?'

Josie shook her head. It had been a shock when Stewart had lashed out at her, but even before that she'd known the marriage was dead on its feet. There was no point going back to that.

'Good, it will give him something to worry about for a change.'

But Josie wasn't sure that Stewart would worry about that. She assumed he'd think she was putting the house on the market so that she could pay him his half when it sold. However, if it gave her a bit of time and kept him at bay for a while, she would certainly give it some thought.

'I'll definitely think about it.'

She went to check on the food and came back a few minutes later to find Livvy staring into space. Livvy had been reluctant to open up the first time they'd met – maybe she needed to talk now.

'Want to tell me what's weighing you down?' she asked.

Livvy sighed. 'You remember I left the association to work with my family?'

'Yes, I do.' Libby's parents owned their own franchise of recruitment agencies. 'I thought you were doing well. Did something go wrong?'

'Leyton Goldstraw.'

'Ah.' Josie pulled her legs up beside her. 'A man.'

'I'd been going out with him for six months. My parents and my brother and sister never took to him. They didn't like the way he pestered me for money all the time. So, after one almighty row, I quit.'

'You left the family business?'

Livvy shrugged. 'It was hard, I know, but they were never going to approve. I would have thought twice about it, had I known how Leyton would react.'

'Oh?'

'He was far from impressed. My brother and sister had both been given their own branches to run and, being the youngest, I was in line for mine. My dad had picked out the office space and was just about to sign the lease on the building when we fell out.

'I managed to find work with an agency before getting back on at head office but the money was nowhere near what I'd been earning before. And then, over the next year, Leyton bled me dry.' Livvy pushed her long hair behind her ears and sighed. 'I was a fool, Josie. I loaned him money towards starting his own business, yet his promises to pay me back never materialised. Eventually he just upped and left, leaving me with all his debts. I couldn't face asking my parents to help me out because I felt so humiliated.'

'I don't believe it.' Josie felt angry about Livvy's quandary. It never failed to amaze her just how similar people were. No matter what beginnings they'd had in life, it only took one event to turn everything upside down. 'So what did you do? I mean, they would have been okay with you, surely?'

'Yes, without a doubt I know they would have bailed me out. But me, being pig-headed Livvy, carried on with life as I did before – a life I could no longer afford, I hasten to add. I don't go out much now but when I do, I still have to spend to keep everyone in the dark.

'At least the argument with my family blew over almost immediately and I still see them regularly. We're really close and I like that. They do still think I'm seeing Leyton, though.'

'What?' Josie was surprised. 'You haven't told them he's gone?'

Livvy shook her head. 'Maybe I hate the words 'I told you so'. But they'd be right.'

'And what about the flat? Are you behind on your rent?'

Livvy shook her head again. 'I lease it from my parents. I pay hardly anything so I've managed to keep up with those payments. It's the other things I'm having trouble with, like my credit cards and the instalments on my car. I can't let them take away my Bessie.'

'I can help, if you like?' Josie volunteered. 'It's part of my job to offer debt advice.'

'If you can sort me out, I'd be eternally grateful.' Livvy laughed, but it was tinged with sadness.

'Okay.' Josie thought it was time to throw in a compromise. 'Providing you tell your parents about Leyton.'

Livvy paused before speaking. 'Okay, providing you at least think about putting the house up for sale.'

'I'm not sure. I'm not usually any kind of risk taker. I'm more your average Joe, anything for a quiet existence. Does that make sense?'

Livvy nodded slightly. 'It does in a strange kind of way. I think what you're trying to say is that you feel trapped living here. Like a bird with clipped wings – never knowing what's out there, but you're too frightened to take a gamble.'

Josie was impressed. 'Wow. You have me down to a tee. I think I've fused my home life with my job. I always feel the need to be looking after someone.'

'Can't you specialise in that for your work?'

Josie wasn't quite sure what she was getting at. 'My job is specialised,' she said.

'I mean, more dedicated to one subject. You seem good with people. You coaxed all that out of me.' Livvy referred to their earlier conversation. 'I've never told anyone about my debt problem, but you're so easy to talk to. You listen and you don't judge. That's the difference.'

'You won't thank me when I cut up your credit cards,' Josie said with a wicked grin.

Livvy shook her head. 'No I won't, but it has to be done.'

'Right then, you go and get them – all of them – and I'll get the scissors.'

'What?' Livvy shuddered. 'Right now? Can't we do it later?'

Josie raised her eyebrows. 'You see? I said you'd hate me.'

*D*espite worrying what Scott was getting up to at the flat without her there, the photograph of Stewart was still playing on Kelly's mind.

Behind a Closed Door

During her tea break that evening, she searched out one particular person in the staff canteen.

'Hey, Robbie,' she pulled out a chair and sat down opposite him, giving him her best smile. 'Where's your friend tonight?'

'You mean Phil? He's on the day shift.'

Kelly shook her head. 'Not him. The one they call Mummy's Boy?'

'You're interested in Mummy's Boy?' Robbie frowned. 'What the fuck for? He's a boring bastard, just a hanger-onna.'

'I'm curious to know where his nickname came from, that's all.'

'It's because he's thirty-nine and still lives with his mum.'

Kelly tried to hide her surprise as she ripped open her chocolate. The guy on the photo was definitely Josie's husband, yet here at work it seemed he was a single man living at home with his mum. It didn't make sense.

Robbie reached across the table and pinched the second bar. She slapped his fingers and he dropped it, moving back and folding his arms.

'So what's his real name?' she asked.

'What's with all the questions?'

Kelly waved to get Sally's attention as she came into the room. She slid across the chocolate that Robbie coveted. He took a bite before continuing.

'All the time he's worked here, no one's ever seen him with a woman. That's not to say that he's gay: no one's seen him with a bloke either. All we could find out was that he's never been married, doesn't go out, he just stays at home. I reckon he's too tight to waste money renting or buying anywhere else.'

'What are you doing with the Robster here?' Sally asked as she took the seat next to her friend.

'She wants to know about Mummy's Boy,' Robbie explained. 'I've just been filling her in.'

'I could have told you about him if you'd asked. I've worked here so long I know everything there is to know.'

'They say he'll be loaded when his old woman meets the grim reaper,' Robbie continued, not one to be dismissed.

'Who will?' queried Sally.

Robbie sighed in exasperation. 'Mummy's Boy.'

'Oh,' Sally nodded in recognition. 'You mean Stewart Mellor.'

361

20

The following week, Emily had gone to the shops with Dot, and Kelly had a rare chance to put her feet up and drink her coffee. Scott – well, he'd gone out about an hour ago; Kelly had no idea where to, but she was eternally grateful that he was out from under her feet.

For the past two hours she'd been cleaning. She'd forgotten how untidy Scott was. He'd leave the mug wherever he finished with it, he'd drop soggy towels over the side of the bath thinking they'd miraculously dry themselves and last night she'd come into a tip when she'd eventually got home from work.

It was obvious that someone else had visited. Two of every dirty dish were stacked in the kitchen sink and a pile of empty cans shoved into the pedal bin. Most probably it would have been Philip Matson: Jay would have tidied up.

Needing some unbiased company, she texted Josie to let her know the kettle was on if she was free.

Her shoulders sagged spectacularly. Was it really only a week since Scott had been released? It seemed like a lifetime already – and as if nothing had changed. Life for Scott had gone back to normal, just in another place.

The fiasco with the spiders had caused another problem. This morning, Emily wouldn't take a bath until Kelly had checked every single inch of the bathroom while she stood on the threshold of the door. In her mind, she could still hear Scott's teasing laughter. How could he taunt a four-year-old about her fear of spiders when there were lots of adults who felt the same way?

What annoyed Kelly most was the fact that Scott had agreed to look after

Emily while she went to work, yet he'd waited until he thought she'd be gone and sneaked into the flat. Yes, sneaked, she realised, that's what he'd done.

But this was *her* flat; *her* name on the tenancy agreement. Was he too stupid to think that nothing would change while he was inside? Because she had – she'd changed into a responsible adult. She went to college and she held down a part-time job. She was still reliant on some benefits, but she was enjoying herself as she learned new skills and, once she managed to get a full-time job, she'd be laughing.

Or rather Kelly would be, if it weren't for one thing. She missed Jay. Jay had made her smile, made her forget all her troubles, made her feel like she could conquer the world. Was she ever going to think rationally again?

Her mobile phone beeped, breaking into her melancholy mood. With Josie on her way, she went to unlock the front door.

'I was only around the corner when I got your message,' Josie said. 'I have a few phone calls to make during my lunch break so I only have time for a quick cuppa, if that's okay?'

Kelly smiled, still marvelling at their unlikely friendship.

'So how are you getting on now?' Josie asked, once Kelly had made coffee.

Kelly took a sip of her drink. 'Okay, I suppose,' she replied.

'What about Emily? Is she coping?'

'She seems okay,' Kelly fibbed, but then thought better of it. 'Actually, she's not okay. At first she was all over him, Daddy's back, but now that the novelty's worn off, she wants to be with me all the time. If I leave the room, she's right behind me. Even if I'm only popping to the loo, she'll go and fetch a toy from her bedroom and wait for me in the hallway.'

'I suppose that's to be expected,' Josie sympathised. 'But hopefully she'll get used to having him around again.'

'I'm not so sure. Before he went inside, they used to get on great. Since he's come back, it's as if he doesn't want to know her – nor me, really. He's continually having a go at me for giving up on Patrick Street. He moans at every opportunity: when I go to work, when I get back from work, when I go to college, when I get back from college. In fact, he's turned into a right nag. I suppose I didn't think it would be this hard.'

'It might not be,' Josie tried to reassure her. 'This time next week you could be feeling much better about things.'

'I know, yet… maybe I hadn't realised how much time I was already spending on my own before he was locked up. Maybe I put him on a pedestal while he wasn't here because I was lonely and not because I missed him. I don't – I don't want to live like this anymore.'

'Do you think the relationship was over before he was sent to prison?' Josie probed gently.

Kelly nodded. 'Possibly. And now I feel trapped. Because he gave up Patrick Street –'

'Lost it, more like.'

'He's got nowhere else to go. I can't abandon him.'

'No one's asking you to. Despite the fact that I think he's a loser, maybe you need to give yourself time to adjust. If everything is still iffy after another couple of weeks, then that'll be the time to do something about it.'

With the sound of the radio playing in the background, they finished their drinks in a comfortable silence. Josie looked over at Kelly, wishing she could do more for her but knowing that it was up to her what happened next. Kelly had to make her own decision; she wasn't going to influence her in any way.

'How are you doing at college?' Kelly asked.

'I'm finding it hard to fit in,' Josie grimaced. 'I've already missed two weeks but I only have a few sessions left. I'll be back on track soon – though that's only an introduction to counselling. If I want to take it further I have to commit myself to four and half hours a week and it's double the length of this course. I need to think about it – but I would like to go further with it. What about you? Passed any more assignments lately?'

Kelly smiled for the first time that morning. 'Yes, another two. I've only got two more to do and I've finished the course.'

'And then?'

Kelly sighed. 'I haven't got a clue what's going to happen. And I'm not sure I even want to think about it.'

Over the next two weeks, life changed dramatically for Josie and Kelly. Every evening as Josie got home from work, she wondered if she would get a letter from Stewart, or even a solicitor acting on his behalf, but there was nothing. Every night as Kelly got home, she let herself into the flat with a dread in her heart, knowing full well that it would be in a mess and that she'd have to prepare her own supper. That was if Scott was even at home: already he'd slipped into his old routine, often coming home after midnight.

Every day Josie got used to her freedom, being able to go out with friends whenever she liked.

Every day, Kelly missed her times with Jay, finding out that it hurt more as time went on. She'd only seen him twice since Scott had come home.

Every morning that Josie woke up alone, Kelly awoke with trepidation, sharing the bed with a loser.

The old Josie had gone; the old Kelly had gone. Josie didn't want to be with Stewart; Kelly didn't want to be with Scott.

Little did these two women realise when their friendship evolved that they would eventually wish for the same things to happen in their lives.

'Hey, Kelly. Wait up!'

Kelly turned to see Lynsey, Jay's sister, wobbling towards her across Vincent Square from the direction of the Post Office. She pushed along a buggy, a child either side of her holding onto the handles. It was Monday, benefit collection day for most of the residents of the Mitchell Estate.

Kelly hadn't seen Lynsey in ages. As ever, she was devoid of make-up, her garish blonde hair tied off her face in a severe ponytail. The warmer weather always brought out strange sights on the Mitchell Estate and Lynsey was no exception. Wearing the shortest denim skirt with a skimpy vest, there was flesh oozing out at every opportunity. But was it still fashionable to have your belly hanging over your waistband? Kelly hid her look of astonishment as she grasped the fact that Lynsey was pregnant.

'Hiya, Lynsey, how are you doing?' Kelly greeted her with a smile.

Lynsey ran a hand over her bulging stomach. 'Up the duff again by the same useless prick that got me pregnant with the first one. You'd think I had learnt my lesson by now. How about you? I heard Scott's out.'

'Yeah, he is.'

Emily tugged at Kelly's hand as Lynsey's two boys ran towards the bench that sat forlornly in what was meant to be a garden area in the middle of the square. Kelly reached in her handbag for the sweets she'd bought earlier.

'Share them out,' she shouted after Emily's little figure as she raced after them.

'It takes some getting used to,' Lynsey added knowingly. 'My Steve has gone down again. He's been ringing cars, got six months – left me holding the baby.' She roared with laughter at her joke. 'Literally!'

Kelly tried to keep her facial expressions impartial. Deep inside she was horrified. There was no way she was sticking around if Scott got sent to prison for the second time.

'Things seem to be getting back to normal,' she decided to say.

In a sad way, it was true. Kelly cast her mind back to yesterday as she watched Emily busy handing out sweets to the boys. Sunday evening, one of only two nights off that she had, and Scott had disappeared again. He'd eaten his tea, grabbed his keys and said he was going to see a man about a dog.

No amount of nagging had stopped him. He'd gone out regardless, coming back after midnight when she'd been lying awake in bed. He'd tried to cuddle up to her but the smell of ale had repulsed her and he'd finally got the message.

'Kieran. Gerrof that wall. You'll break your bleeding neck if you fall!' Lynsey screeched at the top of her voice. She turned back to Kelly. 'You should think about dropping another one.'

Kelly managed to stop her head shaking from side to side. Emily was always pleading for a little sister, but there were no plans on her behalf to increase the family.

'How's Jay?' she asked, to change the subject.

Lynsey threw a thumb over her sunburned shoulder towards the car park. 'Ask him yourself, he's over there waiting for us. He might cheer up when he sees you. Your name always did make his eyes sparkle. He's been a right moody bastard lately, don't know what's got into him. Unless it's something to do with that bird he's been seeing. Frankly, you'd think a few dates would cheer him up.'

'Anyone we know?' Kelly tried to sound casual.

Before Lynsey could reply, the boys came rushing over and Emily followed shortly afterwards.

'Mummy, can we go home now?' she wanted to know.

Lynsey turned the buggy around and started to walk towards the car park. 'Come over with me,' she said. 'Jay will give you a lift.'

Kelly shook her head but it was too late. Lynsey was away before she had time to decline. Quickly, she rubbed a finger underneath both eyes to remove any trace of rogue mascara.

By the time she got to the car, Lynsey was collapsing the buggy and had the baby shoved precariously under her arm as she ushered the boys into the back seats.

'Taxi for Winterton?' Jay said with a smile that made Kelly's insides do something weird. She noticed his sideburns were slightly longer and his hair a little shorter.

Jay clucked Emily under the chin as she hung onto the open window. 'Can we come with you, Jay?' she asked.

'Of course you can, monster, but you'll have to sit on your mum's knee until we drop the kids off.' Jay looked up at Kelly. 'It's only a couple of streets, though. She'll be okay.'

'Kelly's been asking how you are,' Lynsey informed her brother as he reversed out of the parking space once they were all in. 'I told her I've fixed you up and you don't seem very grateful.' She leaned forwards and nudged Jay's shoulder. 'Lisa's really nice. She'll do until something better comes along, won't she?'

Behind a Closed Door

'Although I'm grateful for your help, little sis,' Jay flicked his eyes upwards towards the rear mirror, 'I'm quite capable of finding my own dates, thanks very much.'

'But you've been moping around for ages.'

'I haven't.'

'You have.' Lynsey nudged Kelly this time. 'Want me to tell you what I think? I think someone we don't know about has broken his heart.'

'Lynsey,' Jay cried. 'Do us a favour and shut your mouth.'

'You've only got yourself to blame. You won't tell me what's going on.'

Once the tribe had been dropped off, it was only a few minutes' drive to Clarence Avenue. Almost immediately, the friendly banter that had been present disappeared.

Jay turned the radio up to drown out their silence and Kelly concentrated on looking at the passing gardens. Emily was busy singing to some rapper song. Kelly felt slightly alarmed that she knew most of the words.

'So how are tricks?' Jay spoke first.

'Strange,' Kelly admitted. 'I feel like I've been taken over by an alien.'

Jay eyed her with a frown.

'I mean... it's...' She sighed. How could she explain to Jay, of all people, that she couldn't get used to having Scott around again? 'I mean that it's weird. I suppose things will settle down eventually.'

Jay nodded. 'I thought you seemed low. You don't seem your usual sparkly self.'

Another silence fell between them. Kelly wound down the window to let in some air but it wasn't simply the sun that was making her feel warm. Here she was talking to a man who two weeks previous had told her that he loved her and then picked up his best mate from prison. A man who she now couldn't get off her mind; a man, she was mortified to grasp, who had moved on to someone else to forget her.

Kelly wanted to ask him everything about this new woman. She wanted to know what she looked like, how old she was. Did she have any children? Did she live locally?

Did he share pizzas with her and laugh at episodes of *Dad's Army*? She wanted to know if they had the same tastes in music; if she made him smile.

Kelly wanted to know everything, but she wasn't going to ask – although she couldn't resist asking one question. She kept her tone as even as a friend to a friend would.

'So, this woman you're dating, is she nice?'

'You mean Lisa?' Jay laughed. 'That's my baby sister's way of saying I'm a saddo. As if I'd want to be with anyone at the moment. She's okay, I suppose, but I need to sort my head out first.'

Kelly studied the gardens again, not knowing if she was relieved or jealous. Either way, she had no right to be feeling like that. She was going home to Scott.

Jay pulled up outside the flat and got out of the car.

'Coffee?' Kelly checked her watch to see that it was almost eleven o' clock. 'Scott will probably still be in bed though, but if you come in he's bound to get up.'

Jay shook his head. 'I'd better not. I'm...'

Emily rushed around and threw herself at his legs. 'I miss you.' She squeezed Jay as hard as she could.

Jay picked her up and hugged her back. 'I miss you too, my little angel. I hope you're looking after your mum.'

'When are you coming to see us again?'

Jay glanced at Kelly long enough for her heart to skip a beat.

'Jay's a busy man,' she told her. 'He can't keep calling on us every two minutes.'

Emily shrugged herself down Jay's body. She tugged down her red T-shirt that had risen up to expose her midriff. 'He used to,' she said with a sulk.

As Jay ruffled Emily's hair, Kelly gathered up her shopping bags. 'Come on, Em.' She held out a hand.

Emily huffed. Watching her reach up to Jay for a goodbye kiss, Kelly only wished she could do the same. Jay caught her eye and she felt her cheeks burning.

'I'll see you, then.' She left him standing there, in case the urge to follow through took over.

*A*cross the estate, Josie had other things on her mind as she tried to concentrate during their staff meeting. All the housing team had crammed into one of the tiny cubicles to have their monthly catch up session. It was the one time they'd be guaranteed to see the office manager.

Unlike the others, it wasn't on the tip of her tongue to let Kay know that the staff rota system she'd come up with was pathetic and wouldn't work in a month of Sundays. Josie was thinking about Stewart. She'd finally received contact from him, in the form of a handwritten letter delivered through the post. She fingered it in her skirt pocket as she recalled his words.

During the first few paragraphs, he wrote that he was sorry, that he wanted to try again, but then his tone changed. It was as if he knew she wouldn't agree to him coming back so he wanted to turn the knife. Maybe it was time to get in touch with a solicitor.

'Finally, I'm sure you'll all be pleased to hear – especially you, Josie – that the local council have given the go ahead to convert the old sheltered housing block into an enterprise centre.'

Josie sat forwards in her chair as she heard the words she'd been longing to hear for ages. 'How many units have they agreed to?'

'Let me see.' Kay flicked noisily through her paperwork. 'Ah, here it is. There will be twenty-seven individual offices. That'll be easy to plan as the building was originally self-contained flats. The designers thought the idea to rip out the interiors was a waste of time. They think the fact that each unit will come with its own tiny bathroom and kitchen area will be a good rental point. I happen to agree. I think people will like that.'

Ray burst into laughter. 'If you're talking about people living on the Mitchell Estate, you must be joking.'

Kay shot him a filthy look. 'As usual, you see the brighter side of things. It will give people on the estate something to work towards, something to aspire to.'

Ray slid further down into his seat. 'You're forgetting one thing. There's no work in anyone who lives on the Mitchell Estate. That's *why* they live here.'

'That's why *you* work here,' Doug mocked. Even Ray laughed at that.

But Josie hadn't been listening to the bickering. She'd wondered why the gates had been open the other day as she'd driven past the site. She'd been meaning to report it to one of the community wardens so that they could check it out but, once back in the throes of the office, she'd forgotten all about it. All of a sudden, her mind had gone into overdrive at the possibilities of things to come.

The Workshop had been something Josie had been passionate to move forward. About six months ago, the local council had approached Mitchell Housing to see if they were interested in helping out with funding or expertise when the centre was open. Josie had been chosen as a representative to speak on behalf of the association. With every meeting she'd attended, she'd come away more enthusiastic than the last. This could be a perfect chance to get the estate a better name for itself.

Never mind what the likes of Ray thought, there were lots of people who wanted to work but, with all the factories and skilled jobs disappearing at a steady rate, there were less opportunities. This centre could be a lifeline for a lot of them, and Josie would see to it that one of her tenants didn't miss out on her big break. This was perfect for Kelly.

'Josie?' Kay clicked her fingers.

Josie shook her head and had a guess at what she'd been asked. 'I'm not sure?' she attempted.

Kay grinned. 'I asked you if you'd like to represent us still. Yes?'

Josie nodded, looking a little sheepish. She checked her watch and made a mental note to try and concentrate on what was being said for the rest of the meeting. It was eleven-thirty: they'd be finished by lunch, and then she could nip round to see Kelly. She had some seeds to plant.

21

'Bloody hell, Josie, I thought you were going to bang the door down,' Kelly cried. 'Where's the fire?'

Josie followed her up the stairs. 'I've got some fantastic news.' She paused as she set a foot on the landing. 'Scott isn't in, is he? I forgot to check.'

Kelly huffed. 'I haven't spoken to him since last night. He went out after he'd eaten and I was in bed by the time he came in. He was in bed when I went to the shops this morning and gone by the time I got back. Passing ships we are, but it's better than arguing, I suppose.

'So, what's got you so excited?' she asked, after Josie had shared an imaginary cup of tea with Emily. Kelly swapped it for a mug of coffee and sat down next to her.

'You know the old housing block on Davy Road?'

Kelly shook her head.

'No, I don't suppose you would. Anyway, it's been empty for over a year now. It used to be a sheltered housing block until the local authority deemed it too expensive to maintain. All the residents have moved out now into another purpose-built block – Poplar Village, it's a fabulous place – which leaves the whole building for developing. I've just been told that the council have finally agreed to develop the site into business units for the people on the estate. All the units will come with reduced rates and a grant to set up any new business for the first twelve months.'

Josie paused for breath as well as dramatic effect, but it was completely lost on Kelly. She pointed at her.

'You,' she said, 'could open your own secretarial business. There will be room for twenty-seven individual businesses. Those businesses will all need letters typing, telephone calls answering, photocopying, filing etc. You could provide all these things at a low cost.

'You could do it on a part-time basis until all the units are full, which will give you time to learn your skills and gain confidence. You'll be able to –'

Kelly held up a hand for Josie to stop. 'Slow down, will you? Emily, turn the television down for a minute, please?'

'But I'm watching –'

'*Dora the Explorer* will have to wait, sweetheart. Mummy needs to hear this.'

With the volume lowered yet Emily still engrossed, Josie slowed down long enough to explain it all to Kelly again.

'It's a perfect opportunity,' she said afterwards. 'You'll be able to base yourself in one of the rooms. Your clients –' Josie noticed the hint of a smile at the word – 'will come to you. They'll be able to divert their phones to you so that you can take messages for them. It means that they won't miss important calls because they aren't in the office. You can be everyone's personal secretary at the same time.'

'Do you really think I could do that?' Kelly latched on to Josie's enthusiasm. 'Wouldn't it be beyond me?'

'Of course not. I'd help you wherever I could. Once you've set it up, it'll be a doddle, you'll see.'

Kelly certainly did see. Immediately, she pictured herself in her own office typing into a computer. She'd be taking messages for the printing firm, typing letters for the catering business, making up invoices for the plumbers. Maybe she'd need her *own* personal assistant as the business grew and grew.

But then reality hit Kelly with a thud.

'I'm not sure I can convince Scott it will be a good idea.'

'Then don't tell him until it's too late. He'll have to deal with it, then.' Josie put down her coffee. 'You can do this. It's a perfect chance for you to get off benefits completely and run your own business. How does that sound?'

'Like a bloody nightmare, if you ask me.' Kelly stood up. 'I can't do it.'

Josie wasn't perturbed as she'd been expecting some resistance. 'Then tell him,' she said. 'Tell him the truth, tell him a lie, tell him anything but don't miss out. This could be your chance.'

Kelly's shoulders drooped.

'I'll be there every step of the way, if you let me,' Josie urged. 'Just tell me you'll think about it.'

But there wasn't time to talk anymore as they heard the front door open and close. Before either of them could react, Scott came bounding into the living room.

'What the fuck's she doing here?' He locked eyes with Josie.

'Morning to you too,' Josie replied sarcastically.

'She came to bring me a new rent card,' Kelly improvised, throwing Josie a warning glare. 'I've lost mine.'

'Hiya, Daddy,' said Emily. 'I'm watching *Dora the Explorer*.'

Scott ignored his daughter and grabbed the TV remote control. 'You shouldn't have to pay any rent.' The room erupted with the sound of music. Emily folded her arms and frowned.

Josie stood up. 'Some people like to earn their keep, Mr Johnstone. What have you done towards yours today?'

Kelly groaned inwardly. The last thing she needed was Josie antagonising Scott. She could tell by his face that he was after a fight and, by the colour of his skin, he looked like he was still in hangover mode.

'Josie was just leaving.' Kelly nodded towards the door.

'More likely she's checking up on me.' Scott threw Josie a look of revulsion. 'I'm surprised to see you here at this time of day. I have housing officers for dinner.'

'I'd spit the likes of you out if I had to eat you,' Josie threw back. 'I'm sure you'd be bitter to your core.'

'Are you mad?' Kelly whispered loudly once they were out of the room. 'Don't make it worse for me than it already is.'

Josie coloured. The sight of Scott Johnstone alone was enough to make her blood boil but she hadn't for one moment thought how her actions could affect Kelly.

'I'm sorry.' She gave a half smile in apology. 'But sometimes I wonder what you're doing with the likes of him. You're far too good for him. Surely you can see that?'

Kelly sniggered. 'That's rich, coming from you. You ought to try getting your own house in order before you start telling me what to do.'

'What?'

'Oh, go, will you. I've got enough problems of my own to deal with at the moment.'

'Call me, if you need me,' were the last words Josie said but Kelly had already closed the door.

For a moment, Josie stood on the step. What a waste of an opportunity if Kelly didn't think about what she'd said.

She was intelligent and determined; she had absolute faith in her. Still, she could just need a bit of time to think it over. Kelly might deduce that it was a good idea and that she did have the necessary skills to follow it through. It was only her job to plant the seed.

Suddenly she stopped as she went back over Kelly's words. What did she mean by getting her own house in order?

'What the fuck was she doing here?'

'I told you before,' said Kelly. 'I needed a new rent card. Where have you been this morning?'

Scott grabbed her wrist as she bent to pick up Josie's mug. 'Don't change the subject. I don't want her calling again. Do you hear?'

'Yes, I hear you but it isn't going to happen.' Kelly shrugged her arm loose. 'This is my flat, remember?'

'No, it's *our* flat. I let you stay at my house for years, now you can do the same.'

'I stayed at *your* house to look after our daughter. A daughter you seem to have conveniently forgotten since you've got back.'

Scott slouched down onto the settee. 'Don't bring that up again. I told you, I don't like how she's wary of me. It's taking me time to adjust, too. Everything's changed since I went inside.' He pointed at her with the remote control. 'You, for starters. You used to be so... so –'

'Gullible?' Kelly finished the sentence for him.

'I was going to say trusting.'

'Isn't that the same thing?'

Scott pursed his lips. 'You're pushing me away with all this namby-pamby, goody-goody talk. I hardly know you now.'

'That's because I've had to fend for myself for three months,' Kelly snapped. 'Where were you then? And if you're so bothered about looking after me and Em, where do you keep disappearing to?'

Scott refused to look at her as she continued.

'How the hell do you think I felt when I was told I had to leave Patrick Street? I saw this place and thought my life was over. But do you know what spurred me on? I wanted to make it nice for when you got back. I was hoping things would be okay again.'

'You put the dampers on that when you started working.' Scott spat out the word as if it were a disease. 'Do you know how many years it's taken me to get the social off my back and stop sending me to job interviews?'

Kelly shook her head in frustration. 'What's wrong with getting a job?' she said. 'What's so wrong with having a bit of spare money?'

Behind a Closed Door

Scott stared at her, wide-eyed. 'Have you ever gone without when I was here?'

'No, but –'

'You had new clothes, a nice house, furniture, a flat-screen TV. Half the people on this estate will never have as much.'

'I went without you. Why can't you get that into your thick skull? I went without you for three months. I don't want to do that again.'

Emily's face appeared around the doorframe, her bottom lip trembling. Kelly ushered her over, sat down and pulled her daughter onto her lap. Emily sunk into her chest and began to suck her thumb.

'Look at her,' Kelly urged Scott. 'The only reason she won't get close to you is because she's frightened you might leave again – and so am I.'

'I won't get caught next time.'

'And that's supposed to make me feel better?' Kelly eyed him with disdain. 'There will always be one more job, and one more after that. You know there will.'

'I don't know why you keep moaning, you'll both benefit from them.'

'I don't want your kind of hand-outs,' Kelly hissed.

'It's never stopped you before.'

'I had no choice then.'

Suddenly, Scott leaned forwards. 'What's up? Lost your faith in me?'

Kelly wanted to tell him she'd lost faith in him a long time ago, but knew it would do more harm than good. She knew no matter what she said, he'd bite back. Instead, she stared at him. It was like looking at a stranger. How could two people change so much in three months?

Scott stood up. 'Fine,' he said. 'Have it your own fucking way.' He glared at her for a moment before storming out of the flat.

Only then did Kelly feel Emily relax in her arms.

That evening, most of the Mitchell Housing Association staff had been out for a meal to celebrate Debbie's birthday. It had been pleasant with lots of light-hearted banter, and exactly what Josie needed. She'd laughed so much that her cheeks had ached. By the time, she'd dropped Debbie and Irene off at their homes, it was past midnight.

It had felt so good to have a night out on her own without all the feelings of guilt, knowing that she wouldn't be coming home to Stewart's miserable face, even though she knew she had that to contend with tomorrow. Earlier, on the way to the restaurant, Josie had called at Miles's Factory and left a letter with his foreman to give to him. Rather than get a solicitor involved straightaway, she'd decided to offer him a lump sum.

As she got to the front door, Stewart stepped out from the side of the garage.

'You idiot!' Josie pressed her hand to her chest. 'You nearly gave me a heart attack.'

In two more strides, Stewart stood in front of her. 'What the fuck is this?' He held up the letter.

Josie took another step towards the door while she gained her composure. 'If you're referring to the amount,' she said, 'it's all I'm prepared to offer.'

'Ten grand? It's not enough.' Stewart's fists clenched and unclenched. 'Five fucking years I stayed with you. I want half of everything.'

'Don't be ridiculous,' she told him. 'You may have contributed a little but the house was *mine* to begin with.'

'I want my half.'

'You're not entitled to half.'

'I'm going to sue you for every penny.'

'Fine, you'll have to find the money to fight me for it. I am not giving *you* half of what my parents worked for because you happened to see another opportunity to exploit me.'

Stewart's chin nearly hit the tarmac. 'I never exploited you,' he said.

'You never loved me, either,' Josie muttered. An uneasy silence descended between them. 'Did you?'

Stewart slowly shook his head from side to side. 'Do you think *I'd* love someone like *you*?' He picked up a mound of Josie's hair, and then let it go. 'Your hair's like straw.' He stepped back and looked at her from top to toe. 'Your body's like a twelve-year-old and your sense of style – well, let's say you haven't got one. Face it, Josie, you're a dowdy bitch.'

Josie faltered. It was all right for her to think these things, *know* these things, but never, ever, had Stewart voiced his abhorrence. What made it worse was the fact that she thought she'd dressed accordingly for a night out.

She wore faded jeans, black shoes with a small block heel and a plain red t-shirt. Her hair, although she had tried to do something with it, hung loose and forlorn. She'd attempted to wear make-up but knew she didn't have the know-how to make a good job.

'Well,' she spoke shakily in her defence, 'you haven't got that much to offer yourself. Look at *you*.'

Josie knew she'd lost the fight even as she pointed at him. Stewart had obviously been spending some of his money because he was wearing jeans she hadn't seen before, his shoes were the most wanted brand of many a teenager and his T-shirt bore the name of a well-known designer. Even his hair had been cut recently.

'Yes, look at me,' Stewart smirked. 'You thought I'd shrivel up and die but I'm doing all right without you.' In one quick movement, he screwed up the letter and threw it at her feet. 'So, there's no way I'm leaving you alone until I get what I deserve. Got that?'

Josie's tears fell as soon as she closed the front door behind her. Her breath coming in huge gulps, she ran into the living room and flung herself onto the settee.

What had she done to deserve this treatment? All she'd ever wanted was to be loved and to give that love back in return. Even her huge heart couldn't bat away Stewart's insults – and because she knew he was right, they hurt all the more.

She knew she was a mess. Meeting up with Livvy again had made her more aware of that. And if Livvy wasn't enough, there was always Kelly to look at: Kelly with her stylish hair, her curvy figure and her youthful complexion. Josie had never looked that good, no matter what her age – and at thirty-seven she was never going to.

On a whim, she decided to ring Livvy.

'I'm sorry,' she sobbed. 'I know it's late but I needed to talk to someone.'

'What's the matter, hun?'

At the sound of Livvy's comforting tone, Josie started to cry again. It was some time before she'd calmed down long enough to explain what had happened.

'He's trying to wind you up,' Livvy comforted. 'You shouldn't take him so seriously.'

Josie sniffed. 'So you think I look okay, then? My hair looks wonderful and shiny? My clothes don't hang off my body? I never wear make-up for fear of looking like Coco the Clown.'

Livvy pooh-poohed her thoughts. 'You have so much else, though. Number one, you have a fantastic way with people. Number two, you have a heart – that's always a good thing. Number three, you have personality. You've a knack for making me feel happier since we got back in touch, which leads me to number four: you are a caring person.'

Josie smiled at Livvy's efforts to cheer her up. It didn't alter the fact that she had scarecrow hair, but what the heck.

'And number five, you have me. I can give you a makeover, if you like?'

Josie paused for a moment. 'Would you?' she sniffed.

'You should try a new hairstyle. I think a little shorter would suit you, perhaps stopping at your shoulders, and a fringe, maybe? And you need to make the most of your figure. So what if you're only five-foot and a fag end? That's what heels are for. You need to buy the highest pair you can find and totter around indoors until you feel comfortable in them. Believe me, there is nothing that can give you more of a confidence boost than a pair of 'fuck-off' heels. And I have plenty of tops and shirts that will fit you.' She laughed a little. 'I won't be able to help you in the trouser department, unless I can find some cropped ones. I have boxes of spare make-up, too. Luckily, you're dark, like me. Well, you will be once you've visited my hair stylist.'

Josie's eyes filled with tears again. Livvy had changed into her fairy godmother.

'You need to stick up for yourself and show that useless bastard what you're made of.'

Josie nodded, even though Livvy couldn't see her. 'He caught me off guard, that's all. He's never been so... so personal.'

'He's beginning to realise that little old Josie is stronger than he thought she'd be. You'll be fine. Did you think any more about selling the house?'

'I did look into it but I'm not sure it would stop him, if I'm honest.'

'It would mean closure though if you did move. He wouldn't know where you were.'

'He'd find me.' Josie recalled how she had seen Charlotte after Nathan had attacked her; he'd found her easily enough. And it wouldn't be hard to follow her to somewhere else once she dropped her guard. Still, the idea to sell the house was one that she'd been thinking about.

'Supposing I did put it up for sale, what if it takes a long time to sell?'

'I don't think it will. It's in a good area and you have it lovely inside. Do you think he means what he says when he wants half of everything?'

Josie wiped away the tears that had escaped. 'No, I think once he sees a cheque, he'll take it and run. He won't want to wait around. He'll want to find another pathetic woman to look after his welfare.'

'Hey, less of the 'pathetic woman',' Livvy cautioned. 'You're a survivor. Don't let the likes of him get you down. I'm surprised you've stuck with him for so long, though. You're far too good for him.'

Left with her thoughts as they hung up, Josie remembered saying something similar to Kelly last week. She wondered if she was feeling any better yet. Although she'd probably made it unbearable the other day by provoking Scott, Josie genuinely hadn't thought of the consequences. She hoped that Kelly was okay and made a mental note to text her later that night.

. . .

Behind a Closed Door

Kelly was okay. As Josie predicted, she'd thought of nothing else but setting up her own business – so much so that it was heading for three thirty in the morning and she was tackling the ironing. Not bothering to toss and turn like she'd done for the past two nights, she'd decided to do something productive to take her mind off things. As she plodded through Emily's vast pile of T-shirts, trousers and skirts, she ran through the things she could do and the things that were stopping her.

Her own business: it sounded so cool. She'd have to design a logo to display on paperwork and business cards. She'd have to practice speaking on the phone in a professional manner. She'd have to send out invoices for the work she'd carried out and, hopefully, cash up the huge amounts of money that she'd earn every week.

She could take minutes at meetings. Later, if she continued to go to evening classes, she could provide a book-keeping service; do weekly, monthly accounts.

She could offer a complete business service for the small business entrepreneur. 'You do the hard work: I'll do the sums.' Eventually she could take on her own staff and loan them out to work in the other units. They could provide a portable office service by saving everything on a laptop. The options were endless.

Suddenly, she lay down the iron and reached for last week's copy of *Heat* magazine. She tore a scrap off it and wrote on it. OFFICE OPTIONS – that could be the name of her business. Her stomach flipped over and she sat down on the settee with a thump.

But then the problems started to break through her optimism. Who would look after Emily during the day if she was working now that she couldn't trust Scott? Kelly wouldn't take liberties with her mum and even though Dot and Emily were firm friends, it was hardly fair to put on the elderly woman's good nature. An odd hour here and there to keep Dot company was one thing, but anything else would be taking advantage.

But Emily was due to start school in September. If everything was up and running with the units by July as planned, Emily's child minding would only be a problem for a few weeks at the most. She could always set her up in the centre with a colouring book. Emily would love that.

No, the biggest hurdle to overcome would be Scott. Kelly sighed. She could almost hear his mocking laughter, his look of disdain, if she as much as mentioned that the thought had even crossed her mind. He'd be convinced that *she* was the one to have gone mad.

But surely she could dream? Why couldn't he be more sympathetic towards her feelings? Since their argument last week, he'd hardly looked after Emily while she was at work anyway, but as soon as she'd got back he'd had his coat on in minutes and was out of the door. Hard habits died slowly, she surmised. Had she really let him go out this much before he'd gone to prison?

Had it taken a spell inside for her to realise that she didn't like what he did, but was used to it regardless? From the moment he'd returned, all she'd wanted him to do was stay in with her and watch a DVD; share a bottle of wine and a pizza; laugh with her at some stupid sitcom.

No, no, no. Kelly shook her head to rid it of the thought that had suddenly wedged itself there, but it stayed lodged firmly in place. It wasn't Scott that she wanted to do these things with – it was Jay.

22

*D*espite her nocturnal ironing session, Kelly was still up early the next morning. While Emily was messing around in the bath, surprisingly Scott was up too.

'Don't forget I'm doing that job today.' He slurped up the leftover milk from his cornflakes. 'You'll have to stay in this morning. Jay's calling round for some gear.'

Kelly picked up Emily's pyjama top that she'd left on the settee, before snapping at him. 'What gear?'

Scott sighed dramatically. 'Chill out, woman, it's only some tins of paint I got from Fosters. I had a job lot for fifty quid, sold it on for a ton.'

Kelly eyed him in disbelief. 'You sold it on to Jay and charged him *more?*'

'Don't be stupid. Jay's just dropping it off for me.' Scott dived into Emily's bedroom. Moments later, he came out tucking something into the pockets of his jeans.

'But I've got to go to the shops this morning,' Kelly added.

'He isn't coming 'til eleven. You'll be back by then, surely?'

Before Kelly could complain any more, Scott had gone.

*A*s she checked her diary ready for her next appointment, Josie noticed Ray's car at the bottom of Clarence Avenue. She shook her head in frustration and sighed loudly.

Her first call that morning had been to Martin Smith, one of the troublemakers on the estate who hated any type of authority and had a mouth like a sewer. He always made out that she was scum. His wife was no better and ever since the couple had accused Josie of being rude and abusive towards them, she'd long ago stopped going on her own.

Yesterday, she'd asked Doug if he'd come with her, but he was going to the dentist first thing so wouldn't be around. So when Ray had come in this morning, she'd asked him to go with her, but he'd told her that he was too busy.

'But you know how he was with me last time,' Josie had protested as he sat down with his coffee. 'I'll make it quick, fifteen at the most. I need to sort out an alleged complaint that his youngest son's getting involved in the vandalism at the health centre.'

Ray shook his head. 'No can do. My diary's full this morning and I'm working at the bottom of the estate for most of it.'

'Ah, come on Ray. I'm not asking you to do a thousand miles, turn round for half an hour and do the same again,' Josie persisted. 'I just need you first thing, then you can shoot off.'

But Ray wasn't having any of it. Try as she might, he wouldn't be swayed. Hence Josie's annoyance at seeing his car on her patch. He'd gone out of his way for something. She started her engine and moved away from the kerb.

Ray's car was outside Amy Cartwright's flat. Glancing around as she drove past, Josie couldn't spot him anywhere, so assumed he must be in someone's home. When she rounded the bend into Penelope Drive, curiosity got the better of her. She did a quick turn around in her car.

Something was going on: why would he be around here? Amy had been really off with Josie whenever she mentioned his name. She'd thought it was because Amy had done something wrong, but now she wondered if there was more to it. She'd always thought Ray was a creep but...

Oh no. He couldn't be capable of...

Goosebumps rose all over Josie's body. She quickly locked up her car, ran up the path and knocked on the door. Her intuition had been right as she could hear shouting from inside.

'Amy?' she cried. 'Are you there?'

Josie tried the door handle and, finding it unlocked, faced a dilemma. She hadn't been invited into the property but she couldn't stand there and let something happen to Amy. The shouting became louder and, as she recognised Ray's voice, she knocked again, but this time she opened the door and went in.

The commotion was coming from inside the living room but the door was shut. To her left, Amy's bedroom door was wide open. Baby Reece was screaming but Josie couldn't see him anywhere. Amy was sitting at the top of the bed, a blank expression on her face. Her knees were drawn up to her chest and she'd pulled her nightie over them.

Josie's heart went out to her. Whatever had happened, Amy was trying to blank it out of her mind.

'Amy?' she asked gently, sitting down beside her. 'It's Josie, sweetheart. What's going on?'

Amy shook her head. Josie could still hear voices from the other room. She popped her head back into the hallway but the living room door was still shut.

'Who's in there with Ray?'

Amy shook her head again. Josie moved back to her.

'Has Ray hurt you?'

Amy's head went from side to side and she began to cry. 'Where's Reece? I want Reece.' She looked up at Josie. 'Get me Reece.'

Josie gulped. She couldn't go into the living room unless she knew what she was going in to. As hard as it was, she had to question Amy to find out more.

'Why is Reece in there, Amy? And why are you in here?'

Amy's face crumbled again. She fell into Josie's arms as the living room door flew open.

'Come here, you little shit.' Ray shouted. Josie moved to the doorway again, just as a young lad ran past it, but Ray was quick on his tail. He jumped on his back and they both went down onto the floor.

'Ray,' Josie shouted.

Ray turned to her, a look of relief on his face. 'You have to help me out here. This bastard was –'

'He's gone mental,' the lad shouted, turning his face towards Josie. 'He's a fucking nutter. Get him off me.'

As Amy pushed past her to go to Reece, Ray shouted again. 'For fuck's sake, Josie, give me a hand.'

Josie suddenly came to her senses. Even though she hadn't got a lot of time for Ray, intuition told her that he was trying to help. She pressed her knee into the lad's back and grabbed his arm.

'Call the police.' Ray moved out of the way as booted feet flailed around, his captive struggling and kicking in his efforts to get away.

'No, don't do that. I'll stop. Don't get the cops involved.'

'What's going on, Ray?' Josie demanded. She'd recognised Sam Pearson the minute he'd turned his head. He hung around with Amy's younger brother, Ricky.

'Ray!'

But Ray was in a different zone. 'Lock the door,' he ordered her.

'But –'

'Lock the fucking door!'

Shocked into action, Josie did as she was told.

Ray grabbed the back of Sam's neck. 'Now are you going to calm down long enough to talk?'

Sam nodded and Ray's grip lessened. He fought to catch his breath and it was then that Josie noticed he was bleeding.

'Your mouth,' she said. 'Are you okay?'

Ray wiped away the blood with the sleeve of his shirt. A nudge of his knee in the side of Sam's ribs got the lad to his feet. He pointed to the living room door.

'In there, you, and this time no funny business.'

Sam did as he was told. Amy was sitting on the settee with Reece, who now that he'd been given a teething biscuit was quietly munching away, his feet bobbing up and down as he sat with his mum.

Amy, however, wasn't happy. Her body stiffened as they came into the room.

Ray pointed to the chair in the window. 'Sit there,' he said to Sam. 'That way you can't do a runner again.'

Josie noticed bruising appearing around Sam's right eye. For all of his big man attitude, and the large amount of meat he had on his frame, Sam was barely seventeen. The fight had gone out of him. He was like a shrinking violet.

She sat down on the settee next to Amy and took Reece from her. Amy immediately pulled up her knees again, pushing her nightie over them.

Josie looked at Ray, then Sam, then back to Ray again.

'Is someone going to tell me what's going on?' she said.

'This evil little bastard has been making Amy have sex with him.'

Sam was looking scared now. Underneath his pock-marked skin, it was clear to see that the colour on his face had faded. His right hand was tapping away on the arm of the chair.

'I didn't force her, if that's what you're getting at,' he said.

'So Amy looking away while you're pumping into her isn't forcing yourself on her?' Ray scorned.

'That isn't what happened.' Sam looked at Josie. 'I swear I didn't force her. She was up for it all the time.'

'Is this true?' Josie asked Amy. 'Did you want to have sex with Sam?'

Amy wouldn't look at anyone but she did nod her head.

'How long have you been calling around, Sam?'

Sam shrugged.

Ray tutted and folded his arms. 'I've caught him here before, once or twice. I said the last time that if I caught him here again, I'd lamp him one.'

'But Amy likes it, don't you, Amy?' said Sam.

Amy saw all eyes on her and nodded again.

Behind a Closed Door

Josie sighed. The poor girl was too traumatised to tell the truth.

'I think you'd better go,' she said to the men. 'Both of you.'

Ray sat down on the arm of the settee. 'You must be joking. I'm not –'

'Ray.' Josie motioned her head in Amy's direction. 'Can't you see she's distressed? Leave me to sort her out.'

Sam stood up pretty sharpish and moved to the door.

'And don't think you're getting away with this,' Josie told him sharply. 'I'll deal with you later.'

When Jay arrived, Kelly was in the back garden. It wasn't looking too bad now, even if it did consist of a rectangular lawn with a border. She'd done her best to add some colour by planting mixed lobelias around its perimeter but not a lot of them had flowered yet.

She sat on a checked picnic rug that Dot had given to her. The weather had been good for over a week now, giving Kelly's skin a golden flash of colour. Her charity shop halter-neck top looked far more inviting with a push-up bra and she'd teamed it with a skimpy pair of cut-off jeans.

'Hiya,' she greeted Jay with a wave. 'Hot enough for you?'

Jay wiped a hand across his brow. 'Yeah, I love it when it's like this.'

'Em's inside. She's been running up and down the path like a blue-arsed fly waiting for you. Her thing at the moment is making ice cubes. The second she saw your car, she dashed to fetch you a cold drink, though I'm not sure how much will be left in the glass when she gets down the stairs.'

Jay sat down next to Kelly on the rug. She flinched, his bare legs inches away from hers, and waved a hand in front of her face. Was it her or had it got hotter all of a sudden?

'Yoo-hoo,' shouted Dot from behind them. 'I was wondering if a certain young lady would like to nip into town with me. I need to pay a few bills and I think ice-cream will be on order.'

'Ooh, yeah, that would be great,' smiled Kelly, getting up. Now she'd be able to relax in peace for a couple of hours and top up her tan. Emily never sat for longer than two minutes at a time when it was hot.

Jay was lying on the rug with his hands behind his head and his long legs crossed at the ankles when she got back. He'd slipped off his shoes, his toes busy waggling back and forth in the grass.

'Where's Scott gone?' he asked.

Kelly dropped down beside him on the rug. 'He's doing some kind of job, painting, I think. I haven't seen that much of him really. He's been out more than he's been in since he came out of prison.'

Jay rested on his elbow. 'I think you're amazing,' he said.

Kelly blushed. 'Jay, please. I don't –'

'Oh, no,' Jay cut in. 'I wasn't talking about... you know. I was talking about Stephanie and Luke. I think it's great how you've accepted it.'

'Accepted what?'

'Well, you never mention them, especially Luke, so you must be cool with everything.'

Kelly frowned. 'You've lost me, Jay. Who the hell is Luke?'

Even though Jay's skin had tanned rapidly during the hot spell, Kelly watched him pale.

'Fuck,' he said at last. 'I thought you knew.'

'Stop talking in riddles. *What* did you think I knew?'

Jay looked away, knowing he'd never find the right words to articulate what he'd started. Kelly, deep in thought, was adding some of her own.

'You mean there's another reason why Scott keeps disappearing? That he isn't always at the pub so he can get away from me? That –' She broke off suddenly. 'Who the hell is Stephanie?'

'I – I –' Jay stammered.

Kelly wrapped her arms around her knees. Despite the heat of the day, she'd suddenly gone cold. 'Tell me,' she demanded. 'Tell me everything and don't miss anything out.'

For the next few minutes, Jay told Kelly about Stephanie, Scott's eight-year-old daughter and Luke, his three-year-old son.

'You're lying,' she said when Jay had finished. She eyed him with suspicion: Jay, who she thought would never hurt her; Jay, who had said he loved her – Jay, who had every reason to break them up.

'I'm sorry!'

Kelly stopped, tears pouring down her face. 'You think you know me but you have no idea. If you did, you'd never think I'd be happy about my bloke having kids with someone else. A kid from a previous relationship I could handle but...' she gulped, 'but a kid who's a year younger than Emily? What do you take me for – a fucking mug?'

'I'm sorry,' Jay said again.

'And why tell me now? You could have told me when Scott was inside so I could deal with it before he got out.'

'Until five minutes ago, I wasn't aware that you *didn't* know,' he replied. 'You never mentioned them so I thought you weren't comfortable talking about them. But when you said he'd started staying out again, I thought you meant he was with Anne-Marie and the kids.'

Behind a Closed Door

Kelly backed away as his words sunk in. *Anne-Marie and the kids.* No, there couldn't be another woman as well. Could there?

'No... No! For fuck's sake, Jay, what are you trying to do to me?'

Jay held up his hands. 'Whoa, don't take it out on me. I'm not the one who's got another family stashed away.'

Kelly could see from the look of anguish on his face that Jay regretted saying that as soon as the words were out, but she couldn't let him get away with it. If he wanted to get his own back on her for letting him down, then he'd done it in style. Her body started to shake as shock began to set in.

'No,' she spoke quietly. 'You're the bastard that let it slip for your own means.'

Kelly got up and ran inside. She could still hear Jay's cries as she slammed the front door shut behind her.

While Kelly's life was falling apart, Josie made two cups of tea, settled Reece down on the floor with a few toy building bricks and then sat down next to Amy on the settee.

'Do you want to tell me what's been going on?' she asked gently.

Amy shrugged. 'Nothing.'

'It certainly doesn't seem like nothing. What did Ray see when he came to your front door?'

'I wasn't doing anything wrong,' Amy spoke out immediately. 'Sam calls every day, sometimes twice a day. We have sex and then he goes.'

Josie flinched. Amy didn't seem bothered by what had happened. This was going to take some working out. Ray had seen something to make him react the way he did, but what was it?

'Do you like having sex with Sam?' she asked next.

Amy wouldn't look at her.

'It's okay. All I want to know is if you enjoy it. If you do, then that's really good. It's nothing to be ashamed of, if that's what you're thinking. Sex is good, it should be fun.'

When Amy stayed quiet, Josie wondered if she'd got the wrong end of the stick. Maybe she should try a different tack.

'But when it isn't fun, that's when it's bad. Do you understand?'

Amy nodded.

'So is sex for you good or bad?'

Amy looked up and Josie's heart lurched. Would she trust her enough to tell her the truth?

'I don't like it. Sam's not nasty to me but sometimes it hurts.'

'Did it hurt today?'

Amy nodded again.

Josie kept her anger locked deep inside. 'Now, Amy, listen to me very carefully. You don't have to have sex with Sam. You mustn't let him in again, unless you want to. Can you do that for me?'

Amy smiled then.

Moments later, tears brimmed in Josie's eyes as she watched Amy playing with Reece, seemingly forgetting the past hour. She wondered what to do. She'd never be able to prove that Sam had raped Amy because she wasn't sure that he had. Amy was nineteen with a mental age of a young teenager. Sam Pearson was seventeen: he wasn't much better, granted, but he was more capable of bending the truth than Amy was of telling it.

No, there was nothing legally Josie could threaten him with. But when she collared him, he wouldn't know that, would he?

23

When Josie left Amy's flat, she felt emotionally drained. She knew her job meant that she was there to sort out problems, but when it involved such intense episodes, sometimes it was more than she could take.

As she made her way to the shops to pick up some lunch, she thought about Amy, sitting on her bed, huddled up like a five-year-old who had lost her favourite doll. The image would stay with her for some time.

She hoped Sam Pearson would leave her alone now that he'd been caught out. He was only a chancer on the estate, low enough down on the criminal hierarchy to not worry about his features after a kicking, but high enough not to want to ruin his street credibility.

And, for once, Josie was so proud of Ray. Ray had really gone up in her books today. Surprisingly, he did seem to have a heart; he'd gone out of his way to help Amy. Lord knows how she'd be able to thank him for that.

She parked her car and walked across Vincent Square towards the sandwich shop. Out of the corner of her eye, she spotted Debbie with Scott Johnstone. They looked like they were having a heated conversation. Josie waved to get her attention and pointed in the direction of the shop. Debbie joined her moments later.

'Sometimes I wish tenants would remember that we're off duty when we come across here,' Josie remarked, as she waited for her order to be wrapped. 'What's he giving you grief for this time?'

Debbie grabbed a can of coke and a bag of crisps. 'Oh, he's moaning about his benefits. Apparently he thinks he should be on more money than he is.'

'He would be if he'd signed Patrick Street over straight away.'

Debbie sighed. 'I've told him that already but you know he won't listen. He thinks he should be able to pay off fifty pence a bloody week rather than the few pounds he is paying. If it was left to me, I'd make him pay the lot in one go or take away his benefits until it was paid in full.'

Josie saw Debbie's hands shaking as she paid for her lunch.

'Hey,' she touched her arm lightly. 'Don't let him get to you. He's a piece of nothing.'

Debbie lifted her head and smiled. 'I'm fine, really.'

'I know, but sometimes it's hard not to take things personally.' Josie pointed to the glassed counter. 'Do you fancy one of those jammy, creamy doughnut things? Something gooey is always good for the soul.'

At half past three, Kelly rang and spoke to her supervisor, explaining that she wasn't feeling well enough to complete her shift that night. Like a robot, she bundled Emily off to her mum's before returning to the flat to wait for Scott. By the time he finally arrived home at quarter to eight, Kelly's suspicions were beyond question. He looked flustered when he found her sitting on the settee.

'What are you doing back?' he asked. 'You're not normally home yet.'

'Where have you been?' she demanded, ignoring his comment.

'I told you this morning I was doing a job. Then I grabbed some food at the pub.'

'And which pub would that be? The Cat and Fiddle, by any chance? I suppose that's close enough for you to visit Anne-Marie afterwards, isn't it?'

Kelly couldn't even take satisfaction from the look of incredulity on his face.

'I'm right, aren't I?' she continued. 'And we mustn't forget Stephanie and little Luke.'

'Kel, I –'

'Don't try and deny it! I know it's true.'

Kelly thumped Scott on his chest, then again and again. But Scott was too strong for her. He pushed her arms forcefully back down to her side.

'Stop it, for fuck's sake, or I'll –'

'How could you?' she sobbed, her legs barely able to take her weight. 'All I ever did was love you, look after you. Did you think of me when you were fucking her and then coming home afterwards? Unless you don't think of this as home now you're with her too.'

Scott let go of her hands and moved away. 'I was fucked up. You know I was using when I met you.'

Behind a Closed Door

'Did you ever stop?'

'You know I did, when Perry died.' Perry Hedley had been friends with Scott since they'd met in nursery school, right through to him dying from a drug overdose aged twenty-three. 'But when Em was born,' Scott carried on, 'you hardly took any notice of me.'

Kelly's face reddened. 'Don't you dare blame this on me! I was twenty years old with a new baby. And you treated Emily as if she was the apple of your eye.'

'She was.'

'Until Luke came along, the baby boy that every man dreams of. I bet you thought you were so wonderful.'

Scott pushed past her and into the kitchen. He came back moments later with a can of lager and sat down. As he took a sip, Kelly hit the can with so much force that it flew across the room, landing on its side by the window. Neither of them stopped to straighten it up as its contents oozed into a fizzy puddle on the floor.

'Back off,' Scott warned, flashing dangerous eyes her way.

But Kelly wasn't listening. 'Are you shagging her?' she wanted to know.

Scott shook his head.

'Liar. You stay away for hours on end and you expect me to believe that?'

'What do you want me to say?' he cried. 'Yeah, I have a daughter. Yeah, I have a son. Yeah, there is an Anne-Marie.'

Kelly wanted to hit him again. She wanted to squeeze every last breath out of his body. In the space of ten hours, her life had taken a dramatic turn for the worse. Yesterday, she'd been dreaming of setting up her own business. Today, she'd found out that her partner had set up another family.

The more she glared at him, the more bile rose in her throat. She ran through to the bathroom where she threw up.

In desperation, she grasped the rim of the toilet as all her hopes and dreams went down the pan with the vomit. Afterwards, she sat back against the wall. How could she have been so stupid? The bongo drums on the Mitchell Estate had certainly let her down this time. Scott hadn't even denied what he'd done.

Minutes later, she heard him go into their bedroom. She listened closely, then heard him opening a drawer. Then another. She got to her feet and raced through to the bedroom.

'What are you doing?' she said.

'It's obvious that you don't want me to stay here.' Scott didn't even look at her as he threw balled-up socks into a sports bag. 'I'm just getting a few things and then I'll be back for the rest.'

'You don't get to finish this.' Kelly prodded herself in the chest and screamed. 'I do! You're a cheating bastard and I hate you. How could you do this to me?

Maybe shagging someone else I could get over in time, but to have children with her? And that boy was born a year after Emily, which means... which means...' She paused for a moment. 'Oh, I get it now. That's why you were offered a house in Patrick Street – because you had access to a child.'

Scott shrugged.

'It's the oldest trick in the book, isn't it? Single men don't want flats because of the stigma attached – single bloke equals druggie slash troublemaker – so they say they need more room because they have access rights to their kids three or four times a week. You got that because of Stephanie before I met you, didn't you? You wouldn't have been offered a house so quickly any other way. You would have stayed on the waiting list or had to take a flat.'

'So what if I did? You still had it good while you were with me.'

Kelly was crying openly now but she was damned if she was letting him get away with humiliating her. She moved towards the door.

'Where are you going?' he said.

'I'm coming with you to Anne-Marie's. She needs to hear about this. And I hope she throws you out, because you deserve it. Then where will you go?'

Scott grabbed her arm and threw her down onto the bed. 'Don't fucking threaten me.'

'You're a loser,' she shouted at him. 'A fucking loser! Don't ever think you're coming back.'

'I wouldn't want to come back to you.' It was the last thing he said before slamming the bedroom door on his way out.

Moments later, Kelly heard the front door open and close. She pinched herself and it hurt, prompting yet more tears to fall, not just for the way he'd treated her, but for the chance of happiness she had given up with Jay. Covering her face with her hands, she sobbed.

*A*fter checking up on Amy first thing, it took Josie over half an hour to find Sam Pearson the next morning. She'd driven around all the usual haunts and hangouts before realising it was probably too early for a creature like him to be out of his pit. But just as she was about to give up, she spotted him walking towards the shops. He was alone, a skateboard under his arm. Josie tutted: he couldn't even be bothered to skate, the idle bastard. What a generation was being raised.

Like a scene from a bad cop movie, Josie slammed on her brakes, parked up her car and raced over to him.

'Hey,' She shouted to him. 'I want a word with you.'

'Fucking hell,' Sam cried, jumping away from her. 'You scared the shit out of me, you lunatic.'

'I'll do more than scare you if you go anywhere near Amy Cartwright again, you little creep.'

Sam laughed, even if it was a little uneasy. 'You haven't got a thing on me,' he said. 'Amy was gagging for it. You can't prove anything else.'

'I don't need to prove it. I've got Amy's night-dress with your DNA all over it.' Josie tried to stop herself from grinning. She sounded like a Crime Scene Investigator: Gil Grissom would be proud of her.

'That doesn't mean anything,' Sam spat out quickly. 'I'll say she's up for it with everyone. Loads of me mates will vouch for me.'

'Even Ricky Cartwright?'

At the mention of Amy's older brother, Sam's cocky demeanour changed. Ricky Cartwright was a fighter: they both knew he'd go mad if he found out what had been happening.

'Is Reece your son?' Josie asked next. The thought had been running through her mind all morning.

'No, he's fucking not!' And with that, Sam was off. 'You're not landing me with that one,' he threw over his shoulder. 'I'll say I never touched her at all.'

'But you used that as an excuse to get her knickers off.' Josie ran to catch up with him and yanked hold of his arm. 'She'd done it once, she'd do it again? Is that what you thought?'

Sam shrugged her arm away. 'Gerrof me, you mad woman. Look, I told you it wasn't like that.'

'No, rape never is from the rapist's point of view.'

'Rape?' Sam cowered. He looked up and down the street, as if the word had been shouted, but apart from a car in the distance, there was no one around. 'I never did that. You can't say –'

'Then what would you call it?' Josie prodded a finger into his chest. 'Making mad, passionate love?'

Sam's eyes went to the floor.

'You used her. She's vulnerable and you used that for your own means.'

'I won't go round again.'

'You'll have to think of something better than that to stop me going to the police.'

Josie walked off, but Sam was quick on her tail.

'Wait. Please, I promise I'll leave her alone – I swear.'

Josie opened her car door. 'You've just told me there's no point in threatening you so I don't have a choice, do I?'

'What are you doing?' If it were possible for Sam to go any paler, it happened then as Josie reached for her mobile phone. 'Don't call the pigs!'

'But if I let you off, you'll be round Amy's like a shot.'

'I won't! I swear – please, I'll do anything.'

His words were like music to Josie's ears, but what could she do to make him understand his predicament? Her mind went blank, but she'd think of something in time. For now though, she'd let the hard man-come-mardy-arse stew.

R u ok, Kel? I heard what happened with Scott. Text me if u want to talk. J. xx

Although they'd been out separately on their morning calls, Josie and Ray got back to the office at the same time. After they'd parked up, Ray asked how Amy was doing.

Josie locked her car and shoved her files underneath her arm. 'She seems okay, thanks. More to the point – how are you?'

Ray's hand automatically rose to the split in his lip. 'I'm okay,' he said.

'What happened to make you flip like that?'

Ray shrugged uncomfortably. He moved aside as a car pulled into the space beside him.

'I'd seen Pearson's scooter parked outside Amy's flat quite often when I'd been on my rounds.'

'That's funny,' said Josie. 'I never saw it.'

'It changed on a regular basis. Pearson would have a different one every few weeks or so. They were hot, I reckon. When Amy's heating broke down a while ago, I suppose I started to feel sorry for her. She came into reception in such a panic, as if she was going to get into trouble, so I told her I'd call round later that afternoon. When I got there, Pearson came to the door, I could see Amy was uncomfortable around him, but when I suggested that Pearson leave while I sort everything out, he grabbed Amy's arm and told me to go instead. I just saw red. That little bastard was up to no good but what I didn't know was whether Amy was okay with it. So I barged in –'

'You didn't.' Josie was shocked.

Ray looked uncomfortable again. 'They weren't, you know, exactly having sex, but I still made him sling his hook. He told me to mind my own business, in so many words, so he felt the back of my boot up his arse.'

Josie smiled. That was more like the Ray she knew.

'I meant metaphorically,' he said, clocking her expression. 'A job's a job and

I'm not losing mine over scum like him. I tried to talk to Amy about it and she froze up. And when I next collared Pearson, he practically laughed me off the shops. There were too many witnesses for me to have gone at him.'

'So how did you know when he'd be there again?'

'I kept an eye on those scooters. When I drove past last week, he'd just parked it up and was going up the path. He saw me looking and gave me the finger. That was all I needed.'

'Ray –'

'That bloody kid's not mine,' Ray joked, 'if that's what you're thinking.'

Josie smiled. 'That's the furthest thing from my mind, I just wanted to know why. You always have this big macho attitude about you. Why help Amy?'

Ray looked away for a moment. He seemed to be concentrating on a rose bush popping through the railings, hell bent on pulling the petals off one poor flower.

'She really got under my skin,' he said. 'Her face... it was so... empty. Void of any feeling. She reminded me of a lump of meat. Even prostitutes get paid for it.'

'Amy's not a prostitute,' retorted Josie, annoyed at his insinuation. An elderly man getting into his car turned his head, wondering if he'd heard her correctly.

Ray held up his hand. 'I was comparing, that's all. But you know what I mean. She's just a kid.'

Josie nodded. 'I hope Sam keeps away now. I've got nothing to use on him, except reminding him what Ricky would do if he found out. If that doesn't work, then I'll –'

'It'll work,' Ray said, with a nod of his head.

Josie frowned. 'You seem very sure about yourself.'

They began to walk towards the staff entrance. 'I've been checking into our Mr Pearson,' Ray explained. 'He's been doing a bit of work with Scott Johnstone. Word has it he's trying to get in with the Kirkwells when they get out, stupid bastard. He thinks he's one of the main men around the estate because of it – but he's only a kid. It's a shame to see that he's taking the usual route, but maybe we can catch him early. Or maybe he'll end up in prison. At least he'll be out of our hair then. You certainly scared him, though.'

'Oh?' Josie looked on in perplexity.

'He didn't give me any lip when I saw him yesterday. In fact, he looked the other way, which is unlike him. Usually he mouths off, no matter how far away he is. But yesterday he kept his head down, as if he wanted to be invisible.'

'Funny what power a word like 'rape' can have,' said Josie, feeling better about her little episode with Sam. If it kept him away from Amy, then it had been worth it. Sometimes it was okay to move down a level.

'You'll have to be very careful, Mr Harman,' she continued, wagging her

395

finger at him. 'You're going a long way to ruining your miserable bastard reputation.'

'Don't worry,' Ray assured her with a grin as he took the steps. 'I'll be back to normal tomorrow.'

Kelly pulled herself together and went into work the following night. Now that Scott had gone, she couldn't afford to miss a shift. When Sally heard what had been going on, she threw her arms around her, causing Kelly to burst into tears again. Sally beckoned Leah over to the bench.

'I can't believe that.' Leah was shaking her head after she'd told them everything. 'I know Anne-Marie; she isn't a slag. I wouldn't be surprised if Scott hadn't told her about you either. The sneaky bastard.'

'But all this time?' Kelly sniffed. 'What an idiot I've been.'

'Don't say that,' said Sally. 'This isn't your doing, you've got to remember that. How's Emily?'

'That's the sad thing,' Kelly replied, as Julia came over with mugs of tea for them all. 'She doesn't seem bothered. In fact, if I'm honest, she seems better now that he's gone.'

'That's good then, isn't it? With him having to pick her up for visits, it means you'll be tied to him, so it might work out better if they don't see each other.'

Kelly looked on in dismay. She hadn't thought that far ahead.

'I can't deprive Em of her father,' she said. 'I'd rather be dead than see Scott on a regular basis but I would do it, for Emily's sake.'

Sally touched her lightly on her arm. 'You know that's not what I mean. If Scott really is a loser, then he probably won't want to fetch her. You've got to prepare for that.'

'So what happens now?' Leah asked quietly.

Kelly sighed and blew her nose. 'I don't know. I haven't heard from him since he pissed off last night. I suppose he'll be in touch soon.'

It was then that she remembered something. In his rush to get out, she wondered if Scott had remembered it too.

As soon as she got home, Kelly popped Emily into her pyjamas and they settled down together on the settee. It wasn't long before Emily was asleep. Careful not to wake her, she moved her to one side and went through to her bedroom. In the cupboard over the stairs, she moved some of Emily's toys and looked to where she had last seen the box that she'd collected for Scott. To her surprise, it was still there. She pulled it out.

Scott must have been in it because some of the tape had come away now, making it easier to get her hand inside. She searched around, stretching into all four corners but there was nothing in it. Typical Scott, she thought, leaving me to tidy up his mess. She put the lid back on. Taking the box with her, she stepped backwards into Emily's room.

It was then that she saw a small plastic bag shoved inside a game that her daughter didn't use anymore. She pulled it out and looked inside. Then she gasped.

Inside it were an old gentleman's watch, two gold bands slipped through a gold-link chain, and three wallets. They weren't the only items in the bag. They were on top of piles of twenty-pound notes.

She sat on Emily's bed and counted the money. Once she'd finished, her hand rose to her mouth. The total came to six thousand, two hundred and eighty pounds.

24

*K*elly sat on her settee in a daze. Where the hell had all of that money come from? This was more than the odd knock off bargain or earning a bit on the side that she was used to Scott doing. He must have done more than a burglary here and there to have thousands stashed away.

Then another thought struck her. Had the money come from more than one job? And if so, how long had he been keeping it away from her? And why the hell had he left it behind? Surely he still didn't think she trusted him? Not after what he'd done.

She was desperate for someone to talk to, but there was no one she could trust. She couldn't say anything about this to her parents.

She couldn't ring Jay. He probably knew about it, although he hadn't mentioned anything to make her suspicious of him.

She'd definitely have to keep it a secret from Josie. If Kelly was right and the money was from lots of jobs, then she might have given him an alibi. She used to cover for him all the time, say he was home with her when he'd been out until all hours.

Before she could think herself into a sleepless night, she hid the bag under the sink unit in the kitchen.

*A*fter a quiet weekend, Josie started off the week at a planner's meeting discussing The Workshop. Her head, fit to bursting full of facts and figures, dates for completion and unit sizes, couldn't spare any room to think of

Kelly until lunchtime. It had shocked her to hear what Scott had been up to. She really wanted to call to see how Kelly was doing, but instead she sent a text message, reiterating that she'd be right over if she needed her.

Her mobile phone beeped moments later. Kelly had replied to say that she was holding it together for Emily's sake and that she'd be in touch soon. Josie felt relieved. She'd always thought that Johnstone was a creep, but what he'd done to Kelly was far worse than she could put into words.

Yet, even if it had been terrible to hear Kelly so upset when she'd last visited, inside Josie had been jumping up and down with glee. If Scott did stay away for good, she was sure she'd be able to keep her on the straight and narrow. It could be the best thing that had happened.

Josie felt so proud of her: she wasn't even the Kelly *she'd* met in January, never mind who Scott had made her into over the years, resigned to her lot and not prepared to fight for anything else because she felt she didn't deserve any better.

Josie knew she'd have a hard job to get rid of Scott – you don't lose scum like him without a fight. She only hoped that Kelly would be strong enough to stand her ground, whatever she decided. She made a note on her pad to check out the benefits he was getting. He wasn't going to get away with anything if she could help it.

Her office phone rang next. It was one of the revenue officers asking her to visit a tenant who had rent arrears. Before she knew it, Josie was thrust into her work again. She had another eviction pending, one that she didn't want to happen and was going to do her best to stop – the family had been torn apart by the death of their six-year-old son from leukaemia and, since then, everything had gone to pot. Josie hoped they would see her first. Maybe she could make things more comfortable for them over time.

Next, she conducted an interview with the Bradley twins. They were acting as if they owned Stanley Avenue again. Neighbours had been complaining about the teenagers shouting foul language, throwing bricks and bottles, scratching cars. Luckily for her, getting Gina Bradley onto her turf always subdued her, so it hadn't been too much of an ordeal.

Then she gave Amy a quick call. She hadn't seen her for a couple of days and wanted to know if she was okay. Amy had surprised her by answering the phone in a chirpy manner, letting her know instantly that she was feeling happier. It seemed like Sam Pearson was keeping his promise.

It was four thirty when Josie next checked her watch and she gasped at the lateness. Livvy had made an appointment for her at the hairdressers for five fifteen. She switched off her computer – stuff the groaning in tray and the overflowing desk; she'd better get a move on.

Despite the initial shock of being handed her own fairy godmother, Josie had been pleasantly surprised to find that Livvy hadn't wanted to railroad her into anything she didn't want to do. 'One step at a time', she'd said to her when she'd told her about the appointment. 'First it's a good cut and colour and then I'll take you shopping.' Josie felt nervous about it, but trusted Livvy not to fit her out like a teenager. Besides that, she had never shown an interest in what was fashionable, so she wouldn't know where to start.

Home at last a few hours later, she retrieved her things from the back seat of her car before messing with her new fringe for the umpteenth time. The stylist had done wonders with her thick matt of straw.

After telling him exactly what she didn't want, Josie had left him to decide on a longer version of a geometric bob with a short fringe and, after straightening and smoothing for quite some time, she'd been left with a shine that would compete with any supermodel on any television advert. Add to that an all-over chocolate colour strewn with honey highlights, and her transformation was complete.

She ran a hand down the side – it felt really peculiar to stop at her shoulder – and grinned. Now all she needed were the rude heels that Livvy talked about.

There was a whistle from behind her. Josie turned to see James at the end of her driveway.

'Wow, you look amazing,' he said.

Josie's hand shot up to her hair again. 'Do you think so?'

James nodded.

'Thank you.' Not used to compliments, she felt the colour rising to her cheeks.

'I think I might have to take you out to celebrate.' James threw her a flirty smile.

Josie blushed even more when she caught a whiff of his aftershave in the slight breeze. Because she was drawn to the twinkle in his eyes, she noticed a different pair of glasses, this time with a thicker frame in navy blue. A recent television advert sprang to her mind and she grinned. He must have gone to...

'What's so funny?' James asked.

'Nothing,' she told him. 'I was just admiring your glasses.'

'And I thought you were admiring me. Hey, I don't suppose you fancy joining me tonight?' he questioned. 'I'm going out with a few friends for something to eat. It's a kind of farewell meal as I'm off to America tomorrow for a while. I'm overseeing a project there – bit annoyed that I'll miss the birth of my first nephew or niece as Louise shows no signs of having the baby yet. I'm sure one more bum on a seat wouldn't make a difference.'

Josie was taken aback. It would be so easy to say yes. She hadn't eaten since dinner time and she felt as if she wanted to show off her new image. But to go out with someone she barely knew, in the company of his friends? She'd feel like a fish out of water.

'I've got a lot to do tonight,' she smiled, hoping that he wouldn't be offended by her refusal. 'Some other time, perhaps?'

James nodded. 'I'll hold you to that – in exactly two months.' He pulled out his wallet and handed her a business card. 'Maybe we could keep in touch via email? Do you have a card with your details too?'

Josie stood rooted to the spot long after James had gone. She ran a finger over his name on the card. There might not be anything in it, and she might not want to go out with another man so soon after separating from Stewart but it was certainly nice to be asked to join him.

A huge grin erupted across her face as she went into the house.

The following morning, Kelly flung open a wardrobe door and dumped the remainder of Scott's belongings on to their bed. It had been a few days since he'd left and, after badgering him with text messages telling him to pick up his things, he'd finally agreed to call round. If she packed all his stuff now, at least he wouldn't have to stay there longer than was necessary. And she knew it would be showtime over the money. Even though she wasn't surprised he hadn't come back for it – she realised now that he was using the flat as a safe place to keep it – she knew he'd want it eventually. But she wanted answers first.

She pulled out a drawer and sat down on the edge of the bed next to it all. Tears pricked her eyes again. Pants and socks were one thing but what else would he want to take with him? The television? The fridge, the microwave, the settees; even the bed she was sitting on Scott had provided. She wouldn't put it past him right now to make things as awkward as possible – even though she knew Anne-Marie would probably have it all too.

Emily chose her moment to bring out the devil. She wouldn't eat her breakfast and the cereal in her bowl ended up in a clutter on the floor. Then she refused to eat the toast that she'd wanted instead. Kelly nibbled her bottom lip to stop from yelling at her.

Scott knocked on the door less than an hour later. He bounded past her and up the stairs, leaving a sheepish-looking Jay standing on the doorstep.

'Thought I'd come as the peacekeeper,' he forced a smile.

Kelly forced a smile too as she held open the door. They could hear Scott banging drawers and opening wardrobe doors from where they were standing.

'I don't know what he's doing up there,' she said. 'I've already packed up his things.'

They went upstairs into the living room.

'Do you want to show Jay your new books, Emily?' Kelly asked. She wanted her out of the room for a moment so she could talk to him.

As Emily raced off, Jay sat down on the settee. 'I'm sorry, Kel,' he said, looking troubled. 'I wouldn't have said a word if I thought you didn't know what was going on.'

Kelly sat down too. 'I'm glad you did tell me,' she admitted. 'I wish it had been earlier.'

'I never did it for my own purposes.'

'I realise that now. It was just such a shock, but I'll get over it.' Kelly placed her hand over his and then drew it away, surprised by the intensity of their touch.

'Of course you will,' Jay replied. 'You're one of life's fighters.'

'Why do you stick with him, Jay?'

The question had plagued Kelly for some time now. Jay seemed nothing like Scott and certainly nothing resembling the reputation of his brothers. It didn't make sense. She wondered if he knew about the money.

'Jay, did you know anything about –'

'I want to watch Pingu!' Emily rushed back in with a DVD instead of the book she'd been asked to fetch. She pushed herself onto Jay's knee. 'Pingu... Pingu... Pingu. Can I, Mummy?'

The door opened and Scott came into the room.

'Daddy, where are you living now?' Emily chirped.

'Nowhere that you need to worry your head about, Em.'

'Can I come and see you?'

'Maybe when I've settled in.'

'When will that be?'

Kelly hid a smirk as her little girl played detective for her. Without being prompted, Emily asked him all the questions she wanted to know.

'Mummy says –'

'Mummy says lots of things, Emily,' Scott cut in. 'It doesn't mean they're all true.'

Kelly's eyes bore into Scott's. 'I'm not the liar in this family,' she said.

His look was cold but she held his stare. Eventually, his eyes moved around the room.

'Take what you want,' Kelly motioned with a flick of her wrist. 'If you want to deprive your child, that is.'

'I don't need any stuff.'

'Yeah, of course,' Kelly acknowledged. 'You've got it all at Anne-Marie's house. I suppose you kitted that out as well. What did you do, steal one and get one for me?'

Scott ignored her.

'Where does she live?'

'What's it got to do with you?'

'I obviously need somewhere to send your giro on to.'

'Don't worry. I'm changing my address as soon as I get out of this dump.'

'Come on, guys. Give the arguing a break, hmm?' Jay nodded his chin towards Emily, even though she seemed oblivious to anything other than the antics of the penguins.

Kelly turned towards Jay. 'He started it.'

Jay sighed. 'I can pick your giro up, if you like.'

Scott nodded. 'I can see I'm not wanted here.' Before he got to the door, he turned back. 'Don't think you're getting a penny of maintenance out of me.'

Kelly gasped in disbelief. 'She's your daughter, too.'

'What's maintenance?' Emily asked Jay. Jay shushed her.

'Your point being?' said Scott.

'You're a creep, a pathetic loser. You'd use Emily to get back at me?'

'I'm just saying, don't come running to me when you haven't got a penny to your name.'

'I managed when you were sent down.' Kelly paused, lowering her voice. 'I can manage again. And you haven't given me any money since you got out.'

'I shouldn't have come back at all,' Scott retaliated. 'It would have saved me a load of bother.'

Kelly pointed a finger at him. 'You came back because you thought I'd be the pushover you left behind.'

'No, I –'

'Come on, youth, let's go.' Jay put Emily on to the floor. 'I'll see you on Thursday, Kelly.'

Scott was already out of the flat when Kelly and Jay reached the bottom of the stairs.

'Call me later,' Jay insisted. 'I'm here if you need me.'

Funny, thought Kelly, that's what Josie had said, Sally too. Altogether it made Kelly realise that she didn't have to be alone. She had friends she could turn to; friends that cared about her wellbeing. It was such a wonderful feeling. But right now wasn't the time to keep contact with Jay. Emotions were running high.

'No strings attached,' Jay added into the silence.

Kelly watched him walk away, her heart hurting to see him so wounded. She pushed her hands deep into the pockets of her jeans to stop them reaching out to him. She wanted to hug him but knew he'd read more into it than he should. She might not let him go either.

As she was shutting the door, Scott reappeared. 'Now Jay's out of the way, I'll get what I really came for.' He pushed past her and ran back up the stairs.

Kelly quickly followed him. When she reached the landing, she knew he'd be in Emily's room. She stood in the doorway with her arms folded.

'Looking for something?' she asked.

Scott threw a pile of Emily's toys across the room. 'You know bloody well what I'm after. Where's my money?'

'Tell me where it came from and I'll tell you where it is.'

Scott took a step towards her. 'Don't fuck me about. Where is it?'

'What did you do to get it?'

'That's none of your business.'

'You must have done something major to get that much. You said you'd changed your ways.'

'I had it before I went inside, remember?'

'Yeah, when I was still weak and vulnerable Kelly.'

In an instant, Scott pushed her up against the wall. His face inches from hers, he clasped her chin tightly with his right hand. Her arms flailed as his pressure intensified. Scott's eyes locked with hers and, for the first time ever, she saw what everyone else saw. Scott Johnstone, the good for nothing, the thief – not fit to be scraped off the bottom of her shoes. But she also saw Scott Johnstone the maniac, who could really hurt her if he wanted to.

'Get. Off. Me!'

Kelly tried to push him away but he was too strong. He held her there with the weight of his torso.

'You think you're the only one who's changed since I've been inside? You're not and if you know what's good for you, you'll keep your mouth shut about what's in the bag. If I hear anyone' – he squeezed Kelly's chin harder – '*anyone* talking about it, I'll rip your fucking head off. Do you hear me?'

Kelly felt tears burning her eyes. She knew she shouldn't cry and give away her weakness but she didn't know how to stop. She nodded slightly and Scott released his grip.

'Right, then. I'll ask you again, where's the bag?'

'Under the sink in the kitchen.'

Scott swiped the back of his hand across her face. Crying out in pain, Kelly dropped to her knees.

'Good answer,' he said as he left the room.

Kelly gasped for air. She cradled her cheek as she fought to gain her composure.

'Mummy, what've you done with my toys?' Emily wailed from behind her. She picked up a doll that had landed on its head in the corner of the room.

'I tripped over the box and everything fell out,' Kelly fibbed, knowing that if Emily had been older the logic of the lie wouldn't have worked.

She stood up quickly. Through the window, she could see Jay sitting in his car, saw him check his watch before glancing upwards. Kelly moved back quickly. She didn't want him to see her. This was nothing to do with him, this was her fault.

Scott appeared in the doorway again, holding the bag. 'I've put it inside another bag. I'll tell Jay it's stuff for Emily.' He sneered at her. 'Now keep your nose out of my business or next time you'll find out exactly how much I've changed. That was for starters. If –'

'Everything okay up there?' Jay shouted from the bottom of the stairs.

'Yeah, I'll be down in a sec,' Scott shouted back. Then he glared at Kelly. 'See you around, babe. And remember,' he tapped the side of his nose, 'keep this out in future.'

As soon as he'd gone, Kelly ran down the stairs and locked the door. She slammed the bolts across top and bottom. Sure that she was safe, she sat down on the stairs and stared ahead at the brick wall. She wanted to bang her head against it to rid herself of all the frustration.

What the hell had gone on between them during the last ten minutes? She'd thought he'd leave her alone now that she knew about the money but her plan had backfired. And now he had the upper hand, he would use it against her.

Soft footsteps and tiny legs enveloping her body alerted her to Emily's presence.

'Mummy, I love you,' she whispered as she cuddled into Kelly's back.

Kelly pulled her around to sit on her lap. 'I love you too, monster.' Through her pain and tears, she smiled. If there was one thing guaranteed to make a parent cheerful again, it was the love of a child. Kelly would protect Emily from anything and anyone, even if that included her father, so if staying safe meant keeping her mouth shut about the money, then she would play ball.

What she needed to do now was to concentrate on a life without Scott Johnstone. Now that he wouldn't be there to stop her following her dreams, making a future for her and Emily, she could do as she pleased. And that meant talking to Josie.

Josie, meanwhile, was up to her ears in paperwork. She'd been updating her case files all morning. Now she was catching up with her emails. She scanned down the list of new ones to see if there was anything demanding her immediate attention, praying that everything could wait until another day.

Suddenly her eyes caught a benefit officer's name. Philip Matson was the subject heading. She opened the email right away. It could mean only one thing: they had a new address for him after his recent eviction. Now she could get on with his re-charge for the water damage.

As she read, Josie gasped and her hand shot to her mouth.

She glanced around the office quickly to see if anyone had noticed her reaction but everyone was going about as they were before.

She read the email again, thinking there must be some mistake. But she'd known that particular benefits officer for years now. Between them they had a great reputation for tying up lots of outstanding debts.

Josie knew that she wouldn't be wrong. She just didn't want to believe what she was reading – because the new address she had for Philip Matson was somewhere that she had visited recently.

It was where she had collected and dropped off Debbie when they'd been out for her birthday meal.

25

As soon as Kelly opened her eyes the next day, she got out of bed on a mission. Papers, pens and files were spread over the living room carpet. All the thoughts swirling around in her head were written down and being worked out, if only to keep Scott away from her mind. So far she had some kind of business plan, an advertising leaflet and a price list – none of which may be viable, but she had tried. She'd drawn a huge idea for a logo, so that Emily could be kept busy colouring it in. Kelly smiled as she watched her daughter, absorbed in what she was doing, tongue sticking out as she concentrated. Two hours later, they were sat in the reception area of Mitchell Housing Association.

'Kelly, Emily. Hello,' Josie greeted her in the reception. 'To what do I owe this pleasure?'

Kelly's look was comical. 'Your hair!' she cried with wide eyes. 'It looks amazing.'

Josie ran her fingers over it again, still not used to the reaction that it got.

'You should have told me that I looked like a scarecrow,' she teased. 'Do you like it?'

'Oh, I do. It's taken years off...'

Josie grinned. 'It's okay. Everyone's put their foot in it, but I don't mind. I feel like a different person.'

They sat down in an interview cubicle. Emily was engrossed in a box of toys in the reception area.

'How are you anyway?' Josie asked, wondering if Kelly would want to talk about Scott yet.

'Okay, I suppose.'

Kelly looked a little awkward as she spoke so Josie didn't push the matter. 'Is this a social call or a business one?' she asked instead. 'I can return the favour and make you a cup of coffee, but it won't be the same.'

Kelly emptied the contents of her carrier bag on the desk. 'I've been thinking about what you said, about the business.' A look of panic crossed her face. 'I'm not too late, am I?'

Josie shook her head, pleased that her earlier seeds had been fertilised.

Kelly slid the file across to Josie.

'Office Options?' Josie raised her eyebrows. 'What a brilliant name.' She flicked through the pages in silence, every now and then catching Kelly's intense stare.

Kelly's hands felt clammy. It was like being back at school again, hoping for a good mark for an essay.

'Wow,' Josie exclaimed once she'd gone through every page. 'You've obviously thought things through.'

Kelly nodded. 'I needed something else to concentrate on. Scott's gone for good. I reckon he's moved in with that Anne-Marie, not that I care. All I'm bothered about is Emily.' Through the glassed walls, she eyed her daughter sitting cross-legged on the floor, happily playing with an abacus. 'I don't want it to affect her.'

Josie nodded knowingly. A lot of her tenants were single parents; a lot of their children had been tearaways by the time they hit their teens.

She reached across the table and squeezed Kelly's hand. 'Emily's a good girl because you've brought her up right. If parents stay together but are always arguing, I think it does more harm than good. She settled in well when Scott left before.'

'I know, but I don't want him to forget her.'

Josie snorted. 'And you think that's a bad thing?'

'Honestly?' Kelly sighed long and loud. 'I don't know. I do think she should see her dad but, on the other hand, I don't want him to use her to get at me. I'll have to play things by ear until everything's settled down.'

'You'll work it out,' Josie assured her. 'You're one of life's fighters.'

Kelly gasped. That was exactly what Jay had said. Were her friends telepathic? Or were they simply looking out for her? She felt that warm feeling rise in her stomach again.

Josie got up as she spotted one of the workmen standing at the reception desk. 'Wait here.'

She was gone less than two minutes. When she came back into the room, she jangled a huge set of keys. 'The keys to your future. Would you be able to leave

Emily at your mum's a bit earlier this afternoon? I have a few things to do but then I can show you what I mean.'

For the first time in a long while, Kelly felt optimistic. 'Thanks,' she said sincerely. 'I couldn't have done all this without you.'

Josie batted the comment away with her hand. 'I'm sure you could.'

'No, seriously, I couldn't. You and me, we come from different backgrounds, yet, in some ways, you were right before, we're exactly the same. You didn't have to help me. I know what people think of me.'

'No,' Josie corrected her. 'You have a preconceived idea of what people think of you. That's different. In my line of work, I never judge a book by its cover. And with you, my girl, I'm following through until I get to The End.'

While there weren't many people in the office, Josie took the opportunity to grab a coffee and sit down with some case files. Something had been bugging her since she'd received the email about Philip Matson's address. She logged on to the computer system and opened her electronic calendar. Then she wrote a list of all the tenant support calls she'd carried out over the last few months. Next she opened Debbie's calendar and wrote down the dates she'd been along to visits with her. Then she began to cross-reference them. She had to be sure before she decided what to do next.

Finally, she checked the list of burglaries and cross-referenced those dates also. When she got to Mrs Lattimer, Josie's blood ran cold. She and Debbie had visited her two days before she was burgled. But then she remembered the conversation she'd had with Debbie the day after it had happened. '*Send her my love,*' Debbie had shouted to her as she'd left the building. Maybe she was reading too much into this notion of hers.

She paused for a moment. Was it too much of a coincidence that four other tenants had been burgled shortly after she'd taken Debbie out on calls with her? Josie held her head in her hands and sighed. It couldn't be anything to do with her, could it? Not Debbie, who she'd taken under her wing? Because if it was, she wouldn't be able to live with the guilt that she had taken her into their homes.

A few hours later, Josie pulled up in front of a long building. It stood behind a grassed area, overgrown and neglected. Metal sheeting covered the windows and doors on each of its three floors, graffiti slapped across the ones on the ground floor.

'This is it?' Kelly turned to Josie with a grimace.

'Yes. Don't look so worried. It will be great when it's spruced up. It doesn't need much doing to it. All this grass,' Josie pointed in front of her, 'is coming up and it's going to be made into a car park. Access will probably have to be from Brendan Street, around the corner, as long as we don't have any objections from its residents about the extra traffic. We're consulting with them at the moment.'

Kelly followed Josie up the weed-ridden path to the entrance. Once the locks were undone, they went through double doors into a large room. With their eyes refocusing amongst the gloom, Josie walked over and flicked on a switch. The tiny strip light barely made an impact.

'I hate this vandaglaze but it does serve its purpose,' said Josie. 'I suggested that it went on the minute the building was empty, but the council said it'd be too costly – they have to pay weekly rental for it. You won't believe the amount of times they were called out because another window had been broken. In the end, it would have been cheaper to go with the original idea. They've been boarded up for six months now and the council have hardly had any problems.'

Kelly cast an eye around the depressing room. The walls were painted some kind of pale pink colour, with occasional chunks of plaster missing and black scratches around the room at knee level. The cord carpet underfoot was so thin that it felt as though it wasn't there. There was a serving hatch covered by a metal shutter on the far wall.

Kelly followed Josie through the doorway into another room similar to the one they had left.

Josie pointed at one of the walls. 'This is coming down to make the area into one huge reception. There'll be a receptionist on duty to man the desk, employed by the local council.' She pointed again. 'This will be a seating area where prospective clients can wait, with a coffee machine and a few comfy chairs, a bit more relaxing. And there'll be leaflet racks on the walls, over here, and a floor plan showing where every business is situated.'

They made their way down a long corridor, which seemed to have a door every three metres. Josie opened the first one and walked in.

'They used to be one-bed, self-contained flats,' she explained as she watched Kelly's face light up. 'Perfect, aren't they? They come at a fixed price, no matter what the size, and will be let on a first-come first-served basis. They each have their own bathroom and kitchen. We're going to leave in the loos and take out the baths – some of them are pretty disgusting – and add a partition to make a storage cupboard. The living room and bedroom are going to be converted into one room.' She pushed open another door. 'I thought you'd like to see the room that's perfect for Office Options.'

Although inside was dark because of the metal sheeting outside, Kelly turned her head to the right and, all at once, could see herself sat at a desk by

Behind a Closed Door

the window. She turned to the left where she saw herself sat with a client, having made them coffee in her kitchen. The walls would be painted white for extra light and she could imagine the perfect pictures to decorate them. And a rug and ...

'It's right next to the main reception area,' Josie's voice broke into Kelly's thoughts. 'Outside, we're going to have small signs erected in a uniformed place on each window, which will be another form of advertising. There's also going to be a walkway directly underneath your window, so your sign will be the last one they remember as they walk in.'

Kelly smiled, daring to feel a little hope. 'It's amazing,' she said.

Josie smiled too. 'I was so pleased when I was let loose with the architect. He toured the building with me for two hours and noted down everything I said. More to the point – he acted on most of it.'

'No wonder they asked you to the meetings. I can't imagine planning anything like this. It's really cool.'

'You should give yourself more credit. I've studied your paperwork again. By the look of all the sample work in there, you've part of a marketing strategy already.'

Kelly nodded. 'After you first told me about the centre, I couldn't stop thinking about it. I really wanted to do it – believe that I could do it, rather – but Scott was in my way.'

'And now he's out of the equation?'

'Most definitely.'

'That was said with conviction.'

'I want to show him I can survive on my own but I want a dream too. So I went to the library and borrowed some books. There are so many things to look into. Do you really think I can do it?'

Josie guided her back out into the main corridor. 'Of course you can do it. I can be your mentor if you like. And I've found a grant that you can apply for. Once I have everything sorted out, I'll have even more time. It will be like a home from home.'

Kelly paused. Maybe now she could slip in a subtle question.

'Talking of home, how's that going?' she asked.

Josie shook her head. 'You don't want to know and I don't want to ruin my day by talking about it.'

*S*ubject: Hey there
From: Americanboy@bluememory.com
To: J.Mellor@MitchellHousingAssociation.co.uk

. . .

*H*i Josie,

I hope you're well. Thought I'd pop you a quick line. New York is a fabulous place, even though I'm working. I'm staying with a guy called Darwin who works for the same company. I feel like I've been here for far longer than ten days. It has such a buzz about it: no wonder they say it's addictive.

I have had time for a little sightseeing too. I've been to Central Park – it's huge: 843 acres, covering 51 blocks. It's awesome (oh my, I'm getting the lingo already)! We also went on a 9/11 Memorial Walking Tour. They're provided by people directly affected by 9/11. It was really eerie, I can tell you.

Anyway, enough of me and my love affair with New York. How's that project of yours coming along? I would love to hear all about it, if you have the time.

PS I hope you like the photos. My favourite is the Wall Street Bull, but I'm not going to go boring you with the history of how it first arrived without a permit...

Bye for now, James

*S*ubject: Hello
    From: J.Mellor@MitchellHousingAssociation.co.uk
To: Americanboy@bluememory.com

*H*i James,

Thank you for the photos. Central Park looks amazing! I'd love to see the Big Apple, maybe one day. I'd also like to visit Ground Zero, morbid I know, but that's life.

Hope you enjoy the rest of your visit.

Bye for now, Josie

*J*osie's index finger hovered over the send button as she pondered whether to let it go into the ether or not. Only last week, Louise had mentioned that James was asking for information about her – not that he was being obsessive or anything. Louise said she'd known that he had a soft spot for Josie for some time. So it had been quite a thrill to get James's email.

But Josie didn't know what to make of it, nor how much to write to seem sociable but not too friendly. She reread her reply again. Had she been too forthcoming or not open enough? There was hardly any meaning to it. She didn't know why she was worrying really. It was a message from a friend to a friend. But...

Should she send it? Should she leave it?
Should she send it? Should she leave it?
Oh what the heck. Josie pressed the send button.

26

On Friday morning, Kelly answered the door to find Jay standing on her doorstep.

'Great timing,' she commented. 'Scott's coming to fetch Em. I've rung him three times and he's finally agreed to make an effort.'

'That's good, isn't it?' said Jay.

Kelly shrugged. 'I'm not sure. I suppose time will tell.'

'Do you want me to stay until he's gone?'

Kelly nodded appreciatively. Jay followed Kelly into the living room where Emily lay on the settee. He ruffled her hair but she batted his hand away, too busy watching the television.

They'd had two mugs of coffee each by the time Scott finally arrived, over an hour late. Immediately, he turned on Jay.

'What are you doing here?'

'Fixing my knackered iron,' Kelly said quickly. 'You never had time, remember?'

'I was busy, remember?'

'Don't seem to recall that.'

'I only came to pick up Em, so don't start your nit-picking again.'

Jay sighed. 'Come on, Em,' he said. 'Let's get your bag while the grown-ups act like kids.'

Emily shook her head. 'I don't want to go with Daddy. He smells of beer.'

'Don't be stupid,' said Scott, unaware that he'd filled the room with his rancid breath. 'Come on, get your things. We're going.'

Emily rushed to Kelly and pushed herself between her knees. 'No, I want to stay here with Mummy and Jay. Please don't make me go, Mummy.'

Kelly's eyes filled with tears as her daughter clung to her. Exasperated, Scott grabbed for Emily's rucksack but Emily snatched it back.

'That's mine,' she sobbed and then ran to Jay. 'Can I stay here with you, Jay? We can play dominoes – you can win again.'

Scott's eyes narrowed. He looked at Jay, who by this time had Emily on his knee. Then he looked at Kelly. 'Oh, I get the picture. Quite the happy family, aren't we?'

Kelly shook her head. 'I don't know what you mean.'

'Don't deny it. I can see it in your eyes.' Scott looked back at Jay. 'You back-stabbing bastard. You're supposed to be my mate.'

Jay put Emily onto the floor but she still clung to him. He bent down and tilted her chin up.

'Em, go and play in your room for a bit, there's a good girl.'

'I... I don't have go with Daddy?'

'You don't have to do anything if you don't want to.'

Emily wiped her nose on the back of her hand before giving Scott an extremely wide berth as she left. Jay closed the door behind her.

Scott moved towards him. 'You'd better tell me what the fuck's going on, youth, or I'll –'

'Or you'll what?' Jay interrupted. 'Come on, Johnstone. I'm sick of you and your empty threats. What are you going to do?'

Kelly watched anxiously as they squared up to one another in the middle of her living room.

'You've been screwing my lady, haven't you?' Scott's face creased with rage.

'That's not true,' said Kelly.

'She's right,' said Jay. 'I've wanted to, but Kelly wasn't interested. She waited for you – fuck knows why. I've tried to persuade her otherwise but she stayed loyal to you. And what did you do? Go off and shag someone else.'

'That's got fuck all to do with you.'

'Do you know what she's gone through these past few months? I've had to watch her suffer while her whole life collapsed at her feet. She lost her home, she lost you, you dickhead, and she had no money. But did you see it break her?'

Jay looked at Kelly with such love in his eyes that she was momentarily breathless. Gulping back tears, she stood up, but Jay indicated with his hand for her to sit again.

'She stood by you.' Jay pulled back his head and laughed. 'Yes, you, you scummy bastard. I don't have a clue why the hell she'd have you when she can have me.'

Scott's top lip curled. 'You'd better back off, *mate*, or I'll kick your face all around the estate.'

'Will you two calm down?' Kelly tried, but again she went unheard.

'You think you're so fucking smart, don't you?' Scott goaded Jay.

Jay nodded. 'Yeah, I am, because I get to spend time with Kelly. I'm not sure she'll have me yet, but I'll wait.'

Scott turned once again on his friend. 'Haven't you forgotten something? Something I know about you that she doesn't? What about *your* little secret, Kirkwell? What will she think when she finds out about the other woman in *your* life?'

Jay's fist connected with the corner of Scott's right eye. It knocked him back but he stayed on his feet.

'Stop,' Kelly shouted as Scott lunged back, scarcely missing Jay's jaw.

But she needn't have worried. A fury erupted inside Jay and he caught Scott full in the face before landing a blow in his stomach. As Scott bent double, Jay drew his elbows down onto his back and, along with the cups on the coffee table, watched as he went crashing to the floor.

'Stop it,' Kelly screamed, as Jay went to punch him again. She pulled him back. 'He's not worth it.'

Jay stood for a moment while his breathing calmed. On all fours, Scott wheezed and held on to his stomach. He wiped the blood away from his top lip and spat onto the laminate flooring before getting to his feet.

Kelly felt bile rise in her throat. She stood behind Jay, knowing that he would protect her.

'I'd watch your back if I was you,' Scott threatened. 'I'll have my day.'

'Yeah, yeah, I've heard the rumours, big boy. Let's see how tough you are next month when Stevie gets out. My brother will be more than pissed off when he hears what you've been up to. So I'd watch *your* back if I were you.'

A staring competition began but it only lasted for a few seconds before Scott sloped to the door. He turned one last time to Kelly.

'You think you're something special now that you're involved with him, don't you? And that Mellor woman, that stupid housing officer that put all these pathetic ideas into your head. But you can't get away from your roots. You might think you've changed but you're nothing but scum really – you always were and you always will be.'

Before Jay could catch him again, Scott was out of the door.

*B*ack at the office, as Josie waited for her computer to load up the system, she noticed Debbie at her desk. As she watched her, she still couldn't understand how she would be involved with Matson. Were they in a relationship or had Debbie just taken him in when he had nowhere to go? He certainly didn't seem partner material to her.

A thought crossed her mind as her eyes travelled around the office. Ray and Doug were out on the patch. Irene was covering the reception. Craig and Sonia were deep in conversation about last night's television. Josie realised it was now or never. She might not get another opportunity like this for a while.

'Debbie,' she shouted over. 'You wouldn't be a darling and make me a drink, would you, please? I'm parched.'

Debbie came over to Josie's desk. 'I'll do anything to stop the monotony of this bloody spreadsheet I'm working on.' She picked up Josie's mug. 'Coffee?'

'Thanks.' Josie nodded, trying to avoid eye contact for fear of blushing with embarrassment.

The second she was out of the room, Josie picked up a folder from her desk and sidled over to Debbie's. She grabbed her mobile phone and slid it inside the folder on the pretext of scanning the paperwork. As quick as she could, she navigated to the contacts screen.

Suddenly the office door opened and Irene popped her head around the frame. Josie threw down the phone as if it were a hot piece of coal.

'Mrs Summers is asking for you in reception,' said Irene. 'Shall I say that you're in or out?'

'I'll be there in a minute. She'll probably only want some form or other.'

'She won't let me get anything for her. She only wants to see you, I don't know why. I'm capable of doing that for the old –'

'I'll be there in a minute!' Josie reiterated.

With a melodramatic sigh, Irene retreated. Knowing she was running out of time, Josie grabbed the phone again, pressed a few buttons and wrote down a number. She put the phone back in its original place and sat down at her desk.

Moments later, Debbie came in with two drinks. Once they, and Josie's heartbeat, had settled down again, Josie opened Matson's file on the computer. She queried a search for his contact details – and there it was.

Philip's telephone number was stored on Debbie's mobile phone.

As she casually flipped through a magazine, Kelly glanced at Jay. She'd been trying to read an article about the reasoning behind plastic surgery but her mind had been elsewhere. It was eight thirty, the rain of a summer storm had recently stopped and the sky promised another warm day tomorrow.

They sat either end of the settee sharing a bottle of wine, Kelly with her legs along most of its length. Emily had gone to bed less than half an hour ago. The soulful tones of Adele played in the background: a favourite of them both, Jay had bought Kelly the CD when he'd found out.

'The other woman Scott was talking about ...' Jay began.

Kelly looked up immediately.

'My mum's not well. She suffers from bronchial asthma and is riddled with arthritis. Her hands are the worst. Her fingers are twisted and they won't go back to normal now. She sleeps downstairs in the living room so she doesn't have to tackle the stairs.

'I help her out as much as I can. I do all her meals, I clean the house, I do the shopping, that kind of thing, and she has carers come in twice a day to help with personal stuff. If we didn't have those women she'd have to go in a home, and I can't let that happen.'

Kelly sighed. 'So that's why you don't go to work. But I thought –'

Jay shook his head. 'That's why I have to leave in a rush sometimes. I'm a carer too. That's why I had to go this afternoon, to check if she's okay. I don't like to be away for too long. And that's the reason why I still live at home. My dad died when I was fifteen. Mum's sixty-eight this year and most of her life she's lived in fear of my brothers. It's better for her – for both of us, really – when they're away.'

Kelly's brow furrowed. 'So why hang around with Scott? I always thought you looked out for him.'

'He tricked me into helping him out one night. It was ages ago – I know he'd only recently met you. He'd arranged to do over a cash and carry. A guy who worked there told him where the money was kept and what time to hit the place – for a cut, of course. Nobody does something for nothing around here. Anyway, it wasn't a big place so there had hardly been any security on the site. Scott rang, asking if I'd pick him up from Daniel Street in twenty minutes.

'I was waiting for him on the road outside. I thought he'd been in The Black Horse around the corner to get an early start.' Jay pointed to his half empty glass. 'As you know, I'm not a big drinker, so I was everyone's taxi. I didn't mind so much, I suppose.

'I got there, with time to spare. Good old Jay, always reliable. A few minutes later, Scott walked out of the place as calm as anything. He said he wanted to go home first to get changed. On the way back, I worked out what had happened. I flipped and swung for him but Scott threatened to tell my mum that I was involved.' Jay looked on in anguish. 'Call me what you like, but I couldn't let that happen. I didn't want her to think that I was turning out to be like my brothers. It would have killed her.'

Kelly finally realised what had been troubling her for ages, the reason why everything hadn't slotted into place.

'He blackmailed you?'

Jay shrugged. 'Emotionally, I suppose. Scott said he'd tell my mum I was into everything, the same as Stevie and Michael. I didn't want her to find out I'd been a stupid prick. She felt safe with me. I'd never lie to my mum, so if she'd asked me about it, I'd have told her the truth.'

'But she would have believed you'd been conned,' said Kelly.

'Probably, but I couldn't chance it. I love my mum, I feel responsible for her. Lynsey doesn't go to see her unless she wants something. I'm all she has.'

'Why didn't you just deck him one and have done with it?'

'Stevie and Michael have always looked out for Scott. He'd do anything they asked him. Oh, he thinks he's one of the boys, but you should hear what they say about him when he's not there. They call him their 'lackey lad', 'the fetch-and-carrier'. So I thought I'd be better off if I stuck with him. I know Stevie and Michael look out for me but there's a fine line to tread between keeping them happy and showing my true feelings.'

'So that's why every time I've mentioned her, you've never opened up?'

'Don't be daft, that's because I'm a bloke.'

Jay's attempt at a joke was feeble. All at once, shame washed over Kelly. She remembered when Scott had first been sent to prison and Jay had been there for her. She'd thought that he lived off benefits and hand-outs from lucrative jobs his brothers carried out, even though he told her he couldn't stand what they did. But why would she think any different? Jay was Scott's friend, his partner in crime, surely?

It wasn't until Kelly started to spend more time with him that things hadn't tallied. What was it Josie had said to her – never judge a book by its cover? How could she have done that to Jay?

'I'm sorry,' she said. 'I put Scott up on a pedestal, settled for the life he had in mind. I had a roof over my head, a beautiful baby girl, someone to be around. Until I had to move from Patrick Street, I had stability. But he changed.' Kelly thought better of telling Jay how Scott had lashed out at her when he'd come back for his money. 'I don't like him that much now. I certainly don't feel safe with him anymore.'

They sat in silence as Adele sang of love and hurt and happiness and moving on.

'When Scott was here, I was silently screaming at you to carry on punching his lights out,' Kelly admitted.

Jay gave Kelly's toes a squeeze. 'I wish you'd yelled it out.'

'What exactly did you hear going around the estate?'

'Nothing,' sniggered Jay. 'But he looked worried about something or other, didn't he?'

Kelly smiled and shuffled along to him. Jay's eyes were telling her all she needed to know, but all the same she needed to hear it.

'Did you really mean all those things you said about me?'

Jay kissed Kelly's forehead, a light yet tender flutter of his lips. 'Do you know what, Kel? I think we've had enough surprises for tonight.'

27

'Push me higher, Mummy. I'm going to fly!'

Emily had been on the swings for several minutes now. Kelly wanted to talk to her about Scott but her plan had gone wrong. For starters, the hot weather at the weekend had brought everyone out. There were kids everywhere: all six swings were full, both seesaws were in use and there were numerous kids hanging upside down on the monkey bar frame.

Because it took her so long to get onto the swings, she decided to let Emily stay until she'd had enough. Then she would sit her down and explain things.

Once Jay had left the other night, Kelly had stayed up late, trying to get her life into some sort of order. It hurt her deeply that Scott had been sleeping with someone else but it hurt her even more to think that because of it, she'd missed her chance with Jay. Jay Kirkwell was worth a million Scott Johnstone's – why had she been the last to see that?

However, the most important thing for her at the moment was to reassure Emily. Kelly could only guess at how traumatic this had been for her daughter. She was only four years old after all, no matter how grown up she pretended to be.

Kelly pushed Emily a little higher, enjoying listening to her screams of joy. When do children start to gain their inhibitions? She wondered, was it life that took over and made things rough, got in the way of the good times, making every pleasurable memory disappear in a puff of smoke with one dreadful act?

Kelly didn't find the words to tell Emily while she played in the sandpit for ten minutes; while she skipped all the way home holding on to her hand; while they made jam sandwiches for lunch. In the end, Emily brought up the subject for her.

'Mummy, is Daddy ever coming back to live here?' she asked, spreading the gooey mess across a slice of bread.

'Would you be upset if he wasn't?' said Kelly.

Emily raised her head and frowned as if deep in thought. 'No, I like it better when there's just you and me.'

'That's good, monster, because Daddy's never coming back to live with us.'

'Where will Daddy live now?'

'He's staying with a friend of his. But don't you worry, you'll be able to see him whenever you like.'

Emily's bottom lip started to tremble. 'You won't send me to live with him, will you?'

Kelly shook her head. 'Of course I won't.'

'Not even when I'm naughty?'

Kelly bent to Emily's level and drew her tiny body into the comfort of her arms. If she squeezed a little hard, Emily didn't protest.

'Mummy and Daddy don't love each other anymore, Em, but it doesn't mean that we don't love you. You'll still be able to see Daddy, but you'll always come home to me.'

'I like it when Jay comes to see us, Mummy.' Emily seemed to be through with the subject of her father. 'You do too, don't you?'

Kelly swallowed. 'Yeah, monster, I do.'

'Jay won't stop coming to see us, will he?'

Kelly squeezed her tight again and let out a huge sigh. 'Now that I don't know the answer to.'

Josie had worried about finding Matson's phone number stored on Debbie's mobile all weekend. She'd gone over and over the details until, unable to sleep on Saturday night, she'd got up and began to write things out. She couldn't make her mind up whether it was circumstantial evidence or the real deal. Each time she came up with the same scenario: she wasn't being stupid. She needed to speak to Andy.

As soon as she got to work on Monday morning she called him. He was there within half an hour. She led him into an interview cubicle and they sat down across the table from each other. She handed him the list of addresses that she felt suspicious about and told him everything she had found out regarding Debbie.

'This doesn't look good,' Andy said with a shake of his head.

'I'm right, aren't I?'

Andy scanned over the paperwork again. He sighed loudly before shaking his head. 'But *Debbie?*'

'I was fooled, too.' Josie lowered her eyes briefly in embarrassment. 'She's such a devious cow. I'm struggling to look at her at the moment, never mind speak to her. All the people they've hurt. I want to slap her.'

'You need to stay calm for now. Keep this to yourself and I'll do a bit of digging, see if we can link it all up. We haven't got a scrap of evidence from any of the burglaries, nor any fingerprints or sightings.'

Josie decided to tell him what she had been thinking about at the weekend. 'I'm not sure if this will work, but maybe we could set something up. If it is down to Matson, we've never known where he's going to strike next, until now. I have a bungalow that's come empty over in Ryan place. It's quiet there. How about I set it up as if someone has moved in and give Debbie clues when I'm in the office?'

Andy gnawed on his bottom lip. 'Go on,' he said.

'You know how we have a few weeks to collar tenants if they don't move in right away?'

'Because they claim benefits and then sometimes don't move in at all?'

'Yeah, or they use the address to apply for loans, white-goods and the likes – no matter how much we've pre-checked them beforehand.'

Andy nodded.

'I could say something to Debbie like, 'I've just called to see Mrs Marley but she hasn't moved in yet. I'll have to get in touch with her daughter. She hasn't put curtains up and there's a bloody TV and a microwave all still boxed up. She's asking for trouble with all these burglaries lately.' Something like that – what do you reckon?'

'Don't mention the burglaries because it might be too obvious,' Andy suggested. 'Say that she's asking for trouble or something similar.'

'Right,' said Josie. 'Then if Debbie tells Philip, it will be over to you then. Would your lot be able to set up some sort of surveillance? Catch them in the act?'

'Yeah, it's worth a shot. I'll speak to my sergeant. It would be great to clear up this case. People are so frightened on the estate.'

Josie gave him a half smile, glad she had finally got the weight off her shoulders. 'So you don't think I'm mad, then?' she asked.

Andy shook his head. 'Sadly, I don't. Though I do think you should become a police community support officer. With your mind, we'd solve far more crimes.'

Josie smiled properly this time, even though she hadn't thought of how to solve her own problems yet. 'Not for me, Andy,' she told him. 'I like to stop the crimes on the estate *before* they happen.'

But as Andy stood up to go, Josie thought of something else.

'You don't think he could have had anything to do with Edie Rutter's murder, do you?'

Andy sighed. 'It's highly likely, given what you've just told me.'

'But you don't have evidence from that either.'

'Not yet.' Andy shook his head. 'But leave that with me.'

As Andy left, Josie shuddered at the thought of Debbie being involved in all this – because if she was and Josie hadn't reacted quickly enough, not only would she have Edie's death on her conscience but, she realised, she could have stopped the rest of the burglaries and assaults on the estate too.

*E*ven though the transformation of The Workshop wouldn't take many weeks to complete as most of the layout of the building would remain unchanged, fascinated by the on-going makeover, Josie took it upon herself to visit the site every day. Since she'd had a word with the project manager from the local authority and found out he was up to his ears with other work, Josie had volunteered to oversee most things. Every now and then he'd ring in to check on something, but other than that, it had been pretty much left up to her. It felt like her project now, and she'd had more input because of it – a fact that she loved. She decided to invite Kelly round to see how things were progressing.

'You'll need to wear this,' Josie handed her a yellow hard hat before they set foot inside the building.

Kelly gazed around in awe, shocked by the amount of work that had been done already. Now that the wall had been removed in the reception area and the metal sheeting taken down from the windows, it was easier to picture a bright and airy reception area.

The stained burgundy carpet had gone and there were three men plastering the walls, ready for decoration. In the main corridor, workmen walked its length and breadth, carrying all sorts of tools and accessories.

Kelly beamed at Josie. 'It's amazing,' she said. 'It looks much bigger than before.'

Josie nodded. 'It's really coming on but I've spent so much time here that I've hardly been into the office. Lord knows how much work will have piled up on my desk. Still, do you know what? I've enjoyed every minute of it. Can I get you a coffee for a change?'

Kelly rummaged inside her bag and pulled out a thermos flask and a packet of biscuits. 'I bought some, just in case.'

They made room for two little ones in the makeshift kitchen.

'So what do you think?' Josie asked, as she dunked a digestive into her drink. 'Are you pleased so far?'

Kelly nodded enthusiastically. 'But I'm still worried that I won't be up to doing it.'

'You'll be okay,' said Josie. 'And I'm sure your business grant will be approved.'

'How many applications have you had so far?'

'Fourteen at the last count.'

Kelly clapped her hands eagerly. 'Great. That means fourteen possibilities for me to work my charms on, too.'

Josie smiled. 'It's good to see you excited. So come on then, tell me what's been happening with you lately. It seems ages since I saw you. Last week flew by.'

Kelly explained the falling out between Scott and Jay and about Jay's mum and the predicament he found himself in.

Josie was flabbergasted. 'It goes to show, doesn't it? Gut feelings can be right. I always thought more of Jay. There was something I couldn't quite put my finger on.'

Kelly thought back to the conversation. 'It shocked me too at first but once I knew, everything started to make sense. Is there any way you can help them out?'

Josie nodded. 'The hardest part will be persuading Mrs Kirkwell to accept it. People are so proud. But the trick I use is to suggest a solution, plant a seed – I usually hear a ton of excuses – and then I wait for the idea to sink in. Sometimes it takes a matter of hours, sometimes days, but it always comes out in my favour.' Josie waved a hand around the room. 'I did the same with you about this place.'

Kelly laughed at her audacity. Josie was a mastermind: she *had* come round to her way of thinking eventually.

'If you ever need a favour you know where I am,' she volunteered.

'Now that you mention it, I've put you down as a member of the task-and-finish group to get this place right from the very beginning.' Josie rushed for her mobile as it vibrated across the worktop. 'There's a meeting to attend, once a week for the next month, until we open. You're the perfect person to put forward an idea for a crèche or after school club. It'd be great for clients and unit holders alike. Hello, Josie Mellor speaking.'

Kelly smiled as Josie moved away to take the call. Josie was so full of confidence at the moment. She seemed happy, more positive. Surely it couldn't only be a haircut and a change of environment. Although she was working in dusty, messy rooms, Josie was dressed in new clothes. She wore black tailored trousers and a fitted blouse, the jacket to the suit draped carefully over the back of her chair. Kelly had also spotted a pair of heels in the corner by the window. Josie had her work boots on now but she must have brought them here to change into whenever necessary.

Josie, however, wasn't looking happy when she disconnected the call. Momentarily, she gazed out of the tiny window to her right. It overlooked a brick wall, something she thought she might hit again and again over the coming days.

'Bad news?' Kelly questioned, noticing her distress.

'Just another nasty phone call from my bloody husband. He's now threatening to move back into my house until he gets half of everything – *half* of everything, idiot. I don't know where he got that notion from.'

'But...' Kelly was confused, 'it's your house, isn't it?'

Josie nodded.

'So he can't do that.'

'He's intent on fighting me for every penny. Stewart's really tight where money is concerned. He's told me he's willing to pay a solicitor to get what is rightly his, so I know he's serious.'

'But what about his mother?' Kelly had to bring the subject up now.

'His mother died a few years ago. I'm sure I've told you that already.'

Kelly watched as Josie stared ahead deep in thought, a frown on her face. In a matter of seconds she was faced with her worst nightmare. Should she tell Josie what she knew about Stewart? Was it really any of her business to interfere?

But how *could* she tell her?

Then again, how could she *not* tell her? How would she feel if it was kept from her?

Josie turned to her with a smile but she could see her eyes brimming with tears. Before she gave herself time to bottle out, Kelly spoke out.

'Josie, I have something to tell you.'

'When did you find this out? More to the point, *how* did you find this out? You're telling me that his mother is alive? That he pretends he isn't married to me, like I don't exist? They think he's a single bloke at the factory?'

The questions all came out at once. Kelly hardly had time to answer one before Josie fired another at her. She watched the colour fading from her face.

'It can't be true.' Josie clasped her hands together to stop them shaking. She sat down with a thump.

'I wouldn't have told you without checking everything out first,' Kelly said.

'It's not that I don't believe you.' Josie shook her head. 'Quite frankly, I wouldn't put it past Stewart to do such a thing the more I've seen of him lately. It's just that I don't want to believe he would do it to *me*.'

'I'm sorry, but I couldn't let you give away half of your house to a fuckwit like him.'

'How long have you known?'

'Since I saw that photo, the one that fell out of the books you gave to Emily.' Kelly gulped. This was the moment of truth, the moment where she'd find out if Josie hated her for not telling her sooner.

Josie's right eye twitched. 'But that was weeks ago. Why didn't you tell me then?'

'I... I... didn't know how to.'

Josie was lost for words. Her mind formed question after question. What Kelly had told her would make perfect sense to anyone who knew Stewart. He was sneaky enough, she knew that. But would even he do something as bitter and twisted as this? And why, what would be his reasoning?

'I'm sorry,' said Kelly.

But Josie didn't blame her. 'This isn't your fault. I'd have done the same thing in your predicament.'

'Really?' Kelly didn't sound convinced.

'Absolutely. Besides, knowing this allows me to be one step ahead for a while until I figure out what the hell is going on.'

As soon as Josie got home that evening, she raced up to the spare room where she had stored all of Stewart's belongings. He hadn't collected them, no matter how many times she had asked. She wondered if he thought that the longer he left them there, the more chance there was of him coming back, when in actual fact there was no chance at all. If what Kelly had told her earlier turned out to be true, his stuff would be thrown at the gates of Miles's Factory.

She checked through the things she'd bagged up for him, and inside the boxes that she had filled with items from the drawers of his desk: lots of papers, magazines, notepads and car brochures, old bill reminders.

Then she paused for a moment before dashing downstairs to the hallway. Rummaging through the recent pile of mail that had accumulated, she found the envelope she was after. With shaking hands, she reached inside it and pulled out the letter.

For what seemed like forever, she stood in the hallway. Still in denial, she read the salutation again.

Dear Mrs Sarah Mellor.

Was it any wonder the bank hadn't stopped sending the statements out after she'd complained? There hadn't been any mistake in their wording. The letter shouldn't have been addressed to Mr S Mellor.

Stewart's mother was called Sarah.

Mrs Sarah Mellor.

Mrs S Mellor.

Josie looked down to the bottom of the letter. The balance on the enclosed statement was twenty-two thousand, seven hundred and twenty-nine pounds. And twenty-one pence. Mustn't forget the pennies.

She stared at her reflection in the full-length mirror. A deflated Josie stared back at her. A destroyed, disillusioned Josie. A bruised, a battered Josie.

An enraged Josie that was ready to erupt at any second. She went through to the living room, put on a CD and switched the volume up high. Then she screamed.

Stewart had lied to her. He'd told her his parents had died, how despicable was that? He'd used the 'death' of his mother to find common territory to play his little game. He'd conned – there could be no other word for it – his way into her life, pretending to love her. Josie couldn't work out the whys and wherefores yet, but there had to be some reason behind what he'd done.

Her mind flipped back to the night when Stewart had accused her of having an affair. He hadn't been jealous at all – just simply worried that he'd lose his place to live. How had she let him get away with it?

Josie threw herself onto the settee. Her marriage had been a sham, bogus – a set-up, if you like. And she'd fallen for it. She felt humiliated, hurt, angry and upset. Still the tears came.

Suddenly remembering their wedding album, she ran into the kitchen, pulled the photos from their cheap-plastic coverings and slashed at every one of them with a pair of scissors. Twenty six-by-fours from a disposable camera. She often wondered why she'd kept them: they'd been cheap and nasty, a reminder of the day itself. It hadn't been what she'd wanted; the marriage had been no better.

Ten minutes later, Josie pulled herself tall and turned down the CD before Mrs Clancy next door complained. From a bottle that had been open for some time, she poured a large brandy, allowing herself a moment's pleasure as it made its way down her throat. Then she gathered up her wits and sat down. She needed to think about what to do next.

28

Poplar Village was on the outskirts of the Mitchell Estate, nearly into the city centre of Stockleigh itself. The building was a little over four years old and set up into self-contained flats, one hundred and ten of them to be precise. Josie stood in the entrance with Kelly. They were waiting to meet Jay and his mum.

'There's an electronic door system,' Josie explained as she pressed buttons marked 'reception' and 'call' consecutively at the entrance. 'You can't get in unless you're invited or with an electronic key fob.'

Josie had found that she hadn't needed to plant a seed in Cynthia Kirkwell's mind when she'd called round to see her. Once Cynthia had seen the colour brochure that advertised Poplar Village, she'd practically packed her bags there and then.

'She's driven Jay mad going on about it,' Kelly told her, while they waited to be let in. 'It does look great, though, doesn't it?'

'Yes,' agreed Josie. 'I'm tempted to add my name to the waiting list every time I visit, ready for when I retire. I think it's the most practical use of space under one roof that I've ever seen.'

A buzzer went off and Josie grabbed for the door. 'I've found out that three people have died over the past month – sounds harsh but it's the only reason flats become empty. There's a pretty high turnover here, as you'd expect. I've blagged my way into viewing two of them. Unfortunately, it's taken me three days to get the necessary transfer paperwork filled in. I've had to put other work on hold and go back to the office to do this so you owe me big time.'

Josie had arranged to borrow a wheelchair from reception. She told Kelly to wait by the door with it while she checked her mobile to see if she had a message or an email from her solicitor. After her recent discovery plus the fiasco when she'd sent the letter by herself, she wanted to see where she legally stood before she decided what to do next about Stewart. But there was nothing yet.

Looking up, she spotted Cynthia being wheeled over by Jay and went to meet them.

Cynthia waved her welcome. 'Hello, Josie. Have you got the keys? I can't wait to see them.'

'She hasn't shut up about it since you came to see her,' Jay muttered to Josie through clenched teeth.

The first flat was decorated throughout, with curtains and carpets left behind too. Josie always marvelled at the way residents looked after new-build properties far better than older ones. She couldn't smell a single bad odour in here.

Cynthia touched Jay's arm. 'Help me out of this chair, son. I want to see everything standing up.'

They spent ten minutes there before moving onto the next flat. While Jay wheeled his mother along the brightly lit corridor, Josie held back and grabbed Kelly's arm.

'You and Jay seem a little close,' she said.

'He's helped me through a lot lately.' Kelly shook her head. 'We're just mates.'

'Hmm.'

'What's that supposed to mean?'

'Correct me if I'm wrong, but I thought fleeting glances were shooting across the room?'

Jay looked back over his shoulder and they both quickened their pace – but not before Josie spotted Kelly blushing.

'Tell him,' she urged, nudging Kelly a little harsher than she'd intended.

'Tell him what?'

'That you *love* him, you want to *kiss* him, you want to *marry* him.'

'You sound like a teenager.'

'You're acting like one.'

Kelly stuck her tongue out at her before flouncing off dramatically.

Josie hurried ahead too; she had the keys to the next flat. 'Right, Cynthia, wait until you see the décor in *this* one.'

This flat was slightly larger than the first one. The kitchen units were a pale lemon and the walls had been painted a peach colour. The living room had a picture window at its far end and the view out of the bedroom window was of so far undeveloped fields.

Behind a Closed Door

'I can see cows out of the window!' Cynthia clapped her hands in delight. With Jay's help, she got out of the wheelchair again. 'It certainly beats looking at old Mrs Morrison's huge knickers on the washing line next door.'

Josie smiled. 'Old Mrs Morrison' was sixty-two, six years younger than Cynthia.

'Everything's so new,' Cynthia exclaimed next. 'Are you sure I can afford to live here? It looks pretty pricey to me.'

'Your housing benefit will cover most of it,' Josie explained. 'And the money from your allowances that you save on personal care now that it's provided here will go towards the rest.'

With a huge effort on the part of her knees, Cynthia sat down in the wheelchair again. She watched Jay, who was checking over the bathroom facilities. 'I'll be able to have a shower by myself,' she sighed.

'I think she'll have this one,' Kelly whispered to Josie. 'I know I would. It's nicer than my flat. And that indoor garden is amazing.'

'What do you think, Mum?' Jay shouted over to Cynthia.

'I love it, son,' Cynthia answered. 'When can I move my stuff in?'

'Don't you want to think about it first?' said Josie. 'It's a big decision.'

Cynthia shook her head. She reached for Jay's hand as he walked past. He stooped down to her level.

'I don't know how I would have survived this long if it wasn't for your help, Jay. At least I have one good son.'

Josie noticed Kelly and Jay sharing that look again and sniggered. Kelly threw her the evil eye before sniggering herself.

'But it's about time you lived a little,' Cynthia continued, oblivious to any goings-on. 'You deserve it after looking out for me for so long. And there are people here that I can mix with.' She winked at him. 'I'll be able to fend for myself. It's not right for me to burden myself on you. You've got your own life.'

'Are you sure, though, Mum?' asked Jay.

Cynthia smiled up at her youngest son. 'You're a good boy, Jay. I'm so lucky to have you.'

Tears glistened in Jay's eyes as Cynthia's face lit up. Josie went into the kitchen to stop her tears from falling. For so long she'd been in Jay's position being a carer, taking the rough days with the smooth. It ate at your soul every day they deteriorated. At least Josie could make things better for Cynthia – and for Jay.

Cynthia looked up at Josie expectantly when she'd gathered herself together and re-joined the group.

'He will be able to stay at the house?' she wanted to know. 'Because if he can't, I'm not moving.'

MEL SHERRATT

Josie nodded. 'Yes, he can stay. I can transfer the tenancy over into Jay's name once you've moved in here. He's been living there far longer than necessary.'

'Then I'll take it,' Cynthia said firmly. She pinched Jay's chin; this time, he knocked her hand away in jest.

Kelly hung back to wait for Josie while she locked the door once they were all out in the corridor.

'Do you want me to come with you?' she asked.

Josie turned towards her with a frown. 'What?'

'To see Stewart's mum. I'll come with you, if you like. That's what you want to do, isn't it?'

Josie was amazed at Kelly's insight.

'I'm not sure it would make any difference.' She sighed.

'Me neither.' Kelly shrugged. 'But it might put your mind at rest, for one thing. And it would give you more evidence to use against him. I'd want to know if it was me.'

Subject: It's me again!
From: Americanboy@bluememory.com
To: J.Mellor@MitchellHousingAssociation.co.uk

Hi Josie,
I thought I'd let you know where I've been on my latest excursion. I was taken on the Staten Island Ferry, where I had a perfect view of The Statue of Liberty and Ellis Island. The weather was so hot though. Last weekend we barbequed with some of Darwin and Jorja's friends and also some of the people I've been working with. The couple have adopted me – they've made me feel so welcome.

Tata for now, James.

PS I've attached more photos, this place is so picturesque. The one with me and the two boys in the park - that's the twins, Warwick and Caleb. What great names!

By the middle of the week, Josie was kept busy as she surveyed the work continuing at the Workshop. Most of the sub-contractors had finished but there were still the odd painting and decorating jobs to be done before all the flooring could be fitted. Kelly was helping out too. It was good to get another opinion on how things were progressing. Eddie, the architect who had been overseeing the building work, had a great eye for walls and wood and window frames, but he had no idea on colour schemes and desk shapes, storage units and comfortable chairs.

Josie's mind, however, was buzzing with other things. There was the visit planned for Friday – she felt anxious about it already but everything at the bungalow was ready to go: empty electrical boxes on display looking as though they were still full, the odd bits of furniture but no curtains.

Andy had told her that the police were setting up a 'capture house' – putting cameras in place at the bungalow for all of next weekend rather than having to keep watch. All she needed to do now was give Debbie a few subtle clues – and hope that she took the bait. Or, perhaps, hope that she didn't.

She'd already arranged to take her out on a few visits on the pretext of closing as many cases as possible before The Workshop opened. Her intention was to show Debbie the goods clearly on display through the window and tell her that Mrs Marley was definitely moving in the following Monday. It would mean that Philip Matson would have to do the robbery that weekend or miss out.

She also still had Stewart to deal with. Her solicitor had returned her call, urging her to refer him back to them if he came to the house or sent any more letters. But she still needed to see for herself.

An hour later, she picked Kelly up during her lunch break. In less than ten minutes, they were driving along a road, looking out for a number to indicate whereabouts Stewart's mum lived. Kelly had managed to find out her address pretty easily: Leah Bradley's current boyfriend was a postman.

'What if she knows all about it?' Josie said, peering at the houses. She spotted a plaque with a brass number nine on it and drove on, realising she needed the other side. 'What if there's a reason why he's kept her a secret from me? That they're in this together somehow?'

'Although I wish that was true for your sake, I very much doubt it,' Kelly said. 'Twenty-six, twenty-eight... Oh, she's there! I can see her.'

Josie pulled into the kerb quickly. She turned to look again just as Kelly wriggled down her seat.

'What are you doing?'

'She's in the garden. I don't want her to see me.'

'Why?'

Kelly thought about it and then pulled herself up again. 'I'm not sure, really.'

'Look, we aren't on a surveillance job for *Scott and Bailey*. Where is she? Oh shit, she's there!'

Josie wriggled down in her seat.

When she had got over the initial shock and sat upright again, for the next few minutes Josie watched the woman she assumed to be her mother-in-law winding a few straying clematis stems around a wooden frame. Then she unclipped her seatbelt.

'Where are you going?' said Kelly.

'Over to talk to her.'

'No, you can't!'

'I can't sit here and do nothing.'

'But you might upset her. And it's not her fault.'

'For all I know, she could be part of the scam.'

'What scam?' Kelly looked over at the woman and then back to Josie. 'You've lost me. Is there something that you haven't told me?'

Josie floundered. 'No, but you have to admit, something weird is going on.'

'Yes, but she might not know anything. Imagine how upset she'll be then. She probably thinks Stewart's a devoted son. God knows how she'll feel when you tell her he's married to you. Even worse, he's been lying to you both for years.'

Josie stared through the windscreen. Mrs Mellor was standing up now, rubbing at her back. It made Josie realise that, although age must have shrunken her slightly, she was still tall. Like Stewart.

She reached for the door handle. 'I've got to find out the truth.'

Kelly unclipped the buckle on her seatbelt. 'Then let me come with you.'

'No. Don't worry, I won't say anything to upset her, but I do need to know.'

Josie crossed the road and stopped in front of a neat privet hedge. Her heart was beating so loud she thought everyone would be able to hear it.

The woman was bending over, tending to a rhododendron bush this time. Josie watched her as she carefully dead-headed the stems, tenderly moving each branch to stop it from bouncing back to damage another.

'Excuse me?' Josie started. 'I'm sorry to trouble you, but I think I'm lost. I was wondering if you know of a Sue and Stewart Smith who live in this road.'

The woman turned towards Josie with a frown. Then she shook her head. 'I don't think I do. My son's name is Stewart but he isn't married. And our surname is Mellor – Smith, did you say?'

It took all of Josie's strength to nod her head. While the elderly lady continued to talk, surreptitiously she studied her smart appearance, hair and make-up used to enhance rather than detract from her age. But apart from that, there was no mistaking it. Josie could see Stewart's nose, his dark eyes, his long arms and fingers.

'No, I'm sorry,' the woman added, after naming most of the families in the surrounding houses. 'I don't think it's this road. Are you sure you've got the right address?'

Behind a Closed Door

Josie gathered herself together and smiled politely. 'I thought I had. Perhaps I'll give them a quick ring to make sure. Thank you for your time.'

Josie got back into her car, drove to the next street out of view and parked up again.

'Aaaaarrrrrrgggggggghhhhhhhhhh!' She banged her fists on the steering wheel. 'Oh, Kelly, I've been so stupid.'

Kelly looked as shocked as Josie. 'I thought it would be a rumour,' she said. 'It seemed too far-fetched, too nasty, to be true. But –'

'It's her.'

'– it is her? Shit.'

Josie couldn't believe it. Stewart Mellor's mum was alive, which meant that Stewart Mellor was a lying, two-faced bastard. Josie felt sick to the pit of her stomach. How could he have done that? And not just to her, but to his mother. All in the name of money – for that's the conclusion she had drawn from this. There could be no other reason but greed.

'At least you found out now before parting with any of your money,' Kelly tried to soften the blow.

Josie nodded, tears welling in her eyes. 'You've just read my mind.'

'What are you going do now?'

'I'm not sure.' Josie started the engine again. 'But if Stewart Mellor thinks he's getting as much as a penny from me now, then he's very much mistaken.'

Subject: Home Sweet Home
From: Americanboy@bluememory.com
To: J.Mellor@MitchellHousingAssociation.co.uk

Hi Josie,

Well, it had to happen. I've been here, what, weeks, and I'm... homesick. I can't tell you how much I miss baked beans, mugs of coffee without labels of 'extra skinny' or 'decaf' attached to them, EastEnders and good old fish and chips. Even though I hardly ever eat them, I'm craving them! Talking about cravings, I can't wait to meet my new nephew, too. Hell, I'm even fed up of the sun, although I know you're having a run of hot weather over there.

I'm fed up of being with people most of the time. I'd like some space of my own. Ah well, at least it's only a short contract and then it's back to good old Blighty.

I haven't heard from you so I can only presume things are hectic. Either that or I'm boring you with all of my photos. I'd love to hear from you.

Tata for now, James.

Subject: Hello
From: J.Mellor@MitchellHousingAssociation.co.uk
To: Americanboy@bluememory.com

Hello James,

I'm sorry it's been such a long time before I've replied. I've had a lot to deal with, on a personal and professional level. The Workshop deadline date for opening is still on target for the first week in July. Things are running smoothly, so I guess something will go wrong soon! That's usually the case, isn't it? I hope you're doing well with your project.

I loved your photos. You're right, New York looks so inviting.

Bye for now, Josie.

Josie wasn't even sure if she should be replying to James's emails or not, but she didn't want him to think she was deliberately ignoring him. Besides, it had been nice to receive them, and if it stopped her thinking about Stewart for a moment, it was worth it.

But as Stewart's face kept pushing its way to the front of her mind, still she couldn't get over what he'd done. She wanted to smash her fist right into it, make him hurt, make him bleed; make him cry out in pain. She hated him, hated everything about him.

She was annoyed with herself too, the way she'd been so gullible, the way she'd been tricked. Then again, Stewart Mellor was a con man. He'd used her. He'd probably never loved her.

But Stewart Mellor was going to get his come-uppance… if she could hold her nerve. She knew what she had to do.

29

Before heading over to The Workshop on Friday morning, Josie made her first port of call the office. Noticing Debbie wasn't in the main room, she found her eventually in the staff room.

'You still on for our visits this afternoon?' she asked, as she rummaged in the cupboard for her mug.

'Yeah.' Debbie pulled a sandwich box out of the fridge and sat down at the table. 'What time will we be back, though? I'd like to leave at four tonight.'

'Well, I might need to do a bit of detective work on Mrs Marley. She should have moved into Ryan Place by now but when I called to check, the bungalow was still empty. She's moved some of her stuff in but it's all on bloody show because there are no curtains up yet. Actually,' she turned to Debbie, praying that her face wouldn't redden too much, 'would you do me a favour and find her daughter's phone number? If the place still looks the same when we visit, I'll give her a ring.'

'Will do.' Debbie nodded.

Josie turned her back to her as she poured hot water into a mug, thankful that it seemed to have gone as planned. She sighed, knowing full well that the next thing she had to do wasn't going to be easy at all.

After work that evening, Josie switched off the car engine and sat in silence as she looked across the road towards Sarah Mellor's house. Stewart's car was squashed onto the driveway. She could imagine him now, his scrawny body flat out on the settee, mug of tea by his side after a home-cooked meal with his mum. Before she could change her mind, she took out her phone.

'We need to talk,' she told him.

'I've got nothing to say. My solicitor said not to –'

'But things have changed since we last met, dear husband. I'm in my car across from your mum's house. I suggest you come out to me, unless you want me to knock on the door and introduce myself.'

She ended the call and got out of the car.

Stewart appeared in seconds. 'What the fuck are you doing here?' he cried as he crossed the road towards her. Then, 'Your hair. I –'

'Not so much of a dowdy bitch now, huh?' Josie said calmly, recalling his spiteful words. She was glad she had her new clothes on. She'd swapped her work boots for higher shoes too. 'High heels, red lipstick and a push-up bra,' Livvy had told her. 'Forget diamonds: those are a girl's best friends, by far.'

'No wonder you've stayed away from me a lot more than I thought you would since I told you to leave,' she added. 'And now it makes perfect sense why, when we met, you never took me to your place. You said you were embarrassed of it, when actually you wanted to keep everything secret.'

'How did you find out?' He reached her side of the pavement.

'About the twenty-three grand in your mum's bank account? Or the fact that she was alive and well and not dead and buried like you'd told me?' She prodded him in his chest. 'You piece of shit.'

'Keep your voice down.' Stewart looked up and down the street furtively.

'Or that no one at the factory knows of my existence and they think you live at home with your mother?' she added. '"Mummy's Boy", isn't that what they call you at work?'

He grabbed her arm. 'How?'

'It doesn't matter how. I just want to know why.'

'Why what?'

'Why you hid me away, why you never told anyone you were married and why you were so ashamed of me.'

'You, you, you, it's always you, isn't it?' Stewart pointed a finger close to her face. 'What about me?'

'What about you? I'm not interested in you anymore.'

'I'm still your husband.'

Josie frowned in disbelief. 'You still have the audacity to call yourself that?'

'It's true and I have rights.'

She shrugged her arm but he held her steadfast.

'You think you're such a clever bitch working it all out, don't you?' he seethed. 'But I've still been married to you for five years and I want my reward. I

Behind a Closed Door

haven't done anything wrong to stop me getting it, either. If you don't cough up, I'll sue you for every penny.'

'Fine, I'll go and chat to your mum,' Josie snapped. 'I'll tell her what an evil, selfish bastard she raised as a son. Sarah, that's her name, isn't it? Mrs Sarah Mellor.'

'You wouldn't do that.'

'Let go of me.'

'You wouldn't do that!' he repeated.

'Take your hands off me.'

Josie shrugged her shoulder but Stewart dug his fingers in deeper. Using all the force she could muster, she recalled what she'd been shown on a self-defence course last year, caught hold of his free hand and yanked back his fingers.

Stewart yelped. His grip tightened on her arm.

Josie bent his fingers back.

'Let go, you mad bitch.'

'Okay.' She did as he asked – but then she brought up her hand and swiped the back of it across his face.

Taken by surprise, Stewart stumbled and fell to the pavement. He pressed his fingers to his lips and lowered his eyes to see blood.

Josie didn't stick around to see his reaction. She was halfway into her car when he caught hold of her again and swung her round to face him. Her body rigid, she waited for him to hit her but he never moved. Seconds passed before she realised he wasn't going to do anything.

From the corner of her eye, she saw Mrs Mellor rushing up her driveway.

'Stewart?' she shouted. 'What's going on across there?'

'Nothing, Mum,' he shouted back to her, having the decency to look embarrassed. 'Go on in, I'll be across in a minute.'

Josie felt her chest rising and falling rapidly. Had she really drawn blood? She had! Feeling braver now, she challenged him one last time.

'I don't think I'll ever understand why you did what you did. Staying in a marriage for five years just for convenience is weird – it's beyond belief, really. It's also devious and calculating when all the time you knew you were going to inherit money and a house from your mum. And to tell me that she had died? I wonder what she'd think about it all.'

'She won't disown me, if that's your plan.'

'I'm sure she won't. But if you don't want her to find out, then you'd better do things on my say-so from now on.'

'What are you going to do?'

'I want a divorce – you can pay for that – and I'll decide, with the advice from my solicitor, on a figure that you may be entitled to. One that I think will be reasonable for five years of marriage – perhaps on the basis of how much you paid towards the running of the house.'

'But –'

Josie held up her hand to stop him.

'Take it or leave it,' she said calmly, 'or I will tell her everything. You have my word on that.'

Once she was safely back at home with the door locked to the world, Josie sunk into her settee and sobbed. She wondered if it was really over now that she'd had the courage to face Stewart, or whether it would all kick off again.

Was she mad to have reacted in that way? But she couldn't let him get away with it, and going to his mother's house was the only shock tactic she could think of.

She glanced around the living room, wondering if she would ever recognise this house as her home. She cast her mind back to distant memories, long before Stewart had arrived on the scene – like the time her mother had surprised her with a birthday party when she'd been ten. The time when she'd fallen off her bike and landed in the ornamental pond at the bottom of the garden – it had been filled in shortly afterwards. She remembered coming home with a prize for being the best history student that year in junior school. She'd been as proud as punch, even if she had already read the book twice.

But then she remembered the constant moaning, the whining and groaning as she tried to reach out for her independence. Brenda had been livid the first time she'd worn make-up, stating that no daughter of hers was wearing lipstick and mascara that made her look like a prostitute rather than a fourteen-year-old girl. Unlike most of the pupils at her school, Josie was never given pocket money to spend as she wished. A trip to the local library had to suffice for her Saturday morning jaunts.

Yet sitting here, Josie felt calm, peaceful even. She sensed a huge weight being lifted from her shoulders as she looked ahead towards a brighter future. She had some challenging days ahead – especially when sorting out the fiasco with Debbie – but, right then, she knew the new Josie could cope.

The Workshop was on schedule to open in two weeks and she knew that would mean extra duties for her, which she was looking forward to, even if they would also challenge her current workload.

When she went to bed that night, Josie felt her fears and anxiety float away into the warmth of the night. Maybe she was free of Stewart at last.

Behind a Closed Door

. . .

Subject: Hello
From: Americanboy@bluememory.com
To: J.Mellor@MitchellHousingAssociation.co.uk

Hey, not to worry. It's just great that you found the time to reply eventually. I saw an article about it in your local news online last night. You look like you have a mammoth task on your hands. I wish you luck. It's a pity I won't be back until after it has opened.

PS. You look like a million dollars (no pun intended).

Subject: Hello
From: J.Mellor@MitchellHousingAssociation.co.uk
To: Americanboy@bluememory.com

Why thank you, kind Englishman. I hate having my photo taken but I suppose it is in the name of advertising. We have over sixty per cent of the units filled now – only another forty per cent to go. And guess who's left doing all the grant applications?

PS. Surely you like the new Josie better than the old one?

Subject: Re: Hello
From: Americanboy@bluememory.com
To: J.Mellor@MitchellHousingAssociation.co.uk

Are you flirting with me, Ms Josie?

Subject: Re: Hello
From: J.Mellor@MitchellHousingAssociation.co.uk
To: Americanboy@bluememory.com

. . .

Are you flirting with me, Mr James?

Subject: Re: Re: Hello
From: Americanboy@bluememory.com
To: J.Mellor@MitchellHousingAssocition.co.uk

I might be.

Subject: Re: Re: Hello
From: J.Mellor@MitchellHousingAssociation.co.uk
To: Americanboy@bluememory.com

Well, I might be then, too. Goodnight James.

Subject: Re: Re: Re: Hello
From: Americanboy@bluememory.com
To: J.Mellor@MitchellHousingAssociation.co.uk

Goodnight? It's three o' clock in the afternoon here! So I'll leave you with a message for tomorrow. Have a nice day. I'll be thinking of you.

All that weekend, Josie kept her phone on, waiting for a call or a text from Andy. He said he'd ring her if anything happened as soon as he could. When she arrived at the office on Monday morning having heard nothing from him, the first thing she checked was the weekend call-log to see if anything untoward had been reported. But there was nothing apart from one entry about the kids playing football over on Vincent Square. Debbie's desk was empty, too.

She'd just sat down at her own desk when her phone rang.

'Please tell me it worked,' she said – caller ID told her it was Andy. 'I've hardly slept this weekend.'

'It worked,' Andy told her. 'We got him.'

Josie grinned. 'I can hear you smiling down the phone.'

'Can you talk?'

'Yes, there's only me and Ray in at the minute. He's gone to make a drink.'

'No sign of Debbie?'

'No.'

'Good, I'm heading over there after. But there's something else. We got Scott Johnstone too.'

'What?' Josie cried, and then lowered her voice. 'At the bungalow?'

'Yes, they've been in on it together. Johnstone's admitting his part right now.'

'Bloody typical of him,' Josie retorted without thinking. 'Grass everyone else up to save his own skin.'

'Josie, we want him to cough.'

'I know, but you'd think he'd have some sort of respect or honour amongst thieves or what have you.' Then, knowing how it sounded she added, 'Oh, you know what I mean. What a result though.'

'I have to go. We're still questioning them both but Johnstone has mentioned something else that needs checking out. I've been asked to go along.'

'What do you mean?'

'I can't say yet but it might become clearer soon. If it does, I promise you'll be among the first to know. Are you still there?'

Josie had gone quiet because she didn't believe what she was seeing.

'Yes, I'm still here,' she whispered. 'But Debbie's walked in.'

'Keep cool. Don't do anything that might make her suspicious. It'll be better for us with her out of the picture anyway. Does she look any different?'

'In what way?'

'Worried? Nervous? Does she look as if she suspects anything?'

Debbie was checking her mobile phone as she waited for her computer to load up. She smiled as she caught Josie's eye.

Josie smiled back. 'I don't think so,' she whispered to Andy. 'But I'd better go in case she comes over to me.'

'Okay, but remember what I said. Keep cool. Oh, and keep her there if you can. If she does do a runner, then ring me straight away.'

For the next hour or so, Josie observed Debbie furtively while trying to keep her happy demeanour. She wished she had a bit more fight in her, as she wanted to march right across there and slap her hard. Maybe then she would get rid of this rage burning inside.

Debbie was being her usual chatty self. The only thing Josie particularly

443

noticed was that she was checking her mobile phone constantly to see if she had any messages.

Finding out that Scott Johnstone was involved in the burglaries had blown Josie's mind. It was going to be hard to break that to Kelly too. Josie was certain that she had no idea what had been going on, but she also realised that she'd be mortified that she had been lied to about something else.

She picked up her pen and glanced across at Debbie again. She had her head down, working on something or other. She didn't seem to be bothered about anything.

Unable to concentrate, Josie was thankful when Andy finally walked in, along with Mark.

Andy came across to Josie first. 'You won't believe what we've found,' he said. 'I can't wait to get her into custody.'

Confused by his remark, Josie quickly followed him and Mark across to Debbie's desk. It took a few moments before Debbie looked up. Her eyes ran over the three of them suspiciously.

'Debbie Wilkins,' said Andy, 'I'm arresting you on suspicion of obtaining information under false pretences and aiding and abetting a known criminal. You do not have to say anything, but it may harm your defence if you do not mention when questioned something which you later rely on in court. Anything you do say may be given in evidence.'

A silence fell across the room.

Debbie stood up. 'You can't arrest me,' she said defiantly. 'You don't have anything on me. I might live with him but I had no idea what he was doing and that's my final word on the matter.' She folded her arms.

Josie half admired Debbie's stance as all eyes fell on her. She hadn't even bothered to question the whys and wherefores.

'What's going on?' Irene asked. She'd been joined by Ray; Doug wasn't too far behind him. Sonia and Craig were already close by.

'She's involved with Philip Matson and she's been passing on addresses for him to burgle,' Josie told everyone.

'I never did,' cried Debbie.

'You used me to get information – you used us all for your own means. Have you any idea how much damage you've caused? How long it takes for the victims to get back on their feet, if they ever do?'

'I told you,' said Debbie. 'It's got nothing to do with me.'

'Save it,' said Mark. 'We have bigger fish to fry.'

For a split-second Debbie froze, but then she regained her composure. 'You can't prove anything.'

'So you haven't been supplying Matson with addresses of vulnerable people?' said Andy.

'No, I haven't been supplying *Phil* with anything.'

'And you had no idea that he was a thief and a murderer?' said Mark.

Debbie sighed dramatically. 'I had no idea.'

Andy reached into his pocket and pulled out a small evidence bag. He held it up to Josie.

'I need you to verify this for me until I can check with the family.'

Josie gasped as she spotted the pearl necklace with its unique butterfly clasp. She held on to the desk for support.

'What's that?' asked Debbie.

'You bitch,' Josie seethed. 'That necklace belonged to Edie Rutter.'

Debbie frowned. 'But what's that got to do with me?'

'It was found at your house less than an hour ago,' said Andy.

'But that was missing from –' Debbie paled as she worked out its significance. 'You don't think that Phil did... no, he wouldn't do that.'

'Scott Johnstone reckoned he did,' said Mark.

'No.'

'He told us where to look for it, inside the rose of the light in the hallway. Not every thief goes to so much trouble to hide things and we would have found it eventually, but it was great to know where to go.'

'No.' Debbie shook her head vehemently. 'He wouldn't do that. He wouldn't!'

'Don't give me that,' said Josie. 'You knew perfectly well what he'd done. He left Edie Rutter to die in a pool of her own blood. You might as well have been there with him.'

'Josie's right,' said Ray. 'How could you do that? We trusted you.'

'But I wasn't involved in her murder. I wasn't there!'

'You set her up though, didn't you?'

'No... please.' Debbie faltered. 'I didn't know he'd left her there to... to...'

Josie moved past everyone to stand in front of her. 'And to think that I helped you out when you first started here,' she hissed, prodding her in the chest. 'I could slap your face for what you've done. But that would make me just as bad as you.'

'I didn't know!'

Not a sound was heard but a ringing phone as Debbie Wilkins was handcuffed and escorted off the premises.

30

*A*ndy was ensconced on one of three new settees in the reception area at The Workshop while Josie tried out the coffee machine again. She was looking forward to the opening next week, but dreaded the pace upping further as the day drew nearer. Still, Andy turning up made her find time for a break: any excuse to rest her legs at the moment.

'Who would have thought it, though?' Andy shook his head yet again. 'Debbie Wilkins giving out inside information to that creep Matson so he could then go and rob them all blind.'

'Yep, she conned me good and proper,' Josie replied. She handed him a plastic cup and sat down beside him. 'And I thought I'd exorcised vulnerable Josie over the past few months.'

Andy stretched out his legs as his radio crackled in the background. 'It wasn't your fault. She seemed so nice every time I saw her. I would have done the same things in your position.'

Josie sighed. 'I suppose so, but when I look back I wonder how it went on for so long. She was always so keen to learn anything about my job. I just thought she aspired to be a housing officer. But all the time she was gleaning information from me, using me to scope out which tenants to rob. And because of that, I told her everything *and* took her into their homes.'

'But you would have done that with any housing assistant, wouldn't you?' Andy tried to ease her conscience.

Josie nodded. 'If they expressed an interest, yes. Not everyone wants to do this job – and who can blame them? Sometimes I wonder why I've done it for so long.'

'Because you're good at it. And because you care.'

'And look where that got me.' Josie snorted.

'I hope they throw the book at her when she's up in court again next month.'

'I reckon that's why she was so keen to go on Matson's eviction, too,' Josie acknowledged, going off at an angle slightly. 'She thought it'd take the scent off her.'

'I bet she didn't think the greedy prick would register for benefits from there afterwards,' Andy added. 'Which indirectly linked us to her.'

'And directly linked her to him,' Josie noted.

'But if he hadn't registered to claim his benefits, you might never have twigged what was happening, unless he really did slip up.'

'I'm glad that he did. It was his downfall after all.'

'That and the fact that Johnstone grassed him up.'

'Hmm.' Josie thought back to the time she'd seen Debbie across the shops talking to Scott Johnstone. She'd thought Debbie had been taking grief for doing her job when she was probably handing out addresses of vulnerable tenants that she'd been to visit.

'And with Matson and Johnstone on remand,' she added, 'the Mitchell Estate is that little bit safer.'

Andy laughed. 'The Mitchell Estate will never be safe.'

Josie smiled. 'What I can't work out, though, is why she turned up for work that last morning. I know if it was me and my boyfriend hadn't come home from the take the night before, I would have gone on the run immediately. Where to, I don't know, but I wouldn't have come into work.'

'She denied everything on the day, though didn't she? And Johnstone told us that Matson often stayed with him after a robbery, to take the heat off Debbie if they did get caught. So she had no idea we had him in custody.'

'That's why she was constantly checking her phone,' Josie nodded again. 'She must have been waiting for him to text her.'

'Yep,' said Andy. 'And if Johnstone hadn't come forward with that little gem – or rather, necklace – we would have been none the wiser for Edie Rutter's murder.'

Josie involuntarily shuddered. 'I still can't believe he left Edie to die. I mean, why didn't he call an ambulance after he'd left the property?'

'Perhaps she could identify him?'

'Sadly, we will never know,' Josie said. 'I still miss calling round there for a cuppa.'

Andy pointed to the room. 'But you have this place to concentrate on now. It looks amazing, by the way.'

*K*elly had decided to take a few days off between leaving her job at Miles's Factory and the opening of The Workshop. Now on her last shift, she was helping Sally to remove the wrappings around the many plates laid out in the staff canteen. As a leaving gift, everyone had provided an item of food for a buffet. About a dozen people had come into the room so far.

'I can't believe you're leaving today,' Sally moaned.

'Well, I can't believe all the fantastic presents I've had,' said Kelly, eyeing the flowers she'd received along with other personal gifts. 'I feel like I've only been working her for five minutes.'

Sally gave her a hug. 'I'm going to miss you so much, but I know you'll do okay with Office Options. If anyone deserves to, it's you.'

'Are you going to miss me as well?' Leah swapped places with Sally, not to be outdone.

'Like a hole in the head,' muttered Sally, then looked away all innocent. Leah frowned at her for a moment before grinning.

'Course I'll miss you, you big nerd,' Kelly told her. 'I'll miss you both. And you can always pop over and see me.'

'You'll be too arty-farty-in-your-new-office for us, won't she, Sal?'

As Robbie was warming up, threatening to sing another cover version from the real Robbie Williams, Stewart walked in. Kelly took immense pleasure in the fact that 'Mummy's Boy' looked miserable. It was laughable really, but it still shocked her to think that he could have been so cruel.

She couldn't help herself when she beckoned him over to join them.

'I think you're in need of some cake to cheer you up,' Kelly said, handing him a plate. As he was about to take a bite, she turned down the radio and spoke again. 'Does your wife bake cakes?'

Stewart's fork hung in mid-air. Everyone stopped what they were doing amidst the silence.

'It was you.' Stewart slatted the plate and its contents down onto the table.

'Christ, Kel,' said Robbie. 'Have you been upsetting our Mummy's Boy?'

'He's not a mummy's boy,' Kelly remarked. 'Until last month, he lived with his *wife*. This snide creep has been married to my friend for years.'

There was a gasp around the room.

Stewart launched himself at her. Kelly stood her ground but Robbie and some of the other male workers watched her back regardless, blocking him access to her.

'He told her that his mother was dead,' she continued. 'He never told his mother he was married, either. I reckon he was waiting to inherit all of her money, live with my friend rent free and then do a runner when his mum really died.'

'You sneaky bastard!' Leah was the first one to speak out.

'What does she mean, you're married?'

'When did this happen?'

'That can't be true! It's like something from Jeremy Kyle.'

'Why didn't you say anything?'

'You've ruined everything, you stupid bitch.' Stewart pushed into Robbie but was held back again.

'Back off,' he was told.

'Or fuck off,' said Robbie. 'We don't want you in here. You're not invited to this party.'

Knowing he was beat, Stewart stormed off.

'And don't come back, you sneaky prick,' one of the packers shouted after him.

Sally gave Kelly a hug. 'Well done, girl. You certainly put him in his place.'

'Yeah,' said Leah. 'I bet he'll be looking for another job soon. Those boys can be bullies when they all gang up on someone. You make his life hell, Robbie,' she shouted over to him.

The lively atmosphere of the party soon came back again and, with the undercurrents of the rumour spreading like wild fire, everyone had a good time. Sally changed the music from radio to a CD and turned the volume up again.

'Let's make a toast: to Kelly.'

'To Kelly!' cried everyone.

'To Office Options,' added Kelly.

With one week to go, all stops were pulled out to get The Workshop ready to face its public. On Monday, Josie and Kelly returned after the weekend to a burst pipe. Two of the rooms had been completely flooded; carpeting had to be ripped up and replaced. Luckily, the water had been dripping rather than gushing, so the walls had been spared.

On Wednesday, the caterers turned up. Great news – but they weren't due until Friday, the scheduled date for opening. Even though it was clearly written on Josie's confirmation order, the woman had gone off in a tizzy, insisting the date was correct. But when Josie had checked with the owner of the business, she hadn't been able to apologise enough. As it had been their mistake, she said everything would be redone on Friday without a further charge.

Even their last day had its moments, with items going missing and turning up unannounced, but by five o'clock everything was in its rightful place. Now they were sitting on the chairs behind the reception desk. The last workman had gone roughly an hour ago and, after checking every room was exactly how they wanted it to be for the big unveiling tomorrow, they'd opened a bottle of wine to celebrate before going home.

'Here's to The Workshop. I can't believe it was finished on target.' Josie chinked her wine glass with Kelly's. 'And here's to our futures in it, too.'

'Did you ever think we'd get this far?'

'Are you referring to the building or us?'

Kelly grinned. 'I suppose I mean both.'

'Things have certainly changed since the beginning of the year,' Josie acknowledged.

'For me too,' said Kelly. 'I lost my home – which, while we're on the subject, you forced me out of –'

'For a very good reason.'

'– I survived on my own in Clarence Avenue, found a job to tide me over, passed a secretarial course, sacked a loser, applied for a grant and got ready to set up my own business – that goes live tomorrow.'

'Yes, and once it does, maybe you and Jay could share some quality time together afterwards. You've worked so hard lately.'

Kelly blushed. 'I don't know about that.'

'You've a lot of catching up to do.'

'I... maybe ...' Kelly didn't want to say anything aloud in case it all went wrong. Jay had been shocked when she'd told him about Scott, even more shocked when he realised how guilty she'd felt.

'What?'

'I think it's too late.'

'It isn't. You're mad about him, anyone can see that. And you know how he feels about you, don't you? Lord knows, he ribs you about it often enough.'

Kelly puffed out her cheeks and then blew out her breath. 'Would it sound stupid if I think that he's too perfect?'

Josie shook her head. 'Not at all.'

'I knew Scott wasn't right for me but it was only when he went inside that I realised exactly how much.' Kelly began to tick things off with her fingers. 'He blamed me for everything. Then there was all that business with Anne-Marie. And then to find out that he was involved in all of those robberies makes me wonder exactly what he was capable of. I suppose until he threatened me, I thought he'd never lay a finger on me.'

'But Jay's not like that,' insisted Josie.

'I know.' Kelly's face lit up as she thought of him. Sweet, loyal Jay, who'd become her saviour over the past few months. Loving Jay who she realised she loved back with every atom of her being. He'd stood by her through everything, even when she didn't think she'd deserved it.

'I still think that too much has happened,' she added.

Josie disagreed. 'He knows Scott's an idiot and he doesn't blame you. And he adores Em. That's something extra special, isn't it?'

'But when things seem too good to be true, they usually are.' Kelly's face crumpled. She'd been an idiot letting Scott do what he wanted, but maybe she did have time to put it right now.

She twirled her chair round to face Josie more and rested one elbow on the desk. 'I hope Scott goes down for years rather than months this time. I can't believe the amount of times I covered for him. I hate him more now. He'll never change.'

They heard a car horn beep to announce Jay's arrival.

Josie drained her glass and got to her feet. 'Are you going to give him the grand tour or let him wait until tomorrow?'

'Tomorrow will do,' said Kelly, anxious to get home now that he was here.

'Come on, then, let's lock up and go.' Josie smiled. 'I suppose neither of us will get much sleep tonight.'

In the middle of the room, Kelly and Josie hugged each other. There was no need for words. Both women realised how far they had come.

Once back at the flat, Kelly couldn't stop thinking about Josie's advice. They'd dropped Emily off at her mum's so that they could go out for something to eat. She was staying overnight.

'I fancy a hot curry to celebrate the opening of Office Options. What do you reckon?' Jay asked as he walked into the living room behind her.

Kelly turned to face him, reached for his hand and drew him close. 'I thought we could stay in and celebrate, seeing as we have the place to ourselves.' Smiling shyly, she slipped her hand inside his jumper and ran it over the length of his back, nervous at the feel of his skin for the first time.

Jay grinned, his eyes darkening with lust. 'And what did you have in mind to get the party started?'

Kelly held up her other hand. In it was a DVD.

'It's a girlie flick,' she said. Then she threw it onto the settee. 'But first, there's something we need to clear up.'

Before she could say anything else, Jay cupped her face and kissed her lightly on the lips. 'Kelly Winterton, I don't give a flying fuck about anything right now. I just want to get inside your knickers.'

Kelly giggled. 'You don't understand, do you? That's exactly what I want to clear up. Now get your kit off, Jay Kirkwell.'

Jay's jumper was over his head in a flash.

31

Subject: Good Luck
From: Americanboy@bluememory.com
To: J.Mellor@MitchellHousingAssociation.co.uk

Hi Josie, I just wanted to say all the very best for your big day. I'm sorry I can't be with you. I would have loved to have seen everything as you've planned it.

I'll be thinking of you when I get up (only because you'll be getting ready to open the doors when I am eating my breakfast...!)

Tata for now,

James x

Josie was awake earlier than the birds the following morning. She'd been mentally going over her to-do list all night. There was so much to think about if the day was going to go as planned.

She propped up her head with a pillow in order to see her clothes laid out on the chair: plum-coloured jacket and matching pencil skirt, black sling-backs that instantly seemed to lengthen her legs, cream short-sleeved blouse with a low neck line. On the chest of drawers, a beaded necklace that Livvy had brought as a good luck present and a bottle of new perfume that she'd treated herself to.

She hoped today was going to be a new beginning for her. She had so much to be thankful for recently. Despite everything that had happened with Stewart, she'd found a good friend in Kelly and hooked up with Livvy again, so she wouldn't be lonely – and maybe, in time, she'd get to know James better. That might be nice.

She stretched out every muscle in her body. Then she threw back the covers. Today was going to be so special that she didn't want to waste a moment of it. Within forty minutes, she was heading out of the door.

'Wake up, sleepyhead,' Jay whispered into Kelly's ear. He slid a tray towards her. On it was a bowl of cereal, a boiled egg complete with toast soldiers, and a mug of coffee. A pink flower Kelly recognised from her garden stood proud in a half pint glass of water.

Kelly's smile widened. Jay gave her a lingering kiss before pulling back the duvet and climbing in beside her. Once he'd settled, Kelly picked up her mug – then put it down again.

'I'm so excited, Jay.' She clapped her hands like a toddler. 'Today I am going to open my own business.'

Jay's torso disappeared down the side of the bed. From underneath it, he pulled out a large pink envelope and sat up straight again.

'I hadn't realised Em wouldn't be here, this morning – not that I'm complaining after last night.' He raised his eyebrows lasciviously. 'So I'd better give you this anyway.'

The envelope contained a handmade card. The words good luck had been outlined and filled with silver glitter.

'We made it yesterday,' Jay explained as she opened it.

To Mummy, it read inside. *Good luck tomorrow. Love from Emily and Jay.* Hearts and flowers had been drawn everywhere and a shape which Kelly later found out to be a horseshoe. A lump came to her throat.

'It's lovely.' Kelly put it down on the bedside table. Then she moved aside the tray. 'And so are you.'

Jay drew her into his arms, where she now understood she truly belonged. She kissed him long and hard. Thank goodness he'd waited for her.

At ten thirty, on a fairly dull, yet extremely dry day at the beginning of July, The Workshop was officially opened by The Lord Mayoress, her consort, and two local businessmen. Rapturous applause and short speeches were followed by a surge of people through the doors.

Josie posed for numerous photographs, dragging Kelly and some of the other unit holders into most of them with her. Kelly became Josie's unofficial deputy, showing everyone around the building, remarking when appropriate on what a massive team effort it had all been. Josie worried that they'd cope: Kelly told her she worried too much.

By lunchtime, the place resembled one of Josie's garden complaints. Discarded leaflets were scattered over table tops and chairs, at least four helium balloons had floated up to the ceiling, and people young and old stood around in groups. Some of the dignitaries were hanging around, waiting for the buffet to be unwrapped.

Kay, the office manager who was never there to manage the office, stopped by with Ray and a new girl who had yet to learn the joys of housing. Andy rushed in and out, due to a call coming through just as he was about to sample a cake that Dot had made for Kelly to bring along.

Livvy showed up around two thirty, closely followed by James. Josie's eyes nearly popped out of her head. He looked relaxed, if a little jetlagged, in jeans and designer T-shirt. His hair had lightened slightly: his skin had tanned dramatically.

'Hi,' he waved.

'Hi! You were the last person I expected to turn up,' Josie said. 'I thought you weren't back until next week.'

'I thought I'd surprise you,' he smiled warmly.

'But the email...'

'I asked someone to send it for me this morning.'

'Oh, I...' Consciously, she ran a hand through her hair, remembering her tumble in the bouncy castle earlier with Emily.

After introductions, Livvy went to grab a cup of tea.

'This place looks great,' James enthused as he skimmed the room before quickly turning to her.

'Yes, it's been a lot of work but well worth the effort.'

'Maybe... maybe I could take you out for something to eat this evening and celebrate your success?'

Josie smiled shyly. 'Yes, I'd like that very much.'

She heard a giggle behind her and realised that Kelly and Livvy had obviously been listening. As James wandered off to fetch coffee and Livvy moved to talk to one of the councillors, Kelly whispered to her.

'He's a nice dude. Where have you been hiding him?'

'Nowhere,' said Josie in her own defence. She watched as James added milk to her drink and chatted to everyone around him. 'He's my neighbour's brother and has just come back from America.'

Josie smiled, then turned abruptly. Kelly had gone. She realised she'd been left on her own again as James walked back to her. Nerves fizzled up in her stomach – or was it a tiny bit of excitement?

James moved closer and spoke to her in a whisper. 'So, tell me, Ms Josie, how do you like your eggs in the morning?'

'In the words of Dean Martin,' she replied cheekily, 'I like mine with a kiss.'

'Hmm, Ms Josie,' he wagged a finger at her and grinned. 'Now you're definitely flirting with me.'

Once everyone had helped themselves to lunch, Josie moved over to where Kelly was sitting with Jay. James and Livvy had left half an hour earlier. Emily had gone back onto the bouncy castle with some of the other children.

'I've got something to show you.' Josie handed an envelope to Kelly. 'It's yours if you want it.'

Kelly flicked through the photographs of a semi-detached house. Her hand rose to her mouth and she gasped. It looked a bit tatty, but it was huge. And the living room was big too, not to mention the kitchen that looked onto the garden. She knew she could do so much to improve it.

From the last shot, she recognised where it was.

'It's in Norman Street.' She handed the photos to Jay.

Josie nodded. 'That's right. You won't be 'living on the hell' anymore. You'll be on The Mitch, the *better* half of the estate, and around the corner from Jay. I take it that won't be a problem?'

Kelly looked at the photographs again. 'Why didn't you tell me last night?'

'I wanted to wait until today, make it more special. And I can certainly vouch for you in saying that you've been a model tenant.'

'I'm hoping that the tenancy might become a joint one soon,' Jay broke in. He slung an arm around Kelly's shoulders.

'Ohmigod.' Josie's eyes widened as she looked from one to the other and back again. 'Don't tell me that you two have finally got it together?'

Kelly smiled and nodded.

Josie clapped her hands in glee. 'Wow, I can finally say, 'case closed'.'

Jay grinned. 'I couldn't let this one get away now, could I? You're a right pair of clever broads. And this place is amazing. But if you're looking after it, won't you miss working on the streets, Josie? All that crime and grime?'

'Oh, I'm sure I'll get to hear about everything, one way or another.' Josie smiled. 'Besides, I've got loads of unfinished cases to keep an eye on. You know as much as I do that there's never a dull moment on the Mitchell Estate.'

. . .

A LETTER FROM MEL

First of all, I'd like to say a huge thank you for choosing to read Behind A Closed Door. I hope you enjoyed my second outing to the fictional town of Stockleigh and the Mitchell Estate. I had so much fun creating characters such as Kelly, Amy and Debbie and I hoped you enjoyed reading their stories as much as I did writing about them.

If you did like Behind A Closed Door, I would be grateful if you would write a small review. I'd love to hear what you think, and it can also help other readers to discover one of my books for the first time. Maybe you can recommend it to your friends and family.

Keep in touch,

Mel x

FIGHTING FOR SURVIVAL

1

*G*ina Bradley swallowed two tablets with the help of a mouthful of water, knocking back the rest afterwards. It spilled over the rim of the glass and down her chin in her haste to get rid of the pounding inside her head. Bang, bang, bang.

It took her a moment to realise that the noise was actually from someone knocking at the front door. She shuffled through the living room, careful not to trip over Pete's boots splayed in the middle of the floor, and squeezed around the boxes of knock-off paraphernalia piled up along the narrow hallway.

'What the hell do you want?' she snapped, looking down at Josie Mellor from her vantage point of three steps up.

'Good morning to you too,' said Josie. 'Don't say that you weren't expecting me. Are the twins at home? I need to talk to them about–'

'All right, all right, keep your voice down.' Gina opened the door and moved to one side. 'You'd better come in. I don't want the whole of Stanley Avenue to know my bleeding business.'

Josie moved past her. Before shutting the door, Gina looked up and down the road to see who was nosing at her. She watched for curtains twitching: it was bound to be one of the neighbours who had complained, although for once, it didn't seem to have anything to do with her and Pete making a racket after a late night argument.

She followed Josie into the living room and dropped onto the settee, not bothering to move the pile of magazines and a pair of men's jeans. Josie sat down on the armchair next to the gas fire.

'What do you want to know?' Gina asked as she reached for a packet of cigarettes from the coffee table.

'Where were your girls last night?'

'That depends.' She lit a cigarette, snapped the lighter shut and took a deep drag.

'In that case, you can't be certain that they weren't involved in the altercation across on the square.'

Gina leaned back and placed her feet onto the dusty coffee table. 'In that case,' she mimicked Josie, 'they were here with me all night.'

Josie sighed. 'Mrs Bradley, have you any idea of the serious nature of the attack?'

'Nope.' In truth, Gina hadn't a clue what Josie was referring to. She'd fallen asleep on the sofa, long before the twins had come home. They might have mentioned some sort of a fight when they'd nudged her awake and she'd gone up to bed but she couldn't recall anything now.

'There were two incidents, in fact,' said Josie. 'At half past seven, Rachel and Claire were seen riding their bikes along Davy Road after a woman was knocked to the floor and her handbag was stolen.'

'Not my girls,' said Gina with a slow shake of the head. 'Besides, they know better than to get caught on CCTV.'

Josie frowned: damn the government cutbacks. Manning the cameras on the Mitchell Estate had been the first thing to suffer after the local council cut their staff by twenty per cent. Since then, things had started to slide again; people realised they couldn't be seen as much as before.

'The woman suffered a broken nose and a dislocated shoulder, Gina,' she said.

'And you think my girls are capable of that?' Gina stared back at her.

'They're not girls anymore, they're sixteen. And the mess they made of Melissa Riley last year, I dare say they are more than capable.'

'That was a teenage misunderstanding. You know how catfights can start when boys are involved.'

'Actually, I don't recall any when I was their age.'

'No, you would have been Miss Fucking Perfect at school, wouldn't you? I see you haven't changed now, apart from becoming a jobsworth.'

'At least I have a job,' muttered Josie.

'What?'

'Nothing.'

Gina watched as Josie lowered her eyes. Josie hardly ever retaliated, no matter what she spat out at her. What had rattled her cage?

'You mentioned two episodes?' she said.

'Yes.' Josie tried to regain her professionalism. 'There was another mugging half an hour later. This one was particularly brutal. A young lad was pushed down the steps on Frazer Terrace. He says he fell but–'

'He must have fallen if he said he did. Bleeding hell, Josie, can't you take anything at face value?'

'Not when I know he's lying.'

'And exactly how do you know that?'

'I just do, that's all.'

Gina glared at Josie, wondering as she did what she really thought of her – not her professional opinion but deep down inside.

Josie was thirty-seven and had been working on the sprawling Mitchell Estate for the past eighteen years. More recently, she'd been splitting her time between the role of housing officer and manager of the new business enterprise centre, The Workshop.

She was known as a fair, firm person, always offering a word of encouragement. But she wasn't a pushover; Josie would help for a while, giving anyone the benefit of the doubt until she realised that her advice wouldn't be taken, and then she'd resort to stronger methods to get things done. All the time, she would try; often she would fail. But she still cared, whatever the outcome.

There were fifteen hundred houses on The Mitchell Estate. Until recently, Josie and her work colleague, Ray, had shared the responsibility of the properties that belonged to Mitchell Housing Association, but since The Workshop had opened, Josie was mostly based there. However, she always liked working out in the community and couldn't wait to get back to more casework when the time was right. For now, she was keeping old cases open and only visiting when requested to – like today.

Gina put herself in Josie's place and imagined what she would see. A small, fat woman who had let herself go - someone who looked much older than her thirty-five years, someone who couldn't be bothered to move her fat arse from the settee. She knew she looked a mess compared to the woman sitting opposite her, with her perfectly styled bobbed hair, fresh make-up, and the waft of perfume filling the room.

'Give me a break,' Gina pleaded. 'You ought to try living my life for a week. I have a lazy bastard for a husband who's never done a day's work in his life. My eldest son is heading the same way – either that or he'll end up inside again. I have daughters who happen to be the bane of everyone's life. Wherever they go, they cause mayhem. It's not exactly a barrel of laughs for me.'

'My life is in no way perfect,' said Josie, 'but I do try my best to get things right.'

Gina yawned. 'I'm bored with this conversation. Have you finished?'

'No, I haven't. Your girls are heading for a big come down. You know they think they rule the roost with this stupid gang they're part of.'

Gina giggled. 'Yeah. The Mitchell Mob, they call themselves. So funny.'

'It isn't funny at all.' Josie's voice rose slightly. 'Do you want them both to be locked up like Danny was last year? Then you'll be on your own and...'

'And?' Gina taunted when Josie had been silent for a few seconds.

'You know what I mean. They're both heading for a meltdown.'

Gina stood up quickly. 'I think you'd better sling your hook. I'm sick of you poking your nose into my family's business all the time. Who do you think you are?'

'I have a file on your family this thick,' Josie indicated an inch between her thumb and index finger, 'so you need to be careful. I can't keep shielding you and your girls from eviction.'

'Eviction?'

Josie said nothing.

'You can't be serious?' Gina continued. 'I've been a tenant here for seventeen years. You can't just turf us out.'

'I – I can,' said Josie, 'and I will, if I have to.'

Gina grabbed Josie's arm and pulled her up roughly. 'Get out of my house. And don't come back accusing my family of all sorts until you have the proof that they were involved.'

Josie tried to shrug Gina off but she held on tight. 'Could you at least try and talk to them?' she asked. 'They might listen to you.'

Gina sneered. 'What makes you think they'll listen to me? Like you said, they're sixteen now.'

'Which means we have more rights to lock them up if they're caught.'

Gina pushed Josie across the living room and along the hallway. She yanked open the front door and shoved her through it. Josie just about kept her balance as she flew down the steps.

'I'm warning you, Josie Mellor, stay away from here. Stay away from me and stay away from my family. Because if you don't, I'll come after you. Just you remember that.'

'Gina, you're making a big mistake. I can help you if–'

'Just keep your nose out of my business.' Gina slammed the door so hard that paint chips fell to the floor. She stomped back through to the kitchen, grabbed the whisky bottle from where she'd left it the night before and took a huge swig. Then another. And another.

She wiped her mouth with the back of her hand and took in a huge gulp of air. How dare Josie come round here and accuse her girls? Oh, she knew deep down that they must have had something to do with the drama last night. If not two incidents, they would more than likely be involved in one of them – probably the boy falling down the steps.

Damn that Josie Mellor. And damn that stupid housing association and its rules. No one would turf her family out. They wouldn't dare mess with the Bradleys.

Caren Williams shivered involuntarily, her legs feeling heavy as she leaned her back against the windowsill. She glanced around the large, family kitchen that she'd painted a welcoming yellow earlier that year but its brightness was wasted on her: this was the last morning she'd be walking into it.

Holding back tears, she realised that in less than three hours she and John had to be out of there. The bailiffs were calling at 2pm: neither of them wanted to be there when the locks would be changed and a notice pinned to their front door.

Even though they'd voluntarily given the keys back to their mortgage company rather than wait for the inevitable, it still amounted to the same thing. They were being slung out because they couldn't afford to pay. Besides, Caren didn't want to see the pitying looks that were bound to come from their neighbours.

Bankruptcy – not a word she thought she would ever need to speak aloud in her life. She cast her mind back two years. John's plumbing and heating business had been going strong. It had been a struggle at first, as were most businesses during their first years, but as time went by, regular customers came on board and gradually it grew into a resounding success.

Caren, who had worked full-time with John, taking care of the administration, the accounts, a little sales and a lot of PR, had even been able to reduce her working days to four a week, freeing time up to think about starting her own business.

But then one of John's major clients had gone under. Not only did it leave them being owed thousands of pounds, it created a cash flow problem that the bank wasn't willing to help them out with. The business also lost a vast percentage of its incoming work. John cut staff down to the bare minimum but in the end, the loss was too much to bear. Within months, everything they'd worked so hard to achieve was gone.

John walked into the room a few minutes later, sagging shoulders indicating his mood. Caren felt her heartbeat quicken again. She watched as he buried his face in his hands.

'John, don't–'

He opened his arms and she ran into them. He smelled of shower gel, his short, dark hair still wet. It was so comforting.

'I can't believe this is happening,' he cried. 'I'm so sorry.'

'It wasn't your fault,' she told him, tears running down her face.

'I should have seen it coming; shouldn't have put all my eggs into one basket. I should have reached out for more clients when I had the opportunity but I didn't think it would get this bad – to the point of no return.'

'We weren't to know that Carrington's would go into administration.'

'I know, but–'

'We'll get through this; in time you can start up again and I can get my business idea up and running.'

'It took us years to build up what we had. And now, look at us – at the bottom of the pile again.'

'Look on the bright side,' she encouraged. 'The only way is up; we can't get any lower than this.'

Despite their gloomy prospects, John smiled. 'You can always see the positive,' he said. 'I wish I shared your optimism.'

'We'll pick ourselves up and start again, you'll see.'

But John's buoyancy soon died. 'Sure, we only need a few thousand pounds that we don't have.'

'We'll find it again.' Caren wouldn't let him slide down – because if he did, she would no doubt go down with him. 'Besides, anything is better than sitting rocking in a corner thinking nothing will change. It will – eventually, it has to.'

John shook his head. 'Where would I be without you?'

There was so much pain in his eyes that Caren had to look away for a moment. She and John had been an item during her last year at high school. He was two years older than her at thirty-seven and she'd had a crush on him since the first time she'd seen him. Once she'd walked out of the school gates for the very last time, she'd done her utmost to keep him on the straight and narrow. The Mitchell Estate could drag even the most positive of people down with it after a while. She wasn't going to let that happen to them.

It took them two years to save for a deposit on a house and as soon as Caren finished her hairdressing and beauty course at college, they were on their way.

Their first had been a two-up, two-down in a long row of ex-miners houses. Four years later, they'd swapped that for a semi-detached property that was hardly bigger but had three-bedrooms. Next had come the three-bed pre-war semi, closely followed by the four-bedroom detached house they were going to lose today. It was her pride and joy, and it had all gone in a blink of an eye.

John looked at her. It was twenty years ago that she'd first fallen for those eyes; the blue-grey speckles in the dark ponds of sapphire, and those long, black

Fighting for Survival

lashes. There were a few faint laughter lines around them – not that she'd heard him laughing much since the eviction notice had arrived. Until recently, he'd always been her knight in shining armour. This had ruined him – it wasn't fair – but she wouldn't let it ruin them.

'We'll get through this,' she reiterated. 'You and me. We'll survive.'

Gently, he cupped her face in his hands. 'Do you think so?' he whispered.

'I know so.'

Caren lowered her eyes then, before she gave away how tense she was feeling. John enveloped her in his arms again, where she felt strong in his embrace.

She loved him with all her heart.

No matter what happened, they'd get through this mess.

2

Gina lay in bed, the rain lashing down outside her window hardly giving her any incentive to get up. She hadn't got anywhere to go anyway. She turned over, hoping to get more sleep.

If it weren't for the noise going on downstairs, she would have stayed there much longer than an extra few minutes. But there was no chance of that because Rachel and Claire had been bickering for fifteen minutes now. She covered her head with the duvet, praying they would stop.

'It's mine, you cow. I got it first.'

'I only want to wear it today. Then you can have it back.'

'No, I want to wear it. Mum got this one for me; you've got the blue one.'

'I want the pink one.'

'Well, you can't have it!'

Gina stormed to the top of the stairs and hung her head over the banister. 'If you two don't stop screaming at each other, I'll take both T-shirts from you.'

'Chill out, Mum,' Rachel shouted up to her. 'Claire is just being a moody cow.'

'No, I'm not.'

'Yes, you are.'

'No, I'm not!'

'For crying out loud.' Gina dressed in whatever piece of clothing came to hand from the floor before marching down the stairs. 'Are you two six or sixteen? Why can't you ever act your age?' She looked at the clock. 'Actually, why aren't you two at school?'

'Free period,' said Rachel, the lie rolling off her tongue with ease.

'You're only two weeks into a new term.' Gina clipped her shoulder as she walked past. 'More like you've skipped it again. Move your arse, the pair of you. I'm not having that school woman on my doorstep, going on at me as if I'm not capable of looking after my own kids.'

'You're not,' muttered Claire. It earned her a clip too.

'Ow. What was that for?' Claire rubbed at her shoulder while Rachel laughed at her.

'Less of your lip, young lady.' Gina pushed past them, into the kitchen. This morning's and last night's dishes were piled precariously in the sink, congealed grease swimming in the murky water that they soaked in. Her hand moved to cover her nose. 'It stinks in here. Has someone killed a cat?'

'We would have killed it by now if we had one,' giggled Rachel.

Claire nudged her. 'Don't be stupid. I wouldn't do anything to hurt an animal. They're defenceless creatures.'

'That's not what you said when Loopy Leonard's dog nearly had hold of your ankles last week.'

'That was your fault. If you hadn't been a stupid cow and told me to–'

'Girls, put a lid on it.' Gina lit up a cigarette and took a huge drag, coughing and spluttering the side effects of twenty years on the weed. 'Where's your father?' she asked once she'd caught her breath. 'Is the idle bastard in or out?'

'Left about an hour ago,' stated Rachel. 'Which you would have known if you'd bothered to get out of bed earlier.'

Both girls ran out of the room as Gina lunged towards them, her hand raised again. Their laughter followed them out of the house with a bang of the back door. Gina sighed: peace at last in the Bradley household.

She wondered what work on the side her husband was up to today as she made herself a mug of milky tea. Then, without another moment's thought, she settled down in the chaos of the living room to catch up with the shenanigans on *Jeremy Kyle*. Today's show was about a mother who'd had a family early in life and was now having a mid-life crisis by sleeping with a boy of sixteen.

Gina switched it off after a few minutes. It reminded her too much of her own life to be called entertainment. She felt much worse than the woman with the huge boobs and mini skirt that looked no wider than a belt, because at least she was having sex. Gina couldn't remember the last time she and Pete had got down and dirty. Was it last month, August? Was it July or June? Nope, she couldn't recall any special occasions.

She pushed a pile of magazines off the coffee table to make way for her feet. Then she put them out of sight. Even her white socks were the colour of dirty dishwater.

What was going on with her? She'd chosen this life so she didn't have to go to work so why the long face all the time? Just lately, she found she could raise her hand easier than a smile.

Mind you, what had she got to show for her life so far? She had a wayward husband who didn't know the meaning of working legally for his money, a twenty-year-old son going the same way and sixteen-year-old twins who were regular visitors to Mitchell Housing Association to be interviewed by the local police. Gina hardly had time to live her life for the worries of the ones she'd brought into this world to fend for themselves. That woman on the TV had nothing on her.

She hauled herself up from the old and worn settee and went upstairs to the bathroom. The broken mirror above the sink showed a scary reflection. She ran a hand through red, greasy hair, not bothering to brush her teeth or wash her face. The clothes she'd picked up from the floor were two days old – or were they three?

Gina sniffed cautiously at her armpits. She pulled away sharply – no wonder Pete wouldn't come anywhere near her with that smell.

She sat on the side of the bath while she filled it to the brim with hot water. She could do with a long soak and at least she could lie back in her muck alone for once. Only on rare occasions would the house be this quiet.

A few minutes later, submerged in the water, she tried to remember what had gone down last night to make her head ache so much. She remembered having a few cans of lager and a couple of whisky chasers but she was at a loss after that. Oh, yes, she recalled. Pete had phoned for a takeaway; that had been the smell from the kitchen and the mess down the front of her jumper. Not for the first time, she wished she could turn back the clock and start her life again.

Gina had lived in Stanley Avenue, on the bottom half of the Mitchell Estate, all her life. Her parents lived across the road; her sister Leah and her son, Samuel, lived next door but three. Even her brother had lived there until he'd given up his flat to live courtesy of Her Majesty's pleasure for the past year.

She often wondered if her parents hadn't moved onto the estate, would she have turned out this way? Would it only have taken another street, on another estate somewhere to make her life turn the happy way, rather than the path to nothing she was following now?

From the moment she had seen Pete at high school, she had wanted him. Very soon, she'd had him. Very soon, she'd become pregnant by him. At fifteen, when all the other girls at school were discovering cigarettes, cheap cider and ecstasy tablets, she'd discovered the joys of sex behind the bus shelter.

A quick blow job, a quick fumble and a quick fuck; that was all it had taken for Pete to belong to Gina. Yet she often wondered why he'd stuck with her. After all, she wasn't a catch. She was a plump, thirty-five-year-old mum of three who didn't give a shit about herself anymore.

Gina slid down beneath the water and lay there. If she could hold her breath long enough, she could slip away without anyone noticing. Because she knew as sure as night was night and day was day that no one would miss her.

'Where do you want me to put this?' John asked as he heaved a heavy box up the steps to their front door.

'In the kitchen,' said Caren. 'It's written on the side of the box if you look.'

John lifted his arm slightly whilst keeping a grip on the box. 'Oh yeah.' He grinned. 'It's bloody heavy. What the hell's in it? A dead body?'

Caren picked up a box marked dining room and sighed - there wasn't a dining room here. Lord knows where she was going to put all of their belongings. The house was tiny compared to their old home.

Tears sprang to her eyes. No, she wouldn't think about that, she chastised herself. Onwards and upwards was her mantra. This was their new home; it would have to do until something better came along.

Twenty-four, Stanley Avenue. Of all the places she would end up, she hadn't thought it would be here. Stanley Avenue epitomised everything she had fought so hard to get away from when she was younger. Bloody typical she would end up right back where she had started.

A crash made her hurry through to the kitchen. She put her box down and ran to help John as he grappled with cups and saucers smashing to the floor.

'It wasn't my fault. The box split.' He looked on in dismay, waiting for the wrath of his wife. But Caren grinned.

'I hated that bloody tea set,' she laughed. Then she couldn't stop laughing, knowing full well that when she stopped she would start to cry again.

John put down what was left of the box and hugged his wife. 'It'll get better soon,' he said. 'You wait and see.'

Caren hugged him. Since she'd found out they were about to lose everything, there had been so many times that she'd hated him. It had nothing to do with apportioning blame. She'd been the one who had taken control. She'd been the one who had gone to Mitchell Housing Association to explain about their predicament. She'd been the one who'd phoned all their creditors, assuring future payments, even if they had to be the minimum payment for now. But then again, she'd always been the pushy one in their relationship. If it wasn't for her, she doubted John would have left the estate in the first place.

She watched him now as he bent to pick up the pieces of broken crockery. To her eye, he was still as gorgeous as he'd been in his early twenties. He was clean shaven, with a receding hairline. He wore the latest in designer clothes, fitting his T-shirt and jeans well, with pert buttocks and biceps. Her husband: John Williams. The man who went to the gym three times a week, to the barbers every three weeks and shopping for designer clothes on a regular basis. All that would have to stop now, though. Caren wondered if he'd realised that yet.

'We'll make it work, Caz,' he said. 'Then we can move again, get our own place. Start the business up again. Buy even better cars. We can do it if we stick together.'

She nodded.

'I suppose there's a box for rubbish marked up, Mrs Organised?'

'Of course, what else would you expect?' Caren opened a kitchen cupboard and reeled at the smell. 'God knows who lived here before us, but I've a good mind to complain. It smells as if someone has died in here and it's bloody filthy.'

'Relax, babe.' John nudged her on his way out. 'It's just to remind us of how shit life will be on the Mitchell Estate and how we need to get out of here as soon as.'

'Which means you getting back to work as soon as,' Caren replied. 'Have you rung Daryl yet?' John's friend had promised him some labouring work for a few weeks.

'No, there's plenty of time. Let's get settled first. Then we can get on with creating a new life for us.'

Funny, thought Caren, as she watched him until he was out of sight, that's what I thought I'd started to do all those years ago.

'About bleeding time.' Barbara Lewis told her eldest daughter, when she finally answered the door after three loud knocks. 'I thought even an idle cow like you couldn't still be in bed at eleven thirty.'

'I am not an idle cow,' snapped Gina, 'and as you can see I'm up.'

Even though it was on the tip of her tongue to say something about Gina still being in her pyjamas, Barbara kept her mouth shut, knowing better than to get into a fight.

'Do you fancy coming into town with me?' she asked. 'I'll treat you to coffee and a jam doughnut.'

Gina flopped back down onto the settee where she'd been sprawling for the past two hours. 'Which is usually code for you want me to do something that *I* won't want to do,' she replied. 'Especially if you're buying cake.'

'Well, there's a party coming up and I don't fancy going on my own.' Gina's dad had died two years ago. 'I thought you might–'

'Me?' Gina snorted before lighting a cigarette. 'You must be joking.'

'They won't all be old fuddy-duddies.'

Gina threw her another look.

'So?' Barbara tried again.

Gina took a drag of her cigarette. 'I can't,' she said, smoke coming out of her mouth and down her nose. 'Even if I had something decent to wear, you know Pete wouldn't like it.'

'It's at the weekend – would he even be back to know?'

Gina ignored her sarcastic tone. Pete usually played cards on Saturday nights and didn't come home until the early hours. Often he didn't come home at all until the next morning. Gina wasn't stupid: she knew sometimes he was with other women but she couldn't prove it. Despite the Mitchell Estate being great for spreading rumours, she only ever got to hear who he was with if someone was out to cause trouble.

'Come into town with me anyway,' Barbara urged, not wanting to give up so easily.

Gina perished the thought. It would mean that she'd have to get dressed and washed and she didn't have it in her – not after drinking the remainder of a bottle of Jack Daniel's last night.

'Can't be bothered,' she said. 'Besides, I still feel rough after a heavy session.'

Barbara sat back and folded her arms across her thin body. 'You have a heavy session most nights, that's nothing new. I'm worried about you, you know. All that alcohol you knock back isn't healthy. I think–'

'Mum, zip it, will you?' Gina snapped. 'You're getting to sound like a right nag.'

'And you're a right moody cow.' Barbara stood up. 'I only stopped by so that you'd make an effort once in a while to get out of the house.'

Gina pulled her feet up beside her. 'What's the point when I've got no money to buy anything?'

'I'll lend you a twenty from my pension.'

'I'll never be able to pay you back.'

'Can't you get anything off Pete?'

'No, I can't.'

'But he always seems to have spare cash.'

Gina wondered how she could stop this chat. What she and Pete did with their money – or how he came across it – was nothing to do with anyone else. And why did everyone think they knew what was best for her? Couldn't she be trusted to make her own mind up about things?

Desperate to be left alone, she reached for the remote control and turned up the volume on the television. They sat in silence for a few minutes until her mum finally got the message.

'If you won't come with me, then I'll go on my own. I can't sit around on my arse all day even if you can. It's not healthy.' She stormed out of the room, slamming the door behind her.

Gina sighed with relief: peace at last. She was just about to settle in for another kip when the door opened again. Barbara was back, green eyes sparkling with excitement.

'You'll never guess who I've just seen,' she cried.

'No, but I'm sure you're going to tell me anyhow.' Gina knew it would most likely be one of her old cronies that she hadn't seen for a while.

'Caren Williams – you know, that girl from your school. You and Pete used to go out with her and her fella.' Barbara paused, one hand on her hip. 'Didn't you fall out with her over something and nothing?'

Gina said nothing. Of course she remembered Caren, but she wasn't going to register a flicker of interest. Her mum was right: she and Caren had hated each other at school.

Barbara grabbed her daughter's hands and tried to pull her to her feet but Gina resisted.

'I'm telling you, I've just seen Caren Williams,' she said. 'And get this... she's moving stuff into the empty house across the road from you.'

Gina was up from the settee in a flash.

3

'That's the van emptied, Caz,' John said, carrying in the last box of their possessions. Even though it was marked 'bathroom' in black capital letters, he slid it onto the kitchen worktop. 'It didn't take long to unpack everything, did it?'

'All the contents need to be unpacked too, you dope,' Caren told him. 'That's going to take ages. What time does the van have to be returned by?'

'Four thirty. I'll drop it off and walk back through the estate afterwards. It'll only take me half an hour.'

'No. Someone might see you.'

'So?'

'I don't want anyone to know we're living here!'

'What makes you think anyone else will be interested in our lives? We've been gone too long. People won't even remember us.'

Caren knew that wasn't true. They'd lived their lives on this estate and, even though she had saved hard to get them away, most of their school friends had remained here, not knowing any better. She didn't want to be associated with any of them ever again if she could help it, especially now.

John kissed her lightly on her cheek. 'I won't be too long.'

A minute later, he was back. 'I've picked up the wrong keys,' he said, throwing down a bunch on the table and picking up another set before leaving again.

Caren set to work cleaning inside the cupboards. She filled another bowl full of hot water and bleach, popped rubber gloves on to her hands to save her nails and got down on all fours. She opened the first of nine cupboards and started to scrub at its base.

A few minutes later, John was back again.

'What have you forgotten this time?' Caren kept her back towards him as she continued to scrub. 'Honestly, you'd forget your–'

'Look who I bumped into outside,' he interrupted.

'Well, hello there, Caren.'

Caren took a sharp intake of breath before slowly backing out and turning to face them. No, it couldn't be...

Shit: it was.

'Pete!' She put on a false smile as she stood up. 'What are you doing in Stanley Avenue? Heard we were back and come to say hello?'

'No, I was just getting home and I spotted John pulling off in the van.'

Caren's heart sank but her smile remained firmly in place.

'Yeah,' said John with a smile that was in no way false at all. 'You'll never guess where he and Gina live? Right opposite us – number twenty-five. How cool is that? It'll be just like old times.'

Old times? Caren shuddered involuntarily. She'd worked hard to forget those. There had been no love lost between her and Gina at school and, even though people change, she'd heard that Gina had remained the same small-minded bitch that she'd always been. She knew that she'd had three kids in quick succession; knew that she hadn't worked a day in her life.

She'd heard that Pete was known around the estate for not keeping his dick in his trousers, though looking at him now, with his clothes hanging off him, his scruffy hair and skin in need of a good wash, she wondered why any woman would take a fancy to him.

Oh, God, this was going to be a nightmare.

Turning away, she cast her mind back to when she'd last seen Gina Bradley. She'd been in Woolworths a few years ago, getting presents for Christmas. Gina had come walking – no, waddling – towards her, looking like she expected her to stop and make small talk as their eyes locked.

She recalled being thankful that she'd made an effort to keep in shape over the years and took great pleasure in seeing Gina's resigned look as her eyes then swept from Caren's head to her toes and back again quickly.

Caren had then walked straight past as if she didn't know her, a smile playing on her lips. She wasn't a vengeful person but it had felt so good, so liberating.

Once she heard John and Pete leave the room behind her, she let out the breath she'd been holding. Trying not to cry, she forced herself back down onto the floor and began to scrub away with vigour.

This situation was going from bad to worse. What had she done to deserve this?

*G*ina stood in her bedroom window, hoping that no one could see her as she watched the goings-on across the road. When Mum first told her about Caren, she'd had to see for herself. The two of them had stood at the window, gawping at the items of furniture that had come from the van. There had been some proper posh stuff, things Gina and Barbara had only ever been able to dream of owning.

And although Barbara had lots of fun imagining what items were going into what rooms, every time something else came from the van, Gina's heart sank at the realisation that Caren must be loaded. But then again, she was back on the Mitchell Estate. She would have to find out why.

Since Mum had gone at about one o'clock, her trip into town forgotten, Gina had stood there but still she hadn't seen Caren. That was hours ago; her legs were aching but she didn't dare move in case she missed anything.

She couldn't believe it – her archenemy, moving in directly opposite; their front doors practically parallel to one another. They would see each other every day. Gina quivered at the thought.

Rewind the years and Caren Williams had been Caren Phillips. They'd known each other since infant school but they'd never really liked each other. Gina could still remember Caren looking down her nose at her when she'd become pregnant at fifteen. She had just left school – well, she hardly went to school really – when she gave birth to Danny. She was barely sixteen.

Caren was going out with John then, boasting about how she planned to marry him and buy a house before *she* started a family.

It had been worse when she'd had the twins three years later; she and Pete married hastily when they were three months old. Gina had thought she'd have time to get her figure back after the birth but she was fat and round on the one wedding photo they had. She hated it.

Everyone thought she and Pete wouldn't last but they had proved them wrong. Sixteen years later and they were still married, although Pete had hardly been the loving, doting husband.

Rumours around the estate were that he'd shag anything that moved but Gina wasn't sure if they were true or not. He'd confessed to a couple of affairs and she'd seen off the women each time with a good fist fight. Despite that, no one really knew whether or not they were happy and Gina wasn't telling.

Suddenly, she jumped back from the window as the front door opened. She watched as John jogged down the path and opened the boot of a small white car. Within seconds, he closed it again and ran back into the house.

Gina had seen enough for her heart to start racing. Back when she was fourteen, she'd had an enormous crush on John and that bitch Caren had got to him first.

But why would John have looked at Gina when he could have Caren?

Caren was tall and svelte with long, blonde hair and fair skin. She was an only child – not like Gina being the eldest child of three – and had the latest trainers, the latest school bag, the latest everything.

Gina always had the cheaper brands. She remembered crying for two weeks over a pair of Adidas trainers she'd coveted and being mortified when her mum came home with something similar but with two black stripes instead of the trademark three.

Gina, her sister Leah and brother, Jason, had been called names throughout their school years. It hadn't been a happy time for any of them. Scruffy Gina, she'd been known as. Along with smelly Gina, thick Gina, stupid Gina, ginger Gina. And the worst ones: slapper Gina, scrubber Gina, shagger Gina.

It had been horrible getting pregnant so young, but it was her mistake and she had stood by it, even when she'd come away from school without an exam to her name. She hadn't needed qualifications anyway; she'd never worked since leaving school.

When Pete showed an interest in her, Gina had thought all her Christmases had come at once. It didn't matter that her coat was brown when everyone else's was red. It didn't matter that she had no money to go shopping for the latest clothes and make-up. At fourteen, Gina fell in love.

Yet as soon as John had shown an interest in Caren, Gina had wanted him too. To the point that she'd got very pissed on cider and threw herself at him. When he wouldn't kiss her, she offered to give him a blow job. But John hadn't wanted to know: he'd laughed at her, embarrassed by her actions. Besides, Caren had stolen his heart anyway. Gina had felt so humiliated seeing them together. John would always be sitting by Caren; her legs would be draped over his as she sat on his knee. Or he'd be standing behind her, arms encircling her tiny waist, pulling her in close.

She sighed heavily. Where had she gone wrong? Three kids and a useless pratt of a husband wasn't much to shout about. Back at school, she'd wanted to be a hairdresser. She had intended to go to college, get her own vehicle and go mobile.

Unfortunately, she hadn't reckoned on a thin blue line changing all of that, shattering her dreams, breaking her illusions. And everything continued to go wrong from that day forward.

Was it any wonder she was trying to come up with a reason for Caren to be back on the estate? It couldn't be by choice. No one would ever return to here if they didn't have to. Something must have gone wrong in her oh-so-perfect life. Bizarrely, even that thought couldn't summon a smile.

Even though she had seen John earlier when Pete came home, Gina still couldn't drag herself away from the window. Curiosity was burning up inside her to see if Caren looked as good as she remembered.

The last time she'd seen her in town, Caren had blanked her as she'd walked towards her in Woollies. Gina hadn't been bothered – there was nothing worse than seeing your rival looking a million dollars in a long, black winter coat, leather, knee-length boots, skinny jeans and a white jumper that actually looked white. Even more so when you were wearing shabby old jeans and manky trainers, with no make-up and mop hair. Caren had strode past her in a cloud of musky perfume as she'd slinked away to hide behind the greetings card stands.

That had been about three years ago. It was going to be strange to see her again after so long – and on a regular basis too. Whenever Gina needed to go to Vincent Square, Caren could be in the garden. When she went to collect her benefits, Caren could be in the post office sending parcels to friends overseas. When she went to the chemist to pick up her asthma inhaler, Caren might be there treating herself to a new lipstick or body lotion. When she went to the butchers for the cheap cuts, Caren might be buying the best pieces of steak.

Gina pushed her nails into her palms. Now she would always have a reminder of how appalling she looked against Caren. Gina with the mop of ginger hair; Gina with the body of an Oompa-Loompa – a waist measurement that was way past the healthy limit.

Gina with the lines of a smoker prominent around her mouth, Gina with the clothes that looked like they came from a charity shop. Gina with the husband who didn't give enough of a shit to try to cajole her into doing something about it.

Suddenly, Caren appeared in the doorway. Gina felt tears prick her eyes: Caren hadn't changed one iota since that day in Woollies. Her skin was tanned, her nails painted. She still had the long, flowing hair but it was tied out of the way with a pink scarf that matched the shade of her lipstick precisely. She wore light-coloured tight jeans, Chelsea boots popping out from beneath them. Checked shirt sleeves were rolled up out of the way.

She watched Caren glance up and down the avenue. Her arms were folded and she seemed to be drinking in the mood of the place. It was clear that she didn't look very happy. Gina could almost see an invisible cloak of anxiety shrouding her.

For the first time that day, she smiled. If Caren Williams thought that Gina was going to welcome her into the avenue with open arms, she was wrong. Her family had the monopoly on Stanley Avenue, and nothing ever got past them for long. She'd make it her business to have the low-down on why Caren and John had come back.

And then maybe it was time to have some fun.

'How come you get to be the boss again?' Claire asked her twin sister as they walked to their usual hangout – the car park of Shop&Save across on Vincent Square. It was nearing eight o'clock; they were off to meet up with the rest of their gang. Now the nights were drawing in there were more opportunities to cause mayhem once it was dark.

Rachel peered from behind her hood, her face barely visible to the outside world. 'What do you mean?'

Claire faltered, unsure what to say now that she had voiced her feelings. 'I mean, since Stacey got sent down, you think you're in charge of the gang. Why can't it be both of us?'

Rachel grinned and threw an arm around Claire's shoulder, pulling her close. 'Don't be daft, you nutter. I don't run the gang – we do.'

'It doesn't feel like that.'

Rachel pushed her away playfully. 'We could have some real fun with them, if you like?' When Claire frowned, she continued. 'We could play one against the other; get the low-down on who they like best.'

Claire looked away.

'What's wrong with that?'

'You always want to know who's the best.'

'Don't go all moody on me,' Rachel whined. She held a ten-pound note at each end and wiggled it about. 'I've lifted this from Mum. Let's go and get some lager.'

As they ran across Davy Road towards the square, they made a car slow down by running in front of it, giggling and laughing. Looks wise, if it wasn't for a small scar to the right of Rachel's eye where their brother, Danny, had pushed her from the seesaw at the age of five, it was hard to tell them apart. Compared to their mother, who was five foot and a dot, they were a few inches taller. They both had short, red hair. Their trousers were always baggy, always inches too long and bunched up at the ankles. They wore no jewellery, no make-up: no bling was allowed in the Mitchell Mob, except for piercings. Sometimes it was as hard to tell their gender as it was to tell them apart.

Gang wise, it was hard to distinguish them from any of the other girls. The Mitchell Mob, as they called themselves, dressed in a uniform of dark hoodies, top of the range trainers and baggy jeans or tracksuit bottoms. They all rode mountain bikes, swapped around consistently to hide their identity further. If any of them were in trouble, it was hard to prove.

As a gang, each one of them had their own identity, but to an outsider, they were a bunch of girls out to cause mayhem. Pack mentality almost always took over and any innocent bystander walking past could become their latest prey.

Tonight, there were five girls waiting for them in their usual spot outside the doorway of Shop&Save. It was the perfect place for them to cause maximum trouble. They could also scrounge cigarettes and the odd can of lager from people coming out. That was, until they were moved on – they were always moved on eventually, either by the store manager or the local police. It depended on how rowdy they became.

The girls were sitting on the low railing separating the car park from the walkway. So far the promised rain for the evening had failed to materialise but that, and the added menace of darkness falling, meant that it was fairly quiet.

'What's up?' Rachel asked as she stood in front of them, her hands shoved deep in her pockets.

'Nothing really,' said Ashley Bruce. She was small and thin, with black hair cut into a severe bob, several earrings dangling from both ears. 'It's boring. There's no one about yet.'

Rachel glanced up and down Davy Road, wondering if Ashley meant victims for them to taunt, or the boys. Rachel had arranged to meet Jake Tunnicliffe at quarter past eight – unless he stood her up again like last week, the bastard.

'Heard about Stacey?' Louise Woodcock chirped up from the end of the railing. Her right foot swung back and forth in a semi-circle over the crumbling surface of the path.

Rachel's green eyes narrowed at the mention of Stacey's name. Stacey Hunter was her enemy. 'What about her?' she asked.

'She gets out soon.'

'Already?' said Claire. 'I thought she had at least another three months to do.'

'Let out on good behaviour.'

'More like she's been sucking up,' Rachel said deliberately.

The other girls laughed. Even so, unease at the revelation could clearly be sensed. Stacey Hunter had been sent down for nine months for getting caught after mugging a woman and leaving her with a front tooth missing.

For Rachel, it had been pure poetry as her biggest threat was locked up for a while. After battling it out with Louise, she and Claire had taken over and made headway with the membership. Now, instead of five members, there were seven of them – soon to be eight, if the rumours about Charlie Morrison were true. Rachel had been working on her for a month to join the Mitchell Mob.

'I suppose she'll take over again when she's out,' Louise said with a taunt in her voice.

Rachel shook her head. 'I don't think so. This is mine and Claire's patch now. Right, girls?' She stared at each one of them. Sitting together they looked like a line of blackbirds on a telephone wire.

One by one, in uncomfortable silence, they nodded in agreement.

'Good.' Rachel squeezed in between Shell Walker and Hayley Jones. 'Anyone got any fags?'

'Naw,' said Hayley.

'Me neither,' said Shell.

'My old man only had two so I couldn't lift any,' said Louise.

'So whose turn is it?' As all eyes went to the ground, Rachel sighed. 'I suppose it'll have to be me then. Claire, watch my back while I get some, would you?'

Claire nodded, catching the disrespectful look that came from Louise. Even though she and Rachel had the upper hand, it made her feel uneasy. Louise had brought up Stacey getting out next month, and if it was obvious to her that she was looking forward to it more than she was letting on, it would be obvious to the others.

She ran to Rachel as she stood outside the doors of Shop&Save, hoping to blag the odd cigarette here and there until she had enough.

She glanced back at the gang again, huddled together in a circle now. They looked like they were in deep discussion about something or other – or someone or other. A shiver ran through her body.

It wasn't easy being Claire Bradley when your opposite had nerves of steel.

4

On the Sunday evening of their first weekend on Stanley Avenue, Caren was snuggled up on the sofa watching television when John appeared in the doorway. He was dressed in a white long-sleeved shirt over the top of dark jeans. Freshly showered, she could smell the tang of his aftershave from where she was sitting. All at once she felt a tingle of excitement – maybe she could entice him into having a quickie before he went out. But her smile morphed into a frown when he picked up his wallet and put it in his back pocket.

'Surely you're not off out already?' She looked at the clock: it was just past eight thirty. 'You said it would be for a quick pint.'

'I thought I'd make a night of it.' John avoided her eye as he piled loose change into his pocket. 'Haven't been out in a while and it'll be good to catch up with Pete and a few of the old crowd.'

'Nice of you to ask me along too,' she sulked, knowing full well that she wouldn't have gone regardless.

John bent down, resting his hands on her thighs. 'It's only the one night.' He stuck out his bottom lip, looking very much like a five-year-old. 'I've been a good boy lately, haven't I?'

Caren tried not to smirk. He smelled so good. She ran her hands up and over his back.

'Don't be too late,' she told him, not wanting to start another bickering match. They'd been doing their fair share of that since the move – silly things over something and nothing.

'I won't.' John leaned forward to kiss her.

'And don't make too much noise when you come in,' she yelled just before the door shut.

She went through to the kitchen, cursing again as she eyed the bare walls stripped and ready to be wallpapered with something more decent than the ancient woodchip that had taken an age to remove: the ghastly stuff had come off like chewing gum.

Now that the units had been cleaned, they were fairly decent, despite the one drawer handle hanging on precariously, but they were nothing compared to the kitchen in their last house. Caren had been so proud to show it off to friends, host dinner parties there, drinks after work – now she wouldn't dare tell anyone her new address. Call her a snob but she'd rather let people think she'd dropped off the face of the earth than tell them she was back on the Mitchell Estate.

She reached a bottle of wine from the fridge and poured a large glass. At least they could pay for small luxuries, although she knew they wouldn't even be able to afford those if John didn't get some sort of work soon.

This past week, they'd spent a lot of time doing the vast list of odd jobs needed to get the property to a decent standard. Everything else, she was sure, would mostly be completed over the next few days. At least then they could both start looking for work. And maybe John would meet new people: there was no way she was going to make tonight's meet with Pete something that happened on a regular basis. Pete would bring John down and she wasn't going to have that.

She rummaged in the cupboard for a bag of crisps, thinking that she'd get the local newspaper tomorrow evening and they could scour it together. She wasn't afraid to go out to work for someone else again. She'd cook, she'd clean, she'd shine shoes, wipe up the muck from... well, maybe not that last one.

Caren took a quick look at her manicured nails, splaying one hand out in front. They were her pride and joy. Personally she thought a woman wasn't dressed properly if her nails were shoddy.

She wondered: maybe now it was time to get the business she'd been planning up and running.

*A*cross at number twenty-five, Gina was flat out on the settee when John walked into her living room. She'd been watching some reality TV crap but her eyes flitted from top to toe in a second to take in his clean shoes, designer clothes and the crispness of his white shirt. Immediately, she felt her cheeks burn, the smell of his aftershave having the same effect on her as it had on Caren a few minutes earlier.

'Hi, Gina,' John said, moving aside a pile of magazines before sitting down on the armchair. He stared at the overflowing coffee table, before putting them down onto the floor.

'Hi, John.'

Pete handed John a can of lager before rushing upstairs to get changed. He'd only got in minutes earlier. It was obvious what today's cash-in-hand job had been: he smelled of petrol.

Gina swung her feet round to the floor, trying to pull in her stomach as she sat upright. 'How are you doing?' she asked, running a hand through hair she knew hadn't been washed for five days. 'Getting settled now?'

John nodded after taking a slurp of his drink. 'It's not so bad on Stanley Avenue. Caren was dreading coming back, though.'

I bet she was, the snotty cow, Gina thought but kept it to herself.

'I suppose it will take a while for you both to settle,' she said instead.

John shook his head. 'Not me. I feel like I've never been away.'

'Oh?' Gina sensed an information giveaway.

'I've always liked the Mitchell Estate. It feels like coming home again to me.' He grinned. 'It's great catching up with Pete and seeing old friends.'

Gina sat forward more, hoping to feign polite interest rather than curiosity. 'What does Caren think? I heard you had a lovely house.'

'We did. It was a corker, I have to admit. Caren is a real homemaker.'

Ouch.

'She can turn anything into a better place. I suppose in theory we can live anywhere and she'll make it into far more than it is.'

'So Caren isn't happy about the move, then?' Gina dug deeper, cursing the fact that she was talking to a man. Hadn't he got any idea what information she was after?

John took another swig of lager. 'No, she hates it right now – says something about us moving off here within twelve months but I can't see that happening.'

'Why's that?'

'Well, we're in far too much debt and–'

'Right, Johnno,' said Pete, appearing in the doorway. 'Sorry about that – didn't get in from work until late.'

Compared to John, Gina didn't even want to look at Pete in his farmer-checked-shirt that hadn't seen an iron since she'd bought it for him from the market, jeans that weren't faded for style but from age and white, dirty trainers. His hair was gelled back like a clone of Dracula.

'Work?' She huffed. 'Siphoning petrol and diesel from vehicles isn't earning a decent living like normal people do.'

'Pays for your fags, doesn't it, you moody cow.'

Pete leaned forward to take one from amongst the detritus on the coffee

485

table but Gina slapped his hand. 'Piss off. It looks like the girls have already helped themselves, the cheeky mares. And you can get your own after that sarcastic comment, Pete Bradley.'

'Suits me.' Pete smirked as he pulled out a handful of notes, throwing a tenner into her lap. 'Here, I'm feeling generous. Buy yourself another pack.'

John laughed and stood up. 'Nothing's changed with you two, I see? Still bickering all the time.'

'She wouldn't have me any other way,' Pete replied. 'She knows where her bread is buttered.'

Gina faked a yawn. 'Oh please,' she said. 'Go now before I slice you in two with my razor sharp tongue.'

The door closed behind them a few moments later and the house felt instantly gloomy. Gina pulled her feet up onto the settee again, reached for the remote and switched the volume up on the television. Well, that had been embarrassing. Trust Pete to try and make a fool of her. You'd think that over twenty years together, she'd be used to his put downs by now but still they hurt – especially when said in front of John, who she hadn't seen for so long. Who, she realised, she still had a massive crush on.

But then again, that wasn't hard when you stood him next to Pete. To Gina's eyes, John had got better with age.

It wasn't fair.

*I*t's quarter to nine. Do you think she'll show?' Claire asked her sister as they sat on the low railing outside Shop&Save with the other girls. Although it had been raining for most of that day, it had stopped now but the wind had picked up instead. Crisp packets and chocolate wrappers over by the doorway created a mini tornado. They closed their eyes momentarily as a cloud of dust flew up into the air.

'She'd better, if she knows what's good for her,' Rachel said with a scowl.

Just before nine, Charlie Morrison came running around the corner, not stopping until she was level with them. She sat down on the railing next to Claire, holding her side as she caught her breath.

'Soz I'm late,' she said eventually. 'Mum wanted me to look after my baby brother. I told her to get lost so she clouted me one. I ended up getting locked in my room.' Charlie ran a hand through short, blonde hair, messing up her carefully styled spikes. 'I waited 'til I heard her on the phone and legged it through my bedroom window, out onto the porch.'

Rachel grinned. 'Nice one. Won't she wait up for you, though?'

'Don't care – I'm always getting lamped when I get home anyway, so I might as well have some fun while I'm out.' She smiled shyly at the others, suddenly her nerve deserting her. Her gaze dropped to the floor.

It didn't go unnoticed by Rachel. She stood up and nudged her sharply. 'You still up for it?'

Charlie nodded. 'What do you want me to do?'

'Ever robbed anyone?'

'No.'

'Then that's what you can do.'

Charlie swallowed. 'Can I pick a victim?'

Rachel shook her head slowly. 'No, we'll choose.' She looked at the others. 'Won't we, girls?'

Some of the group nodded.

'Yeah, let's not make it too easy,' said Ashley. 'I remember my initiation. It was hell.'

'Only because you were such a wimp,' Claire teased, squeezing in between her and Louise on the railing.

'Me? A wimp?' Ashley faked a hurt expression. '*You*,' she pointed to Rachel, 'chose a hard knob for me and I got a good kicking.'

'We got our hands on some good booze though,' Shell sniggered, 'while you were on the floor.'

As the girls continued to cajole and laugh, Rachel watched the shop doorway to see who was coming and going. It was a good fifteen minutes before she spotted two girls, one of whom had given her lip at school, and she knew the initiation could go ahead. Time to kick ass as The Mitchell Mob.

'Charlie, get their bags and see what's in them,' she told her.

Charlie grinned when she saw who Rachel had picked out for her. She interlaced her fingers, pushed them back and stretched them out in anticipation. 'Which one shall I do first? Or shall I do them both?'

'Both!'

'Okay. Oi, you two,' Charlie shouted as she ran towards them. 'Care to join us for a moment?'

The two girls stopped in their tracks as Charlie reached them, the others not far behind.

'It's Sarah, isn't it?' Charlie spoke to the younger one. 'Sarah Syphilis.'

The girls burst into laughter and circled the sisters.

Sarah glanced at her older sister, just before her bag was whipped off her shoulder.

'Whatcha doing out here, all alone, at the shops?' asked Charlie.

'Give that back to her,' the older girl said.

Charlie grabbed the collar of her jacket and pulled her close. 'Don't push your luck, Jill Crawford, if you know what's good for you.'

'If you know what's good for you, you'll back off right now,' Jill dared to speak again. 'I'll get my brother on you and then you won't be so sure of yourself.'

Charlie slapped her hard across her cheek. 'Do you think I'm scared of a brother coming after me?' She punched Jill in the stomach, watched her face crumple a second before her knees.

While Sarah's bag was searched and the contents thrown into the road by Claire and Hayley, Charlie laid into Jill. Twice she elbowed her in the back, then she brought her fist up underneath and caught her in the chin.

Jill tried to grab Charlie's hood but Charlie was too strong for her. Another punch in the stomach and she curled up in a ball, trying to fend off the remaining blows. All the time, Sarah screamed as she watched what was happening to her sister, the rest of the girls in the gang egging Charlie on.

People began to appear at the doorway of Shop&Save. Someone shouted over angrily at them.

'Punch her lights out,' said Louise, ignoring them.

'Yeah, kick her in the head so that she can hear bells ringing,' added Hayley.

'Give her one for me,' cried Claire, tossing Sarah's purse on the ground in disgust. 'There's hardly anything in here, just a few measly coins. Next time, Rachel, we need someone with a wallet.'

Rachel shot her twin a warning look. 'Don't tell me what we need to do,' she hissed. 'Or you can take down the next victim.'

'No way. It's not my turn again. I did–'

'Well, shut the fuck up then.' Rachel moved towards Jill, who by now was crawling away, and pulled her head up sharply by the hair, delighted to see fear in the girl's eyes. It was a perfect time to reiterate what they were all about.

'So, your olds – who do you tell them attacked you?' she asked.

'I – I didn't see who it was,' Jill muttered.

'And who do you tell everyone else who attacked you?'

'The Mitchell Mob,' Jill sobbed.

Rachel shoved her forward head first and Jill fell to all fours. For good measure, she kicked her up the backside. 'Now, get out of my sight, you pathetic loser.' She turned to Charlie, who had returned after chasing Sarah away, and grinned.

'You're in.'

5

Caren padded across the dark red quarry tiles, being careful to avoid the chunk missing from the corner of one right in the middle of the kitchen floor, and yanked the cold water tap clockwise as much as was physically possible. The bloody thing wouldn't stop dripping. Drip, drip, drip, all day, every day since they'd moved in. She leaned on the kitchen worktop and sighed loudly.

Two weeks they'd been in this dump and, despite the jobs they'd carried out, she hadn't begun to make a dent in making it feel like home.

She looked out at the tip of a rear garden: she could just about make out a pathway through the jungle of grass and overgrown hedges. A mass of green, apart from the huge pile of rubbish left by the previous tenant – she'd been on to Mitchell Housing Association and been told that she'd have to shift it herself. Compared to the house they'd left behind, this garden could have fitted onto her decking area before heading towards the well-maintained, landscaped gardens.

Even the late September day was trying to be cheery. She squinted as the autumn sun peeked out from behind a rain cloud. It was ten thirty. After coming in at 2 a.m. the night before and waking with a hangover, John had taken the car to have two new tyres because it had failed its MOT.

Unable to stand another minute alone with the few remaining boxes left to unpack, she grabbed her keys and bag and headed for the door. It was too depressing to face right now; she had to get out. A trip across the shops would do her good, even if just for a bit of fresh air.

She walked down the front path and came face to face with Gina Bradley. She cursed silently underneath her breath.

. . .

*G*ina spotted her at the same time. Shit! If she'd known she was going to bump into Mrs Frigging Perfect, she would have made more of an effort before she'd left the house. As it was, she was only nipping out for some fags to get out of Pete's hair. They'd been arguing for well over an hour, and she'd stormed out with a slam of the back door. So, wearing antique leggings that sagged absurdly at the knees, slippers and a black T-shirt, her hair unkempt and not a flicker of age-defying make-up on, she was looking dire to say the least.

She walked slowly down the path, glancing in Caren's direction but trying not to make eye contact. Damn, she looked as good as she had when she'd watched her moving in. Her hair hung straight like a velvet curtain, framing her face on either side. She wore make-up to enhance her beauty, black trousers and a smart jacket that looked like it had cost a fortune.

Gina could hear her heels tippy tapping down the steps from here. Finished off with a Burberry scarf knotted around her neck, to Gina, she oozed class.

They reached the street at exactly the same time.

*C*aren knew it would be awkward when they first met again but she wasn't going to be the one who was discourteous. Brought up with manners, she knew it would give her the upper hand if she used them. Gina would assume she wouldn't want to bother with her. Well, she didn't, but she could at least hide it well.

'Hi, Gina,' she smiled falsely.

'Hello,' said Gina, giving her the once over in as intimidating a manner as she could muster.

A silence followed as both women stood still. Caren wondered what to say next while Gina stared at her.

'Where are you off to?' asked Gina sharply.

'To the shops. I fancied a bit of fresh air.' Another silence. 'You?'

Gina shrugged. 'Off to my mum's – you remember, she lives at number twenty-eight? My dad died but she's going strong, the old doll.'

'Oh.' Twenty-eight was next door but one. Caren hoped there wouldn't be any more of the Bradley clan in Stanley Avenue. One was more than she could bear right now.

But Gina picked up on the 'oh' like a dog with a rabbit.

'What do you mean, *oh?*'

Fighting for Survival

'Nothing.' Caren took a step forward, wondering how quickly she could get away.

'I suppose this avenue is too low-down for you and your precious John,' Gina spat out nastily. 'Me and my family have quite a few houses here. My sister, Leah lives at number thirty-three – not that she's home much now since she started seeing her fella. So, that's three of us. Is that enough scum for you in one place?'

Even though she'd half expected it, Caren was taken aback by Gina's hostility. 'I didn't mean anything,' she said.

'Good, because there's nothing to worry your little head about. We won't be bothering with the likes of you.'

'And what exactly is that supposed to mean?'

Gina pointed at her. 'You... you think you're so high-and-mighty but you're as low as the rest of us. What brought you back to the Mitchell Estate, hmm? Remember what you said? Because I do. 'I'm never coming back to this shit-hole', you said.'

'I wouldn't be back if it wasn't for...' Caren's words faltered as she realised she was about to give away more than she'd intended.

'If it wasn't for you going bankrupt?' Gina smiled, loving the look on Caren's face.

'How did you find out?' Beneath her make-up, Caren paled. She couldn't believe John had blabbed about that. How dare he tell everyone their problems.

'John told me and Pete last night, when they came home pissed.' Gina smiled even more when she saw Caren's eyes widen. 'Didn't he tell you that he stopped by our house afterwards? I was going to go to bed because it was so late but I'm glad I stayed up now. They brought back fish and chips and shared it all with me. I did loads of bread and butter and we opened some cans. You're not mad with him, are you?'

Trying to keep her emotions from spilling out, Caren shook her head. 'No, I'm not his keeper. And you know John, he can look after himself.' She made a big deal about checking her watch. 'Look, I'd better be going, I'll be late back else.'

Gina popped up a hand and waggled her fingers. 'Ta-ra for now,' she said to Caren's disappearing form. Watching her scurry away, she smiled and congratulated herself. Even looking like she did as opposed to Caren's picture of beauty, she'd managed to get the upper hand. She opened the gate to her mum's house and practically ran up the path. Suddenly the need for a cigarette had gone.

Ruth Millington turned the key in the lock of number thirty-two Stanley Avenue, pushing open the door quickly so that she could put the bags she had carried down. She stood upright and rubbed at the small of her back. God, they had been heavy. She shouldn't have tried to carry that many but she hadn't realised how far away she was here from the bus stop. Her fingers had ridges where the bags had dug into them. She clenched and unclenched them to get back their circulation.

Tears welled in her eyes as she gazed around the dismal hallway, at the yellow stripy wallpaper that was peeling off more than it was stuck onto the walls. The carpet had seen far better days, worn and grimy with some spectacular dirty marks, but it would have to stay down. Either that or they could all walk on bare floorboards. There was no money to spend on flooring.

She dragged heavy feet into the living room. It was a bright space, a large window at either end. The fireplace was made from old, cream tiles and probably worth a fortune now if it wasn't chipped in a dozen places. There was no carpet in there. Ruth looked above the windows: there were no curtain rails. There wasn't even a bulb in the electrical fitting hanging pitifully from the ceiling.

Feeling familiar panic bubbling up inside her, Ruth tried to keep it at bay. She went upstairs.

Directly in front of her was the bathroom. Although she'd seen the property the week before, the only thing she could remember about the room was the state of the bath and the toilet.

Tentatively, she pushed open the door, hoping to find that the cleaning fairies had taken pity on her, but no such luck. There was a rust mark between the hot and cold taps down the white-enamel bath where the water must have dripped for years. It swirled down into the plug hole. Ruth doubted that would come off, no matter how much bleach and elbow grease she used.

She peered into the toilet, gagging at what she saw, and knocked down the lid. The force of it slamming made it slide to the right, only one hinge keeping it in place. Ruth flushed it, wishing it would take her away into the deepest, darkest depths of nowhere. But then again, wasn't she already there?

The eerie silence suddenly became welcome as she stepped in and out of the three bedrooms. At least the boys had separate rooms, even though they were now living in Stanley Avenue.

She hadn't wanted to move here but she'd had no choice. There were no more empty properties with three bedrooms. Two bedrooms would have been a challenge. Mason and Jamie would never give her a moment's peace if they'd had to share a room.

And all this because that bastard Martin Wallace had decided that he needed some space. Three years she'd given him and what had he given her, apart from the odd backhander and a huge dose of depression and anxiety?

Fighting for Survival

Nothing. He hadn't even had the decency to help her move, and she'd had to fork out for a removal van.

Finally, she made her way back downstairs and into the kitchen. The units were made from white Formica, the cheapest you could get on a job lot, she reckoned. A front of one drawer was missing and two doors hung lopsided.

She ran a hand over the grubby worktop before bursting into tears. The house would take ages to get right, especially with her arm playing up again. She pulled up her sleeve and picked at the scab forming there. Then she dug her nails into it. It stung like hell, but she scratched until it was bleeding again. Quickly, she rolled down her sleeve before she did even more damage.

A knock came at the front door, echoing around the hallway: she could almost feel the emptiness from where she stood. Ruth wiped her eyes before moving to answer it.

'Morning love,' said a tall, thin man, carrying two small boxes. 'Where do you want these going?'

'Mason's room. Turn right at the top of the stairs, back of the house.'

The man nodded. 'Right you are. Ooh, is that the kettle I hear boiling?'

'I doubt it,' said Ruth. 'It's in one of the boxes on your van. Couldn't carry it on the bus, could I?'

The man wouldn't be deterred. 'I tell you what,' he nodded his head towards the door. 'I'll find the kettle, you make a drink and I'll share my digestives with you. What do you say?'

Ruth nodded: anything to get him gone and on his way so she could be alone. She couldn't bear to be among cheery people at the moment, especially ones whom she was paying to do a job for her.

Alone with her thoughts, her feelings, her sorrows – that's what she needed. Even if it was ten minutes before she had to fetch the boys from school; before all hell broke loose again.

'I've just bumped into that stuck up cow, Caren Williams,' Gina said to Barbara as she let herself into her mum's house and found her in the kitchen. 'She's already getting on my nerves with her high-and-mighty attitude.'

Barbara was sitting at the table, three curlers in the front of her grey hair, sipping at a cup of tea.

'At least she made an effort to work and move off this estate,' she replied.

'She thinks she's too good for Stanley Avenue. I'll show her if she doesn't watch with the attitude.' Gina slid her hand across towards an open packet of biscuits. Barbara slapped her fingers away. 'Ow. What was that for?'

'I'm ashamed of you, Gina. Why couldn't you be nice to Caren? She must be feeling really vulnerable right now, what with losing her house and all.'

Gina folded her arms. If she knew she'd get this much grief, she wouldn't have bothered to escape from Pete. 'Bloody hell, Mum, you've changed your tune. You said she'd had her come-uppance when she first moved in.'

'Yes, but that was before I'd seen what she's done to that house.' Barbara looked up from the magazine she was scanning. 'She's cleaned every window, all the sills, cleared the front garden of rubbish and John's cut back all the hedges. You can't walk up your pathway without getting soaked when it's been raining – and there's enough rubbish in *your* garden to have a three-metre bonfire.'

'You know we haven't got any hedge cutters,' Gina offered lamely, already anticipating her mother's reply.

'You could borrow mine at any time – even at my age, I still use them. And stop making excuses for that lazy bastard you call a husband. Why can't he be like John?'

Why indeed, thought Gina.

'Mum, don't start all this again.' She pushed herself out of the chair and switched on the kettle.

'Hit a nerve, have I?' Barbara smirked.

'Well, you've never worked a day in your life, so I don't see how you can go on about me.'

'I didn't need to work because your Dad provided for this family. Not everyone was on the take. I had my morals.'

'Yeah, morals you forgot when you were arguing or fighting with someone from the estate. Honestly, Mum, it's like the pot calling the kettle black. You were no better than me.'

Barbara relented as she looked over at her daughter. 'I suppose you're right. But I really wish you'd make more of an effort with your life. You need to do something with your time instead of waiting for your next benefits payment to come through.'

'That's not all I live for,' Gina retorted. 'I have my family.'

Barbara frowned. 'Your bloody girls have been up to no good again, though. I heard Mrs Watson talking about them earlier.'

'You don't believe anything she says, do you?'

'They aren't exactly saints.'

'I know but they're kids. I bet me and Leah were the same when we were their age.'

Barbara smiled then. 'You were. And I had your brother too. I don't know how I coped with the lot of you.' She pointed at Gina. 'Remember that time when you were going through your punk stage and you went beating up anyone who didn't like the same music as you?'

Gina giggled. 'What about Leah with that old man she was seeing? I remember you and Dad being livid.'

'Of course we were. He was a bloody pervert, if you ask me. I mean, our Leah was fifteen and he was nearing on thirty. It should never be allowed.' Barbara reached for her daughter's hand and took it gently in her own. 'Seriously, Gina, I worry about you. You're getting old before your time.'

Gina stared at her mother. She knew she was being compared to Caren Williams and that hurt. She made coffee and plonked the mugs down onto the table with a thud. Tears stung her eyes but she refused to let them fall.

'Hey,' Barbara squeezed her hand quickly, 'don't get upset now. You know I only want the best for you – for all of you, really.'

'Don't compare me to her, then.'

'I'm not. I couldn't possibly…' Barbara stopped, the unspoken words saying so much regardless.

'You see,' Gina pulled away her hand, 'even you think I'm a slob.'

'No, I–'

She clasped the hem of her T-shirt. 'So you think I look good in this?' Then she pointed at her head. 'You think my hair looks like I've stepped out of a salon? You think I make an effort every day?'

'No, I just think you should make more of an effort every now and again. Our Leah makes an effort and she's–'

'She's thinner than me? Is that what you were going to say?'

'Don't be silly, I was going to say she's younger than you.'

'She doesn't have three kids or Pete for a husband,' Gina pouted. 'She's not–'

'If there's anything going, you could work the twilight shift with her.'

'I don't want to work in some stupid factory doing menial tasks, thank you very much.'

'So you'd rather be supported by that useless layabout of yours?' Barbara folded her arms. 'All those knock off jobs he does? They'll catch up with him one day, like they did with your brother.'

Gina stood up, the chair scraping across the floor beneath her. 'I'm sick of everyone thinking that my family are lowlife. And I can cope with all the jibes and the stares from everyone else, but to hear it from my own mother? That really stings.'

'I didn't mean–'

'Yes, you did.'

Gina turned and left the house, another bang of a back door reverberating behind her that morning. Would her family ever think she was good for anything?

6

As soon as John came back with their car and she'd closed the back door behind him, Caren laid into him.

'You had no right to tell them that we're bankrupt,' she shouted. 'Or anyone, come to think of it. It's our business.'

'I'm sorry. I didn't think it was such a big deal.' John pushed past her into the kitchen.

Caren prodded him forcefully in his back as he stood over the sink. 'I don't want everyone knowing that we have no money.'

John ran the tap before filling the glass with water. He took a huge gulp.

Caren prodded him in the back again. 'Are you listening to me? I didn't want anyone to know.'

'They would have found out sooner or later. You can't keep anything secret around here.'

'Not where Gina Bradley is concerned. She'll take great pleasure in blabbing her mouth off and then...' tears formed in her eyes, 'everyone will know that we're stuck here.'

John put the glass down onto the drainer. 'Do you have to keep dragging it up at every opportunity?'

'It's the truth. It's not going to get any better and I–'

'I've had enough of this.' John sighed loudly. 'I'm going out.'

'But you've only just got in.'

'For your information, I'm going to carry on tidying up the back garden. You can help, if you like. Or is your love of gardening supposed to be a secret too?'

Fighting for Survival

'I'm surprised you're not going across to the scummy side of the street. I bet you'd prefer it over there, slumming it with Gina and Pete.'

John slammed the back door on his way out.

Tears pricked at her eyes again. What was happening to them? Was this house always going to bring them down? Ever since they'd got here they'd done nothing but argue. Caren needed John's support as much as he needed hers, but he didn't seem able to offer it.

Why, oh why, hadn't they been quicker on the uptake of that tiny two-bedroom flat she'd found, just on the outskirts of the city? If they'd seen it a couple of days earlier, they could have been in there, but someone had beaten them to it. It wouldn't have been ideal – it would have meant living in each other's pockets but it would have been in a nicer neighbourhood – far away from the Mitchell Estate.

But the real thing that annoyed her was that she'd been left with everything to sort out. She now had full control of their finances – not that they had a lot of money, but what they received from now on, what pittance was left over after all the debt payments had been made at the end of each month, was due to go into an account in her sole name. John wasn't good with money so every week she intended to draw out a set amount of cash and nothing else; once it had gone, there'd be no more until the following week.

It would be like being sixteen again, when she'd made sure they'd saved every penny for a deposit towards getting off the estate. It had taken a lot of hard work to get where they were. She wasn't going to lose everything as well as that, no matter what.

Caren couldn't bear the thought of anyone else being with John if they were to split up due to the pressure they were under. Like most couples they had their ups and downs but they got through them.

Could she cope without him forever? And then to know that he'd be in the arms of someone else? She wasn't even going to think about it.

She wiped away the lone tear that had fallen, sniffed and went to join John in the garden.

Feeling well and truly stressed after her disastrous morning, Gina slumped in front of the television and lit another cigarette. The house was empty now. It was eleven thirty – Pete had most probably gone to the pub, seeing as he had no work on at the moment.

Looking around the living room made her even more upset. Faded white paintwork; the ceiling a nicotine yellow colour. Cheap wallpaper that had been up since they had moved in sixteen years ago – well, what remained of it – torn off or scuffed in so many places, drawn on when the kids were younger.

The door leading to the stairs had a huge hole in the bottom of it where Danny had kicked it in temper and it hadn't been replaced because they'd have to pay for the damage.

And she didn't even want to look at the state of the threadbare carpet. What colour it had started its life as she could barely remember – which added insult to injury as she'd watched the vast array of wallpaper rolls and paint tins that had gone into Caren's house over the past couple of weeks. She'd seen John a couple of times with paint splattered jeans, Caren with the same. Pete would never dream of doing any DIY, no matter how much she nagged. That's what had started the argument this morning.

She recalled the last time she'd had a go at him to do something around the house. That disagreement had turned into a full-blown row, and Pete had thrown his ready-meal across the kitchen. There were still remnants of the artificial colourings on the grout in the tiles around the sink that the housing association had fitted. Despite her best efforts at trying to get it white again, it looked like the grout had gone rusty.

Gina clenched her teeth. Was she going to be compared to Caren fucking Williams all of the time now? Even her mother thought she could do better.

Idly, she switched on the television. There was a talk show on featuring a bunch of male strippers.

She stared a little closer. One of the men looked a bit like John. Gina suddenly felt a rush of heat as she recalled how she was infatuated with him at school. She wished she could get his attention again.

Suddenly, she had a thought. She quickly turned to the television menu and scrolled down through it. Sure enough, there was a makeover programme on. Perhaps there was a way she could improve herself. It was never too late, surely?

Engrossed in the programme, she jumped when the back door slammed and Pete came rushing into the room. She grabbed for the remote but he'd already seen the television screen.

'What are you doing back?' she stammered, this time her face flushing through embarrassment.

'I need my tool bag and my steel toe caps – a job's come up. What the hell are you watching?'

'Nothing.'

'You'll never make anything of yourself sitting on the settee resting that fat arse of yours.'

Gina glowered at him. 'Thanks for the vote of confidence,' she snapped. 'And why would I make an effort for you? You don't give a shit about me anymore.'

'That's because you look like you do.' Pete searched out his boots behind the settee. They were caked in mud, which he brushed off onto the carpet. 'You need to do some exercise if you want to look good, before that arse stretches from here to Blackpool. I keep telling you not to stuff your face.'

'Shut up.' Gina turned the volume up on the television. 'You'd never notice if I did change myself. You'd be far too busy down the pub.'

Pete laughed. 'Don't be daft, woman. If you made more of an effort I wouldn't have to spend my time at the pub.' He snorted. 'You are so stupid.'

'So why do you come home to me?' Gina taunted.

'Ah, that's easy.' Pete ran his tongue across his top lip. 'You do a mean blow job.'

Gina flung a cushion at him as he headed for the door. Pete stood in the doorway, pushing his tongue into his cheek simulating fellatio. Gina threw another cushion but he'd gone before it fell to the floor.

She turned the television back to the previous channel. The credits on the programme were rolling: damn, she'd missed the end. Now she'd never see what Stephanie Lathisha from Chester had been transformed into.

She picked up one of the twin's magazines and flicked through it. Maybe there was something she could do to get Pete interested again. She was tired of solo sex and her batteries were running low on her vibrator.

It was too ambitious to lose three stone in three days and the thought of exercise made her shudder. So what about a new image: clothes, shoes, underwear? But that would take money and she hadn't got any of that. Neither had she got the figure to put into it to look attractive.

She turned the page to see an article about the latest trend in hairstyles. Fingering her own hair as she looked at each one, she brought the magazine nearer to study picture two. It was a short, choppy, extremely of-the-time hairstyle. The model had the same red colour hair as she did and she didn't look much younger than Gina so she might be able to pull it off. Actually, she looked about sixteen but Gina ignored this fact.

Maybe a different hairstyle could be the start of her new image. All it took was one step, then maybe she could go on a diet and then she could pick and choose what clothes she wanted to wear.

And maybe John Williams would fancy you.

Gina shook her head to rid herself of the image that had invaded it. She and John, bodies entwined on Madame fucking Williams's settee, having sex right under her nose, as John was unable to resist the new Gina. She felt that familiar tingling between her legs as she imagined where he would kiss her, where his hands would be, how his body would feel on top of hers. That would show stuck-up Caren that she meant business.

Without further ado, she picked up her phone and rang Tracy Tanner, the local mobile hairdresser.

'I'm bunking off school this afternoon, Claire. Fancy coming into town with me?'

'Yeah, I'm sick of this course already. Shall we have lunch out?'

'Why of course.' Rachel put on a posh accent. 'I think we can run to a *Mac-o-Donald's*. What do you say?'

'Indeed, indeed.' Claire nodded. She gave a royal wave. 'And one might run to a strawberry milkshake too.'

Rachel grinned before breaking out into a run, her sister following closely behind. They charged through the school gates and out into the rabbit warren of streets that made up the Mitchell Estate. In minutes, they were on a bus heading for the shopping centre in Stockleigh.

'Mum will kill us if anyone sees us today,' said Claire.

'Don't be so whiny,' said Rachel, stretching her legs across the seat behind Claire so that no one could sit next to her.

'I'm just saying.' Claire turned back to face her. 'She'll go mad if we're caught again.'

'We won't have to get caught then.' Rachel looked up as the bus pulled into the kerb at the next stop and a short, squat man got on. He looked to be in his late fifties.

'Ooh, here comes moaning Archie Meredith from Christopher Avenue,' said Rachel.

The girls watched as he paid his fare and marched down the aisle to a seat a few rows in front of theirs. Before he sat down, he scowled at them.

'Did you see that?' said Rachel incredulously. 'He looked at us as if we were shit.' She got to her feet. 'Come on, Claire. Let's have some fun.'

Claire slid along the seat and followed Rachel as she sat behind Archie. He was reading a newspaper.

Rachel leaned forward. 'What're you doing on the bus, Archie? Is your car knackered?'

'Mind your own business,' he grunted.

'What're you reading?' asked Claire.

'I bet he's only looking at the pictures,' nodded Rachel.

Archie glanced over his shoulder and frowned at them.

'I bet he's staring at tits on page three.'

Claire laughed loudly.

Archie ignored them and turned over the page.

Fighting for Survival

'Tits. Tits. Tits.'

This time, Archie took the bait. He turned to Rachel. 'Act your age, you stupid girl.'

'Who are you calling stupid, you old fucker?' Rachel glared back at him.

'Why, you cheeky little cow. I suppose you're bunking off school because you're too stupid to see the benefit of a little education?'

As Claire giggled, Rachel glared at her.

'What are you laughing at? He's dissing us, you moron.'

'I'm not a moron.'

'You are a moron,' said Archie. 'You and your sister. And your brother and your mother and father. You're all a bunch of morons.'

'I'd watch what you're saying or else I'll–'

Archie roared with laughter.

'I'm not a moron,' Claire repeated. 'I'm sick of you making out that I'm stupid all of the time.' She got up and sat nearer to the front of the bus.

'I didn't mean anything, you stupid cow,' Rachel cried after her. 'Hey, wait for me.'

'Run along, now, little girl,' said Archie. 'Go and annoy someone else. That's all you're capable of.'

Rachel stopped and turned back to him. She leaned in close, smelling old-fashioned aftershave and a fresh scent of soap. 'I'd shut the fuck up if I were you,' she told him.

'Or else you'll what?'

Rachel smiled sweetly, leaned forward and whispered in his ear. 'I'll tell everyone I saw you fucking Melissa Knight behind the shops on more than one occasion.'

'You lying little bitch.' Archie's face began to turn the colour of a tomato. 'I've never–'

'That's not what I heard.'

'It's a lie. I'd never do anything like–'

'*I* know that.' Rachel leaned back a touch so that she could look him in the eye, 'but no one else does. And you know how quickly rumours spread on the Mitchell Estate. So I'd watch who you're calling a moron, if I were you, or I'll have that rumour doing the one hundred metres in less than ten seconds.' She stood up abruptly. 'Whoops, here's my stop.'

'Come back here, you little cow.' Archie stood up too. But Rachel was already off the bus and hoping to make amends with Claire.

. . .

501

'What the fuck have you done–'

Gina stopped Pete mid-sentence with a raised hand and an icy stare. 'Don't you dare say anything else,' she muttered. 'It was your fault I did it in the first place.'

'Me?' Pete stared back wide-eyed. 'What did I do?'

'You said I should make more of an effort, so I did.' Gina pointed to what hair she had left on her head. 'And this is what I ended up with.'

'I didn't tell you to shave your head.'

'I haven't shaved my head.'

'You could have fooled me. You look like a–'

Gina flounced out of the room, eager to get away from his spiteful comments. She headed for the safety of the front room, only to find the girls sitting on the settee.

'What the fuck have you done to your hair?' said Rachel, eyes as wide as her father's.

By this time, Gina was close to tears. 'Don't you have a go as well,' she snapped, storming past them to run upstairs.

In her bedroom, she slammed the door shut and threw herself onto the bed. Damn that Tracy Tanner. It should have been a simple haircut to get right: a short, inverted bob with a block fringe.

But Tracy couldn't get both sides to an equal length, and in a fit of frustration as she watched her hair getting shorter and shorter, Gina had snatched the scissors and snipped away angrily. Tracy could then only make a bad job of a terrible mess – short back and sides with a round face was not the trendy and sexy look she had envisaged.

What was wrong with her? Gina sobbed – couldn't she get anything right? Tracy was cheap and all she could afford. Damn her mother for getting on to her this morning. Damn Pete for catching her watching the makeover show. And damn that fucking Caren. If she hadn't moved in across the street, there wouldn't be a need to make herself feel attractive.

There was a knock on the door. 'Can we come in?' asked Claire.

'Not if you're going to take the piss.'

'We're not,' said Rachel. Both girls sat down on the bed beside their mother.

Gina sat up so they could check out her hair. Immediately she saw the look in their eyes, she began to cry again. 'You see?' she sobbed. 'I look like a bloke.'

Neither of them said that she didn't but Claire gave her a hug. 'You might have known, asking Tracy to do it. I heard she got a slapping last month when she butchered Mandy Flannigan's hair. Didn't you hear about it?'

Gina shook her head.

Fighting for Survival

'She wanted to go blonde. Even I know you can't put a blonde hair dye straight on to dark hair. She ended up green, it was awful. Tracy got a bloody nose for it – and Mandy paid over a hundred quid to put it right and made Tracy cough up for it. I'm surprised she hasn't stopped; I'd never use her.'

'Thanks for telling me now,' sniffed Gina.

Claire raced through to the bathroom and came back with a handful of toilet roll. She gave it to Gina before sitting down again.

'Maybe we could help you do something with it?' she proposed.

Gina huffed as she wiped her face. 'What on earth could you do with this? I'll have to wear a hat for months until it's grown back.'

'That's a great idea.' Rachel nudged her and grinned. 'How about I lift you a pink baseball cap when we next go into the town?'

'You'll do no such thing,' Gina admonished. 'If you get caught again, you'll end up in real trouble; not just from me and your father.'

'Mum, I was kidding, right?'

'It doesn't look that bad,' added Claire. 'And you can pretty it up with a hair band or some sparkly clips.'

'And it'll grow again,' said Rachel.

Gina gave them a weak smile. It would get better in time – or by downing a bottle of whisky in the interim.

'I think I need a drink.' Gina looked at them both before shuffling to sit at the edge of the bed. 'If you can sneak the bottle past your dad, I'll let you off about why you weren't at school this afternoon.'

Claire and Rachel shared a look: how did she know?

'I saw you running for the bus.'

'I'll get the bottle.' Rachel got up quickly, followed by her sister, just as eager not to be told off.

With a huge sigh, Gina dared to face the mirror. She stared at herself for a moment before starting to tug at the short strands. They were far too short for the shape of her face: she did look like a tomato, an overripe one at that. Tracy had cut a fringe into the so-called style and her ears were on show. She tried to smile and look on the bright side; at least she could wear earrings now.

But the smile faded as quickly as it had arrived. All she'd wanted to do was to look a little smarter, make an effort for a change but she'd got it wrong again.

Maybe it wasn't worth the effort anyway, she mused. Maybe she *was* destined to be fat and ugly with a man's hairstyle for the rest of her days. Maybe in a cruel twist of fate her hair would never grow again and she'd have to change her name to Gerry.

. . .

'Here.' Rachel passed Claire a small bottle.

Claire sniffed. 'Mum's whisky. How did you manage that?' she asked before taking a sip.

'It was easy; I took it into our room before giving it to her.' Rachel snatched the bottle back from Claire. 'She won't notice that some of it's missing.'

The girls were on their way to the shops to meet up with the rest of the gang. Rachel was looking forward to it immensely. Tonight they had another initiation test. Leanne Bailey wanted to join the Mitchell Mob and Rachel had lined her up with something special, providing her timing went to plan.

'I bet Mum's still pissed off,' said Claire. 'Her hair looks a mess, doesn't it?'

Rachel nodded, throwing the now empty bottle over the hedge of a garden they were walking past. 'She should be taught a lesson, that Tracy. Maybe there's something we can do to get her back.'

'Like what?'

'I'm not sure; we'll have to think about it. But first, some fun.' Rachel turned to Claire. 'Let's do over Archie Meredith.'

Claire stopped. 'No, Rach, you can't do anything to him. We'll be in big trouble if we–'

Rachel sighed. 'You're whining again, Claire.'

'No, I'm not. I'm just saying–'

'We won't be doing anything – Leanne will – so chill out.'

'What will she have to do?'

'That depends. If Archie comes to the shops like he usually does, then she can wreck his car.'

Despite her misgivings, Claire felt her insides do an excited somersault.

'If he doesn't come to the shops, then we'll go to his house.'

'And do what?'

'We're gonna throw a brick through his front window.'

'Now who's being stupid,' said Claire.

'What do you mean?'

'All Mitchell Housing Association's properties have UPVC windows.'

Rachel sighed impatiently. 'So?'

'So, they're all fitted with double-glazing. The brick might break one glass pane but it probably won't go through two.'

'How do you know?'

'Danny told me. Completely fooled him once; he thought it would go right through. Problem was, he was trying to smash his way out of the factory he was nicking from so he got caught by the pigs.'

Rachel snarled before walking on. 'I didn't know that.'

Fighting for Survival

'But at least you know now. And it'll stop us looking like idiots.' Claire ran to catch her up.

They were nearing the shops now. Rachel could see the gang up ahead waiting for them to arrive. It was getting dark; even so the car park on the square was fully lit. CCTV cameras were in operation but there were certain places that they couldn't reach. Many a time, Rachel and Claire had been questioned about some crime or other that they'd been seen nearby, before or after. They were the queens of keeping quiet and, so far, age had been on their side. Claire had been concerned about this once they'd turned sixteen but Rachel said they would continue to get away with things if they kept their mouths shut. No one would crack the Bradley girls, she was fond of saying.

Just like clockwork, Archie Meredith turned up as he did every night at nine. He parked his car, scowled at them all as he walked past, and headed into Shop&Save. The moment he was out of sight, Rachel pulled up her hood and nudged Leanne.

'Now,' she cried.

Leanne picked up a large brick from the side of the car park and ran over to Archie's car. First, she smashed it into the right headlight and then the left. Next she twisted back both of the windscreen wipers. Then she took out her front door key and ran it along the whole length of the nearside, across the boot lid and right along the passenger side.

When she saw another car pulling in, she legged it back to the gang who then split up in a regimented manner. Louise went with Rachel and Claire and ran across Davy Road, down the steps into Roland Avenue. Leanne, Shell and Hayley headed for the site where The White Lion pub had been until it was burned down the previous year. Charlie and Ashley stayed near the shops as advised.

'I wish we'd stayed at the shops now,' sighed Rachel as she bent over to catch her breath. 'It would have been fun to watch Archie when he sees his car trashed.'

After twenty minutes, they sauntered back. Archie was standing by his car, a policeman taking down his details.

'What's up, Archie?' Rachel shouted as she walked past them. 'Someone do you over?'

'Mind your own business,' Archie shouted back.

'Looks like you've upset someone. I wonder who that could be.'

Archie frowned then his face began to contort. 'Why, you little bitch. It was you.' He turned to the policeman standing next to him. 'It was her and that bloody gang of girls she hangs around with.'

'Why would you think that?' PC Mark White asked as he took down the names of the girls he could see.

'She,' he pointed to Rachel, 'had a go at me on the bus this morning. Said she'd seen me somewhere I wasn't... with–'

'You want to watch yourself, Archie,' Rachel said as she drew level with him. 'Rumours have a nasty way of flaring up on this estate.'

Archie moved forward but Mark put out his arm to stop him. He stared at the three girls. 'Move along now. I'll be over to talk to you soon anyway.'

'Why?' asked Rachel. 'We weren't even here.'

'That's what I aim to find out. Because I saw you here no less than half an hour ago when I drove past.'

'So?'

'So... I'll be over in a minute.'

Rachel strutted off to join the others. As she got to them, she turned and gave Archie Meredith the bird.

'You should have seen his face when he saw what had happened,' Charlie laughed.

'I don't want to know about it,' snapped Rachel.

Claire turned to her with a frown. 'What's up with you?'

'Nothing.'

Rachel perched on the railing and glared at PC White. Tonight hadn't gone to plan because of him. Why did he have to turn up so quickly? Most of the time, people complained about the lack of policing. Oh, he just happened to drive past half an hour ago? Yeah, right.

And now she'd missed her fun with Archie. She'd wanted to laugh and laugh in his stupid podgy face and let him know who had done the damage and him to be unable to prove it. Now, because the law had turned up quickly for a change, she hadn't been able to do that. And it irked her.

'I did what you said, Rach,' said Leanne. 'Am I part of the gang now?'

Rachel glared at her, until Leanne lowered her eyes. 'There won't be a fucking gang if we don't get a little more savvy.'

'What do you mean?' said Claire, the only one confident enough to stand up to her.

'I mean him.' Rachel pointed over to Mark. 'I'm sick of everyone thinking that we're just a girl gang. He's laughing at us and I don't like it. The sooner people on this estate realise they can't mess with the Mitchell Mob,' she added, 'the better. And that includes the coppers.'

7

Josie had been about to visit one of her tenants, Cath Mason, who lived in Christopher Avenue when Archie Meredith shouted her over.

'It's not on,' he said as she sat on his settee, having coffee with him and his wife. 'It's going to cost me a fortune to put my car right. In fact, I can't afford to do it all in one go. The paintwork will have to stay damaged.'

'There isn't any evidence to say exactly who it was,' Josie told him, although it pained her to say. 'The CCTV cameras barely picked the girls up anyway. They've been questioned but you know as well as I do, they all say they didn't do it and they are so hard to tell apart. I'm really sorry.'

'They're a bunch of animals.'

'The only thing I can do is see if I can get more of a police presence over there,' she said. 'I doubt it with resources how they are, and I know it won't help you now, but–'

'But they're never there, are they?' Archie folded his arms across his protruding belly. 'I know they're needed elsewhere, I'm not complaining in that sense, but there aren't enough coppers to go round this godforsaken place because it's getting worse.'

'I wish we could move away from here,' Mary Meredith said quietly.

Josie looked across at her. Mary was in her mid-fifties. She could tell from looking at her that she had been a beautiful woman in her earlier years. She'd put a bit of weight on due to being struck down with multiple sclerosis several years ago and was now confined to a wheelchair. But she still took pride in her appearance; her clothes were clean, her hair washed and styled.

Josie knew both of their children: Patrick who was now twenty-seven and Amanda who was nearing thirty, if she remembered correctly. They had never been in trouble with the police and always kept themselves to themselves. Patrick had family of his own now and, although Amanda had moved off the estate, she came to help out with Mary every other day.

There was no mistaking the tears glistening in Mary's eyes. Seeing them made Josie well up too.

'I wish I could help you,' she said to both of them. 'But you know as well as I do that there's nothing I *can* do.'

'You could talk to their parents,' suggested Archie. 'Before I get myself into trouble down the pub when I lamp Pete Bradley.' Archie squeezed his index finger and his thumb together. 'I was that close to it on Sunday night. But knowing my luck, I'd get locked up for it.' He smiled affectionately. 'And who would look after my Mary, then?'

Mary smiled too, but the tears were still there. Josie's heart went out to them. They were a lovely couple. Archie had worked all his life, and provided for them both when Mary had been taken ill. Despite her best intentions not to, Josie relented.

'Let me have a word with Mrs Bradley and see if we can ease things for a while. Sometimes she keeps them away from the square. I'll talk to–'

Archie shook his head. 'Thanks, Josie. I know your hands are tied, and I know you mean well, but it won't work. They'll only move on and cause trouble elsewhere. Trouble breeds trouble. They're better on the square, where people can see them, I suppose.'

Josie knew what he meant. How could she give them peace when a man built like Archie Meredith didn't feel safe going to fetch his wife a bottle of cough medicine from the shops after dark? Archie wasn't very tall but what he lacked in height, he gave back in muscle. His job as a roofer kept him fit. To know that he was wary of the estate after dark gave Josie the creeps in itself.

But what could she possibly do for them?

'Let me talk to Mrs Bradley first,' she tried again. 'I'll check in at the police post and see if they have anything to link the girls to the crime. But you know as well as I do that those bloody girls are too clever to get caught out.'

Archie smiled a little. 'I know you'll try your best for us. You're one of the good guys, Josie.'

. . .

'Oi,' a voice bellowed from behind as Josie got out of her car in Stanley Avenue thirty minutes later. She locked the door before turning around. When she saw who it was, she cursed under her breath.

'Yes, you,' cried Barbara as she drew level with her. 'I hope you're not off to moan at our Gina again.'

'What I say to Gina is confidential, Mrs Lewis.' Josie turned and began to walk away. But Barbara followed her.

'She's my daughter, you cheeky cow. She tells me everything.'

I doubt that very much, Josie thought. She continued up the pathway towards Gina's front door as quickly as possible.

'She'll have done nothing wrong,' Barbara continued, marching behind her. 'She's always in trouble for something someone else has done. If it isn't the twins, it's Danny. If it isn't Danny, it's that useless layabout of a husband. Why can't you give the poor girl a break?'

'Mrs Lewis,' Josie turned on her heels so abruptly that she narrowly missed knocking Barbara to the floor, 'why don't you let me do my job? I'm sure Gina will tell you all about it once I'm gone.'

Barbara marched back to her own house as Josie knocked on the Bradleys' front door. Cath hadn't been in after she'd visited Archie Meredith – what she'd give for another sit down at a respectable tenant's home rather than being about to enter the lion's den.

She'd almost given up when the front door opened.

'What do *you* want now?' Gina cried. 'My family haven't done anything wrong as far as I am aware.'

'Can I come in and chat for a moment?' Josie said. It wasn't a question, more of a statement.

'I'm not interested in anything you have to say.'

'Can I come in or are we going to tell the whole of Stanley Avenue what's going on?'

Gina let out a huge sigh and walked into the house, leaving the door open for Josie to follow. As usual, she manoeuvred herself past boxes stacked in the hallway: four of bottled lager, one pack of 32 toilet rolls, several boxes of crisps, and a fair number of cigarettes.

'These things are a hazard in here,' said Josie as she squeezed through into the living room. 'I've told you before to move them. If you ever have a fire, you'll be–'

'If I ever have a fire I bet you'll be the first to say it was an insurance scam.' Gina retorted angrily. She flopped down onto the settee, lit another cigarette, threw her lighter down onto the coffee table and took a long, unhealthy drag.

'And you should be doing something about that Reynolds's family. Their music was blaring into the early hours again last weekend.'

'I've come to chat to you, not take a complaint from you.'

'So it's all right for them to be anti-social, but not my family?'

Ignoring her, Josie sat on the armchair, first moving the pile of washing to one side.

'Are the girls at school?' she asked.

'Of course they are.' Gina folded her arms.

'Were they over on Vincent Square on Tuesday evening?'

Gina cast her mind back to Tuesday. Ah, yes, the hair disaster day. Well, she'd be damned if she could remember anything after finishing off the whisky before starting on the lager – apart from the hangover the following day.

'I'm not sure,' she replied.

'Mr Meredith from Christopher Avenue had his car trashed. Your girls were seen near to, as well as–'

'You see, you're blaming my girls already!' She moved in closer to Josie.

'No, I only want to talk,' said Josie. 'Things do seem to be getting out of hand with Rachel and Claire. And I'm not just talking about the damage to the car. There have been some really nasty catfights lately.'

'That sounds more like it.'

Unexpectedly, Josie noticed a tear in Gina's eye. She supposed it must get to her every now and then. How could it not do?

'All I'm really bothered about is what it might lead to,' she spoke more softly now. 'I'm sure you remember when Stacey Hunter ended up in juvenile detention and–'

'My girls won't end up *there*.'

'If you let me finish, I was going to say since she's gone, Rachel and Claire seem hell-bent on taking her place at the head of this stupid gang they've created. I heard they've been getting the other girls in their group to do initiation tests.'

'That's my girls.' Gina couldn't help but smile.

Josie ignored her sarcasm. 'I'm actually more concerned about what will happen when Stacey gets out.'

Gina frowned. 'What do you mean?'

'Don't you think there's going to be trouble if she doesn't get her place back at the helm? I doubt that Rachel and Claire will back down, so there may be what we'd call a turf war.'

'A turf war? This isn't exactly the East End of London.'

'You know what I mean. Stacey Hunter is a nasty piece of work. Having a stepfather like Lenny Pickton means she's grown up in a world of violence. She

Fighting for Survival

thought nothing of the attack she carried out that got her locked up in the first instance. If Rachel and Claire don't watch their step, who knows how far things might escalate?'

'My girls can hold their own.'

'But what if they can't?' Josie paused. 'It isn't Rachel that I'd be worried about as much as Claire. She doesn't seem as strong as her sister and if Stacey wants to make trouble when she comes out, you know she will. She won't be bothered about going down again and she won't be bothered about taking your girls with her.'

Gina finally caught on to Josie's meaning. Christ, she didn't want to lose the girls too, despite how much grief they caused her. She sat back with a sigh of resignation.

'What can I do?' she said. 'Neither of them listens to me anymore.'

'Can't you try and talk to them?' Josie urged. 'I know it was a bad turn of phrase when I said a turf war but it's highly likely if Stacey hears they're trying to rule her out as coming back as their leader. I'm not sure the police will be able to stop them. They're like animals when they get going.'

Gina frowned – that was her daughters she was referring to. But she realised that Josie meant no harm.

'I'll see what I can do,' she told her.

'Maybe Mr Bradley could have a word?'

'Pete?' Gina snorted as she reached for another cigarette. 'He's bloody hopeless. I'll try and talk to them.'

Josie stood up. She looked at Gina with a heavy heart. Even though her family troubles were of her own making, she couldn't help feeling sorry for her at times. No one would take any notice of Gina: Josie had seen it so many times on the estate. Her brood were too strong-willed.

But she had to admire her for wanting to try. And she hoped that Rachel and Claire Bradley would take note of the bollocking their mother was about to dish out.

'Will you two keep the din down in there?' Ruth shouted through to the living room, almost making as much noise as her sons, Mason and Jamie, combined. The screeching was getting on her nerves. They'd been playing soldier games for near on an hour now. She wished they would settle down and watch a DVD but there was no television set up yet. As it was, she only had the portable television that she'd had for years now. Although she'd paid towards the widescreen television at Martin's house, there was no mention of it coming with her when he'd chucked them out.

How could he have been so cruel, after all that time? She'd spent three years with him, and for what? So he could sling her out on the streets at the first opportunity that some new skirt came along.

It had been that Tracy Tanner's doing, she knew it. As well as being a mobile hairdresser, Tracy worked a couple of nights down at The Butcher's Arms. Ruth had only been in there on one occasion with Martin – babysitters were hard to come by when you didn't have any friends – but she'd noticed immediately the effect that he had on Tracy. Martin was tall, not too scrawny, with a lush of black hair and denim blue eyes. They were the first thing to attract Ruth when she'd met him at the job centre.

He'd been seeing Tracy for over a year on the side when she'd found out they were an item. England had been playing and Martin had gone to The Butcher's Arms to watch the match. He'd only been gone an hour when Jamie had been taken ill. She'd rushed round to a neighbour's and asked them to keep an eye on both boys until she had fetched Martin. She'd run most of the way to the pub, arriving breathless and red-faced.

But she'd been even more red-faced when she'd spotted him in the corner with Tracy Tanner. At first, she hadn't been able to tell who the woman was because Martin's tongue was down her throat.

As she'd stood over them while they continued, Tracy had opened her eyes eventually and pulled away. The look Martin gave her when he turned around was one she would never forget. He sneered; then he laughed. Then he turned back to kiss Tracy Tanner. Ruth had run out of the pub.

Two days later, while Jamie was recovering from what turned out to be no more than a nasty virus, Martin dropped his bombshell. He wanted them out and he wanted them out as soon as possible. He was moving Tracy Tanner in.

Ruth hadn't got a leg to stand on: the property was rented in Martin's sole name. He was the one who was in the wrong, yet she lost her home and what she looked on as her security.

'Mum, can I have some chocolate?' Mason asked as he ran up to her.

'There isn't any left,' said Ruth, as she tidied the work surface. 'You and Jamie had the last of it yesterday.'

Mason kicked the kitchen cupboard, the bang reverberating around the room. 'Why can't you go out and fetch some more?'

'I'm busy.'

Mason raised his voice. 'You're a stupid mum.'

Ruth sighed. 'Don't start all that again. What have I told you about calling people stupid?'

'You are. Stupid, stupid, stupid.'

'Not now, Mason, please.'

Fighting for Survival

'Stupid, stupid, stupid!'

Ruth raced towards him, narrowly missing him as he ran through the door. She could hear his laughter as he tore up the stairs to join his brother. Why did she have to have two boys? All she'd ever wanted was a girl that she could dress up; that she could take shopping; that she could help do her hair. God had been cruel to her in so many ways. Not only had he taken the boys' father away far too early, but he'd then turned her little horrors into eight and ten-year-old fully blown nightmares.

The house now quiet, for a moment at least, she settled down to wash the kitchen flooring. It looked like it had been there long before either Jamie or Mason had been born. She scrubbed frantically at the black scrape marks until her arms ached, but they wouldn't budge.

She sat on her haunches while she caught her breath, wiping her brow with the back of her hand. 'Ow.' She pulled back her arm. Her wrist was covered in a bandage: there was blood seeping through at the edges.

The cut on her arm was her latest torture. If she didn't watch what she was doing, it would become infected and she'd have to seek medical attention and then all the questioning would begin again.

Ruth pulled up her sleeve, ignoring all the scars that ran across her arm. Scratches, wounds of yesteryear. Some were deep, some faint and some scabbing over nicely. But it was the one on her wrist that was giving her problems. It hadn't stopped throbbing for days. In frustration, she unravelled the bandage. As the wound came closer to being unveiled, she winced. The gauze had stuck to the congealed blood. She pulled at it gently, millimetre by millimetre, wincing again with every move. Then the mess was revealed in all its glory – or should that be gory.

Ruth felt the tears building up: how could she do this to herself? She was such an expert on cutting now, how could she have gone that deep? She wasn't even giving the wound time to heal over before she started at it again.

But she knew why – feeling that hurt took the pain of her everyday life away. While she was cutting, hurting herself, no one else could. The pain was part of her, yet she felt detached as she pushed a craft knife into the open wound night after night and sliced away a little more. She glanced down at it, the blood steadily increasing from where she'd pulled away the gauze. Then, hearing banging footsteps down the stairs, she quickly covered it up.

'Mum.' Jamie bounded in this time. 'Mason's hit me.'

'No I haven't.' Mason came in behind him. 'I never touched the little squirt.'

'Yes, you did.'

'No, I didn't.'

'Yes, you did.'

'Shut up, the pair of you,' cried Ruth. 'If you can't play nicely together, I'll split you up.'

Jamie started to cry. It was then that she noticed the red mark on his cheek. She pulled him close, bent down to his level and then addressed his brother.

'For God's sake, Mason,' she started.

'I didn't hit him hard.' Mason walked past her to the sink. 'He's a wimp.'

'You'd be a wimp if I hit you like that.' Ruth wiped away Jamie's tears as the red patch turned to scarlet.

'You wouldn't dare.' Mason glared at her. 'You're a wimp too.'

'Why, you little...' Ruth stood up straight again, grabbed Mason roughly by the neck of his jumper and turned him to face her. She bunched her hand into a fist, raised it high and...

She stopped it in mid-air. Seeing the fear in his eyes had pierced her heart.

'Don't you touch me,' he shouted.

Ruth put her fist down and let go of his jumper. She didn't know who was shaking the most.

'Say sorry to your brother,' she said quietly.

'Sorry,' said Mason.

Ruth turned back to Jamie, only to catch him pulling faces behind her back. The little bastard.

'Get out of my sight,' she said. 'Both of you. Now!'

Jamie turned and ran. Mason followed quickly behind him. When he got to the door, he turned back.

'I hate you,' he said.

Ruth started to cry. She sat down in the middle of the kitchen floor and put her head in her hands.

This was hopeless. It was too much for her to cope on her own. She pulled at her hair sharply. 'Bad mother; bad mother; bad mother,' she repeated over and over.

It wasn't fear that had stopped her from lashing out at Mason. It was the fact that she knew once she started, she wouldn't have been able to stop.

8

*C*aren awoke the next morning when she felt an arm encircle her waist and pull her across the bed. She found herself spooned into John and she closed her eyes to snuggle down again.

'What time is it?' she whispered as his hand sidled up and down the outside of her thigh, then changed to his fingertips.

'Early but I'm horny,' he whispered back.

Caren shivered as she felt his breath on her neck. He moved her hair and kissed her bare shoulder. Sleepily, she sighed and let him. His hands moved lower and around to her breasts, and he stroked a nipple through her vest. Then his hand found its way inside the top.

Caren took it, parted her legs and pressed it to her. She could sense John smiling as his fingers slipped inside her. She gasped and opened her legs a little wider. The sound of her breathing invaded the room as he moved over her, getting her wet and excited in moments.

Eventually, she turned towards him and he kissed her with fervour. She manoeuvred her body beneath his and ran her hands over his back as he continued, down over his naked buttocks which she pulled in closer to her. His kisses were sharper now, deeper, his tongue exploring her mouth. And then he was gone.

He circled her breast with the tip of his tongue, his hand in between her legs again. Caren grasped his hair as he bit down hard on one nipple before running his tongue over her chest to find the other one. Once that was standing erect, he moved further down her body, massaging her, teasing her, tantalising her. As the unmistakeable waves of passion engulfed her, she arched her back, moaning slightly.

John looked up at her as he took her over the edge, waited for her to subside enough for him to push himself gently inside her. They kissed a long time before gaining an easy rhythm and moving together as one. Slowly, slowly. Faster, faster. Caren grabbed John's buttocks as he thrust deeper and deeper into her.

Then they were still.

John lay above her as his breathing returned to normal. Then he kissed her lightly on the nose, pulled her near again and snuggled into her.

Caren entwined her legs with his, sighing contentedly as a smile played on her lips

Well, that was good.

Gina was woken by a loud bang as the back door slammed yet again. She glanced at the clock on her bedside table. It was quarter to nine: most probably it was the twins going out, hopefully on their way to school.

Pete rolled over beside her and she pushed him away. 'Move, you moron,' she said. 'I'll be on the floor in a minute.'

She lay still as she waited for him to settle again. But then the snoring began.

Gina nudged him sharply. 'Shut the fuck up, will you? I can't hear myself think.'

'We're in bed, what's there to think about?' Pete mumbled. 'Mind you, what else is there to do in here but sleep?'

'Don't be so disgusting,' Gina snapped. 'It's all sex with you.'

'I can't remember getting jiggy with you in ages.' Pete grinned. 'We could always squeeze in a session now, if you're up to it?'

She was about to protest when she wondered what the new, improved Gina would do. Even though her hair had turned out to be a disaster, she still wanted to be different; live her life a little more.

'Okay then.' She cuddled up to him but moved away as quickly. 'God, booze breath.' She flapped her hand in front of her mouth. 'You'll have to brush your teeth first.'

'Aw, come on, Gene,' Pete protested. 'You don't have to have fresh breath to do what I want you to do.'

Gina sighed as Pete rolled over on his back. He placed his hand on the bulge that had appeared in his pants. 'Come on, girl. Do us proud. You know you want to.'

'You'd better return the favour, Pete,' she said as she disappeared beneath the covers. She nearly gagged as she got to his pants. God, the man was filthy. 'You need a bath too,' she told him but it came out as a muffle.

'Can't hear you,' said Pete, reaching inside for his cock and flashing it out. It hit her in the face.

'Oi! You'll give me a black eye if you're not careful. Now lay back and be quiet.'

While she took him in her mouth and concentrated on the task in hand, she imagined that John was lying beneath her. She heard Pete gasp – no, it was John that gasped, stupid, she scolded herself.

Pete began to tense his legs and thrust upwards, taking her out of her daydream.

'Fuck, Gina, that's good,' he said.

Gina wished that he'd shut up. How could she imagine it was John she was giving pleasure to if this idiot wouldn't be quiet?

She moved up and down faster, faster, moving her hand to the base of the penis and up and down the shaft. Finally, she heard an almighty groan and his body went rigid with pleasure. Gina sighed: thank God for that – mission accomplished for another month. Now it was her turn.

She emerged from underneath the covers, slipped out of her T-shirt and wriggled her knickers down. Turning towards him, she leaned on one elbow. 'Right, me now,' she said expectantly.

But Pete jumped out of bed. He grabbed the pants from off the floor and sniffed them before pulling them on again.

'I have to be out for nine,' he replied, reaching for the jeans that he'd left on the floor the night before. 'I said I'd meet Barry over on the square. We're doing a job today.'

Gina picked up his pillow and threw it at him as he headed out of the door. 'You self-centred git,' she cried. Then she pummelled her feet on the mattress.

John wouldn't have left her feeling frustrated like that. John would have made sure her horny mood was taken advantage of. Damn Pete, the selfish bastard.

With resignation, she took her vibrator from the drawer. Well, that was shit.

After tea that evening, Gina made her way upstairs to have that talk with the twins. The girls shared the large bedroom at the back of the house. Gina had tried to give them their own bedrooms from an early age, changing the parlour room downstairs into a bedroom for Danny. It wasn't ideal; they really needed somewhere to eat but as they couldn't afford a proper dining table, they always ended up squeezed into the kitchen anyway.

When they were ten, she'd tried to install in them a sense of individuality, but it had become quite clear that they didn't want to be separated, not even at night time.

When she'd check on them before going to bed herself, she'd go into Rachel's room and find Claire snuggled up beside her. Or she'd go into Claire's room and find Rachel sleeping top to toe. So it had made more sense to take back the parlour room, move them in together and let Danny have his old room back.

She knocked on the door. 'Girls, I need to talk to you,' she said, marching in and turning down the music blaring from the tinny CD player they shared.

Rachel was lying on her bed, reading a magazine. Claire was sitting next to her.

'Don't you ever knock?' Rachel sighed.

'I have knocked,' Gina told them. 'I've also had a visit from Josie Mellor yesterday.'

'Whatever she says, we haven't done it,' said Claire. 'She's always blaming us for everything.'

'That's because you're usually in the thick of things.'

Both girls spoke in unison. 'No, we're not.'

Gina sat down on the edge of Claire's bed. 'It's what I want to talk to you about. I need ammunition for when she next comes round asking all sorts of questions. I need to know that you haven't been involved in any of the incidents she mentioned.'

'We don't know anything about Archie Meredith's car getting bashed up,' said Rachel.

'How did you know I was going to ask about that?'

'I– I just know that you'll blame us for it anyway. You never stick up for us.'

'I do!' said Gina. 'I get a roasting for it most of the time, too.'

Claire put down her magazine. 'What do you really want, Mum?'

'What I *don't* want is you two going the same way as your brother.'

'Huh, like we'd ever.'

Rachel nodded in agreement with her sister. 'We're far better at getting away with things.'

'That's not what I mean. Danny chanced his luck and he got caught last year.'

'Yeah, well, Danny's a knob,' said Rachel. She lay back on the bed and sighed. 'And an idiot. I mean, he got away with that murder charge when Miles's Factory got done over and then he gets caught nicking stuff from Halford's. What a comedown he had.'

Fighting for Survival

Claire laughed and turned to Gina. 'We won't get caught. We're far too clever.'

'You mean getting other girls to do your dirty work for you?'

Both girls glared at her then.

'You think I don't know what's been going on?'

'Nothing's been going on,' snapped Rachel.

'So when Stacey Hunter gets out, she won't be bothered by the fact that you seem to have taken over as gang leaders.'

Rachel sat upright. Claire nervously looked her way.

'You have no idea how hard it is to survive on this estate, Mum,' said Rachel.

'*Survive*?' Gina tried in vain to keep the incredulous tone from her voice. 'We don't live in the ghetto.'

'Dur,' said Claire. 'Take a look out of the window. Yes we do.'

'You've been watching too much television.' Gina shook her head in exasperation. 'I know living on the Mitchell Estate isn't exactly a barrel of laughs, but there are worse places.'

'Where?'

Gina stood up and raised her hands in the air in surrender. 'I give up with you two,' she said. 'Do what you want. But I'm warning you both,' she pointed at Rachel,' you, madam, in particular, be very careful what you do. These things have a habit of coming back and biting you. Don't say you haven't been warned.'

As soon as Gina left the room, Claire turned to Rachel. 'Stacey will want to take over, won't she?'

'Well, we're not going to let her.'

Claire looked away. Quite frankly, the thought of Stacey getting out next week was enough to start her worrying about it already.

Rachel shot forward, grabbed Claire's chin and yanked her neck round so that she was facing her.

'We're not going to let her take over, *are we*?' she repeated, staring at her intently.

'No,' Claire managed to say.

Rachel pushed her sister away. 'Good.'

Claire went to sit on her own bed. She hated it when Rachel got all mouthy with her. And why did she have to cause trouble all of the time?

'We need to come up with a plan,' Rachel told her, the leg perched on her knee swinging violently from side to side. 'Stacey won't be content with second in command.'

'I thought I was second in command.'

Rachel ignored her. 'If she wants to get back on top, she'll have me to put down first. I'm not letting go of the lead, no way.'

'I thought I was second in command,' reiterated Claire.

'Shut the fuck up. I'm thinking.'

I've been thinking,' Caren said to John as they ate their lunch together the following week. 'I'm going to start working for myself.'

John looked up from his pasta dish with a frown before shoving in another forkful.

Caren held up a hand and waggled her fingers at him. He looked blankly at her.

'Nails, dur. I'm going to set myself up mobile. It might not bring much in but it'll be a start. And it'll get me out of the house.'

'Great.' John continued to eat.

'So that only leaves you to fix yourself up now,' she added.

Yeah, Pete's been telling me about–'

'You're not doing his type of work.'

'What do you mean by that?'

Caren put down her fork. 'I know what he gets up to. He's never earned a decent day's pay in his life.'

'He gets by all right. Him and Gina–'

'It's nothing legal. He's a bad influence and knowing you, you'll get sucked into his way of life. Before you know it, you'll be doing time for some petty crime or another.'

'It's easy money. Besides, I've been too busy to start making contacts.'

'You already have contacts. Some of *them* might have work for you.' Caren stood up. 'It's only pride that stops you. You need to stop being so picky.'

'So picky?'

'Yes.' Caren moved to the sink and shoved the plate into the washing up bowl. 'There's work to be had out there with people you already know. Go and beg if you have to but we need to–'

'You think it's so easy, don't you?' John said quietly.

Caren turned to him. 'Of course it isn't easy, but you have to do it. I'm willing to give it a go too.'

John huffed. 'Anyone can paint nails for the scabby bitches on this estate. You'll make a frigging fortune. None of them ever get their hands dirty.'

John stood up quickly, his chair scraping across the tiles. Not bothering to put it back under the table, he marched towards the door.

Caren threw down the dishcloth. 'Where are you running off to now?'

'Away from you and your nagging. Maybe my best will never be good enough for you,' John continued. 'Maybe I'd be better off on my own.'

'So you can shirk all your responsibilities?'

'Like I said, I'm doing my best.'

Caren burst into tears. 'I hate living like this,' she cried. 'We don't have any money in the bank to call our own – we can hardly afford to pay the bills. And if we weren't living in this hell hole, we wouldn't be bickering all the time.'

John stared at her for a moment before walking across and taking her into his arms.

'What are we going to do?' she sobbed, his hands soothing her as he rubbed her back. 'I don't want to fight all the time but I feel so vulnerable living here.'

'It won't be for long.' John tilted her chin up. 'I'll make more of an effort, I promise. If you want to move off here straight away, I'll start looking for somewhere to live too.'

'One step at a time,' Caren sniffed. She smiled through her tears. 'I don't want us to break up over this. We've come so far through the years. We can't quit now.'

John continued to stare at her. 'Who said anything about quitting?' He kissed her lightly on the tip of her nose.

'I'm bored,' Claire said to Rachel as the girls congregated outside Shop&Save that evening. 'Who can we irritate?'

Rachel took a noisy slurp from her can of lager before replying. 'I can't be bothered tonight.'

'Aw, come on.' Leanne circled round on her bike in front of them. 'I fancy some fun too.'

'Shut up, Leanne,' said Rachel.

'What's with you, you moody cow?' Leanne snapped back. 'Anyone would think you were worried about something.'

Rachel glared at her. 'I said shut it.'

Leanne shrugged and continued to circle them on her bike.

'Ohmigod,' squealed Charlie. 'Looks who's here.'

Rachel glanced in the direction that Charlie was running to see Stacey Hunter walking towards them.

'Fuck.' Claire's hands gripped the railing they were perched on, twisting and turning quickly.

It didn't go unnoticed by Rachel. 'Quit looking scared of her,' she retorted.

'I *am* scared of her,' whispered Claire.

Rachel shook her head. 'You'd better not be.'

The rest of the girls crowded around Stacey as she drew near to the car park. She was a tall girl, with deep-set eyes and a small nose. Brown hair was cut so close to her head that it was hard to tell her gender. Her face was void of any colour, several earrings dangling from an ear. A small tattoo on the back of her right hand spelled out the word 'sinner.'

She approached Rachel with assurance. 'Hi,' she said.

'Hi yourself.'

'How're tricks?'

'So, so.'

Stacey thrust her hands deep into her pockets and pulled out a packet of cigarettes. 'Anyone want one?'

Suddenly she was the star attraction.

'I could murder a fag,' said Leanne.

'Me too,' Louise pulled one out. 'Ta.'

Stacey handed them out before addressing the twins.

'Claire?' she offered the packet to her.

Claire shrugged, unsure what to do. She looked at Rachel, who with a slight nod of her head, indicated that it was all right for her to take one.

Stacey shoved the packet into Rachel's chest. 'Do you want one?'

Rachel purposely took two. She placed one behind her ear and the other one went in her mouth. Charlie lit it for her and she took a drag before looking up again.

Stacey and Rachel stared at each other like a pair of gunslingers ready to duel. The atmosphere turned to one of mixed tensions. Some of the girls couldn't wait for the showdown: some of them were worried about its outcome. All of them were wondering who to pledge allegiance to once things started to get rough.

It was Stacey who finally broke the silence as she spotted a navy blue BMW driving towards them.

'Here's my ride. Thanks for watching over my patch,' she told Rachel, 'and my girls, but now I'm out, I've come to claim back my turf.'

Rachel glared at her. 'Over my dead body,' she replied.

Stacey nodded her head slowly. 'I'm sure that can be arranged.'

Rachel only had time to fume as Stacey ran towards the car. From where she sat, she could see the driver was Sam Harvey, a well-known troublemaker from the estate. Stacey slid into the passenger seat and he sped off quickly.

Rachel walked off then, kicking over an advertising board outside Shop&Save as she drew level with it.

'What's up with you?' Louise shouted after her. 'You're not losing your bottle, are you?'

Rachel stopped in her tracks and turned back. 'No, I'm not losing my fucking bottle. For your information, I think we need to move on to bigger things – not just nicking stuff from easy targets. It's a joke. I want everyone to be afraid of the Mitchell Mob; I want everyone talking about us. And for that we need to go up a gear.'

'What do you mean?' Louise was the first to challenge. 'We cause enough mayhem already.'

'If I get into any more trouble, my olds will ground me,' Charlie spoke out.

'Me too,' said Ashley. 'I got a backhander after we did Meredith's car. My olds knew I'd been involved even though I denied it.'

'Sounds like some of us are getting cold feet about belonging to the Mitchell Mob.' Rachel folded her arms in defiance.

'I don't want to get locked up like Stacey,' said Louise.

'You have to take chances in this game to survive, so if we get sent down, we get sent down,' reiterated Rachel.

Had Rachel noticed the wary looks travelling between the girls, she might have chosen her words better. Instead, to hide how nervous she felt, she went in guns blazing, pointing at them.

'You lot need to decide your loyalties. I'm not giving in to the likes of Stacey Hunter so things will get tough for a while. She might think she's hard but I'd smash her face in any day. And none of you need to make me into an enemy, or I'll start on you too.'

She paused but no one spoke out. Great, just how she liked it; they were quaking in their trainers.

So there was absolutely no need for anyone to know that she was too.

9

As Caren tackled a pile of ironing, she thought more about the idea she'd had about going mobile to do nails. When she'd spoken to John about it, he'd said to hold fire and to see what came up for him. But that had been over a week ago and he still hadn't sorted anything out – although she knew something was going on. She'd hardly seen him for the past couple of days. Every time she asked him what he'd been up to, he'd tap his finger to his nose and smile. She wondered if he was doing a trial for a company to see if he was what they were after.

'Hey, gorgeous,' he said when he came in twenty minutes later. He wrapped an arm around her waist and kissed her on the cheek. 'You okay?'

'Yes, you?'

'I am indeed.' John threw a wad of notes down onto the ironing board.

Caren stared at them, then at him. She put down the iron. 'Where did you get that from?'

'I've been working.'

Caren smiled, noticing that his jeans and boots were covered in white powder. 'I knew you were up to something.' She pointed to a chair. 'Sit down and you can tell me all about it. I'll make coffee.'

'Don't get your hopes up. It was only for a couple of days.'

'It's a start, isn't it? Was it a trial for someone?'

'Not exactly.' John sat down. 'I've been working with Pete. A mate of his needed some plastering doing. I've been labouring for him.'

Caren's smile dropped away.

'You wanted money, didn't you?'

'Yes, but–'

John sighed. 'Then get into the real world. Jobs don't come along ten a penny. So I thought I might as well get some money coming in while I try to find something permanent.'

'You said you wouldn't get involved with his dirty deals.'

John sniggered. 'Plastering is hardly a dirty deal.'

'You know what I mean.'

'I'm trying my best, Caz.'

'No, you're not. Working cash in hand isn't what we do.'

'It'll put food on the table.'

'Yes, I know, but–'

'I thought it would make you happy.'

'Well, it won't. I know it's only a plastering job now, but what next? Pete's a taker. He'll use anyone he can to make a quick buck.' She pointed to the money. 'How much do you think he got, if he gave you a hundred?'

'He got the same.'

'Did you see him pocket his share?'

'No, but he wouldn't–'

'I wouldn't put anything past him. He's a loser, John, and hanging around with him, no matter what your best intentions are, will do you more harm than good.'

'Okay, little miss fix-it. You tell me how to get a job.'

'Get out of Pete's pocket and start acting like a–'

'For fuck's sake.' John grabbed the money from the ironing board. 'I'll take this, shall I? I might as well gamble it away because it won't be good enough for you.'

'That's not going to solve–'

'You've got to face up to things. We've been here for over a month now. I've not had a sniff of a job so I've done what I thought was best.'

Caren stopped then. There was nothing she could say to that.

John's brow furrowed. 'I'm not sure if I'll ever be good enough for you.' He threw the money down onto the floor and left with the slam of the door.

Caren flinched. Why had she pushed him into an argument again? She knew he had their best intentions at heart but what she didn't want was him getting used to the amount of money he could get on the side while claiming benefits.

There was always someone in the papers who thought they'd get away with it but, inevitably, they got caught out. And that was beside the point: they were not, and never would be, benefit cheats.

Upstairs, she heard John in the bedroom. At least he hadn't gone out. She

525

knew he'd calm down by the time he emerged from the shower. That was one good thing about him; he could never stay angry for long.

How she detested Pete Bradley. He would be their downfall if she let him.

Caren sighed. Yet another day in paradise.

As soon as Rachel and Claire turned the corner into Davy Road that night, they saw Stacey. She was talking to Hayley and Shell, huddled up in discussion. None of them noticed as they approached.

Rachel had seen this coming but she didn't think Stacey would act so quickly. First, she'd caught her talking to Louise a couple of nights ago. Louise had run over to Rachel as soon as she'd spotted her and when questioned had said Stacey was after the tenner she owed her before she got sent down. Now, here she was again, determined to get her gang back.

Rachel pulled up the hood of her jacket. Well, one way or another, she was going to find out how determined she was. Even though she was wary, she'd have to show her who was boss.

'What the fuck do you want?' Rachel asked as she drew level with them.

'Nothing.'

'Back off my girls, then.'

'They're not your girls.'

'No?'

'No.'

Rachel turned to Hayley and then Shell. 'Maybe you two need to think about loyalties,' she snapped.

Shell dropped her eyes immediately but Hayley stared at Rachel for a while. At last, with a quick glance at Stacey, she too looked away.

Claire, hanging round in the background like a spare part, finally moved forward.

'Right, that's sorted,' she threw into the tense atmosphere. 'Now, let's get some fags. I'm dying for a drag.'

As Rachel and Stacey strutted their stuff like two peacocks, she grabbed hold of Hayley's arm and dragged her nearer to the entrance of Shop&Save. 'Come on, you're better at scrounging than me.'

Eventually, Stacey moved away.

'Bye, bye,' Rachel shouted after her. 'See you again soon – I don't think.'

Stacey turned back. 'You won't win, redhead,' she spoke coolly before continuing.

'Want to take a bet on it?'

'No point when the odds are stacked against you.'

Once Stacey was in the distance, Rachel turned to Shell and punched her on the upper arm.

'Ow,' Shell cried out.

'Show me up again and you'll get a lot more of that.'

Ruth woke up with another headache. Was it any wonder with the vodka she'd knocked back last night? She tried to focus on the bedroom, still not familiar enough to feel at home in. The nights were drawing in now – soon the clocks would be going back and the dark would descend in more ways than one. Ruth hated winter. In summer, it was much easier to rid herself of a bad mood if the sun was shining and she could sit in the garden. In winter, when it was cold and raining and windy and icy, it took all of her strength not to pull the duvet over her head and stay there all day.

'Mum, there's no bread left,' Jamie shouted up the stairs.

Ruth sighed: couldn't that boy do anything quietly? She dragged herself downstairs to face the day.

'You'll have to have cereal for your breakfast,' she told Jamie as she joined him in the kitchen. She opened the fridge to pull out the milk. Damn, there wasn't a lot of milk either. She'd have to call in at the shops on her way back from school.

'But I want toast.'

'You can't have any.'

Jamie threw down the empty bread packet and stamped on it. Without a second thought, Ruth leaned forward and slapped him across the face.

'Shut up with the moaning,' she told him. 'You'll have what you're given. Now, go and see where your brother is.'

Ruth ran a hand through her hair and began to pull at it. Then she heard the scream. She looked at Jamie in confusion. He was sobbing, and holding his face. For a moment, she froze. Then she rushed over, pulling him into her arms quickly.

'I'm so sorry,' she whispered. 'I didn't mean to hurt you.'

It was the truth: in actual fact, she couldn't remember *hitting* him. But as she saw a red mark appearing on his cheek, she hugged him again.

What had made her do that? She was tired, of course. She hadn't had more than a couple of hours sleep the night before. Trying to drown her sorrows with the vodka, she'd ended up wide awake and weepy. But usually tiredness didn't make her lash out like that, especially not at one of the boys.

'What's up?' A sleepy Mason appeared in the doorway, rubbing at his eyes.

'M-mum hit me,' Jamie said through his sobs.

Ruth looked at Mason. 'I didn't mean to. I–'

Mason ran at his mother, his fists grabbing handfuls of her hair.

'Don't hurt my brother,' he screamed.

'Ow. Mason, let go!'

But Mason held on, long enough for Jamie to run past his mum and out of the room.

'I hate you. I hate you. I hate you.' shouted Mason.

With every word, he pulled her hair a little harder. Ruth forced one of his hands away and then the other. In moments, she had the better of him.

'Let me go, you little horror,' she yelled in his face. 'I've had enough of you and Jamie. You think I like looking after you two every day of my life? You think it's easy to do this, when you two misbehave like you do? You should show some respect. I'm your mother.'

Breathing heavily, Ruth only came to her senses when she heard the rush of his bladder releasing itself. She looked down.

'Mason, I–'

Mason stood still, unable to speak. His bottom lip started to tremble as he tried hard not to cry. He hardly ever cried. Jamie was still a baby at eight so he could cry, but Mason? He was ten and saw himself as the head of the family.

Mason burst into tears.

Ruth looked at her ten-year-old child, a snivelling wreck who had peed his pants and was now too afraid to speak. Over in the doorway, his brother watched on in horror, the mark on his cheek reddening with every second that passed.

What was she going to do about her temper?

Ruth stood up and turned away from them before they could see her crying.

'I think you'd better get ready for school,' she said. 'We need to leave in half an hour.'

*R*uth worried about her behaviour as she took the boys to school. What on earth had gone on this morning? It was one thing to get drunk and have a go at bringing pain to herself. But she had never lashed out at her children in temper. Not like that. And it scared her to think what she might be capable of. She decided to check up with Doctor Morgan, see if any of her tablets needed changing.

After calling in at the surgery to make an appointment, she stopped off at the shops to pick up some chocolate before heading back to the house. But halfway along Stanley Avenue, her morning got decidedly worse.

'Ruth? Ruth Millington?'

Fighting for Survival

She turned to see who had shouted, her shoulders sinking immediately. 'Hi, Gina,' she replied.

Gina opened her gate and walked over. 'I thought it was you,' she said. 'I heard you'd moved into number thirty-two.'

Ruth nodded but Gina didn't give her time to speak.

'It looks a right dump. How are you going to cope with that on your own?' Gina folded her arms across her coffee-stained T-shirt and smirked. 'You are on your own now, aren't you?'

'No, I have my children with me.'

Gina smirked. 'You know that's not what I meant. Your fella's been shagging around, hasn't he?'

Ruth turned to walk away. 'That's none of your business.'

'That's where you're wrong. Everything on this avenue is my business. I make it that way, so you'd better get used to it.'

Ruth closed her eyes for a moment as she tried to blot out Gina's words. A ranting neighbour, one she'd known vaguely at school and disliked, having a go at her in the middle of the street was the last thing she needed right now. She took a step away.

'Hey.' Gina grabbed her by the arm. 'Don't walk away from me when I'm talking to you.'

'I'm sorry, Gina, I'm tired. Why don't we catch up later?'

'You think I want to catch up with you?' Gina moved closer. 'I don't think so. I'm just letting you know the rules that you have to abide by so that you can survive on Stanley Avenue; so that you settle in okay and don't give me any trouble.'

Ruth sighed. 'What are you after? Because if you're after a fight, I don't have it in me.'

'Oh, chill woman. I'm not out for your blood yet. But I will be if you step a foot wrong – or take a shine to my Pete. I know that your husband died but mine is off limits, do you hear?'

At the mention of Glenn, Ruth felt like she'd had a knife thrust into her heart and twisted savagely. Her eyes filled with tears as his face flashed before them.

'Involved in a car accident, wasn't he?' Gina added. 'I heard he was drunk when he–'

'You heard wrong,' Ruth interrupted. 'Another driver hit him head on. He– he died instantly. It wasn't his fault.'

Gina raised her eyebrows. 'You'll tell me anything. I suppose you'll tell me next that your Martin wasn't getting his end away with Tracy Tanner.'

Ruth couldn't cope with any more verbal abuse. She began to walk away quickly. But Gina followed her.

'I know your sort, Ruth Millington – if that's still your name. You've lost your husband and you couldn't keep the next fella in check. So just you keep your hands off mine.'

Ruth walked faster.

'If I hear that you've as much as looked at my Pete, I'll knock your fucking head off. Do you hear me?'

Ruth was at her garden gate now. She ran the last few steps to get away from the screeching behind her. Once inside the house, she drew the bolt across the front door and sat behind it, trying to calm her breathing before she had a panic attack.

The letterbox clattered open.

'You're only a few doors away from me,' Gina yelled through it. 'I can find you anytime, remember that.'

Ruth jumped as the letterbox snapped shut again. She ran through to the kitchen and slammed the door. Her back to it, she slid to the floor and sobbed.

Although they should have been at school that morning, it was ten thirty and Rachel and Claire were still lying in bed. Claire was reading the latest edition of *Heat* Magazine. Rachel was messing about on her mobile phone. Suddenly, it beeped as a text message came in.

'Not meeting u 2nite. Hanging round with Stacey. Shell is 2. No hard feelings? Hayls.'

Rachel bit down hard on her bottom lip. Those cows. She knew they were up to something the other night. She should have punched Stacey Hunter when she had the chance.

She thought back to the other members in the gang, wondering who she could keep on side for the longest, Louise or Charlie? Louise had been with Stacey from the beginning. Now that Hayley and Shell had jumped ship, it would seem safer for her to gravitate towards Stacey too. And Stacey had been making headway to get Charlie to join her before she got sent down.

Suddenly, Rachel saw her little empire falling down before her. She glanced across at her sister, knowing she'd be no use if it came to a full-blown war. She'd have to do some planning; see if she could get Hayley and Shell back on side, because if she didn't, she and Claire would end up as sitting ducks. Despite the big attitude she portrayed when they were out with the gang, it was only an act. She knew Stacey would come out on top.

In frustration, she threw her phone down onto the bed. 'Fucking bitches,' she hissed.

'What's up?' asked Claire.

Fighting for Survival

'Hayley and Shell have gone back to Stacey.'

Claire gasped. 'But, I thought they were with us.'

'So did I.'

'What shall we do?'

'We'll have to get them back.'

'How?'

Rachel sighed. 'I don't know. What do you think?'

Claire shrugged. 'Why can't we go back to how it was before?'

'What do you mean?'

'When we were all together, it used to be a laugh and I reckon –'

'Are you saying that I'm a shit leader?' Rachel picked up a slipper and threw it at her.

Claire dodged it. 'No, I'm –'

'You'd better not be. You're my sister. You're supposed to stick up for me and think my ideas are good. You're supposed to fight with me.'

'I know that, but –' Claire ducked as another slipper flew past her head. 'Back off, will you and let me speak.'

'Piss off.' Rachel pulled the duvet over her head.

'Why is it that you always have your say but you won't listen to me?'

The duvet flipped up again. 'Because you talk so much shit.'

'I only talk as much shit as you do.'

'Shut up.'

'I'm just saying that if you don't want to be leader any more, it's a perfect time to say. Stacey would take us back right now, but if we start messing around with the others, then we'll be the ones hunted down.'

'And you think that bothers me?'

'It bothers me.' Claire paused. 'And if you must know you've become really nasty and I'm not sure it suits you.'

'Ha, that's a laugh, coming from you. We've always been known for being nasty.'

'We've been known for causing trouble, and wrecking things and nicking things, but not beating people up.'

'Well, you're part of this so you'll have to do what I say.'

Claire sighed. It was her turn to pull the duvet over her head. She knew Rachel wasn't listening.

But she had tried.

10

Ruth reached for her wine glass again, sighing when she saw it was empty. She staggered through to the kitchen to fill it up, only to find the bottle empty too. She couldn't afford to drink wine but after the day she'd had, it had gone into her shopping basket as if it were an everyday essential. Three for a tenner that she hadn't really got: one of them must work out as free, surely? So, in theory, she was really only about to start on her first bottle, not the second.

It was nine thirty on a very murky, very lonely, Tuesday evening. Ruth opened the bottle and took it back into the living room. She poured a glassful and drunk it immediately. She wanted to be smashed, over the edge; pass out paralytic as soon as possible. She couldn't take the pain caused by the images flashing through her mind since she'd bumped into Gina that morning.

Tears pricked her eyes as she thought of Glenn. They had been married for seven years when he'd been killed. He'd been an electrician for one of the major electricity suppliers. The money was good, giving them a lifestyle far better than any tenant of Stanley Avenue could expect.

But good money also meant overtime and being on call. That night, Glenn had been called out to fix a broken power line. Afterwards, he rang to say he'd be home soon and to get the kettle on because he was chilled to the bone. The winter temperatures had dropped to minus five. Ruth told him she'd be ready with hot chocolate and cheese on toast.

Glenn never made it back. He'd been driving the work's van. Another driver in a truck coming towards him had lost it on a bend, sliding straight into him

Fighting for Survival

and pushing him over the side of a bank. According to the police, the van had rolled over a couple of times but Glenn wouldn't have known about it as a bump to his head seemed to have killed him outright.

Going to the front door and finding two policemen with bad news had been the worst thing that had ever happened in her life. At twenty-eight, her world and her future had been crushed. Everything she knew had been taken from her, and she had two small boys to look after.

After the funeral, over the next few months she spiralled further and further into depression. As the money stopped coming in, the mortgage went into arrears, the bills started to pile up, and eventually the house was repossessed.

She and the boys went to stay with her parents. During this time, Ruth struggled to get on with the day-to-day mundane things and it was only a matter of time before she cracked.

Luckily, her parents took control of caring for Mason and Jamie. Ruth couldn't look after herself: there was no way she could see to two demanding boys as well.

But slowly, she began to cope again. Eventually, she moved into a flat – the boys moving in with her on a permanent basis a month later – and she began to enjoy spending time getting to know them again. Being a mother was an important job, one she'd loved before she lost Glenn, her soulmate.

Oh, Glenn. She picked up the photo frame she'd been hugging to herself for most of the day and then took another swig of her wine before trying to focus on the room. She'd made it as homely as possible with what she had but still it seemed sparse. It looked, and felt, like a house not a home. And that was her fault because she'd gone and lost the only man who had shown an interest in her since Glenn had died.

Ruth had started to self-harm about six months after she'd moved in with Martin. She could remember the day quite clearly: it had been the first time he'd hit her. He came home from the pub to find his dinner in the oven, shrivelled up because he was late, but he lashed out at her when she'd moaned at him.

A crack across the mouth and a face-full of mashed potatoes had made her run to her room. She began to pick at a scar that she'd got from a burn on the oven door. Bit by bit, she picked at it until the half inch scar became a two inch mass of pus and blood. She ended up going to the doctors and he gave her some antibiotic cream.

She remembered clearly the sting of the cream, putting it on every hour rather than the intended twice a day. Hurting herself blocked the pain she was feeling. For those few minutes, the anguish she felt took away everything else.

The pain sometimes became so intense that she cried, but she didn't stop. It was meant to try and wipe out her abysmal existence; it was her punishment.

She couldn't cope with Mason; she couldn't cope with Jamie; she couldn't cope with herself. Hell, she couldn't even cope with life.

She took another gulp of the wine, the urge to self-harm becoming stronger with each passing minute. She slapped at her face, trying to ease the throbbing inside her head. She needed to hurt herself: she knew it would make her feel better. Stuff the do-gooders who thought it was a terrible thing to do. Stuff the people who stared at her arms as they caught a glimpse every now and then.

She picked at the most recent scar on her arm. It hadn't had time to heal yet: she doubted it ever would at this rate. She dug her nails in, then picked, picked, picked until she saw the blood ooze out. There was blood underneath her fingernails: it satisfied her somewhat. But it wasn't enough. She fetched her craft knife.

'Mum, don't do that.'

Ruth looked up a few minutes later, trying to focus on the figure standing in front of her. Was it Mason or was it Jamie? And what the hell were they doing out of bed?

'Mason?'

'Put down that thing. I hate it when you do that.'

'Do what?'

Mason pointed. 'That.'

Ruth looked down at her hand. She'd bought the knife from a craft shop in the town; it had been a godsend, perfect for the job at hand. As she looked at it more clearly, yet again it was covered in blood. She smiled; it made her feel so good.

'Oh, that,' she said, putting it down on the table. 'It's nothing. I've just found it down the side of the cooker. It must have been left behind by the people who lived here before.'

'I know what you do.' Mason stepped towards her. 'I know you cut yourself. I've seen you lots of times. Why do you do that, Mum? Why do –'

Ruth grabbed Mason's arm and pulled him nearer. She didn't notice her son pull away from the stench of her breath.

'You've been spying on me, you little creep.'

'No, Mum. I –'

'Have you told anyone?'

'No. You're hurting me!'

'You'd better not say anything to anyone. ANYONE, do you hear?'

'I haven't.' Mason was crying now.

Ruth pulled him nearer still; she was having trouble focusing on him. Why wouldn't he stay in one place?

'If you do tell someone, they'll put you and your brother into care. You'll end up in a children's home, with lots of other naughty kids and you and your

Fighting for Survival

brother will be split up. Because it's your fault that I do this. You and your brother. You won't behave yourself. You're always up to mischief. Always doing something that you shouldn't. There's no way anyone would want the two of you, anyway. You're nothing but a bloody liability.'

Mason stood still now, tears pouring down his face. 'I – I only wanted a drink of water,' he whispered.

It was enough to bring Ruth out of her trance. She pushed him away from her. 'Go on then and be quick about it.'

Mason did as he was told and was gone in seconds.

Ruth grabbed for the craft knife, picking it up by the blade and relishing the feel of it pressing into the skin on her fingers. Stuff them, she thought as she settled back into the settee. Stuff Mason, and Jamie. And Martin. And that fucking Gina Bradley.

As she drew the craft knife across the inside of her arm, for a second as she saw the red line getting thicker and thicker, she felt that little bit better.

While Ruth watched the blood drip out of the cut and onto her T-shirt, Gina was trying to focus on the cards fanned out in her hand. She peered at them with resignation. They weren't good enough to win. She contemplated whether to call it a day or have another lager.

Pete put his cards down onto the table one by one, a triumphant grin on his face. He reached for the pile of coins on the table in front of him, but John placed a hand over his.

'Not so quick, my friend.' John spread out his cards. 'Look at 'em and weep, my son,' he grinned, pulling the money towards him. 'I win again.'

'You lucky git,' Pete cried as he shuffled the cards again. He looked at Gina. 'Another game?'

Gina shook her head. 'You've had all my fag money so far.'

There was a knock at the front door. All three of them looked up in surprise. It was way past midnight.

Gina got to her feet just as another knock rang out, this time much louder. 'All right, all right, I'm coming.'

'Where is he?' Caren pushed past her and into the house.

'Well, hello, to you too,' Gina smiled lazily. Oh, she was going to enjoy this.

'Jeez, what a mess,' Caren muttered quietly as she walked through the living room and into the kitchen.

'Oi, I heard that, you cheeky cow.' Gina followed close behind her.

'Caren!' John smiled at her before returning to look at the cards in his hand.

Caren stood over them, folding her arms. 'John, it's gone midnight again. How long are you going to be this time?'

'As long as it takes to win this fat fucker's money.'

'Less of the fat, you cheeky bugger,' Pete laughed. He flicked his eyes up to Caren and then back to his cards. 'He won't be long now, so hurry back home, little wifey.'

John fanned his hand out on the table. 'Beat that, loser.'

Pete looked back at his own cards before admitting defeat. He threw them down. 'You are one hell of a lucky bastard.'

'He won't be, by the time I've finished with him.' Caren waved a hand in front of John's face. 'Remember me? I'm standing by your side.'

'Chill out,' said Gina, sitting back down at the table. 'We're playing for ten pence pieces, not ten pound notes. He won't bankrupt you again, if that's what's worrying you.'

'I knew you shouldn't have opened your mouth about it,' Caren hissed.

Looking awkward, John shrugged the comment off. 'I'm having a night out with friends. A few beers and a laugh, that's all.'

'Have you no sense of pride?' Caren lowered her head to his level. 'Why would you ever call these two friends?'

'Hey,' snapped Gina.

Pete shuffled the cards again. 'I'd quit while you're ahead, if I were you, Caz.'

'All I'm saying is you've got to get up early in the morning and –'

John sniggered. 'What do I have to get up for? All you do is nag, nag, nag.'

Caren baulked. 'This isn't the time to get into a full-blown row.'

'No, I suppose not.' John sighed. 'You'll more than likely keep that for tomorrow.'

Gina sat grinning as she watched the exchange with intrigue. A plan began to form in her mind, just exactly how she could get one up on Caren after all.

Silence engulfed the room as Caren stood fuming. When John didn't look up for a few seconds, she snapped. 'Fine, have it your way. But if you're not home in fifteen minutes, the bolts will be across and you'll have to sleep here.'

John looked up in alarm but Caren was already heading out of the room. He went to shout after her but noticing Pete staring at him, shrugged and grabbed the cards. He began to shuffle out a new game, hardly jumping at all as the front door slammed moments later.

'Another beer, boys?' Gina rushed over to the fridge.

'Now, you see?' Pete slapped her bottom as she went past. 'That's how a woman should treat you – with respect.'

John said nothing. He picked up his hand and gave it the once over. Typical; his luck had changed.

As Gina removed the bottle tops, leaving the one that dropped to the floor, she turned back to the table and noticed the scowl on John's face. Bleeding hell, she hadn't realised how hen-pecked he was.

Maybe she should try and persuade them to do this more often. Then, if she could get Caren to lock him out again, maybe she could take advantage of the situation.

She smiled deviously. Caren had handed her husband over on a huge serving platter. Pretty soon, he'd be hers for the taking.

She held up her bottle in the air. 'Cheers,' she cried.

11

Caren was in the kitchen when John came downstairs the next morning. It was nine thirty: she'd been up since six.

'Can I come in?' he asked, holding his hands up in surrender.

'If you must.'

He tried to touch her arm as she moved past him but she slapped it out of the way. She piled the dishes in the sink, glad that the radio was on to avoid the inevitable silence.

'I'm sorry, I was out of order. I had too much to drink. I'm a total idiot.'

'You missed off selfish bastard.' Caren wiped at her hands with the tea towel. 'And don't forget the "I'm with my mates again so fuck off wifey bastard". You made me look like a right nag.'

'I didn't mean to.'

'You could have fooled me. Gina was relishing every second of it. I wish I'd leaned over and wiped that smug look off her face.'

John smirked. 'That's never going to happen. Your tongue is lethal but a fighter you're not.

'I am sorry,' he added. 'Sometimes I want to forget things for a while. And where better to forget normality than across the road. It really is a weird place: all those boxes of stuff everywhere. And clothes piled high, magazines and mugs everywhere and... I couldn't wait to get out, if I'm honest.'

'I can't understand why you have to forget things by going over there. I mean, why can't you sit with me in the evening?'

'After the mood you'd been in all day?' John scoffed.

Caren sighed. He was right: she'd been in a foul temper yesterday. She hadn't got a particular reason to feel angry, but she'd been really crabby with him. In fact, she recalled, ashamed at herself now, she'd wanted to pick a fight with him because she was so fed up. No wonder he'd slammed out to get some peace.

'How about I make it up to you this evening?' she offered. 'I'll cook up something special and we can check out the television, watch a film.' She grinned. 'I'll even let you choose.'

'I thought you'd be really mad.'

'I am really mad, but I don't want to fight. So...' she reached for his hand and placed it on her breast. 'A film and good food – unless you can think of anything else you might like to do?'

Rachel put a finger to her lips and turned to look at Claire. 'Over there.' She pointed into the distance. By the side of Shop&Save car park sat two girls, their backs towards them.

'Ready?' she whispered to Claire.

'Ready.'

It had taken five nights of stalking, coming out early to check on their prey, before they'd managed to get Hayley and Shell alone without Stacey Hunter. They knew Stacey wouldn't be far behind but she didn't need to be in this fight. This was payback for the two of them running to Stacey the minute their backs were turned.

They weaved in between the parked cars and across to where they were sitting. Before they could react, Rachel and Claire grabbed a girl apiece around the neck, pulled them backwards and down onto the gravel. Rachel tackled Hayley, the stronger one of the two. She sat astride her and punched her in the face. Hayley struggled to gain ground but it was a no-win situation. All she could do was buck her legs to see if she could knock Rachel off balance.

Claire, however, had failed to keep Shell down on the ground. As Shell landed a punch to the side of her head, she rushed at her, fists and feet flying at the same time.

Rachel aimed another fist at Hayley's face and struck her in the mouth. She noticed a splattering of blood across her knuckles and looked up. Hayley's top lip had split. Knowing she had the upper hand, Rachel took a moment to catch her breath. Then she punched her one last time before getting up to help out her sister.

Claire was pulling Shell around by the hood of her jacket, trying to knock her to the ground again. Rachel grabbed Shell's hair as she swung past her and thumped her in the face. Shell dropped to her knees in an instant. Rachel drew back her foot to kick her but Claire put a hand on her arm.

'No!'

Rachel turned with a glint in her eye that Claire had learned to recognise as the danger zone.

Ignoring it, Rachel kicked Shell in the stomach.

Claire pushed Rachel to one side. 'Back off, Rach.'

'Move out of my way.'

'No. There are people everywhere.'

Rachel looked around her. A group of lads at the far end of the car park stood watching. A man and his dog walking past stopped to wonder what was going on. An elderly couple hurried to the safety of their car.

Claire held her breath, knowing enough to recognize the situation was hardly under control. She'd been there so many times before, thinking that Rachel had calmed down only for her to turn back and kick the unsuspecting victim and continue with the fight. But the lull in action was long enough for Shell to pull herself up, and stagger off with Hayley.

Rachel stared after them but didn't move to follow. Claire let out her breath again. She clenched and unclenched her hands, felt the ache. Her left eye was swelling by the second; Shell had caught her good and proper.

She glanced in their direction but they'd already disappeared out of sight. No doubt one of them would be on the phone to Stacey, telling of how the Bradley twins had caught them off guard.

She wondered how long it would be before someone jumped the two of them. She sure as hell wasn't looking forward to it. But for now, it was over.

Rachel, suddenly more calm and collected than she'd been in a long time, felt that feeling of superiority wash over her. 'What the fuck are you lot staring at?' she shouted to the lads who were still watching. They all turned away. One thing she knew, not a one of them would dare speak out, talk about the incident. They were too scared of what she'd do to them. She pulled her sister close and they walked off together.

'So what shall we do now?' she asked her.

'I might go home and get cleaned up. Mum will kill me if she sees me like this.'

Rachel shrugged, knowing when she was beat. As they walked off, she felt that familiar stirring inside. The fight of their lives was brewing: she knew this was the beginning. It was going to be tough, for Claire especially, but right now, all she could think about was that she was ready.

Bring it on.

. . .

Fighting for Survival

The following afternoon, Ruth sat at the kitchen table. The darkness was falling. Although she could feel and see the warning signs, she knew there wasn't anything she could do to stop it. Being with Martin meant she'd had to hide it, control it; keep it well hidden. But since she'd moved to Stanley Avenue without him, it had begun to control her again. She knew it was going to consume her completely soon.

It was half past two: another half hour and she'd have to make the trek to fetch the boys from school. Well now, wouldn't that be exciting? Yeah, a real bundle of laughs. Mason had hardly said a word to her since her outburst the other night, no matter how much she'd smiled, cajoled, apologised and pleaded with him. Jamie hadn't been too bad. He was too young to understand why his mum was cheerful one minute and screaming at him the next. In his own little world, he was just glad when she was happy.

But Mason ignoring her made Ruth realise how terrible it must be for them. She ran a hand through unwashed hair. What must they think of her – a drunken mother who cut herself, screamed at them all the time when all they were doing was enjoying their childhood? Would they compare her to the mothers of the kids at school? The perfect mothers with their perfect lives, their perfect homes, their perfect husbands.

Glenn, Glenn, Glenn. That stupid cow Gina had brought him hurtling to the front of her mind again. She tapped a foot on the floor persistently. What would he think of her now? Would Glenn hang his head in shame? Would he grab her by the shoulders and shake her? Would he talk some sense into her or would he realise that it was too late?

All she wanted was to feel his arms around her, be drawn into his embrace and held there. It was the only place she'd ever felt safe. Without that, there was nowhere to hide.

She reached for the small plastic bottle in front of her as the oppressive silence began to draw her in. Her hand clasped around it tightly. Next to it was the rest of the vodka that she'd started the previous night. She pulled that nearer too.

It would be so easy. A pill: a swig of vodka. Another pill: another swill of vodka. How long would it take? She peered at the clock: twenty to three. Who would care enough to see why she hadn't turned up to collect Mason and Jamie? Who else knew of her existence? She thought of her mum, alone since her dad died two years ago. They'd fallen out over something so stupid, so trivial that she couldn't remember what. It was probably about Martin, it usually was.

The knock on the front door made her visibly jump. She turned her head slightly. Through the open kitchen door, she could see through to the hallway. It was her way back into the real world.

She stayed sitting at the table.

Another knock: she ignored that too, watching as a white card came through the letter box and fluttered to the floor moments later.

There wasn't another knock after that. But, for now, the spell had been broken. Ruth hid the bottle and the pills, wiped a cloth quickly around her face and reached for her keys.

She picked the card up on her way out. It was from the housing officer, that bloody Josie Mellor again.

Ruth threw it in the wheelie bin as she left the house.

Josie had her suspicions that Ruth was at home that afternoon. But, then again, it was near time for the school run. Maybe if she'd got there a little sooner as planned, she would have caught her. But she'd been dragged into another discussion about Susan Harrison in Derek Place, the state of her welfare as well as her two kids and the property. She'd tried to get in there too, on several occasions, but each time had been, well, shooed away, to put it politely.

With a sense of dread, she walked up the path towards Gina Bradley's front door. She rapped on it sharply. As usual, Gina opened it in her own time.

'For fuck's sake, not you again,' she cried.

'Yes, it's me –'

'What have they done this time?' Gina didn't wait for an answer. She went back into the living room.

'Do you know anything about the fight on the square the other night?' Josie asked as she followed behind.

'Nope.' Gina sat down and pressed play on the TV remote control.

Josie perched on the armchair and sighed – the place was a tip as usual. 'Gina, I don't know how many times I'm going to sit here and warn you about the girls' behaviour.'

'Then don't.'

'You're happy if they end up in a detention centre?'

'It would get them off my back.' Gina glared at Josie. 'And it would get you off my back too.'

Josie leaned forward and pressed the mute button on the remote control.

'Hey,' Gina protested, raising her hands in the air. 'You can't do that.'

'I need you to listen to me. The CCTV camera clearly shows the fight but not which two girls dragged the others to the floor. However, there were lots of people around to witness the event.'

'And?'

'And the police are going to be talking to them.'

'And these witnesses are going to make statements, are they?'

Josie sighed. 'I'm not sure, but –'

'Thought as much.'

'The police can charge without witness statements now there is evidence on film.'

'If they can distinguish one girl from another, like you say.' Gina closed her eyes and pinched the top of her nose. 'I do my best. What more do you want from me?'

Josie's silence spoke volumes. She knew she wouldn't get through to Gina, nor her layabout husband, but she couldn't let go. If she could make Gina see sense, if she could change her attitude, then maybe it would rub off on the girls. Even if Gina got to one of them, they were so close they could both change. She decided to switch tactics.

'Have you ever thought about coming along to any of the sessions at The Workshop or the community house?'

Gina snorted. 'And join your goody-goody tribe? I don't think so.'

'Why not? I reckon it'd be good for you to get out and do something different.'

'Happy doing what I do, thanks.'

'Are you really?'

Gina shrugged.

'But don't you ever get bored?'

'There's plenty to watch on the telly.'

'Well, maybe if you got involved in The Workshop sessions, then the girls might come along too. I'm always crying out for volunteers and someone like you, who knows the estate, might –'

Gina laughed then. 'You have no idea.'

'Well, I –'

'You don't have kids, do you?'

'Not yet,' she replied.

'Leaving it a little late, aren't we?'

'That's none of your business.'

'And what me and my girls do is none of your business either.'

Josie sighed in frustration. 'Clearly it's not worth me visiting to see if I can help out.'

'Clearly.' Gina was already reaching for the remote control.

'Okay, have it your way. No doubt the next people to call will be the police and they won't take any crap from you. You've had your chance to get involved and start acting as you should. I can't do any more for you if –'

'See yourself out, will you?' Gina interrupted.

'Fine,' snapped Josie. 'But don't say that I didn't try.'

Once Josie had gone, her words hanging heavy in the air, Gina felt tears prick her eyes. She knew Josie was only trying to help but what the hell did she know about her life really?

She folded her arms and put her feet up on the coffee table, flicking through the TV channels again. The programme she was watching before she was so rudely interrupted had finished.

Damn that woman. How come every time Josie Mellor came knocking, the minute she left she'd start getting all weepy? Hadn't she got anything good to say about Gina? So what if her girls were the scum of the estate – how was that her fault? Weren't all teens hard to control? Every time she picked up a newspaper, there was always some story or another to be read about it. What made her girls so different? And this was the Mitchell Estate – did Josie really expect anything to change?

She knew she sounded defeatist but living this life for so long had taken its toll on her. She would never have any faith, any belief that her life could change for the better. It would only get worse, year after year after year.

She glanced at the clock to find it was nearly teatime. Her stomach felt like her throat had been cut. What did she fancy? A nice fresh chicken salad with crusty bread? A nice bowl of homemade soup?

She stretched her arms above her head, her tears long ago banished. Stuff it: she'd never change. It wasn't in her to lose weight and look all girlie. Better to welcome her inner fat demon with open arms.

She'd go down to the chippy later on.

12

After their triumph two nights earlier, Rachel and Claire were on a high. Shell and Hayley had kept well away from them and the rest of the gang. The other members had been in awe of what they'd done. Rachel still felt that her rightful place was at the head of the gang. She was top dog.

So when the counterattack came, they were completely caught off guard. It happened when they turned the corner of Stanley Avenue onto Davy Road. Feeling safe in their own territory, they hadn't expected anyone to assault them there.

Fists went flying, feet kicked out. Claire took a punch to the nose and dropped to her knees. Rachel was dragged to the floor by two girls: it was hard to tell who, their hoods tied up by their chins. She took punch after punch, two on to one overpowering her.

Claire jumped at the nearest girl. She pawed at the hood, finally managing to pull it back. Wondering which bitch she'd got hold of out of Hayley and Shell, she was shocked at who she revealed.

'Charlie!'

'You traitor.' Rachel punched the side of her head.

Charlie staggered back. As a natural lull came, the two of them stood side by side, wondering who the hell was hidden by the other hood. When Leanne revealed herself, Rachel gasped.

'You.' Claire launched herself at her. But Rachel stood in front of her to block her way.

'Leave it,' she said.

'But they can't get –'

'I said leave it!'

Claire stood glaring at them. She finally calmed down enough for Rachel to let go of her.

'Why?' she turned to Charlie. She'd thought Charlie was a true friend. How could she have done that to them?

'It's our initiation test,' said Charlie.

Rachel understood then. 'You've gone back to Stacey, haven't you?'

'I was never with her in the first place.'

'But you're with her now?'

Charlie nodded.

'And you?' Rachel looked at Leanne.

She nodded too.

'Which means the gangs are equal now.'

'Which is exactly what Stacey intended,' said Leanne. 'She wants us all back, in one gang, or...'

'Or?' said Rachel.

Leanne shrugged. 'Surely you can work that one out for yourself. Come on, Charlie. We're finished here.'

With all the noise as the girls let themselves in through the back door, Gina jumped clean out of the forty winks she was having between episodes of Coronation Street. She rushed through to the kitchen to see what all the commotion was.

'I'll kill her,' Rachel said, reaching for a tea towel. 'I'll fucking kill her. Charlie, of all people.'

'What the hell's going on?' Gina demanded.

Rachel kept her back towards Gina as she ran the tap and wet the towel underneath it. Claire looked down to the floor. She knew it had been a bad idea to come home but Rachel's top lip had split. There was blood all down her jumper.

'Rachel?' said Gina.

'It's nothing,' she said.

Gina marched over and tilted Rachel's chin up to the light. 'You've been fighting again.' She sighed. 'Will you two ever learn/'

'It wasn't our fault,' Rachel protested, folding her arms. 'We didn't start it.'

Gina raised her eyebrows. 'No, but I bet you started the fight that got you this beating.'

Rachel held the cloth to her mouth. 'It wasn't us.'

'It doesn't matter.' Gina pointed to the table. 'Sit, both of you.' No one moved. 'I said sit!'

The two girls flounced across the room and sat down. Claire pushed aside the dirty tea plates that wouldn't be washed until they were needed again. She sniffed: her nose was beginning to swell already.

Gina sat down across from them. 'What's going on with you two?' she asked. 'All of a sudden you've grown into monsters. More than that, you're acting like animals. Not much better than a pack of wild dogs.' She pointed at Rachel, holding the towel to her mouth. 'It's horrible to see you looking like this, but what's worse, is how you got like that. Fighting in the street – where were you exactly?'

'At the bottom of the avenue. The bitches were waiting for us when we turned into Davy Road.'

'Have you any idea how nasty that looks – to see girls fighting?'

'It's common, Mum,' said Rachel. 'You need to get with the times.'

'I don't give a shit if it's common. All I know is that it's disgusting and you need to pack it in. You leave school in a few months. Who's going to employ you if you continue to act like children?'

'Like anyone will employ us anyway.' Claire sniggered. 'Just think, Mum, come summer time, we'll be here and under your feet.'

Gina stared at Claire, trying not to give her inner thoughts away. That wasn't something she'd ever look forward to but she knew it would probably be the reality of the situation. Both girls spent more time away from school than in lessons so she knew they most probably wouldn't make the grades for their exams – that is if she could get them to turn up to take any.

'But don't you have any ambitions? Anything you want to do when you leave school?'

'The only ambition I have right now is to ram my fist into Stacey Hunter's face.'

'Rachel!'

'She's dead when I get hold of her. I'm going to rip every hair from her head if she comes after me. But not before I've thrown a few punches at her and –'

'If you don't shut up with the big talk, I'll reach over there and give you a crack myself.'

Rachel stood up so quickly that her chair fell to the floor. 'I've had enough of this. I'm off out.'

'No, you're not.' Gina looked at each one of them in turn. 'You two are grounded.'

'That's not fair,' Claire protested.

'Until you can go out without causing trouble, I think –'

'But we didn't start anything!'

'They'll get back at you though and… have you any idea what can happen in the heat of the moment? It could all end in tears.'

'The only tears will be coming from Stacey when I punch her lights out,' declared Rachel. She moved towards the door.

Gina followed her, pulling her back before she made it outside. 'Where do you think you're going?'

'Out.'

'And I've just told you that you're grounded, for the rest of the week.'

'Let go of me,' said Rachel.

'Come on, Rach.' Claire stood up. 'Let's go listen to some music.'

But Rachel was intent on staring her mother down. 'Let go of me,' she repeated.

When Gina didn't relinquish her grip, she saw Rachel's free hand curl up into a fist and aim it at her face. In the nick of time, she blocked it with her forearm and then slapped Rachel across the face.

Rachel's eyes widened and filled with tears.

Gina moved her head closer. 'Don't you dare, do you hear me? Don't you fucking dare! I may be smaller than you, I may be older than you, but I am your mother and you will respect me for that. When I say you're grounded, I mean it. Now get up to your room, and I don't want to see you,' she turned to Claire, who was looking visibly shocked, 'either of you, until tomorrow morning. Is that clear?'

Hearing their footsteps thundering up the stairs, Gina sat down at the table again and reached for a cigarette. She finally controlled her shaking hands enough to light it. The nicotine hit calmed her down momentarily.

She ran a hand through her hair: it was like watching Danny growing up all over again, but this time she had two of them. She inhaled again and again as panic struck her. Would she be able to stay in control when they got that little bit older?

It was ten to nine: where was Pete? She hadn't seen him since that morning when he'd gone out to sign on for his benefits. Damn the man for not being around to help her deal with this.

She didn't dare risk nipping around to her mum's to talk about what had happened because she knew the minute she disappeared, they'd be out again, seeking revenge on Stacey. It was bound to happen. She wasn't stupid enough to think otherwise. But for now, the hope was to calm down the situation. If Rachel and Claire went after Stacey, one of them could end up getting seriously hurt.

Gina sighed into the empty room. She took a last couple of drags from her cigarette before putting it out. Then she dropped to her knees on the kitchen floor, opened the door to the sink unit and fumbled about at the back of it. Hidden behind numerous cleaning materials that went untouched, she found half a bottle of vodka. Not bothering with a glass, she twisted off the cap and knocked back a considerable amount in one swig.

She wiped her mouth with the back of her sleeve. Then she waddled through into the living room with the rest of the vodka. She flopped onto the settee and reached for the remote control.

Damn those bloody girls.

'What's *wrong* with you?' Claire asked Rachel as they went into their room. 'Have you gone totally barmy?'

Rachel flung herself down onto her bed. 'Leave me alone.'

'But you were going to hit Mum!'

'So?'

Claire gasped. 'You should never hit your olds. I know she can be a pain at times, and an idle cow, but she's our Mum.'

Rachel buried her head in her pillow and pummelled the mattress either side. 'Argh!'

Claire sat down beside her. 'You were way out of order.'

'It's that bitch's fault, that Stacey Hunter. She started all of this.'

'Maybe but you don't have to be so nasty to Mum. She's on our side. She just doesn't want us to get involved in any more trouble.'

'You're only saying that because you're scared of what Stacey might do.'

'No, I'm not.'

'Yes, you are. You're scared of your own fucking shadow.'

Claire got up and left the room then. There was no talking to Rachel when she was in this sort of mood. She'd have to wait for her to calm down. Instead, she went to the bathroom to inspect the damage done by Leanne. In the cracked mirror above the sink, she saw what a mess she looked.

She pressed a hand to the swelling on her nose and winced. Charlie had thrown a really good punch: she'd never gone down so quickly before.

She peered a little closer: there was a tiny cut at the side and one eye had started to discolour. She was going to have a right shiner tomorrow. Still, it meant legitimate time off school. They weren't allowed to go in looking like they'd done ten rounds in a boxing ring.

Besides if she did, it would probably be her who got detention for fighting, even though she hadn't been the instigator.

She cleaned herself up and went back to their room. Rachel was lying on her side, her face towards the wall. As she lay back on her own bed, Claire listened intently but she couldn't hear anything. She knew Rachel wasn't asleep but she didn't seem to be crying either.

'Rach?'

Nothing.

'Rach?' A little louder but nothing again.

Sighing, she grabbed a magazine from the floor and lost herself in a world of celebrity.

*R*achel wasn't sleeping. She'd turned her back as soon as she heard Claire come out of the bathroom because she didn't want her to see that she'd been crying. But even though she'd been expecting something to happen, she'd had enough tonight.

Although she'd known that Stacey wouldn't take things lying down and she'd been ready for a fight, she thought it would happen across on the square. So both she and Claire had been unprepared. They weren't even on their bikes, or else they wouldn't have caught up with them.

But the way she was feeling was more to do with hitting out at her mum. She felt guilty. Claire was right; she shouldn't have lashed out at her. Even though she always gave her lip, respect was respect. There were some things you didn't do on the Mitchell Estate. Hitting your olds was one of them.

Was she out of control, like Mum said? Was she going to end up going off her head like Stacey Hunter?

She looked over at Claire. Her head was in a magazine, her right foot tapping away. She turned on her side to face her.

'You have to stick with me on this,' she said.

'Meaning?'

'Meaning that I'm going to stay top dog. I just need to get rid of Stacey.'

Claire closed the magazine, threw it onto the floor and lay on her side, facing her sister. 'How?'

'I'm not sure. I'll have to think about it. Have you got any ideas?'

Claire thought for a moment, then shook her head. 'I'll have a think too. But you'd better make sure that whatever it is, you take Stacey out or she'll be the one that's always top dog.'

'You don't think we can do it?'

Claire shrugged. 'I'm not sure it's worth bothering about, if I'm honest.'

Rachel raised herself to one elbow. 'But we –'

'I'm not saying that I won't help you. I'm just saying that we could go back to how it was.'

'No.'

'But it used to be a laugh.'

'I said no, all right!'

'Okay, okay, calm down.'

'I need to know that you'll be with me.'

'Of course I'll be with you, but –'

'Good. We'll sort her out and then we'll take control again. It'll be a doddle, you'll see. Once we take Stacey down, the rest will follow. It'll –'

'What do you mean, once we take Stacey down?' Claire interrupted.

'It's the only way. They got us tonight, they think we'll retaliate. So instead we go for Stacey. She'll never suss that out, until it's too late.'

'But we can't fight her. Well, I can't anyway. She'll beat me to a frigging pulp.'

Rachel frowned. 'We can do it together.'

'But that's not fair.'

'Was it fair what they did to us tonight?'

'It was only because we did it to Hayls and Shell.'

'But we're known for doing everything together. If we attack Stacey so that she knows we mean business, she'll be shit scared of us catching her again, she'll back off and –'

'– and then you'll be top dog,' Claire said.

'Exactly.'

Claire looked away. Everything was always about Rachel. It was Rachel who wanted to get back at Stacey. She'd come out head of the gang. Claire, however, having done some of the dirty work with her, would then have to play second fiddle.

It wasn't fair. That's why she liked Stacey being in charge. For her, it meant not being undermined by her dominant twin.

Rachel glared at her. 'You're not going to help me?'

'Sure I'll help you. I'm just not sure that I should.'

'Because you are my sister. That should be enough.'

'You're my sister, too, but you never listen to me.'

'Yes, but I look out for you.'

Claire said nothing. There wasn't any point.

*A*cross the street, Caren shuddered as she opened the back door and took out the rubbish. She lifted the lid of the bin and jumped as she heard a noise behind her. The only light coming from the kitchen window, she peered into the darkness.

'Hello?' she ventured.

'Why, hello, gorgeous.'

Caren sighed as Pete came out of the shadows.

'John's inside,' she told him.

'It's not John I've come to see. It's you.' He grabbed her upper arm, roughly jerking her towards him. 'What the fuck are you playing at?'

'I don't know what you're –'

'You told John to keep away from me, didn't you?'

'Let go of me.' Caren tried to shake off his grip as he pushed her up against the wall of the house. He pressed against her, his leg between her thighs forcing her feet to widen. Then he grabbed her chin.

Caren's breath began to come in rasps. She banged her foot on the wall, hoping to alert John. But she knew he'd be watching the television. She'd only gone in the kitchen to make a cup of tea before the late evening news began.

'I could have you,' Pete said.

Caren froze.

'Right here. No one would see us. I'm sure we could be quiet.'

'Leave me alone.' Her arms stuck down by her sides, she felt her knees beginning to give way.

Pete moved his face towards her. Caren squirmed as he kissed her. She clenched her teeth when she felt his tongue against them.

He pressed roughly on her breast. 'Don't be a prick tease, now. I know you want me. I can tell every time I see you.' He reached for her hand and placed it on his crotch.

Oh, God, she could feel his hardness.

'See what you do to me.'

Caren whimpered in fright. 'John will be out in a minute,' she whispered.

Pete kissed her again. This time she moved her head to the side. He thrust his tongue into her ear. Then he grabbed her chin again.

'If John wants to see his mates, catch up on old times and play a few card games, you won't stop him. Do you hear?'

Caren nodded.

'And I don't want John to know about this, or else there'll be more where that came from. As you can see, there's always a time when I can get you alone.'

She nodded again, this time fervently.

'Good girl.' Pete kissed her one last time before moving away.

13

Caren sat in the living room, trying not to spill the tea she was attempting to drink. Instead of leaving after he'd groped her, Pete walked into their house as if nothing had happened and invited John out for a late drink. Caren faked a smile and told John to go out. Even though he looked on in surprise, he jumped to his feet and ran upstairs to get changed, leaving Pete in the living room with her.

A frosty silence lingered in the air as they watched the news. Pete kept glancing across at her but her eyes stayed firmly on the television screen.

It was a long ten minutes before John appeared again. She sent him on his way with a kiss. As soon as the front door closed behind them, she rushed upstairs and took a shower. She scrubbed her skin until it felt raw, shaking as she recalled what Pete had done, what he'd said, what he'd touched.

Sitting on the settee afterwards, she realised that what had happened could easily happen again. Pete lived right across the road. If he wanted to, he could watch the house, see when John disappeared and come hurtling across. She'd have to lock the doors all the time from now on. There was no way she could leave them open, in case he showed up unannounced again.

She wondered – had he been waiting for her or had it just been good timing on his part? Had he been watching for her routine?

She thought about telling John but immediately dismissed the idea. What if Pete denied it – what would she do then? Who would John believe? She'd like to think it was her, but after their recent arguments about the time he was spending over there, John would have his doubts. Who wouldn't?

Caren began to cry again. She was in a no-win situation. Damn that man and his family. What chance did she have of keeping John on the straight and narrow now?

Further down Stanley Avenue, Ruth was trying to get her boys to go to bed. She hadn't realised the time after falling asleep on the sofa. After having a glass or two of wine, she felt exhausted, drained, a dark mood coming down quickly but she couldn't be bothered to move.

'Come on you two,' she said. 'You've school in the morning.'

'Don't want to go to school,' Mason said, banging his feet against the wall as he lay on his back in the armchair.

'You have to go to school.'

'No, we don't. We can stay at home and look after you.'

Ruth smiled absent-mindedly. 'That's nice.'

'We need to look after you because you're mad.' Mason made a circling motion by his temple. 'You're a mad mum. You're a mad mum.'

'You're a mad mum,' Jamie joined in, banging his toy car in time to his syllables.

Ruth closed her eyes and pinched the bridge of her nose. 'Bed, you two. Now.'

'No,' said Jamie.

Ruth stood up quickly. 'How many more times do I have to tell you?' She pointed to the door. 'Bed, now!'

They scurried away quickly.

Ruth sat down again. Once they were asleep, she could break out the bottle of Bacardi she'd bought. Get pissed on her own, fall asleep here on the sofa and end the day as she'd begun it. Jeez, her life was so exciting.

The noise of the boys stomping around upstairs soon escalated. Jamie started to scream. Ruth pressed mute on the remote control.

'Pack it in, you two,' she shouted up to them. But the noise continued.

'Mum,' screamed Jamie, rushing into her. 'Mason is hitting me.'

Ruth ignored him. 'La la la.' She turned the sound up on the television, notch by notch by notch, until the sound distorted. Stuff them, she thought. She too could play stupid games.

Suddenly, there was a bang on the wall beside her. Ruth jumped out of her trance and switched the volume down.

'Are you fucking mad?' a voice shouted from next door. 'Pack it in or I'll put your windows through.'

Fighting for Survival

Ruth switched the sound off completely. Jamie's screams had turned to sobs now but she didn't comfort him. They'd sort themselves out: they always did.

In the kitchen, she reached for the Bacardi. Not bothering with a glass, she twisted off the top and swigged it neat from the bottle. Faster, faster, the liquid poured down her throat, spilling over her lips, down her neck in her hurry to get it all in there.

Block out the pain.

Block out the hurt.

Block out the darkness.

She stared at the bottle before throwing it at the wall. As it smashed, she screamed. It was much louder than Jamie.

As soon as Gina's back was turned the following evening, Claire and Rachel sneaked out of the house. They were on the prowl for Stacey. When she wasn't across on Vincent Square, they waited outside her house until she came out.

'Hunter,' Rachel shouted when she spotted her. 'A word.'

Stacey tutted loudly. 'What do you two want?'

'You.' Rachel punched her in the face before she had time to do anything about it. But it didn't have the desired effect. Stacey stayed on her feet.

'Is that all you've got, bitch?' She taunted. 'Or do I have to fight you both?'

Rachel punched her again. Claire rushed at her.

Stacey fell to one knee but stood upright again immediately. She screamed as her fists flew out in every direction.

'Oi! What's going on out here?' A man in his thirties appeared behind his garden gate next door. He pointed down the street. 'Fuck off out of here, Stacey. You wake my kids up and you'll know it.'

Rachel took the opportunity to catch her breath, holding on to her ribs where Stacey had caught her a blow. This wasn't going to plan. They were supposed to take her down, kick the shit out of her and then drag her over to the shops where the rest of the girls would probably be waiting for her by then.

Except Stacey wouldn't *go* down. Even with the two of them, she stood her ground. Blood trickled from her nose but she had her fists up, ready to hit out again at any moment.

'I said fucking move!' The man opened his gate and ran towards them, a piece of wood in his hands raised in the air.

All three of them ran. At the end of the street, Rachel and Claire headed toward the square. Stacey doubled back and ran down the steps and along Peter's Walk.

'You fucking coward,' Rachel shouted after her.

'That was close,' said Claire.'

'I know. He was a nutter waving that wood around like that.'

'I didn't mean him.' Claire turned to her. 'We were lucky to get away then, Rach. Stacey took us both on and she was winning. If he hadn't come out, she'd have hurt one of us and then have started on the other. *She's* the nutter.'

Rachel knew she was right. They'd have to think of another plan – and quickly. Other than that, Stacey would win the battle.

'Let's get over to the square,' she said, 'and put our side of the story out first.'

'Which is?'

'We were winning, right?'

While her twins were out fighting again, Gina lay soaking in the bath. A glass of wine balancing on the ledge, she ran a cheap razor over her legs. She found it tough going to get rid of the pale hairs growing there. They hadn't seen a blade in ages. The water was turning positively murkier as she dipped the razor in and left the scum behind.

'Shit.' She cried out as the blade nicked her again. She wiped away the blood as it emerged. At this rate, she'd need to cover up her legs and, for once, that wasn't on the agenda.

Tonight she'd be wearing easy clothes for easy access, because tonight she was going to have John Williams. She was going to sleep with him right underneath the nose of that snotty bitch he called his wife.

She rubbed a hand over her right breast. Just thinking about what she was going to do was turning her on. Her hand moved lower as she imagined more of what they would be doing.

John would take her in his arms and pull her onto his lap. She'd feel his hardness beneath her, rub herself up against him while they kissed. Long smoochy kisses that she and Pete had given up years ago.

Then she'd move his hands to her breasts and he'd knead them while she climbed on top of him. He'd kiss her while he moved her up and down, up and down, up and down. The image in her mind became tuned into her body and as she felt the ripples of pleasure engulf her, she said his name aloud.

Afterwards, she lay in the cooling bath water and smiled. She knew John wanted her. She'd seen the looks he'd been throwing her. Sly, secretive looks that only she would have noticed. Pete was going out with John again so, once they'd come in from the pub, she would keep them drinking.

She'd have to be careful though – she didn't want him to suffer from brewer's droop – but she needed to get them drunk enough so that he'd fall asleep on the sofa and Pete would head off for bed. It was a perfect plan, really.

She reached for the shampoo, rubbed a dollop in her hair, and ducked beneath the water. Had she seen the scum forming, she might have thought twice about it.

But things didn't go to plan for Gina. Pete and John arrived back just after midnight and had wanted a fry-up. Although Claire had gone to bed, Rachel was up and sitting on the settee chatting to John as he gobbled down a bacon buttie.

Pete slapped Gina's bottom as she came back into the room with a sandwich for herself.

'Great grub,' he spoke with his mouthful. He laughed and looked across at John. 'I suppose she's useful for something.'

'Hey, do you mind?' Gina glared at him before knocking Rachel's feet off the coffee table. Then she squeezed herself into the space between her and John.

'Jeez, Mum,' Rachel complained. 'You're too fat to sit on here.'

'Oi!' Gina felt her skin burning up. But when John joined in with the laughter, she smiled then, glancing surreptitiously at him. She knew it was an act to keep everyone from guessing what he really thought.

'You like me just the way I am, John, don't you?' she couldn't help asking.

'Erm, yeah, course I do,' said John.

Pete and Rachel burst into raucous laughter.

Pete checked his watch, stood up and stretched. 'I'm off to bed now my belly's full. I need to be up early in the morning. Got some work on at the builder's yard. You up for it, John?'

John sighed. Even knowing Caren would give him hell didn't stop him nodding. They needed the money.

'Need to be gone by eight.'

John looked aghast. 'Eight? I'd better be off.' He stood up but had to steady himself on the arm of the settee. 'Bloody hell, Bradley. How many have we had?'

Pete sniggered. 'Dunno, I lost count.'

Rachel stretched her arms above her head. 'I'm off too. Do you need a hand upstairs, Dad?'

'Cheeky cow.' Pete grinned. Then he looked at John. 'Why don't you crash down there tonight? You look a bit green.'

'I'll be fine in a minute.' John held his head in his hands like it was going to fall off.

'Sit there for a while. Gina will look after you, won't you, bird?'

'Sure.' Gina tried to sound nonchalant. This was turning out to be perfect after all. John faking his head hurting was genius.

John stood up once the other two had gone. 'I need some water.'

Gina followed him through to the kitchen.

John steadied himself on a cupboard door as he looked for a glass. He staggered back before opening another one.

'Here, use this.' Gina handed him a mug.

He belched noisily and grinned like a naughty schoolboy. 'Ta.'

The sound of water gushing rang in her ears. It spurted everywhere as John tried to put the mug underneath the tap. 'Fuck!'

Gina turned it off quickly.

John looked down at his soaked T-shirt and laughed.

She began to laugh with him. Daringly, she took hold of the hem and shrugged the garment up and over his head. John laughed some more. Gina was a little put out then. He was more wasted than Pete. And the only way she could get to kiss him was if he leaned down. Five foot nothing against nearly six foot didn't quite work out. Still, an opportunity was an opportunity.

She reached for his belt buckle, undoing it quickly. 'I think these need to come down too,' she said, ignoring the fact that John's eyes were closing and he was leaning on the worktop as if his legs were going to give way.

She slipped her hand in and around him. Leaning forward as she began to stroke him to life, she dared to kiss his chest. Gentle butterfly kisses.

John gave out a groan. At long last, he began to come to life. Gina glanced up and saw him throw back his head. She laughed inwardly: at least he could get it hard enough after all that booze.

'Oh, that's good, Caz,' he said.

And the magic was spoiled.

Gina's shoulders drooped and she stepped away from him. 'I'm not Caren,' she snapped.

John's eyes opened. For a moment, he looked dazed as he struggled to figure out his whereabouts. Then he saw Gina.

'You have got to be joking.'

'It's no joke.'

John went to speak again but he couldn't find the words. Gina smiled as he left in a hurry. She had him exactly where she wanted him. Although she recognised the shock on his face, she knew it was good for him. He'd sleep with her soon, she was certain of it.

14

The next morning, Ruth awoke from her nap as the door knocker banged down heavily. She checked the time: ten fifteen. After taking the boys to school, she'd slept on the settee, last night's hangover taking its toll.

She sat up but didn't go to the door; she wasn't in the mood for visitors – and it would more than likely be that Josie Mellor again. She'd tried to get in twice more since the last time she'd left a card. At this rate, Ruth would have a full deck soon.

'Ruthie?' A voice came through the letterbox. 'Ruthie, it's me.'

Martin!

Ruth staggered to her feet and rushed to the door. 'Martin.' She flung her arms around his neck. 'Oh, it's so good to see you.'

'Good to see you too. Can I come in?'

'Yes, I'll make coffee.'

'Great, although I'd prefer something stronger.'

She smiled at him. It was then that she saw what he had with him.

Martin stepped into the hall, chucking down the black bag full of his belongings. He shrugged off his holdall, leaving that to fall too. 'I've got nowhere to go, babe. It's only for a few days.'

Ruth frowned. 'You can't stay here. It's not –'

'Relax, I'll be as quiet as a mouse. No one will know that I'm here.'

'But –'

Martin leaned forward and put a finger over her lips. 'Put the kettle on, there's a good girl.'

As bold as brass, he took the stairs two at a time and disappeared. Ruth sighed and made her way through to the kitchen. By the time she'd boiled the kettle, Martin literally had his feet underneath the table.

'What happened?' she asked him.

'Got evicted. Couldn't manage without you.'

'What are you going to do?'

'Stay here for a couple of nights until I get settled somewhere else.'

'You'll have to leave then.'

Martin sighed. 'Chill out, Ruth. I won't be here for long.'

'And you'll have to sleep on the sofa.'

'Don't be daft. I'll shack up with you until I find another bed.'

'You'll do no such bloody thing.'

Martin reached across for her hand, giving it a firm squeeze. 'You've become quite the brave lady since we split up.'

Ruth pulled her hand away. She stared at him, wariness clear in her eyes. Martin hadn't even tidied up his hair that morning. His clothes looked as though he'd been wearing them for a couple of days, his facial hair saying the same thing.

In his heyday, he'd been a looker. Now, nearing forty, his dark hair was receding rapidly, his teeth decaying slowly. Prominent crow's feet were visible even when he didn't smile; eyes wide and beady like an owl.

Martin reached for her other hand. This one, she didn't move away. She knew she wasn't strong enough to fight him right now. And maybe he'd stop her from self-harming, or from hurting one of the boys.

Suddenly, she could see the positive to having him back for a while – providing he hadn't bought Tracy Tanner along with him.

She smiled. 'Something stronger now?'

Once she'd settled Martin in, Ruth realised she'd have to go to the shops. She needed food: she couldn't remember the last time she'd cooked something that hadn't come from a packet. Martin had given her twenty pounds – it wouldn't go far after she'd bought him the cigarettes and lager he'd asked for as well, but it would get them something decent to eat.

Deep in thought, she hadn't been prepared to bump into Gina.

'You!' Gina screeched as she spotted her. 'I want a word with you.'

Ruth put her head down and continued, walking past another neighbour in their garden.

But Gina wasn't going to be ignored. She let the gate bang shut as she rushed over to face her. 'You want to watch your step, ignoring me like that.' She grabbed Ruth's arm. 'I might lose my temper.'

'What do you want?' Ruth asked.

'My mum said she saw you hit your little lad last week.'

'I – I – we all do it,' she replied. 'He was obviously being naughty.'

'But he's too little to stick up for himself. You shouldn't hit him.'

'I didn't hit him hard,' Ruth decided to say, unsure of what anyone had seen her doing.

'It doesn't matter. You shouldn't –'

'Surely your children had a smack when they were naughty.'

'This isn't about me.' Gina folded her arms. 'This is about you.'

'Haven't you got anything better to do than have a go at people?' someone shouted from behind them.

Gina swivelled on the spot and came face to face with Caren. 'Mind your own business,' she snapped. 'This has nothing to do with you.'

'Do you get a kick out of bullying people?'

'I'm not a bully.'

'Yes, you are.'

Gina took a step nearer to Caren. 'Say anything else and I'll ram my fist into your face.'

Caren sighed. 'That's you all over, isn't it? You *and* your family. Threatening behaviour is the coward's way out.'

'Quit while you're ahead,' she warned.

'Or what? If you hit me, beat me to a pulp even, I'll be here tomorrow. If you hit me again, I'll still be around.' She took a step nearer to Gina, hoping to intimidate her with height as well as words. 'I knew you were a nasty piece of work when we were at school, and that I could understand because we were sixteen and didn't really know any better. But we're in our thirties now. You should try growing up a little.'

Gina felt her skin reddening and she raised her fist. 'Bitch,' she seethed.

As the two women glared at each other, Ruth took the opportunity to continue on her journey. When Gina noticed, she shouted to her. 'Don't think I've forgotten about you. You might have got away this time, but you'll keep.'

Caren sighed. 'Will you listen to yourself? You sound like one of those wayward daughters of yours – they're always fighting from what I hear around the estate.'

'Leave my daughters out of this.'

'Well, it's obvious where they get their traits from. You're hardly a role model – nor that husband of yours.'

Gina narrowed her eyes. 'You ought to get your own house in order first before you start knocking mine. You and John aren't so perfect.'

'Are we going to do tit for tat over each other's family now?' Caren folded her arms and leaned on the garden wall. 'Come on, then. Bring it on.'

'I'm not bringing my family into this discussion.'

'Why not? You're happy to slag off everyone else – like Ruth who's doing her best – but no one can say anything about you. Doesn't seem fair to me, that.'

'If you want to bring families into it, you haven't slept with my husband so I think I win that round.'

Caren faked raucous laughter. 'Like I'd want to do that.'

'For all your cleverness, you are a little thick at times. You don't understand, do you?'

'Understand what?'

'Listen to what I said.' Gina proceeded to pronounce her words like she was speaking to a toddler. 'You may not have slept with my husband but I've slept with yours.'

Gina had Caren's full attention then – and a fair few neighbours who had come out to see what was going on too.

'Tuesday night, pub night,' she continued. 'John came home with Pete. I cooked them a fry-up. Pete was smashed and went off to his bed. And your fella and me got down and dirty on the kitchen floor.'

Caren's eyes widened in disbelief. 'You're having a laugh. No one in their right mind would crawl around on your kitchen floor. They don't know what they'd catch. Can you see the pattern on your tiles anymore?'

Gina played her trump card. 'When did he have his appendix out? That scar on his groin looks fairly old to me.'

Caren visibly paled. How would she know about John's scar? Her mind told her it was something as simple as it being discussed in a conversation: her heart had them shagging away on the kitchen floor.

Suddenly she lurched forward, hand raised high in readiness to slap Gina good and hard. But Gina blocked her. She grabbed her wrist and held on to it tightly.

'Tut tut. Fighting isn't the answer to everything, Mrs Williams.'

'You're lying,' said Caren.

Gina shook her head. 'No, I'm not.'

'You must be. He wouldn't... he wouldn't do –'

'Ask him.' Gina knew she was in the prime position. Caren wouldn't ask him: John would deny it anyway. But it would put doubt into her mind and her cosy life.

'Ask him,' she repeated.

Fighting for Survival

. . .

Once in the safety of her home, Caren stood in the middle of the living room and gulped back tears. Don't let her get to you, she told herself. She's lying: John wouldn't do that. She searched out her mobile and rung him.

'Is it true?' she snapped.

'Is what true?'

'You and Gina Bradley?'

A pause.

'I can't talk to you now.' Another pause. 'Not here.'

'Why? Is that stupid fucker Pete there with you?'

'Yeah, can we do this later? I'm in the middle of plastering a wall and I need to –'

Caren disconnected the call.

No.

No!

She thought back to last week, when Pete had taken John out after he'd molested her in the garden. Were he and Gina in this together somehow? She knew it sounded irrational but surely there couldn't be any truth in it?

Calming down quickly, Caren wiped at her cheeks where a few tears had fallen. That was it: Pete and Gina were doing their best to get back at her. John wouldn't sleep with Gina. Moving here had tested them to the limits over the past few weeks but, apart from Pete's visit, everything had been okay for a few days.

Yes, she knew John was working on the side, but the cash was good, and it wouldn't be forever. He had an interview for a job next week. If he got that, all their prayers would be answered and Pete would be out of their hair, unable to lead John astray – at least in theory anyway.

No, she would ignore them. Their sort hated that.

Her mobile phone beeped the arrival of a text message. It was from John.

Its not wot u think. I was drunk. She tricked me.

Caren stared at the tiny display screen. She sat up abruptly and read it again.

Its not wot u think. I was drunk. She tricked me.

She frowned.

Its not wot u think. I was drunk. She tricked me.

She gasped. Gina was telling the truth.

. . .

*G*ina lit a cigarette as soon as she set foot in her kitchen. She sat at the table, busily puffing away, pleased with her little outburst – for all of a few minutes before doubt began to creep in.

What would happen if Caren said anything to John? Gina would have to deny it, even though half the neighbours had heard her say it. One of them was bound to say something to Pete down at The Butcher's Arms.

Nothing stayed a secret on Stanley Avenue. She should know; she was usually the one spreading the rumours. Then again, maybe people would hold their tongue. The Bradley family were not to be messed with. Everyone knew that.

Gina sighed loudly. Sometimes she could be so stupid. Pete would kill her if he thought for a moment it was true – he could stop John from coming over and where would that leave her?

And if Caren did start a row with John, Gina would have some lying to do. She'd have to think about it this afternoon, get her story right or she could end up with more than a red face. More likely she'd get a backhander from Pete.

But the one thing that riled her most was that she should have saved the information for later. Once he'd slept with her a couple of times, the story would have been more convincing, more hurtful too. It would have wiped that smug look off Caren's face. Everyone would know that Miss Fucking Perfect couldn't keep her man satisfied.

Gina sighed again and took another drag of her cigarette, a long drag that made her cough loudly. Now he'd never sleep with her and she'd come so close.

*F*rom the minute she'd scuttled off down Stanley Avenue with Gina Bradley screeching obscenities after her, Ruth had dreaded returning home. With every footstep back, she became more and more agitated, feeling the stickiness on her recently heeled scar oozing blood as she dug her nails in over and over.

She practically sprinted past Gina's house, expecting another torrent of abuse. But all was quiet, on both sides of the road. Wondering if the woman from number twenty-four had given Gina Bradley more than she'd bargained for, she relaxed a little.

Martin was lying on the settee in the living room watching the television when she put down her shopping on the kitchen table.

'Make us a brew, would you?' he shouted through to her. 'I'm parched.'

And I'm knackered after lugging your lager home, thought Ruth. Still, it would be good to have someone around to talk to; someone to belong to.

Fighting for Survival

There had been no mention of an apology, why he'd done what he'd done. Neither had there been any explanation about Tracy Tanner. She wondered who had finished the affair: it was obvious that something had happened.

'Where's that tea?' Martin shouted through.

'Coming up.' Ruth frowned. How had she thought she could do this? Now she had three of them to cater for and she didn't feel capable of looking after herself.

The kettle switched off. Ruth popped tea bags into two mugs and continued to put the shopping away.

'Where are you getting the tea from? China?' Martin appeared in the doorway.

'It's nearly ready.' Ruth opened the fridge. 'Just getting the milk.'

He leered at her. 'Bloody hell, Ruth. You've got a right pair when you bend down.'

Ruth peered down at her chest. The neckline of her jumper wasn't showing that much.

Martin came behind and put an arm around her waist. He pressed himself to her. 'Can you feel that? You've made me hard already.' He kissed her neck. 'Might as well not waste it.'

Ruth squirmed. 'Don't do that, Martin. Not now.' He caught her by the wrist. 'Ow!' She grimaced.

'I'll make the other arm hurt too unless you let me fuck you.'

Ruth swallowed. 'I don't want –'

Martin swept a hand over the kitchen table. Mats and coasters crashed to the floor. He bent her forwards and shoved his hand up her skirt.

'You're having it, whether you like it or not,' he told her.

Ruth knew it was easier to get it over with. She heard him open his zip and then he pushed himself inside her. She groaned in pain.

He pushed in further, holding on to her shoulders. 'I know you like it rough, don't you?' He thrust into her.

Ruth held on to the table as he did it again and again. The table screeched across the tiles. Still he held on to her, thrusting, swearing, thrusting, swearing.

Then it was over. Martin pulled out of her and tucked himself up. She felt his sperm running down her leg and stopped herself from gagging as she grasped the worktop, this time for support. Her legs didn't feel able to sustain her weight.

Martin grabbed her injured wrist and twirled her round to face him. She flinched as he squeezed it harder, intent on hurting her.

'I will have you whenever I want you,' he said, an inch away from her face. 'Got that?'

It took all of her strength to nod back at him.

'Good. Now, where's my tea?'

Ruth watched in a daze as Martin squeezed the teabag, threw it into the kitchen sink and added a dollop of milk to the drink. Then he winked at her before taking a noisy slurp.

Once he'd left the kitchen, Ruth closed the door. Then she rushed to the sink and threw up all over the teabag. The bastard. How could he force himself into her like that? Already she could feel the hurt he'd caused between her legs.

Still clinging to the worktop, she managed to calm her breathing and stop herself from going into full panic mode. Her arm was burning. Instinctively, she began to pick at the scab a little more.

How had she forgotten how cruel he could be?

The minute she spotted John coming home in their car, Caren was out and down the path without another thought. She flung the overnight bag she'd packed with his clothes at his feet.

'Have you any idea how humiliating it is to know that not only have you been messing about across the road from where we live –'

'I haven't.'

'– but you've been messing about with that – that thing.'

'It wasn't like that, I swear.'

'I hate you.' She spoke through gritted teeth. 'It's bad enough that we have to live here but then you go and do *that*?'

'I'm sorry!'

'You will be. You can sleep on *her* settee tonight. You're not coming in here.'

'But I don't –'

'Having a row in the street is getting quite your thing, isn't it, Caren?' Gina came up behind them.

'Piss off, Gina.'

'Ooh, charming. Did you know you had such a foul mouth of a wife, John?'

John turned to her. 'You heard her, piss off. You've caused enough trouble as it is, with all your lies.'

'I'm not lying. Can't you remember? You weren't that drunk now; you managed to get it hard enough.'

'Why, you little –' said Caren.

John held onto her as she tried to get past him.

Gina laughed. Pete hadn't come home yet, which gave her time to do this and then deny any of it once he was.

She looked along the avenue. Mrs Porter was on the doorstep of number seventeen. Julie Elliot was standing with Sheila Ravenscroft. They were both staring their way. She looked the other way to see her mum hanging out of the upstairs window.

'You can always come and stay at our house if she's throwing you out,' she mocked.

'Back off,' said John. 'I've had enough of you insinuating –'

'No,' Caren interrupted. 'She's right. Why *don't* you stay over there? It's where you belong, with the scum.'

'Who are you calling scum?'

John stared at Caren in disbelief. 'You can't possibly expect me to do that.'

Caren glared at him. 'I mean exactly that. You want her, you can stay with her.'

John turned to Gina. 'Now look what you've done.' He looked back to see Caren storming up the path and into the house with the slam of a door.

'She'll come round.' Gina held out a hand to him.

John took a step towards her and grabbed her roughly by the arm. 'You're such a poisonous cow. Just leave us alone.'

Gina was taken aback by his malice. 'But I thought you wanted to –'

'I don't want to do *anything* with you. Not now, not ever. You've caused enough trouble.'

They both saw Pete's car turn into the avenue.

John raced across to his house. 'Caren!' He banged on the front door. 'Caren, let me in.'

Gina moved to her side of the road as Pete drew up.

'What's going on?' he questioned, wiping his nose on his sleeve.

'Caren and John were arguing,' said Gina. 'It was nothing really.'

'Bloody hell,' Pete grinned at her. 'They'll be rivalling us for the most rowing couple.'

Gina looked across the road again. Getting no joy from the front of the house, John had gone round to the back. She'd seen him sneak out of sight when Pete had pulled up.

'Come on, Gina,' Pete said. 'I'm starving. What's for tea?'

Gina sighed and turned towards her house. That had hardly gone to plan either.

15

The next morning, Ruth was struggling to bump her wheelie bin down the path to the pavement when she heard someone shout her name. She looked up to see Pete Bradley coming towards her. Great, what did he want – to start off where his horrible wife had finished?

'Here, let me help,' he said. He took the bin from her, bumped it down the last two steps and wheeled it in front of the garden hedge. Then he turned to her with a friendly smile. 'How are you doing, Ruth?'

'Fine thanks.' Her eyes narrowed.

'I saw Martin here yesterday. Is he on the scene again?'

Oh, here we go, thought Ruth. He must have some beef with Martin.

'He's staying for a few days, yes.' Ruth glanced shiftily upwards to her bedroom window. Martin was still in bed. Luckily, last night he'd gone out and hadn't come back until after midnight so he'd crashed out as soon as his head hit the pillow.

'Is it what you want?' asked Pete, leaning in towards her, touching her arm gently. 'I could move him on, if you like? Make sure he doesn't come bothering you again.'

'He doesn't bother me.' Her look of panic obviously gave Pete something to latch on to.

'Does he look after you?'

'Yes, but he isn't staying for good.'

'That's what they all say, isn't it? When they take advantage of a beautiful woman.'

Ruth pulled her dressing gown around her tightly. She looked up the avenue, hoping that no one could see them. Even though it was only just after seven some people in Stanley Avenue actually got up for work. But she was more interested in whether Gina Bradley was watching them. If she was, she would be in big trouble.

'You're a pretty woman, Ruth. I could make life easy for you. Would you like that?'

Ruth nodded before she had time to think about the implications. She knew Martin wouldn't have any intentions of moving on. He'd want to slot himself back into her life as if the hurtful mess with Tracy Tanner had never happened. Then she shook her head.

Pete raised his eyebrows. 'Oh, I don't mean anything like bump him off. I mean warn him to move on and keep away from you.'

'He's very good with my kids,' Ruth came to Martin's defence.

'But is he good with you?'

Ruth lowered her eyes for a moment, feeling her skin flushing. How come Pete Bradley was being all nice to her?

'I haven't got a hidden agenda, if that's what you're thinking,' he added. 'I've just been watching you lately, and you don't seem happy.'

Ruth laughed inwardly. Well, that was the understatement of the month.

Pete moved closer. 'I could make things happen.'

All of a sudden panic took over and Ruth stepped back. 'I – I have to go in,' she said. 'In case he wakes up and notices I've gone.'

Pete stood at the end of the path as she scuttled inside. Ruth paused at the back door to look again: he was still there. She smiled at him.

Pete's smile widened: perfect.

Later that morning, a sheepish looking John came downstairs. Caren was in the living room. Last night had been dreadful for her. After locking him out, she soon realised he'd have nowhere to go but across the road. She'd waited for him to knock again later in the evening, knowing this time she would let him come in and explain himself.

When he hadn't, she'd gone to bed but as she'd looked through their bedroom window, she'd noticed the interior light on inside their car. Moments later, she'd knocked on the window and told him to come inside. It was only the middle of October but it was still cold to sleep out.

Once he'd come in, however, she'd gone to bed without talking to him – lying awake most of the night because of it.

'Are you going to give me time to explain what happened yet?' he asked.

Caren tried to play it cool. 'Fire away, but it had better be good.'

John sat down opposite her in the armchair. 'I know she must have told you we'd slept together but we hadn't.'

'The bitch broadcast it to everyone.'

'She did try it on but I was wasted. I couldn't stand up never mind get it up.'

'How eloquently put,' Caren uttered.

John gave an embarrassed giggle. 'I suppose I could have put it a better way.' He moved to sit next to her then, taking both her hands in his own. 'What I'm trying to say is that I'm really sorry. She tried it on, that's all. I pushed her away and she didn't like it.'

Caren stared over his shoulder rather than look at him directly. Of course she'd known that John wouldn't sleep with Gina. But she'd wanted him to realise that she wouldn't be standing for this nonsense of him going out with Pete whenever he fancied.

John tilted up Caren's chin. 'Did you honestly think I'd sleep with *her* when I can spend time with you?'

'But you don't want to spend time with me anymore.' Caren looked pained as she said it. 'You want to be with them and get drunk every night.'

'He knows I'm struggling to get a job so he helps me out. I feel obliged to go out with him. He overpowers me.'

Caren frowned. That wouldn't be hard. John had always been a pushover.

'I'm not sure,' she admitted truthfully. 'It's making me doubt whether we can survive this – this mess.'

'We're made of stronger stuff than that, Caz.'

Caren shook her head. 'It won't work – not with them over the road, sticking their nose in at every opportunity to ruin things for us. And if –'

'As if they could ever do that.'

Caren realised how lucky he'd been to interrupt her then. She was about to tell him what happened with Pete.

'They've made a good job of it so far,' she said instead.

'Pete can be very persuasive.'

Caren struggled to keep her face straight. 'He's controlling you, can't you see that? Not only is Gina stirring trouble between us but so is Pete.'

'No, he isn't. He found me work.'

'You can find your own work.'

'It's not that easy.'

'But you've stopped trying. Since you can get cash-in-hand doing odd jobs – which quite frankly goes beyond my understanding as Pete Bradley is bone idle – you think you've found your feet. You need to take responsibility, John.' Caren stood up. 'And until you do, we can't move forward.'

Fighting for Survival

*J*ust after eleven thirty that evening, head full of beer and fuzzy thoughts, Martin staggered across the square in the direction of Stanley Avenue. He laughed to himself. It had been so easy to get Tracy Tanner on side again tonight. Maybe he could get away with seeing her *and* Ruth for the time being. Ruth was stupid enough to think that he wouldn't do it twice to her. What a silly bitch.

Without warning, someone grabbed him from behind and slammed him up against the wall between the post office and the bookies. He felt a fist in his stomach and doubled over.

'What the fuck is wrong with you?' Martin clutched his stomach as he looked up at Pete Bradley. 'Did I spill a drink over you or something? If I did, sorry mate, I'm lashed.'

'This has got nothing to do with the pub.' Pete thumped him in the stomach again. 'Keep away from Ruth Millington.'

'Ruth – my Ruth? What do you want with her?'

'She's not your Ruth and she never will be. I've had enough of you scrounging off her. You'd better back off.'

Pete brought his hand up to strike Martin again. Martin blocked his arm and threw a punch of his own, but he missed completely, twirling round in a circle. As he staggered around, Pete hit him another time. He fell to the floor as another fist found his stomach.

In the quiet of the night, Pete spoke again. 'I want you out of her house and I don't want you bothering her again. Do you hear?'

'I've probably got no fucking hearing left,' muttered Martin, spitting blood onto the pavement.

'There'll be plenty more of that if I see you there in the morning.'

*R*uth woke up to the sound of the bedroom door slamming open and bouncing off the wall behind it. She squinted when Martin turned on the light. Then she saw what a mess he was.

'Ohmigod – what happened to you?'

Martin ignored her and opened the wardrobe. He began to throw his clothes on the bed, hangers clattering against each other.

Ruth scooted nearer to him. 'Martin, what's going on?'

'You're poison, do you know that?' he spat nastily at her before pulling out his holdall from the side of the drawers. 'I've only been here a night and look what's happened to me.'

Ruth spied Mason in the doorway, behind him stood his brother. 'You two – shoo.' She pointed at them.

'Yeah, piss off back to your beds,' Martin yelled at them.

Jamie ran off immediately but Mason stood his ground. Martin pushed a few T-shirts into his holdall.

'Where are you going?' asked Ruth.

'As far away from you as possible. I don't want to spend another minute in your company.' He located a pair of trainers and crammed them into the holdall too.

'But you're hurt. And you're covered in blood.' Ruth pulled off the duvet and rushed to the door. 'Let me get you a towel.'

'No, I'm leaving right now.'

Ruth pushed Mason out of the doorway, shut the door and threw herself up against it. 'You're not going anywhere,' she cried. 'I won't let you.'

'You don't have a choice.' Martin fastened the zip on the holdall and slung it over his shoulder, wincing at the pain in his stomach. 'Move out of my way.'

'No.'

'I said move.'

Ruth shook her head.

Martin raised his hand to strike her but stopped. If he made a mark on her, Pete would come after him again.

'Move.' He pushed her to one side.

Before Ruth had chance to stop him, he was halfway down the stairs.

She ran after him. 'Martin, don't go. Please. Wait for me.'

But it was too late. By the time she got to the front door, Martin had already disappeared down the path. She ran to the pavement and saw him in the distance.

'Martin,' she shouted after him. 'Martin!'

She burst into tears. Why did he have to go now? She wanted him to stay; *needed* him to stay. Without him there, the darkness would descend even more.

She went back into the house a few minutes later to find Mason sitting on the bottom stair.

'Why has Martin gone, Mum?'

But Ruth ignored him and went upstairs. Then she threw herself onto her bed and cried.

*T*he next morning, once she'd taken the boys to school, Ruth climbed back into bed. But at quarter past eleven, she heard someone knocking at the front door. She dragged weary limbs to the window and peeped out. She groaned: Pete Bradley.

He knocked again. She sighed, knowing he wouldn't go away until he'd seen her.

'Hiya,' he said as she opened the front door. 'Christ, you look terrible. Are you okay?'

'I'm fine,' Ruth lied. 'I'm just coming down with a cold. What can I do for you?'

'Nice to see you too,' Pete grinned.

Ruth gave a faint smile. 'I'm sorry. Not with it this morning.'

'Can I come in?'

Ruth paused.

'You can tell me what's wrong,' Pete encouraged. 'I won't say anything.'

Ruth held the door open for him. They went through to the living room.

'Martin left last night,' she said when it was evident Pete wasn't going to speak until she told him what was wrong.

'But he'll come back, right? I mean, he'd only just arrived.'

Ruth shook her head. 'He was acting all weird, said he wished he'd never come back – and he'd been beaten up.'

'Beaten up? Did he say who by?'

'He hardly said a word actually. He just took his stuff and went. He didn't even stay long enough to clean himself up.'

'Something must have freaked him, because if I was your man, I wouldn't leave you.'

Ruth remembered their earlier conversation. 'This wasn't anything to do with you, was it?'

'Of course not.' Pete feigned shock.

'But you said you could make him leave.'

'You never said you wanted me to.' Pete looked around. 'Neat place you have here – much better than the doss-hole I live in. Three women in our house and none of them will lift a finger.'

Ruth smiled a little. She had always been house proud. When she was with Glenn, they'd had the best house in the street.

Pete was in front of her now. He touched her hair gently. 'I can call again, if you like?'

'I – I don't think that's a good idea.'

'Why not?'

'I'm sure Gina would have something to say about it regardless. She has a go at me practically every time I leave the house as it is. I don't want to antagonise her any more than is necessary. She'll flatten me.'

'I'll tell her to lay off.'

'And she will?' Ruth's tone was doubting.

'She'll do exactly what I tell her to do.' Pete looked pleased with himself. 'So, that's that, then. I'll pop round every couple of days and see how you're doing.'

After he'd gone, Ruth sat down and rested her head in her hands. She didn't really want Pete coming around whenever he pleased. She didn't like him that much, felt intimidated by him, but what could she do? Maybe he'd lose interest in her after a week or so and move on to someone not so close to home.

God, what a situation to be in. As quick as she'd lost one man, another came to take his place. And this one was Gina Bradley's husband. Could things get any worse?

But for now, she'd have to play the game. After all, she was in no fit state to do anything else.

Two nights later, Claire fancied some chocolate but Rachel didn't want to nip to Shop&Save with her. It hadn't quite been dark so she'd run all the way there and back. As she got into Stanley Avenue, she slowed down to a trot.

'All alone for a change?' Stacey said, jumping from the shadows. Before Claire could react, she punched her in the side of her face.

Claire took another punch before she managed to throw one of her own. It missed its aim, catching Stacey on the shoulder.

Stacey took another shot at her, causing her to stagger back against the wall. Then she pulled out a knife.

Claire saw the glint of metal. Shit. Stacey and fist fighting were more than she could take. But Stacey with a knife? She wouldn't stand a chance.

'Leave me alone,' she said, hoping to sound more confident than she felt.

'Tell that bitch of a sister to back off or else one of you will get it.'

Claire felt the sting of the blade cutting the delicate layers as Stacey brought the knife up to her cheek, pressing it against her skin.

'This is just a warning,' said Stacey, 'because if she doesn't back down, I'm going to come after you until she does.'

Claire squeezed her eyes shut, praying she wouldn't draw the blade across her face and scar her forever. But she didn't. A car door slamming and an engine starting up brought Stacey to her senses. When Claire dared to open her eyes, she was staring at her.

'If I have to warn you again, next time I won't stop before I mark you permanently.'

Before Claire could answer, Stacey punched her in the stomach.

'Tell her,' she said.

Claire doubled over. By the time she looked up again, Stacey was gone. She gathered her senses and ran. Mum would kill her for getting into this state again.

Rachel was lying on her bed when she heard the pebble strike the glass outside. She went to the window to see who it was, hoping that it wasn't any of the Mitchell Mob as she didn't feel like going out that night.

She was confused when she peered down and saw her sister. 'What are you doing?'

'I'm in a mess,' Claire whispered loudly. 'Stacey got to me. You'll have to get me past Mum.'

'Hang on a moment. I'm coming down.'

Rachel closed the window and crept downstairs. She squeezed herself past the stuff in the hallway, let her sister in and then popped her head around the living room door. Gina was curled up asleep on the settee. Her dad hadn't come in yet.

Quickly, she sneaked through, grabbed a glass, a couple of painkillers and rushed back upstairs.

Claire was sitting on her bed, a mirror in her hand, examining the damage.

'She had a knife, Rach. She had a fucking knife on me.' She started to cry.

Rachel rushed over to her, comforting her while she sobbed. What the hell was going on? This was getting beyond a joke now. They couldn't compete against weapons and she wouldn't use a knife to hurt anyone, unless in self-defence.

There was no option to back off now. Even if Stacey reverted to gang leader, she would never let them be members anymore. Rachel needed the backing of the others, as well as Claire, to stand her ground.

But she was more annoyed with herself. Why the hell hadn't she gone to the square with Claire? This had happened because she'd been in a mood and couldn't be bothered to go out. Stupid, selfish cow.

'I'm sorry,' she said, handing her sister the glass of water and painkillers. 'Here, take these.'

Claire burst into tears. 'What are we going to do, Rach?' she asked again. 'We're in big trouble.'

Rachel tilted Claire's face up to look at the damage Stacey had inflicted. Claire's nose was swollen, again. Her cheek was cut, it hadn't been done to cause any lasting damage, but her right eye was swelling too, bruising already appearing.

'Smile,' she told Claire.

'Piss off,' she replied. 'There's nothing to smile about.'
'I want to check your teeth are okay.'
'Oh.' Claire smiled, wincing at the pain it caused.
'Nothing out of place there,' Rachel confirmed.

Claire looked in the mirror. 'I look a right mess again. Mum's going to mad when she sees me.'

Ruth sat on the settee with her head in her hands. She'd sent the boys to bed an hour earlier, having had enough of them playing up by seven thirty, but she could hear them banging away upstairs as they ran from room to room.

Why did they always act up for her? When she'd lived with Martin, they'd been sent to bed at eight and not a peep would be heard from them. Maybe he had persuasion tactics that she didn't know about, like the bogeyman in the wardrobe or underneath the bed.

Martin arriving and leaving within the blink of an eye had really unnerved Ruth. She couldn't understand why he'd left so quickly. And why had he said that she was poison? At the back of her mind, she knew it must have something to do with Pete. Martin wasn't the sort of man to look a gift horse in the mouth when it came to free food and lodgings, and sex on demand whenever he felt like it. And despite the way he'd treated her in the past, Ruth had enjoyed having someone around before he'd thrown her out. Someone that she could talk to, look after, see to their requirements. For the first time in a while, she'd felt needed and not just as a mother.

She dismissed his rough handling of her: sex was always for his satisfaction; he had no intentions of pleasing her. But just the closeness, the feeling of a man inside her, joined with her, made her feel wanted.

'Mum, can I have a drink?' Jamie popped his head around the living room door.

'If you're quick.' Ruth didn't look up. Emotionally drained from crying all day, she wished she could go to bed and sleep forever. Maybe it would be better if she never woke up, she surmised. The boys would have to go into care but surely that would be better than living with a lunatic for a mother.

One minute she was acting the way she should: the next she'd be screaming at them, trying to stop from lashing out at them. The way she felt wasn't their fault but sometimes she couldn't help it. It was those times that scared her the most.

Suddenly, she heard muted laughter and then coughing coming from the kitchen. She pulled herself up from the settee to investigate. Opening the kitchen door, she saw Mason holding up a glass of wine to Jamie's lips.

'What the hell are you two doing?' She swiped the glass from Mason's hand, catching Jamie as she did so. The glass shattered as it hit the floor.

'We only wanted to taste it,' Mason protested.

'It's not for kids.' Ruth grabbed him by the arm. 'Have you any idea how dangerous that could be, you stupid idiot?'

'But you drink it all the time.'

'I'm an adult.'

'He only had a little bit. Ow, Mum. You're hurting.'

Ruth pushed him away roughly. 'Get to your room, now!'

Mason shot out of the door. Jamie ran behind him but Ruth stopped him. 'Whoa, little soldier. You're going nowhere.'

'Leave me alone,' Jamie wailed.

She reached for the bottle. There didn't seem to be too much gone from it. They had more than likely just had a taster. But she couldn't be sure. She filled a large glass with water and held it to his lips.

'Drink,' she ordered. 'And you piss the bed tonight and there'll be trouble.'

'No.'

'I said, drink!'

Jamie knocked her hand away, the water spilling onto Ruth's feet.

'Why, you little –'

Jamie took the opportunity to run.

Ruth sprinted up the stairs after him, one time touching his heel. Jamie ran into Mason's room and slammed the door shut. Ruth pushed down the handle but they held it steadfast on the other side.

'Get away from the door,' she screamed. She tried the handle again but it wouldn't go down enough for her to get in. She banged on the door for a while before dropping to her knees.

What was happening to her, she asked herself, as the fog began to lift and she started to come to her senses. Why did she turn into a monster when she was with them? Martin had been right. She was poison and she hadn't even had a drink tonight. She'd wanted to wait until later. What little wine she had wouldn't last her long.

She wasn't fit to be a mother, was she?

She never would be, would she?

As she sat crying, all of a sudden, it came to her what she had to do.

16

Gina woke up the next morning on the settee. She sat up slowly, stretching her arms above her head and moving her neck from side to side. It was eight fifteen and the third time that week she hadn't made it to bed after having a drink. It wasn't good for her bones. She wondered what had woken her. Then she heard movement in the kitchen.

'You're up early,' she said to one of the girls, unsure which twin it was until they turned towards her.

'Couldn't sleep,' a voice said.

Gina sat down at the table, reached for her cigarettes and lit one up. 'Make us a brew, will you?' she said.

Another mug was placed beside the two already there, a teabag shoved into it and a spoon of sugar added.

'What's up?'

'Nothing.'

'For God's sake, will you turn around so I know who I'm talking too?'

Claire turned around.

Gina jumped out of her chair and across to her. 'What happened?'

'It's nothing, Mum. It'll heal.'

'Who did this to you? Was it Stacey Hunter?'

'I was in the wrong place at the wrong time, that's all.'

'I bloody knew it. Why didn't you keep away from her, like I told you?'

'I did. She jumped me.'

Gina saw red. This had got to stop.

'I've had enough of this,' she said. 'I'm going round to see Maggie Hunter.'

'No, Mum.' Claire's head turned abruptly. 'Me and Rach will sort it.'

'You'll do no such thing. I'll give her mother what for, letting her daughter attack one of mine.'

'Mum, please.' Claire pushed a mug of tea over to her before picking up the other two. 'We can handle it ourselves.'

'Claire!'

Knowing she wasn't going to listen, Gina let Claire scoot off back to her room. She sipped at her tea and wondered what she had done to get a pasting like that. Was it over some lad or another or were she and Rachel still playing this leader of the pack thing?

She knew she could sort out Stacey's mother if it became necessary. Gina might only be five foot two, but she'd been told she packed a mean punch, especially if her girls were in trouble.

'Do you think this will be okay?'

Caren looked up to see John taking out a jacket from the wardrobe. She watched as he slid it on, fitting into it easily even though it was a few years old.

'I don't see why not,' she replied. 'It'll save buying something new, which we can't afford to do anyway. Here.' She handed him a couple of ties.

'Does anyone bother with these anymore?'

'Maybe not but I think first impressions count.'

John placed one over each shoulder. 'Any preference?' he asked.

She pointed to the blue one with a faint check. 'This one,' she said. 'Do you need a new white shirt? I can get you one from Tesco, if you like.'

'Tesco?'

'You can get anything from there nowadays – good quality too.'

John was in the wardrobe again, pulling another shirt from a coat hanger. 'I reckon this one will be okay.'

Caren sat down on the bed with a thump. This was John's first interview in years, having worked for himself for so long. She wondered if he'd cope with the pressure. The job was only for a service advisor on the parts counter of the local Land Rover dealer but she knew it was what he needed. And what *they* needed to get themselves back on track – and away from that nasty Bradley family.

Since the episode with Gina, things had settled down again. John had spent more time with her. They'd talked about their future, and their worries. She'd told him how scared she was at the thought of being stuck in Stanley Avenue forever. He'd told her that he felt inferior because he couldn't provide for her; didn't feel like a man she'd want around her anymore.

It had done them both good to get their feelings out in the open. And then yesterday, he'd come home with a huge grin, telling her he'd got a job interview.

John twirled round to face her, the shirt underneath the jacket. 'What do you think? Will I pass?'

Caren smiled, feeling her insides responding. She'd forgotten how good he looked in a suit.

'I think you scrub up pretty well, Mr Williams.' She gave him a hug, relishing the feel of his arms as he pulled her near. 'What I actually mean by that is I'd far rather see you with no clothes on at all.'

She began unfastening the buttons on his shirt.

Ruth hadn't slept much the night before. The idea had come to her in a flash and she'd thought about nothing else since. So much so that she'd started to pace the room in the early hours of the morning. It was the perfect opportunity, the only opportunity really. It would certainly be better for the boys.

Then doubt crept in. She knew what she had to do but would she be strong enough to do it? What right did she have to inflict such pain? To walk away from her troubles – pass them on to someone else.

But it would be much better for them all in the long term. For Mason and Jamie, and for her. This way, she wouldn't be able to harm them.

She was in the kitchen bright and early the next day. Mason and Jamie came downstairs, wary after the antics the night before. As she saw them creeping in sheepishly, she realised she was making the right choice.

She gave them breakfast, keeping a cheery attitude that must have confused them after last night's tricks. Then when they had finished their cereal, she sat down with them.

'How would you like to go on an adventure today, boys?' she asked, trying to muster enthusiasm into her tone.

'No school?'

'No school.'

Mason and Jamie looked at each other wide-eyed.

'Cool,' said Jamie.

'Where are we going?' asked Mason suspiciously.

'It's a surprise. I've packed you some clothes and I want you to pick a few of your favourite toys – not the big ones, mind – and I'll put them in your bags too.'

'Are we staying out all night?' Jamie wiggled his bottom about in the chair.

Fighting for Survival

'Can we go to a safari park? I want to see some lions. And wolves. And an – an elephant.'

'We won't be going to a safari park.' Mason's tone was scathing at his brother's ignorance. 'We'll be going to stay with Martin.'

'No, we're not going to see Martin.' Ruth gathered together the breakfast dishes. 'Today we're going somewhere else. And we need to be ready in twenty minutes. Can you do that?'

Jamie and Mason rushed upstairs. She sighed, trying to keep in her frustration. Why were they so bloody noisy all the time? Still, it would be much quieter later when they weren't around to bug her anymore. She squirted some washing-up liquid into the bowl and ran the hot water tap. Then she threw in the dishes, leaving them to soak. She needed to get herself ready quickly. She didn't want her heart to get the chance to rule her head.

Less than an hour later, they were in the town centre. Ruth had taken them into the market to get a bag of pic'n'mix sweets and a comic apiece to keep them quiet.

Then she walked into the Social Services offices, sat the boys down on the settee inside the window and went to speak to the lady on reception.

The office was busy, but she bided her time in the small queue. As she reached the head of it, the woman gave her an unexpected smile.

'Can I help you,' she asked, whipping away her long blonde fringe to reveal friendly eyes.

'I need someone to take care of my boys,' said Ruth.

'In what way exactly?' The woman popped a form onto the counter. 'Can you fill your details in here?'

'No, you don't understand. I'm leaving my boys here with you. The oldest is Mason and he's ten. The younger one is eight and he's called Jamie.' The woman reached for the phone and dialled an extension number as Ruth started to cry.

'Please,' she sobbed, aware that people were beginning to stare. 'Please don't split them up. They don't deserve that. It's my fault, you see. I can't be their mother. I can't look after them. So you must do it for me.' Then she turned away.

'Wait,' the woman shouted as people started to stare. 'Please. You can't just leave them here!'

'What's up, Mum?' Mason asked as she came back to them.

Ruth kneeled down and pulled him into her arms. She beckoned to Jamie and hugged him too. 'I want you to be good boys now,' she said. 'Can you do that for me?'

'Why, where are you going?' asked Jamie.

'I – I won't be a minute,' she said. 'I need to pop out for something. Wait here, will you?' She turned to Mason and touched his face lightly. 'Look after your brother, Mason. You're strong enough to do that. I'm not. Always keep him safe and...' she swallowed her anguish and kept her tears inside, 'look after him. Please.'

'Mum, what are you doing?' Sensing something was wrong, Mason clung to her. She pushed him away gently but firmly.

'I love you both,' she whispered. Then she walked away.

'Mum!'

'Where is she going?' asked a bewildered Jamie. He ran to her.

Ruth hugged him fiercely. 'I'll be back in a moment. Go and sit with your brother.'

She was stopped at the door by a man with a child in a pushchair. 'You won't be back,' he said. 'You can't leave them here. They're too young to understand.'

'I can't...' Ruth fought to control a scream building up inside. She turned to look at them one more time. 'I can't... I just can't anymore.'

Before anyone could stop her, she ran out of the building and disappeared into the shoppers on the high street.

She didn't stop, she didn't look back for fear of returning. Instead, she walked until she could see no more for tears and sat down. She ended up in the bus station, sitting there for over an hour before climbing on a bus and heading back to Stanley Avenue.

She had never felt so alone in her life. But she knew she had made the right decision.

Caren spotted their car returning and went out to John. Desperate to hear how he'd got on at the interview, she ran down the path.

'Well?' she wanted to know. 'How did it go?'

John shrugged. 'It was okay, I suppose. But there were so many guys after it. Some of them were much younger than me.'

'You're hardly an old-timer,' she said, noting his dejection.

'It didn't feel that way.'

'Did they say when they'd let you know?'

John locked the car up and walked up the path with her. 'No, they said they'd contact me in due course.'

Caren tried hard not to show how miserable she felt. It didn't sound too hopeful, especially if there were a lot of men out for it.

'Was the pay good?'

'Not bad, but I doubt it matters now.'

'Don't be too downhearted.' She took his hand.

Suddenly, John grinned. 'Oh, ye of little faith. I got it.'

'What – they told you, just like that?'

'Yep, I was the last one to be interviewed so they made we wait outside while they had a chat and then called me back in to tell me.'

Caren squealed and jumped into his arms. 'That's fantastic. Oh, I knew you could do it.'

'Like hell you did.'

'I did.' She paused. 'Wait a minute! You tricked me, you git!'

'You're so easy to fool.' He kissed her on the cheek. 'Let's go out for lunch to celebrate. I'm starving – all that nervous energy.'

'You mean she left them in reception?' Josie said, her tone incredulous.

'Exactly that, poor mites. They had no idea she wasn't coming back. I haven't been able to get hold of her since.'

Josie was making coffee for Sarah Cunningham, a social worker she had known for about seven years. Sarah had been helping her out at The Workshop since it opened too, and Josie knew if it wasn't for her, some of the women would never have come along. Both known for their persuasion tactics, between them, they were a great team – which is why Sarah had called in especially to see Josie.

Josie handed her a mug of coffee. 'And have you caught up with her since?'

'No.' Sarah shook her head, messy but stylish curls flicking from side to side. 'I've called several times over the past couple of days but either she's not in or she won't answer the door. I'll keep on trying over the next few days but I'm not sure what to do after that. I've taken the case on but I've never had anything like this happen before. She said she wasn't a fit mother and they'd be better off without her.'

Josie sat down at her desk with her drink. She swivelled from side to side on her chair. 'She must have been in one hell of a state to get to that conclusion,' she noted. 'I've been calling for weeks now. I only managed to get in a couple of times before the barrier dropped completely, and I haven't seen her since.'

Sarah sighed. 'It really gets to you when you can't get through to someone, doesn't it?'

Josie nodded.

'How was she when you did see her?'

'She'd only just moved in so I assumed she was busy, and maybe a little pissed off to be moving into Stanley Avenue.'

'It's not that bad.'

'Not unless you live opposite or next to one of the Bradleys,' Josie retorted.

. . .

*T*he next morning, when Sarah Cunningham knocked on her door again, Ruth lay in bed curled up in the foetal position, a photo of her boys in her hand. It was half past eleven and she hadn't got up yet. She ignored the knock but the next one was much louder. She closed her eyes and drew her feet up further. Whoever it was would go away soon.

The letterbox clattered and she heard something drop onto the floor. She wondered who it would be this time – the housing office; the social; the police?

Of them all, she was scared of the latter most. It must be a crime to dump your children in an office and run away, like she had, surely. To leave a ten and an eight-year-old to fend for themselves, chuck them into a new way of family life, or worse, into a children's home because no one would want two brothers. She'd heard stories on the news and read them in the papers. Some adoptive parents only wanted one child; they didn't want to take on the responsibility of two. But then again, what did the media know? Maybe they'd got it wrong.

She pushed the thought to the back of her mind and imagined Mason and Jamie being put into the loving care of a man and woman who would look after them as their own, not for the money as she'd read about people doing too.

She began to cry again. She'd let her boys down, but she'd had to or else she might have killed one of them instead of herself. Yet what right had she to give her children away, like the booby prize of a raffle? How would they feel later, realising that she had abandoned them? Right now, they were probably thinking that she was coming back for them; she'd had a bit of a breakdown and once she was better they'd be home again.

She leaned forward, picked up an empty vodka bottle and put it to her lips. There wasn't even a drop left for her to devour. On the drawers beside it, she noticed the craft knife covered in blood.

She held her wrist up and then dropped it. It too was covered in blood and so were some of the covers around her. She couldn't remember hurting herself last night; couldn't remember the feel of the blade splitting her skin, the blood oozing out. And that upset her, because to take away the pain, she had to feel it. And if she didn't feel it, she couldn't make things better. Hurt heeled hurt. But not this time.

She reached for the craft knife and placed it on her wrist. It would be so easy to draw it across and go to sleep. Really, it was the arm that was a better place. Just above the elbow. She'd seen that on a television programme. It bled just as much as slashing at the wrists and looked easier to do as it was fleshier. Simple, clean, and effective. It was perfect.

But she knew the blade might not be strong enough to do the job properly. Maybe she needed a Stanley knife for that – or a heavy duty pen knife. Or maybe it didn't have to be heavy duty. Maybe it was the action of drawing the blade across her skin that needed to be heavy duty.

She threw the craft knife across the room. It stuck in the wall before falling to the carpet. Next went the bottle. This too hit the wall but fell without smashing.

She screamed in frustration. 'I can't even break a fucking bottle.'

The following day as Josie drove along Davy Road towards The Workshop, she decided to call into Stanley Avenue and see if she could catch Ruth. But after banging on her door three times with no answer she left, disappointed yet again.

She was getting back into her car when she spotted Ruth walking towards the house. She went to meet her.

'Hi, Ruth,' she smiled. 'I've been meaning to catch you but you're always out. I wondered if I –'

'No, I'm not.'

'Sorry?' Josie frowned.

'I said no, I'm not.' She looked up at Josie with glazed eyes. 'I'm not always out. I've just been avoiding you.'

'Oh.' Jose was taken aback. 'Well, I'm here again,' she laughed nervously. 'Might I come in for a chat?'

'Please yourself.' Ruth walked through the gate, letting it fall back in place. Josie sighed, opened it and followed her into the house.

'I heard about what happened with your children,' she said. 'I'm really sorry that you felt that way. I wish I could have helped you.'

'What could you have done?'

Josie paused. Ruth's tone wasn't scathing but she was right. What could she have done?

'Maybe I could have talked to you, offered you a friendly ear? Maybe I could have got some help for you.'

'I didn't need help.' Ruth switched on the kettle.

'Do you mind if I sit down?' Josie pointed to a seat at the table.

Ruth shrugged.

As Ruth made coffee, Josie studied her. It was so obvious she'd been taking something. Not heavy drugs but some kind of a sedative to calm her down. Trouble was, it had calmed her down so much that she was acting like a zombie.

'Why give the boys to Children's Services?' she asked once Ruth was sitting opposite her. 'It must have been a hard decision to make?'

Ruth shook her head.

'Was this place getting to you so much?' Josie clocked the sparse kitchen. 'I'm sorry. I could have done more, got you some help with the decorating. I've been so busy lately and –' she stopped herself. 'Hark at me. Ruth, I don't have any excuses. I should have been here for you.'

'You're not my keeper.'

Josie faltered. 'I know, but I do feel responsible for you. Only in the same way I do for all my tenants',' she added hastily as Ruth began to glare at her.

'It isn't easy living my life,' she spat out.

Josie shook her head. 'No, I don't know. Why don't you tell me?'

'So you can go running back to the office and tell everyone my business?'

'I would never do that.' Josie looked horrified. 'What you tell me is confidential as long as it's within the law.'

Ruth opened her mouth to lay into Josie again but she saw the concern on her face. She was being genuine. Her shoulders drooped.

'I didn't know what to do,' she admitted finally. 'And I was afraid of myself, that I might hurt one of them and live to regret it. Did you know that I'm a widow?'

Josie nodded She'd seen it on Ruth's paperwork.

Tears misted over Ruth's eyes. 'Me and Glenn were so happy. I could cope when he was around. We had a really great relationship. I lost my soulmate when he died, yet I had to go on with my life. I had two children to look after. They took up all of my time, and I was coping, in a fashion, until I had my breakdown. If it weren't for my mum and dad, the boys would have been in care a long time ago.'

'Had you spoken to your parents about how you were feeling?'

'My dad's dead and my mum hasn't spoken to me for ages now – not since I started seeing Martin. She didn't like him.'

Josie sighed. It must be so hard to live the lives of these women.

'I can't have them back,' Ruth said matter-of-factly. 'I can't have it on my conscience that I was the one who ill-treated them. I was the one who didn't look out for them. I was the one who made them into the anti-social thugs they would have turned into. They're a handful now: imagine how they'd be when they got to their teens.' Ruth shook her head. 'It's not fair on them.'

'It's not fair on you, either,' said Josie.

'I don't care about me.'

'But this is –'

'They won't make me take them back, will they?' Ruth rung her hands together. Then she began to pick at the top of the bandage around her wrist. 'I couldn't do that.'

Fighting for Survival

Josie knew that wasn't about to happen. Ruth hadn't even asked about the boys yet.

'But don't you want to know where they are? Who they are with?'

'Yes, but please don't make me have them back.'

It wasn't often in her role that Josie was lost for words. Most of the time she could talk someone around to her way of thinking, but that was easy to do when she wanted them to attend a mother and toddlers club because she knew they were lonely; or when she wanted to help them sort the house out, get it cleaned and decorated to an acceptable standard; or when she needed a tenant to pay their rent or just a little bit more off their arrears every week to stave off eviction proceedings.

But this was different. She didn't know what to do, what to say, to ease this woman's pain. There were only so many words she knew but none of them were good enough for this situation. Sometimes it was best to sit and listen. Make some sense of it when she had left the property.

'Is someone nice looking after them?' Ruth spoke, her voice barely audible.

Josie nodded. 'They haven't been separated and have gone to live with a foster family who I've met several times. There are three girls there at the moment too. Every time I've visited, there's always been a happy atmosphere.'

Ruth nodded through fresh tears. 'I just want them to be happy.' She began to sob.

Josie felt tears welling in her eyes too. How the hell was she going to deal with this case?

On his first morning at his new job, John had been hoping to sneak out of his house early without Pete seeing him but was dismayed to see him in the front garden. He tried not to catch his eye, knowing he wouldn't be happy with him, but Pete spotted him eventually.

'Hey, John, haven't seen you lately,' he shouted across the street to him. 'You up for a cash-in-hand job, later in the week?'

'Can't mate,' John shouted back. 'I'm a bit busy.'

'What's more important than making a bit of dough?'

John stopped before getting into his car. He might as well tell Pete now, get it over with.

'I've got a job, mate. I needed something steady.'

Wearing baggy grey joggers spotted with stains and a particularly nasty scowl, Pete crossed the road. As he reached him, he threw his hands up in the air.

'You're deserting me?'

'It's regular hours.'

'I bet you can make more with me in one day than what anyone will pay you for a week's work.'

'It's not that.' John paused. 'I just want to get into a routine.'

'This is Caren's idea, isn't it?' Pete pointed to his forehead. 'She's put ideas into your head. She thinks she's better than anyone else. I can't believe you've fallen for it.'

'Got to keep her happy.'

'By selling your soul to the devil?'

John laughed nervously. 'It's not that bad.'

'You don't need a job when I'm around. She's got a fucking nerve. You should show her who the boss is. Don't you wear the trousers in your house?'

'It's only a job,' John stated. 'We've been through a shit time lately so I'm trying to make things better. What's wrong with that?'

Pete shrugged. 'You've joined the other side, pal, not me.'

'I need the security,' John shouted as Pete walked off.

'Pussy whipped, that's what you are,' Pete shouted back. 'Under the thumb good and proper.'

As John drove off down Stanley Avenue, Pete glanced across the road. Spotting Caren standing at the front window, he shook his head at her slowly, laughing as she moved away quickly.

Bloody women. He and John had something good going on. He'd never get half of the gigs without two of them going together.

And he'd been wrong about Caren. He thought she'd heed his warning when they'd had their little chat but it seemed not.

He wondered for a moment. There must be a way that he could teach the interfering bitch a lesson; something to upset Miss High and Fucking Mighty over there?

17

Ruth ignored the front door that morning when someone knocked at half past nine. She sat at the kitchen table nursing a hangover: she seemed to have been in constant headache mode for the past few days.

Another knock – why couldn't everyone leave her be?

'Ruth? It's me, Pete.'

Ruth groaned inwardly. What did he want? Because he'd left her alone for a few days, she was hoping he was going to stay away for good.

'I know you're in there. Come on, let me in.'

Ruth dragged herself to the door.

'Hi, I was wondering – Christ, you look rough.' Pete's smiled dropped. 'Are you okay?'

Ruth shook her head. 'I – I –' She felt herself sway, her knees buckle.

Pete stepped in and caught hold of her arm. 'You've gone the colour of pea soup.' He guided Ruth into the living room and sat down next to her on the settee.

Ruth began to gulp in big mouthfuls of air as panic took over.

'You need to calm down. Breathe easy, in, then out. In then, out. Look at me.'

She did as she was told.

'In, then out. In, then out.'

A few minutes later, panic subsiding, she gave an embarrassed smile. 'Sorry.' She eyed him nervously. 'I haven't eaten anything since last night.'

'And that's all?'

Ruth looked away. How could she tell him that she'd drunk a bottle of vodka and taken a few happy-clappy pills? The pills had been prescribed to her a couple of years ago. At the time, she'd stopped taking them because they'd made her act irrationally. Now she'd decided to give them another go – anything to make her feel better.

Pete took hold of her hand. 'You can tell me anything, Ruth. I'm a friend, that's what I'm here for, to listen.'

Latching on to his caring manner, Ruth nodded. Everything came spilling out; about her life, losing Glenn, Martin, and how she hadn't been able to cope with the boys.

Forty minutes and two mugs of coffee later, Pete was still there and Ruth felt like a weight had been lifted from her shoulders. Pete was telling her how taxing it had been bringing his own kids up.

'Little bastards they were,' he said. 'Still are, if you ask me. Those twins are evil. I swear they must have mixed them up in the hospital.' He pointed at himself. 'How could such naughty kids come from such a sweet and innocent man like me?'

Ruth giggled.

Pete nudged her playfully. 'Oi! Are you mocking me?'

'No.' Ruth giggled again. Pete nudged her again.

They smiled at each other shyly.

Pete gently wiped the fringe away from Ruth's forehead. 'You have beautiful eyes when I can see them,' he said.

Ruth blushed.

Pete leaned forward and kissed her lightly on the lips.

'So.'

He kissed her again.

'Blue.'

And again.

'Let me make it better for you,' he whispered.

Ruth stared at him. Up close he wasn't that good-looking but she didn't care about that. Right now, she just wanted to be loved, feel a man's arms around her, comforting her. Surely it wouldn't do any harm? No one would know.

She nodded.

Pete kissed her, gently at first, then more persistent. His hand roamed over her bare legs. Until then, she hadn't noticed she'd gone to the door in only her dressing gown.

He pulled the belt undone, his hand finding her breast this time, tweaking the nipple to erection. Ruth gasped as his mouth followed his hand. She ran her hands down his back, pulling out his T-shirt, urging him to remove it. They pulled it off together, then the rest of his clothes. Coming back to her, he knelt down in front of her and buried his head between her legs.

Ruth was in a daze, headache forgotten. She heard a moan and realised it had come from her.

'Does that feel good?' Pete stopped for a second to look up at her. It was all she could do to nod.

He pulled her onto the floor, gazed for a moment at her nakedness before pushing himself into her. She wrapped her arms around him, moving with him as his thrusts became longer and quicker. Then he stopped.

'Turn over.'

Ruth obliged. He pushed into her from behind but this time he didn't thrust. Instead his hand moved over her stomach and down into her pubic hair. He found her clitoris and gently began to massage it. Ruth gasped again. She pressed her buttocks into him, begging him to thrust.

'You want it, don't you?' Pete said, his fingers never stopping.

'Yes.' His touch was so pleasurable.

Pete thrust into her, taking her to a moment where she could forget all her problems. Who cared what was going on in the world while they fucked? She had love; that was all she needed.

Pete bucked for one last time and then collapsed on top of her. 'You are one horny bitch,' he grinned.

As she turned her head to smile at him, Pete smirked. She'd got the nice Pete today but fast, rough and selfish sex was his thing. From now on, he'd show no consideration towards her needs. He'd have her exactly how he wanted.

For the second night in two weeks, Gina heard a commotion in the kitchen. She rushed through to find the girls in a flurry of banging doors and swearing. She swore loudly when she saw Rachel's face covered in blood.

'What the hell has happened now?' Gina marched Rachel over to the sink. 'If this is Stacey Hunter's doing, I'm going right round to her house.'

'It wasn't anyone,' said Rachel. 'I fell down the steps on Frazer Terrace. I'm a right dozy cow at times.'

'This is serious, you two.' Gina sighed loudly as she tended to Claire's face. 'Someone is going to get hurt if you don't stop playing these stupid games.'

'We're not playing games.' Rachel raised her voice.

'Shut up or you'll wake your father.'

'Too late, you already have.' Pete came into the room. 'What's up?'

Rachel knew there wasn't any point in trying to cover anything up now. Dad could clearly see what state she was in.

He rushed across the room. 'Who did this?' he wanted to know.

'That mad cow, Stacey Hunter,' replied Gina. 'I told you she was trouble last week. She needs teaching a lesson. I'm going –'

'No,' said Claire. 'Leave it, Mum.'

Pete tilted Rachel's chin up to inspect the damage but also to look his daughter in the eye. 'Who was it?'

'I told you, I fell,' Rachel insisted.

But Claire had had enough. 'You're right,' she said. 'It was Stacey Hunter.'

Gina watched Pete's face darken. He'd had many a run in with Stacey's stepfather, Lenny Pickton, over the years but Lenny had a whole bunch of his cronies and a prison reputation to fall back on. Pete wasn't strong enough to fight him. Lenny's methods were evil, cruel and despicable.

Right now, none of that bothered Pete. His face contorted with rage. 'I'm going to kill him,' he said. 'No one does this to my daughter and gets away with it.'

'Don't be stupid,' said Gina. 'I'll end up with two of you to look after at this rate.'

'Stacey can't get away with this.'

'I said no!'

'Mum's right, Dad,' said Rachel. 'We need to think this through first. There's too much shit aimed at us as it is. We don't want to watch our backs every time we set foot outside the front gate.'

'Me neither,' said Gina, although secretly she was counting down the days until she could confront Stacey Hunter's mother. She'd rip her hair out before slapping her around. This had all gone too far.

Pete frowned. If he stood up to Lenny, he'd get his head smashed in. If he didn't stand up to Lenny, then his daughters, and maybe his wife, would think he was a coward. Lenny did scare him but he couldn't sit back and let Stacey get away with it.

'I'm going to find him,' he said.

'No!' Three women spoke in unison.

'Leave it be, Dad,' urged Claire, taking hold of his arm. 'For me, please.'

'I can't.'

'He won't stop if you hit him,' added Gina.

'Maybe not, but it'll give me great satisfaction,' said Pete. 'He's had it coming to him for a long time.'

'Let me speak to Maggie Hunter first; see if I can't calm this whole situation down.'

'If she's anything like her daughter, she won't listen.'

'It's worth a shot before you go and –'

'You don't have faith in me, do you?' Pete glared at her.

'Of course I do,' Gina lied, noting the hurt in his eyes. She moved closer to him. 'But I want my family to be safe. If you go after Lenny, it'll start up something bigger. If I talk to Maggie, then maybe things will settle down.'

'I doubt it,' said Rachel.

Pete stared at them all in turn. Suddenly, he shook his head. 'No,' he said.

'But –' Gina began.

'I'm not having it.'

Gina grabbed for his arm as he pushed past her. He was out of the house before she could stop him.

'Pete,' she shouted after him. 'Leave it for now.'

Pete stopped halfway down the path, turned back for a moment. 'If you think that I'd let anyone get away with doing that to my kids... I'll be back when I've kicked that fucker around.'

'There's some sort of commotion going on over the road,' Caren told John as he came through from the kitchen.

'Oh?' John joined her at the living room window, in time to see Pete marching down the path towards his car. Gina ran after him, but he screeched off before she had time to get to the driver's door.

'Just another day on the scummy side of the street,' said Caren, unable to keep a smile at bay. It was always good to see Gina and Pete arguing, no matter what trivial matter it was over.

John laughed. 'You shouldn't say that,' he told her, wagging his finger. 'One of these days, you'll slip up and have all the neighbours on your back. And then what would you do?'

Caren watched Gina run back into the house, almost glad she looked really upset. If things had been different, she would have gone across to see if she could help, showing genuine concern. But, as it was, Gina wasn't a friend of hers so she didn't really care.

A woman walked past their house. She stopped for a moment at the gate and then pushed it open.

'There's someone here.' Caren watched her before moving to answer the door.

'It'll be a sales rep trying to flog us something we either don't want or can't afford.' John buried his head in the evening newspaper, not the slightest bit interested.

'No, I'm sure I recognise her but I can't quite put a name to her face.'

'I'm looking for John Williams,' the woman said after Caren opened the door. 'I was told he'd moved into Stanley Avenue?'

'That's right.' Caren eyed her warily. 'And you are?'

'Is he in?'

She was a brassy woman – bottle-blonde hair and make-up that didn't suit the age of her face. Her clothes were stylish but far too tight for her small frame. She had a huge bust underneath her cropped leather jacket and thin legs covered by leggings. Her heels were stacked ridiculously high: Ah – now she recognised her.

'Donna?' she said. 'Donna Adams?'

Donna nodded. 'Yes. Well, I used to be. I'm married now.'

'I thought I recognised you.' Caren moved to one side so that she could step in. 'John?' She waited for him to appear before speaking again. 'It's Donna –'

'Donna Adams,' he exclaimed, a little surprised to see her.

'Hi, John,' said Donna. 'Long time no see.'

'She wants to see you,' Caren said pointedly.

John frowned. He glanced at Caren who seemed just as puzzled at her appearance.

Donna paused for a moment. 'I thought you might like to know now that you're back on the estate again, that you and I have a son.'

Caren paled in an instant. Thoughts of the anguish she and John had gone through to try to conceive a child together came hurtling to the forefront of her mind. Christ, no – it was the one thing she hadn't been able to provide him with. Please don't let this be true.

Donna handed John a photograph.

'I had no idea,' said John looking down at it, realising how it might seem different to Caren.

'Let me see.' She took the photograph from him. Then she almost laughed out loud with relief. 'This is a man.'

'Yes, Sam's twenty-one this year,' said Donna.

'Sam?' John's voice came out in a whisper.

'I thought – I thought you meant a little boy.'

'You thought I'd had an affair?' John looked hurt.

'You can't blame me for being suspicious. When someone comes to your house and tells you that your husband is the father of her son, what do you expect me to think?'

'It was a long time ago,' Donna explained. 'We were only kids. I was sixteen when I found out I was pregnant.'

'Me and you weren't together, Caz,' John added hastily. 'It wasn't a long relationship.'

'It doesn't matter,' said Caren. For some reason, she was immediately suspicious of Donna. 'If you were sixteen, you weren't much more than a child yourself.' She turned back to Donna. 'How did you find out that he was back? Or where we lived?'

'I saw you turning into Stanley Avenue the other day. I was going to follow you but I lost my nerve and drove on.'

'How did you know which house we lived at?'

'The car was parked outside,' she said. 'And when I drove past a few minutes ago you were both in the window.'

Caren shrugged. It was a feasible answer: they had been watching Gina and Pete.

'You haven't changed much, either of you,' Donna spoke into the silence that had developed.

'But why now?' John gave the photo back to Donna. 'You could have told me before I left the estate; before I married Caren.'

Donna shrugged.

Caren watched as she spoke to John for a few minutes. Donna had started to look a little awkward at all his questions. Something wasn't sitting right with her – call it a gut feeling but she couldn't help thinking that this whole thing was a set up. Why now, after all this time? She decided to play along with it.

'Does Sam want to meet his dad?'

Donna frowned. 'I'm not sure.'

'It's understandable after all this time. I suppose he'll be nervous and... you haven't asked him, have you?'

'Not yet. I wanted to talk to you first,' she looked at John, 'to see if you wanted to meet him.'

John had been leaning back on the wall but stood upright again. 'Of course I want to meet him. But I'm a little annoyed that you've come to see me without telling him. What happens now if he doesn't want to know?'

'Well, I –'

'John, why don't you give Donna your mobile number and she can pass it to Sam,' Caren took charge of the situation. 'Then he can decide if he wants to see you or not.'

Donna smiled at Caren but it wasn't genuine.

As soon as she'd gone, Caren turned to John. 'What the hell was all that about?'

'I'm not sure.' John scratched his head. They moved back to the living room. 'Do you think she was telling the truth?'

'No, but I'm not sure why.' Caren sat down. 'She looked practically flustered when we didn't start arguing.'

They sat in silence as *EastEnders* drew to a close for the night.

'It was a long time ago, Caz,' said John. 'You do believe me?'

Caren smiled. 'Of course I believe you.' Then she frowned. 'But I certainly don't believe her. We need to work out some dates.'

She headed for the kitchen to find a notepad.

An hour later, Pete stormed up the path to his front door. Despite asking around, he hadn't managed to find Lenny and had come back with his tail between his legs. He supposed that was better than coming home with several broken ribs, which is what he'd probably end up with when Lenny got wind that he'd been after him. But he couldn't let it ride again.

He heard his name being shouted. Turning, he squinted in the dark until the image of John appeared clearer. He sighed. What was up with him now? All Pete wanted to do was curl up in front of the telly and sleep off this godforsaken day.

'You'll never guess who's turned up at our house,' John told him.

'No, but I'm sure you're going to tell me all the same.'

'Donna Adams. You know, she used to be in our year at school?'

'Oh, yeah. Blonde hair, big tits. Skinny legs right up to her armpits.'

John nodded. 'I went out with her a few times before we finished school. Apparently, she got pregnant, never told me and now she claims I have a son.'

'Really?' Pete sounded shocked. 'What did Caren say? I bet she did her nut.'

'That's where you're wrong.'

'But I thought you and her can't – sorry, *she* can't – have kids.'

'*We* can't.'

'Then how did you get away with that?'

'Ah, Caren's the salt of the earth. She was quite calm about it. Besides, I wasn't with her then.'

'I suppose not,' Pete grunted. 'Look, if you don't mind, I'll catch up another time. I haven't had anything to eat yet and I'm starving.'

'But it's nearly nine. I was just off to the shop.' John tried to make small talk. He knew he wasn't fully forgiven for getting a job. 'What've you been up to?'

'Something and nothing.' Pete walked off.

'Is everything okay, mate?'

'Yeah, why the fuck shouldn't it be?'

'I saw you and Gina having words earlier. Wondered if you wanted to chat about it?'

'No, I bloody don't.'

John shrugged. 'Okay, okay. I'll leave you to it then. See ya.'

As soon as Pete stepped foot into the house, Gina was waiting for him. She gave him a quick once over before throwing herself into his arms.

'You didn't go after him then?'

'I couldn't find him.' Pete shirked her off. 'I tried the pubs and the bookies but he wasn't around – probably keeping a low profile knowing that I'm after him.'

Gina smiled, relief flooding through her. If Pete had caught up with Lenny, she'd probably be visiting him in A&E by now.

'Come on, I'll make you something nice to eat. What do you fancy?'

Pete barged past her. 'I'm not hungry. I just want a beer.'

She went to the fridge and searched out two cans of lager.

'Where are the girls?'

'In their room. Rachel went to lie down with a headache. I sent Claire up to keep an eye on her. I haven't heard a peep out of either of them since. But listen to this. Mum popped round and she said –'

'Leave it will, you, Gene. I'm knackered.' Pete took the can she held out to him. He wasn't in the mood to hear Gina's latest tittle-tattle.

'But I don't have anyone else to share it with.' Gina folded her arms and carried on regardless. 'You know that Ruth across the road? She moved into number thirty-two a couple of months back now?'

'What about her?' Pete tried to stop from snapping. Had someone seen him going into her house? No, they couldn't have – Gina was too calm. She would go ballistic if she ever found out.

'Her kids have been taken into care,' she told him triumphantly.

Pete sighed, with relief. 'Is that it?' he said.

'That's big news,' snapped Gina. 'I've been a cow but none of my kids have been taken into care.'

'Why don't you back off for once? Sometimes you don't have the true story and you still go accusing everyone of all sorts.'

'But I want to get to the bottom of this.'

'You're such a bitch,' he told her, before switching off completely.

'I'll take that as a compliment.'

Gina smiled. Already she was looking forward to the showdown with Ruth. She'd try and collar her first thing, when she wouldn't be expecting it.

. . .

Needing some fresh air, Ruth ventured out early the next day. She hadn't had a drink the night before because she couldn't be bothered to go and buy some. Instead, she'd cried herself to sleep and ended up with the same headache she would have had with a hangover.

She might have known Gina would be standing at her front gate when she set foot into the avenue. Ruth put her head down, hoping to scuttle past.

'Oi!' Gina shouted. 'I want a word with you.'

Ruth paled – had she found out about her and Pete? She walked a little faster but Gina caught her up.

'It's not what you think,' Ruth began. 'I –'

'Don't come with your excuses,' Gina spat. 'You've had your kids taken off you, haven't you?'

Ruth sighed with relief that the truth about her and Pete hadn't got out but her eyes brimmed with tears. 'Leave me alone. It's got nothing to do with you.'

'You live in Stanley Avenue so it has everything to do with me.' Gina pointed a finger in her face. 'Your business is my business now that you've moved in here.'

Ruth closed her eyes for a moment and pinched the bridge of her nose. Arguing with Gina again was the last thing she needed right now.

'Why don't you get on with it?' she told her. 'Say what you want to say and leave me alone. I'm tired and I have a headache, so if you don't mind?'

'People like you are not welcome in Stanley Avenue.'

'You don't know the full story.'

'I know that you've had both boys taken into care. That means you obviously weren't a fit mother.' Gina folded her arms, warming up for the onslaught. 'You obviously couldn't take care of them.'

'Well, you tell your gossip source that they're wrong. My kids haven't been taken into care.'

'Yeah, right, like I believe you,' Gina said, but her smile slipped a little. 'Where are they, then?'

'If you must spread malicious rumours, then get your facts right. My boys weren't taken into care. I gave them over to Children's Services myself.'

Gina frowned. 'You *let* them take your kids away? That's sick, if you ask me.'

'No one's asking you.' Ruth looked up and down the street, suddenly not giving a damn who was listening in to their conversation or peeking out from behind their curtains. 'I gave my boys up because it was the right thing to do, so don't you, or anyone else in this godforsaken avenue, pass judgement on me because of it.'

Gina was momentarily stunned but it didn't take her long to gain ground again.

'Why, you cheeky little bitch,' she cried. 'I'm going to see to it that you can't walk back to your house without everyone knowing what's happened. Your life won't be worth living by the time you get back from wherever it was you were rushing off to.'

'Leave me alone.' Ruth burst into tears and ran quickly down the avenue. Gina didn't follow her, but her voice did.

'We don't like cruelty cases in Stanley Avenue,' she heard her bellow. 'If we take a vote on it, you'll be banished. Do you hear me? I'll walk you out of the avenue myself.'

18

Gina Bradley was true to her word. By the time Ruth came back from the shops, she counted no less than six women waiting at their gates for her to pass.

'Bitch,' Mrs Porter from number seventeen shouted across.

Ruth scuttled past, head down.

'Yeah, someone should put you into care, you heartless cow,' said Julie Elliot from number fourteen. 'I've a good mind to slap some sense into you.'

Ruth gulped back tears but she continued. Up ahead, she could see her front door – her sanctuary from preying eyes and heckling women – and wondered if she'd get there without Gina or one of her friends throwing a punch.

Caren was in the garden, clearing a few bits of rubbish that had blown in during the rainy storm they'd had the night before. She stood up to see what all the shouting was about and then sighed – that bloody Gina.

'Take no notice of her evil tongue,' she said as Ruth walked past her garden. 'We're not all out to get you.'

Ruth caught Caren's eye for a moment, noticing the concern as she walked on.

'Don't come past me,' Sheila Ravenscroft shouted. 'You're not fit to tread on the pavement here.'

Ruth ran the last few yards into the house, slamming the door shut behind her. She gulped in air as she tried not to go into panic mode, then dropped to her knees in the middle of the hallway and sobbed. Every day seemed to get worse.

Would she ever get out of this nightmare?

When she heard someone knock at the door half an hour later, Ruth jumped. She couldn't even remember crawling into the corner of the room, but her head throbbed from the number of times she'd banged it on the wall behind her.

The letterbox lifted up. 'Ruth? It's Caren, from number twenty-four.'

'Go away,' said Ruth, realising that she couldn't hide now. Caren had already clocked her sitting there.

'I just wanted to see if you were okay?'

'You obviously don't listen to the gossip. If you did, you wouldn't be here.'

'I don't care about gossip. Look, this is killing my back. Can I come in for a moment, please?'

'This is a trick. I know Gina's standing behind you – and some of them other women. If I open the door, you'll all barge in and kick the shit out of me.'

'Ruth, I can't stand the sight of Gina so there's no chance of me playing her stupid games.' There was a pause. 'Come on, what do you say I make you a cuppa?'

Ruth decided to answer the door. She peeped around the frame, eyes red raw, hair messy where she'd been pulling at it.

'I didn't think you knew my name,' she said, her voice barely audible.

'If anyone stands up to that bully, I make it my business to find that out.'

They went through to the kitchen. 'Sit,' demanded Caren. She put the kettle on, searched around for two mugs and in a matter of moments had made coffee.

'Do you want to tell me the real story behind the rumour?' she asked once she'd sat down opposite her.

Ruth shrugged. 'Most people have already made up their minds about me. What good will it do?'

'I'm not most people.'

'You still want to know what's going on, though.'

'Maybe I do but not for the reason you're thinking. I'm not after gossip.' Caren paused. 'I've watched you since you moved in. I've watched you sink deeper and deeper into a dark hole and it upsets me to think that whatever you have to put up with in your personal life – which you should be able to keep to yourself without it being bawled around the avenue – you have that bleeding Gina Bradley to contend with.'

Ruth's mouth formed into a glimmer of a smile. 'You don't like her either, I presume?'

'She's a nasty piece of work, hell bent on destroying anyone's happiness. If she sees someone smile, she thinks she has the right to wipe it off their face.'

'What did she do to you?'

Caren blew on her drink to cool it down. 'I was unfortunate to grow up with her. I knew her from school. We – that's me and John, my husband – moved off the estate as soon as we could. Growing up on 'the Mitch' made us both want more. We didn't want to end up like the losers on the dole, claiming we had glass backs so that we didn't have to work for a penny.'

'Glass backs?' Ruth hadn't come across that expression before.

'As in you can see right through someone who is putting it on? Swinging the lead; nothing wrong with them really.'

Ruth nodded. 'There seems to be a lot of that around here. I suppose you could say I was one of them.'

Caren tried to backtrack. 'Oh, no, I meant that some people –'

Ruth held up her hand. 'I know what you meant.'

Caren paused again, long enough to take a couple of mouthfuls of her drink. Then she started to talk again.

'I found it really tough when I moved in here too. We – we had everything before John went bankrupt.'

'A business deal gone wrong?'

'Sort of – we lost a major supplier. Not only did they owe us thousands, they took away a lot of his incoming work. John's a plumber by trade and over the years we'd built up a company that allowed us to have a little bit of financial freedom. We had a beautiful house off this estate, and we had a life with no worries.'

'And then you ended up here?' Ruth shuddered.

'My worst nightmare.' Caren nodded. 'But it didn't stop there. That's when I found out Gina and her awful family lived right across from us.'

'And I thought I had it bad when I moved in.' Ruth smiled, warming to Caren.

'What I'm trying to say is that no matter what life, or people like Gina, throw at us, we can get through it. Today will be a shit day for you: tomorrow might be the same. And the day after. But one day soon, it'll get that little bit better, and brighter. Nothing lasts forever.'

'I gave my children away.' Ruth's eyes filled with tears again.

'And you had your reasons.' Caren gave her hand a quick squeeze, ignoring the blood stained bandage around Ruth's wrist. 'You need to work through your problems in your own time and then you'll come out the other side.'

'I – I'm scared that I might not make it.'

'You will – we're all stronger than we think. I know what it's like to move into

Fighting for Survival

Stanley Avenue and feel like you don't belong here. Luckily for me, I have John to talk things over with. He picks me up when I'm feeling low. But you don't have anyone.' From a pocket in her jeans, she pulled out a piece of paper she'd written her mobile phone number on. 'The next time something gets you down, maybe you could text me and if I'm free, I'll pop down to see you.'

Ruth wiped at the tears that had fallen and smiled again. 'Thank you,' she whispered.

Caren smiled too. 'Now, don't lose that slip of paper.'

*P*leased with herself after most of the neighbours had come out to hassle Ruth, Gina lit a cigarette and leaned on the gate, watching out for Pete. He'd gone out earlier, said he'd pay a couple of bills and then come home and take her for a cheapo lunch in The Butcher's Arms. Gina was hoping to get him merry enough so that he'd sub her a twenty so she could get some new shoes. She fancied a treat.

Jenny Webster wobbled her heavy frame across to her. Jenny lived in the corner house with her son and daughter from a previous marriage and an Afro-Caribbean man who made Gina's neck ache when she addressed him. Jenny was the same height as Gina: she often wondered how they got it together.

'Can't believe that about Ruth Millington, can you?' said Gina, the minute she drew level with her. 'I didn't know you could do that, give your kids back.'

'Me neither.' Jenny rested her hand on the gate while she caught her breath. 'I'd have given my Leo up a long time ago if I had known,' she laughed.

Gina did too for a moment. 'She's a sneaky piece of work,' she added.

'She is – I've seen some comings and goings at her place already.'

'Oh?' Gina realised she might be about to hear more gossip.

'I don't trust her.' Jenny glanced up and down the avenue before turning back. 'I was going to tell you earlier, then I wasn't sure but I think you should know. I saw Pete going in to see her the other morning.'

'What?' Gina roared.

Jenny nodded. 'It was early, about nine-ish.'

'Did you see what time he came out?'

'Yes, just after ten.'

'And was it the first time you saw him?'

Jenny paused. 'It's not my place to say – I've said enough already.'

Gina clenched her fists. 'Tell me.'

'I've seen him a couple of times. I don't know what...'

But Gina wasn't listening anymore. She was across the road and heading for number thirty-two. Jenny trotted behind her as quick as she could.

603

'You'd better come outside, Ruth Millington.' Gina hammered on Ruth's front door. 'I know you're in there because I've just seen Caren coming out.' She lifted up the letterbox but she couldn't see anyone. 'I'll rip your fucking head off when I get hold of you. You've had it, do you hear?'

Behind the kitchen door, Ruth sat with her hands covering her ears. Damn that family. If it wasn't Gina spreading malicious rumours and turning the neighbours against her, it was Pete coming to get his end away.

Although she knew they shouldn't have done what they did, he had taken advantage of her at her weakest moment and now it looked like she was going to pay for it in more ways than one.

Still, at least Gina hadn't found out about that yet. It could only be a matter of time but maybe all this other gossip would keep her off their trail for now. Then she could talk to Pete and see if he would back off.

'You have to come out some time and I'll be waiting.' Gina shouted again. 'No one messes about with my Pete and gets away with it.'

Ruth gasped. She *had* found out. Were all the women in Stanley Avenue set up as spies? Pete had only called round twice.

Ruth pushed herself further into the corner of the room as the banging on the door continued. Why couldn't everyone leave her alone?

Gina snapped down the letterbox and stared up at the windows. There weren't any signs of movement but she knew Ruth was in. She picked up a brick from the garden and threw it at the large windowpane in the living room. It bounced back onto the garden, narrowly missing her toes.

'Gina!'

Gina turned to see her mum running towards her.

'Leave me alone, Mum. I'm going to get her. She's been –'

'Never mind her. You'd better come quickly. It's your Pete. He's in a right mess. There's blood everywhere.'

'Pete?' Gina stormed into her house. 'Where the hell are you?' She went through to the kitchen. 'Pete!'

Pete sat on the floor, his back resting on the oven door. His face was a mishmash of bruising, swelling; thick blotches of red blood oozed down his cheeks, his neck, over his T-shirt. He was holding onto his ribs.

'You should see the other guy.' He tried to smile but winced in pain.

Gina wet a tea towel with cold water and dropped to her knees beside him. She held it to his nose.

'Is this Lenny's doing?' she asked.

'Ow, Gene, don't be so rough,' Pete moaned.

'You knew full well this would happen if you went after him. He could have killed you. He's an idiot.'

Pete stopped her hand with his own. 'I couldn't let it rest. I knew he'd be after me. But I saw him across the shops. He shouted over, asking how the young 'un was. Then he laughed. I just flipped. No one laughs at me or my family.' He tried to smile again. 'At least I got the first punch in.'

Gina held back her frustration. What was happening to her family? Were they all hell-bent on fighting to get what they wanted? And since when had it started to control their lives, spiral out of control? No wonder people thought they were scum. They gave them enough reasons to think none the wiser.

'We have to stop,' she said after they'd sat in silence for a while. 'All this fighting, it's not good.'

'If we don't stick up for ourselves, people will walk all over us.'

'People do that anyway. We're the Bradleys. People think we're shit. That's why we fight, to get one in before someone knocks us down.'

'It's a beating, Gina.' Pete withdrew the towel from his nose, trying not to retch at the sight of all the blood. 'I'll get over it. I always do.'

Gina rested her back on the unit beside him. 'But what's it doing to us? Our girls have turned into animals. Even I'm ashamed of them at times.'

'They have your temper.'

'What's that supposed to mean?'

'You'll fight over anything. That's hardly a good example to set.'

'Don't go blaming this on me. This is your doing, not mine.'

'I know.' Pete sighed. 'We should try and talk to them, though. Let's catch them when they come in later.'

But later, after school, Rachel and Claire were causing trouble outside Shop&Save. An elderly gentleman had been going about his business when Rachel pinched his tweed cap and raced off with it on her bike.

'Come back, you little cow,' he shouted, brandishing his walking stick and tottering after her.

'Relax, Granddad,' she taunted him, riding by but not near enough for him to claim back his cap. 'You want it? Go and fetch it.' She threw it into a huge puddle of water.

'That's my best cap!' The man bent down and retrieved his soggy possession. He glared at Rachel. 'You're such an awful generation. This would never have happened in my day. You'd have been locked up and dealt with by the local bobby.'

'Yeah, yeah, and I suppose you'll tell me that you fought a war for me too.'

'I'd have never fought a war for a piece of shit like you.'

'Ooh, Granddad's getting brave.' Rachel beckoned to the other girls. 'Come on over, join in the fun.'

'Leave him alone,' said Laila.

Rachel looked over in disbelief. Laila was always the mischief maker. The scowl on her face said she was definitely annoyed about something.

Ignoring the man, Rachel rode over to her. She was sitting on the railing with Ashley. Claire was beside her, sitting on her bike, a foot down on the floor to steady herself.

'What's up with you, you moody cow?' Rachel asked Laila.

'Nothing.'

'Yes, there is. You've been like this for days now.' Rachel peered at her closely. 'You're not knocked up?'

'No. And keep your bleeding voice down. I don't want any rumours starting about *me*.'

'What's that supposed to mean?' When Laila didn't say anything, Rachel pushed. 'Go on, tell me what rumour is circulating. Is it about me?'

'Or me?' asked Claire.

'Don't say anything,' Ashley told Laila.

Rachel threw down her bike and grabbed the front of Laila's jacket. 'What's going on that I don't know about?'

Laila still said nothing.

Rachel pushed her away in frustration. 'You're all mouth.'

'You'll have no mouth left when Stacey's finished with you this time.'

'Aren't we supposed to be on the same side here?'

Laila shrugged. Ashley studied her feet, running the toe of her trainers back and forth in the gravel.

Then Rachel understood. 'You two are my bessie mates. Surely you don't want to go back over to Stacey?'

'Yes, she wants us to join her again.' Ashley looked up at Rachel. 'I know you'll probably beat the crap out of me when I say this, but I'd rather have Stacey on side. She hits so hard.'

'Tell me about it,' muttered Claire.

Rachel turned to her with a scowl. 'Shut up, Claire.'

'Look,' said Laila. 'Don't you think it would be better if we all joined as one?'

Rachel shook her head.

'She's going to get us together eventually,' said Ashley. 'Whether you two like it or not.'

'She only thinks she's got everyone on side,' said Rachel. 'Once the others get fed up of her childish ways, they'll soon ditch her. That's why we should stay strong now. We'll all be top dogs again and Stacey Hunter will be nobody. Wouldn't you like that?'

Laila nodded. 'But it's not going to happen. Stacey will keep them all on side because they're scared of getting a leathering. She won't stand for anyone deserting her again.'

Rachel sat down beside her on the railing, quiet for a moment while she thought about things. 'We need to stick together.' She looked at each girl in turn. 'All five of us, including Louise. If we stay like this, she won't break us down but if one of you two falls,' she ran a finger across her throat, 'then the Mitchell Mob will be fucked. Are we in this together?' she asked, holding her breath while she waited for their reply.

'I'm in,' said Claire.

Rachel tutted. 'I didn't mean you, you dope. Laila? Ashley?'

Laila and Ashley looked at each other and after a quick nod of her head, Laila spoke.

'Okay,' she said. 'I want to stay with you two. But if it's a choice between you and her, then I think I'd rather go with her.'

'But –'

'Don't complain,' said Laila. 'If I go with her, I want you to come too. And you, Claire. If we go over, we go over together.'

Claire shrugged a shoulder. 'What do you say, Rach? One for all and all for one?'

'What the fuck do you take me for?' Rachel glared at her. 'I'll never side with Stacey Hunter. Not now, not tomorrow, not ever.'

'But –'

'But nothing,' Rachel interrupted her sister. 'It's either her or me.' She picked up her bike and rode off.

'Rach,' Claire yelled. 'Wait up for me. Rach!'

After pedalling fast to release some of her pent-up aggression, Rachel slowed down and let Claire catch up with her.

'What's up?' she asked when she drew level at last.

'Nothing.' Rachel bumped down three steps onto Rowley Green and headed for home. She didn't want her sister to know how upset she was. 'I'm hungry,' she lied.

As soon as they went through the back door, they could tell something was wrong. It was too quiet – even the television was off. In the kitchen, they found their parents sitting at the table.

'Dad!' Claire swallowed as she took in the state of him.

'Wow, Dad, you did it then?' Rachel grinned. 'You stuck up for Claire and took a beating off Lenny.'

'Sit down, Rachel,' said Gina. 'You too, Claire. Me and your dad have been talking and we feel that the fighting has got out of hand.'

Rachel folded her arms defiantly. 'You talk to us about fighting, when Dad comes home in that state?'

'It's *because* I came home looking like this that I feel the need to talk to you both. Things are going to get even nastier if we don't stop now.'

'I agree,' said Gina. 'Your Dad getting beat up today could be the start of things if you continue to fight with Stacey.'

'You mean he won't hurt you again if we behave, right?' said Claire.

Pete nodded. 'I shouldn't have gone after him. He's too strong for me.'

'You'll always be good enough in my eyes.'

Pete smirked, then grimaced. 'I'm a scrap-collector-come-odd-jobs-for-cash man.'

'We want your word that you two will behave yourselves,' said Gina.

The girls shrugged.

'Promise us!'

'Okay, okay!' said Rachel.

'And you need to back off that Ruth woman, from number thirty-two,' Pete spoke to Gina. 'I heard what you'd been up to earlier.'

'That depends if the rumour is true.'

'What rumour?' Claire and Rachel asked at the same time.

'The one that says she's playing around with your father.'

'Dad?' said Claire.

'It's not true,' Pete lied. He scraped back his chair and stood up. 'We all need to stop fighting, before someone gets seriously hurt. Right girls?'

Rachel stood up and marched past him. 'Fine,' she said.

'I'll talk to her,' said Claire, following on a minute later.

'And you?' Pete stared at Gina once they'd both gone. 'No more from you either?'

Despite her earlier thoughts, Gina wasn't going to promise anything yet, not until she'd spoken to Ruth.

'Right?' repeated Pete.

'All right,' cried Gina. 'I'll keep the peace for a while.'

He pointed at her. 'You need to set a good example for them. They look up to you.'

Gina raised her eyebrows. When had anyone ever done that?

19

'Dad looks a right mess, doesn't he?' said Claire as she sat down next to Rachel on her bed.

'Yeah, he's taken a proper pasting. I'm glad he stuck up for you though.'

Claire paused. 'Rach, don't you think they're right, that we should back off?'

'We can't.' Rachel shook her head. 'We're in too deep now.'

'No, we're not. We can always stop.'

Rachel flopped back on the bed. 'If we back down, Stacey will hunt us down and tear us apart. She'll make sure that she humiliates us so that no one will want to be our friends.'

Claire huffed. 'So what? No one wants to hang around with us anyway. Let's face it, Dad's right – we're the Bradleys. Everyone thinks we're scum and that's down to the way we act.'

Rachel said nothing.

'Aren't you sick of it all yet?'

'I hate being the leader of the gang. I hate what it's done to us all. We used to have a laugh over at the shops with the other girls – we used to have fun. Now it's all about who can get one up on the other first. So, yes, I *am* sick of it all.'

'Me too! I dread going out now, wondering who's going to pounce on us next. I want to just have a laugh again.'

Rachel sighed. 'It's never going to happen.'

'But if we don't join in with Stacey and her stupid games, we –'

'Are you mad? She'll never stop coming after us.'

'She will, if we back down.' Claire was warming to her cause now. 'We can do it, Rach. Let's tell Stacey she can be leader again.'

Rachel shook her head. 'It won't work. We'll be a laughing stock.'

'For a week, maybe two, tops. But you know Stacey. She'll move on to someone else. And we'll be with her then.'

'You think she'll let us hang around with her after what's happened?'

Claire shrugged. 'It's worth a shot.'

'And if it doesn't work?'

'Then we have each other. No one can break that up, can they?'

Rachel knew there was no way Stacey would back down. Even if they went to her and said they wanted to join her gang, she'd laugh them off the estate. Stacey was a power freak. They should have known better than to mess with her.

Mum and Dad were right, things had gone too far. The whole family had never been in as many scrapes as they had over the past few weeks.

Rachel knew when she was beat. She couldn't fight the likes of Stacey and win, just as her dad couldn't stand up to her stepdad, Lenny. They weren't tough enough.

'What are we going to do?' Claire asked.

From her muffled tone, Rachel could tell that she was crying.

'I don't know,' she told her. 'But whatever happens, it's going to be nasty for a while.'

Things didn't look any better the following morning. Rachel got up in a mood and fell out with Claire, Gina and Pete within half an hour. She slammed out of the house ten minutes later, leaving Claire to face the sombre atmosphere alone.

Pete's right eye had swollen until he could barely see out of it. Gina tried to make a joke about things but it hadn't gone down well. He stormed off after slamming his mug down on the worktop, spraying remnants of tea all over the tiles.

And it wasn't even nine o'clock.

Claire and Gina sat in silence, finishing off their breakfast.

'Things will get better, Mum,' said Claire. 'They'll both calm down soon.'

'I was talking sense last night, wasn't I?'

Claire nodded. 'But it won't happen, will it? Let's face it, everyone thinks we're shit. So why change a habit of a lifetime.'

Gina felt tears prick her eyes. 'Coming from you, also known as my sensible twin, that doesn't half sting,' she told her.

'I didn't mean anything by it, Mum.' Claire gave her a hug.

Fighting for Survival

Gina hugged her back fiercely to stop herself from screaming. What the hell was happening to their family? Anger welled up inside her.

'We have to stick together,' she said. 'No one bad-mouths the Bradleys, not without getting what they deserve.'

'But we do deserve what we get at times, don't we?'

Gina felt Claire's sobs as her body shook.

'I don't want to fight anymore, Mum.'

'You don't have to.'

'It's not going to be that easy.'

Gina moved back and held her daughter's face in her hands. 'Claire, love, when was anything in life going to be easy for a Bradley?'

By eleven thirty, neither Rachel nor Pete had returned home. Gina hadn't been able to get Claire to go to school either. Exasperated, she decided to have a walk across to the shops, see if anyone was about for a gossip. She was running low on cigarettes and she could do with some lager for tonight.

Maybe, when Rachel and Pete came back, she could persuade them all to have a night in together. She'd get the girls some crisps and chocolates, and a frozen pizza to go with the bag of oven chips she already had. It would do them good to sit down as a family, watch a film together and relieve the tension.

She was there and back in half an hour yet, even as she'd thought about her problems while she walked, things didn't seem any better. She sighed as she got home. Maybe things would start to improve soon.

But then, from the corner of her eye she noticed Ruth coming out of her gate. Without thinking of the promise she'd made the night before, Gina dropped her bag and groceries over into her garden and legged it across the road. When she drew level, she slapped Ruth across the face.

Ruth staggered back but stayed on her feet until the second slap was administered.

'Slut,' Gina cried as she slapped her again. 'Stay the fuck away from my Pete.'

Ruth didn't cower. She knew she deserved what she was getting so she wouldn't fight back.

Gina grabbed at her hair. 'You. Keep. Your. Filthy. Hands. Off. Him!'

'Mum!' Claire shouted. 'You promised. No more fighting and look at you.'

Gina paused for a moment to catch her breath, pointing at Ruth. 'It's all her fault. She's been messing around with your dad.'

Claire gasped. 'Is that true?' she asked Ruth.

Ruth didn't reply. In the background, she could see Caren running towards them.

'Answer her,' cried Gina.

'Stop it, Mum.'

As she was about to hit Ruth again, Caren grabbed her wrist and held it in mid air.

'Enough!' she shouted.

Ruth pulled herself up and leaned on the wall, panting for breath.

'What the hell's going on this time?' Caren hissed. 'Are you always going to act like a child?'

'She started it,' Gina mumbled. 'It was her fault.'

'Ruth started a fight?' Caren looked on in astonishment. 'I don't think so.'

'Mum, let's go in,' Claire said, 'before you get landed with assault.'

'I – I won't say anything,' said Ruth.

The black mist was beginning to lift but as guilt began to surface, Gina fought back with her tongue. She pointed at Ruth. 'Breathe a word of this to anyone and I'll –'

'You'll what?' said Caren. 'Pick another fight? Is that all you're good for? No wonder you've never had a job.'

'Hey,' said Claire.

'Leave it, Claire,' said Gina.

'But –'

'I said leave it. Go inside and mind your own business.'

As Claire marched off, Caren held out a tissue for Ruth.

Ruth took it from her. 'Can you help me home?' she whispered.

'Course I can.' But before she did, Caren turned back to Gina. 'Is this how you get your thrills in your sorry little life, by attacking people? Is this how you *all* get your kicks – you, your kids and Pete?'

'No,' cried Gina. 'We –'

'I have never met anyone so nasty, so vicious, so – so animal like in my entire life. You're nothing short of a thug. I should report you for this.'

'You wouldn't dare!'

'I would and you know it, so back –'

'Please, I don't want this to go any further,' Ruth broke in.

'But you're bleeding. And look at your eye. You'll –'

'I'll be fine,' Ruth assured her.

'Yes,' added Gina. 'She'll be fine, won't you, Ruth?'

'Oh, get out of my sight.' Caren put an arm around Ruth's shoulder. 'Come on, let's get you home.'

. . .

Fighting for Survival

*G*ina stood in the avenue, watching Ruth walk off with Caren. As her anger turned to shame, her eyes glistened with tears. She hadn't a clue what had come over her. She'd just seen red when she spotted Ruth. And now that Claire had seen her, she'd be in trouble with Pete when he finally showed his face again.

Wearily, she gathered up her wits as well as her pride and went back home. So much for a fun night in with the family.

*O*nce inside the house, Caren helped Ruth remove her blood stained jacket. She took it from her and shoved it into the washing machine out of the way.

'You have to report this to the police,' she said.

'I can't do that,' said Ruth. 'I'll have the whole family against me then, as well as all the neighbours. It'll be like signing my own death warrant. I'm going to put in for a transfer.'

'I wish I could. I hate this bloody avenue. Everyone is so small-minded.' Caren looked at Ruth, now sitting at the table. Her face was beginning to swell up like a bruised tomato, nerves as shredded as her bottom lip that had split twice. 'How can one family completely rule a street? If it isn't Gina, it's her bloody mother causing grief, shouting her mouth off.'

'I think the neighbours are okay,' admitted Ruth. 'It's just if they all get together with Gina. You were right. She is an animal.'

'So what started it all?'

'She found out that Pete had called around a few times. One of the neighbours must've grassed me up.'

Caren felt her blood run cold. 'He hasn't – threatened you in any way, has he?'

Ruth shook her head, a little too quickly for Caren's liking. She sighed, sat down across from her and reached for her hand. 'Whatever's going on, you can trust me if you need someone to talk to. I'd cut my own tongue off and shove it up my arse before I'd tell Gina Bradley a damn thing.'

Ruth tried to smile at Caren's joke.

Caren squeezed her hand, urging her to talk. 'Did he force himself on you?'

Ruth shook her head.

'You mean you wanted him to?'

Ruth shook her head again.

'So what, then?'

When Ruth shook her head for the third time, Caren backed off. She was upset. It wasn't fair to push her. Still, she wanted to press the point.

'Please, call me if you need to talk. You still have my number?'

'Yes.'

'I can understand if you don't want to but the offer will always be there.'

'She doesn't get it, though.' Ruth looked up through tears. 'No matter what she does, no one can hurt me any more than I've already been hurt. My life is a mess anyway, because of my own doings.' She flicked her thumb towards the front door. 'I don't need them lot out there to tell me how stupid I am.'

'You're not stupid.'

'You don't have kids, do you?'

'Sadly, no. I'm unable to.'

'Oh, shit, I –'

Caren held up her hand. 'It's okay. I've known for a while now. Dodgy ovaries and I ended up having an early menopause. It couldn't be helped.' For a moment, she thought of Donna Adams and Sam. Donna had finally been in touch. Surprisingly, it seemed that Sam was coming to visit them next week.

'Then you must hate me for what I did, giving my kids up when you can't have any.'

'We all do things according to our circumstances. It's not my style to judge anyone.' Caren paused. 'Maybe once things have died down, you and I could start meeting for coffee once in a while. I could give you a lift into town, share the odd glass of wine in the evening. What do you say? It'll certainly get that lot out there talking.'

'Why are you doing this?' Ruth asked suddenly.

'It's because I know how shit I felt when I had to move into Stanley Avenue – and I had John to help me out. You wouldn't believe the arguments and rows we had when we first got here.'

Ruth was surprised by this. 'You always look so solid when I see you together.'

'That's because I, unlike Gina Bradley, won't air my dirty washing in public. There were times I could have killed him, especially when he started to spend more time over on the scummy side of the street with Pete.' Caren stopped when she heard Ruth giggle. 'What?'

'The scummy side of the street?'

'Oh.' Caren smiled. 'That's my nickname. I shouted it out in temper to John once and it stuck. It's appropriate, though.'

'It is.'

'And if that bloody Pete knocks on your door again, tell him to sling his hook.'

Fighting for Survival

Ruth's smile faded.

'He's a bully too. I think that's where Gina gets it from. She doesn't control that family as much as she likes to think. He does, the tosser. He tried it on with me too.'

Ruth's mouth gaped.

'He threatened me. Said he'd get me if I stopped John from hanging around with him. Well, I stopped him and nothing happened to me.'

'Yet,' muttered Ruth.

'It's too late now. And besides, he moved on to you, didn't he, the bastard?'

Ruth nodded.

'But he won't be coming in again, will he?'

Ruth shook her head. 'I just hope he gets the message.'

'Maybe he won't come round now that someone has blabbed. And I'll get John to fit you some more security on your door, if that's ok?'

'I don't have any money until next week. I can't pay you until then.'

'We don't need money.' Caren waved the offer away. 'Have you any idea of the amount of junk he pulled from our garage before we had to move? He'll have something lying around doing nothing.'

'Thanks,' Ruth said again.

Caren smiled.

'No, really. I mean it. You didn't have to step in this morning.'

'I *wanted* to. Someone has to stand up to that foul-mouthed cow. Although, I must admit, I'm not a fighter. If she had a go at me, I'd have done the same as you.'

'She's got a hard hit.' Ruth touched her nose and winced.

'There is one thing, though.' Caren splayed out her fingers. 'I'd have been annoyed if she broke one of my nails. Hey, I've had an idea.'

Gina stood on the back step, puffing heavily on a cigarette. Although there was a wind blowing and the weather had turned colder overnight, she wasn't about to go inside the house. She knew she'd have to face the music after what she'd done.

She took another long puff. What the hell had got in to her? One minute she was telling her family to back off and behave; the next she was fighting hell for leather in the middle of the street. Some example she was setting.

She recalled every detail of the incident in slow motion in her mind. Ruth had looked like a cornered animal. She hadn't fought back at all and there was only one reason she could think of for that – she must have a guilty conscience.

A few minutes later, Gina took a final drag of her cigarette before stubbing it

615

out, letting out a sigh along with the smoke. Maybe Caren was right: maybe she was fit for nothing except fighting. Gina Bradley – not an exam to her name, not a penny earned by hard work. And if truth be told, she had too much time on her hands. There was nothing to do with her days. They all rolled into one.

She had no purpose to her pitiful life. Pete went out to do some kind of cash-in-hand job most days. Even the girls went to school occasionally. But what did she have? Nothing. Every day was the same. Every day in the future was doomed to be the same – unless she did something about it.

Claire was in the kitchen when she finally went inside. She gave her mother a filthy look.

'I'm sorry, love,' said Gina. 'I don't know what came over me. And after what me and Dad said last night, it isn't right.'

'Then why did you do it?' Claire asked. 'It was horrible to see you laying into her, in front of everyone, not bothering how much you hurt her.'

'It's only the same as you and Rachel having a go at Stacey or one of the other girls you've been fighting with lately.'

'No, it's not. We're not that nasty.'

Gina opened her mouth to snap back an answer but she closed it instead. Her fight wasn't with her daughter.

'I don't know why I did it,' she admitted moments later after they'd sat in a stony silence. 'That's the honest truth.'

'Then maybe you should do an anger management course or something.'

'Anger management?' Gina laughed. 'You must be joking. Living in this house, I'd never get a chance to learn how to be calm. Besides, it's not in my make-up.'

'But have you any idea how embarrassing it is to see your mum beating up a defenceless woman in the middle of the street? To have another neighbour pulling her away?'

'Okay, okay.' Gina had heard enough. 'It's me who should be lecturing you about these things.'

'I didn't start the fight this morning.'

'No, but you'll probably start another one sooner than I will.'

Claire had no answer to that.

Gina left her to sulk in the kitchen. In the living room, she thought about what Claire had said. She hadn't realised how she would look through her child's eyes – she hadn't actually thought any further than punching Ruth's lights out.

She ran a hand through her greasy hair and sniggered. Anger management indeed. But deep down inside, she knew it was what she needed. She had to get rid of all her pent-up aggression or it would ruin her. She'd end up in real trouble – she might even end up in prison – and then where would she be?

Maybe it was time to see if she could get some help, start setting an example to her children instead of being an embarrassment. It was never too late to change, right?

And she knew just the person to go to.

20

'I never expected to see you sitting in my office.' Josie smiled at Gina. 'It's obviously not a call you're making lightly. Trouble at the mill?'

'Isn't there always?' Gina tried to make light of her mood. It had been easy to make out she was nipping across to the shops this morning and sidle into The Workshop and ask to see Josie.

She'd thought of the idea last night after her cosy family night in had disintegrated when Rachel and Pete had given her as much of a tough time as Claire had over the fight with Ruth. Rachel dragged Claire out with her and Pete stormed off to the pub fifteen minutes later, saying she was stifling him.

She'd sat and cried for over an hour before deciding that she needed to get help. But now she was here, sitting in Josie's tidy office, she didn't really know where to start.

'So who do you want to talk about? Pete? The girls?' Josie paused. 'Or is there anything I can help you with?'

Gina glanced up and was embarrassed to find her eyes had filled with tears. 'I don't know where to start. I'm so angry, all the time. I'm arguing with Pete. My girls have gone haywire because I let them get away with stuff. When I do decide to talk to them, I go and...' Gina stopped. She didn't want to alert Josie to the trouble she'd made with Ruth. 'Let's say I let myself down.'

'You're bored, Gina. Your life is empty, your children have grown up and are no longer dependent on you, and you don't feel that you fit in anywhere. And, being frank, you don't, do you?'

If anyone else had spoken so harshly to her, Gina would have followed it with a torrent of abuse. But she knew that Josie was telling the truth. And hadn't Caren said something similar yesterday?

'I feel like I'm not in control anymore,' she admitted. 'I feel like no one listens to me. I feel – I feel invisible.'

'And that's what makes you so angry?'

Gina nodded. 'I suppose.'

'I still think it comes down to boredom.' Josie swivelled on her chair slightly. 'Look, I could really use you right now. I've been asking you to visit The Workshop for months. There are lots of things you can do here to stop you from taking your frustration out on other people. Come and help me.'

'Me?' Gina looked taken aback. 'What would you want me here for? I've just said no one listens to me. I can't –'

'You are part of the estate.' Josie ticked off a list with her fingers. 'You know how easy it is to be dragged down. You'd be great with some of the kids groups, even the teenagers.'

Gina sat wide-eyed. 'No one has a good word to say about the Bradleys. How can that be to your advantage?'

'I'm crying out for help – there's obviously no way I can pay you, I have to make that clear from the start – but you'd be perfect because of who you are.'

'Now you're really talking shit.' Gina sat back in her chair.

'No, I'm not. I think it would work for both of us.' Josie reached for her diary and flicked through it quickly. 'How about you give me a week? You come to the centre, say a couple of hours every morning, and I'll get you involved with different groups. At the end of the week, if you're still here,' she smiled kindly, 'maybe you can choose an area where you feel you could make a difference and come on a more regular basis? I can be around for you, if you like? I could introduce you to people and let you get the feel of the place. It'll become familiar to you after a few days. More importantly, it'll give you something to look forward to.'

Gina felt her spirit lifting. Could she find a purpose here, fit in and do something useful? Maybe she'd stop getting into so much trouble if she was involved with other people. Maybe she could even make a few friends.

But then reality kicked in. Pete would take the piss out of her for volunteering – in his eyes you never did anything without payment. And Rachel and Claire would probably be mortified that she'd be working with some of the kids from their school. They'd start moaning about street cred and that she wasn't home for them when they needed her.

But, no matter how much grief she was bound to get from her family, she knew that she wanted this more. She nodded at Josie.

'Okay, then. I'll give it a go. A week, you say?'

Josie's smile made it all the more meaningful. 'Great. I'm sure you'll find it worthwhile. And, like I said, I need all the help I can get here.'

Gina grinned. 'As long as you remember, I'm as mad as the colour of my hair.'

Caren had dropped John off at work and taken the car to do a shop at the supermarket. When she parked up outside her house afterwards, the first thing she noticed was the Bradley girls sitting on their garden wall.

Hmm – no school again, she shook her head. Then again, they were wearing their uniforms underneath their coats and it was lunchtime. Maybe she shouldn't be so judgmental. She gathered together a few bags of groceries from the boot of the car.

'Damn and blast and bugger.' She grappled helplessly as the handle split on one of them, her groceries falling to the tarmac. She knew the twins would be laughing at her.

But then she noticed a pair of trainers in her line of vision and heard someone speak. She stood up quickly, surprised to see one of the girls holding out the damaged bag and the other putting things back into it.

'You'll have to carry it by the bottom,' said Claire, 'but it should hold.'

'Thanks,' said Caren.

'I'll take it in, if you like,' offered Rachel.

A bit taken aback, Caren nodded. 'Okay.'

'I don't know why you don't have it delivered,' said Rachel. 'I bet it's so much better ordering online and then getting it delivered for you.'

And a luxury I can no longer afford, thought Caren. Gone are the days when she could order all she wanted over the internet and not worry about the cost.

'But this way I get to see all the bargains and BOGOFs,' she replied.

'BOGOFs?'

'Buy One Get One Free,' said Claire. 'BOGOFs.'

They trooped around the back of the house and Caren let them into the kitchen. Claire put the broken shopping bag down onto the table. Rachel added the two that she'd brought in as well.

'Thanks,' said Caren. 'That was good of you to help me.' As they turned to leave, something inside her softened. 'Would you girls like a coffee?' She pulled out a packet of biscuits. 'And a BOGOF custard cream?'

Several minutes later, they were chatting around her kitchen table. Rachel's foot was tapping away to a tune on the radio. Claire was telling Caren about her latest favourite band.

'Your nails are so lovely,' she said, pointing at Caren's hands. 'Are they real?'

Caren nodded. She splayed her fingers to display them to their full glory. 'They're hard work to keep like this but,' she curled up her fingers now to inspect them for herself, 'it's worth it. I love them. I go ballistic whenever I break one.'

Rachel splayed out the fingers on both her hands. They were bitten down, dirt under the tiny rims. 'I'd love to have nails like yours. As soon as mine get long, they start to snap off.'

'But you bite them, don't you?'

Rachel nodded. 'With a life like ours, you'd bite them too.'

Caren smiled inwardly. If only they knew how different, or difficult, life would be for them in ten years time. Then she wondered...

'I'm having a nail party,' she told them. 'Would you like to come?'

'What's a nail party?' asked Claire.

'I've started doing manicures and beauty treatments on a mobile basis. And to get to know the neighbours a little better, I'm going to do free manicures for the evening. I'll get a few bottles of wine and some nibbles. If I have time, I'll do everyone's nails. If not, some will have to settle for a hand massage.'

'We could both come?' asked Rachel.

Caren nodded. 'Yes.'

'What about Mum?'

'She can come too – I suppose.'

Claire giggled. 'You don't like her that much, do you?'

'Is it that obvious?' Caren tried to make light of it. 'You're right. We're not exactly the best of friends but, yes, if she wants to come, she can.'

Rachel shrugged in a non-committal manner. 'We might be busy.'

'No, we bloody won't.' Claire nudged her sharply. 'I fancy having my nails done, especially for free.'

'What about my nan? Can she come too?'

Caren sighed inwardly – and Nan made four. Four Bradleys under one roof. Her fun party atmosphere was beginning to sound like a disaster waiting to happen. Maybe they wouldn't all be able to make it.

But this wasn't about making enemies. This was about breaking barriers down for Ruth and, now that she had them here, trying to get these girls to realise there was more to life than causing trouble. Caren decided to kill two birds with one stone. She opened the kitchen drawer and pulled out a pile of envelopes.

'Would you two like to post these for me? I've already written them out.'

'There isn't one for us,' said Rachel as she flicked through the names of all their neighbours.

'That's because I didn't think you'd want to come,' Caren admitted.

Both girls looked at her.

'I've enjoyed your company today. What do you say?'

Both girls looked at each other.

'Yeah,' they replied.

'Great.' Caren picked out a blank invitation, quickly wrote their names on it and shoved it into an envelope. 'These will be like gold dust. Every woman in Stanley Avenue has been invited but no one else has. I'm hoping once word gets round the estate that I might get a few clients. But this will be a one-off free party.' She gave the envelope to Rachel. 'And you two are invited.'

Caren smiled – how easy was that? Suddenly, her plan to engage Ruth with the women in the avenue had taken a turn for the better. By having Rachel and Claire go on about their invite to the party, Gina might be curious enough to turn up. Then she could really get going on Ruth's return from the dark side. Once Ruth had a friend or two, everything might not seem so black.

*L*ater that evening, Rachel turned the corner out of Stanley Avenue onto Davy Road. She was heading for the shops, a little earlier than usual as she and Claire were hoping to stick to their promises they'd made to their mum and dad. Rachel had sent a text message to Laila and Ashley saying that they needed to talk. Claire had nipped back home because she'd forgotten her phone.

'Frigging hell,' she blurted out as someone came out of the shadows. She held onto her chest. 'Laila, bird, you nearly gave me a heart attack.'

Laila stood in front of Rachel, not realising that, although she appeared to be alone, she wasn't. Behind her, she could see Claire running to catch up.

'What's up?' Claire asked as she drew level with them both. She looked from one to the other.

Laila chewed at a fingernail.

'What's up?' Rachel parroted, although she'd already guessed.

Laila swallowed. 'I don't know how to say this, because I know you're my mates, and I know I'll probably get a good bollocking off you, and I'll probably deserve it for giving up on you, but I don't want to be in the Mitchell Mob anymore. I'm joining Stacey.'

The words were said so quickly that it was hard to decipher where one sentence finished and the next began. Laila stood there, her breath coming in short bursts. She clenched her fists in readiness for the fight to come.

After a few seconds, she realised nothing was going to happen. She dropped her hands.

Claire placed a hand on Rachel's arm as she took a step nearer to Laila.

Rachel looked back with a smile. 'It's okay. I'm not going to do anything.' She looked next at Laila. 'We were coming to tell you that we're not fighting anymore.'

'What?' Laila frowned.

'We've had enough – of all the fighting, of all the ganging up on each other. We were coming to tell you and Ashley first and then go and find Stacey – see if we could have some sort of truce.'

'Are you mad? She hates you two.' Laila pointed at Rachel. 'Especially you. She's only waiting for us all to go back to her and then she's going to beat the shit out of you.'

'I'd like to see her try.'

'Rachel,' said Claire. 'We promised.'

'Promised who?' said Laila.

'Never you mind,' snapped Rachel.

'She'll find out eventually,' said Laila. 'Stacey always does.'

Suddenly Rachel clicked in. 'You're the snitch in the camp. While Stacey gathered together the rest of the mob, you were in on it all the time.'

'Not all of the time.' Laila looked down at the pavement for a moment. 'She's too hard for me, Rach. I can't deal with her by myself. You two will always have each other. Stacey doesn't like that. You know she wants to be top dog –'

'More like top bitch,' Rachel spat out.

'I wouldn't let her hear you saying that.'

'She doesn't bother me,' said Rachel.

They all knew she was lying.

Across the street, music started up from inside the Reynolds's house. Someone inside had cranked the volume to full.

'So what happens now?' Laila shouted above the noise.

Rachel got out her phone. 'I'll text Ashley, see where she is. Then we'll have a meeting.'

*C*aren paced up and down the living room. It was nearly half past eight and Sam was supposed to have arrived for eight. Surprised that he was coming at all, she now had her doubts reaffirmed. Something was wrong.

'He's not coming, is he?' John said for the umpteenth time.

Caren was about to reply when the doorbell rang. John glanced at her before going to the door.

Donna came into the living room first, followed by a man who fitted the image of the photograph they'd been shown last week.

Caren stood up, unsure how to greet him. 'Hi, Sam.' She held out her hand. 'I'm Caren, John's wife.'

Sam shook her hand slightly before slumping down on the settee.

'Can I get you anything to drink?' said John, for want of something to do.

'Lager.' Sam's eyes flitted around the room before turning to watch the television.

'We'll have coffee,' said Donna.

Before Caren could offer to help, Donna beat her to it.

Caren watched her follow John into the kitchen, realising too late that it left her sitting with Sam. She smiled at him as he caught her eye. He raised his chin slightly in acknowledgment before staring intently at the next product that came on.

Bloody typical, thought Caren. An advert for panty liners.

'John says that you live over in Graham Street?' She made small talk. 'Have you got your own place?'

'You have to have kids to get a decent shack on this estate, so I live at home with the olds,' Sam replied, without taking his eyes from the box. 'I ain't got any kids. Well,' he sniggered. 'None I'll admit to, anyway.'

Caren smiled but inside she was horrified. Suddenly all the suspicions she'd had began to rise to the surface again. Surreptitiously, she studied him. Sam was supposed to be twenty-one but he looked younger than that. His eyes were blue: John's eyes were brown. His hair was blonde: John's was dark brown. And Donna's hair was bottle blonde: her roots were dark. He was quite small: John was tall. At a guess, Donna was around five foot four, give or take a heel; neither small nor tall. It wasn't easy to surmise.

Sadly, she realised, Sam's whole demeanour spelled out loser. This didn't look good. It seemed suspicious. Was John being set up to believe this was his son? And if so, what on earth for? She couldn't put her finger on anything.

John and Donna came back into the room, carrying two mugs apiece.

John placed his down on the coffee table.

'Why didn't you use a tray?' Caren asked.

'I didn't know where they were kept.'

Donna giggled. 'Like father, like son. Sam isn't domesticated either.'

'John's not too bad.'

'Sounds like you're under the thumb mate,' Sam snorted.

John smiled a little. 'Where do you work, Sam?'

'I don't.'

'Oh, I see. Finding it tough to get something? I did too. I haven't been at my current place for long but I hated every day that I didn't have a job.'

Sam shook his head. 'I don't want a job.'

'But what do you do with yourself all day?' questioned Caren. 'This estate hasn't got a lot to offer.'

Fighting for Survival

'I do a bit of this and a bit of that.'

'Maybe you could put a word in at your place for him, John.'

'I'd be pleased to, if anything else comes up.'

'I'm happy as I am.'

'Yes, but –'

'I hear you've set up a mobile nails business,' Donna interrupted Caren purposely.

'There's no money here, if that's what you're after,' Caren snapped.

'Caren,' said John. 'Donna didn't mean anything like that.'

'Sorry.'

'I heard you went bankrupt,' said Sam.

'You hear a lot of things about us, don't you, Sam?' said Caren. 'I wonder where you get your information from.'

Sam folded one leg over to rest it on his knee, nudging the coffee table in the process. A mug fell to the floor, hot coffee splattering everywhere.

'For Christ's sake.' Donna sat forward and pulled a tissue out of her pocket. She began to dab at the flooring. 'You're such a clumsy bastard.'

'It's okay.' Caren stood up, face like thunder. 'I'll get a cloth.'

'Stick the kettle on again, Caz, and make Sam another.'

Caren couldn't help herself when she sighed loudly. Why was it always her that had to do everything?

But Sam misunderstood its meaning. 'Don't bother,' he retorted. 'I can see I'm not wanted here.'

Donna stood up too. 'I think we'd better go. Maybe we could call again? Perhaps next time it won't seem so... *awkward*.'

The minute John had seen them both out, he rounded on Caren. 'What the hell's wrong with you? You were out to have a dig from the moment he walked in.'

'She's playing you, John. They both are.'

'What do you mean?'

'Sam isn't your son.'

'Why wouldn't he be?'

'He looks nothing like you. In fact, he's the total opposite to you.'

'No, he isn't.'

'Why can't you see what they're doing?'

But John wasn't having any. 'You had no intention of making him feel welcome, did you? You'd already made up your mind before he got here. You didn't want him in our house, so you went out of your way to be spiteful.'

'*Spiteful*?' Caren hissed. 'Why were you so long in the kitchen with Donna?' Caren watched John's mouth drop. 'You were gone ages and left me having to make small talk with your so-called son. What were you discussing back there in the kitchen?'

'Nothing. I was showing her the coffee maker we brought with us.'

'Like I believe that.'

'What do you think I was doing? Getting re-acquainted with her over the kitchen table?'

Caren's eyes filled with tears. 'No,' she said. 'I didn't think that at all.'

Suddenly the rage was gone. John drew her into his embrace. 'I'm sorry,' he said. 'I'm really disappointed. It didn't go as well as I wanted it to.'

That's because he's not your son, she wanted to add. But instead, Caren stayed quiet. She'd had enough for one day.

Besides, until she figured out what the hell was going on, it was as well to keep it to herself. She'd do some digging of her own.

And she knew exactly where to start.

21

'So how are you feeling now?' Josie asked Ruth as she sat in her living room. After trying on four separate occasions over the past week, she'd finally managed to get in for another visit.

'So, so,' said Ruth. In actual fact, she hadn't set foot outside the door since the fight with Gina. Luckily, Caren had kept to her word and, instead of taking her shopping, she'd brought some essentials back for her when she'd feigned illness.

Quite frankly, she looked too much of a mess to go out in public so it must have been easy for Caren to agree rather than try and persuade her to get a little fresh air.

'Have you been to see the boys?'

'No, I don't want to upset them.'

'I'm sure they'd be pleased to see you rather than be upset.'

'How would you feel if your mother left you in an office for someone else to look after? I'm not going to be the most popular of people.'

'Maybe not, but I bet they'd like to see you.'

'Am I allowed to see them, after what I did?' Ruth ran a hand through her hair, pulled at it. 'Why did I do it? Why did I give them away?'

'Because you couldn't cope at that particular moment in time,' Josie tried to appease her. 'It doesn't mean that you'll never be able to see them again.'

'You have an answer for everything.'

'It comes with the job, I'm afraid. I'm nosy too – are you going to tell me how you got that black eye? I heard there was a bit of trouble with the Bradleys earlier on in the week.'

'Oh? I never heard anything.'

'And you got those bruises by keeping yourself to yourself?'

'That's none of your business.'

'I know,' said Josie, 'but humour me. Like I said, I'm nosy.'

Ruth smiled. She couldn't help it. No matter what, Josie always made her feel at ease. She had a way about her that felt like she enveloped you in a fluffy blanket and smothered you with enough hope and optimism to get you through the day.

'I'm fine,' she told Josie.

Josie raised her eyebrows questioningly.

'Really,' reiterated Ruth. 'I'm fine.'

'So Gina didn't hit you?'

'No, I didn't say that. Please. You won't say anything, will you? I deserved what I got.'

'Why would you think that?' Josie pointed to Ruth's face. 'She's an animal for doing that and she needs locking up.'

'I'm not going to grass on her.'

'I know you're not, and I wouldn't expect you to either. It's just that sometimes I wish someone would give her a taste of her own medicine, make her hurt for a while. Honestly, that woman and her family have been the bane of my life for a –' Josie stopped. 'I'm sorry, Ruth. I shouldn't have said that to you. My feelings got in the way. It was unprofessional.'

'It's true, though, she isn't a nice woman.' Ruth grimaced. 'Mind, I made a mess of my life too.'

'You talk as if it's over.'

'Newsflash – it is.'

'No, it isn't. There's always hope, no matter what.'

Ruth had to stop herself from laughing aloud. Josie Mellor was always so positive. She always thought she could bring out the best in people. It was a good trait to have, but it was wasted on her.

Optimism was something she'd given up on a long time ago.

'This party was such a good idea,' said Caren to Rachel and Claire. They were in her kitchen getting things ready for the evening ahead. 'I can't believe how many women are going to come.'

'It's the talk of the avenue,' said Rachel. She was putting glasses out on Caren's worktop.

Fighting for Survival

'I reckon it'll be the talk of the estate,' added Claire.

'I hope it is. I...' Caren frowned. 'How do I tell you apart?'

'I'm Rachel,' said Claire.

Rachel nudged her. 'I'm Rachel.'

'No, I'm Rachel.'

'No, I am.'

Rachel touched her nose with her finger. 'There's really only one of us.'

'Yeah, she's a ghost.'

Caren shrugged, none the wiser.

Claire pointed at her jumper. 'I'm always in red or white. Rachel is always blue or black.'

'And I have a scar, here.' Rachel pointed to the side of her face.

Caren passed them a multi-pack of crisps. Then she watched as they filled the bowls set out on the worktop. Since moving into Stanley Avenue, she'd always felt intimidated by them – more to do with their surname rather than their behaviour – but as she saw them chatting away, she had to admit that maybe she'd been wrong. Or maybe she'd judged them, as other people did, on the outfits they were wearing. They wore hoodies and tracksuit bottoms, with trainers. Their hair was short, faces void of make-up. Yet, if they made more of themselves, they could be real beauties.

She remembered what she wanted to ask them.

'Do either of you know Sam Harvey?' she asked, trying to keep her tone light.

'Yeah,' said Rachel. 'Why?'

'He's been asking to do some odd jobs. I wanted to check him out.'

'He'll make money any way he can. He's work-shy.'

'What makes you say that?'

'I don't think he's ever had a job in his life.'

'He is only eighteen,' said Claire.

Caren froze. 'I thought he was older than that.'

Claire paused and looked at Rachel for confirmation.

'No, he's younger than our brother. Danny is twenty-one.'

'Have you ever met his parents?'

Rachel helped herself to a handful of nuts. 'I don't know what happened to his old man but his mother, Donna Adams? She works in Shop&Save on the square.'

'And you're sure he's only eighteen?' Caren pressed one more time, hoping she didn't sound too suspicious.

'Positive.' Rachel grinned. 'You're not after a toy boy, are you?'

'In my dreams.' Caren glanced at her clock on the wall. 'Right, you two,

629

thanks for your help. I'm off to have a bath now so I'll see you back here in an hour?'

Once the girls had left, Caren wondered what was going on. If Sam was only eighteen, then he couldn't be John's son unless he really did have an affair.

And if he wasn't John's son, then what were he and Donna up to? Were they after money thinking that John would pay up because of all the missed years? Fat chance they had of that.

As soon as the party was over, she'd have a word with John, try to put things to him delicately because he probably wouldn't believe her, and then she would see what happened next.

In the back of her mind, she hoped that whatever games were going on between Donna and Sam were finished. Sam had clearly been unwilling to play the doting son and Donna throwing cow eyes at John every two seconds had been another dead giveaway. It was a strange predicament.

What had they on John?

An hour later, Claire stood examining her nails while she waited for Rachel to come downstairs. Her sister had been choosing an outfit for the past half hour, something Claire had found highly amusing as she'd done the same – usually they'd grab whatever clothes were close at hand, clean or dirty.

'Are you sure you're not coming over the road, Mum?' she asked.

'No,' said Gina. 'You know I can't be bothered with all that crap.'

'But wouldn't you like to be pampered, make the most of what you've got?'

Gina waved a hand from her head to her feet. 'I'll never be able to make anything out of this blob. It's too late.'

'But it's free,' Claire tried to entice her. 'When have you ever missed out on anything that's for nowt?'

Gina didn't bite. Instead, she lit a cigarette.

Rachel joined them a few minutes later. She wore a bright blue T-shirt over a black long-sleeved T-shirt, dark jeans and ballet pumps. Gina's eyes nearly popped out on stalks. She'd got them each a pair of those shoes for Christmas but she'd never seen them on either girl yet.

'At last.' Claire sighed. 'There'll be no time for us if we don't get over there soon.' Then, as they got to the door, she stopped. 'Wait. I'm going to put my pumps on too. They're better than wearing these manky trainers.'

Rachel tutted. 'Hurry up then.'

'Look who's talking. I waited ages for you to get ready.'

Fighting for Survival

Rachel sat in the chair that Claire had vacated. 'Are you coming across, Mum?'

Gina sighed. That was the trouble with having twins. Sometimes things had to be explained twice.

'No, I'm not,' she replied. 'There's bound to be something interesting on the telly.'

Rachel was old enough to catch the sarcasm. 'She's not the enemy.'

'I never said she was.'

'She's trying to bring everyone together for a laugh. She'll do your nails, if you want her to.'

Gina curled her fingers into a fist so that Rachel couldn't see what a state hers were in.

Claire appeared, saving Gina from snapping a reply. They grabbed the bottle of wine Gina had got for them and in a flurry of giggles, they were gone.

For a few seconds, she sat in silence until curiosity won her over and she ran upstairs. She stood in the bedroom window, hidden behind the grimy nets, watching as Rachel and Claire knocked on Caren's front door. She saw Caren open it and smile, taking the wine from Rachel as they went in.

Over the next quarter of an hour, she watched most of the neighbours troop into Caren's house: Julie and Sheila, Mrs Porter and Jenny Webster. Each time the door opened, she heard the music filter through until it closed again. Then Gina gasped, her mouth hanging open at who walked up the path next. That bloody bitch Ruth Millington had been invited.

Gina fumed in silence. This was Caren's doing. She knew it would wind her up to see Ruth having fun with the neighbours – her friends. It was as if Ruth belonged in Stanley Avenue.

Her mind made up in an instant, she reached for her mobile phone and rang her mum. If Ruth was good to go, then so was she.

The party was in full swing at Caren's house. Before John left them to it, he'd helped to rearrange the furniture in the living room. What could be pushed back was now around the walls. They'd also borrowed dining chairs from next door and brought in the chairs from the patio set.

Looking around, Caren realised that most people who had been invited were there. She picked up a bottle of nail polish from the coffee table. 'Ruby Red. Who'd like this one?'

'Me!' shouted Rachel, practically pushing Claire over to get up.

'Hey, look out.' Claire narrowly avoided spilling her drink. She watched as the liquid settled in the glass again.

631

'She's a live wire, that sister of yours,' Wendy remarked once Caren and Rachel had gone into the kitchen.

'No, she isn't.'

'Relax, honey, it was a compliment. She's nice – and so are you, when you want to be.'

Claire was amazed when some of the other women in the room nodded their heads in agreement.

'I thought everyone thought we were scum.' She became hostile as the other women began to laugh. 'That's not fucking nice.'

Wendy smiled and tapped Claire on the thigh. 'We're not laughing *at* you. We're laughing *with* you.' She waved a hand around the room. 'Everyone in here is known as scum. But we're not, are we ladies?'

'No, we're not,' said a woman with purple hair, a nose ring and a tattoo covering half of her arm.

'Absolutely no way,' said another, wearing a dress short enough for a five-year-old girl. Her hair had been bleached so many times it resembled white candy-floss, black roots peeping through. She wore red lipstick. Claire tried to remember her name but decided to call her freaky instead. She looked scary but at least she was smiling.

'Well, I think they're right,' one dared to say.

A murmur echoed around the room and a cushion was flung at the culprit.

'We are. But we make the most of what we have.'

'And we stick together.'

Claire grinned, finally realising the woman was joking. Then everyone laughed.

'You're new, Ruth.' Wendy turned to her next. 'Tell us how you see us all.'

Ruth coloured instantly as all eyes fell on her. If she had known she'd be the subject of interrogation, she wouldn't have come.

'Well, I, erm, think... I...' she stumbled over her words. 'I don't know you well enough to comment really.'

Wendy glared at her before folding her arms and pulling back her head. She laughed, as did the other women.

'I'm sorry, love, I'm pulling your leg. We only heard what her mother,' Wendy jerked a thumb in Claire's direction, 'had to say about you. And 'scum like us' should really find out the whole truth before taking up a stance.'

Ruth lowered her head. She knew they were referring to the fight she'd had with Gina. She still had the remains of the bruising.

'I wish Mum would change,' Claire admitted, helping herself to a few crisps. 'You might not think it but she can be really cool at times.'

'Yeah, right,' said Julie Elliot. 'And I've got myself a sugar daddy.'

'It's true. She really does care. She just doesn't know how to show it.'

'No, she's more interested in spreading rumours around than love. Isn't she, Ruth?'

'Maybe they aren't all rumours,' Claire said.

Ruth gulped. The spotlight was on her again. Why did they insist on doing that? There was no way she'd admit to sleeping with Pete, especially in front of one of his daughters.

'She shouldn't have had a go at you like that,' said Wendy, noticing her discomfort. 'And, I for one, am sorry that she did – *and* that I joined in.' She picked up a wine glass, a smidgen of liquid left in its bottom, and raised it in the air. 'So, how about we toast to new beginnings?'

Everyone raised their glasses. 'New beginnings.'

'New beginnings,' Ruth joined in cautiously, not exactly sure if she was being swept into some sort of gang ritual to be explained later.

In the kitchen, Rachel sat opposite Caren at the table while she painted her nails. She'd already had her hands massaged, something she'd never had done before yet had instantly loved.

Caren finished one hand and Rachel gasped. 'That colour. It makes my nails look really long.'

Caren smiled. 'You have a lot to learn, my dear. Do you ever wear make-up?'

'No, I'd end up looking like a dog's dinner if I put it on.'

'Have you never experimented?'

Rachel shook her head. 'We haven't got anything to experiment with, although we could lift some.'

Caren looked up momentarily.

'I mean we could buy some,' Rachel said quickly. 'I just don't know what to pick. There's so much of it.'

Caren stopped for a moment before painting Rachel's thumbnail. 'Would you like me to show you afterwards, give you a makeover?'

'Would you?' Rachel felt excitement fizz up in her stomach. 'I'd love to know how to do it all. Some of the girls at school look like shi – look awful but some of them look really nice.'

Caren smiled. 'Let's finish these nails and before I shout anyone else in, I'll do you a quick makeover. No doubt Claire will want me to do the same for her?'

'I suppose.'

'Right then, go and ask her. And see if anyone wants any more wine?' she shouted after her.

. . .

*D*espite her earlier freak out, Ruth was beginning to enjoy herself now. The women in the group were making a conscious effort to get to know her. They'd asked questions about her boys but not in a nasty way, not trying to blame her for it, but in a women-united kind of way. One of them, Denise, had even spoken of her miscarriage and her breakdown trying to cope with her four-year-old son afterwards.

Half of the women were either alone or in unhappy relationships. And every one of them knew horror tales of kids that had gone into Children's Services and why they'd had to. It was as if they were trying to let her know that what she'd done, what she thought was so wrong, was in actual fact right for her, as well as Mason and Jamie.

Tears pricked at her eyes as she dared to bring their faces to the front of her mind. Wendy noticed and came to comfort her. As Ruth cried, she held her.

'Pass me some tissues,' she pointed to a box. Claire passed a couple over to Wendy and she gave them to Ruth. 'Feel better now?' she asked after a minute or so.

Ruth nodded.

'Good. Let's change the conversation and get on with having a good girlie night in. Let's up the tempo of the music and have a sing song.'

'I have a karaoke machine,' said Claire.

'Oh, we don't need any machine to sing, now do we girls?' Wendy grabbed an empty lager bottle and held it an inch away from her mouth. 'This'll do. You can hear my voice over anything.'

*A*s the women in the living room danced and sang along to an ABBA CD, Caren was running around her kitchen. She'd moved the table to one side as best she could in the space provided and told Rachel and Claire to sit back to back. As she added foundation to one and then the other, she wouldn't let them look.

'No peeping,' Caren cried, catching Rachel trying to see her sister as Caren swept blusher over her cheeks. She handed her a small black case. 'Find me some brown mascara, would you?'

Rachel dived into the case. 'Why have you got so much?'

'I used to be a rep, selling it for parties, that kind of stuff. Most of it is old and out of date, but it's great for experimenting on. Help yourself to anything you like. It'll go back upstairs and be forgotten about after tonight.'

'Have you finished after you've put mascara on?' asked Claire, trying desperately not to laugh as Caren added colour to her eyelids.

'Nearly,' said Caren. 'The best bit is always your lippy.'

Fighting for Survival

'Hurry up,' urged Rachel. 'I'm dying to see what we look like.'

'I reckon we'll look like the ugly sisters from Cinderella.'

'Hey,' Caren said and tried to look hurt by Rachel's remark. 'I'll have you know that I'm good at creating something out of nothing. Anyway, I'm done now.' She stood between them. 'Seeing as you look identical, even with make-up on, you can look at each other. On the count of three. One. Two. Three!'

Rachel and Claire turned to face each other and gasped.

'Ohmigod,' said Claire. 'You look *amazing*.'

Rachel sat wide-eyed. She pointed at Claire, no words coming from her at all.

'Say something,' urged Caren.

'I feel so – so grown up,' said Rachel.

'Wow.' Claire clapped her hands in glee. 'I can't believe it's us. Why haven't we done this before?'

'Maybe because you're hell bent on causing trouble across on the square. There are other ways to get attention. I'm sure the boys will be queuing up soon.'

'Do you think?'

'I don't think so – I know so.'

Rachel turned to Caren and smiled shyly. 'Thanks,' she told her.

'My pleasure,' Caren smiled too, glancing from one to the other. 'You really do look great.'

'We'll have to practice,' said Claire.

'Just use the tricks I've shown you. Accentuate what you have and always make the most of everything. Then you can –'

'Bleeding hell, what have we here?'

Caren turned to see Barbara in the doorway. Behind her mother was Gina.

'Nan, Mum, look at us,' exclaimed Claire. 'Don't we look gorgeous? Caren has made us up. She's given us loads of freebies too.' She twirled round. 'What do you think?'

'It's such an improvement.' Barbara nodded. 'Although I've always thought my granddaughters were gorgeous.' She winked at Caren. 'I don't suppose you could do anything with me to hide these wrinkles. Or this one behind me?'

'Mum,' said Gina.

'Mum,' said Rachel, spying her too. 'You came across.'

'I had no choice,' Gina fibbed. 'Your nan dragged me across.'

Barbara tutted. 'I did no such thing. You wanted to –'

'Here, you lot,' Wendy shouted, appearing at the kitchen door. 'If you're not careful, we'll all be pissed in here before we've had our nails done. We've eaten all the crisps too.' She held out a bowl in *Oliver* style. 'Please, miss. Can we have some more?'

635

'Let me join you in the living room for a break first,' said Caren. 'Besides, I need to show off my work. Come on, girls. In you go.'

Gina lagged behind, standing in the living room doorway. Inside, the women were either talking or laughing. As everyone was having fun, the music had gone off momentarily. No one even noticed that she'd come in. She couldn't even take pride in the fact they were too busy admiring her girls.

'You look so grown up,' said Ruth, joining in freely now she felt more confident with the women. 'Your mum had better watch out. The boys will be going wild.'

'Their mother is right here,' snapped Gina. 'I hope you, of all people, weren't insinuating that my girls were going to get knocked up now that they look like tarts.'

'Give over, Gina,' said Barbara.

'Mum!' said Claire and Rachel in unison.

'I – I didn't mean that at all.' Ruth's temporary good mood crumbled in a second.

'Calm down, Gina,' said Wendy. 'The atmosphere was great until you showed up. So either go back out with the chip on your shoulder or leave it at the door and come and join in the fun.'

Gina knew when she was beat. Somehow, in a couple of hours, Ruth seemed to have won over all her friends.

Why hadn't she come across right away rather than take an age to get ready? By the time she'd finally left her house and called for her mother, nearly an hour had passed. It was only just after nine but the party had started long ago. The women were all enjoying themselves so she'd have to do the same, even though inside she hated the thought of having to mingle with Ruth. She hoped Ruth wouldn't speak to her or else she'd have to keep herself in check. She wasn't done with her yet.

She perched on the arm of the chair next to her mother. Caren passed her a glass of wine and she smiled politely. Might as well get the night over with as quickly and pleasantly as possible – drink would make her feel a little bit better about it.

'Let's crank the music up again,' said Wendy. 'Then, you, my lady,' she pointed to Caren, 'can do me next. But don't worry, I won't expect a pedicure as well. The smell would knock everyone out if I took off my shoes.'

*A*s Claire chose another CD to put on, Rachel heard her phone go off in her pocket. It was a text from Laila. It was short and sweet.

Gone with Stacey. So has Ashley. Hope 2 c u around. L&A

Rachel put her phone away and sat quietly as she digested the news. Fuck, they were in trouble. There was only Louise left now to go over to Stacey. Once Louise heard from Laila or Ashley, Rachel knew she'd join Stacey.

She couldn't blame her. If she was Louise, she would join Stacey too. It was too dangerous to be alone – or even around her and Claire now that Laila and Ashley had gone over as well.

She watched Claire as she began to dance, holding onto Nan's hands, swinging her around gently. Nan was laughing and Claire looked so happy. Maybe it would do them good to stay low for a while, watch out for each other.

But would Stacey then think she'd won, without even fighting for top position? And could Rachel back down? For Claire it would be easy. She'd do whatever she told her to do.

What should she do next? Should she fight for the leadership and risk the wrath of Mum and Dad? Or should she back down and let Stacey win? Rachel didn't know if she could let that happen. She was a Bradley through and through – and no one got the better of them now, did they?

22

*G*ina was awake early the next morning. She nudged Pete who was lying on his back and snoring like a train until he turned over in his sleep. She cuddled up into the duvet. The clock said half past five: she needed some sleep before she decided what to do. Today could be the start of a different life for her.

The nail party at Caren's last night had turned out to be a disaster for her, but she seemed to have been the only one who hadn't enjoyed herself. Rachel and Claire had stayed over there when she'd finally found time to excuse herself without fear of being accused of breaking the party up.

They'd come in an hour later, for once high on life and not alcohol, thankfully. Gina had been lying on the settee in a sulk and told them to shut up as they were still singing. They'd tried to pull her up to join in their duo but she'd refused.

Even when Pete returned home from the pub with fish and chips, she hadn't managed a smile. She knew the reason why. It was because she'd seen the inside of Caren's house.

Ever since she and John moved back, Gina had imagined how their home would be, but her imagination was way off with this one. It had felt like walking into a television advert for a furniture store. The house was spotless; it was modern and fresh and inviting... it was all she'd ever wanted.

And all her so-called friends had been there – another thing that had annoyed her. They'd all been quick to accept invitations when something was free, she'd realised as soon as she'd walked into the living room, yet they seemed like they were really enjoying themselves.

Gina couldn't remember a time when the women in the avenue had got together like that. Sometimes there would be an impromptu barbecue when the weather was promising, where everyone's families would join in for the night. But there had never been anything planned.

Worst of all, Rachel had told her they were going to make it a regular thing and go to a different house each month. And Claire had upset her by saying that it was obvious they couldn't come there though – their house was too old-fashioned and even with a good clean wouldn't be inviting enough. Gina had cried the minute they'd gone to bed.

The girls had startled her too – they'd looked so grown up after their makeover. The worry of one of them getting pregnant had popped into her head straight away. She didn't want either of them to end up in the same predicament as her, pregnant by the only fella she'd ever slept with. Gina wanted much more than that for her girls.

And now it was Monday morning, the first day of her challenge to spend a week with Josie at The Workshop. Josie had been true to her word and arranged five, two-hour sessions, one each morning this week, with different groups so that if she liked it, which she doubted already, she could decide which area she'd like to volunteer in.

She hadn't told anyone about her plans. Pete would go mad if he knew she was doing something for nothing. And even though, after joining in last night in a fashion, Rachel and Claire might think better of her for having a go at something, she wouldn't tell them either.

She wouldn't tell anyone until it was over. She would do the week to keep Josie happy. Then she'd either go back to being boring Gina or show an interest in something. She would have to wait and see how she got on.

This morning she'd be helping out with the mother and toddlers group. Tomorrow was the self-assertiveness group. Wednesday and Friday mornings would be spent at the community house with the teenagers and Thursday was pensioners' coffee morning.

Gina glanced at the clock again: ten minutes to six. She decided to get up and make a cup of tea. It was far more productive than lying in bed trying to get back to sleep. Besides, she needed to find some clean clothes if she was going to go out of the house. Leggings, what-used-to-be-white T-shirts and baggy cardigans weren't called for today.

That was if she decided to go at all. She had more than three hours to change her mind yet.

. . .

'Did you leave a window open?' Caren asked John when they got home that evening. She frowned; she could have sworn she heard music coming from their house. But that was impossible.

'I don't think so.' John sighed. 'Neither did I kick the wheelie bin over. There's rubbish strewn everywhere. Bloody kids.' He made his way up the path and stopped dead in his tracks.

'What's wrong?' Caren felt the hairs on her neck rising.

'Some fucker's broken in.' John turned to her. 'The back door's been forced open.'

Caren followed him into the kitchen. Breakfast cereal scrunched underneath their feet. A bottle of milk had been tipped over the kitchen table, left dripping onto the seat covers. Every drawer had been pulled out and smashed up, the contents thrown to the floor.

'Christ, what a mess,' said John.

Caren's hand covered her mouth. A mess was an understatement. It was a pure act of vandalism. And after they'd worked so hard to make it into something decent.

'Don't touch anything. I'll check upstairs and then I'll ring the police.'

Being careful where she stood, Caren went through into the hallway, trying to ignore the lines of aerosol paint stretching from one end to the other. Framed pictures and the hall mirror had been thrown to the floor and smashed. Something, she dreaded to think what, had been crushed into the carpet.

'They've been in every room,' John told her when he joined her a few minutes later. 'It's as if we've been hit by a tornado. The portable TV's gone; so has my laptop. The rest is mess to clean up.'

Caren stepped into the living room, tears pouring down her face. There were spaces where their television and stereo should have been. Both settees had been slashed, the stuffing pulled out in lumps and strewn around. Paint had been thrown over the fireplace and over the carpet. The aerosol can had been used in here too, around the middle of all the walls and the door.

Caren's face crumpled as John pulled her into his arms.

'Who would do something like this?' she asked him.

'I don't know. Let's hope the police get some clues.'

When the police arrived, PC Mark White crunched through the kitchen. He pointed to the open door. 'Any windows broken?'

'No, just the door that's been forced. We'd been out for something to eat – two hours at the most – and we get back to... to this.'

'Have they taken much?' PC Sandra Morton asked, getting out her notebook.

John raised his hands in exaggeration. 'The usual stuff – we'll have to make a list. If I could get my hands on them, I'd break them too.'

'It's easy to put it down to the kids on this estate. There's not much for them to do so they get their kicks out of petty crime and vandalism. But in my experience, they usually take smaller items, things they can offload quickly to make a bit of money. Other than that, on an avenue like this, with no real easy access out if you come home early, I'd say you were targeted.'

'Targeted?' Caren cried. 'No one would do this to us.'

'Sadly most people have enemies, Mrs Williams.'

Caren noted it was said kindly, not spitefully. As the police officer checked the door in the kitchen, she hovered in the doorway, not wanting to enter yet not wanting to go back into the living room. None of it felt like her home anymore; she felt violated.

Suddenly she retched. Covering her mouth with her hand, she managed to get to the kitchen sink where she threw up.

Afterwards, she steadied herself on the worktop as she tried to gain her composure. She wondered about the neighbours but knew they probably wouldn't have heard a thing. They were both in their eighties.

She questioned if it was something else the thieves would have known before they'd broken in. Then she wondered about the women who had been at the nail party on Sunday – no, it couldn't have been any of them, surely? But could she rule that out altogether?

'I suppose it could be kids, getting their kicks out of breaking and entering.' PC Morton held up the plug that had been cut from the wire to the microwave. 'I could understand more if they'd taken things to sell on but blatant vandalism? Nothing like this ever makes sense. Do you have a spare key that you give to anyone?'

'No.' Caren tried to focus on anything in her kitchen that hadn't been ruined. She glanced around: there was nothing. Someone was hell-bent on making them suffer. So far, all she could see was it costing them money, but at least they were insured. Yet it didn't take away the fact that someone had been into their home when they weren't there.

PC White came back into the room. 'I'll arrange to get what I can finger-printed and we'll go from there. If you can provide your prints, we can eliminate you and then see if there are any different ones that might match up on our database.'

'Do you think you'll find anything?'

'It's possible,' he said. 'But from what I've seen so far, I very much doubt it. It's more likely that you're not going to find out who did this.'

. . .

$\mathcal{O}$nce the police left, Caren and John tried to get their house back into some sort of order.

It took Caren a long time to settle down when they finally went to bed. John spooned his body around her. Every window and door had been shut and checked, yet still she lay staring ahead into the darkness, listening to the sound of the house settling.

Damn it – she'd just started to get used to being back on the Mitchell Estate and now this had to happen. Her imagination working overtime as she heard a clank of a radiator, Caren sat up in bed. But John pulled her down again.

'Relax,' he said, his voice husky with sleep. 'You're safe now.'

'There's no way I'm leaving the house until you've changed the locks.'

'Try to sleep.' John kissed the back of her hair. 'You'll feel better about it tomorrow.'

'Are you out of your mind? How can I ever forget what's happened today?'

John pulled her nearer into him. 'The only way I can make you feel safe is to hold you. I don't know what else to do.'

Caren squeezed his hand. Being so wrapped up in herself, she hadn't given a thought to John and how he would be feeling.

'I'm sorry,' she whispered into the silence, even though she hadn't got anything to feel sorry about.

She lay awake for ages wondering who would do such a thing.

$\mathcal{O}$n Thursday morning, Gina made her way to The Workshop. It was her fourth session and the one she was looking forward to the most. Monday had gone okay as she'd helped out with the mother and toddler group. She'd panicked at first, thinking she'd be a glorified babysitter while the mums went off to attend classes. But the mothers and the toddlers stayed together, interacting with each other. It hadn't taken long to get into the swing of things, even though most of the time she'd been making tea for the women.

On Tuesday, she'd helped out at the self-assertiveness class. That had been tougher than she'd imagined. After listening to a young woman from Adam Street talking about the abuse she'd suffered at the hands of her partner, Gina found herself in tears and thanking her lucky stars that even though her family were a little wayward at times, they all looked out for one another.

Josie had been true to her word and stuck by her side. Gina had thought she'd be an irritant but found, to her surprise, that she'd had a laugh with her. On mutual territory, they even shared a smile or two.

This morning she was helping out at the pensioners' coffee morning in one of the back rooms. By chance, she was topping up the tea urns when she heard a snippet of conversation from outside in the corridor.

'Yeah, we trashed it good and proper,' the voice said. 'It was a total wreck when we'd finished.'

'Did you come away with anything to sell on?'

Gina peeped around the doorframe. She thought she recognised the voice. Yes, she was right. It was Sam Harvey.

'A few bits,' he continued. 'I sold them on to Lenny. The place was rich-looking. She was a stuck-up cow considering she lived in Stanley Avenue. She got what she deserved.'

Stanley Avenue? Gina wondered if they were talking about Caren and John. Pete had told her their place had been trashed on Monday evening.

'I bet Pete won't be too pleased.'

Pete? Gina held perfectly still. *Pete who?*

'I'm not walking away if I can make a quick buck.'

'But he paid you, didn't he?'

'Yeah, fifty quid but only to pretend I was the bloke's son. There was stuff there for the taking too. I wasn't going to leave it. Plus if I've been lax with my prints, I've already been there so they'll rule me out.'

Gina stayed quiet, hoping to hear more but when she peeped around the frame again, Sam and his mate were walking away.

She frowned, trying to make sense of their words. Why would Pete set someone like Sam up to visit Caren and John? It must be Caren's place as it was the only one she'd heard of lately that had been done over in the avenue. Apparently, it had been trashed beyond recognition. And although they didn't particularly get on, she didn't deserve that.

The urns topped up, Gina went back to the group, wondering what on earth was going on.

On Saturday, Rachel received a text message from Louise. She and Claire were in their bedroom. They'd been in there every evening since last weekend and hadn't wanted to go out that afternoon either, feeling safe but putting off the inevitable. They would have to face Stacey and the gang soon.

'Who's that?' asked Claire nervously, already dreading her sister's reply.

'Louise.'

'Oh.'

'She wants to meet us on the square in half an hour.'

'But we'll get lynched if we go out.'

'Not necessarily. Louise is still on our side, remember. Maybe some of the others have swapped back again. We might not be on our own.'

'I doubt that very much.'

'Well, we'll soon find out.'

Outside Shop&Save half an hour later, Claire glanced up and down Davy Road but there was no sign of Louise.

'What time did she say she'd be here?' she asked Rachel.

'Ten minutes ago. We'll give her ten more.'

'Maybe we should go now. We did promise not to fight.'

'Yes, I know, but it's only an excuse, isn't it?'

'What do you mean by that?'

'We have to fight, to survive. Stacey will kill us if we don't.'

'She won't *kill* us.'

'Maybe she'll get the message that we're not interested in gangs anymore.'

'It doesn't ring true, though. Think about it. You were hell-bent on being the leader of the Mitchell Mob when Stacey came out of juvie. We've both been fighting all the girls who've swapped sides and then… then we stay in for a week. It doesn't make sense. It seems like we're scared of her.'

'*You* are scared of her.'

'Of course I am.' Claire shook her head. 'But I'm not frightened by any of the others. I think we should finish off what we started or take a beating from Stacey and get on with it. We don't have to hang around with any of them afterwards but at least we'd have street cred.'

Rachel looked away then, pretending to look out for Louise. Claire was right, and it was killing her to know that Stacey thought they'd chickened out. And she knew Stacey wouldn't settle until she'd knocked them both down and taken back her crown.

Rachel sighed and lit up a cigarette that she'd lifted from Mum earlier. It looked wrong with painted nails. Since the nail party, she and Claire had spent a couple of hours over at Caren's house learning more make-up tricks.

Caren had shaped their eyebrows and showed them how to style their hair a bit softer. The result had made them both feel feminine. It'd had a soothing effect on them, far more than any lecture from their mum and dad would have done.

Finally, Louise appeared in the distance a few minutes later. But instead of joining them, she shouted to catch their attention. She beckoned to them with a wave and sat down on a wall to wait for them.

Rachel sighed. 'She keeps us waiting for near on twenty minutes and then she wants us to go over to her?'

Claire put her arm through Rachel's as they walked towards her. 'Chill out,

Rach. At least she wants to know us.'

'What took you so long?' Rachel couldn't help but say when they reached her.

Stacey stepped out from behind the wall, the rest of the girls too.

'What's going on?' asked Claire. Pulling out her arm from Rachel's, she balled both hands into fists in readiness.

'She's done what I asked her to.' Stacey narrowed her eyes. 'What the fuck have you done to yourselves?'

'We thought we'd make an effort for once,' said Rachel. 'I see you couldn't be bothered.'

Stacey laughed. 'You look like a pair of hookers.' She pointed at Rachel's hands. 'You're wearing nail varnish.'

'What's wrong with making the best of what you've got?' Claire spoke out.

Stacey laughed again. 'No one could make anything out of you two – you're Bradley scum, remember?'

'It's better than being Hunter scum,' taunted Rachel.

Stacey took a step nearer to her. 'Say that again and you're dead.'

'What, the part about you being scum? Or the part about you being Hunter scum? It's the same thing either way.'

'Rachel,' Claire warned.

As Rachel turned to address her sister, Stacey punched her in the face. Rachel did her best to fight her off when she came at her again but she was too strong. Claire lunged at them, grabbing Stacey by the hair. While the rest of the girls watched, she managed to pull them apart.

'Stop it,' she cried. 'We don't want to fight anymore.'

'Who cares what you want.' Stacey pulled out a knife.

Three of the girls behind her stepped back, worried looks flitting between them.

'You didn't say anything about a knife,' said Laila, standing her ground.

'Shut the fuck up,' said Stacey.

'Put it away,' said Rachel. 'It's not part of what we are.'

Stacey waved the knife about in front of her. 'You have a new look. Well, this is the new me. It's fair now, don't you think? Two against two. You and Claire.' She stabbed at the air in front of her again. 'Me and my knife.'

'Back off, Stacey,' Ashley spoke out.

Before anyone could dissuade her, Stacey lunged forward. She slashed the arm of Rachel's jacket.

'Watch it.' Rachel looked down at the damage. But not before she'd seen the glint in Stacey's eyes. It was the look of someone who wasn't in control.

Claire nudged Rachel's arm. They turned and ran.

23

*C*aren was in the kitchen wading through a pile of ironing. When the house had been trashed, some of their clothes had been taken from the wardrobe and thrown out of the back window, landing in the garden. Washing them again had meant a bigger pile than normal.

She heard a knock at the door and opened it to find Gina. 'You're the last person I expected to see,' she spoke first.

Gina looked embarrassed but stood her ground. 'I wanted to come across, see how you were doing after the break-in and –'

'You've come to gloat?' Caren folded her arms.

'No, I wanted to see if there was anything I could do to help. I heard it was a right mess.'

Caren baulked. '*You* want to help *me*?'

Gina nodded. Since Thursday, she hadn't been able to get Sam Harvey's conversation out of her mind. She needed to know why Pete had given him fifty pounds to say he was John's son. By coming across and chatting to Caren, she might glean a little more information. Then she'd decide whether to tell her or not. This might be something she wanted to keep from her.

Caren smiled faintly. 'You could come in rather than stand on my doorstep, I suppose.'

Gina nodded. 'Yeah, ta.'

. . .

Fighting for Survival

Claire ran across Davy Avenue and into Winston Green. Behind her, she could hear Rachel close on her heel. She glanced behind them, only to see Stacey and the others on their tail.

'Come on, Rach,' she urged. 'They're catching us.'

'Wait for me, Claire. I'm going as fast as I can.'

'No way.' Claire jumped down two steps, levelled out and then three steps onto the green in between the houses. She could hear Stacey screaming out obscenities as she tried to catch ground. They legged it over the grass, across Graham Street and back into Stanley Avenue.

Rachel yelped. She'd caught her shin on the bumper of a parked car as she ran past it.

Claire turned back to help, saw she was on her feet and continued to run. When she reached Stanley Avenue, she had never been so pleased to see her house up ahead. As Rachel caught up with her, they slowed their pace. Stacey stopped at the top of the avenue. There were only three girls with her now.

'I'm going to kill you, Rachel Bradley,' Stacey yelled. 'I'm going to rip your fucking heart out.'

'Yeah right! When you're strong enough!' Rachel bent over and leaned on a wall as she caught her breath for a moment. When she looked again, Stacey was running at them. She turned quickly and ran, bumping into Ruth up ahead in her haste.

'Sorry,' she said, but didn't stop.

Further in front, Claire had made it and was halfway up the path to the house. But Stacey had caught up quicker than they'd anticipated. As Rachel got to the gate, Stacey pulled her back by the hood of her jacket.

'Claire!' Rachel held out her hand to her sister in front.

Claire saw the knife still in Stacey's hand and screamed. 'Leave her alone!'

Stacey plunged the knife into Rachel's back.

Although Claire could hear herself screaming, time seemed to stand still. She watched helplessly as Stacey thrust the blade into Rachel's back again and again.

Rachel dropped to her knees on the path.

'Leave her alone!' Claire jumped on Stacey but she lashed out with a fist. Losing her footing, she fell down the path, landing with a thump against the gate.

Stacey glowered at her. 'You'll be nothing without her,' she said. Then she turned Rachel to face her and plunged the knife into her chest.

. . .

*R*uth saw the girl grab hold of Rachel and pull her back by her hood. Bloody typical, she thought: the Bradley twins were up to no good again. She continued on her way until she heard Claire scream. The hairs on the back of her neck stood up when she saw the girl had a knife. Without a thought for her own safety, she ran over.

'Stop her!' Claire screamed to Ruth.

Stacey stepped away, for a moment standing with a bewildered look on her face. Then she threw down the knife, pushed past Ruth and ran onto the street.

Ruth watched her go, for a moment wondering if she was dreaming. But Claire's screams were real. There was blood all over her hands. Hearing Rachel gasping for breath, she knelt beside her on the damp path.

Rachel's head lolled to one side.

'Rachel,' sobbed Claire. 'Oh, God, she's going to die, isn't she?'

Ruth didn't want to think about that. 'Go and get your mum.' As Claire ran into the house, she took off her coat and, ignoring the cold weather, removed her jumper. She pressed it to Rachel's chest.

Rachel groaned, causing Ruth to burst into tears. She could see whatever she did would be hopeless. Blood was covering Rachel at an alarming rate. The knife must have cut through a major artery.

Claire came running out of the house moments later. 'There's no one in.' She got out her mobile. 'Do something. Do something!'

Ruth knew there wasn't time for an ambulance.

'Go and get Caren,' she said. When Claire didn't move, she shouted. 'Claire, fetch Caren. Now!'

*G*ina sat down at the table. Apart from the faint smell of paint in the air, the room was fairly void of any reference to the burglary. The conversation she'd overheard with Sam Harvey spoke of all the rooms being trashed. They must have been busy to get it painted so quickly.

'Did they make a lot of mess?' Gina wanted to know.

'Did they ever! They went into every room. Paint tipped over the rug, aerosol paint sprayed everywhere, food chucked out of the fridge. They even emptied our wardrobes and threw the clothes out of the bloody window. It was pure vandalism. It's going to take forever to put right. I cried for –'

'Caren.' Claire burst into the kitchen through the back door. 'You have to come – Mum!'

'Claire? What's going on? You look like you've seen a ghost.'

Claire pointed to the door. 'Rachel – she's been stabbed. Outside.'

They all ran out of the kitchen and across the road. Gina saw three girls outside her gate. As she got nearer, she spotted Ruth, Rachel's legs to her side. Nearer still, she saw her cradling Rachel in her arms.

'Rachel.' Gina pushed Ruth out of the way and took her place. Rachel's arm flopped around as she pressed her body to her chest. 'Stay with me, Rachel. Stay with me.' She looked back to the street. 'Where's the ambulance?' she screamed.' Where's the fucking ambulance?'

'I rang for it as soon as I saw what happened,' Ashley told her, openly crying. 'I saw what happened. She isn't going to die, is she?'

Gina ignored her, turning on Ruth who sat on her knees beside her. 'You had no right to touch her.'

Ruth shivered. She stared down at her hands, her body, her jeans. They were covered in Rachel's blood.

Caren tried to take control. 'Claire, where's your dad?' She turned to John who had followed them across. 'John, go and look.'

'He's not in the house,' Claire sobbed. 'Mum, do something.'

'I don't know what to do,' Gina cried.

'Mum,' Rachel spluttered, her voice barely audible.

Gina stroked her hair. 'I'm here for you, baby,' she said. 'I'm here for you. You're safe now.'

Caren sat down beside Rachel. She took off her jumper and gave it to Gina. Gina removed Ruth's top, soaked through to dripping, and pressed that one to Rachel's chest.

Rachel groaned.

'I'm sorry,' Gina told her over and over. 'I'm sorry.'

A scarlet bubble appeared at the corner of Rachel's mouth.

'The ambulance is on its way,' Gina told her. 'You hang on in there.'

Blood began to trickle from her mouth. Rachel coughed and more appeared. She coughed again.

'Mum,' screamed Claire. 'Do something. She's dying!'

'No, she's not.' Gina stroked her daughter's forehead. 'Now you listen to me, Rachel Bradley. We're made of strong stuff. You're not going to die, do you hear? Don't you fucking dare.'

But Rachel didn't hear anything. She didn't see anything either. Life slipped away from her. Her arm flopped to the floor.

'No!' cried Gina. 'No.' Tears poured down her face as she held Rachel to her.

'Rachel?' Claire dropped to her knees next to them.

Caren's hand covered her mouth; her blood ran cold. She looked back to see

John standing by the side of the three girls who had come into the garden. Ruth sat in shock a few feet away. By now, a few neighbours had come out too.

Gina looked at Ruth with so much hate. 'You let her die, you bitch,' she yelled. 'Not content to steal my husband, you let my daughter die.'

'But I –' Ruth tried to explain.

'I hate you. This is your fault. You let her die.'

Claire grabbed her sister's hand. 'Rachel, wake up.'

Caren gently pulled Claire away and hugged her, hoping to comfort her, knowing that Gina needed to hold Rachel for the moment.

And then, amidst the chaos and the sound of an ambulance in the distance, silence fell on Stanley Avenue. Gina rocked Rachel in her arms. Caren hugged Claire. Ruth sat on the garden, holding her hands in the air, staring at the blood. John stood in shock, three teenage girls crying by his side.

'She's not dead,' Claire sobbed. 'She can't be. I was talking to her just... She can't be dead.'

Caren let her ramble on. She wondered how Claire was going to fare without her twin. Gina was going to have a tough time as her mother, but Claire was the other half of Rachel.

'Where will your dad be?' she asked.

'I don't know.' Claire stared at Rachel, fresh tears falling fast. 'She's dead, isn't she?'

'Let's wait until the paramedics look at her,' Caren replied. 'Look, they're here now.'

'I'm going to try Dad's phone again.'

'He's probably shagging his latest conquest somewhere,' Gina said, never taking her eyes from Rachel, wiping the hair from her forehead.

The ambulance drew up, the sirens dropping off as it parked up. 'Excuse me, love,' said the paramedic as he sat down next to Rachel.

'There's no point,' Gina said. 'She's dead.' She slapped his hand as he reached to check Rachel's pulse. 'Don't you fucking touch her.'

'Mum, let him help.' Claire dropped to her knees beside them. 'He needs to look.'

Gina looked at Claire and gasped. Then she held out her hand. 'Rachel,' she smiled.

'No, I'm Claire!' She moved away, horrified.

The paramedics took over and Gina looked around her. This was a dream. She was going to wake up in a moment. There was Claire sitting beside her and there was Rachel, lying... lying... Gina stared at Rachel before turning to Claire. Oh, there she was.

'Rachel,' she whispered.

'It's me, Mum.' Claire pointed at the lifeless body of her sister, paramedics all over her. 'That's Rachel.'

Gina frowned. She looked at Rachel, and then back at Claire. 'Rachel,' she whispered. 'Rachel.'

'No.' Claire shook her head vehemently and then she ran.

'Claire!' As she ran past, Caren grabbed for her arm but Claire thumped out at her.

'Leave me alone,' she cried. 'I don't want to be here.'

Once the police arrived, everyone was moved from the garden as a murder investigation got underway. Barbara had been asleep until she'd heard the sirens but she rushed across. She stayed surprisingly calm after she'd learned that her granddaughter had been murdered, realising that as a mother, Gina needed her help. She needed her strength.

The police said it would be some time before they would be let back into their property so she took them all across to her house.

Although John had gone home, Caren had stayed with Gina, not really wanting to be there but feeling the need too. She was worried about Claire. She'd been gone a couple of hours now.

She was worried about Ruth too. Ruth had gone into a stupor since Rachel's death. After the police had arrived and taken their details, Caren had walked her home. All she'd repeated was 'I couldn't save her'.

And no matter how many times, she'd reiterated that it wasn't her fault, Ruth had continued, changing to 'I should have saved her'.

Caren had cried with her as she'd made cups of tea. Once she thought Ruth was going to bed, she'd gone back to Barbara's. It had seemed eerie seeing the white tent and the hustle and bustle outside Gina's house. There was a small crowd, several vehicles and lots of police around.

She'd been told someone would need to question her soon. She wished there was more that she could tell them. What a dreadful chain of events. It was such a young age to die.

She'd been at Barbara's house for no more than five minutes when Pete burst into the kitchen. He rushed over to Gina.

'They just told me. She... is she... no... she can't –'

'Where were you, you bastard?' Gina's legs gave way as she slumped into his arms. 'I called you and called you and...'

'I'm sorry,' he sobbed, holding on to her tightly. 'I didn't know what had happened. I'm sorry.'

'Mr Bradley,' said PC Andy Baxter. 'If I could–'

'That bitch Stacey Hunter stabbed her,' said Gina, the words she spoke making her cry again. 'She was home, Pete. She was running up the path but she pulled her back by her hood.'

'But she's just a kid. They're both kids.'

'Kids have weapons too, unfortunately,' said Andy.

'Rachel didn't have a knife, did she?'

Gina gasped. 'Did she? Did she have a knife?'

'I'm not sure,' said Andy. 'We'll know more later.'

Pete wiped at his eyes. 'Did you see what happened?'

'No, I wasn't there.'

Pete looked at Caren who was standing in the doorway. 'Were you there?'

'No, Gina was over at mine.' When Pete frowned, she explained. 'Gina offered to help me with the mess we'd been left in because of the break-in. I suppose when Claire didn't find anyone here, she ran across to get me.'

'You didn't hear anything before that?'

'Sorry, no.'

'No one heard them fighting?'

'She did – that fucking Ruth Millington,' Gina cried out. 'It's all her fault. She was the first person to get to Rachel. She should have stopped the bleeding.'

'There was too much,' said Caren.

'Blood everywhere.' Barbara shook her head from side to side before breaking down.

Gina glared at Pete. 'You should have been here.'

Pete wiped his eye with the back of his hand. 'I'm sorry, Gina.'

'She was too badly injured to survive.' Andy rested a hand on Pete's shoulder. 'I'll leave you for a moment and then I'll need to take a statement from you.'

Noticing how sad he looked, Caren followed him into the kitchen. She closed the living room door and sat down at the table.

'Are you okay?' she asked him. 'I didn't think this sort of thing would upset you.'

Andy sat down next to her. 'Every case is different but it's terrible if you know someone personally. I knew all the Bradleys.' He laughed half-heartedly. 'Who doesn't know the Bradleys? But Rachel was a child, just sixteen.'

'It's Claire I'm worried about,' said Caren. 'She's going to be so lost without her sister.'

Andy nodded. 'This isn't going to be an easy case. The witnesses are all teenagers. They'll be frightened of Stacey Hunter and her family.'

'Claire saw it all, though.'

'Yes, we'll gather what forensic evidence we can from Rachel's body, as well as the knife that Stacey dropped, and the garden area.'

Fighting for Survival

'It's a terrible thing to happen. It's going to hit the family hard.'

'It's going to hit the estate too. Another murder to bring us down; to remind people how shit it is on the Mitchell Estate.'

'It isn't that bad,' said Caren.

Andy raised his eyebrows questioningly.

'It isn't.' Caren shook her head. 'I remember when I had to move back, I cursed the day I set foot in Stanley Avenue. But slowly the people around here, they got under my skin. They made me into a better person – and I wanted to help them.'

Andy listened as Caren continued.

'Rachel and Claire were trouble but did anyone give them a chance because of who they were? They always had the Bradley reputation to live up to. Maybe I could have won them over. Maybe I couldn't. Or maybe it was them that won me over, I don't know. But I changed – I accepted what I have. And...' Caren's voice held a shake, 'until today I thought that no one could take that away from me.'

From behind them came a voice.

'Caren?'

Caren looked up to see Claire. She tried desperately to hide her shock as she saw the innocent face staring back at her. It was literally like seeing a ghost of Rachel, a terrible reminder of what had happened.

'I don't know what to do,' Claire said, her tears falling again. 'I don't know –'

The living room door opened.

Claire ran into her Dad's embrace. 'She's dead, Dad,' she cried. 'What am I going to do?'

'I don't know,' said Pete as he hugged her close. 'I don't know.'

Two doors away, Ruth sat on her sofa, one hand wrapped around the near-empty bottle of vodka, the other turning a craft knife over and over.

She staggered into the hall, knocking into the doorframe as she did. She cursed loudly, rubbing at her arm, but she managed to negotiate the stairs, even if she did have to crawl up the last two steps.

She threw herself face down on her bed. The room had long ago started to spin. But when she closed her eyes all she could see was blood. Rachel's blood; lots of it. Thick, dark blood, the worst kind.

She pecked at the scar on her arm. She needed to see her own blood instead, to take the pain away.

'Argh,' Ruth screamed. 'It's so unfair.' She plunged the craft knife into the open wound, tearing at her skin.

Then just as suddenly, she stopped.

It had made her realise how much pain Rachel must have been in when the blade of the knife went into and through her vital organs.

Ruth threw the craft knife down to the floor. 'I should have saved her,' she cried. 'I should have saved her.'

24

Gina spent the next few days in a haze. Half of Rachel's school turned out to see where she had died, along with lots of local people. Bunches of flowers lay in front of the garden wall, stretching from their gate and halfway to next door's driveway.

Teddy bears, small and large had been left, a T-shirt with dozens of messages written on it in blue biro. An odd photograph; an odd candle. Gina had been across to look at them a few times, finding comfort in some of the words of tribute. Other times, she couldn't bear to look at them.

Everyone was saying what a lovely girl Rachel had been – well liked and great fun. What a bunch of liars, Gina had wanted to shout. It was always the same. Someone taken down in their prime and no one having a bad word to say about them. Well, not in public anyway – behind closed doors, she knew what everyone would be saying, what they were thinking.

They hadn't been allowed home yet. They'd been over to get a few belongings but until the forensics had finished their job, they'd had to stay at her mum's house.

From the window of the spare room where she and Pete were sleeping, Gina gazed down onto the avenue, watching two council workers picking litter up from the pavement. One of them stooped to read a card. He leaned on his brush and then beckoned his colleague over. They read the words together, and then with a shake of their heads, continued on their way.

Gina wiped away tears pouring down her face. Once Rachel's body was released to the coroner, they were planning on giving her a great send off. She'd asked Claire what she thought Rachel would like to wear. Each of them had also chosen something to put into the coffin.

Claire wanted to give Rachel her favourite baseball cap but knew that Rachel would prefer her hair to be spiked up and styled. She'd also asked Caren if she could do her make-up. Caren had looked relieved when Gina stepped in before she'd had time to answer and said that it would be the undertaker's job.

Pete had chosen a family photograph. It had been taken a couple of years ago when they'd all gone to Dorset for a week's holiday.

Gina was going to give her the teddy bear with 'I love Mum' embroidered on its T-shirt that Rachel had won at the fair when she was seven. It was dirty and grubby now and it had an ear missing where Danny had pulled at it. She knew that Rachel would be comforted to have that near to her. And it had to go with her – she couldn't bear to look at it now that Rachel had gone.

Behind her, there was a knock at the door. Pete opened it and came into the room with two mugs.

'I thought you might like a cuppa,' he said, placing them down on the bedside cabinet. He perched on the end of the bed, looking everywhere but at Gina. They sat in silence for a moment. It had been ten days since Rachel had been murdered, yet the question of Pete's whereabouts had remained unanswered long after Gina had held her while her life slipped away. She was going to have to force it out of him.

'Where were you?' she asked outright.

'I was down the pub.'

'No, you weren't. Mum phoned The Butcher's Arms and they hadn't seen you since the day before.'

'I – Christ, I can't remember now. Besides, it doesn't really matter in the great scheme of things. We've far more important things to think about.'

'Like who to invite to the funeral? Michelle? And Donna? And Tracy?' As she turned to face him, Gina couldn't even take pleasure in the look of bewilderment that flashed across Pete's face. Michelle Winters had been the first affair she'd found out about. Donna Adams had been his second or was it his third? Tracy Tanner, however, had been a guess because of her reputation. But from the look of guilt that flashed across his face, she had hit the jackpot.

'You selfish, two-timing piece of shit!' she cried.

'I'm sorry,' he said, 'it was just a fling.'

'While your daughter was dying, you were fucking Tracy Tanner.' Gina leaned forward and thumped his chest. 'Have you any idea how I felt? I knew what was going on when your phone was switched off. Everyone else knew what

Fighting for Survival

was going on when I couldn't get hold of you. Where were you when I needed you?'

'It didn't mean anything.'

'So why did you do it?'

Pete paused and sighed. 'Because I could, okay? She was there – you weren't and we just –'

'Don't you dare shift the blame to me. You have the nerve to screw around and you think it's okay to say it's *my* fault?'

'You're right.' Pete looked shamefaced. 'I'm stupid and thoughtless and should have known better by now.'

'No, *I'm* stupid and thoughtless and should have known better by now. I should have kicked you out after I found out about the last tart.'

'We'll sort it, love.' Pete stretched across the bed for her hand. Gina snapped it away and glared at him.

'Don't 'love' me. We *will* sort it. Once the funeral is over, there are going to be changes around here, whether you agree with them or not.'

Caren left her house to walk the few metres down to see Ruth. As she drew level with Barbara's house, she stole a look at the windows, wondering how Gina was coping with things. She hadn't seen her out and about for a couple of days.

She knocked on Ruth's front door but there was no answer. She hadn't seen her for a couple of days either – usually by now, she'd have gone past her window at least once – and she hadn't answered her phone today. She'd tried several times without any luck.

She knocked again: still no answer. She peered through the living room window but couldn't see anyone. Not one for giving in, she tried around the back, pummelling on the door.

'Ruth? It's me, Caren.'

'In here.'

Caren opened the door to find Ruth sitting at the kitchen table. Her head lay on the surface, one hand clasped around an empty glass. There was a half empty bottle of vodka beside her.

'What time did you start drinking this morning? Or haven't you stopped from last night?'

Ruth's head popped up a second. 'I can't remember,' she slurred.

Caren sighed and switched on the kettle. 'I'll make coffee – black. Lots of it for you, my lady.'

'Don't want any coffee.'

'Tough luck. And you're having no more of that, either.' Caren took the bottle of vodka and put it away in a cupboard.

'Hey, you can't do that,' Ruth griped. Wincing, she held on to her head. 'You can't tell me what to do.'

'And I can't sit around while you drink yourself to death either. Honestly, you have to take –'

At the mention of death, Ruth's face crumpled.

'I'm sorry. It was only a slip of the tongue.'

'It was my fault she died,' sobbed Ruth.

'No, it wasn't.'

'I let her die.'

'No, you didn't.'

'But if I had got to her sooner,' she sat up, 'she might not have lost as much blood and –'

'Bloody hell, Ruth, how long are you going to sit here wallowing in self-pity?' Caren spoke firmly. 'Rachel died. It wasn't your fault – get used to it.'

'But –'

'You can't keep blaming yourself for her death. Neither can you keep feeling sorry for yourself. You haven't lost Rachel. Gina has.'

'Yes, but –'

'Ruth, snap out of it.'

Ruth sniffed. Tears intermingled with snot and she wiped it all away with the back of her hand.

Caren pulled a tissue from her pocket and gave it to her. Secretly, she wanted to slap her. She felt her patience slipping away again. It was hard to talk to Ruth when she was drunk.

'I suggest you sober up and get a grip.'

'I'm not drunk.' Ruth slurred even more. 'Where's my vodka?'

Caren made her strong black coffee and plonked it in front of her nose. 'Drink this and get yourself washed and changed. You smell, Ruth. When was the last time you had a shower?'

'I don't know.'

'I think you should –'

'Stop telling me what to do,' Ruth shouted.

Caren held up her hands in surrender. 'Have it your way,' she said. 'Drink yourself stupid. But don't expect me to come round and check on you later. I have my own life to live.'

'Piss off... and leave me alone.'

Fighting for Survival

Caren frowned but she did exactly that.

Claire lay on her side, curled up on the camp bed set up in her nan's bedroom for her. She hadn't slept much since Rachel had died. It still didn't seem real that she'd gone. And at the hands of Stacey Hunter too. What a nasty, vicious bitch. Who would have thought she would go that far to get even?

Claire could see the attack every time she closed her eyes. Stacey had been caught almost immediately after the assault and was now remanded in custody until the date of a court hearing.

Even that tiny thought didn't console her. She was all alone. She had lost the one friend she thought she would have for life. Rachel was her twin, her equal, her soulmate. For her, she was irreplaceable.

No one knew how to behave around her since it had happened. Her mum was treating her like a five-year-old; her dad barely talking to anyone. Twice she'd gone around to Caren's but had come away before she knocked on the door. Aunty Leah had been around a fair few times but was keeping away now, probably unsure what to say. Claire had even thought about knocking on Ruth's door. Maybe she'd understand. She had been with Rachel at the end too.

She closed her eyes, concentrating to see if she could feel her sister's presence, cuddling into her back, bringing her closer, trying to protect her.

'I'm here,' she whispered into the room. 'Please come back for me. I can't do this by myself.'

Suddenly, she heard screaming outside. She ran to the window. Down below, she saw her mum. She was standing in the middle of the street.

'Mum!' She ran outside quickly.

Gina had dropped to her knees in the middle of the road.

'They took her away,' she cried. 'They took my baby away.'

Barbara appeared in her dressing gown. 'Gina, come on in.'

'She's gone, Mum. I don't know what to do without her.'

'You still have me,' whispered Claire.

But Gina ignored her.

Caren was next to come out. 'Let me help get her inside,' she said to Barbara.

By this time, a few more neighbours had appeared on their doorsteps. But as they turned to go back into the house, Gina spotted Ruth silhouetted in her doorway.

'You,' she shouted over to her. 'You were useless at looking after your own kids and you were useless at looking out for mine.' She prodded her own chest. 'I would have saved her,' she screamed. 'I would have, but – but you...'

Caren looked over at Ruth as they helped Gina back into her house but she had disappeared. Damn – she'd have to go and check on her after she'd settled Gina again. She sighed half-heartedly.

How had she managed to become chief babysitter?

25

The day of the funeral dawned on a cold December day. The sun was high in the sky, but the wind was bitter with it. Ice from the morning frost was still under foot. Gina wore a black suit that she'd bought especially for the occasion; so too did Pete. Everyone else had been told to dress in bright colours. She was sure it was what Rachel would have liked.

Claire had new clothes too. She'd surprised everyone by buying a black and white dress. It came just above her knees and she'd teamed it with black knee-length boots with a slight wedge heel.

Gina had also treated her to a fake-fur coat. Wearing her make-up the way Caren had demonstrated, plus a bright pink lipstick, Gina realised that she didn't just look different. She looked individual. If it hadn't been such a heart-breaking occasion, she would have told her how lovely she looked. She would have complimented her on her choice, how she'd put it all together, the colour of her freshly painted nails.

But she couldn't say anything because she was burying her other daughter. Rachel had been so much the life and soul of the twins, it was hard to put into words how much she was missed once they'd been able to return to the house. With only Claire, there had been quiet.

All of a sudden, Gina realised how selfish she was. With tears forming in her eyes, she smiled and beckoned Claire over. She held her face in her hands and kissed her nose.

'I may be burying one daughter today,' she smiled through the tears, 'but I still have you. You look beautiful, so grown up.'

Claire swallowed and hugged her mum. 'I can't do this, Mum. I can't say goodbye.'

'Yes, you can. We all can.'

Pete knocked on the door. 'The cars are here,' he said softly.

'We'll be down in a minute,' Gina told him, keeping her back towards him until he'd gone. Then she spoke to Claire.

'Rachel will always be with you, in your thoughts and in your memories,' she comforted, wiping away her tears and pointing to her chest. 'She'll be right there, in your heart, no matter how far away you go. You need to make her proud today, and so do I.'

'No more fighting?'

Gina squeezed her eyes tightly together for a moment. Could she get through the day without laying into someone? If anyone said a bad word about Rachel, she'd be right in there. If anyone mentioned Stacey Hunter or her family, she knew she'd be the same. It would be so hard to keep her word.

But she would do it.

She would do it for Claire.

'I promise.' She smiled. 'No more fighting. Let's get through this the best we can.'

Caren and John were waiting in their doorway for everyone to come out of the house. The hearse had arrived a few minutes earlier but so far there had been no sight of the family.

The front door of number twenty-five opened. Caren gave John's hand a squeeze as she held back her tears. Just the sight of a coffin was enough to reduce her to pieces. This funeral seemed so meaningless. It shouldn't have happened.

'They're coming out,' said John. They saw Pete walk down the path and chat to the undertaker in the second of three black cars. Caren blinked away more tears as Pete stared at the coffin in the hearse, and put a hand to the glass for a moment before turning his back to it and wiping at his eyes.

John locked their front door and they walked down their path to the pavement.

Gina came out, holding on to Claire's arm. There were lots of family members behind them; Claire's brother, Danny, other people she didn't know but could recognise as Pete's parents, and a brother and sister on Pete's side.

'Christ, I haven't seen Dave Bradley for years.' John reached for Caren's hand. 'I'd forgotten there was a sister. Can you remember her name?'

'No.'

Fighting for Survival

The two of them stood in front of their gate until all the family were on street level. They got in their car and waited for the cortège to pull away from the kerb. Then they would follow on, just like half a dozen more cars that were waiting.

*L*ike a lot of neighbours who wouldn't be going to the funeral but wanted to pay their respects, Ruth came out to watch. Unlike the other neighbours who were mostly on the pavement, Ruth stayed in the doorway of her house. Somehow it made her feel protected from the outside world. She didn't want to intrude, but neither could she stay indoors and pretend that she didn't care.

She watched Gina get into a car, followed by Pete and Claire and a young man she assumed to be Danny. Then the rest of their family followed.

The engines started and suddenly the street erupted with the sound of music. Ruth popped her head out as everyone turned towards the Reynolds's house. Despite the cold weather and as a mark of respect this time, their front door was wide open, all the windows too – the sound of Robbie Williams singing *Angels,* so apt for the day.

Ruth wiped at tears that slid down her face as the cars moved off.

She should have saved Rachel.

*A*s the funeral cortège pulled out of Stanley Avenue and onto Davy Road, Gina felt Claire grip her arm tighter. She followed her daughter's gaze out of the car window. There were people dotted here and there, waiting at the side of the pavement.

An elderly man took off his cap as they passed. Gina saw two shop workers and the manager from Shop&Save standing in a line. One by one, as they passed a car, an engine would start and moments later, another car would join in at the back of the procession. Some cars had only teenagers in them.

'Do you know any of them?' Gina asked Claire.

Claire could only nod.

'It's such a tragedy,' said Leah, Gina's sister. 'Someone dying so young always upsets people. Rachel hardly had chance to live her life before...'

Claire began to cry.

Gina's heart broke again. She'd been determined to keep it together until after the funeral. But seeing Claire in so much pain was more than she could take. She pulled her into her embrace and they cried together.

'What am I going to do without her, Mum?'

. . .

*E*ver since she'd come to live in Stanley Avenue, Ruth had fallen deeper and deeper into a hole. First she'd lost the boys through her inability to look after them. Then she'd started to drink again. Martin had come back and although he'd taken advantage of the situation, wanting a roof over his head rather than be back with her, he'd gone almost as soon as he'd arrived. That had left room for that business with Pete Bradley – and look at the beating she'd received because of that.

She'd had one ray of sunshine when Caren took an interest in her. The nail party had been a success and a couple of the women had continued to be friendly to her afterwards. One of them had even invited her over for coffee – not that she'd taken up the offer yet.

And then Rachel had died. In the back of her mind, Ruth knew she could have been one of any neighbour to be first on the scene that afternoon. But Gina hadn't seen that. She'd just seen Ruth meddling in her business yet again.

Today had been the last straw. Ruth had really wanted to go to the funeral. She'd wanted to explain to Gina that she knew how empty she'd be feeling. She'd lost her children too. But it was better to stay away. It would have sparked off another fight.

But seeing all the Bradley family together, supporting their own, no matter whether they got on with each other or not, it made Ruth realise she'd completely lost her way. Worse than that, she couldn't think of anything she could do to make amends.

Back in the kitchen, Ruth took out two bottles of vodka she'd bought the day before. She twisted the top from one and, not bothering with a glass, swigged back a large mouthful. Wiping her mouth, she coughed. Then she poured half of it into a large glass and fumbled for her tablets. There was only one thing left to do.

But first she needed a notepad.

*A*s the funeral cortège drew up in front of the chapel at the crematorium, Gina imagined how a movie star must feel at a film premiere. There were no paparazzi, no screaming crowds, no flash photography, but everyone was looking at them – and ironically she could glimpse a red carpet inside the chapel.

'There must be two hundred people here,' said Pete, glancing around at the groups standing in silence. 'I barely know any of them.' He peered through the window.

'Good old Mitchell Estate, give anyone a good sending off,' said Barbara fondly.

The driver came round and opened the door. Gina stepped onto the tarmac. The crowd began to move forward. She noticed a few familiar faces amongst them: Josie Mellor and Matt Simpson – the caretaker from The Workshop – Cath Mason, Andy Baxter.

She spotted some of the regulars from The Butcher's Arms, and the manager of Shop&Save was just driving past in his car to park up. But mostly there were teenagers everywhere. Groups of girls in tears; groups of boys standing stoic.

There were people from Stanley Avenue too. But even as she wondered if she'd come, Gina knew who she was really searching out.

Her eyes raced around the crowd and beyond, finally seeing Maggie Hunter in the distance. She prickled but realised she needed to catch the woman's eye.

When she did, she watched Maggie lower hers to the ground. Gina waited for her to lift them again and gave her a small nod in acknowledgement. Mother to mother, she understood her pain. They were both suffering for the actions of their daughters and Maggie had lost her daughter in a way too. Stacey would be locked up for a good many years to come.

Gina couldn't stay bitter at the thought that Maggie could always visit her daughter, and always see her when she was released. What had happened would change Stacey too. She needed help. Maybe she would get it, and maybe she wouldn't accept it – who knew? But it would be a long time before Stacey came back to the Mitchell Estate, if she ever did.

Maggie Hunter nodded back before disappearing behind a crowd of teenagers who had only just arrived.

Claire took her hand. 'Come on, Mum.'

Gina looked at the coffin in front of them by the chapel doors, even now not wanting to believe that one of her daughters was lying inside it. The family had said their final goodbyes last night and Gina felt more at peace now. She'd kissed Rachel's cold forehead and left her in the hands of the angels.

She wasn't sure whether God existed or not. But she hoped that Rachel had gone to somewhere far better than here. And she hoped to see her there someday in the future.

By her side, Claire took a single red rose from the undertaker. Gina gave her hand a quick squeeze as they waited for everyone in the funeral party to get out of their cars and stand behind them.

'I feel sick, Mum,' whispered Claire.

'Me, too.' Gina took hold of Pete's hand on her other side. Danny stood to his side.

The notes from the chorus of *We are Young* rang out from inside the tiny chapel, their cue to move forward. Gina knew that some people wouldn't have heard of the band Fun but the song had been Claire's choice. It meant a lot to her.

With her remaining daughter hanging onto her arm, Gina swallowed, blinking away tears. Finally, she managed to put one foot in front of the other and go in.

By the time they were back in Stanley Avenue, Gina was drained of emotion as well as tears. She'd refused to have the wake anywhere but the house – didn't want Pete getting drunk and shouting his mouth off about the Hunter family. It would only cause more ill-feeling.

Quite a few friends had come back to the house for the wake. It was nearing six thirty now. Most people had gone but a few of the neighbours were there.

'It's been a tough day for you, our Gina,' Barbara stopped her on the way back to the kitchen with a pile of empty plates. 'You look worn out.'

'I'm knackered, Mum,' she admitted. 'But I'll keep on going until everyone has left.'

Claire was in the kitchen, sitting with Caren and John. They were laughing about something, and instantly stopped when they saw Gina.

'It's okay,' said Gina, understanding their guilt.

'Claire was telling us about some of the things she and Rachel got up to.'

Gina smiled. 'About the times they got into scrapes or the 'just plain silly' times?'

'A bit of both actually,' said Claire. All of a sudden, her laughter changed to tears. Gina rushed over and hugged her.

'It's okay to be happy, love. Rachel wouldn't want us to be sad all the time.'

'I miss her, Mum,' sobbed Claire. 'I can't live without her.'

'Yes, you can. Things will seem different for a while, that's all.'

'But you don't understand. I feel like I'm missing my shadow.'

Pete staggered into the room. He burped loudly, noticing the scowl that came from Caren.

'What's the matter with you lot?' He wiped his mouth with his hand and sniggered. 'Cheer up, why don't you?'

'Don't be so disrespectful,' snapped Gina.

'It was a joke, for Chrissake...' Pete raised his hands in surrender, splashing lager from his can over the floor.

'I can't believe you're wasted. Go upstairs and sleep it off,' Gina told him coolly. 'You're embarrassing.'

'Hey, Miss Fancy Pants,' Pete staggered towards Caren. 'Did you enjoy seeing Sam Harvey?' he stopped within inches of her face.

'Get away from me.' Caren pushed him, trying not to heave at the stench of his breath.

'You think you're so high and mighty across the other side of the road. Well, I showed you, didn't I?'

'Showed me what?'

'Did it shatter your perfect life when you found out John had a kid when you failed to give him any?'

'That's enough,' warned Gina.

'It's – it's none of your business,' said Caren, the word failed hanging in the air.

'But I want to hear. How much did Sam coming back on the scene ruin your happy marriage?'

'We have a strong relationship – something as stupid as that wouldn't have torn us apart.'

'You are so stupid,' Gina said to Pete.

'Huh?' Pete spun round to face Gina, staggering slightly but keeping his balance.

'I *know* your secret, you sad bastard,' she snapped.

Pete frowned as he steadied himself again.

'I knew too – that Sam wasn't John's son,' said Caren. 'One minute Sam was there; the next he never turned up when he arranged another meeting. The girls had told me his age and I was deciding what –'

'I don't mean about John,' Gina interrupted. She looked pointedly at Pete, 'I mean that I *know* who Sam's father is.'

'What's going on?' John was looking from one to the other in confusion.

'Claire, tell them how old Sam is,' said Gina.

'He's eighteen.'

'But Donna told us he was twenty-one,' John said to Pete.

'He tried to trick you,' said Gina.

'Sam's your son,' Pete said to John.

'Liar,' Gina screamed. 'Sam's your son!'

'What?' Caren cried.

'Yuck,' said Claire. 'You mean I've kissed my own brother?'

'So,' John tried to link the pieces together, 'if Sam isn't my son, then why did he turn up with Donna to say that he was?'

'He paid Sam fifty quid to pretend that he was your son, thinking it would cause arguments between you, take away what you had and maybe split you up.

But once Sam, being the loser that he is, saw your house and what he could thieve, he decided to rob it too.'

Pete looked confused. 'I didn't tell him to do that.'

'I overheard him talking when I was at The Workshop. All the damage he caused is down to you.'

'My God, you piece of lowlife.' Caren shook her head in disbelief. 'Have you any idea how we felt after that burglary?'

'That stupid little fucker,' said Pete. 'If –'

John stood up quickly. 'Why, you –' In his haste, the chair scraped across the floor as he lunged at Pete.

'John, no.' Caren pulled him back.

'I'm warning you,' John pointed at him. 'Stay away from me and stay away from my family.'

Gina left them to it. What did she care? Pete had done his worse by her. The neighbours were already standing in the doorway, coming to see what the commotion was about. This new revelation would be all around the estate tomorrow.

'Is it true, Dad?' Claire asked once John and Caren had gone. 'Sam is your son?'

'Of course it's true,' said Gina. 'Your dad can never keep his dick in his trousers.'

'That's because you never give me any. You're like a lump of lard.'

'Zip it,' she told him. 'For years I've put up with you and your inconsiderate ways, your philandering and your selfishness; letting you get away with everything. Good old Gina – why should I give a fuck about her? Well, you were right about one thing. I must have been dim to put up with it. But at least I can make amends for my stupidity now. I want you out of this house.'

'You can't make me –'

Gina launched herself at him. 'Get out of my house!'

Pete wrestled to grab her wrists as she pummelled at his chest.

'I hate you, you useless piece of shit. If it wasn't for you, we –'

'Stop it!' Claire began to scream at the top of her voice, taking a step backwards, and another and another until she touched the wall behind.

Everyone stopped as Claire pointed a finger at her mum and dad.

'You two,' her hand shook visibly, 'that's where we get it from. Rachel's dead and you're *still* fighting. I hate you. I hate you *both*.'

Pete turned away from them. Even drunk, Claire's words had got to him.

All at once, Gina saw herself through her child's eyes. They had to stop all this rage escaping. It wasn't good for any of them. Suddenly, she knew what she must do – the *only* thing she could do. But first she needed to comfort her daughter.

'I'm sorry, love.' Gina put out her arms. 'Come here.'

Claire slapped them away and pushed past her. 'I hate you and I hate him. I'm leaving and I'm never coming back.'

And with that, she ran of the house.

26

Dear Mason and Jamie
    I am sorry for letting you down. I love you so much but I know that you will be better off with people who love you and can take care of you and make you happy. I hope that you find that and I hope that you will always look out for one another. Lots of love always, Mum x

Dear Gina
    I am so sorry that I couldn't save Rachel. She was so young and didn't deserve to die like that. I hope you can find it in your heart to forgive me. I never meant to hurt you. I felt so helpless watching her slip away, knowing that I couldn't do anything to stop the blood. I hope that Claire will find peace, as I hope you will too, one day.
    Ruth

Dear Caren
    Thank you so much for being my friend. You were there for me when I had no one to talk to. I'm sorry to let you down but I can't see a way out apart from this. The dark cloud is back. No one will miss me anyway.
    Ruth

. . .

Fighting for Survival

*R*uth picked up a photo. It had been taken when Mason was two and Jamie was a baby. They were sitting on a bench either side of their dad. She ran a finger down the image of Glenn, remembering his smile, his laughter, the way he made her feel. Tears dripped onto the glass. God, she loved him so much.

Another photo. She was holding a newly born Mason, Glenn had his arm around her. She topped up her glass with vodka and drunk it quickly. Her eyes were getting weary now as she brought the photo closer. It had been such a happy time. But Ruth didn't smile through her tears.

Paper balls were strewn across the kitchen floor. She'd started to write notes to the boys and given up many times before finally settling on what she had written. In simple terms, she loved them and she needed them to know that. What more was there to say? She was sorry but they wouldn't care about that. She'd already ruined their lives; she had no right to ruin them further. They weren't her children now. Someone else was looking after them.

She picked up another photo: another faded memory. Ruth was standing by the edge of the sea, her hand trying to keep her skirt from flailing around in the wind. She remembered how she and Glenn had walked hand in hand into the cold water, then ran out laughing as the waves took their breath away.

'Glenn,' she sobbed. How had she survived for so long when life wasn't worth living without him? Gina was right when she'd told her she was bad through to her core. She grabbed a handful of tablets and washed them down quickly with vodka, coughing a few times in her haste.

'Not long now, Glenn,' she slurred. Her head touched the table and the glass fell from her hand. 'Tired... Not long now.'

*G*ina left it until eight o'clock before she went round to Caren's house. Claire hadn't come home yet but Gina had a sneaky feeling where she might be.

'Is she here?' she asked Caren when she answered the door.

Caren nodded, pressed a finger to her lips and then beckoned her in. Gina followed her through to the living room. Claire was curled up asleep on the settee. Even closed, her eyes seemed swollen. She looked so young and fragile.

'They both told me how much better it was over here than at our house,' said Gina sadly. 'You made a real impression on them.'

'Oh, please.' Caren waved the comment away with her hand. 'All teenagers think someone else's mum is better than theirs.'

'You *are* better than me, in every way.'

'No, I'm not. I've made mistakes too. I just don't go round broadcasting them to everyone.'

Gina tried to look offended but failed. She smiled shyly, knowing exactly what Caren meant. They went through to the kitchen and sat down at the table.

'Can I ask you something?' she started.

'Sounds ominous,' said Caren.

'What do you see when you look at me?'

Caren stared at her. 'Are you trying to trick me?'

'No, I'd like to know.'

Caren paused for a moment. 'Last month I would have said that I see someone in a loveless marriage, who's under the thumb where her husband is concerned; who hasn't got any control of her kids and who isn't bothered how she looks or what anyone else thinks of her.'

'Wow, don't hold back.' Gina almost grunted.

'Like I said, a month ago I would have said all that. But now, you're changing.'

'Changing?'

'Last month, you would have taken great pleasure in telling me what Pete had set up with Sam Harvey. But instead, you kept it to yourself rather than blurt it out.'

'I used it to get even with him.'

'Only because you've finally realised he's a loser and that's a massive step in the right direction.'

'Watch it,' she said. 'I have a great upper cut.' But Gina was smiling.

'And you volunteered at The Workshop – now that I *am* impressed with.'

'It was only a few hours... but I really did enjoy it. I enjoyed the days with the babies but really I loved hanging round with the kids. The ones in their early teens, you know, thirteen or fourteen.'

'I think you should continue with it. They'll listen to you. Maybe you can make a difference on the estate – especially now.' Caren reached across the table and squeezed Gina's hand. It took them both by surprise but none of them moved. 'Through Rachel's death, maybe you could talk to the kids about gangs and fighting and belonging. It all comes down to peer pressure to conform. Make them see there's more to life.'

Gina didn't know what to say.

'I think it's what you need right now,' Caren continued. 'I like Josie Mellor, she's a good sort. I – I thought about offering to volunteer myself actually.'

'You?' Gina sat back in amazement.

'Yes, I have some free time until I get my business up and running. Maybe I could help out.'

'Well, I have to admit, you've changed too.'

'I had to, being back on the estate.'

'Was it tough, to lose your house like that?'

Caren sighed. 'It was the worst thing that ever happened to us. But me and John got through it – it's always a good sign if you can do that.' She laughed and held up a hand. 'And look what we got instead.'

'Yeah, worn out flooring, chipped doors and damp patches.'

'And nuisance neighbours.'

They smiled at one another.

'How about letting me help you get through this?' Caren suggested.

'It's worth a shot.'

'How about me,' Caren paused, 'and Ruth?'

Gina sighed. 'I can't.'

'It wasn't her fault what happened with Pete.'

'I know.'

'But you blame her.'

'I don't really.'

'So, help her. She's grieving too.'

'It's not the same.'

'Of course it's not the same,' said Caren. 'But she has lost two children in a way. What she did was so brave, hoping to give her boys a decent chance somewhere else.'

'But to give them to Children's Services? That's beyond cruel.'

'Can't you see, Gina? Imagine how low she must have felt to have no other choice than that. No one to talk to; no one to get her through it.'

Gina lowered her eyes. She hadn't thought of it like that. In actual fact, until now, she'd never thought of anyone but herself.

'She needs friends,' Caren pushed. 'We all do.'

The kitchen door opened and a sleepy Claire came in. Gina smiled and patted her knee. As big as she was, Claire sat in her lap and wrapped her arms around her mum's neck.

'Would you like a coffee?' Caren asked.

'Please.' Claire nodded.

Caren flicked on the kettle and then picked up her phone, only to find it switched off. She must have forgotten to turn it back on after they left the crematorium. 'Let me give Ruth a quick ring,' she said, 'see if she's okay. She looked a bit upset this morning.'

'And then shall we go home afterwards?' Gina asked Claire.

Claire nodded. 'Mum, can I change bedrooms and sleep in Danny's old room?'

'Of course you can, love. Although, I have plans that we need to discuss tomorrow.'

'Ruth? Hi, it's Caren. Just ringing to see how you are.'

'Am fine.'

Caren sighed. She sounded drunk again. 'Do you want me to pop round for a while?'

Silence.

'Ruth, are you okay?'

Gina and Claire looked up at Caren.

'Ruth?'

'I… want to… time to… time to go. I want to –'

'You're not making sense. Christ, Ruth how much drink have you had tonight?'

'I – I… No, I – Glenn. I –'

'Ruth?'

'I – s'over.'

'Ruth!'

Caren didn't give her time to reply again. She ran out of the house and down the avenue towards number thirty-two. 'Ruth!' She banged on the front door. She raced to the window and banged on there too. 'Ruth! It's me, Caren.'

'Does anyone have a spare key?' Gina had come running up behind her with Claire.

'I don't know. Claire, run round to Mrs Ansell's and see if she has one.'

Claire took off and Caren went to try the back door. 'Ruth!' She tried the handle. 'It's open.' She looked at Gina. 'Should I go in?'

'Of course you should. Something spooked you on the phone.'

Caren knocked and went in. 'Ruth?' She gasped as she spotted the array of things on the kitchen table. A blister-pack of painkillers sat next to an empty bottle of vodka. She noticed the writing on the notepad and picked it up.

'Oh, God,' she covered her mouth with her hand as she read it. 'We need to find her.'

Both women checked downstairs but didn't find her. Caren ran up the stairs two at a time. Into the bathroom, into the back bedroom and then into the front bedroom. Ruth lay on the bed, another vodka bottle on the floor beside her.

'Ruth?' Caren shook her but there was no response. 'Ruth? Talk to me. It's me, Caren. Talk to me. Gina – in here!'

Ruth moved her head and muttered something unintelligible.

'Get her to her feet and walk her around.' Gina pulled on her arm. 'We need to keep her awake.'

Claire appeared in the doorway. 'Ohmigod, is she okay?'

'She will be,' said Gina. 'Ring for an ambulance.'
'No.' Ruth muttered again. 'No – blance.'
'You don't have any choice in the matter.'
'No...' said Ruth. 'No choice.' Her head flopped to the side.
'Ruth.' Caren slapped at her face and took another few steps around the room, dragging her along with Gina. 'Stay with us, Ruth.'

27

Josie pushed opened the gate to number thirty-two Stanley Avenue. As she walked up the path to the front door with trepidation, she wondered what sort of welcome she would receive. Was it too early for a support call? Would she be accused of poking her nose in again? Would she even be allowed in?

But she needn't have worried at all.

'You look better than the last time I saw you,' she smiled widely as Ruth led her into the living room. 'How are you feeling now?'

Ruth smiled too. 'I'm feeling good, thanks,' she acknowledged.

In actual fact, Ruth was feeling exceptionally well. It had been two weeks since her suicide attempt. She wasn't self-conscious about it, more embarrassed by the fuss she'd caused.

People around her had been so nice, kind even, afterwards. She'd had her stomach pumped and a stern lecture off a doctor half her age. But the nugget of information that she'd left the hospital with – hope and a reason to survive – had re-enforced how precious life could be.

Josie held up her hand. 'I've got the paperwork you requested. Sorry it's been a while for me to get it to you.'

'Oh, that. I don't need it anymore.' They moved into the living room and sat down before Ruth replied. 'I've decided to stay here,' she said.

'Here?'

'Yep.'

Josie shook her head. She frowned and then she smiled. 'I'm shocked. I thought you hated living in Stanley Avenue.'

'I did, but the grass isn't always greener and all that malarkey.'

'I'm glad because I would have only been able to get you transferred into a flat anyway. And I think you'd be better staying in a house, in case things change in the future.'

Ruth knew she was referring to the boys coming to stay. Last week, she and Josie had gone to see the social worker with a view to meeting up with them for a one-off visit to start off with. It wasn't going to be easy. She didn't know if they'd want to see her again and rejection would hurt like hell, but she felt she had to give them the choice and then to stand by their decision.

'I'm scared of it not working out,' she told Josie, unaware she was wringing her hands.

'But you'll never know if you don't try and that would be much worse,' said Josie.

'I don't mean for me. I mean for them. What happens if one of them doesn't want to see me? Jamie might be able to be won around because he's younger but Mason probably won't ever forgive me. And it's not just that, it's upsetting their new routine by imposing myself on them again.'

'Imposing yourself on them?' Josie sounded shocked. 'You're their mother.'

'Yes, but I gave them away.'

'Only because of how you were feeling at the time. Now you're back on the straight and narrow, anything's a possibility.'

Ruth sighed. 'I suppose so. I'll just have to take one step at a time.'

'Talking about steps,' Josie stood up. 'I'd better be making a move. I can see my work here is done before it's even started.'

Alone with her thoughts again once Josie had gone, Ruth flopped back in the settee and hoisted her feet up onto the coffee table. She rested a hand on her stomach, feeling the tiny bulge that had started to form over the past week. Now wasn't the time to tell Josie, or anyone else. She needed to be sure there weren't any side effects from her suicide attempt first. Not for another couple of weeks at least, or until she could hide the little life growing inside her no more.

What a predicament to be in. She wasn't sure if the father was Martin or Pete, but she knew she wouldn't be making the same mistakes with this one. She was going to be a better mother to this child, try her best and give her or him her undivided attention.

And now that she had a friend in Caren, she didn't feel so alone anymore.

. . .

Ruth took the plate of chocolate muffins through to the living room and slid them onto the coffee table. She wondered if Gina and Caren would like the cake that she'd made especially for them or would it be over the top? She had never hosted a coffee morning before.

She'd been surprised when Caren had told her she'd invited Gina along too. Surprised because Gina Bradley was the last person she'd thought would want to walk through her front door, even with an invite. It would be the first time she'd seen her since she'd been taken away in an ambulance.

The knock on the door had her heart pounding in her chest. She checked her appearance quickly in the mirror, smoothing down her hair.

'Hi,' said Caren, handing Ruth a carrier bag. 'We have cake, biscuits and more cake. And before I go home, I'm going to have one of everything.'

'I fear we have enough cake to last us a month.' Ruth smiled shyly as Gina hovered in the doorway. She beckoned her in.

Coffee made, Caren started the conversation off.

'How are you feeling today, Ruth?'

'I feel a little delicate, I suppose, but other than that, I feel great.'

'You gave us a real fright,' said Gina, wanting to join in but not sure how much she should say.

'I think I frightened myself a lot more.' Ruth picked up a cake and began to nibble at it before replying again. 'I had no idea that I was going to do something so stupid.'

'It's stupid, all right,' said Caren. 'But I happen to believe that suicide is really brave. Just think how hard it must be to end your life. I can't imagine throwing myself in front of a train or hanging myself.'

'Or taking tablets and getting blotto, like I did? I suppose it was the easy way out but I wasn't thinking of anyone but myself. It was selfish, really.'

Caren paused. 'It might have felt like that, but it was a cry for help.'

Ruth shrugged.

'Did you want to kill yourself?' asked Gina.

Caren tutted. 'Trust you to come out with the one question I needed an answer to but wouldn't have dared to ask.'

'I'm a Bradley,' said Gina. 'It's my job. Unless,' she glanced at Ruth, 'unless you don't want to talk about it.'

Ruth shook her head. 'It's okay. I've thought about nothing else since.'

After Caren and Gina had found Ruth near unconsciousness that night, at the hospital she'd stayed in overnight to be observed. What she'd found out while she was in there had been her saving grace.

'The worst thing was that I can't remember doing it,' she admitted, her cheeks colouring. 'I must have been so drunk that I wasn't thinking straight. I was really upset about not going to Rachel's funeral and you blaming me for it.'

'I'm sorry,' Gina said quietly.

'No, I'm not blaming you,' Ruth said quickly. 'But I think, in a way, I was still grieving for the loss of my family.'

Ruth launched into her past. When she'd told them about Glenn and how devastated she'd been by his death, how she'd thought she was being punished by losing him and how she found it hard to cope with life without him, Caren and Gina finally understood why she had given her boys over into the care of the local authority.

'That's some story,' Caren said, wiping a tear from her eye. 'And I thought my life was shit when we lost our house. Have you ever thought about getting the boys back?'

'Lots of times, but I know it's not the right thing to do.'

'Says who?' asked Gina. 'A bunch of social workers? They don't know what's best for you.'

'They're not interested in what's best for me,' said Ruth. 'They're interested in the welfare of Mason and Jamie, and so they should be. They are the most important people in all of this mess. I – I miss them so much but I think what I did was for the best.'

'Maybe for now, but you should see what you feel like in a few months when you're more able to cope.'

Ruth nodded. She had been thinking about her future a lot over the past week.

'How's Claire doing?' she asked to take the heat away from her.

'She's starting to attend school on a regular basis. Seems she doesn't want to waste her life now. I think she might be finding her feet more as an individual.'

'Wow, that's great.' Caren picked up a biscuit and raised her cup in the air as a toast. 'I do hope she settles down. It must be so hard for her.'

Gina felt her eyes brim with tears. 'It's so hard to be in that house every day without Rachel. Everywhere I look, there's a reminder of her.'

'But that will be a great comfort in time,' said Caren.

Gina wasn't so sure. 'It feels so empty now.' She smiled. 'I hadn't realised how much she and Claire argued. The noise was deafening but the silence without it is so much worse.'

'I was such a bad mother,' she added, moments later.

'I bet you weren't.' Ruth smiled. 'We always feel that everyone else's life is perfect, that we're the only ones that aren't doing it right?'

'Human nature, I suppose.'

Caren held up her cup. 'Any chance of another.'

Ruth stood up. 'I have a bit of Tia Maria left if you fancy adding a tot to it? There's enough for the two of you.'

'Aren't you having any?' Caren teased.

'No.' Ruth placed her hand on her tummy discreetly. 'I think I need to look after myself a bit better from now on.'

She re-joined them minutes later with fresh drinks. She gave them each a mug and then raised her own high in the air.

'Here's to new beginnings,' she toasted, smiling shyly.

'And new friendships,' said Caren.

Gina laughed and raised her mug in the air too. 'And here's to no more fighting for survival.'

EPILOGUE

'Is that the last of everything?' John asked as he packed another suitcase and a box into the back of his car.

'I think so,' said Gina. 'Everything else has gone ahead in the van – unless Claire has anything to come.'

'I'm done.' Claire came up behind her. She placed both of her hands on Gina's shoulders and rested her chin on them. 'Feels strange, doesn't it?'

'Yeah.' Gina saw her mum walking towards her. Across the road, Ruth was rushing over. Some of the neighbours were already standing on the pavement. Surely they weren't all coming to see them off? Oh, God, she was going to cry.

'Bleeding hell, I'm only moving a few streets away.' She waved her hands in front of her face and blinked back tears.

As everyone crowded around to say goodbye, Gina noticed Pete in the doorway.

'Ready to go then?' Caren asked a few minutes later.

Gina held up her hand. 'Give me a minute?' She made her way back up the path.

'You off then?' he asked.

She nodded, seeming a little shy with him.

'You don't have to leave.'

'Yes, we do.'

Pete stepped down to her and took hold of her hand.

'Please stay.'

Gina had never seen him looking so forlorn. He looked like he hadn't eaten much for days – actually she knew that he hadn't. My God, she realised. He really was going to miss her. But she wasn't backing down now. The hardest decisions had been made. She turned to leave.

'I'll always be around,' he told her.

But I won't always need you.

'I know,' she replied.

Claire was already in the car. Before she joined her, Gina stopped and looked back at the house.

'Goodbye, Rachel,' she whispered. She continued to stare, as if she expected the ghost of her daughter to run across the garden and stop them from leaving.

'Goodbye, Stanley Avenue,' Claire said as John drove off.

Gina smiled at her daughter and squeezed her hand. Good riddance more like, she thought.

She'd lived her life on Stanley Avenue, moving only from number twenty-eight to number twenty-five. Moving to a flat in Harrison Court was a whole new journey for them both. She was frightened, yet excited; nervous yet intrigued. Could they make it on their own?

Caren thought they could.

Ruth thought they could.

Her family thought they could.

Even Josie Mellor thought they could.

So she'd have to give it a damn good try – even just to prove them all wrong. She'd never done anything on her own before, and neither had her daughter.

'Here's to our future.' She smiled at Claire. 'We're finished with the scummy side of the street. From now on, it's Happy Road for me and you.'

***

A LETTER FROM MEL

First of all, I'd like to say a huge thank you for choosing to read Fighting For Survival. I hope you enjoyed my third outing to the fictional town of Stockleigh and the Mitchell Estate. I had so much fun creating characters such as Gina, Caren and the twins, Rachel and Claire, and I hoped you enjoyed reading their stories as much as I did writing about them.

If you did like Fighting for Survival, I would be grateful if you would write a small review. I'd love to hear what you think, and it can also help other readers to discover one of my books for the first time. Maybe you can recommend it to your friends and family.

Why not join my book club? I send out a newsletter every 4-6 weeks, keeping you up to date with when the next book will be out, what I've been writing. I also run regular competitions to win books and goodies and talk about other books I've read and enjoyed.

Please click here to join

Keep in touch,

Mel x

*R*ead the next book in the Series
Written in the Scars

ABOUT THE AUTHOR

Ever since I can remember, I've been a meddler of words. Born and raised in Stoke-on-Trent, Staffordshire, I used the city as a backdrop for my first novel, TAUNTING THE DEAD, and it went on to be a Kindle #1 bestseller. I couldn't believe my eyes when it became the number 8 UK Kindle KDP bestselling books of 2012.

Since then, I've sold over 1.5 million books. My writing has come under a few different headings - grit-lit, sexy crime, erotic crime thriller, whydunnit, police procedural, emotional thriller to name a few. I like writing about fear and emotion – the cause and effect of crime – what makes a character do something. I also like to add a mixture of topics to each book. Working as a housing officer for eight years gave me the background to create a fictional estate with good and bad characters, and they are all perfect for murder and mayhem.

But I'm a romantic at heart and have always wanted to write about characters that are not necessarily involved in the darker side of life. Coffee, cakes and friends are three of my favourite things, hence I write women's fiction under the pen name of Marcie Steele.

ALL BOOKS BY MEL SHERRATT

Click here for details about all my books on one page

DS Allie Shenton Series

Taunting the Dead

Follow the Leader

Only the Brave

The Estate Series

Somewhere to Hide

Behind a Closed Door

Fighting for Survival

Written in the Scars

DS Eden Berrisford Series

The Girls Next Door

Don't Look Behind You

DS Grace Allendale Series

Hush Hush

Tick Tock

Liar Liar

Watching over You

She Did It

All characters and events featured in this publication, other than those clearly in the public domain, are entirely fictitious and any resemblance to any person, organisation, place or thing living or dead, or event or place, is purely coincidental and completely unintentional.

All rights reserved in all media. No part of this book may be reproduced in any form other than that which it was purchased and without the written permission of the author. This e-book is licensed for your personal enjoyment only. No part of this text may be reproduced, transmitted, downloaded, decompiled, reverse engineered, or stored in or introduced into any information storage and retrieval system, in any form or by any means, whether electronic or mechanical, now known or hereinafter invented, without the express written permission of the author.

Cover image by paperandsage.com

The Estate Series © Mel Sherratt

E-edition published worldwide 2014

Kindle edition Copyright 2014 © Mel Sherratt

Printed in Great Britain
by Amazon